MORE PRAISE FOR ROBERT BARNARD

"Robert Barnard remains one of the wittiest of the mysterians."
—*Los Angeles Times Book Review*

"Robert Barnard['s] wit and invention have enlivened many a murder investigation." —*Washington Post Book World*

"One of the deftest stylists in the field. . . . It is the writing that counts here. Mr. Barnard goes about it with a quietly malicious sense of humor."
—Newgate Callendar, *New York Review of Books*

"Barnard [has] an eye for the self-delusion and hypocrisy in all of us . . . and the result is a growing series of mysteries that are entertaining, often quite funny . . . and acutely observing."
—*Boston Globe*

"The wryest wit and most scathing satire in today's mystery."
—*Chicago Sun-Times*

"Few writers are better equipped to handle the intricate plotting and larger-than-life characters." —*Denver Post*

"There's no one quite like Robert Barnard in his ability to combine chills and chuckles and then sprinkle the whole with delicious irony." —*San Diego Union*

"Excellent and enjoyable." —*Cincinnati Post*

ROBERT BARNARD

— FOUR COMPLETE MYSTERIES —

ROBERT BARNARD

FOUR COMPLETE MYSTERIES

DEATH BY SHEER TORTURE
DEATH OF A PERFECT MOTHER
DEATH IN A COLD CLIMATE
DEATH OF A MYSTERY WRITER

WINGS BOOKS
New York • Avenel, New Jersey

This omnibus was originally published in separate volumes
under the titles:

Death by Sheer Torture, copyright © 1981 by Robert Barnard.
Death of a Perfect Mother, copyright © 1981 by Louise Barnard.
Death in a Cold Climate, copyright © 1980 by Robert Barnard.
Death of a Mystery Writer, copyright © 1978 by Robert Barnard.

This edition contains the complete and unabridged texts of the original
editions. They have been completely reset for this volume.

This 1993 edition is published by Wings Books,
distributed by Outlet Book Company, Inc., a Random House Company,
40 Engelhard Avenue, Avenel, New Jersey, 07001, by arrangement with
Charles Scribner's Sons, an imprint of Macmillan Publishing Company.

Random House
New York • Toronto • London • Sydney • Auckland

Printed and bound in the United States of America

Library of Congress Cataloging-in-Publication Data

Barnard, Robert.
[Novels. Selections]
Four complete mysteries : Death by sheer torture, Death of a
perfect mother, Death in a cold climate, Death of a mystery writer /
Robert Barnard.
p.   cm.
ISBN 0-517-09329-4
1. Detective and mystery stories, English.   I. Title.
II. Title: 4 complete mysteries.
PR6052.A665A6   1993
823'.914—dc20   93-11296
                                                                    CIP

8 7 6 5 4 3 2 1

Contents

DEATH BY
SHEER TORTURE

CONTENTS

1

OBITUARY

I first heard of the death of my father when I saw his obituary in *The Times*. I skimmed through it, cast my eye over the Court Circular, and was about to turn to the leader page when I was struck by something odd in the obituary and went back to it.

'As reported on page 3, the death has occurred . . .' was how it began. That was odd. Famous actresses, disgraced politicians, exploded royalty might get their deaths reported on the news pages, but why should my father? Even the obituary had admitted that his achievements were few—had implied, indeed, that had he not been a member of a family whose fame verged on notoriety they would hardly have paid him the compliment of an obituary at all. 'Though now rarely heard, his song-cycle *Dolores* . . .'—that kind of thing. My father's death would shatter the world no more than it had shattered me. And in that case there must be something unusual about the death—a spectacular accident, suicide (no, not that), or . . .

Going against all my principles (for like all right-thinking people I read my paper backwards) I turned to page three. And there it was, tucked away down at the bottom: 'Police were called to Harpenden House late last night after the death was reported of Leo Trethowan, youngest member of the famous Trethowan family . . .' Well, well: so the old boy had gone out with a bang.

I turned back to the centre pages, but I found it hard to concentrate on the first leader (which was about changes in the Anglican liturgy, never a subject of urgent personal interest to me). In spite of myself, in spite of the affectation of total indifference which I assumed even when alone, it had to be admitted that I was interested. My mind was already toying with various enticing speculations: a spectacular accident was of course a possibility, but it seemed to me that, knowing my father, it was odds on he had met his unexpected death at the hands of someone or other. Certainly he would not have committed suicide: he was never one to do anybody a favour. No, on the whole murder seemed . . .

It was then that the telephone rang.

'Perry Trethowan,' I said.

'Hello, Perry,' said my superior at the other end. 'Have you read the paper yet?'

'Yes,' I said cautiously. 'The Common Market summit seems to be sticky going.'

There was a second's pause. I have a nasty vein of dry facetiousness that a lot of people find trying, and my boss was one of them. He was trying to decide whether it was operational now. 'I was referring to the death of your father,' he said cautiously.

'Oh yes, I saw that.'

'But of course, they must have telegrammed you last night anyway.'

'No.'

'You'll be going down for the funeral, I take it?'

'I hadn't thought to,' I said. 'I wouldn't be expected.'

'Isn't this a time to let bygones be bygones?'

'That's what I try to do. I finished with my family years ago.'

'Perry, you're being difficult. You know we've been called in?'

I pricked up my ears. 'Ah. So it was murder?'

'Yes, it was. Almost definitely. Of course there's no question of sending you down—'

'No, thank God,' I said. 'Who are you sending?'

'Hamnet. What's your opinion of him?'

'Perfectly decent chap. Excellent choice.'

'It just seemed to me that perhaps he's a bit lacking in . . .

well, imagination. And with your family imagination might be exactly what is wanted.'

'Personally I'd have said a thoroughly nasty mind was the first requisite for anyone investigating the murder of a Trethowan,' I said incautiously, giving him an opening.

'Well, you should know. That's really why we'd like to have you down there—'

'I do not have a nasty mind.'

'But you do know all the inside secrets. You are on their wavelength. Of course, I'd heard you weren't close . . .'

I laughed. 'A nice way of putting it.'

'Do you have any financial interest in the death, may I ask?'

'Certainly not. I was cut off without a penny. If there is anything much to inherit (which I wouldn't bank on) it will go to my sister, which is quite as it should be: she is precisely the sort of person odd legacies do go to.'

'He could have changed his mind, of course.'

'My father never, but never, changed his mind.'

'Well, that's all to the good as far as we're concerned.'

'Thank you.'

'I mean if you have as little as possible personal interest in the matter.'

'Joe,' I said, addressing the Deputy Assistant Commissioner in a way I would usually not do except over an off-duty pint, 'we are both agreed, aren't we, that I cannot have any part in the investigation of this murder? I can brief Hamnet, I can even put in an appearance for a couple of hours at the funeral. But surely nothing more can be asked of me than that?'

'I thought,' said Joe Grierly, 'that since you could be down there for perfectly natural reasons over the next few days, you could be given something in the nature of a watching brief. There are features in this case . . .'

I groaned audibly. 'There would be features,' I said.

'The personalities involved, for example, present problems: I don't know whether you knew, but one of your father's sisters—Catherine, I think the name is—went off her head last year.'

'How did they know?' I asked.

'Eh?'

'My Aunt Kate has been teetering on the edge of insanity for fifty years. One would hardly notice when she actually toppled over.'

'Wasn't there something about the war?' Joe asked, cunningly vague.

'My aunt had various mad crushes in her teens, on people like Isadora Duncan and D. H. Lawrence, and she capped them by becoming a besotted admirer of Adolf Hitler. She used to spend her summers attending Nuremberg rallies and consorting with Hitler's *Mädchen* in Bavarian work camps—some sort of Butlins plus ideology, I gather. They interned her in Holloway during the war.'

'Oh I say—that seems rather hard.'

'Not a bit: I've every sympathy with the authorities. If the silly . . . buzzard had kept quiet everything would have been forgotten. Instead of which she went careering round the village on her bike distributing pamphlets calling for a German victory. They really had no option. She had a highly privileged life in Holloway with others of like mind. As far as I can gather they all sat around complaining about the quality of the port.'

'Poor old thing.'

'She was thirty or so at the time,' I pointed out.

'I can see I'm not going to rouse any sympathy in you for the difficult position your family's in at the moment.'

'No.'

'How did you and your father come to disagree?'

'We never agreed. How did we come to fight? Well, you know how in the past families like ours expected their sons to go into the army, the church, manage the estate and so on, and there was a great stink if one of them wanted to go on the stage or something?'

'Yes.'

'Well, our family's cussed in this as in everything else. If I'd said I wanted to go to ballet school, or train to be a drop-out, or go to the States and graduate in dope-peddling, they'd probably have patted me on the head and given me the family blessing and a couple of thou. When I said I wanted to join the army, all hell broke loose. My father said it was a pathetically conformist way of life, Aunt Sybilla said it showed a dreadfully coarse nature, and Aunt Kate said I'd be *on the wrong side*.'

'It was no better when you switched to the police?'

'I didn't enquire. But I assure you, no—no, they would *not* have looked more favourably on the police.'

'Your Aunt Sybilla, she's some sort of artist, isn't she?'

'My Aunt Sybilla is or was a stage designer; my Uncle Lawrence is a poet and writer of *belles lettres* sort of stuff; my father was a composer and my Aunt Kate is—well, I suppose you could call her a politician.'

'Well, you see the problems Hamnet is going to face when he gets down there.'

'My sympathy goes out to him,' I said.

'Look, Perry, it'll be much the best thing for all of us if you go into this voluntarily. After all, they are your family. Blood is thicker than water.'

'So my professional experience tells me,' I said. 'Personally, taking it metaphorically, I've never been able to extract much meaning from that saw. Blood is certainly *stickier* than water—that I do know.'

'Christ, I don't want to have to *draft* you—'

'Oh, hell's bells, all right. I'll go down for the funeral.'

'You'll go down today. And you'll stay down there as long as Hamnet needs you.'

'No wonder men are resigning from the Force in droves,' I said. 'This is nothing but jackboot tyranny.'

'Have fun,' said Joe, registering my surrender.

I was just banging down the phone when I remembered something I'd forgotten to ask. 'Here, Joe,' I shouted, 'you haven't told me how he died.'

Joe obviously resumed the conversation with reluctance. 'I was afraid you'd ask that,' he said.

'Not nice?' I asked, now really curious.

'He died,' said Joe cautiously, 'while subjecting himself to a form of torture which I believe is called strappado.'

'Oh, no!' I howled.

'He had it arranged, I gather, so that he could stop it at will. As far as we can see, someone fiddled with the ropes.'

'Joe, listen,' I gabbled, 'you can't send me to that snake pit. That is *just* how one of my family would die, and *just* how one of my family would murder. This is appalling. The press will have a field day. I'll be the laughing-stock of the CID for the rest of my life. You can't send me there, Joe—'

'There's a train at ten fifty,' said the Deputy Assistant Commissioner. 'Oh, and there's one more tiny detail—'

'What?'

'He was wearing gauzy spangled tights at the time.'

2

HOMECOMING

The inconvenient, and slightly ludicrous, house which my great-grandfather finished building in the last years of the Old Queen's reign must, over the years, have brought a small fortune to British Rail and its predecessor companies from successive generations of my family, and in its heyday, their numerous guests. Perhaps this was why the Beeching axe quivered with compunction in the early 'sixties and spared the nearest station of Thornwick, and why subsequent carve-ups of the public transport system designed to force more and more cars on to the roads have left it standing and (with reduced services) functioning. It's not every day you meet a large family of lunatics ready to travel from Northumberland to London at the drop of a hat.

Not, I suppose, that the state of the family finances, or the state of the family limbs come to that, encourages that sort of genteel hoboism nowadays.

Anyway, I caught the ten fifty Edinburgh train (because, when all is said and done, you may wrangle and grumble, wriggle and chafe with your superiors in the Force, but you don't disobey their orders) and after changing trains at Newcastle I chugged into Thornwick some time around four. I was oddly touched when the stationmaster, after all these years, said 'Sad business, Mr Peregrine' as he took my ticket, though no one had used the appalling full form of my Christian name with my permission for years.

When, twenty minutes later, my taxi swung through the gates of Harpenden House and up the curved approach, I was cured of any lump-in-the-throat nostalgia by the sight of the house itself. (You are getting all this stuff about trains and stationmasters and ancestral piles because I don't think you're strong enough yet to meet the Trethowan family *en masse*. Did you think you'd heard all there was to hear about them in the first chapter? Oh no, dear reader: you haven't heard the half of it yet.)

The house, Harpenden, has just nothing to recommend it—except its size, and even that is more than a trifle ridiculous. My great-grandfather had few qualities to plead his case at the Judgment Seat except a very great deal of money, but even a filthy rich Victorian was expected to build with a modicum of discretion. Pevsner, who is searingly honest about the building, names the architects as 'Hubert Selby-Grossmith, succeeded at a late stage in the enterprise by Auberon Biggsworth,' and he might have added that my great-grandfather aided, abetted and tyrannized over the enterprise from beginning to end, having the infernal good fortune to die between completion and moving-in day. The architects, chivvied, bullied and finally swapped midstream, were told to impose the Trethowans on Northumberland: they did so in the form (roughly) of an enormous lowish central block with four turretty wings at each corner. Does that sound regular and sane to you? Well, I should add that each wing is a fantasy based on a different style and period of architecture, that the massive central block acquired certain accretions, that . . .

In fact, even John Betjeman, faced with it on arrival for a house party in the early 'thirties, could only stutter 'It's jolly . . . jolly *arresting.*' And when he tried to write an impromptu verse about it during his visit, the future Laureate's feet moved in classical metres, and the result was so lugubrious it has appeared in none of his collections. The house has affected most of its visitors in pretty much the same way. It depressed me no end, even now, and as we drove up the sudden swerve in the drive which led to the front door (the result of a last-minute geriatric whim of my great-grandfather's) and I was disgorged on to the main steps, I fancied that the taxi-driver shook his head in sympathy. Or perhaps he had heard about the death. Or had driven some of the inhabitants.

It seemed funny to ring, but ring I did. The taxi sat there, the driver separating his tip from his fare, unnecessarily slowly, I thought, and I wondered whether he knew who I was and was interested to see my reception. Was this the beginning of the hideous general public interest that I had foreseen? Eventually the door opened on a smallish, sandy-haired manservant with a manner that (perhaps assumed temporarily) seemed set to repel invaders.

'Good afternoon,' I said, feeling slightly ridiculous. 'I'm Perry Trethowan . . . Mr Leo Trethowan's son.'

His face changed, but only to cautious welcome. 'Oh, Mr Peregrine.' (His voice was gentle, Lowland Scots, and made a meal of the r's in Peregrine.) 'Won't you come in, sir?' Once in the hall he turned on the soft sympathy. 'A terrible business, sir. You have my wife's and my sympathy, indeed you do. Would you . . . would you wait while I inform Miss Sybilla . . . and Sir Lawrence?'

And without waiting for an answer he left me in the hall, while he made off in the direction of the main drawing-room. I reflected on the order of the names: would it not have been natural to mention my Uncle Lawrence first? I stood there, looking around the entrance hall, four times the size of a family council flat, its ceiling five times a man's height, looming in some brown cobwebby heaven up there. It was exactly as I remembered it—its gloom, its stuffed heads of animals slaughtered for the size of their antlers, its monstrously large picture of my great-grandfather, executed (the picture, I mean) by Sir Harold Hardacre, RA, in 1887. Many painters of the period have long ago recovered from the rock-bottom prices they fetched in the 'twenties, but my great-grandfather selected, to commit him to posterity, artists whom no amount of recovered piety could render desirable. One had the impression that he paid them by the square yard.

Nevertheless, since the little Scotsman did not return, I went to the far wall to gaze irreverently on my great-grandsire. He had been, like me, a large man, and the size therefore had a certain appropriateness. Mill- and mine-owner, captain of industry, were written on his face. He had been as well in his time a 'useful public figure,' and that was there too. Believing in the untrammelled freedom of Capital, in the absolute right of men such as himself to pay their men as little as possible and to take no thought whatsoever to their safety at work, he had naturally entered Parliament as a Radical. In the course of time he had become an orthodox Liberal; then he had split with his leader over Home Rule and become a Liberal Unionist. It was very easy, then, to move to the Right without giving anyone the opportunity to label you turncoat. He had held minor office in weak governments that needed the broadest possible basis of support, and had been a great trial. Lord Rosebery had called him, under provocation, a pig-headed nincompoop, and in spite of the best efforts of Sir Harold Hardacre, RA, that had got into the picture too.

Still the little Scot did not return. An impossible hope rose in me. Could it be that they were refusing to see me? Was I being barred from the ancestral door? Could I not then return quite justifiably to Scotland Yard and report to Joe the satisfactory failure of my mission? I was just weakly nourishing such hopes when a door softly opened.

'Sir Lawrence is in the drawing-room, Mr Peregrine, with your two aunts,' said the ingratiating voice, 'and they'll be pleased to see you now.'

My heart sank again. 'Thank you—I'm sorry, I don't know your name.'

'McWatters, sir. Shall I take your case to one of the guest rooms?' He gestured towards the tiny case (suitable for a *very* short stay) which I had set down by the main door.

'No, McWatters, better wait a bit,' I said, ever the optimist. Squaring my shoulders I marched across the vast expanse of hall and into the drawing-room.

My eye was met, first of all and inevitably, by my great-grandfather again, in position over the mantelpiece in the version of himself perpetrated, for just that position, by Sir Richard Fairweather, RA, in 1896—very much the same as the one in the hall, except that nine more years of pig-headedness and nincompoopery had lined their way on to the face. Around the other walls were large masterpieces I remembered, by Maclise, Frith, Waterhouse and others, as well as newer ones, portraits, by my Aunt Elizabeth, the real artist of the family, who died when I was still a child. Dwarfed by all this oil and varnish, in two uncomfortable arm-chairs and a wheelchair, were my Aunt Sybilla, my Aunt Kate, and my Uncle Lawrence. Sybilla rose, somewhat unsteady on her pins, to greet me.

'Good afternoon, Peregrine,' she said. 'This is quite a surprise. Oh dear, still so *large*? . . . Even *larger,* I think?' (Six-feet-five, seventeen stone, enthusiastic amateur weightlifter and shot-put-ter, I could only nod agreement that I was even larger. She shook her head regretfully, as if shrinking would have been the best sign that I repented my odd notions.) 'Your Aunt Kate, your Uncle Lawrence.'

I kissed Aunt Kate, who stood to attention to allow it, and then burst into a disconcerting chuckle of laughter. I had to take Uncle Lawrence by the hand to shake it, since he seemed immobile, but as I did so he shouted, 'Who? Who?', and then seemed to relapse into a doze. To relieve the awkwardness of the situation Sybilla said 'Would you like some tea?' but she seemed displeased when I accepted. She was forced to ring for McWatters and order tea and, after a pause, sandwiches and cake. The prodigal son, I felt, got a much more wholehearted culinary welcome.

'Er . . . you've come about your poor father, I suppose?' said Sybilla, unusually uncertainly for her, I felt, since she was so sel-dom less than mistress of any situation.

'Of course he's come about Leo,' bellowed Aunt Kate. 'Don't be a blithering ninny. Give him the details, then! Give him all the details!'

'Kate!' shrilled Sybilla. But Kate's parade-ground tones had unfortunately woken Uncle Lawrence, who immediately started up with his 'Who? Who?' routine again.

'*Pere*grine,' said Aunt Sybilla in her loud, hard tones, like a malignant bell-bird. 'Your nephew Peregrine. Leo's son, you re-member.'

'Oh, Leo's son,' nodded the patriarchal head. 'Well, what are you wasting time for? Show him up to Leo!'

At which, mercifully, he nodded off again, and McWatters came in with the tea-things.

Perhaps I should take advantage of the pause to describe the surviving members of my father's generation, grandchildren of the imperious, frock-coated numbskull staring down at us in all his eight-feet-high splendour from over the marble fireplace. My Uncle Lawrence's most remarkable physical feature was his shaggy, venerable man-of-letters head: its mane of white hair might have been (in fact, probably was) combed outwards to emphasize its size and distinction, to provide a striking frame for the classic lines of the face, the shaggy moustache, the keen (though now senseless) eyes. Lawrence Trethowan, his appearance proclaimed, was a Literary Man. He had survived the First World War and had written some agonized sonnets on it, much praised by Eddie Marsh and other literary gents of the era. After that (for want of subject matter, I take it) he had declined into writing rather feeble nature lyrics, stuff about country lanes and whatnot, and this was hardly attuned to the public mood. But he had also written occasional essays—'delightful' was the usual way of describing them—for declining periodicals, and in collected form they entranced the Boots library subscribers of the 'thirties and 'forties. He had been inexplicably knighted in 1964, by which time he was unread if not forgotten (my family, alas, has never been forgotten.)

My Aunt Sybilla had aged less gracefully. In her youth she had been known for her spry, sharp, gamine qualities—qualities which easily grow sour with age. She had designed the sets and costumes for that bright young review *Wits!* in 1929, and its nearly as successful successor *Quits!* in 1931 (both revues still affectionately remembered by old ladies in St John's Wood and their older flames in Highgate). She had designed things for Coward (who had seen through her), for the young Rattigan, and had even done a spry, witty *Orfeo* for Sadler's Wells, which nobody who understood the opera had really liked. Her career had collapsed with the war and had never got going after it, though Covent Garden, notoriously prone to pick lame ducks when it comes to designers, did employ her on a couple of misconceived ballets. She was now—and had been as long as I can remember—a vinegary, pretentious bundle of egocentric extravagances, a succession of ghastly, ill-fitting artistic poses. It's living with people like Aunt Sybilla makes a man take up weightlifting.

Aunt Kate, as ever, was square, gruff and ludicrous, but now she had—perhaps regained from her childhood, and the result of last year's breakdown—a dreadfully hockey-stick schoolgirl roguishness peering through the heartiness. I never could actually dislike my Aunt Kate, but she exasperated me thoroughly: plenty of people were silly enough to admire Hitler before 1939, but to persist in that admiration forty years later seemed to call for a superhuman kind of silliness that was all but repellent.

Anyway, there we sat, over tea and cress sandwiches, one big happy family.

Lawrence ate little. He woke, looked at me, muttered 'Oh, yes,' and was handed a cress sandwich, which he wolfed down. Kate handed him another, but after one bite he fell asleep, and she took the rest of it from his hand with surprising gentleness, then went back to stolidly munching her own.

'I apologize for Lawrence,' said Sybilla sharply. 'He is *not* always like this. In fact, this is what Mrs McWatters calls "one of his off days"—which is a very vulgar phrase, but it does rather sum it up, doesn't it?'

I did not respond to this invitation to ridicule my Uncle Lawrence (though only, probably, because it came from my Aunt Sybilla). Aunt Kate, by this time, was positively bouncing with suppressed puppyish enthusiasm.

'*Syb!*' she said. 'You haven't told him. Oh, go on, Syb! Tell him the details!'

I found this—even *I* found this—rather ghoulish. 'I think I know the main outlines.'

'*Really?*' said Sybilla, clearly affronted at being cheated of her story. 'But no. You can't possibly. You can't have talked to Cristobel, and nothing has appeared in the public prints.'

Deliberate archaisms were one of Aunt Sybilla's favourite forms of affectation.

'I'm not dependent entirely on the public prints,' I said. 'I heard it from my superior in the police force.'

'The P*olice*! Have you joined the P*olice*? I thought you were in the army! Kate, did we know Peregrine was a Peeler?'

'I knew,' said Kate, chomping vigorously at her sandwich like a young horse. 'I've known for jolly ages!'

'I left the army eight years ago,' I said. 'I went into the police. I'm a detective-inspector with the CID. I expect to be a superintendent before long.'

'Spare me the details of the promotional ladder in the Metropolitan Police Force,' said Aunt Sybilla, flapping an aesthetic claw. But I thought she was interested too, because, nibbling delicately at a piece of seed cake, she said: 'Well, well, so you're in the police. Really, you must forgive me, Perry dear—not knowing, or forgetting. But the fact is, your father did not . . . very frequently . . . *talk* about you, you know!'

'I'm sure he didn't,' I said. 'We each went our own way a long time ago.'

'Yes, indeed—thirteen years, is it? Or fourteen? A long time. And now you'd be—ah, yes, thirty-two. So you heard about our little problem in . . . in the course of duty, as it were?'

It struck me, momentarily, that the Aunts were taking this with a quite chilling degree of calmness. Then I realized that sensation, public clamour, the scorn of *vox populi,* these were meat and drink to a Trethowan: the legend had been a pure publicity creation, and if my father at his death had been recognized as an obscure minor composer, he would have been a totally unknown one had it not been for the Trethowan PR machine. And much the same went for Lawrence and Syb.

'I was officially informed of my father's death,' I said stiffly, 'and of some of the details. You can probably tell me more, I imagine.'

Kate bounced anew. She made an odd, soaring gesture with her hands to signify being hauled up, then, with relish, a great swooping one to signify being dropped down. 'Bump! Ouch!' she guffawed.

'Catherine! Any more and you leave the room!'

'Oh Syb, you are a spoilsport.'

'Your father,' said Sybilla gravely, turning to me (but I thought

I detected a certain enjoyment in her, too), 'met his end while conducting one of his little experiments. Of course, you know all about them . . .'

'To be frank, Aunt Sybilla, I don't. You forget the last time I saw him I was only eighteen. I had some . . . inkling . . . about his tastes. But the fact is, I really don't think he was actually . . . experimenting, at that time.'

She thought, her scratchy little face, all crow's-feet and old chicken skin, puckered in malicious calculation.

'You know, I think you must be right. The experiments came later, I think. With age. Probably he needed more . . . stimulation. Anyway, the fact is, Peregrine, your father was exceedingly interested in the tortures of the Spanish Inquisition (among others), and he began to experiment to see whether he might not . . . reproduce their effects . . . if you understand me . . . on himself.'

At this point Aunt Kate could not repress another chortle.

'I see. Now, was this something that was generally known—I mean in this house?'

'Oh, yes. We're a very unconventional family, as you know, Peregrine. We are *not* censorious: we can encompass human variety. No, give your father his due: he wasn't like those poor little men who shop furtively in Soho. He never made a grubby little secret of it!'

I was seized with a conviction that the best thing to do, if you have inclinations like my father's, was to make a grubby little secret of the fact.

'When you say you all knew,' I said, trying not to make this sound like a police enquiry and not succeeding very well, 'what does that mean? Did he invite you all to exhibition performances?'

'You are being a teeny bit vulgar, Peregrine dear. No, he did not. Though I'm quite sure he would not have minded. I would not have thought twice of breaking in on him, if anything important had come up. He talked about it quite openly, even at meals.'

'I watched him through the keyhole once,' volunteered Aunt Kate. She was going to do a repetition of her pantomime, but thought better of it.

'I see,' I said. 'So the whole household would have known. And so what happened?'

'Well, of course, it was just a *little* unwise, at his age. And I suppose he overdid it . . .' She averted her eyes. 'They say a thread snapped, or a pulley broke, or something, and he just . . . couldn't stop it.'

'I see.'

'That's really all there is. Your poor sister—' she looked at me conspiratorially, to see whether we mightn't have a snigger together over my poor sister, but I maintained my professional policeman's poker face—'your poor sister woke towards midnight, wanted some water or something; she heard the machine still going, and she went down and . . . found him, poor thing. She had hysterics all over the house. And it's a big house to have hysterics all over.'

'Poor Cristobel,' I said. 'And at the moment the police are in possession of father's wing, I take it.'

'Exactly. Though why they should have been called I don't know. Anyway, they're infesting the entire house.' A thought transparently crossed her face, and she leaned towards me. 'Now, Peregrine, dear boy, let me have your candid opinion. What is the best thing for us to do?'

In a flash I understood that Aunt Syb was on the horns of a dilemma. On the one hand there was the aristocratic (well, upper-middle, with oodles of the necessary) instinct, bred into her, that at times of family crisis one sat tight, closed ranks, said nothing, and waited for things to die down. On the other hand there was the newer Trethowan feeling (fostered by her and her siblings) that everything ought to be capitalized on, everything done to the clashing cymbals of publicity. The Trethowan legend, the creation of publicity, had been kept alive by periodic injections of it (including one hideously embarrassing libel action I remember from my adolescence). Now my father's death could perhaps be the latest in a long line of front-page spreads. She rather nauseated me, did my Aunt Syb.

'Well,' I said, cautiously and reluctantly, 'the first thing to say is that, even if it was an accident, it can't—the strappado business and so on—be kept quiet. There will have to be a coroner's inquest—'

At this point my Aunt Kate clapped her hands with happy anticipation and woke Uncle Lawrence, who began to shout: 'What am I doing here? Gross negligence on somebody's part! Why haven't I been put to bed?'

'Take him up, Kate,' said Sybilla. 'No, this minute! You brought it on yourself!' And Kate, dragging her old feet, began the long wheeling of Lawrence's chair towards the door. I rose to help her, but Sybilla's arm restrained me.

'No. It does her good. Gives her something to think about. You know she was Not Well last year?'

'I heard she had some kind of . . . breakdown,' I ventured.

'All that *wonderful* strength of mind—gone! As you can see. Now, you say there is no chance at all of keeping all this *absolutely* quiet?'

'None at all, I'm afraid.'

'Well, then, we'll have to make the most of it,' said Aunt Sybilla, with something like a happy smile on her face.

'I don't quite know what you mean by that, Aunt Sybilla, but . . .'

'Now never you mind, Peregrine. You leave this to me. I *know* the press! I've been dealing with them for years! Meanwhile *you*—since you are here, by happy chance—can help me by being my *liaison* with the gentlemen of the Police! You must know this man they've sent. Get in with him! Find out what he's up to! And I can feed judicious fragments of information to my friends. Oh, by the way, you will stay for the funeral, won't you?'

'I—'

'Then that's settled. I'll go and tell McWatters to get a spare room ready. Your father's wing—?'

'Well, there are places I'd rather—'

'Splendid, that's settled. And I'll tell Mrs McWatters there'll be one extra for dinner. I'll try and get *all* the family there for dinner, a real reunion. That will be nice, won't it?'

'Yes, well, perhaps I'd better go and see Superintendent Hamnet.'

'No hurry, Peregrine dear. Do finish those sandwiches. You do look as if you need an . . . awful *lot* of food.'

And she tottered out with the tinkling laugh that had echoed through the smaller London theatres on dress-rehearsal days in the 'thirties. I took another sandwich and was just stuffing it into my mouth (to get a healthy sized bite) when she surprised me by putting her birdlike head round the door again.

'Oh, by the way, are you married, Peregrine?'

'Yes, I am actually. But—'

'Splendid. Thought I ought to know. I didn't want to make another *false step*—like about the police. Do gobble up all those, won't you? Dinner's not until eight thirty.'

I cursed her, but I did as I was told. I took up the plate and stood with it in the centre of that enormous room. Chomping away, with Trethowanian irreverence, I gazed at the portrait of my great-grandfather. I winked at it, but it was one of those portraits that could never, by any stretch of the imagination, seem to wink back. I looked at the enormous, wonderfully literal Victorian story-telling canvases: *The Love Potion*; *The Capulets' Ball*; *Bank Holiday on Hampstead Heath*. They had been on the family walls over a period so long that their critical esteem must have done a graph rather like a political party's between general elections.

Then I looked at the portraits—by my dead aunt, Elizabeth Trethowan. The witty, affectionate one of her father (my grandfather, the first actual occupant of this elephantine monstrosity of a house). Then the little group of pictures of her brothers and sisters, done just after the war: Lawrence, posing like mad as the Man of Letters; Kate—stern in greens and khakis; my father, looking every inch a minor composer. And my eye came to rest on the picture of Sybilla—all bright modern blues, greys and pinks, colours which highlighted the crow's feet around the eyes, the discontented droop of the mouth, the souring of the bright little talent of ten or fifteen years earlier.

I have always said that Aunt Eliza was the only one of the family with talent. I'd go further: there was a touch of genius about the work of Aunt Eliza at her peak. And she was dead these twenty years or more, leaving behind the brood of siblings that had swung merrily into the glare of publicity on the skirt-tails of her gifts. 'That enormously vital and gifted family,' *The Times* had generously called them. Us. No, it was wrong. There was really only one Trethowan.

3

THE PAINFUL DETAILS

Eventually it had to be faced up to. I supposed that Hamnet was still at work in my father's wing of the house, and before dinner I would have to meet him and face the appalling *professional* embarrassment of my father's death.

I left the drawing-room, crossing the gargantuan hall on my way to the Gothic wing where my father and sister, and myself when young, had had their home. But as I passed through the hall my eye was caught by a lectern standing near the door, on which was placed an enormous book well remembered from my childhood: Great-Grandfather Trethowan's Family Bible. It had always stood, before, in the chapel—now, I presumed, not merely disused but abandoned. I went over and opened it, curiously, for here were entered all the family births, marriages and deaths—things Hamnet would no doubt expect me to have at my fingertips, though in fact of all that had happened in the family over the past thirteen years or so I had merely the haziest of notions, culled from occasional meetings with my sister, or the inevitable newspaper paragraphs.

So here (in thick black Gothic script) they all were: on the first page JOSIAH BENTHAM TRETHOWAN, 1828–97; his entry the thickest and blackest of all, with details of his marriage and his three children—my grandfather and his two maiden sisters, who spent the first half of their lives ministering to their father's every wish and whim, and on his death, suitably rewarded, took up their residence in a Mediterranean country, where they lived happily if respectably to a ripe old age, upholding the Protestant religion and fighting cruelty to animals.

The next page was assigned to my grandfather, CHARLES ALBERT TRETHOWAN, 1870–1946, in much smaller letters. My grandfather, I believe, was an inoffensive, loving man, who tended the family fortune as best he could and devoted himself to his wife, his duties as magistrate, and his garden. He married Charlotte Victoria Matcham, 1877–1939, the daughter of a Yorkshire baronet. She was a gay, witty creature—as a hostess much loved by Edwardian society and on several occasions by King Edward himself. Her husband doted on her, obeyed her every whim, and turned a gallant blind eye when necessary. She loved children, but mainly, it was said, when they were little: she tended, I believe, to lose interest when they were six or seven. A psychiatrist might make something of this to explain the family. I'll leave you to do your own diagnoses. The offspring of this marriage were: ELIZABETH ALEXANDRA, 1898–1955; LAWRENCE EDGAR, 1900– ; SYBILLA JANE, 1905– ; CATHERINE SIEGLINDE, 1908– ; and LEO VICTOR, 1911– . The date of my father's death had not yet been inserted, but no doubt Sybilla, with the zeal of the survivor, was already scrabbling around for the printer's ink.

From now on one got a page to oneself only if one produced offspring. Aunt Eliza, for all her honours and talents, missed out. On Lawrence's page, however, it was recorded that he married first in 1918 Florence Emily Horsthorne, 1901–34, and produced a son, Wallace Abercrombie Trethowan, born 1919, missing, presumed dead 1944. And, second, in 1946, Lily Beatrice Cowper, born 1920, divorced 1954, by whom he had issue Peter Clement Trethowan, born 1947. My cousin Pete. Lawrence's page also recorded worldly honours—his election to the Royal Society of Literature, his knighthood (both ludicrous but very British elevations).

My Aunt Syb's page was shorter. It recorded her marriage in 1936, her divorce in 1942, and the sole offspring, Mordred

Winston Foley, born 1941. My cousin Morrie. The page also recorded the most notable of her theatrical works.

My father's page recorded his marriage in 1945 to Virginia Godrich, and her death in 1958. You will observe that he was already in his mid-thirties by the time of his marriage, and you may like to connect this marriage with Lawrence's loss of an heir in 1944. My father, naturally, denied any connection, and claimed that my sister and myself were not afterthoughts but long-delayed intentions. In any case, as you will have seen, Lawrence stole a march on him by marrying in the following year and producing a replacement heir before he did. Anyway, my birth was recorded, Peregrine Leo, 1948– and that of my sister, Cristobel, 1951– , but I did not get a page to myself on which my marriage was recorded, or the birth of our son. I did not expect it: I had not, as you may say, paid my subscription. My father's page also recorded two or three of his less unsuccessful musical works, and the fact that he had served on the Arts Council Music Panel, 1958–60. Wowee!

My Aunt Kate got no page to herself: she had never married, nor ever done anything with her life except make a fool of herself before one hundred thousand people at Nuremberg in 1938. The last page belonged to my cousin Peter, Lawrence's heir, recording his marriage to Maria-Luisa Gomez da Silva, and the birth of children Pietro 1971, Elena 1973, Mario 1975, Alessandro 1976, and Emilia 1978. My God! I thought. And all done in singles!

I closed the bible and went on my way, down the gloomy wide corridors hung with portraits and occasional etchings of industrial England in my great-grandfather's time (Hepplethwaite's Mill, Preston, 1854, and the like). Finally I reached the door that opened into the Gothic wing of Harpenden—my father's wing, my once and nevermore home.

I had figured out already which room my father was likely to have used for his 'experiments'—the high-ceilinged sitting-room on the ground floor. Ideal for the purpose, and much too large for him and Cristobel alone—no doubt they had moved their living quarters up to the first floor. I needn't have bothered figuring this out, for the entrance to the whole wing was guarded—by, happy memory, PC Smith, of my childish apple-stealing days; still PC Smith, but heavier and slower.

'You can't come in here, sir, not unless you're sent for. Special,' he intoned, looking immensely complacent. I showed him my card. 'Oh, sorry sir, Mr Perry, isn't it? Well, well . . . sir. I wouldn't ever have believed . . . The Superintendent is expecting you. In the old sitting-room. Straight through there, sir. But you'll remember the way, I s'pose.'

Yes. I remembered the way. I thanked him, and marched in.

My father, of course, had long since been taken down and hauled off to the morgue, so you will be spared horrific descriptions of purple faces and . . . well, do it yourself, if you fancy that kind of thing. All I saw was a splendid array of ropes, belts, pulleys and hooks—rather like something out of a museum of early industrial objects. There were other things in the room, whose nature I could only guess at, but it was the strappado which caught my eye and dominated the room. Standing by the apparatus, pensively, looking in urgent need of recourse to *Varieties of Sexual Experience*, or some such tome, was my colleague Superintendent Hamnet, Tim.

'Hello, Tim,' I said.

'Perry!' The relief and welcome which lit up his face were immediately replaced by professional sympathy: 'I say, old boy, I really am sorry.'

'So am I,' I said. 'I don't expect I'll ever recover from it.'

He lost the expression at once, and looked suspicious. 'But I thought you weren't close?'

'We weren't. I'm not talking about the death of my father. I'm talking about my professional reputation.' I began expatiating aggrievedly on a theme which had been nagging at me all the way up on the train. 'Do you realize, Tim, that whatever I may do in the future: if I save the President of the US from a bomb attack, catch a whole posse of Mafia hit men, wipe out the international drug traffic, banish hard porn and soft porn and four-letter words from our streets—still when I retire everyone in the force is going to say: "That was old Perry Trethowan: it was his Dad who got done in while he was practising medieval tortures in chorus-girl's tights". And they'll guffaw, or snigger, or hide their grins behind their hands, depending on the type of chap they are. That's me, fixed, for all eternity.'

Tim Hamnet was an honest man, so he didn't attempt to argue with me.

'Well, as I say, I'm deeply sorry,' he said. 'Bit of a facer, I can see that. Best thing for all of us is if we can get it all over and done with as soon as possible, eh? The Chief mapped out your role, I suppose?'

'Hmm,' I said. 'Our conversation was brief.'

'Naturally all the heavy stuff I'll be doing myself,' said Tim. 'All the interviews, the on-the-spot stuff, getting the lab reports. And of course I'll keep you informed about that. All we wanted you to do really was—well, ingratiate yourself with this lot—sorry, with your family, get their confidence, nose out all the background stuff, the little family tensions and so on—'

'*All* you want me to do!' I expostulated. 'I tell you, in comparison infiltrating all the rival Middle East freedom fighters would be a piece of cake. But I'll do what I can. I've made the first hurdle: I'm invited to stay for the funeral.'

'I took that for granted,' said Tim.

'You shouldn't have. Take nothing for granted with this family. It *never* does the conventional, as a matter of principle. Well, you'd better give me the basic low-down.'

As I said it, I sighed, and Tim himself gave a grimace of distaste. He turned back to the apparatus that dominated the room.

'Well, this, as you'll have gathered, is a sort of do-it-yourself strappado. Know anything about strappado?'

'I've educated myself since Joe called,' I said. 'It's a Spanish Inquisition torture, still used by a few enlightened governments as late as the last century. Not that we can afford to feel superior these days, I suppose. Anyway, what you did was you strapped the bloke up by the wrists, usually tied behind his back, you drew him up to the ceiling, then either you left him, or—the real refinement —let him down with a great big wallop till he nearly hit the floor, practically wrenching his arms out of their sockets in the process. If he was unwilling to recant his heresies, or shop his liberal friends, you repeated the process, *ad nauseam* or, as in this case, *ad mortem.*' I paused. 'Poor old bugger. Still, you can't say he didn't bring it on himself.'

Tim tried hard to be tactful about the whole business. 'Did you . . . did you know he went in for this kind of thing?'

'I don't think it had gone anything like as far as this while I was around. It was mostly books then, I think. I remember once having lunch with him in Soho, and after lunch as we were walking along he plunged into a dingy little bookshop and came out with a parcel in plain brown paper. We were on the way to a matinée of *Peter Pan* at the time.'

'He doesn't sound such a bad old buffer.'

'He just wanted to see Captain Hook. Anyway, when he went for the raspberry fizz at the interval I opened the package. It was a book called *Secrets of the Torture Chamber*. Vividly illustrated. I had dreams about those illustrations for months afterwards. I've been against third-degree methods ever since. I later found he had a whole shelf of them: histories of the Inquisition, books on the birch, the cat. Most of them were presented as serious social histories, with frequent implied tut-tuts. The hypocrisy was almost as nasty as the practices described. I suppose it had to be presented in that way then. Nowadays you can probably get much the same info in any number of the *Beano*.'

'So he'd only taken up with this sort of experiment in the last few years?'

'So my Aunt Sybilla tells me.'

'Hardly a very wise recreation for a man of seventy.'

'You said it. Still, pensioners get some funny ideas, and my papa was a bundle of nothing but. Come on, show me how the thing works.'

'Well,' said Tim Hamnet, going over to a pair of heavy leather wristguards on the end of two strong ropes. 'The first thing is to strap your arms into this, right? Not altogether easy if you're on your own, but these were no doubt designed specially and it's perfectly possible—I did it myself a minute or two ago. Your dad at least had the sense not to tie his hands behind his back first.

Now, once you've done that, you can start the motor with your foot.'

He flicked the switch of the motor on the floor, then walked two paces away and grabbed hold of the heavy wristlets. The apparatus of ropes and belts moved slowly but inexorably, and gradually Tim was lifted, inch by inch, to the high ceiling, the weights on the other ends of the ropes being aided by the power-driven belts from the motor. When Tim was hanging full-length at the highest point there was a pause of about a minute. Then, as the machine momentarily cut out, Tim's weight immediately exceeded that of the balancing weights and he plunged to earth—but, letting go of the wristlets halfway, he landed nimbly on the floor.

'Christ, be careful, Tim. I never knew you were a gymnast.'

'No harm done. I tried that out before you came. But I wouldn't want to do it too often. Now—see the position of the wristlets now? Seven feet or so from the floor. Your father was a smaller man than you, Perry. His feet didn't quite touch the floor, however nasty the wrench he'd given himself. Hear that machine? It's starting off again. We're going through the whole process again. Now—note that when he's dangling, he can't switch the machine off with his foot. The only way to do that is when you're up at the ceiling—with that—'

He pointed to a white cord, which should have stretched from the on-off switch on the motor to a pulley in the ceiling.

'He could pull that when he was at the top, and he'd just be given one last bump.'

'Bloody daft idea!' I said. 'Practically inviting himself to have one more than he ought.'

'Not entirely daft, though,' said Tim. 'Since it was operated by the hand it was probably more reliable than something operated by the foot. Except that—'

And he pointed to what I already could hardly fail to have noticed: the cord from the ceiling had been neatly cut, and was dangling free. The other end trailed like a dead snake across the floor. I went over.

'Boffins finished?' I asked.

Tim nodded. I took the cut ends and brought them together. It had been sliced at a height of two feet or so from the floor. I looked at the ends: the cord was depressed into the centre, as if cut with scissors rather than a knife. I looked up again at the apparatus of belts and weights, and at the sturdy little motor.

'It's homemade,' said Hamnet.

'Really?' I said. 'I thought he might have picked it up at Harrods toy department.'

'Tell me, Perry, what sort of chap was your father?'

'I suppose you mean apart from the sado-masochistic cum transvestite kinks he had?' I rested my foot on the little motor, and thought for a bit. 'Well, first of all, he was a very, very minor composer—so minor as to be virtually an amateur. I'll tell you what I think: he was the youngest, and I think he looked at the elder ones in the family, found we'd already got two artists and a writer and decided a composer was all there was left to be.'

This idea had first come to me as a boy, in the school holidays. HMV had just issued, with British Council support, an LP of my father's song-cycle *Dolores,* to words by Swinburne. Despite the best efforts of Alexander Young and a group of chamber musicians, it had received lukewarm reviews. But my father was delighted with it, absolutely chuffed. Listening to it, perforce, over and over again, I decided first, that my father had no feeling for words, then that he had no aptitude for music either.

Anyway, I gave Tim a run-through of my father's career, which necessarily touched at several points on the careers and fame of the family as a whole. I mentioned their first scandalous success in 1929: it was called *The Somme,* and it was a sort of mixture of words, music, décor and scenic effects to which they all contributed. The intention was to lampoon the leaders of the First World War and crucify them for their conduct of it—by then hardly a new theme. But the way they did it was certainly novel: my Aunt Eliza painted some scarifying murals for the Wigmore Hall, which remained spotlit throughout; Sybilla organized some terrifying battle effects; my father (still in his teens, and at the Guildhall School) provided satirical settings of patriotic poems by Brooke and Julian Grenfell; Lawrence read his own poems from the ceiling (as if he were one of the better, dead, First World War poets).

The newspapers loved it, and them: they were copy, to be applauded or pelted with journalistic mud. They went on loving them through the 'thirties, when they threw a succession of bohemian house-parties (my grandfather presiding benevolently, if bewilderedly) and put on two more examples of what I suppose today would be called 'total theatre'. Though their reputations waned, as far as the newspapers were concerned their star never entirely faded. Lawrence produced nothing of interest after the Second World War, Aunt Sybilla went into acidulated retirement, Aunt Eliza (admittedly still at the height of her powers) died in 1955.

Meanwhile my father never recovered from being an infant prodigy. His Stravinskyish settings of Brooke were followed by works derivative of other composers. I think he is seen at his best in his incidental music for a revival of Wilde's *Salome,* starring some 'thirties vamp whose name I have forgotten. True, he challenged Richard Strauss on his own ground, and was resoundingly beaten, but still, there was something in the subject that brought out the best of his meagre talents. And that something was something really very nasty. But this merely relative failure was no more than a flash in the pan. Of recent years he had produced nothing much at all: the last I heard of was a *Hymn of Tribute* on the occasion of the Silver Jubilee—it was commissioned by nobody and as far as I know played by nobody either, so the Monarch was spared.

All this I told Tim Hamnet.

'That's very interesting—' he said.

'Liar. It's the pathetic record of a ninth-rate talent.'

'—but what I really wanted was some idea of his . . . his personality. What sort of chap he was.'

'He was a snivelling little scrap of humanity, without a generous bone in his body. He was jealous of other people's success, always wanting to make a splash in the world but lacking the talent, guts and perseverence needed to achieve anything. He was a bad husband, a bad father and a frightful composer. Anything else?'

'I won't come to you next time I need a reference,' said Tim, who looked genuinely shocked. 'If I were you, Perry, I wouldn't go around saying that kind of thing.'

'Why not? I was at a lecture on "The Use and Abuse of the Laws on Sus" last night—at Scotland Yard, surrounded by policemen. I don't have a twin and it wasn't my double—doubles don't come easy at six feet five and seventeen stone. I talked to at least twelve people I know well and went for a pint with them afterwards. If you know of a better alibi, I don't.'

'I didn't mean that,' said Tim. 'I meant with the family. I should play down your opinion of him, if you want to get in with them again.'

'*You* want me to get in with them again. Apart from Cristobel, I shall rest happy if I see nary a one of them again for the rest of my life. As far as what I say or don't say is concerned, I'll play it by ear. It's perfectly possible that by the time he died my father was loathed to desperation by everyone in this house—in which case I won't get far by applying the soft soap. As I see it, the whole case probably hangs on the state of family relationships at the time of his death.'

'Agreed. By the way, you've never told me how you broke with him. Was he brutal?'

'I'd like to have seen him try. I was bigger than him by the time I was thirteen. And to be perfectly fair, as I always am, there was never much of that, even when I was small. His nastiness within the family was always of a much more subtle sort than that. No, the break came partly because I chose a career which did not measure up to the family's standards of eccentricity. This caused a running battle that went on for several months. Then one day, in the course of this, I came upon my father listening to a rather peculiar record. Remember the Savernake mob?'

'East Enders. Particularly nasty lot. Violent.'

'That's them. Most of 'em got life about fifteen years ago. There was a lot of gang warfare, and they specialized in getting hold of their opponents and using especially nasty forms of violence on them. Of course nowadays they've all got Open University degrees in Sociology and write incomprehensible letters to *The Times*. Well, my papa had got hold of tape-recordings of their torture sessions, things that were produced at the trial. And when I came on him, listening to them, and gloating, I—'

But we were interrupted by the chiming of the clock from the Elizabethan wing, a sound well remembered from childhood.

'Well, I suppose you can guess the sort of thing I said. I've got to go. If habits haven't changed in this house, it's now that The Family gathers for sherry. Sherry and Dinner are always taken together, otherwise they go their own ways. This is my best chance to catch them in the same place, so I shall consider myself on duty, as it were. By the by, do you know how my sister is?'

'Well, she was pretty hysterical, as you can imagine, after she found him. We got a few things out of her—about the time she found him, and so on. But she kept breaking down, so the family doc sedated her and she was put to bed. I think she's woken up since, but she's still a bit groggy, I gather.'

'OK. Sister can wait. I'll go and pour dry sherry and tepid epitaphs over my father's corpse.' I looked around the room. 'Really, after all this, I can't think of much pleasant to say about him.'

'You haven't seen the half,' said Tim. 'Just come and look at this.'

He led me over to a far corner, to an apparatus obviously still under construction. It didn't need much esoteric knowledge to conclude that this was a rack, and probably the work of the same ingenious gentleman who had designed the strappado. But I wasn't going to let Tim expound the workings of the rack to me: I'd had about as much embarrassment from the extended family as a man wants in one day. I made for the door, but I turned there and said:

'Watch it, Tim. One can develop a relish for that kind of thing. What's a well-brought-up policeman like you doing, getting involved with a family like mine?'

4

TRETHOWANS AT MEAT

'I've been looking,' said Aunt Sybilla, while Aunt Kate poured me a large sherry, 'for the printer's ink. To record your father's sad death, you know, Perry dear. And it occurs to me that we have entries to mark up about you too, isn't that right?'

So: I was helping them; I had paid my subscription. I sipped my sherry (which was wine-seller's bulk, the sort of thing I drank at home, but decidedly not what used to be drunk in this house) and did my best to respond in friendly kind.

'That's right, Aunt Sybilla. I am married, and we have a son. But at the moment we are—'

'Oh dear—not separated?'

'Only physically. My wife is doing a degree at Newcastle, and our little boy is with her because my working hours are so unpredictable.'

'Really?' Aunt Sybilla's voice resumed some of its usual vinegarish tone. 'A policeman with a wife doing a degree! Quite original. What is it in—something *worthy,* and socially *rel*evant, I suppose? Like eco*nom*ics, or soci*ol*ogy?'

'Arabic,' I said.

Even Aunt Sybilla could make nothing of Arabic, and she retired for the moment defeated.

Not all the family had arrived yet. Lawrence was there, and showing some signs that he might be getting over his 'off day'; at any rate, though saying little, he was managing to clutch a sherry glass and convey it stiffly to his lips now and then with obvious enjoyment. Kate was standing to attention by the mantelpiece, a stance I remembered well, and the only other occupant of the room was Sybilla's son, my cousin Morrie (which is a ghastly name, but not half so ghastly as Mordred, the name that was inflicted on him at birth).

Mordred was a smallish man, dressed with a degree of pernicketiness, with a smiling, ingratiating, permanently youthful manner. He was, indeed, very much as I remembered him, on holidays from school—always looking as if he cleaned his teeth three times a day, and worried about ingrowing toenails. Morrie had had, I gathered, various short-term engagements in foreign universities, teaching English, but was now at leisure. What he was doing with his leisure, apparently, was vaguely researching for a book on—alas—the Trethowan family. And the awful fact is, it would probably have quite a good sale. I confess I could never actually *like* Morrie, but I came close to it when we shook hands and he said: 'Awfully embarrassing for you, old chap,' because he was the only member of the family who did seem to understand that.

It was Morrie who resumed the conversation now.

'It's terribly good to see you again, Perry, back with us all. I suppose it wouldn't do to ask you how things are going—over there—' and he jerked his head in the direction of the Gothic wing.

'I can't tell you much, I'm afraid. You realize I'm in rather a difficult position—neither fish nor fowl.'

'At least,' said Sybilla, 'they will have realized by now that it was an accident.'

'Well, no—' I began. But Lawrence had suddenly burst into spasmodic life.

'Accident? What was an accident?' He was so agitated he spilled sherry down his shirt front.

'I'm talking about Leo's going,' said Sybilla, her acidulated distinctness intended to contrast with his own slurred articulation. 'I'm saying that Leo's going was an accident.'

'Yes. Of course it was an accident. Pure accident.' Uncle Lawrence subsided slowly, then suddenly said: 'Has Leo gone, then?'

'Yes, dear. You'll understand in the morning,' said Aunt Kate.

I stuck to my guns after this interruption, and resumed: 'I'm afraid you'll have to put the idea of an accident out of your minds. Almost definitely it was murder.'

'Oh, goody,' said Aunt Kate.

Aunt Sybilla, however, showed her displeasure. She retreated into the gauzy drapes which were her habitual costume, and sipped her sherry in a pouty way, as if it wasn't mother's milk to her. 'There's something awfully un-Trethowan about having a *policeman* in the house, and one of the family, too, talking about *murder* with such *hor*rible calm.' She sighed. 'It's like one of those television serials, about Liverpool or somewhere. Well, I won't ask any more tactless questions, but I shall rely on you, Peregrine, to see that the whole thing is *over* as soon as possible. We are none of us young. Lawrence, in particular, is not younger than the rest of us. We simply can't stand the fuss and vul*gar*ity of investigations of this sort. Meanwhile, after dinner I shall ring up my friends in Fleet Street.'

At this point we were interrupted. A door opened somewhere in the distance and there hit the ears a screaming, thumping din, which gradually came nearer and nearer.

'Oh dear, the Squealies,' said Aunt Sybilla. 'Peter's brood, you know, Perry. They're only allowed out of their part of the house once a day, at sherry time, so they won't worry you, or hinder your friend's investigations.'

'They're always getting out,' said Aunt Kate. 'They need a bit of discipline.'

I was inclined to agree when the hideous din, like an armoured regiment crossing a railway line, finally landed up with a bump at the sitting-room door, which opened to admit a screeching, fighting, filthy mass of half-clothed juvenile humanity. Each one was passionately conducting three quarrels at once at the top of his voice, the elder ones pushing the faces of the smaller, the smaller kicking the ankles of the elder. As they got into the room their language suddenly changed from street Italian to English. One of

them shrilled 'There's Gran'pa', and they swarmed over him like
the locusts over Egypt, crying 'Give me a sweetie, Gran'pa,' 'Me
too, Gran'pa,' and the like. And the odd thing was, Uncle Lawrence seemed to like it: he woke up, patted them on the head, said
a few 'Who? Who?'s (understandably, I thought) and began scuffling around in his pockets for sweets. This was clearly a nightly
ritual: Aunt Kate had taken Lawrence's sherry glass and held tight
to his chair as soon as the sound of the infant army had been
heard in the distance. I confess I did not regard them with anything like Lawrence's benevolence, except in one vital respect: this
ghastly brood, three of them male, made it quite certain I would
never inherit the family abode. And that was quite a lot to be
grateful for.

Bringing up the rear of this invasion were the parents. My
cousin Peter strolled lazily along, oblivious of the row. He was
wearing a denim suit (Oh God! a denim suit!) which he bulged out
of fore and aft, over and under. Though hardly a year older than
me he had a general surface flab that was nasty—as if he were an
Italian *paterfamilias* of forty or so, of whom years of pasta and sweet
cakes had taken their toll (which no doubt *was* part of the problem
with Pete, too). His flab was probably white and jellyfishy, though.
His face was set in a self-satisfied sneer: he came over, nodded,
said: 'Heard you were back, Perry,' with a notable lack of enthusiasm, then went and poured himself a drink.

He was followed by his wife. You won't need to be told that she
was pregnant again.

All I'd heard about Maria-Luisa was of her origins: her father
had been a Spanish or Portuguese gypsy, her mother a Sicilian
peasant, bastard daughter of a German tourist. All Europe had
contributed to the making of Maria-Luisa, and you'd have
thought all Europe could have made a better job of it. She was fat,
slovenly, foul-tempered, with a large vocabulary of Latin abuse
but not, apparently, a single word of English. She understood it,
though, giving Sybilla yet further chances of employing her condescending, over-distinctly articulated tone of voice.

'Grappa Julia, Maria-Luisa? Oh dear, we're out. I must tell
McWatters to reorder. Will you have a Cinzano?'

Maria-Luisa muttered bitterly, then said: '*Sì.*'

We were not introduced. But over her drink she stared at me with frank peasant curiosity.

So here I was, in the bosom of my family. That is all the family you will be introduced to for the moment, except for my sister Cristobel, and I can tell you, standing there with the whole lot around me—not to mention the family portraits alternately lowering and simpering from the walls—made me as uneasy as a mouse at a cat's tea-party. This was what I had been running away from for fourteen years, and now suddenly I found I had run full circle and here I was again in the middle of them, being watched, appraised, and no doubt found wanting. It wasn't that I felt they were a whole lot more intelligent than I am: it would be false modesty to pretend I did. But I did think they were a whole lot more cunning, and what's more they were a whole lot better in the picture as far as the murder was concerned. What if they were all in it—had ganged up together for some odd Trethowanish reason? I think my cousin Pete sensed my uneasiness, because he said nastily: 'Well, it takes a death to bring the family together, doesn't it?'

Two of them, at least, felt the need to cover this over a bit, and Mordred said, 'Anyway, it's good to have you back, Perry,' and Aunt Kate said, 'It's just as if you never went away.' (Oh, no, it's not, Aunt Kate. Not for me.)

'Life is strange,' mused Sybilla, who was a dab hand with a platitude. 'Who would have thought, last evening, that within twenty-four hours we would have lost one, and gained one!'

Maria-Luisa, for some reason, let out a raucous, spiteful laugh.

'What had my father been like, these last few days?' I asked. 'Perfectly normal?'

'Perfectly well,' said Sybilla, understandably rejecting my adjective. 'In the pink of health. Otherwise he would hardly have—'

'No. Quite,' I said. 'What had his life been like, in the years since I was here? You must remember that I know very little of his routines.'

'Oh, not much changed. He pottered a little in the garden—we only have two men there now. He liked a trip to London now and

then: his club, the bookshops—you know. He did a little composing—he was never one of those *fertile* geniuses, though, was he?
Then we all have to chip in a bit in the house these days. Really a
terrible bore, but what can we do? The McWatters are all we have
living in, and they *insist* on two days off a week.'

'Awfully inconsiderate of them,' I said.

'We take it in turns to cook,' put in Kate.

'That's right,' resumed Sybilla. 'Maria-Luisa gives us some of
her *in*teresting Italian and Iberian dishes. The oily tang of the
South—so refreshing! Then Mordred was in Sweden for a time,
you know, and he does some enchanting things with herrings.
And then Kate, too—'

'I cooked last night,' burbled Kate, full of herself. 'I go in for
interesting combinations. Most cooks are so unadventurous. I
gave them meat-loaf with caramel sauce. Everyone said it was
scrumptious!'

For the first time I felt a twinge of pity for my father. To go to
Hell with a belly full of meat-loaf and caramel sauce was a fate
worse than even I would wish on him.

'It was *quite* delicious, Kate dear,' said Sybilla, winking at me.
'So your father had his day as well—'

'It was always tinned ham and salad,' said Kate, pressing her
superiority. 'That was almost cheating. And Chrissy had to wash
the salad things.'

'Well, he did his best. As we all do. Except poor Lawrence, who
since his stroke really *can't* manage his arms and legs well enough,
even on his good days.'

'My poor old Pop, he ain't what he used to be,' said Pete, with a
wholly synthetic sympathy. 'My poor old Pop has been through it.'

'Been through it?' suddenly boomed Lawrence from his wheelchair, where he had apparently been dozing happily. 'By God,
yes. By God we went through it. Nobody who wasn't in the
trenches can have an idea of what it was like. That's what I tried to
convey: "The mud, the mud, the blend of earth and gore!"; "The
shrill, demented choirs of wailing shells". That's what it was like! A
living hell! You young people know nothing! Nothing!'

It was my uncle's habit, as the observant of you may have

noted, to mingle a line or two of his own turgid sonnets with lines by more talented poets of the First World War. It was only years after I left home, when I started dipping into histories and memoirs of the time, that I discovered the true authors of lines I'd known from boyhood, and had been convinced were the work of Lawrence Trethowan.

Lawrence's reawakening did not go unnoticed by the Squealies, who had been fighting happily among themselves in the far corner, but now regathered to clamber all over him and pick his pockets of 'sweeties'. Luckily, in the midst of this nauseating performance McWatters came in to announce dinner, and their mother collected them up in her brawny arms and removed them to their own wing, squeaking and bawling until the door was finally shut on them and it felt like Armistice Day, 1918.

As we all trooped in to dinner, Sybilla took my arm in her bony claw and whispered: 'You needn't worry. None of us is "on" tonight. Mrs McWatters is a jewel.'

And certainly the food, though traditional, was first rate. But we were an ill-assorted gathering to eat it. Maria-Luisa talked only to her husband, keeping up a constant stream of comment, complaint and imprecation in what sounded like gutter Italian, probably with bits of something else thrown in (at any rate, it certainly didn't sound to my ears like the Tuscan language spoken by a Roman tongue). Pete just said 'si' and 'no' and 'basta', and looked bored and contemptuous, though he forked his food in with enthusiasm. I had relieved Aunt Kate of the job of wheeling Lawrence in, and when I had placed him at the head of the table he had looked round and said: 'Capable young chap. Who is he?' Then he had relapsed into concentrated eating. McWatters had left two tureens of soup on the table, and we served ourselves.

'Not what you were used to in other days, Perry dear,' said Sybilla, leaning over almost intimately. 'We thought it was difficult with servants then, but now it's simply impossible!'

'It wouldn't be like this if we had won the war!' suddenly barked Aunt Kate.

There was an immediate silence round the table, even from Maria-Luisa, who evidently understood more than might have been expected. They all looked at me, to see how I would take it. Me, I was used to my Aunt Kate, and her unorthodox arrangement of loyalties. I went on eating my soup. The atmosphere relaxed.

'*Dear* Kate!' sighed Sybilla. 'There's a touch of her old self back tonight!'

I smiled briefly. 'You're all very much as I remember you, you know. And it sounds as if my father hadn't changed greatly. You don't think he had any special worries when he died, do you?'

'Dear me, no,' said Sybilla, vaguely, the drape around her wrist trailing in the soup. Then she perked up. 'But he might easily have had some that we didn't know about. Do you think he took his own life?'

'No,' I said firmly. Then I went on in my plodding policeman-like fashion: 'Had there been any tensions, dissensions, disagreements over the last few days?'

'He's inquisiting us!' chortled Kate. 'Just like in a book.'

'Not that I know of,' said Mordred, who was turning out to be easily the most sensible of the lot. 'But then I'm a bit out of it. If it wasn't brought to table here, I wouldn't have noticed.'

I turned to Aunt Sybilla. 'You probably saw more of him. Was there anything that you noticed?'

'Well, no, Perry dear. Otherwise I'd have said. Of course, you know us. We're very much creatures of instinct.' (Oh yes—pure children of nature: with resident butler and cook, a dozen cleaners, two gardeners, and several acres of house to be natural in.) 'If we *feel* anything, we say it out. So much better to be *open*. So if there had been any *major* row, I'd certainly have heard of it . . . Certainly.'

The fact is, the way this bear-garden is arranged, with each group going its own way in its own wing, and each wing miles from the other wings, it was perfectly possible for major rows, wide-ranging conspiracies or out-and-out cold war to take place and yet be kept secret, provided a moderately good face was put on on 'public' occasions. Which meant, I took it, at sherry time and over dinner. I chewed over this as I enjoyed Mrs McWatters's excellent steak and kidney pudding.

I chewed over something else as well, and that was the feeling I was beginning to get that the family, and Sybilla in particular, was welcoming me back into the happy group, reinstating me in the family Bible and all, because they thought that I could protect them in some way from the consequences of having a murder in the family. Nobody loves a policeman these days except when a crime might occur or has occurred, and the Trethowans were less 'law and order' people than most. But now I was a friend in high places, to make sure their cosy little world was not shattered. As you can understand, I imagine, this sort of protection was one thing I had no intention of giving them. So as we gracefully spooned our syllabub into our (not noticeably impaired by the tragedy) digestive systems, I made a frightfully official-sounding clearing-of-the-throat noise, and started actually to address them all:

'If you don't mind, Aunt Syb . . . and, er, Uncle Lawrence . . . there's just one thing I'd like to say, now we're all together. I'm very grateful to you for welcoming me back home as you have. And of course for your sympathy. And I shall certainly do all I can to advise you in the present difficult situation. And if possible to help you. But what I can't do—'

But I was interrupted. From the distance there came once more the hair-raising sound of infant strife, a yowling, rolling, thumping sound that seemed to be approaching us irresistibly like the armies of Genghis Khan, spreading havoc and destruction in their wake. Peter and Maria-Luisa compounded matters by screaming at each other in their own queer linguistic modes of communication, and it ended by Peter going disgruntedly out just as the Squealies were at the door. Aunt Sybilla raised her eyebrows.

'You were saying, Perry dear?'

But at that moment there was yet another interruption. The door to the hall opened, and in came PC Smith. Looking more than a little overwhelmed (for this was not just gentry, remember, but his own particular gentry), he crossed the great open space of the dining-room and, standing by Aunt Sybilla's chair, said in a low voice:

'Superintendent Hamnet would be glad to see you as soon as possible after dinner, Miss Trethowan.'

It was as if he'd made an indecent suggestion.

'Perry!' squawked Aunt Sybilla, her eyes bulging with outrage. 'I do think I might have been spared this!'

I banged my fist on the table with a force that raised the glassware and crockery an inch.

'What I was just about to say was that the one thing I cannot and will not do is protect you from the normal processes of the law in a case of murder. Nothing can protect anyone from that— except diplomatic immunity.'

'Then I must set about getting it with all despatch,' said Sybilla, throwing down her napkin and stalking from the room.

The meal, not surprisingly, more or less broke up after this. Maria-Luisa poured herself another large glass of wine and stomped out after her maniacal brood. Aunt Kate wheeled a mumbling, dribbling Lawrence off to bed with a reproachful 'He's *not* to be upset, you know.' Only Mordred seemed inclined to linger. He poured us both a glass of port, and I was about to settle down to a little chat before going up to my sister when McWatters came in with a little servant's cough (so different from a policeman's magisterial clearing of the throat) and said: 'Oh, Mr Peregrine, sir, there's a phone call for you.'

'Probably the Yard,' I said, getting up. 'You're sure it's not really for Hamnet?'

'Oh yes, sir. It's for you. Actually sir, the leddy said she was your wife.'

'My God!' I said. I hurried out to the extension I'd seen in the hall, then changed my mind and asked McWatters if there wasn't anywhere more private.

'There's Sir Lawrence's study,' he said doubtfully. 'But mebbe it'd be best if you were to use the one in the old butler's pantry.' He led me down a corridor, through the great baize door, down a staircase, and into the well-remembered, high-ceilinged domestic palace which my great-grandfather Josiah had deemed suitable to minister to his needs. You could have cooked the Coronation dinner in here. But McWatters went to a side door and showed me into a considerable and well-equipped apartment, suitable to the dignity of an Edwardian butler.

'If you'll take up the receiver, sir, I'll put you through in a moment.'

Within thirty seconds I heard a click and said: 'Jan?'

'Perry! Home is the sailor, home from the—'

'Cut that out! How did you know I was here?'

'I read about the death in the papers. It sounded fishy. I knew it was your day off, so I kept ringing home. Then suddenly I put two and two together. The sentimental little lad has gone back for the funeral baked meats.'

'Nothing of the sort. I am here under orders and under protest.'

'That's exactly what I guessed, actually. Knowing Joe. So my deduction from the newspaper report that all is not quite quite, so to speak, was right?'

'Nothing is ever quite quite with my family. You've no idea how dire it all is.'

'Never fear. Help is on the way. Daniel and I are coming for the weekend. You know how I've always wanted to meet your f—'

'*No,*' I said. 'No, you are *not.*'

'Don't tell me they'd refuse to meet me?'

'*I* refuse to let *you* meet *them.*'

'There's obviously room for us. I bet we could both fit into your bedroom.'

'There's room for the Eighth Army in my bedroom. That is not the point.'

'Perry, I know you can't be officially on the case, so why are you being so appallingly stuffy?'

'Because,' I said, 'I do not choose to bring my wife and son to a house where a murder has just been committed and in which a murderer is still at large.'

This stumped her a bit. There was a long silence.

'So long as it's not that you're ashamed of me in front of your family,' Jan said, rather feebly.

'You know perfectly well I'm ashamed of my family in front of you.'

'Well, that's all right, then. That's as it should be. Perhaps it is best if we actually stay in the village.'

'You'll have a job. "The Village" is about ten houses.'

'And a pub. The Marquis of Danby.'

'That fleabitten hostelry. I had my first pint there.'

'Probably it'll be some kind of anniversary, then.'

'Don't be deceived by the grand name: it's a tiny country inn with two cramped bars. They certainly won't take guests.'

'They certainly do. The AA book says so.'

'My God. It's probably been tarted up.'

'Better that than fleas, anyway. Well, so I'll collect Daniel after lectures are over, give him something to eat to keep him happy, and then drive over in the early evening. Wasn't it lucky I got a place at Newcastle?'

'Jan, I still—'

'See you tomorrow. Love to the aunties and uncles!'

And she rang off. I sometimes win arguments with my wife, but never those conducted over the telephone. I shrugged my shoulders in irritation, and decided to go and have a good talk to Cristobel.

5

CRISTOBEL

Cristobel—that's a bloody silly name to start with. Or silly spell-ing. Because it's pronounced perfectly normally, as in Pank-hurst. That sort of silly-buggery runs in our family. Would you believe that my cousin Pete was supposed to be called Pyotr? Only the clergyman making a deliberate mistake at the font and stand-ing Uncle Lawrence out that it couldn't be rectified saved him from that fate. And look at Kate. I sometimes wonder whether she wasn't conceived in a private box at Covent Garden, during one of the more missable sections of *Die Walküre*.

You mustn't think I'm not fond of Cristobel. I am in my own way. And she's worth all the rest put together. So bear this in mind if I am occasionally a little negative about her. She could irritate me—and she certainly irritated me in the course of this case. For a start she is a Girl Guide. I suppose she got this from Aunt Kate. Did I tell you that when Kate attended the Nuremberg Rally of 1938 she did so in Girl Guide's uniform? There was a great flurry of Brown Owls about that, and they were just getting down to a delicious Discussion of Principle on the subject in the highest Guiding circles when Hitler invaded Poland and out she had to go. They all thought it very unsporting of Hitler. Well, Cristobel is by now a Brown Owl or a Grey Squirrel or something of the sort, and she is rather a lumpy, earnest, well-meaning sort of girl, one of those people who can probably light a fire with twigs but might well destroy acres of national parkland by doing so.

After that rather unsatisfactory conversation with my wife I went up through the green baize doors and into the main part of the house. McWatters was just entering the dining-room as I passed through the hall, and I wondered whether he'd been listening in on the hall extension. Then I went up the great staircase (which seemed to have been conceived for corpulent fin-de-siècle monarchs to make an entrance down, arm in arm with their consorts) and to my bedroom. Dear Aunt Sybilla had told McWatters to put me in my old room, but he had had the sense to realize I would not much want a room in the Gothic wing, even had the police allowed it, so I'd been given the principal guest bedroom in the main block—an enormous room, inevitably, big enough to erect a circus tent in, with its own bath and shower and, of all things, John Martin's *The Destruction of Sennacherib* taking up most of the inner wall. I have grown up with nineteenth-century painting, it's very much part of me, but still I decided that *The Destruction of Sennacherib* was not under present circumstances the kind of interior decoration best calculated to cheer the faltering spirit. Alas, there was no question of taking it down, or turning its face to the wall. I walked round the room for a bit, tut-tutting at the thought of Jan's and Daniel's arrival; I got out my notebooks (part of my personal equipment for a case) but wrote nothing in them; then I decided to go along and have my talk to Cristobel.

Cristobel, after her hysterics, had been put in another guest-room only three doors from mine—hardly more than the length of Liverpool Street Station away. I tapped on the door. There was a long pause, and I stood picturing her there, frightened out of her wits. I had just reached down to open the door and put her out of her misery when there was a small 'Come in.'

She was lying in bed, very white against the sheet, and in that big room oddly and unusually small. She managed a frightened smile.

'Oh, hello, Perry. Is it you? I'm glad you've come.'

'Hello, Chris. How are you, old girl?'

'Getting over it. I hope to be up and about tomorrow.'

(Up and about is the sort of phrase Chris uses. She probably barges round the Guides' camps bellowing 'Rise and Shine'.)

'Don't you think about getting up yet. There's nothing you can do: the police have taken over the whole wing. Just you try and make a proper statement to Hamnet—he's the CID man—then stay put where you are.'

'The CID? Then it's definitely murder?'

'Oh yes, I'd say so. But you knew that, didn't you?'

Chris shook her head. 'I didn't know. I just couldn't believe—I mean, who would do anything like that? I mean—*like that*?'

'Somebody, my lass. So we'll just have to face up to it. Would you like to tell me what happened?'

'I suppose I can try, if I've got to tell the—*them*, tomorrow. Well, I went up to bed at my usual time.'

'When's that?'

'About half past ten. I have to get up early to do most of the housework before Daddy gets down. Got down. Anyway, when I went to bed, Daddy went . . . downstairs. To . . . well, you know. When he did it, it was always after I'd gone to bed, in case I was disturbed by the . . . bumps. He was awfully considerate like that.'

Charming olde-worlde courtesy, I thought. But I just nodded.

'Well, about a quarter past twelve I . . . er . . . still hadn't got to sleep—'

'Why?'

'No reason, I just hadn't. And so I came down to the kitchen to get an aspirin or something. It's on the first floor of the wing, you remember, and you can . . . hear. And so I heard, and I thought: this isn't right. He *never* did it for that long. And I ran downstairs into the Gothic room and—'

'Were the lights on?'

'Yes, very bright. And I saw—'

She stopped, sobbing, and I sat on the bed and put my arms around her, like I did when our mother died. Eventually she calmed down and wiped her eyes.

'Did you notice the cut cord?' I asked.

Chris nodded. 'I dashed over and switched the thing off, and it

—he—came down with a last bump and he seemed about six inches away and it was—horrible. I screamed and ran out of the wing into the house, and screamed and screamed.'

'Who came out to you first?'

'Oh dear. McWatters, I think. Did you know he wears a night-shirt? Oh no, you don't know him. Then Mrs Mac. Then—Mordred, I think, and later Sybilla.'

'What did they do?'

'Someone—McWatters, I think—ran to the Gothic wing, then dashed back and called the police. He told them to bring a doctor, but he must have known . . . *I* knew.'

'I see. Then they put you to bed?'

'Yes. They tried slapping me, and water, but Mordred said it was barbaric and the doctor would be here in a minute. So they got me to bed, and I don't remember much more. Eventually I talked a bit to the police, but I kept—'

'I know. Well, it's over now. Perhaps Hamnet won't need to talk to you again about that. I'll report back to him. Chris, what had things been like in the family recently?'

'Oh, you know, much as usual. We each lived in our own wings, but still—it isn't an easy house to live in, Perry.'

'I know,' I said.

'But I don't complain. It's always the way, isn't it? The men go off and do the glamorous and exciting jobs and the women get left behind looking after the older generation. It's always been like that and I suppose it always will be.'

Hmmm, well, I thought. I'd been getting stuff like this in letters from my sister recently, showing, I suppose, that this kind of low-est-common-denominator feminism has at last filtered down into the kind of magazine my sister reads. As the bandwagon grinds slowly to a halt, my sister hears of the movement. Now, the fact of the matter is that my sister stayed home with my father because she had no aptitude for any kind of interesting job and wanted to inherit what was going. Highly sensible reasons, of which I heart-ily approve, but no basis for a good feminist whine. My great-aunts, daughters of the redoubtable Josiah, may not have had much choice, but Chris did, and made it. And if anyone by some laughable contingency had offered Chris a glamorous and exciting job, she would have cast a pall of the humdrum over it within hours of signing on. Still, this wasn't quite the time for saying things like that.

'You say it wasn't easy. What especially do you mean? Had there been any rows, any big problems?'

'Nothing out of the ordinary, really. Aunt Kate has been very odd since her breakdown, as I suppose you'll have noticed.'

'Yes. But hardly *odder*. Better on the whole, I thought.'

'Perhaps. But you never know where you are. What else? Oh, people were always complaining about the Squealies. Then there was a great fuss over some picture or other—'

'Oh?'

'Aunt Sybilla was going to redecorate one of the guestrooms. You know she sometimes feels her artistic talents aren't stretched to the full these days.' (When my sister says things like that there is not a hint of irony. I have heard her refer to our father as a great composer. She is a true Trethowan.) 'She went looking for something that was put up in a lumber-room when they first hung Aunt Eliza's pictures of the family in the drawing-room. But you know how it is. That was twenty-five or thirty years ago. They couldn't find the picture.'

'I see. What was it?'

'I don't know. Rossetti, or Holman Hunt, or somebody.'

'Did she think it had been stolen?'

'Oh—you know: she went around saying it was very *odd,* and telling Mordred he ought to do an inventory of the whole house— as if poor Morrie hasn't got enough to do with the family history. It would take years. Anyway, I wouldn't be surprised if it didn't turn up, in some room or other.'

'Very likely it will. There must be some nobody's been in since the builders moved out. So Father wasn't really at the centre of any of these rows, was he?'

'No, not really. He sort of stirred things up, now and then. Helped them along. Of course, it's awful to say things about him now he's dead . . .'

'If you don't, we'll probably never find out who did it.'

'No. Well, he said he thought we should get somebody qualified to do the inventory—implying poor Morrie wasn't, and that was a red rag to Aunt Sybilla. In any case, it's almost all Uncle Lawrence's property, in fact.'

'And he didn't want an investigation?'

'Oh, I think he did say it would be a good idea. But then I suppose he had one of his days, or something. Anyway, one way or another the whole idea got forgotten.'

'Chris, you've been with Father these last fifteen years. He wasn't an easy man to get along with, I know. Which of the family would you say hated him most?'

Chris thought for a bit. 'Well, I suppose you, Perry.'

'Apart from me,' I said impatiently. 'Let me tell you I have an absolutely cast-iron alibi, otherwise I wouldn't be here.'

'I wouldn't say anybody actually hated him,' said Cristobel, resuming her pensive pose. 'It sounds so melodramatic. I mean, he and Maria-Luisa sometimes had words about the Squealies. They're lovely children, but they must have been particularly trying to someone *musical*, don't you think? And Mordred was a *little* bit put out when he wanted the professional art-historian in to do the inventory. Nothing more than that. He and Syb jogged along much as they always did.'

'And how did you get on with him, Cristobel?'

'All right. We went our own ways. I did most of the cooking and cleaning in this wing, but I had a lot of free time. I have the Guides and that. And I'm great friends with the vicar's wife, and I sing in the choir. He didn't interfere. Most of us in this house go our own ways, you know. On the whole it works very well.'

I got up with a vague feeling of dissatisfaction.

'There's precious little to go on so far. Precious little in the way of possible motive. It just seems senselessly cruel and pointless.'

'Senseless? Do you mean a . . . a lunatic might have done it? Someone from outside? Or Aunt Kate?'

'I wasn't pointing at Aunt Kate,' I said. 'If she did it, I'd bet it was for a very good reason. Well—you'd better get some sleep now, Chris. I'll pass all this on to Hamnet, to spare you as much as possible tomorrow. If I were you I'd stop there and get a bit more of your strength back.'

I kissed her and moved over to the door. It was just as I was opening it that Cristobel came out with her most interesting idea so far.

'Perry,' she said, 'has it occurred to you that one of the Squealies might have done it? In play, I mean?'

6

NIGHT PIECE

I went back in and closed the door.

'Do you think that's possible, Chris? Could they have got through the house without being seen?'

'I think so. It's a big house, and we each live in our separate wings. You can hear people coming miles off and get out of the way. Uncle Lawrence would be the one they'd be most likely to meet, and you can certainly hear his wheels. Anyway, he's often in Kate's wing these days—he certainly was last night. She's the one who looks after him.'

'Kate implied they often got out.' (I realized this sounded like caged animals, but so be it.)

'They do. Not all that often, but they do. Mostly they play together. They're not . . . terribly well behaved.'

'So I noticed. They struck me as complete monsters. But do you think one of them might actually—'

'Well, of course, they wouldn't *realize* what they were doing. It would just be in fun, they'd think. But they are *awfully* naughty sometimes. They just don't think.'

'Do you think anyone could have used them? Put the suggestion into their minds? One of their parents . . . ?'

'Oh Perry! Of course not! Nobody could be so *wicked* as to use a little child like that!'

Poor innocent Cristobel! I saw I had distressed her. 'I expect you're right,' I said. 'Now you get a good night's sleep, Chrissy, and I'll see you in the morning.'

I went back to my room. I didn't feel ready for bed yet, and certainly not for sleep. I showered in a luxurious flow of water (none of your miserable modern trickles for Harpenden House) and soaped vigorously, as if to wash off the slime of such a home-coming. That was marvelous, but it was while I was doing it that my mind, still over-active, started to grapple with an odd feeling of dissatisfaction—something niggling away at the back of my mind that refused to come forward, you know how it is. Of course the whole day had not been of the sort to make me pirouette for joy, as you will have gathered, but there was something else—something that had not been quite . . . it was something, yes—that was when the feeling had begun—something connected with my talk with Cristobel.

It was while I was towelling myself down that it came to me: she wasn't relieved enough that I had come.

Now don't get the wrong idea about this. I suppose you're thinking that this is a big *macho* thing on my part: he wants little sister to sob on his chest and say 'Now you've come, Perry, I feel safe,' and all that stuff that flatters the male ego and may have some truth in it or no truth at all. He thinks she should have made him feel tough and capable and in control.

No, it's not that at all. But I know Cristobel, and just think yourself of the situation: here is a girl, not very bright or very confident, who has just found her father murdered in a peculiarly horrible manner; she is surrounded by nuts whom she cannot find very congenial or put any great trust in; along comes a brother, a policeman, whom she is fond of and who is (on the surface) pretty sure of himself and who ought to be a pillar of strength and relia-bility to her. You would expect her to be pleased, to feel a load off her mind—in short, to be relieved.

Now, I think Chrissy was pleased to see me as a person. And yet . . . I pinned it down: I wasn't convinced she was pleased to see me as a policeman.

And that was odd, and thought-provoking, and disturbing.

For some reason my mind went back to a talk I'd had with

Cristobel ten years or so before. It was while I was still in the army, when I was thinking of going over to the CID. And it was four years after I had flung myself out of this house, shouting at my father that he was a dirty-minded, sadistic mediocrity. I was giving Chris lunch in London, and I could see that she was lonely and unhappy, and rather nauseated by my father's tastes and habits. I urged her to get a job, but she resisted, and I could see that she was counting on the money from Father—such as it would be—to give her some kind of independence when he died. Anyway, I was a bit upset by her position in the house, and I actually suggested I try for a reconciliation with Father, so that I could visit her more often.

'Oh, I don't think that's at all possible,' Cristobel had said. 'He was *deeply* wounded.'

'What, at my calling him a sadist?'

'No. At your calling him a mediocrity.'

Well, that figured. Or had seemed to at the time. Still, I recalled that conversation now, and wondered if Cristobel had ever wanted a reconciliation between me and the family. At times like this, you know, nasty thoughts even about the comparatively near and dear do occur to one.

I put on pyjamas and went over to the desk, where my note-book lay, white and inviting. I opened the window: the night air outside was warm, even heavy. It was early autumn—season of mists and mellow fruitfulness. Or of decay and death, if you are in that frame of mind. I sat at the great Victorian desk, big enough to store a couple of bodies in, drew my notebooks towards me and took up my pen.

'Why *that* way?' was the first thing I wrote.

I'd told Joe that that was *just* the way one of my family *would* kill somebody, and I held by that. Still, almost any other way would have been quicker, cleaner, safer. Whoever did it must surely have been *seen* by my father to do it. And there was no guarantee that my father would not be heard, crying for help. I jotted down: 'Lights on'. It was a spectacular but exceedingly dangerous way of getting rid of anybody, and it almost suggested that the method

was part of the point—that the murder was some kind of appropriate revenge, some ghastly tit-for-tat affair.

Which in its turn suggested some victim of my father's peculiarly perverted mind.

I next wrote: 'Scissors? Knife? Where are they?'

Whatever it was had been used, it was in effect the murder
implement, and would have to be found, even if it brought us no
closer to any particular individual. And that, to a practical policeman, immediately suggested an army of PCs swarming through
the house. If a proper search of the house were to be made, let
alone of the grounds, it would take days. Which would *not* please
Aunt Sybilla. But perhaps I could suggest they search for the missing picture at the same time?

I wrote. 'Picture. Get description. Painter.'

Then I wrote: 'Financial situation. Not just Father's. Lawrence's. All the rest too.'

That, surely, Tim Hamnet would do. I hoped Chrissy would be
left fairly well off—a tidy sum would be only her just deserts. My
father, though, when I knew him, was not careful with money,
even though he had always hated to be swindled. He was the last
person in the world to care whether anybody else would be well
off or hard up after he died. Lawrence *should* be very comfortably
off. With the house, in the male line, went a hell of a lot of money.
But these days, none of the whacking fortunes were quite what
they were. There had been inflation, the house itself must be a
terrible millstone, there was Peter, who seemed to have no visible
means of support. Day-to-day living in the house seemed much
more frugal than in my time. Was Lawrence becoming miserly in
his old age, as so frequently happened, or were there solid reasons
for the frugality? At least the house—that is, Lawrence—had tremendous assets, of every kind.

I wrote down: 'Pictures. Worth how much?'

The Times kept me informed of saleroom prices. Little-known
Victorian painters were often fetching quite fantastic sums these
days. Not to mention the moderns—and under Aunt Eliza's super-
vision quite a lot of first-rate stuff had been bought for Harpenden
in the 'twenties and 'thirties. Interesting.

On the other hand, it was not immediately apparent how the financial state of the head of the family could have any bearing on the death of my father.

I got up and walked around a bit. There was this to be said about Harpenden: it gave you room to move about. Hour by hour, in fact, I felt myself expanding. Space itself took on a new dimension, and I felt in a relation to things quite different from the one I was in in the little flat in Maida Vale, where the three of us lived. Thinking about us I thought about Daniel, and thinking about Daniel I (most unfairly) thought about the Squealies. There was the possibility that one of them (*not* all together, surely—I could not imagine all five of them moving through the house with murderous stealth) had crept over to the Gothic wing and snipped through the cord. This would argue, I thought, a certain mechanical aptitude, or that the Squealy in question had watched my father 'at it' before. Not impossible. The eldest Squealy was—what? —about ten. Still, I didn't find it altogether probable. There was also the possibility that the murderer (or the Trethowans in general, closing ranks under attack, as was their wont) would put it about that that was what had happened. Even persuade one of the Squealies to confess. Though that might prove a highly dangerous course.

But so would be the other possibility: persuading a Squealy to do it and instructing it how. Hideously dangerous. But perhaps not quite so dangerous if the persuader were one of its parents.

It was just at this point in my perambulations about the great guest bedroom that I thought I heard something. I crossed to the window and stuck out my head: undoubtedly I had heard something, and what it was was sounds of fury, of altercation. And it wasn't difficult to guess where they came from. I stuck my feet into slippers and quick as a flash I was out of the room, down the great staircase, and out of one of the back doors. I pulled the door to: McWatters had given me all the necessary keys, so I could get back in. I made off through the garden, finding to my pleasure that I knew every tree, every flower-bed. The air was warm and still, the garden a mass of looming, menacing shapes, the moon through the trees highlighting the nearly bare branches. The leaves on the

ground were like a pillow under my slippered feet. I skulked towards the Elizabethan wing.

The two wings on the back of the house were the Florentine
wing (occupied by Sybilla and Mordred) and the Elizabethan (occupied by Peter and his brood). It required no great deductive
genius to guess that if anyone was bawling their lungs out at twelve
o'clock at night, it was likely to come from the Elizabethan wing. I
darted from tree to tree, hugging the shade, shunning the moon-
light. In no more than a couple of minutes I had landed up safe
under an oak, hardly twenty feet from the lighted living-room
window.

And boy! they were really going at it. There was Pete, standing
in a filthy old sweater and baggy trousers, his foot resting on a
chair, his whisky glass in his hand. And there was Maria-Luisa,
hands on her hips, if there were still hips under that great bulging
front, tossing her head, bending forward to give point to her
hisses of hatred and contempt—looking, in fact, for all the world
like Anna Magnani in one of those post-war neo-realistic films.
And they were really handing it out, both of them. She, louder
and shriller, but he really with considerable expertise and relish. I
had to hand it to him: he was holding his own, all right.

As far as I could make out, of course. Because ninety per cent of
all this was going on in Italian, which is really the only language to
quarrel in. They made such good use of it that I don't think I
missed all that much, artistically, by not understanding: this wasn't
an exercise in logic. Still, as a policeman I would dearly like to
have known what it was all about. Now and then Pete would let fly
with a phrase or two in English: 'You stupid bitch, you've got it
wrong as usual' was one; 'Why don't you fucking learn English,
then you might understand what's going on?' was another. These
were phrases principally for his own satisfaction: it was like shouting insults at a Lambretta. On and on she went, higher and
higher, working herself up to a final orgasm of fury.

I noticed, while this process was at a point of screw-turning
tension, that her eye was suddenly caught by her own whisky glass
standing on the table, and if Pete hadn't been shouting so hard he
might have noticed too. Advancing a step, she seized it in her

capable kitchen hands and launched it with its contents straight at his head.

'*Bruto! Barbaro! Seduttore! Assassino!*'

It didn't need even as much as holiday Italian to understand that last one, and to wonder whether it was part of Maria-Luisa's normal repertoire of abuse, or a statement of fact or opinion.

7

THE YOUNGER GENERATION

I awoke on Friday morning to the sound of policemen in the house. The sound is quite unmistakable, at least to a policeman: heavy men trying to move discreetly. I poked my head round the bedroom door: hordes of them—down in the hall, up the staircase, on the landing. Hamnet was really intending to take the place apart.

McWatters brought me breakfast on a tray, a substantial and traditional bacon-and-egg affair. He was too sensible to apologize to me for the infestation of policemen. I ate well, then I shaved and dressed and went to see what was going on. If the police were everywhere, the family was not: only Aunt Sybilla seemed to be around in the main part of the house. I expected her to be creating merry hell, but in fact she was sitting, robed and turbaned, in a small study off the hall, in pensive attitude, as if going through her Blue Period. I slipped in to have a word with Hamnet, and said I thought she was unusually quiet, given the circumstances.

'Used it all up last night,' said Tim in his phlegmatic way.

'Bad?'

'Incredible. Stood me out it was suicide, or accident, or possibly both. Said she was going to get on the phone to the Home Secretary who was a personal friend, but it turned out she was thinking of the last one but seven. But phew! I think she must be what they call a *grande dame*.'

'She'd like to think so,' I said. 'Did you get anything out of her in the end?'

'Not a thing. As far as movements were concerned, she was in bed. No doubt they all were. As far as motive is concerned, she knew of nothing whatsoever. Everything was hunky-dory.'

'Hmm,' I said. 'Can you imagine this lot living together and everything being hunky-dory?'

I told him about the hypothetically missing picture, suggested his searchers should keep their eyes open, pending more details, and then I drifted off into the grounds.

My idea was that, since it was a fine day, the Squealies might be playing outside, and that I might detach one of the older ones and talk to it in an uncle-like fashion, and perhaps get things out of it that a policeman could not. A pretty fatuous idea, actually, because they did not know me as an uncle and I do look awfully like a policeman. And anyway, as Tim Hamnet found out later, they are only to be detached from one another by the strength of three men. In any case, they weren't in the grounds—I would have heard them—but I wandered around for a bit, partly for old time's sake, partly to see if anyone would spot me from the window and come out for a chat. I was just standing on the edge of a spinney down by the lake, now thick with weeds, when along came Mordred. I don't know if he had seen me from the window, but he came purposefully, all bright-eyed and bushy-tailed, neat and dapper in a tailor-made suit, and looking as if he'd just washed behind both his ears, and felt all the better for it.

'That's the tree you fell out of when you were five,' he said, pointing, 'and that's the lake you pushed me into when you were ten.'

He was full of beans, and doing none of the House of the Dead stuff. Still, none of them were.

'What a memory you have,' I replied in kind. 'I can see you're the family historian.'

'For my sins,' he said with a wry grimace. 'And until some academic job comes up in somewhere other than Qatar or Abu Dhabi. The damnable thing is, what with the general family publicity mania and now this, if I did ever get the thing finished it would probably be a best-seller. It would sell better than Pete's *magnum opus,* anyway.'

'Pete writes, does he?'

'What else?'

'What on?'

'Let him bore you with it. He'll be delighted. I hear your wife's coming tonight.'

'Now, how in God's name—?'

'Calm down. I haven't been listening in to your calls. I heard at the Marquis of Danby when I slipped down for a double Scotch last night. I can see why you don't want them here, but do bring her up for a meal, won't you?'

'If she sets her mind on it, I don't see how I can stop her,' I said gloomily. 'Short of its being one of Aunt Kate's nights.'

'She was on on Wednesday. It'll be another ten days before she's on again. With a bit of luck even you will avoid her spinach blancmange.'

'How do you stand it?' I asked.

'You mean the family in general, I take it, rather than the spinach blancmange?' He considered for a moment—really, I thought, he is quite nice, and not unintelligent. 'Well, I suppose the brute fact of the matter is that it's better than teaching. Teaching in an ordinary school, I mean. Almost anything is better than that. So long as I'm part of the great army of the unemployed I can stand it here. I'm used to my Mama's little ways, and as for the rest—well, they must appear appalling to you because you've been so long away, but I find I can put up with them.'

'I hear you're looking into this notion your mother has got that a picture has disappeared from the house.'

He raised his eyebrows to heaven. 'Just what I was going to have a chat to you about last night. If it was only *one* picture, though . . .'

'She thinks a lot have gone?'

'Once she got the idea, she started thinking of things she'd known as a child—pictures, furniture, Great-Grandfather Josiah's christening spoon, God knows what. Then she'd scream they were missing, cry blue murder—and then of course she'd find them and go quiet. On the Rampage and Off the Rampage, as Joe Gargery says. Personally I don't know what to think.'

'You mean not everything's been found?'

'No, alas: we'd get some peace if it had been. Of course, stuff gets lost, furniture breaks, things get given away. But certainly there seem to be things missing.'

'What picture was it that set all this off?'

'It was a thing by Holman Hunt, called *The Rustic Wedding*. A sort of companion piece to *The Hireling Shepherd*.' I shuddered. 'Yes, indeed. I remember it dimly from childhood, and it too has greens that sear the eyeballs. Which makes it odder that it can't be found. Likewise a picture by William Allan entitled *Lord Byron Reposing in the House of a Turkish Fisherman After Having Swum the Hellespont*.'

'Christ.'

'Exactly. But if I remember it rightly, it's not something you could just tuck away somewhere.'

'But you remember it framed.'

'True. That's a point. Anyway, the fact is that these, at least, seem to be gone. Then there are Aunt Eliza's—that's another problem. Nice old thing, as I remember her, but not the most methodical of women, and her will, I hear, was a mess. Who owns the ones that are here, were there more here when she died? The fact is, I agree there should be a proper inventory made. Because the security in the house is far from impressive, and it could be that any one of us is taking them off and popping them, one by one. As my dear mother, in her nice way, made us all very much aware.'

'I gather it was suggested a professional might do the inventory.'

'Exactly. Your papa's bright contribution. Now, the advantage of this suggestion—you don't mind if I abuse your papa, do you?'

'Be my guest.'

'Well, the advantage of this suggestion was that it *looked* as if your papa was keen to get the job done properly and insisting it be done by an outsider. And it *is* work for an expert, not for a dilettante like me. But the fact is, the expert could only deal with what

is here now. He wouldn't know a thing about what *should* be here
but isn't. So the proposal, to my ears, smelt just the tiniest bit
fishy.'

'I see your point. Or it could have been pure mischief-making.'

'Of which your late papa knew a thing or two. Precisely. Anyway I did a bit of work on it, from the family papers and that, but
by then it had all begun to die down and I dropped it. I might
have done more if Uncle Lawrence had been willing to pay me,
but *that* would have been out of the question, knowing the dear
old phoney.'

'Are the family finances rocky?'

Mordred turned his eyes in the direction of the horizon: we
could see Thornwick in the distance, and some prosperous housing estates of a private kind in between.

'I don't see how they can be, do you? It's all ours, all that. Still
ours. Lawrence should be bathing in the stuff.'

'That's not quite the impression given.'

'You noticed the inclination to pinch the odd penny, did you?'

'I never expected supermarket sherry in this house.'

'Precisely. Though we're all good children and say we prefer it.
If you'd like a guess at the reason for all this, I'd say it's because he
hasn't been able to bring himself to make the house and all the
doings over to Pete.'

'Of course!' I said. 'So the death duties—'

'Will be colossal. The only time I ever remember the subject
coming up, he muttered: "Heed the Bard. Remember King
Lear." I suppose he foresees himself being turned out into a Cor-
poration old people's home—our modern equivalent of the heath.
I imagine he's penny-pinching in anticipation of death duties—
though that doesn't quite make sense either, unless he's salting it
away somewhere secret. The fact is, Uncle Lawrence is only passing fond of Peter, but he absolutely dotes on the Squealies.'

'So I noticed. He's totally senile, I take it.'

'Only so-so. He can tell a hawk from a handsaw when the
wind's southerly. Anyway, the fact is, it could be Lawrence putting
the pictures up for sale, as is his perfect right.'

'And being too embarrassed to say?'

'Exactly. So what you've got here is either a fine old can of worms, or conceivably a storm in a teacup.

'Had all this caused much trouble—for example, between my father and Uncle Lawrence?'

'Not that I noticed. There was no more than the normal quota of sniping, heavy ironies, double-edged innuendoes and so on— the usual currency of communication in this house.'

We had been walking through the golden trees, under falling leaves, and we now arrived back at the lawn behind the house. Mordred paused in the shade of a tree.

'See that window in the Elizabethan wing?' he said. 'That's Peter's sitting-room.'

'I know. I spied on him last night. I saw Maria-Luisa clock him with a whisky glass.'

'Good for her. Now, in that window is my cousin—our cousin— Pete. And I bet you anything you like that if you walk across this lawn alone he will call you in and pump you for all you're worth.'

'How do you know?'

'I know Cousin Pete. Inheritor of Harpenden House, and future head of the Trethowan family.'

He started off in the direction of the Florentine wing, but I caught his arm and kept him a moment longer in the shadow.

'Morrie—if my wife comes here, can I rely on you?'

'What? To see they all behave themselves?'

'No—to make sure they don't. I want her to see them at their worst. I couldn't bear a big reconciliation, with family visits in the summer hols.'

'I'll do my best, but I should hardly think it will be necessary. With nerves all tensed up as they are now, anything can happen.'

With which prophecy of ferment Morrie trotted off happily in the direction of the Florentine wing—his tie as straight as when he had emerged, his shoes as spick and dust-free. There are some men nature can't touch.

But he was dead right about Pete. Because I was just strolling, oh so casual, in the direction of the main block, when he appeared in his sitting-room window.

'Oh, I say, Perry—' I turned coolly. 'I say, are you at leisure, or on the beat, as it were?'

'Pretty much at leisure,' I said.

'Could I have a word with you, old man? Nothing frightfully important, but—'

I strolled over to him. 'But—?'

'But . . . I'd just like a word,' he concluded feebly. He was in that denim suit again, which made him look ten years older than his real age. Have you noticed it's only aging phoneys who wear denim suits? Well, it is, exclusively. This phoney had a bad bruise over his left eye, and I asked with concern: 'Been in an accident?'

'My marriage is one long accident,' said Pete gloomily. The sound of the Squealies, playfully scalping each other several floors up, lent point to his remark. 'I say, I'll come round to the side door and let you in.'

'Don't bother,' I said, easing myself up on to the window ledge and swivelling my legs round into the room.

'Maria-Luisa's all het up about security. Every door locked, and bolts on the one through to the main house. Crazy bitch. That's what comes of being born and bred among the Mafia.'

Peter and Maria-Luisa's sitting-room was a fairly comfortable affair, with a lot of 'thirties furniture retrieved from the main house, or perhaps left in this wing by Aunt Eliza. There was no great impress of personality on the room, however, unless it was the untidy scattering of books and papers around the place, which could have been strewn for my benefit.

'Excuse the mess,' said Peter perfunctorily. 'This is the overflow from my study.'

'I hear you write,' I said. (I would never have dreamt, by the way, of giving him an opening like that if it wasn't that I knew I had to find out something about him and his life.)

'Mmmm,' said Peter. 'At the moment I'm reviewing. A load of sex books, for the *New Spectator*.' He gestured towards the sofa, where lay a disorder of books, among them such surefire American best-sellers as *Sex and the Stock-Market* by Theodore S. Rosenheim and *Is There Sex After Death?* by Dr Philip Krumm-Kumfitt.

'I'm pretty much the *New Spectator*'s sex man these days,' said Peter contentedly.

'Really?' (Well, you think of a reply to that.)

'What with that and the novel, I've got my hands full,' he went on, with killing casualness.

'Novel?' I said, playing my part like a ventriloquist's dummy.

'Ye-e-es,' said Peter, as if reluctant to speak of it, but since I'd brought the topic up . . . 'A really big one, something on the scale of the old three-volume affairs.'

'Have you got far with it?'

'Oh, so-so.' He gestured with his hands, as if to indicate a thick pile. 'I write reams and discard a lot. Discard the whole time. I'm a perfectionist.'

'What . . . sort of thing is it?'

'Well, you know, novels today are all niminy-piminy little affairs, written by housewives between the nappy-changes, or academics in their summer hols. God! British novels these days are so unambitious! They're positively anaemic.'

'Yours will have blood, will it?'

'I see it as a sort of sexual odyssey, if you see what I mean, combined . . . com*bined* with an enormous social conspectus, a sort of diagnosis of current social ills, get what I mean? *Bleak House* was the model I had in mind.'

'I should have thought *Nightmare Abbey* might be a more appropriate model for someone living at Harpenden,' I said.

He looked at me closely. 'You don't like us very much, do you, Perry?'

I shrugged my shoulders. 'I only meant this house can't be the most peaceful place for a writer to work in.'

Peter wagged a fat finger at me. 'It's having the leisure that counts, it's not being a part-time writer. It's *only* the old upper classes—the *rem*nants of the upper classes—that have the *time* to conceive anything really *big* these days. Look at your father—'

'He never conceived anything bigger than a musical fart in his whole life,' I protested.

'Well, he was a bit different,' Pete admitted. 'What I meant was, he had *leisure*. He could *wait* on inspiration.'

'He certainly waited,' I agreed. 'What was it you wanted to talk to me about, Pete?'

This chat was not going very well, and I wasn't helping it to go any better. Wasn't I supposed to be worming my way into their confidences? Hearing their artless, gushing confessions? I was hardly going to succeed in that if I made it so abundantly plain I couldn't stand any manjack of them. And my direct question had very obviously embarrassed Pete, who had clearly intended to come round to this topic via several B-roads, public footpaths and back alleys.

'I just wondered . . .' he muttered, '. . . you know . . . how the police were . . . regarding the case. How it was going . . . Whether they were getting any leads.'

'You'll no doubt have a chance to ask Superintendent Hamnet that yourself before long.'

'Well, yes, that's partly the point . . . You're the expert, Perry. I was wondering how to approach that . . . interview. Wondering what line I should take.'

I raised my eyebrows. This really took the biscuit. What could one do but take refuge in cliché? 'What can you expect me to say but that you should tell the truth?'

'Oh, come off it, Perry. Don't be so bloody Dixon of Dock Green. There's truth and truth. Now, take this suggestion that one of my kids may have done it.'

'Ah! Whose suggestion is that?'

'Oh, it's . . . going around. Now, what line am I supposed to take on that, for example?'

He grinned, as if somehow he'd made a point I was incapable of seeing. 'You don't have to take any line,' I said, exasperated. 'All he'll want to know is whether it could have happened. Could they have got out of this wing, for example?'

'We *usually* lock them in their bedrooms,' said Peter. 'On the other hand, we sometimes forget.'

'Did you forget the night before last?'

'How should I remember? It was chaos that night. The suggestion hadn't come up then.'

'And Maria-Luisa? Does she remember?'

'Oh, she'll swear herself black and blue it was locked. She'd do that if everyone else had heard them rampaging through the house. Perjury isn't a crime in Sicily: it's a family duty.'

'There probably wouldn't be any question of perjury. The case could hardly come to court. They're obviously too young to know what they're doing.'

'That's rather what I thought,' said Pete speculatively.

'Unless, of course,' I proceeded weightily, 'someone put them up to it.'

Pete darted a sharp glance at me. 'Oh, come off it. You've seen my kids. Can you imagine them doing something they'd been put up to?'

I spread out my hands. 'Perhaps. If the idea appealed to them. If they thought it was fun. It might depend on their relationship with whoever it was.'

'Meaning me or Maria-Luisa, no doubt. Hmmm. Yes, well I can see there are dangers in that line.'

'Why,' I asked nastily, 'are you trying to take a line? What are you trying to cover up?'

'I'm not trying to cover anything up, I'm just trying to get the whole silly business over and done with.' He bent forward in his chair opposite me, in a gesture of intimacy I shrank back from. 'Look, Perry: you know what your father was. He was an insignificant little troublemaker without an ounce of talent. I'm not particularly happy he's been done in,' (he said this rather quickly, as if he realized he was laying himself open) 'but I'm not going to pretend I care a button either. Even if it was, say, McWatters or Mrs Mac. They do a good job, and we couldn't cope if we lost them. If admitting one of the kids might have done it—and they might have—will get us back to normal so that I can get on with some work, then so be it. I still might, if you forget this daft idea they might have been put up to it, and if I can knock some sense into their silly cow of a mother. You know us, Perry. You can't expect any conventional law and order stuff in this house.'

'Even if it means leaving a murderer at large among you?'

'I can take care of myself,' he said, puffing out some flab.

'Well,' I said, getting up, 'you're obviously going to take your own way, whatever I advise. But I'll tell you one thing: if it was one of your children, doing it in a spirit of youthful fun, you can be pretty sure Hamnet will find it out.'

'Will he interview them?' said Pete admiringly. 'Christ, I wouldn't be in his shoes.'

'Obviously he'll have to, since this has come up. I'm sure he'll know the best way to deal with them.'

Pete narrowed his eyes: 'What do you mean by that? I know you police: he'll try and bully them into saying one of us put them up to it. I tell you, if he lays a finger on one of them, I'll get my lawyer on to him and have him up for assault.'

'Good to know you think the law has its uses,' I said, vaulting out of the window.

And I walked back to the main block, happily chewing over the notion that Pete was willing to dub one of his own kids in, if it would win him a bit of peace and quiet. Which no doubt was what the quarrel was about last night. All things considered, I thought my cousin Pete was as nasty a specimen of humanity as I had met in years of treating with the criminal classes, and it was good to know that the Trethowan estates were to go to such a worthy inheritor.

8

LUNCH WITH UNCLE LAWRENCE

When I went back into the house, Aunt Sybilla called me into the dark little study off the entrance hall, once, I believe, my grandfather's business room where he dealt with all the estate accounts, now a rather unattractive writing-room. I doubted whether much writing went on there as a general rule, and was quite sure Aunt Sybilla had spent the morning in it because it gave her a good view on to the hall, and hence on to the comings and goings in the house as a whole. Something seemed to have happened to put her into a better humour than when I saw her earlier.

'Well, Peregrine, I gave all possible help last night to your nice friend from the Force.'

When Aunt Sybilla lies, she does so with total conviction, and when she is found out lying she can summon up a truly Pecksniffian self-righteous outrage.

'I'm sure he's grateful,' I said.

'I hope so. Have you seen the papers today?'

'No,' I shuddered. So this was the cause of the beam of sunlight that had brightened her morning.

'Well, I got on to my friends in Fleet Street. Not all of them. Some of them had died!' She said this in a tone of affront, as if they had deserted their posts. 'As a result, there's only a silly little piece in the *Grub*. But otherwise we've been done proud! They've given us a really good spread!'

'Aunt Sybilla, do you think—?'

'I shall give them further *dribbles* of information from time to time. And, of course, exclusive interviews when it's over and the monster is caught. *Who* can it be, do you think, Perry? *Who* could wish to kill your father? A man without an enemy in the world. A verray parfit gentil knight, or the younger brother of one, at any rate.'

'I'm afraid, Aunt Sybilla, you should face up to the fact that it's most likely to have been someone in this house.'

'Impossible! Unless it was a Squealy. I do think that's a definite possibility. If it was, he'd be packed off to a Reformatory, wouldn't he?' Her face expressed delighted anticipation, but then it fell again. 'Not that it would make much difference. They keep coming all the time.'

'Did you want me for anything, Aunt Sybilla?'

'Did I what? Oh, yes. I've told Mrs McWatters that you will lunch with Lawrence. He's in good form today, thank heavens, so you should seize the chance. A good head-to-head, as the French say. Of course, we'd love to have had you ourselves. Mordred said especially to ask you because he really finds you quite interesting, but . . .'

'Thank you,' I said. 'I'm looking forward to a talk with Uncle.'

'Exactly. Get in while the going's good. Because tomorrow he could have Gone Off, as it were.'

So that was that. I was doomed to lunch with the famous Survivor of the Trenches. (I never found out, by the way, whether my Uncle Lawrence ever did any actual fighting in the First World War, or whether he so much as saw a trench. He was not eighteen until July 1918, and he certainly didn't lie about his age to get in early. Of course one could get killed as easily in the last days of the war as in the first, as Wilfred Owen found out, but malicious family rumour, fostered by my father, suggested that Lawrence's closest view of the war, like Hemingway's, was from the front end of a stretcher while serving in the Ambulance Corps. It was on leave in

December 1918, in the euphoria of peace, that Lawrence met and married his first wife, a chorus girl.)

I went along to have a bit of a natter with Tim Hamnet. He had been interviewing Aunt Kate, and looked dazed. I told him about the paintings, and he sent a message through to his men to keep their eyes open for any rustic scene in liver-congealing greens, and any picture with Turkish overtones. We discussed the Squealy idea, which seemed to possess such attractions for the various adult occupants of the house: we weren't really sold on the notion; though, as Tim said, there was something about the method of the murder which suggested a naughty child. To fill in the half-hour until lunch I went off and glanced at the papers. And then wished I hadn't. FAMOUS FAMILY'S TORTURE CHAMBER shrieked one. TORTURE HORROR IN STATELY HOME yelled another. The stories were in kind, and I began to get rather angry until I suddenly decided that really you couldn't blame the journalists: when they blew something up from nothing and persecuted inoffensive citizens—that's when you should get angry. But this was hardly nothing, and it had been handed to them on a plate by publicity-crazed Sybilla. One would have to be a saint not to rub one's hands a bit at a story like that, and Fleet Street seldom runs to saints.

Lunch was simple, mostly salad, and it was served by Mrs McWatters.

'McWatters is in with the policemen, helping with Mrs Trethowan,' she explained, and I couldn't remotely think what she meant.

She was a stern-faced, rigid woman, the sort who look as if they go around singing 'Their land brought forth frogs' under their breath all day. I wondered how someone whose soul seemed to have been entered by the iron of Presbyterianism could bear to live day by day in the vicinity of the Trethowans.

Uncle Lawrence was in a little motorized chair, and he got himself into the room and up to the head of the table with a good deal of dexterity. On his good days he could easily do without Kate, which was worth remembering. On ground-floor level, anyway, he was as mobile as if he had the use of his legs. At least now he knew who I was, and he greeted me expansively.

'Ah, Perry, m'boy. How are things? Sorry I wasn't at m'best yesterday. These things happen at my age, y'know. They looking after you all right?'

'Very well indeed, thank you.'

'You'll have to come more often, now your father's gone, eh? See to—what's her name?—Cristobel, now she's on her own. I suppose she gets the loot, eh?'

'I sincerely hope so, if there is any.'

'What? If there is any? 'Course there is. Rolling. Must be. What did he have to spend it on, eh?'

'Do-it-yourself strappado machines,' I suggested.

Lawrence roared with laughter. 'Dear me. Most unseemly. Brother's going, and all that. Still. When you think of it: those that live by the sword shall perish by the sword, what? eh? Same principle.'

There was a dreadful cheeriness about Uncle Lawrence's discussion of my father's death that was hardly decent. After all, he could scarcely have disliked him as much as I did, otherwise he'd have booted him out of the house long ago. In the intervals of his wheezy chuckles he was tucking heartily into his meal. Salad wasn't the easiest thing for a man partly paralyzed by a stroke to eat: he intently got a few bits of this and that on to his fork, then effortfully raised it to his mouth, the last few inches—past his oh-so-Bohemian cravat—being particularly painful. Still, he managed, and chatted on in his old way the meanwhile.

'Have any contact with y'father, Perry, after you left?'

'None whatsoever.'

'No reconciliation, eh? What was the trouble?'

'I believe he objected to my calling him a mediocrity.'

This delighted Lawrence. 'Seriously? How splendid! Well, he wasn't much, was he? Dried-out little talent, that's about all you could call it. You'd've thought setting Swinburne might have inspired him, eh? chap like that. But it didn't. At the end there was even less. It just trickled away and he wrote nothing. Too busy with his infernal machines, what?'

'Did he have any—what shall I say?—accomplices in his special tastes? I mean—' this was horribly awkward—'he didn't pay people to beat him, or anything?'

Lawrence guffawed again. 'No, he was essentially a man of solitary vices.' But he thought, and I think he perceived that the drift of my question might have led the search away from the occupants of Harpenden. 'Mind you, I don't know what he did when he went to London. You can get all sorts of people to do things for you there, what?—sort of thing you wouldn't want to ask one of the gardeners to do. Soho's still what it was, eh? And then there's the little man who made his machines.'

'Did he come here?'

'Think so. Organized the installation and all that, don't you know. Never saw him m'self.'

'Did he go to London often?'

'Not so much in recent years. Too damned expensive. Still, I imagine he still had contacts.'

'You didn't have any quarrel with him yourself?'

'Quarrel? No. Didn't like the man. Couldn't be bothered to quarrel with him.'

'You didn't think he'd been taking pictures and selling them?'

'That damnfool idea of Sybilla's? No—nothing in it. Silly buzzard gets these bees in her bonnet. Not that there's not some valuable stuff in the house.' He fumbled stiffly in his pockets. 'Got a letter today. Some place or other in America. Philadelphia, that's it. Some damn woman writing. Setting up some kind of museum of female art. Ever heard such nonsense, eh? Lot of rubbish they'll have, eh? But they want some of Eliza's stuff. Got one already, want more. Hmm. Think I'll hold out on them for a bit. Make 'em more eager. They can't have much stuff as good as hers.'

I had looked into Germaine Greer's book on women painters and their wrongs, and remembering the dire assemblage of illustrations I could only agree. I didn't know which would be worse, the collection of paintings, or the sort of person who would go and see it. Still, it was all rather interesting. I noted that Lawrence was far from ruling out the idea of selling.

'There seems to be some idea going round,' I said casually,

'that one of Peter's children might have cut the cord—completely in play, of course.'

That really set Uncle Lawrence off. Obviously no one had dared broach the idea to him before.

'What? Whose idea was that? Absolute poppycock. Never heard such bilge in m'life. Little darlings! Have you ever seen such little sweetlings? Wouldn't enter their heads, not for a moment. They like a bit of fun and games, but they'd never do a thing like that. You stamp firmly on any talk you hear. Absolute balderdash.'

'I'm not madly keen on the idea myself,' I said calmly.

But Lawrence had clearly been upset, and now began to toy fretfully with his ice-cream. He seemed to be getting tired, because there was little more in the way of conversation to be got out of him, and he sat there muttering 'Poppycock' and 'nasty nonsense' and things of that kind, making me feel the most utter louse even for mentioning it.

Luckily, after a bit Mrs McWatters appeared and came over to whisper in my ear: 'The Inspector says, they've found the scissors, sir.'

'What? Speak up! No secrets here. What's that you're saying?' bellowed Uncle Lawrence.

'The Inspector,' said Mrs McWatters in a deep Clara-Butt-ex-horting-Britain-to-rule-the-waves voice, 'said to tell Mr Peregrine that the scissors have been found.'

'Scissors? What does he want scissors for? I could have lent them a pair of scissors if they'd asked,' said Uncle Lawrence.

9

PAPA'S PAPERS

The finding of the scissors that had cut the thread of my papa's destiny raised my spirits no end. It seemed to suggest—quite irrationally—that at last we might be getting somewhere, that before long there might be an end to this nightmare, and I might shake the dust of Harpenden House off my feet and head back to real life. Perhaps I wouldn't even stay for the funeral: no one had asked me to it, after all, and I had only come under the sternest call of duty. Almost without realizing it, I burst into song as I made my way through the hall and down the corridor to the Gothic wing:

> ' "Come down and redeem us from virtue,
>   Our lady of Pain." '

'Christ Almighty,' said Tim Hamnet, meeting me at the door of our wing. 'What's that?'

'A section of my father's masterwork, the song-cycle *Dolores*,' I said. 'To words by Swinburne. It should be sung by a tenor, but it doesn't make it sound any better. Come on, Tim, spill the beans. Where?'

'Stuffed down the side of a flowerpot. The earth was only slightly disturbed—bit of luck our chap noticed it. A London copper probably wouldn't have. I'll show you.' He led the way back to the hall, and then down the corridor leading (past numberless small, dark and totally useless rooms) to the Florentine wing. On an old, low occasional table was a pot containing the plant known as mother-in-law's tongue. I raised the bladelike leaves gently, and looked at the place where the scissors had been pushed down.

'Hmm. Interesting. What sort were they?'

'Largish pair of nail-scissors. Sharp—very good quality—German-made. You don't get that class of article from Sheffield these days. McWatters says they belonged in one of the downstairs bathrooms. I've sent them off to the boffins, but it's pretty obvious they did the job, isn't it?'

'For the moment I can't think of a hundred and one other reasons for stuffing a pair of nail-scissors down a flowerpot,' I said. 'Well, we're a step or so for'arder. We can certainly knock on the head the idea that it was one of the Squealies having a bit of childish fun. They'd just have dropped the scissors, or put them back where they found them.'

'Whereas anyone else—?'

'Would, I guess, have seen that the scissors, if they belonged to the house, and if the forensic bods could prove that they cut the cord, would have brought the murder home irrevocably to one of the inhabitants. Or at the very best to someone who knew the house well.'

'Your family have many friends these days, Perry?'

'Friends in the area? I don't get that impression. They don't seem to have been deluged by phone-calls of sympathy. I'm not surprised. Can you imagine old Jack 'Obbs from the village tottering up to have a natter about his rheumatiz with one of this lot? Of course, the McWatterses may have friends.'

'Remarkable chap, that. Engaging, too.'

'What on earth was he with you at lunchtime for? His better half—who is *not* engaging—said something about Mrs Trethowan. Sybilla calls herself Miss Trethowan these days, so I suppose she must have meant Maria-Luisa?'

'Yes. He was translating.'

'He was *what*?'

'Translating. Unorthodox, but since they didn't seem to be able to get anybody locally, and thinking of the time it would take to get someone from London, I decided to take the risk. She obviously had enough English to protest if he misrepresented what she said. Just won't speak it, the lazy bitch.'

'And how come the Admirable Crichton is fluent in gutter Italian?'

'War service, so he said.'

I calculated. 'The war's been over thirty-five years or so. That makes McWatters at least fifty-five. I'd have put him five or ten years younger myself, but he is sort of ageless. The quiet, withdrawn type that time doesn't line. Still, his wife looks all of mid-fifty, so I suppose it's probably true. Interesting in the circumstances, I must say. Did you get anything out of Maria-Luisa?'

'Protestations of the innocence of her infants, swearings to God and the Holy Virgin that they were locked in, maledictions—I learned the word *maledetto* without any trouble—on those who tried to pin such an atrocious crime on her innocent angels. Nothing of any substance, in other words.'

'Predictable, I suppose. Still, a bit more engaging than their ghastly father, whose first thought was to shop them for the crime.'

'Doing anything this afternoon, Perry?' said Tim. 'If not, I've got a job for you.'

'Interviewing the Squealies or something dangerous like that, I suppose? I think you should call in the Specials.'

'Actually, I'm doing that myself, with assistance. No, I'd like you to go upstairs into your father's quarters and go through all his papers and things. You know your way around up there, know where he kept all his stuff, I imagine, and it's possible you might come across something we might pass over.'

'I suppose I could. What am I looking for?'

'Well, obviously anything that could have caused trouble between your father and the family. Money, those pictures, anything of that sort. And possibly anything connected with his nasty little sexual practices. The person who made the machines, any pals with similar tastes—I'd like to know about them. Do you think he had contacts with others of his kind?'

'For all I know they held a von Sacher-Masoch memorial dinner once a year at the Savoy,' I said. 'Or else they got my Aunt Kate to cook one for them. Actually, that's what put me in mind of that song . . .'

'What song?'

> ' "When thy lips had such lovers to flatter;
> When the city lay red from thy rods," '

I bellowed.

'Don't do that, Perry, please.'

'That song-cycle *Dolores*. I wondered whether it wasn't some sort of covert announcement—of his tastes, I mean, and an appeal to others of his kind to make contact. It makes it pretty bloody obvious. On the other hand, Uncle Lawrence said not: implied it was very much a solitary thing with my papa.'

'Well, keep it in mind while you're looking around, eh, Perry?'

And so I climbed the stairs and at last went back to my childhood home. I can't describe the sensations I had: for minutes on end I just pushed open doors and wandered through the old rooms—so well remembered, and hardly changed. The drawing-room, my mother's little sitting-room, my father's library and study, my cosy round bedroom in the turret, and Cristobel's room just beside it. I imagine everybody going home after a long time away feels a bit like me. But I suppose most of them have a lot of happy memories. It wasn't that I had none; on the other hand, it wasn't those that came back to me. The oddest thing of all was that, though my father and Cristobel had lived here alone for fifteen years, it wasn't their presence I felt here at all: it was my mother's, investing every room with memories: I came upon her as I turned corners, I saw her back as she sat at her writing-desk, I imagined her lying on the sofa with a rug over her, I heard her thin voice calling to me. My mother—whom I'd barely thought of twice a year since I'd grown up and left home.

I think my mother was a sort of survival, one of a species that could not fend for itself in the modern world but had clung precariously on in tiny numbers. I suppose you'd call her well born:

she came of a very old Cumberland family with a splendid pedigree and lots of in-breeding. My mother drifted through life—thin, Roman-nosed, kind and remote—with not a thought of how to grapple with realities or fight battles for herself. Things were done for one, weren't they? It was an odd world she lived in—one where she had family, 'birth', a place in society, appointed duties, the respect of the peasantry. Even in Jane Austen's time such people ought to have known the world was changing; my mother never seemed to learn. My father proposed. She was thirty and unmarried. Her family was hard up, as an old family always is that has not sent representatives into the big worlds of banking and commerce and industry. They told her she should accept, and she accepted, drifting into marriage as she had drifted into everything else she had done in life.

I don't suppose she was marked down for happiness, but in some other marriage, or in respectable spinsterhood, she might have got through life with some dignity and contentment. My picture of her is of sickness, and bewilderment, and a sort of helpless and impractical love for me and Cristobel. She was an ailing body, probably from my birth, or even before. I remember in the 'fifties her taking long cruises for her health—cruises to the West Indies, cruises round the world, in the belief that what she needed was sun and change. Nothing helped. She lay, almost throughout my childhood, on the sofa in her little sitting-room, flickering, angular, sad.

I remember her taking me to her one day and telling me that if anything happened to her—as if I didn't know, at ten, exactly what was going to happen to her—I was to look after my small sister. It came to me now with a pang that I hadn't made much of a fist of it. I'd walked out on the job.

The memories got on top of me. To get away from them I went through into my father's study, a room where I never remember my mother going. It was the room with fewest personal associations for me, too: not a place we were called into often, or to which we went of our own accord, though it opened out into the little library, where I spent many hours. Dominating the room, on the wall that got most sunlight, was a painting by Salvador Dali, a picture of various things melting into various other things, a purchase of Aunt Eliza's in the 'twenties: it was vaguely nasty, but it went with the room. Also dominant was the grand piano over by the leaded windows, where my father would go and try over the inspirations that crowded in on him. It was very dusty. I tried it and it was out of tune. On the table nearby was a pile of music, including a few of my father's own compositions in manuscript. I took up the Jubilee *Hymn of Tribute*, written in my father's thin, quavery musical notation: a page of it looked like the death-throes of a consumptive spider. It was a setting of some bilge by John Masefield, and I wondered whether it had in fact been written for the 1935 Jubilee, and resurrected for the more recent one. I moved over to the desk.

In spite of his apparent openness about his amusing little vices, my father was in many ways a secretive man: he certainly didn't 'give himself' (thank God) to his family, nor, I imagine, to his friends. On the other hand, he was meticulous in his habits, and I found evidence in the desk that my Uncle Lawrence's condition of intermittent senility had frightened him and made him take precautions. For example, he left a notebook labelled 'Apparatus', with precise details of what had been ordered for his games room, and how much had been paid for it. It was clear that almost all the equipment had been devised and constructed by one Ramsay Percival, of 118 Reform Street, Newcastle. I went through the book, marvelling at the scrupulous recording of the progress of the various machines, often with little diagrams. He had noted down the sums paid to Percival—'to prevent fraud in the event of my death or incapacity'. I totted up the various amounts relating to the strappado: it came to about the cost of a second-hand Mini. Well, I suppose we all have our own forms of self-torment. The rack, unfinished, looked as if it would have cost considerably more.

The stubs of my father's cheque-book also bore the name of Percival pretty frequently, but otherwise were unrevealing. Mostly they were to Cristobel, presumably for housekeeping purposes. There was nothing else around on the desk that was at all personal —no blotters with letters that could be read in reverse, no letters *to* him either (but who would write?). I tried the drawers: little clipped bundles of bills, unrevealing except for some from Soho bookshops and a receipt from a theatrical costumier (for the tights, no doubt).

In the bottom drawer was my mother's will. I thought of it fondly: it had left everything to be divided equally between Cristobel and me, and what it came to was about a thousand pounds each. It's rather a neither-here-nor-there kind of sum, but I thought of it with gratitude, because it had tided me over when I slammed out of the house, before I got myself into the army, and it had paid for a fortnight's honeymoon in Portugal, more or less. It hadn't gone astray, my mother's thousand. I took a bet with myself that Cristobel had just saved hers—a pretty lunatic procedure these days, but she is the sort that tries to be farsighted and falls into a gravel pit whilst being so.

As I opened my mother's will, a little slip of paper fell out—the sort of slip that you tear off a pad and write messages to yourself on. It just said, in my father's anaemic script; 'Letter WOAF.' I puzzled over it for a bit. No doubt one of his hedges against mental decay, but what did it mean? Had it just fallen into my mother's will, or did it for some reason belong there? There was nothing about a letter in the will itself, which was simple and touching in its references to Cristobel and me, and did not mention my father at all. And what on earth were the initials? It looked like some female branch of the armed services, but if so I'd never heard of it.

I got up and shook myself: how my mother seemed to be coming back to me, like a courteously reproachful ghost, getting a gentle revenge for all those years when I'd shoved her to the back of my mind. It was my father that was my business, though. I walked over to the bookcases in the study. There were the tall shelves with his favourite scores: wispy composers like Fauré, Poulenc and Hugo Wolf. There were the books of musical reference. And then there was the case devoted to his own special kink: much loved works like *Salammbô*, *Justine* and (oddly in such company) various novels by Harrison Ainsworth. Then there were two shelves of those distasteful pseudo-scientific studies of torture which had haunted my childhood, shoulder to shoulder with sev-

eral gloating studies of all varieties of corporal infliction. I flicked
through the torture books and found the fullest possible description of strappado: it was much-thumbed, and had clearly formed
the basis for the streamlined, motorized version downstairs. I put
the book aside to show Tim Hamnet.

I felt unclean. That sounds like a piece of evidence given by a
respectable lady witness to one of the Whitehouse commissions on
porn, but it's exactly how I felt. I wanted to get out of that room,
and I pushed open the door to the library and went quickly
through. It was dark and musty and unused. Perhaps like the
chapel it had outlived its day, had now only the stale whiff of an
old habit, discontinued. I had spent many happy hours here in
childhood—when I was a small child, that is, in the days before the
apple-stealing and the sportiness and the general anti-Trethowan
rumbustiousness. When I was small my mother worried about me
—roaming around, climbing trees and fells, playing with the
rough village boys. She liked me to be where she could call me,
from her sofa. When she saw I was substantially there, she would
fade away quite happily again into the chintzy background, and I
could go off—to sit, as often as not, in this library and read. That's
the paradise of children with too much time on their hands. I read
books much too old for me (or so librarians today would say, but
how can they have been too old for me if I enjoyed them?). I read
Oliver Twist and *Nicholas Nickleby*—I always loved the Dotheboys
Hall scenes, till my father put me off them by reading them aloud.
I suppose I sensed the relish. I read *Jane Eyre* and *The Mill on the
Floss*, and I even read bits of books ridiculously old for me: *The
Ordeal of Richard Feverel,* and *The Way Of All Flesh.* Here they all
were, in their musty, dull bindings: heavy, three-volume editions
that I had difficulty heaving off the shelves and propping up on
my small lap. Here was my absolute favourite of all: *Dombey and
Son.* Why had I loved that so much? There never was a boy less
like Paul Dombey than I was. I suppose it was just the vague
general resemblance which gave it its special relevance: the boy
and his sister, the antipathetic father, the frail, distant mother
floating gradually into eternity at the end of the first chapter.

My mother . . .

I sat there, with all my thoughts, and impressions, and the ideas that danced and jeered and tantalized by refusing to come forward. Only connect . . . I had an odd feeling that I had connected momentarily, and it had flown from my mind. I pulled myself together. It must be an illusion. In fact, I had spent the whole afternoon and early evening wallowing in my past, and not at all doing what I was supposed to do. Still, I doubted if there was much here to discover that I had missed. I made a quick decision. I would go down and report to Tim Hamnet, and then I would go and tell the family (God! what an awful expression! As if they were mine!). I would go and tell the Trethowans that I would not be dining tonight. Then I would hijack a police car—the place was crawling with them—and go off to the village and spend the evening and night with Daniel and Jan. Since they had come, I might as well take advantage of it. I looked at my watch. Half past six. They could even have arrived by now.

Tim was still on the ground floor, and boy! was he looking frazzled. His collar and tie were askew, and there were big, dark blue sweat marks under his armpits.

'Sweet little kiddies, aren't they?' I said. 'Talk about trailing clouds of glory . . .'

'God! Don't talk to me about them, Perry.'

'How did it go? Did you talk to them all together?'

'Do I look crazy? I sent three men to prise them apart, and a fourth to cope with their mother. I saw them one by one, and only the three eldest. Frankly, I couldn't take any more.'

'What did they do?'

'Screamed abuse, ran at me and started scratching my face, yelled blue murder and started pounding on the door.'

'Is there a magic recipe for dealing with them?'

'I'd *like* to slaughter the lot of them.'

'Ah, the Herod approach. Not allowed in the Book of Rules, unfortunately. What did you actually do?'

'Made friends, cajoled, flattered, bribed, threatened, bullied—pretty much in that order.'

'And what did you get out of them?'

'Nothing. They had never done such a thing, never thought

about it (but wish they had), were locked in their bedrooms all night, didn't know Great-Uncle was dead until the morning, and would I tell them all the details? That was the oldest, and actually he asked for the details first: it was only by promising them I got the rest out of him.'

'Do you believe them?'

'Don't altogether know. Their stories agree.'

'Good sign, or bad?'

'With that lot I'd be inclined to say good. I think if anyone had tried to spoonfeed a story to them, it would have had the opposite to the desired effect. What about you, Perry? Anything of interest?'

'Meagre,' I said. I showed him the notebook about the various torture machines, the book with the description of strappado, the meaningless slip of paper from the will—and that was about it. I really felt ashamed it was so meagre. We nattered things through for a bit, and then I told him in no uncertain terms I was going off duty. I don't think he liked that, but I laid down the law (so to speak) to him: since I was down here quite unofficially, there was no way he could hold me to a twenty-four-hour working day.

My spirits heightened perceptibly as I left the Gothic wing. At least for a night I was going to get out of this hell-hole, this Victorian gaol. I nearly sang as I strode across the hall—something nice, not *Dolores*. I'd drive to the village, and I'd have Jan and Daniel in my arms, and I'd play games with Daniel until his bedtime, and then we'd have a pint or two together in the Saloon and take whatever was offering in the way of food at the Marquis, and after that . . .

I opened the door to the drawing-room. There they all were, assembled for sherry. There was Sybilla, in her usual flimsy drapes, with Mordred standing beside her. There was Lawrence, with Kate at attention by his chair. And there was Cristobel, very white and all too obviously trying to be brave.

And there, looking ravishingly pretty, holding a sherry glass and talking animatedly, for all the world as if she were at home, was Jan. And clutching shyly to her skirts was Daniel.

'Ah, do you know each other?' said Uncle Lawrence.

10

FAMILY AT WAR

Now the fact is, I had prepared in my mind all sorts of injunctions and prohibitions for Jan as to how to behave when she finally came face to face with the awful shock of my family. Such as not admitting for a moment to the slightest twinge of interest in anything artistic or cultural: not even such things as singing in choirs, or Adult Ed. courses in batik. I had it all worked out: say you're doing Arabic to help oppressed Middle-Eastern shop-lifters in London, or to write a book on conditions in the modern harem that will cause the Saudi-Arabians to break off diplomatic relations —anything except an interest in tenth-century love poetry. Give the Trethowans an inch and they claim four thousand acres and build a mansion on it: admit to the merest murmuring of an aesthetic sense and they rope you in on the family act, claim you as a spiritual soul-mate, invite you to participate in poetry readings with them.

And it was all thrown away. For here was Jan swilling *good* sherry (I could see the bottle) with them, and talking—if my ears did not deceive me—about Harrison Birtwistle or some such OK name. Nevertheless, I folded her and Daniel in my arms, because after all it wasn't their fault they hadn't had the benefit of my good advice. While I was about it, I kissed Cristobel too, who was looking wan but serviceable and obviously benefiting from the Guiding instinct to keep hitting the trail.

'What a lovely surprise for you, Perry,' cooed Aunt Sybilla. 'As soon as Mordred told me they were coming I knew you'd want to see them as soon as possible, and I sent down a little missive to the Marquis of Danby.'

Since she obviously imagined I'd be delighted, I muttered my thanks, and shot Morrie the sort of glance a schoolboy gives the class sneak.

'It's awfully nice, Peregrine,' pursued Sybilla, 'that you at least *married* a truly spiritual person—I mean *spirituelle*. Alas, that is *not* always the case in our family. For example, Lawrence's wives—'

Uncle Lawrence burst out into a shout of complacent laughter: 'Sluts! What I wanted. What I got. Sluts!'

'Yes, well . . . And dear Maria-Luisa, though an *excellent* mother as far as quantity is concerned, does just a teeny bit lack *esprit*. But Janet, so she tells us, is studying Arabic love poetry! What a fascinating subject!'

I deliberately let that remark fall into a dead silence, for I knew that Aunt Syb knew even less about Arabic love poetry than I did. Jan however was obviously not enjoying the Trethowan habit of treating an outsider as if he were not quite *there*—of talking at, around, above and below him as if he were a novice gymnast to whom they were awarding points. She said:

'What have you been doing today, Perry?'

'Going through my old home, actually,' I said. 'I've been snuffling around in the Gothic wing.'

'Ah!' said Sybilla, brightening up. 'And did you find anything? Make any Holmesian discoveries? I have wondered whether your father didn't have some *fascinating* but not entirely reputable secrets that he did not see fit to confide even to us.'

'If he did, I found out nothing about them,' I said. 'As a matter of fact, I was thinking most of the time more about my mother than my father.'

At this sudden mention of our mother, I saw Cristobel react—something between a blink and a flinch. But Sybilla ploughed on:

'Your mother! How extraordinary! You know, I'd really forgotten all about your mother, though of course I knew you had one. You know, she was a case in point to what we've just been talking about. *Charming* woman, but not a grain of aesthetic feeling in her body. Sometimes it was difficult to remember she was there, when we were all talking!'

'She was always nice to me,' said Kate.

'I'm sure we're all nice to you, Kate dear. I don't see the point of that remark. I suppose, Peregrine, you've been sitting up there thinking that your father was a bad husband to poor Virginia, and no doubt you're right in a way, but the fact is that a little neglect was all your mother asked for, she just wanted to be left alone, so it worked out quite for the best for all parties.'

'All the Trethowans make terrible husbands,' pronounced Lawrence complacently. 'Except m'father. And he was a fool.'

It was at this point that once again the sort of noise that must have assailed Davy Crockett's ears as the Alamo fell sounded from a far corner of the house and came threateningly nearer. Daniel's eyes (which had been gazing with mildly contemptuous curiosity at the present company) now grew round with fear, and he clutched convulsively to his mother's skirts. I went and took his hand as the infant Assyrians burst in like wolves on the fold, and once more threw themselves, screaming and pummelling each other the while, into the lap of their fond grandfather.

Today it wasn't sweets they were after. They had something much more novel in their appalling little heads. As they climbed all over Lawrence's chair they screamed: 'G'anpa, we fought the policeman,' and 'G'anpa, he tried to beat me up, but I hit him back,' all crowned by the oldest boy, who let out a great crow of 'We won! We ground him in the dust!'

This din of claim and counterclaim, complaint and rodomontade, went on for some minutes, during which Peter and Maria-Luisa sauntered in, nodded to Jan (not even that, actually, on Maria-Luisa's part) and helped themselves to drink. Lawrence was drooling (literally: there was dribble coming down from the side of his mouth) over his monstrous grandchildren, telling them how clever they'd been, how the idea of questioning little children was scandalous, how he'd see some questions were asked in the right quarters, and so on, until finally, by some unspoken collective decision, they swarmed off him again and went to dispute in a far corner as to who had hit the policeman the hardest. Only then did Daniel, wonderingly, come out from behind Jan's skirts and my leg.

'Not much spirit, your boy, Perry,' said Uncle Lawrence.

That got me. That really got me. 'We've tried to teach him some manners,' I said.

'Dear Perry,' cooed Sybilla. 'Such a conventional streak. I can't *think* where it comes from.'

'Probably from my mother, whom you never noticed was there,' I said.

Well, things really did seem to be starting badly: here was I working up to a right little session of snipe and countersnipe with them, whereas what I wanted was for the Harpenden Trethowans to wrangle among themselves, maul each other. I wanted to be quite out of it. One's wife so easily decides that it is you in the wrong, rather than all the rest. You may have noticed that yourselves. Fortunately, Mordred changed the subject.

'I've got you to thank for a very busy day, Perry.'

'Oh?'

'Yes. Quite a change to feel needed. Your men have been coming to me all afternoon with pictures of a vaguely Turkish character, or else with rustic scenes in horrendous greens.'

'Any luck?'

'No. I've had *Lady Mary Wortley Montagu at the Court of the Sultan.* I've had *The Death of Tamerlane.* I've had some designs Mother-dear did for *Hassan.* And some really frightful rural scenes that are simply jungles of sentimentalized farm animals. But not a trace of the Hunt or the Allan.'

'At least they're doing something *useful*,' said Sybilla, 'something that will save us hiring somebody to do it. One feels that at last one is getting something back for all the imposts that the government inflicts on one.'

'It's a point of view,' I said. 'Though I'm not sure policemen make the best art detectives.'

'Those designs for *Hassan*,' pursued Sybilla meditatively. 'It was a revival that never actually came off. Your father was to do the music, Perry—lots of cymbals and wailing wind instruments. But tastes had changed, and it was too expensive. A little too blatant, too, perhaps. I wonder now if one mightn't hold a little exhibition of one's theatrical designs.'

When we had all penetrated Sybilla's use of the impersonal third person and the negative conditional tense, Lawrence said: 'You're not having an exhibition here, Syb. I've always stood out against letting in the public.'

'I didn't say *here*, Lawrence dear,' said Sybilla waspishly. 'Though, when you come to think of it, it would be appropriate. And we have to bear in mind that there is going to be a great upsurge of public interest in *us*—in us as a *family* of artists—' (especially in one of us, I thought) '—and an exhibition actually in our home would be a tremendous attraction. Quite apart from the quality of the designs themselves.'

She looked around, her head cocked like a fledgling bird waiting for a nice portion of worm. Most of us looked a bit glum, but Cristobel, who can be relied upon in the sweetness and light department, said: 'What a lovely idea, Aunt Syb! It would give you such an interest!'

Kate said: 'Shouldn't have thought we'd want *hoi polloi* all over the place.' But I thought she sounded a bit wistful. It couldn't be much of a life here for Aunt Kate, without a monster-sized ego to keep her warm.

At last it was dinner-time, and the Squealies, who had been re-enacting the snipping of the strappado cord with yells of delight all over the available floor-space, were bundled off back to the Elizabethan wing. We most of us breathed sighs of relief, and as the din finally faded and died Jan said:

'Golly, I can hear myself speak.'

Lawrence chuckled: 'Full of life, what? Aren't they little sweeties, eh?'

But Daniel, gazing perplexedly at the door through which they had disappeared, said: 'Daddy, are those *children*?'

It was a good question. Kate and Syb and Mordred thought it very amusing, but Lawrence muttered something about his being a queer sort of kid, and Pete reactivated his sneer.

'Aren't children *funny*!' said Cristobel brightly.

As we all sat down to dinner, Daniel seemed to have regained confidence. He sat next to me on a raised chair, and looked round at the assembled oddities as if they were a Punch and Judy show set up especially for his benefit. I had to keep shovelling bits of food into his mouth because he forgot to eat, in anticipation of something happening. He didn't have long to wait.

It was Mordred who started them off, after a covert wink in my direction.

'Well, it will be fine for me if there *is* a big new public interest in the family. I could probably get some publisher or other to commission my book on you all.'

'Oh darling—money in advance!' said Syb.

'Precisely.'

'Bit parasitic all this, isn't it?' muttered Peter.

'If so, all the more necessary to suck the blood. The good thing is that this is all coming at a time when everyone is also waking up to the real quality of Aunt Eliza's work.'

'Dear Elizabeth,' breathed Sybilla. 'Dear sweet muddle-headed soul. You know, I never felt the tiniest twinge of jealousy at her success.'

'Y'fought like cat and dog when she was alive,' said Lawrence.

A vein in Sybilla's forehead twitched. 'If we fought, we fought as *sisters,* not as fellow artists,' she said grandly. 'I'd have thought you of all people would have understood that.'

'Don't see it makes a scrap of difference, m'self,' said Kate, at her most downright tonight. 'You fought all the time anyway.'

'Being sisters is *awfully* difficult,' said Cristobel.

'Never really understood what they saw in 'Liza's stuff,' said Uncle Lawrence. 'Not that later stuff, anyway. All wispy lines and dots. Went bonkers, I'd say. Just slightly bonkers. I'll be glad to get rid of it.'

'*Rid* of it?' said Sybilla.

'Oh yes,' said Mordred, happily heaping on the coals. 'You had an offer today, didn't you, Uncle?'

'Had an enquiry. Not the only one. Had several galleries on to me these last few years. I string 'em along, keep 'em panting. The galleries mostly wanted the late stuff. They must be bonkers too. Whole world's gone slightly off-beam, what?'

'And who,' asked Sybilla coldly, 'was this enquiry *from*?'

'America. That's different. They've got the cash. Some damn-fool lot of women in America somewhere. Philadelphia. They're starting a Museum of Women's Art, or some such nonsense. They've got one of Eliza's already, want some more.'

'How *fas*cinating!' said Sybilla, thawing visibly as the possibilities of the idea struck her. 'I wonder if they'd like some of my designs.'

'Shouldn't wonder,' said Lawrence, raising a portion of meat painfully to his mouth. 'Was saying to Perry this morning, must be mostly rubbish they've got. No wonder they want more of 'Liza's.'

Kate had been listening greedily, while shovelling food in with hearty, open-air relish. 'I've got five of Eliza's,' she said. 'Left me in the will. I could sell one and have a holiday again. I haven't seen Bavaria for jolly ages. Dear old Berchtesgaden!'

'I shouldn't be *quite* sure they're yours, Kate dear,' said Sybilla, the twitch active again. 'Eliza's will, as you will remember, was a terrible mess.'

' 'Course they're mine. What do these Americans want, Lawrence?'

'All her periods. Early, middle, late. Comprehensive survey, they said. She was "one of the focal pioneers of" something or other, so they said. God, what tommyrot people talk these days!'

'Oh, goody!' said Kate, swallowing half a potato in her delight. 'I could sell them all. Eliza wouldn't mind. She always preferred her things to be seen. Apart from the portraits of us, the only things we've got here are the ones she couldn't sell.'

'Which is mostly the late stuff,' complained Lawrence. 'They got dumped here. Bits o' nonsense. I had 'em put in the rooms nobody goes in.'

'Those are the ones people want these days,' said Mordred, meditatively. 'They fetch . . .'

'And which,' interposed Sybilla, edging her troops in slowly, 'is the picture of Eliza's that they've got already?'

McWatters was serving the second helping of roast lamb, and

seemed to be doing it extraordinarily slowly. Perhaps he knew the signs of approaching convulsions, and was hoping to circumvent the family's tendency to throw breakables at moments of stress (they'd all once visited the D. H. Lawrences in Italy, and watching them at it had decided it was an awfully jolly game).

Lawrence begun scrabbling in his pocket, with great difficulty, and Sybilla continued: 'Not, of course, that there's any question of *selling*. We are, after all, *custodians*—'

'Speak for yourself,' roared Lawrence. 'I'm not a custodian, I'm the bally owner.' He drew out a crumpled bit of paper, now wrapped up with one of the Squealies' sweet-papers. 'Ah yes, here it is. Where is it? Ah: they've got something they call *First Night at Covent Garden*—"wonderful confection of reds and golds and gauzy greens" the damnfool woman writes. Ever heard such rubbish?'

There was a moment of loaded silence, which I saw Mordred conducting with his left hand. Then Sybilla took off.

'She never in her life painted a picture with that title. That's *Crush Bar, Covent Garden, May 1952*. I know it! The description fits exactly!'

'Don't know why she bothered with titles,' grumbled Lawrence. 'Never looked like what they're supposed to be. I can understand abstracts, but I never got what Eliza was getting at.'

'But she was a wonderful painter,' protested Jan. 'There's a splendid late one in the Tate—'

'She was a wonderful painter, in her way,' interrupted Sybilla, and turning to Jan as if momentarily unsure who she was, 'but you're all missing the point. Whether she was good or bad is neither here nor there. She is in demand, and *Crush Bar, Covent Garden* is one of *our* paintings. One of the late ones that was here at the time of her death. When she was going through a trough, and very little was selling. The point is, they've got one of ours!'

'Y've probably got it wrong as usual, Syb,' said Lawrence.

'I have not got it wrong, Lawrence. Peter, you must remember —it used to hang in the hallway, by the Elizabethan wing—'

'Oh God, Aunt Sybilla, I can't remember every damn thing of Aunt Eliza's there is around the place. I don't take to them, quite frankly. You got it wrong about Great-Grandfather's christening spoon, so I expect you've bombed again.'

'I have not bombed! Mordred. You must remember. We moved it after her death to the south writing-room.'

'Good Lord, Mother. I was only twelve or so at the time. I don't suppose I've been in the south writing-room in the past twenty years.'

'Exactly. That's what the thief banked on. We just never go into those rooms. It's been all too easy for him! Surely *someone* remembers that picture?'

'Oddly enough, Aunt Syb, I think I do,' I said. 'It's sort of all lines and suggestions—'

'That's it. Like all the late ones. A line here, a dash of some new colour there, and the whole scene was before you.'

'You didn't think much of them at the time,' said Kate.

'As I remember it,' I said, raising my voice, 'it wasn't any sort of Impressionist thing. It's almost abstract when you first look at it, and then it begins to take shape.'

'Exactly!' said Sybilla.

'Aunt Eliza talked to me about it. She often used to talk about her paintings to me, I suppose because I was small and quiet, and hadn't much to do. She said that one was done . . . oh dear, I was so young . . . was it when Callas was singing, or something?'

'Yes! That's right! The first night of Callas's *Norma*. Lawrence, that proves it. They've got one of *our* pictures.'

'*Mine,*' said Lawrence. 'Anyway, you haven't proved anything, Syb, you old fool. You haven't even seen a photograph of the thing they've got.'

'We can soon remedy that. Perry, that policeman of yours with the Shakespearean name, he can telegraph for a photograph, can't he? This is important! The family substance is being dissipated!'

'There is no such thing as the family substance,' shouted Uncle Lawrence, getting red in the face and looking as if he would like to loosen his collar. 'There is what is mine and what is yours. You've got no sense of *meum et tuum,* you foolish creature. That damn confection in pink and gauzy whatever-it-is is mine, and I tell you now I forbid the police *or* any hysterical old women poking their overdeveloped noses into my affairs.'

'I'm afraid it's not quite as simple as that, Uncle Lawrence,' I put in. 'If this is connected with the murder, it may be necessary to look into it.'

'I forbid it. A man still has his rights, eh? Against officialdom's poking and prying, what?'

'I think Lawrence has popped them himself,' said Kate, voicing the general impression, I suspect, 'and if he can, I can. I'll sell all mine.'

'The question is, which *are* yours?' said Sybilla sharply. 'You were left the pictures in your possession. You've swapped the pictures in your wing with pictures in other wings over and over again since poor Eliza died.'

'I had to find something to go with my collection,' said Kate defensively. She turned to Jan. 'I've got an absolutely ripping collection of SS mementoes. You must come and see it. Daniel would love it. The trouble is, nothing of Eliza's really *went*. Finally I decided on *Coventry Razed, 1940*. I know I own that because Eliza gave it to me.'

'Kate! She did not! That was a personal gift to me!'

'Oh rot, Syb. She never gave you anything. You were always so sniffy about her work. The only reason you had several when she died was because you went and grabbed things from the house while she lay dying.'

'Catherine! Such lies!'

'You knew what was in the will. The only thing you had of your own was a little abstract called *Shifting Planes* which you'd bought to spite her because you knew she was no good at abstracts.'

'She's deranged,' announced Sybilla.

'No, I'm not. I'm the only one who really knows what's been going on in this house. Leo had hardly any paintings either, because he didn't like any member of the family being more talented than he was. He grabbed more when she died, too. I saw him smuggling them up to the Gothic wing.'

'They'll all have to be given back,' said Lawrence with a malignant relish. 'They're all mine.'

'I know *Festival Scene* is ours,' said Cristobel, with a trace of family spirit, not to mention family acquisitiveness. 'Mine, I should say. Because Daddy told me that Aunt Eliza gave it to him.'

'Hardly evidence,' said Lawrence. 'It'll all have to be given back. And that Dali you've got.'

'I certainly won't give it back. Daddy bought it, with his own money. He told me so.'

'Nonsense. It was bought by Eliza when he was still in short trousers. If it's not back tomorrow I'll go and see m'lawyers!'

I foresaw an eternity of litigation, a Jarndyce and Jarndyce case that would outlive us, the fourth generation of Trethowans. Sybilla seemed to sense the danger too, for she began to draw in her horns.

'This is all too silly,' she said. 'If there is one place for Eliza's paintings it is here. Nothing will be sold. Of course.'

'Suddenly become head of the family, have you, Syb?' enquired Uncle Lawrence. 'That's something no woman will ever be, thanks to Grandfather Josiah. Sensible chap. Well, as far as I'm concerned there's no reason why Eliza's daubs should be here. She didn't even like the place.'

'Lawrence! What nonsense! She loved Northumberland!'

'She hated Harpenden. She said it was a festering sore on the body of the county. She said it got bigger and uglier every time she came back. Hardly ever did come back till the end. Lived in London. Well, London can have her.'

'She never lived in Philadelphia.'

'Well, I don't want her around me here. It's like living in the Turner rooms of the Tate. We're not a damned Museum. I prefer those Victorian things she used to sneer at. At least they're lively, what?'

I began to think that on the whole I preferred Uncle Lawrence senile: he could be a right Josiah Trethowan if he really set his mind to it. Without the strength that comes from a truly bullish stupidity, of course.

'Well, of course we all love the Victorian pictures now,' said Sybilla. 'We've come round to them, as no doubt Eliza would have, too. They're part of the house, too; part of the Trethowan heritage. It's simply not up to you suddenly to make a decision to get rid of parts of it. You're robbing us of our common patrimony.'

'It's not common! It's mine!'

'When, after all, you're not going to live forever—'

'I'll outlive you! I'll outfox you, too, if you try anything! I've still got my wits about me!'

'On occasion,' said Sybilla.

'The main thing is, it's mine. The house is mine—you're all here on sufferance, remember that. Don't even pay me a penny rent. The grounds are mine, the pictures are mine, the furniture is mine, the money is mine. None of you can alter that. And it will all go to little Pietro—'

'Via me,' said Pete.

'Via you. *If* you outlive me. Talk about custody of the family heritage! I'm the custodian! And I'm not answerable to *any* of you. D'ye hear me, Syb? I've been too soft! I'm the head of the family! One word from any of you, and out you all go!'

I saw Aunt Syb's hand reaching towards a side plate, and I pushed back my chair and made moves to go. Much more of this and Uncle Lawrence would have another spectacular stroke and the third generation Trethowans would have suffered further decimation in the course of a couple of days. It was all quite deplorable. Daniel had been so fascinated he had forgotten to eat his caramel custard, absolutely his favourite sweet. You can't blame him: as an exercise in geriatric awfulness I remember nothing like it since *Whatever Happened To Baby Jane?* or the last years of President de Gaulle. As we all broke up in disorder I muttered our excuses to Uncle Lawrence, and said we had to get Daniel back to the Marquis of Danby and off to bed. Lawrence didn't seem to hear. He was puckering his old lips in triumph and looking round as if he'd won a famous victory. I dashed off to Tim to acquire a car, and while I was about it, I tipped the wink about Philadelphia, and suggested he get a photo by the fastest possible method. He tried to show me details of my father's financial affairs, and his will, but I said I had to get out of this madhouse, and made my escape.

The funny thing is that by the time I got back to the main block, they were all having coffee in the drawing-room, and palsy-walsy as could be. Sybilla was telling Jan some funny story from Aunt Eliza's death-bed. Morrie grinned at me conspiratorially, and I had to be friendly back. He had done a marvellous job, and quite unobtrusively. I suppose if you live with them you know every sensitive spot, and can effortlessly put your finger on it in a way that sets them howling. Maria-Luisa saw the exchange of glances between us, and lowered.

Anyway, driving back to the village I was quite irrationally proud of the evening's performance, especially since it was put on without benefit of rehearsal. It was Daniel who had enjoyed it most: no sooner were we out of the house than he started jumping up and down with delight at the spectacle he had just witnessed.

'Daddy, Daddy—they behaved very badly, didn't they, Daddy?'

I thought this was no time to beat about the bush with specious excuses.

'Yes, they did, Dan.'

'Can we go and watch them do it again tomorrow?'

'No.'

'Poor old dears,' said Jan, 'they—'

'Cut that out, Jan. Don't give me the "poor old dears" line. They've been like this as long as I can remember. They're a thoroughly repulsive collection of crazed egotists, and always have been.'

'Well, at least they're individuals,' she retorted.

'Oh my God, individuals. If there ever was a ghastly warning against cultivating your ego, aiming at total self-fulfillment, doing your own thing regardless—the Trethowan family is it. If they'd given them their own television show twenty years ago, the 'sixties would never have happened.'

'Well, it's better than my parents. Stuck in front of the telly the whole time, and if you drop round to see them they complain they missed one of Annie Walker's lines because they had to open the door.'

'Your parents scarcely exist. There must be something between being like them and being like the Trethowans.'

'Aren't we going to see them again?' asked Daniel, downcast.

'No,' I said.

'Yes, darling,' said Jan. 'I told Aunt Sybilla I'd go and see the gardens tomorrow.'

'Oh, God!' I said. 'Well, keep in the open where you can be seen. I don't trust any of that lot an inch. I'd put your old jeans on. She'll get you doing the weeding. The grounds are obviously too much for two men. Just to look at it has me itching to get at a spade.'

'You see? You're feeling at home there already. I can just see the way you've been settling in.'

Well, we started a good old slanging match over that, but as a matter of fact we had a very nice rest-of-evening: we played with Daniel and I heard all his news; we put him to bed and went and had a pint in the bar, where the landlady deferred to me in a way that tickled Jan pink; and then—well, there isn't any more of the day's doings that you need to know of for this story.

Except that in the middle of the night I woke up, and sensed that Jan was awake too. And as I put my arm around her, she said:

'Perry, are you awake? There's something I've been meaning to say to you all evening since we got away.'

'What's that, love?'

'You do realize that Cristobel is pregnant, don't you?'

11

BROTHER AND SISTER

Breakfast was served next morning in a poky little dining-room in the new extension to the Marquis. (I disapproved of the extension, of course, as all returned travellers disapprove of things that have happened since their time, however much they disliked what was there before.) Mrs Killigrew, the new landlady, waited on us with a quite killing deference, which she no doubt thought was our due as part of the family at the Big House. Coming from Birmingham, she was living in the past, I suppose. Jan, I am ashamed to say, lapped it up.

'Any moment now she'll be calling you the Young Master,' she whispered.

'Is Daddy the Young Master?' demanded Daniel.

'No, dear. He's not.'

'Who is, then?'

We thought. 'Well, Peter, I suppose,' I said, and Jan and I collapsed choking with laughter over our poached eggs. Mrs Killigrew, returning, seemed to be noting down that seemly grief in times of mourning was no longer *de rigueur* in the best families.

'Are you sure?' I asked Jan, when she had gone out. 'About what you said last night?'

'Of course I'm sure.' She put on her wise-family-friend look. 'A woman always knows.'

'What does a woman always know?' asked Daniel.

'Everything, darling. Are you going to have a big-brotherly thing with her, Perry? Demand she go into seclusion at Ostend and conceal the family shame?'

'Oh, don't be crass, Jan. Of course, I feel a bit responsible for her, but she's all of thirty, and in fact I think it would be a really good thing for her, if not for the kid, and I'd be quite pleased, only—'

'Only?'

'Well, I'd be quite pleased if I thought it was one of the gardeners, or the vicar, or somebody.'

'She sings in the choir. Perhaps it is the vicar. They're awfully liberated these days.'

'Only the homosexuals. The rest keep it all in, same as ever. But I know who it is. I've been remembering our first chat, and it was "poor Morrie's got so much to do" and "Daddy kept picking on poor Morrie" and all that kind of thing. I know what's been happening. He's been working on her pity. The neglected spaniel approach.'

'Mordred? Are you sure? Anyway, she may like him.'

'Hmm. But she would keep it in the family, wouldn't she? All those healthy, normal people out there in the big world, and she goes bedding down with Cousin Morrie. It would be so much better if she got right away from Harpenden. But I bet she won't. Not just when she's come into what she's been waiting for.'

'She doesn't inherit the wing, does she?'

'Sounds like shares in a chicken. No, of course she doesn't. You heard Uncle Lawrence doing his "Mine—all Mine!" stuff last night. But she'll stay on—she's part of the family circus by now, even if she doesn't do much more than show people to their seats. Besides, she obviously has a strong sense of her rights. It'll take her longer than a pregnancy to establish her claim on what's in the wing. I wouldn't give much for her chances of keeping the Dali, I'm afraid.'

'You're assuming that Mordred won't marry her?'

'I suppose they'd have gone and done it already if they were going to. What would they marry on?'

'There's Morrie's book.'

'I don't know much about publishing, but I should guess that anyone who married in the expectation of royalties these days would really take a prize in the foolish virgin stakes.'

'Is our family royalties, Daddy?' asked Daniel, and brought this conversation to an end.

After breakfast Jan said she'd wander round the village and see if she could pick up any gossip. I gave my blessing to this project with an inward chuckle. The village of Harpenden had done nothing but gossip about the Trethowans for the last ninety-five years, ever since the first workmen had arrived to dig foundations that would have been more appropriate for a Crusader castle. The villagers had got more hand-outs and free drinks out of British newspapermen than anybody in the world, except perhaps the islanders of Mustique. That should keep Jan happy for the morning.

When I got myself to the Gothic wing I was met by an interesting sight. Tim Hamnet and Constable Smith were having a right old one-twoer with two men whom I took to be the gardeners. They had been caught trying to remove the Dali from my father's study. They were under orders, apparently, to take it to the main block. Uncle Lawrence, it seemed, was having another of his good days today, and was acting firmly on the principles enunciated so brutally last night. However in this case, at least, he was frustrated: nothing was to be touched in the murder wing (as—if he'd had a grain of sense left—the silly old bugger should have realized for himself). In the end the gardeners saw they were on to a bad wicket and sloped off. No doubt they had several calls of a similar nature to make in the other wings.

Anyway, Tim and I went up to the library, as being more comfortable than the big room on the ground floor which I was increasingly coming to think of as the Torture Chamber, and we sat around and had a good old natter about the case. I won't go into it in detail, because I've given you most of the stuff already, one way and another, and I want to get this story over within a reasonable time, but there were a couple of interesting things emerged from Tim's side of the conversation. The first of these was the will. No great surprises there. I half suspected I was going to be left some derisory object to underline his contempt for me: a pair of old socks, or his musical manuscripts or something. But no. I was not so much as mentioned. I was pleased: it seemed to keep our mutual antipathy pure and abstract, as it had been since the day I left. Everything went to 'my daughter Cristobel' (he didn't even bother with a 'dear'): money, investments, possessions—many of the last being specified, including the Dali. In fact, I had a feeling that one look at that list would have given Uncle Lawrence apoplexy. The scientific apparatus in the Torture Chamber was not mentioned. Presumably it went to Cristobel. Suitably adapted, it might form the basis of a good little gymnasium for her.

The other thing of interest was the money. My father's financial state. Here I admit my earlier guesses were proved wrong. I was surprised—and no end pleased, for Cristobel's sake—to learn that he was worth all of thirty thousand pounds, quite apart from shares, pictures, furniture, and rare editions of nasty books. Not at all bad, for my papa.

'Anything shady about it?' I asked Tim.

'Hmm, well, I'm not entirely happy, let's put it that way. I'll tell you why. You see, I've got his bank accounts for the last ten years or so. Now, on the face of it, it's a perfectly dull little record, with nothing in the least suspicious there—'

'I saw his last book of stubs upstairs,' I said.

'Precisely. Booksellers, this Percival character—'

'The wondrous artificer.'

'—whatever you like to call him. And cheques to your sister for the housekeeping. Pretty generous ones, too, so they obviously included pocket-money-cum-wage for herself. Nothing wrong with that. Now, the trouble is, they keep being interrupted for long periods. No housekeeping cheques. Then they start up again. Then there's another long break.'

'I see. Meaning, you think, that my papa somehow or other came by largish sums of cash, which he stashed away (it being difficult to account for them otherwise) and used for the housekeeping and personal expenses for a bit, till they ran out. Later on he got access to more. Is that how you see it?'

'Pretty much like that.'

'Meaning, conceivably, pictures—is that what you think? What does Chris say to that?'

'That's the trouble. She denies it absolutely. She stands me out that she was paid every week by cheque for the housekeeping expenses. Perhaps once or twice in cash, she concedes, but otherwise always by cheque. I keep telling her this can't be so, she keeps telling me it is. I don't like to say this, but she's not too bright, your sister, Perry.'

'She's all right,' I said defensively. 'She's got more sense than most of this lot.'

'That's another of your faint compliments, I suppose. Well, if you talk to her again, would you try to convince her that if she'd been paid by cheque regularly, I'd have a record of it?'

'Oh, I'll be talking to her,' I said. 'I'll try. But you know my family by now. As the lady says in Thurber: "Mere proof won't convince me." '

Chris was apparently up and about, as she called it, and I finally came upon her on the far side of the lake, sitting in a little ornamental summerhouse that no doubt seemed to Great-Grandfather Josiah to add a Marie-Antoinette touch to his grounds, but now merely augmented the general sense of neglect and decay. Chris was deep in thought, but now and then she leant out and pulled at the branches and creeping tentacles of shrubs that threatened to take over the summerhouse.

'Chris,' I said.

'Oh, hello, Perry.'

'Why didn't you tell me, Chris?'

'Tell you?' The words jumped out of her mouth, and she tensed up in a terribly defensive posture.

'That you were pregnant.'

'Oh, that . . . I didn't want to worry you, on top of all this. It'll have to come out soon. But not yet. Wait till all this has . . . died down. Did Janet notice?'

'Yes. I suppose Sybilla has, too.'

'Oh, no, I don't think so. She never notices people.'

'You don't think you ought to tell her?'

'Oh, no, Perry! I couldn't! If I told anybody, it would be Kate.'

'Yes, I suppose she might be better. You really ought to get away from Harpenden, Chris. You've got money of your own now. You could manage it, and it would be much less . . . unpleasant.'

'Oh, no, I wouldn't want that, Perry! Harpenden's my home. It's where . . . everyone is. They'll all understand when they get used to the idea. We're a very unconventional family.'

'Hmmm. So the theory goes. The point is, it's the most unrestful place in the world to have a baby in, particularly in these circumstances. Oh, why did you have to keep it in the family, Chris?'

'The family's all I've got,' she said. 'You hate them. I wouldn't expect you to understand.'

'It's nothing to do with whether I hate them or not. In any case, I don't hate Mordred. But it doesn't seem right for the kid, growing up in a house full of elderly maniacs, with his father around, doing nothing, and not married to his mother . . .'

Chris had shot me a glance, but her mouth still was pursed into an obstinate line. 'Family patterns are changing these days,' she said, as if it were something she'd learned by rote. Suddenly her voice broke: 'Oh, Perry, you don't think it will matter, about being cousins, do you? I've been so worried about that . . .'

'No, no, Chris. It's an old superstition,' I said (without having much idea whether it was or not, but Chris is so helpless and pathetic at times that she makes you want to soothe her down at any price).

'Then I don't see why things shouldn't turn out all right,' said Chris, setting her chin high in the air. 'And you never know . . .'

Marriage, I thought. One could be quite sure that what Chris would really want, in these circumstances, was marriage. Well, I'd better keep off that subject till I'd investigated the ground a bit further. For all I knew it could eventually be possible. Golly, I thought, I bet Aunt Syb's been stashing it away over the years. To change the subject, I said: 'Chris, why did you lie to the Inspector?'

'I did not, Perry!' All her defensiveness came back, and she reacted with irrational pugnaciousness.

'Look, love, you can't have been paid the housekeeping money each week by cheque, otherwise we'd have a record of the cheques in his account. There are long gaps, Chris.'

'He must have had more than one account.'

'In that case, there should have been more than one kind of cheque that he paid you with. Were there?'

'Yes . . . Yes, I think there were.'

'What was the other bank's name?'

'I . . . I can't remember, Perry.'

'Chris, what on earth *is* this? What are you trying to do? There's no reason on earth why he should not have paid you in cash. Why are you denying it?'

'Because he didn't! He paid me by cheque, every week. You've got a cheek, Perry, coming and questioning me like this, and saying I've been lying. I'm the one who looked after him. I'm the one who knows. You resent my getting his money!'

That was so irrational it floored me. 'I do not resent it, Chris. It's what I've always wanted for you. We just stopped the outside men lifting off your Dali, by the way.'

'The Dali!'

'You're going to have to fight to keep that, I'm afraid. But you should have a better chance with the Aunt Elizas. The trouble is, if you're going to fight Lawrence, you'll have to stay here. I still think it would be better to get out. In fact, I think you'd have done better to get out long ago.'

'How could I? Who would have looked after him? It was my job. Mummy said so.'

'Mother? When did she say that?'

Chris, for some reason, looked as if she could have bitten out her tongue.

'In . . . before she died. Before she died she said it was up to me to look after Daddy after she'd gone. Oh, go *away*, Perry. You said you'd save me from all those questions, and now you're doing it yourself. I'm not well, you know. I shouldn't . . .'

'OK, OK, Chris. I'm going now. Look, just one more thing: remember, if there's any trouble here, Jan and I are always there to help.'

She looked rebellious. Then, to get rid of me, she said: 'All right. I know you mean well, Perry.'

But you blunder in in your copper's boots where angels ought to fear to tread, seemed to be the general implication. I got up and wandered away round the lake and back to the house, deep in thought. What was it eating Chris? One thing I was pretty sure of: our poor mother had not commended Father to Chris's care just before she died. For a start, Chris was only eight at the time. And secondly, we were about as close as it was possible to be, Chris and I, just before Mother's death and in the years immediately after. Naturally. And she would have told me of a thing like that, because it's the sort of trust Chris would take very seriously, and get a big conscientious thing about.

And yet I didn't get the idea she was lying. In fact, it had come out seemingly involuntarily, regretted immediately. And though it might seem a pretty repulsive thing to do, calling on a girl like Chris to devote her life to looking after a nasty old crackpot like our father, nevertheless, the idea was perfectly typical of my mother: she was still emotionally in the world of 1750 or thereabouts, and the pious hope that Chris would devote herself to her father's well-being would have seemed entirely natural, indeed only right, to her. I asked myself how the wish had been communicated. And I came up with the answer: by letter.

I walked round and round the garden, thinking about this and other things: the pictures, the *mise-en-scène* of the murder, the scissors in the plant-pot. I spoke to the gardeners, who had finished their deeds of retrieval around the house, and were busy rehearsing the story of Aunt Sybilla's pink fits for later retelling in the Marquis. I recognized one of them as being the most junior of the outdoor staff in my young days. We talked about the grounds, and what needed to be done, and how you couldn't get the labour, in spite of all this unemployment, and how you couldn't expect two men to do the work of eight, and so on. I began to feel like a member of the gentry, being matey with the peasantry. I was glad Jan wasn't there to overhear. Finally I landed up round the front of the house and was hailed from the Gothic wing by Tim Hamnet.

' 'Morning, Perry. Back on duty, I hope? By the way, no luck with Philadelphia. The Museum's closed until Monday, and no power on earth's going to get them to open up and let the police photograph the thing. That's the message; I suspect the cops themselves aren't putting their backs into it.'

'Damn their hides. I suppose with their murder rate the odd country-house killing seems an epicurean luxury. By the by, I had an idea about those pictures—bit of a long shot, but—'

'Give.'

'Well, if you'd got pictures like those to dispose of, who do you think would be interested?'

Hamnet was a bit at sea. 'National Gallery?'

'Wrong. They've got nothing British later than Turner.'

'That other one—the Tate.'

'Right. But if there was anything shady about the deal, you'd be a bit wary at approaching anywhere so well known. Their purchases tend to be well publicized. Then there're several provincial galleries with a strong line in Victorian stuff—Birmingham, for example—and of course we ought to approach them. But on the whole the same applies. What would be better would be to approach somewhere a bit less . . . how shall I say? . . . exposed. See what I mean? Somewhere not quite so well known.'

'I get you. Could a small place afford them?'

'They could afford the Allan. He has no particular market value. And it occurs to me that the place that would be most likely to be interested in *Lord Byron Reposing in the House of a Turkish Fisherman After Having Swum the Hellespont* would be—'

'Yes?'

'Newstead Abbey. Byron's home.'

'Where's that?'

'Not far from Nottingham. Do you think it would be worth while giving them a tinkle?'

'Surely. We don't lose anything by it. I'd do it myself, but I'm waiting to interview little Mordred. Anyway, you know your stuff on that sort of thing. You'd do it better.'

So I trolled off quite happily and entered the house. Then I was presented with a poser. Where did I phone from? I had intended using the phone in the Main Hall, but if there was an extension in the kitchens, as I suspected, that was about the last thing I ought to do. I ruled out Sybilla as too agog, and Peter as all too conceivably implicated, and I landed up with Aunt Kate. So I made for the Georgian wing, and of course found her thoroughly delighted to be of help.

'Ring from here? 'Course you can, Perry! tickled pink, really. Don't trust the others, I suppose. Is it top secret? Anyway, come on in.'

I went in, averting my eyes from the signed photograph of the late German Führer, given a place of honour in the cluttered little hallway.

'It's not exactly top secret, but I would like it to be private. It's not just an extension you've got here, is it?'

'Not on your life. We each have our own phone, pay our own bills. Old stingyboots Lawrence sees to that. You can have the study phone if you like. Come on, we'll take the lift. Upsadaisy!'

I'd forgotten the lift. Lifts had been installed in the Georgian wing after the car accident in 1939 which killed my grandmother and left my grandfather an invalid for the rest of his life. Kate was the only child at home, and she had taken care of him, at least until her internment, in this wing that had later become her own (or rather her own, subject to the whim of Lawrence, or—rather more dangerously—Peter, in the not too distant future). We got out at the third floor, and she popped me in through the study door.

'There it is,' she said cheerfully. 'You can have a look at my collection while you're talking. Be worth a lot When The Time Comes. I'll be downstairs. Toodle-oo.'

No wonder she made a quick escape. Her 'study' in fact housed her proud collection of Nazi mementoes. As I got on to Directory Enquiries my eye rested on medals from the desert campaign, Iron Crosses, and pictures of the heroic action against the Polish ghetto. I closed my eyes. Really, I had to try to think of Aunt Kate not as she was now, an overgrown product of St Trinian's, but as she had been for much of her adult life, a besotted admirer of a regime that even the most morally undeveloped could perceive as

evil. Could that old Kate have been totally obliterated by the
'breakdown' of last year?

I got the number of Newstead quite easily, but after that things
did not go quite so well. I was answered by a helpful but rather
hesitant male voice, which was obviously not at all pleased when I
said I wanted to ask a question about the house.

'Look, could you ring back Monday? There'll be someone
around then. I'm just a student, sitting in, you know, and none of
the regulars will be back till next week.'

'It's quite a simple question, about a picture. It's a big one, I'd
guess, so you ought to be able to locate it.'

'Yes, well, you see I'm a student of psychology. My mum knows
one of the gardeners. The fact is, most of the visitors here know
more than I do.'

I sighed. I knew that sort of literary shrine. 'Look, my name is
Trethowan. I'm a policeman and it's an urgent matter.'

'I say, are you *the* Trethowan? Whose dad got done in when he
was getting himself a bit of sado-masochistic fun? That case is just
killing me. I've just been reading all about you in the *Excess*.'

'Oh, God,' I said.

'They call you Big Perry. Your aunt told the *Excess* you gave her
the most wonderful feeling of safety.'

'My aunt gives me the most wonderful feeling of a pain in the
arse,' I said.

'Would you like a snap diagnosis of your father's mental condition?' asked Little Brightness at the other end.

'I understood my father's mental condition without benefit of
psychiatry before I was into my teens,' I said. 'Look, about this
picture—'

'OK. But I don't see what pictures have to do with it.'

'Yours not to reason why. Read next Monday's *Excess* and you
might find out. It's a picture called *Lord Byron Reposing in the House
of a Turkish Fisherman After Having Swum the Hellespont*. It must be
fairly easy to identify.'

'Hell, it's not even easy to say! How am I supposed to identify
it?'

'Well, he can't have much on, I would imagine. And there must be a sort of Turkish element in the picture.'

'I suppose you're right. Hey, wait: there is a picture like that. Sort of sexy, in an ethereal Victorian kind of a way. Where is it, now?'

'Could you trot round and have a look for it?'

'Sure thing. Hold on.'

I hung on, and cast my eyes around my aunt's loathsome souvenirs. The Turks and the Nazis—both rapists of Greece. There was a picture of tanks entering Athens. Before long my budding Freud came back on the line.

'Yes. I've found it. It's like what you said. Lots of white flesh. Hey, you'd have thought he'd have had a tan, wouldn't you?'

'Gentlemen didn't tan in those days. White was sexy.'

'Is that for real? I thought sexy was always sexy.'

'You can't have seen any silent films. Keep to the subject. Is there anything about the picture in the catalogue?'

'Catalogue? . . . Oh yeah, wait a tick . . . Yes, here it is: *Lord Byron* etc by William Allan. Painted, 1831. Acquired for Newstead in 1979.'

'It doesn't say who from?'

'Nope.'

'Any idea who would know?'

'Not a clue. Why don't you ring Monday, eh?'

'Look, is there a list in the catalogue of the Trustees, and the committee, and such like, for Newstead Abbey?'

'Haven't a notion. Where would it be?'

'Try the first page.'

'Oh yeah. Here they are. Local bigwigs and some professors.'

'Could you dictate their names to me?'

And so, finally, I got them, and the other end rang off, very cheery, saying if I wanted more help, just to ring back. I decided that the checking of the list of trustees to see if they could help over the buying of the Allan could be done by Tim or one of his team. The main thing was, I'd established that one of the pictures missing from Harpenden had indeed recently been sold (I was

damn sure it hadn't been given to Newstead!). Now we had to
decide where to go from there.

I went down the stairs. I'm never entirely happy in rickety old
lifts: they sometimes give the impression that my weight is something in the nature of a last straw. When I got down to the hall,
Kate was waiting, like a well-set-up vulture.

'Get what you wanted?'

'Yes, Aunt Kate, I think so.'

'I say, Perry?'

'Yes?'

'You haven't inquisited me yet.'

'I haven't inquisited anyone, Aunt Kate.'

'Oh, you fibber. You've talked to people. You've talked to Mordred and Peter, I know. The other one inquisited me, but I didn't
tell him much. There are things one doesn't talk about outside the
family.'

'Well, we could have a little chat, Aunt Kate,' I said, thinking
she wasn't so entirely round the bend that she couldn't be useful.

'Oh, spiffing! When?'

'Well, I've just got to deliver this list to the Superintendent. I
could be back in twenty minutes or so.'

'Oh, goody,' said Kate. 'Then you can stay to lunch!'

12

LOW CUISINE

Of course, I had to admit to myself that I'd asked for it. Walked straight into it with my chin out. One look at the clock, then showing after twelve, should have warned me of the danger. Even then I could have said I'd come back at half past four, and she could have given me afternoon tea and we would have both been happy. You can't do much with afternoon tea. But I was caught off balance, and all I could do was to produce a ghastly grin of acquiescence.

I went and shared my bit of news about *Lord Byron* with Tim Hamnet, and he set one of his men on to ringing round the various Trustees of Newstead to see if any of them had been involved in the buying of the picture. I also procured one of those little plastic bags that policemen use for sending specimens along to the forensic labs. I felt an awful coward. It was obvious that eating with Aunt Kate was an essential part of the Trethowan experience. One ought to face up to it, as to one's first beating at public school, one's first taste of fire in battle. It wasn't as if I had a particularly delicate stomach: after all, I'd been eating in army and police canteens for most of my adult life. One develops a certain toughness of the gut.

Still, I have to admit that as I strode resolutely back towards the Georgian wing, I was in a moderately filthy mood. And it wasn't improved by my coming upon Mordred in the main hall: quite apart from the business with Chris, I was irritated by the mere look of him: he had no business to go around with that air of oh-so-appetizing agelessness, like an academic Cliff Richard.

He said: 'Hello, Perry. Bloodhounds still hot on the scent, are they?'

I just snapped: 'I want to talk to you later.'

He looked hurt and injured, like a favourite courtier spurned by the Sun King.

I steamed ahead, the battleship *Resolute* preparing for an engagement, and rang the doorbell to the Georgian wing. Kate was all over me, of course, and beside herself with the unaccustomed pleasure of being hostess. She was wearing one of her inevitable suits (I remember her confiding to me that as fashions changed she took the hems up two inches, or let them down two inches), and over it a magnificent flowered apron. She looked the very embodiment of *Kirche, Küche, Kinder*. She marched me into the sitting-room—normally decorated, thank God, without tributes to the heroes of the Third Reich, though I noticed gaps on the walls caused, no doubt, by Lawrence's depredations—and she sat me down in a capacious, comfortable armchair. All the time she fussed over me in her gruff way, like an Old English Sheepdog penning up a prize ram.

'Won't be a sec,' she bellowed, darting off to the kitchen. 'It's nearly ready. I love risotto, don't you? You can put absolutely everything in!'

Well, I suppose that is the theory. I had an awful feeling that even the most exuberant of Italian housewives would still exercise a modicum of discretion that was beyond my Aunt Kate. I sat there, helpless, a lamb to the gastronomic slaughter.

Kate poked her head round the door.

'Dandelion or parsnip?'

'I beg your—'

'Wine, you chump! I've got the parsnip chilled.'

'Oh,' I said, being fiendishly cunning. 'The parsnip, then.'

She bore in the wine, in superb nineteenth-century goblets. She bore in a great tureen and served out the risotto with a liberal hand, ignoring my gestures to stop.

I received my plate, and tried not to look too closely. The rice was soggy with overcooking, but it was in any case a minor component. The major part consisted, if my eyes did not deceive me, of scraps of beef, bits of turnip and beetroot, hacked up sardines and diced tinned peaches. And some squares of what could very easily be dog food. I shut my eyes and thought of England.

'Lawrence sent the gardeners today,' announced Aunt Kate. She had seized a fork in her large paw and now began shovelling in with gusto, as once she must have gobbled camp food in the Bavarian mountains, while Czechoslovakia bled. 'After my pictures.'

'Did they take any?'

'Took two. When they came back for more, I'd got my Mauser out of the Collection. Scared 'em silly, and they took to their heels. Wasn't loaded, but they weren't game to risk it. World's gone soft!'

'Uncle Lawrence certainly seems to be concerned about his property.'

'Got a fit of the meanies,' said Aunt Kate complacently. 'Happens when you get old.'

'I suppose so,' I said. 'I never remember him being miserly when I was young.'

Aunt Kate shook her head vigorously. 'Wasn't. Didn't care about money. Above it. Paid out oodles to that second wife of his. Pete's mother. What do they call it? Alimony.'

'Why did he do that?'

'Keep her quiet. He was having an affair with a Marchioness or somebody. Paid out so she wouldn't be named as co-respondent, so he said.'

'Doesn't sound like a Trethowan. I'd have expected him to revel in the publicity.'

'Yes, you would, wouldn't you? We are a bit blatant, aren't we, Perry?'

'The tiniest bit, now and then.'

'Anyway, he didn't have to shell out for long, because she died.'

'Had he paid alimony to his first wife too?'

'Oh, no. They were never divorced. She was a Catholic. She died before the war some time.'

'Didn't have much luck with his wives, Uncle Lawrence.'

'They didn't have much luck with *him*,' said Aunt Kate emphatically. 'Always sniffing round someone or other. Wouldn't think it, to look at him now!'

'How bad is Uncle Lawrence? In health, I mean.'

'Has his off days, as you saw. He'd had three days like that when you saw him. Sleeps here with me, these days. Think he puts it on a bit, sometimes. Like a child. Wants attention. Likes to be fussed. Knows more about what's going on than he lets on to. Still, I play along with him. Not like Syb and Leo—'

'Oh?'

'They're crazy, the way they provoke him. Provoked, in one case. Ought to think of the future. He'll pop off if he has another of those strokes. Then where will we be? Awful swine, that Peter. Wouldn't think twice about throwing us all out into the snow. You enjoying this? It's scrumptious, isn't it?'

I was masticating thoughtfully a forkful that seemed to include a bony bit of kipper and a lump of marshmallow. I washed it down with a great gulp of parsnip wine and said: 'This wine's awfully good.'

'I'll fill you up,' said Aunt Kate, and trotted off to the kitchen, while I transferred a judicious amount of the nauseating goo to my little forensic bag, and stuffed it into my trouser pocket.

'What did you mean,' I asked, as she settled herself down again and resumed her enthusiastic fork-lift job on her plateful, 'about Father provoking Uncle Lawrence? Did they have any big rows?'

'Not out in the open. Too cunning for that. Of course, your father sniped. He couldn't help that, you know, Perry. He was a sniper by nature. But they kept the row under cover.'

'What makes you think they had one?'

'Because,' said Aunt Kate triumphantly, 'he took him walking!'

'What?'

'They went walking together—a long tour round the grounds. Well, Leo walking, Lawrence being wheeled. Can you imagine your father wheeling that chair? He *never* did it. Not his style at all. But he had to do it, because it was the only way they could be alone. So they could row.'

It made sense. 'Did it happen often?'

'Just once since the stroke. About ten days ago. I'd've trailed them if I'd known. I used to be a marvellous tracker! Put on weight a bit since, but I bet the twigs wouldn't crack under me!'

'You've no idea what it could be about?'

'Not a notion. Chrissy, perhaps?' She looked at me in a side-ways way to see if I knew, and was disappointed when she saw I did.

'I see you've noticed, Aunt Kate.'

' 'Course I've noticed. Got eyes. Saw it start. Saw what they were up to. Glances across the table. Footsy. Trotting off to the summerhouse.'

'Did you discuss it with anyone?'

' 'Course I didn't. Kept it to m'self. Silly gel, though. Got no pride.'

'It's going to be difficult for her, though, Aunt Kate. She may need a bit of support.'

'I'll support her. Can't blame a girl for going off the rails once in a while. Drive you a bit potty, looking after a little squirt like Leo all day long. I know. I did it for my father. And he was *nice*.'

'Cristobel says it was our mother who charged her to look after Father. I don't see how it could be . . .'

' 'Course it was. Cristobel got this letter thing.'

'Ah! She did, then.'

'That's right. You know, sent by the lawyers, marked "to be opened when she is twenty-one" or something like that. Bit soppy of Virginia, I thought. Old-fashioned. But then she was. Anyway, your mother—God rest her soul, because she was a *good* woman, Perry, I don't mean to speak against her—said she should regard her father as a sacred charge. I couldn't see Leo as the Ark of the Covenant m'self, but you know Chrissy. Went around for days after she got it, telling everybody about it.'

'Was there anything else in it?'

'Lot of guff. Embarrassing. About a mother's love. You know. People shouldn't write stuff like that. When you're gone, you're gone. Nobody gives a damn what you say. Look at Franco!'

'It's odd she should write a letter like that to Cristobel, but not one to me.'

'Post Office's gone all to pot these days,' said Kate, who seemed a bit distracted. 'I say, more wine?'

Blessedly she bore my glass to the kitchen, and I had recourse again to my bag, at the same time managing to extract from my mouth something that seemed to be nutty fudge. Look, I won't tell you anything more about that damned risotto. I don't want to be accused of writing gastronomic pornography.

I wasn't willing to let the subject of the letter drop, so when Kate came back waving another bumper of parsnip wine (the only good thing about which was that it did not taste of parsnip), I said: 'I wonder if my mother did send me a letter. And I wonder what happened to it.'

' 'Spect Leo destroyed it,' said Kate cheerfully. 'Lawyers probably sent it here. I can just see him. Probably read it over, smiled his nasty little smile, tore it up and put it in the fire. Bet that's what he did.'

Yes, I could see him too. Except for that little note in his drawer. I said: 'But if he were to hide it . . .'

'Plenty of room to hide it,' said Kate, in the understatement of the year. 'But I think he'd destroy it, unless it contained something important. He hated you, you know, Perry!'

'Yes, I think he did,' I agreed. 'I wondered at one point whether Cristobel wasn't exaggerating, but I think it must have been true. All because I called him a mediocrity!'

'That's the one thing none of them will admit!' said Kate. 'Got to be plumped up the whole time. Like cushions. Calling him a mediocrity was worse than hitting him. He hated you, I tell you. He certainly wouldn't have put a postage stamp on a letter from your mother to you.'

'Yes, I see that. Nevertheless, I do think he kept it. If only I knew where. Or, for that matter, why.'

' 'Course, he was a secretive little man,' said Kate. 'If he thought he could use it . . . Against you, for instance. Silly old Sybilla says he wasn't secretive because he was always boasting about those torture games he played. But he was. He liked gloating over things—having knowledge, enjoying the thought of what he knew. Crackers, if you ask me. Dangerous.'

'So it seems. Still, if it was something that concerned me, that was surely no reason for killing him. Do you think he was the one to pinch the pictures, Aunt Kate?'

'Leo? No. Not the type. No gloaty fun in that. Too risky, too.'

'Who do you think it was?'

'I think old Lawrence popped them himself. Stashed the money away somewhere the Inland Revenue won't find it. For the Squealies. Or else it was Peter, and Lawrence is covering up for him. Or McWatters.'

'That's three,' I pointed out. 'Which do you really think took them?'

'McWatters knows Iti,' said Kate. 'Bit suspicious, what? Ever heard of a butler who knew Iti before? Must be an art buff, or something.'

'How did you know that he knows Italian, by the way, Aunt? Is he open about it? Did you all know?'

'Don't suppose the rest knew. Not interested, except in keeping him. I get around the house a bit. Trailing. Heard him talking one evening to Mrs Mac. Maria-Luisa had been shouting insults at us over dinner. Does that periodically. Comes from the gutter. Scum. *Untermensch.* Anyway, old McWatters heard 'em all, and was translating them to his missus. Singed my hair, I can tell you!'

'So you'd pick McWatters—getting in with the household and progressively robbing it of pictures?'

'Makes sense. Rather have that than one of the family.'

I sighed. That was no argument. Aunt Kate was not the logical thinker of the family. I put down my fork with every appearance of regret, leaving a little mountain of food as if I thought it the polite thing to do, and stood up.

'Well, I'd better be getting back to work, Aunt Kate,' I said.

Unluckily her eyes were on the level with my waist, and she peered disapprovingly at the bulge in my trousers.

'Shouldn't stuff things in your pockets like that, Perry,' she said. 'You young people don't know how to treat good clothes!'

'Er, is there anything else, Aunt Kate?' I said hurriedly, 'anything else you would like to tell me?'

She was still chomping away, unwilling to miss a mouthful, but she became pensive and finally she said: 'Don't know if you realize how much we hated Leo. Well, we did. We didn't have rows with him, but we all hated him. He got to our weak points and he twisted the knife in. We're all failures in a way, him most of all. But he made us all feel it. He made us squirm.'

'He certainly made me squirm.'

'You were just a boy. It's different when you're old. Worse. He was a man who would have hated to be loved. Because he couldn't love. Think of your poor mother. He despised her. Ignored her. Even you children. He hadn't an ounce of feeling for you. And you were a lovely little boy, Perry! Golly, you were nice!'

I blushed purple.

'But he hated you by the end, and he'd have done anything to spite you. He tolerated Chris because she looked after him, but he despised her too, and he'd have made her life hell when he found out about the baby. He was a *horrible* little twerp, Perry! You can't expect any of us to feel sorry he's gone,'

'I don't,' I said. 'Even Chris, I don't think—'

'Oh, Chris, underneath, doesn't care. And she'll have the baby now. It'll be better for her, you know, when she has that to look after.'

'I know. But I wish she could have been married. Chris is the sort that ought to get married. And it'll be much worse with him in the same house. That I do feel bitter about. Of course I know things aren't easy for him either. Without a proper job, and no outlets . . .'

Aunt Kate let out a great whoop of laughter. 'No outlets!'

'Well, I don't imagine Morrie has a wildly exciting sex life, stuck here in Harpenden—'

'Oh Perry, you are a chump! It's not Morrie, it's Pete!'

13

IN WHICH I HAVE AN IDEA

Chump was as good a word as any for it. I had been the most complete and utter chump. I had remembered Cristobel's expressions of sympathy for Morrie and jumped obediently to the wrong conclusion. I would have done better to ask myself whose name Cristobel *didn't* mention once during the course of that first interview: Peter's. And what really got me as I strode through the house and up to my bedroom was that when I had talked to her a couple of hours before she had known I had fixed on Morrie as the father, and she'd let me go on thinking it. Worse, I had the feeling that she'd been playing with me, like an angler with a big and not very bright fish, ever since I arrived. We had been too dismissive of Cristobel's intellect. She clearly had depths of animal cunning I had never hitherto plumbed.

What was still more worrying was the feeling that she was quite simply holding back on me. That she knew something she was not telling. Knew what had been going on in this house, but for some reason or other—and I could think of some—was keeping mum. I didn't like that. It was foolish, it was unsisterly, it was dangerous. One thing I was quite sure of: there had been a letter to me, and Chris knew about it. Why else hold back on the subject of her own letter from our mother? Something she had, according to Kate, burbled on about quite happily at the time she received it. The fact was, she must only recently have found out about my letter.

Somehow found it and read it. And my letter, from Chris's point of view, was obviously a hot potato.

When I got to my stateroom, I flushed the little pile of risotto from my bag down the lavatory, and cleaned my teeth vigorously to get the taste of Aunt Kate's efforts out of my mouth. Then I went over to the desk, to the notebooks that had been sitting there since the night I arrived, and I scrawled 'Peter, Peter, Peter—damn him!' all over a new blank page. That relieved my feelings a bit. I sat down with the intention of being more rational, and I wrote: 'Pregnancy—significant, or just carelessness?' And then I asked: 'Did Cristobel tell Father?'

But no train of thought could bring Cristobel's pregnancy from being a side issue to occupying the centre of the stage. I could not see how the answer to the murder could lie there. I was just about to put down a query on the baffling subject of the letter and its whereabouts when I glanced out of the window and saw Jan and Daniel being shown around the grounds by Sybilla and Mordred. They were near the tree where two nights before I had stood watching Maria-Luisa launch her marital missile, and they started off down towards the lake. Well, it was a lovely afternoon, and the fact is, I couldn't resist. Damn the case, I thought: they're my family. (Ignoring the fact that so was the case.) I went out to them.

Daniel—we seldom call him Dan, by the way, because Jan and Dan sounds like some ghastly cartoon film, with people who talk in funny voices—Daniel was capering around, beside himself with delight. The Trethowans went tremendously up in his estimation for owning such an enormous expanse of ground. And I could see his point. It was a pretty good feeling to know you could get all the exercise you could possibly need without danger from cars or muggers, and without passing beyond the confines of your own domain.

'Daddy! Daddy!' Daniel screamed as I came up. 'I can run for miles and miles and not have to turn round!'

And he suited action to words. I strolled up to the little sight-seeing party—Jan all modest and a-watch, like Elizabeth Bennet being shown over Pemberley—and I greeted the others and put my arm around Jan.

'He loves the space,' she said.

'Children do,' said Sybilla.

'You like space too, Perry,' said Jan.

'Of course he does,' said Sybilla. 'He grew up here.'

I was beginning to get a nasty feeling of being accepted back in the fold.

'Don't the Squealies ever get out into the open?' I asked.

'Sometimes,' said Sybilla, with a downward curve of her discontented mouth. 'Sometimes they're locked in the tennis court. But the eldest are beginning to be able to climb the fence. Today they're all at the dentist.'

'Poor things!' I said. 'I mean the dental people.'

'They have to go to a new one each time. They're known over a wide radius, and they're having to be taken further and further afield. Luckily their mother cuts their hair herself. Now *this*, Jan, is the lake.' (I have commented before on Sybilla's capacity to state the obvious.) 'This is the lake Perry threw Mordred into in the year 'fifty-eight. It was over there . . .'

As Sybilla seemed about to expatiate on this not-very-interesting topic, and still seemed to nurse a motherly sense of outrage, I took Morrie aside.

'Mordred, I'm sorry—'

'Oh, for heaven's sake, Perry. It was twenty years ago.'

'Not for throwing you in, you ass. Since I was ten and you were sixteen I'm rather proud of it. For snapping at you this morning. The fact is, I'd got the idea that you'd done something, and now I find you hadn't.'

'Oh? Denuding the family picture collection?'

'No—making my sister pregnant.'

'Is she pregnant? That would be Pete.'

'Yes,' I said grimly. 'That would be Pete. Did they make it that obvious?'

'Not at all. At least, I never noticed anything. It's just that it's the sort of thing he does. Getting people pregnant makes him feel good.'

'Well, if he must scatter his maker's image through the land, I wish he wouldn't do it via my sister,' I said. 'It makes me puke. It's worse than when I thought it was you. Quite apart from anything else, what's Maria-Luisa going to do when she finds out?'

'Hmmm. If I were Chris I certainly would avoid coming to dinner on the nights when she's cooking what my mama calls her delicious Mediterranean specialities. Though in point of fact it's not the first time our little Neapolitan child of nature has had to face news of that kind.'

'Really? Who else?'

'Oh, there was the wife of a filthy-rich Yorkshire industrialist. Then there was the literary editor of the *New Spectator*.'

'So that's how he got the job. Interesting variant on the old-fashioned interview.'

'He likes the sort who are not likely to sue for maintenance. None of your barmaids or local peasant wenches for Pete. He's very calculating where he dips his wick.'

'Peregrine! Mordred!' came the vulturine voice of Aunt Sybilla. 'What are you so deep in converse over? I will not be left out, Peregrine. Tell me all. Have you found those pictures?'

We were at the far edge of the lake, not far from the summer-house. We stopped, like tourists, to look back at that monstrous house, that heavy load of architectural pretension burdening the strong back of Northumberland.

'Well, actually, yes, Aunt Sybilla,' I said. 'We've found the *Lord Byron,* anyway. It's been . . . at any rate acquired, probably bought, by Newstead Abbey.'

Sybilla was ecstatic. 'You see! You hear that, Mordred? I was right. You've all been mocking me, saying things weren't *really* missing—'

'Half of them were *found,* Mother dear,' said Mordred.

'*Put back!* I was right all along. Somebody is dissipating the family heritage. Peregrine, I really think you have been *quite* clever. It may be we have been misjudging you a teeny bit all these years. So appropriate, too! What a Trethowan has dispersed, a Trethowan recovers!'

'Well, we're not sure of the legal—'

'We shall demand it back. Of course. Now, perhaps if you've

seen enough of the garden, Janet, we could go into the summerhouse and Peregrine can tell us *all*.'

But I didn't want that. I wasn't going to be a police mole,
feeding the gutter press through Aunt Sybilla. Besides, I had seen
through the thick skirting of shrubs a scrap of blue material in the
summerhouse, telling me that Chris was there (she loves that sort
of middling blue that suggests nothing so much as one of the
Women's services). Presumably she had not left the place since we
spoke, or else had come back. Perhaps it had memories of a sentimental or erotic nature for her. Luckily the rest of the party was
headed off by Daniel, who was gazing at the modified jungle
stretching for miles beyond the lake in the direction of Thornwick
and demanding (in a rather grand-seigneurial voice, I thought):
'But I want to see it all!'

Sybilla rather reluctantly consented. 'Perhaps we could go a
little further. He is really rather a *nice* boy, yours, Peregrine.'

Of course I agreed. But with the current standards of comparison available to Sybilla, it was a bit like winning a gold at the
Moscow Olympics. Jan obviously had not yet exhausted her curiosity any more than Daniel had, so I let them go off quite happily
through the undergrowth and made my way over to the summerhouse. I was not welcome. As soon as Chris saw me she set her face
in an obstinate line.

'Go *away*, Perry. You're hounding me. You promised you
wouldn't. I will *not* talk to you.'

'Very well, then, I'll talk to you, Chris,' I said, sitting down
beside her. 'First of all, let me say I've been an absolute fool about
the father of your baby, but you must admit you led me on.' She
looked mulish and kept her mouth shut. 'Now I know it's Pete,
and of course that makes it much worse. Chris, you must leave this
place. Adding another Squealy to the pack is really carrying wild-
life preservation a bit far. Think of the fuss Maria-Luisa is going to
make, and I can't say I'd blame her. I thought you might want to
stick around in the hope that he'd marry you, but now of course
there's no question of that—'

'Who says there's no question?' Cristobel burst out. 'There's
such a thing as divorce.'

'Has that come up? Has he said he wants to marry you?'

'He said wouldn't it be wonderful if we could . . .'

Oh, my God! Don't they teach you *any*thing in the Guides? I held my temper with great difficulty.

'Right. That's the first thing I've at last got straight in my mind. Now for the second. You received a letter, Chris, from Mother, sent by her lawyers, I'd guess on your twenty-first birthday.' She looked obstinate, but shifty. She also looked scared of what was coming. 'I think it very unlikely that Mother, when she was dying, would have written a last letter to you, but not one to me. I believe that a similar letter had also been sent to me, earlier, on my twenty-first birthday. It must have been sent by the lawyers to this house, where it was intercepted by Father—out of spite, or for some other reason. He could have destroyed it, but I don't believe he did. Chris, I think you know of this letter, and I think you know where it is.'

'You're talking in riddles,' said Chris shortly. 'I've never heard of any letters.'

'Chris, don't be entirely dim. When you got yours you went around talking about it to people. Naturally. Everyone in the house knows you got it. I've only got to get on the phone to Mother's lawyers to confirm it.'

'I don't know anything about any letter to you.'

'I think you do. That's why you lied about receiving one yourself. You knew I'd wonder why she hadn't written to me too. Chris: she was our mother. We both loved her. I've got a right to know what she wrote to me. How would you feel if yours had been kept from you? Where is it, Chris?'

I could see that I had got to her. She had flinched when I spoke. But still she remained obstinately dumb.

'Chris, what do the letters WOAF mean?'

'I think they're some kind of United Nations organization.'

'God in heaven, Chris—Father didn't send our mother's letter to a United Nations agency! Come on: tell me what it means.'

But she would say nothing, and sat there obstinately looking ahead of her, her eyes wet but determined. When she gets that Christian martyr look on her there's nothing can shift Chris. I

spent a few minutes battering away at her silence, like waves on
Beachy Head, but after a bit I had to give up. I stormed off. But
it's not very satisfying to shout 'You haven't heard the last of this!'
when you know you've been well and truly worsted.

I suppose it was this feeling of frustration that made me open
up to the McWatterses when I found them in the hall. They were
puzzling over a pile of wreaths that for some reason had been sent
to the house. As it was by no means clear when my revered father
('An Ornament to British Music' as one of the wreath-cards put it)
would be consigned to the earth, it was difficult to know what to
do with them. Finally we decided to ring the family undertaker
and get him to come and take them away. But when we'd done
that we stood around in the hall for a bit, chewing the cud.
McWatters was gently, courteously amused by the whole business,
Mrs McWatters was displaying what is usually called a grim relish
for the misfortunes of Harpenden.

'Did either of you know,' I asked, deciding this was one family
secret it was quite useless to hide from the domestics, 'that my
sister was pregnant?'

They looked at each other. 'Hmmm,' said Mrs McWatters. 'We
had an idea that Something was Up.'

'The summerhouse,' said McWatters roguishly, 'was becoming
more popular than its attractions seemed to justify. Even in summer.'

'I see. I guessed they might have met there. Do you think my
father knew about it?'

'I'd take a wee bet—were I a betting man, which I am not—that
he'd be among the last to hear. There was not much confidence
between the young leddy and her father, particularly not in recent
weeks.'

'McWatters, Mrs McWatters, you can be frank with me: I really
don't count as a member of the family anymore. You must have
overheard a lot of things in this family—'

'Oh, aye,' said McWatters.

'Mek you hair currrl,' said Mrs Mac, descending practically into
the bass clef.

'Always something going on,' said McWatters. 'And us being the only regular staff, not counting the leddies who came by day, we heard a goodly lot of it. I've often said to ma wife that a good book could be made of it. But my tastes run more to the visual arrts. And my wife's religion teaches her to disapprove of fiction as lies.'

'Then *what*,' I said, 'was going on in the weeks before my father died?'

McWatters shook his head regretfully. 'I get your drift, sirr, but as I had to tell the other policeman, I don't rightly know. There was something, right enough. Of course, there was the wee matter of the pictures—you've heard about the pictures, I believe?'

'Aye,' I said. 'Yes. Who would you think took them?'

'We-e-ll,' said McWatters, 'I wouldna' mek accusations, but talking it over, the two of us, we cam' to the conclusion that, psychologically speaking—'

'It was Master Peter!' said his wife triumphantly. 'Not a scruple in his body! As your puir sister has no doubt found out!'

'I'm not quite sure she's faced up to that discovery yet,' I said. 'But you don't think the pictures were the root of the trouble?'

'Naw, I do not. Because the pictures thing had begun to blow over. But your late father—God rest his soul, but I ha' ma doots—certainly had something on. He was all excited. Pleased as a cock sparrow wi' himself, he was. He got like that, periodically as you might say. Chuffed was the word we used to use in the army. And he was chuffed in those last few days before his life was terrminated. But *why* he was chuffed, we havena' been able to put a finger on.'

'You say this happened periodically?'

'Aye. Just now and then. It was a real mystery to us. I'll not be denying we were itching to find out. Natural human curiosity, you might say. But it was no go.'

I sighed. 'Ah well. I suppose neither of you would know anything about a letter my mother wrote to me—wrote before she died, to be given to me when I grew up?'

They shook their heads regretfully. 'It's a good old-fashioned notion, that,' said Mrs McWatters. 'But it would be well before our time, wouldn't it?'

'Yes, it would. Well, never mind—'

'Ye'll excuse my asking, sir, but is there anything actually found out about the pictures?'

'Yes. One of them has definitely been located.'

'Ye'll understand, it's been a mite awkward, since the discovery that they were missing. They've been looking a mite askance, both at my leddy wife and maself. The firrst thing they think of is that the staff is thievin'.'

'I'm sure, McWatters, they trust you absolutely.'

'I'm no' so sure about that. We've had some experiences, ma wife and I, in a previous situation. We were accused by a noble lord of stealing his silver, when we knew his wife was pawning it to spend on immorrral purrposes I would na' like to put a name to. So we've been conscious that there's been talk, that we've been regarrded with the eye of suspicion . . .'

'I think you can be sure that the picture business at least will be cleared up in a day or two,' I said. I added (though I was not sure they really minded being suspected, but really rather enjoyed contemplating the bottomless depravity of the Trethowan mind): 'You mustn't take it too hard, if the family did for a moment wonder . . . After all, living in a disorganized house like this, full of valuable paintings, it wouldn't be surprising if you'd felt the temptation . . .'

'You think so, sir? Pairsonally, since my time in Italy I've never fancied anything later than the Rococo.'

And, conscious that he had said something that was unlikely to be capped, McWatters led his leddy wife back to the servants' quarters. I slowly made my way up that long flight of stairs, so wide and so lonely-making—I always felt like the sole person in some megalomaniac's private opera-house when I walked them. In my bedroom the notebooks and the questions remained, looking reproachfully at me for my dereliction of duty. All the old questions were there, unanswered—or, if I had some provisional answers in my mind, they needed that cornerstone, the establishment of motive, before they could be brought out into the daylight. I wrote:

'Why has Chris been lying?'

and I put down some possible answers: 'to protect herself?' 'to protect her inheritance?' 'to protect Peter?' 'to protect me???'

I had seen when I spoke to her that last time that the only thing that really got through to her was when I spoke of our mother, of my right to know what she had wanted to say to me, to tell me. Chris is like that: she's the sort of person who can only be appealed to on a direct, close, personal level. Larger issues, abstractions, mean nothing to her. Such concepts as Justice are meaningless to her, but the bond between mother and child is the sort of thing that goes straight to her heart. Still, she had resisted it, stuck it out obstinately, and no doubt now she was strengthening her fortifications against future attack.

And the thing was, in a sense, urgent. If Chris knew where the letter was, she could destroy it. Not, probably, while there were policemen all over the house—and certainly not if, as seemed likely, it was hidden somewhere in the Gothic wing. But when they moved out, and things began to return to normal, then she could get at it again, and then she might simply burn it. I didn't want that. Not just for the sake of the case. I did want to know what my mother had written to me. I smiled sadly as I thought of her— poor, pale, ill-adapted creature, lying on that sofa, perhaps, and penning some preposterous injunctions totally out of tune with the world of the 'sixties and 'seventies that I in fact grew up into. No doubt it was something along the lines of Christina's dying letter in *The Way of All Flesh*, which I had read as a boy, and taken seriously, been moved to tears by. A child could not see the deadly irony behind the letter, anymore than he could see the way Christina's egotistical fantasizings were laid bare. But I didn't think my mother's letter would be like Christina's. She might well have been a fantasist, but unless my childish perceptions were totally awry she had none of the egotism of poor Butler's parents whom he so joyously delivered over to public crucifixion. Butler was a very special case, even if he did regard it as the way of all . . .

The Way of All Flesh! Oh my God, what a fool I'd been! WOAF! Just like my father's sense of humour, to hide it snuggled next to Christina's letter. The obvious had been staring me in the face— throwing itself at me only yesterday as I sat in the library, remembering. And I hadn't tumbled to it, even when I looked along the shelves. I jumped up, dashed from the room, and took those gloomy corridors as if I were pacemaker for Steve Ovett. I was down the stairs three at a time and then through the corridors to the Gothic wing like a flash.

'I've had an idea!' I bellowed to PC Smith as he tried to bar my way.

I raced up to the library and stood there looking distractedly along the Thackerays, the Dickenses and the George Eliots. There it was, Butler. First edition of 1903. I pulled it down, and as I held it in my hands it fell open at Chapter 25, at Christina's very letter.

But the letter from my mother, which had been there, was gone.

14

IN WHICH I HAVE
ANOTHER IDEA

It was a blow, but when I thought about it I felt pretty sure I knew what had happened, though I hadn't a scrap of evidence to prove it. The letter had been there, and it had been filched by Chris. She had heard about it, or perhaps she had seen father gloating over it, had investigated, found it and read it. Then she had taken it. *Why?* I did not know, but I did feel gut-sure she had taken it.

I sat there, on the arm of the library sofa, looking at the volume of Butler open at Christina's letter to Ernest. Suddenly an extremely interesting idea occurred to me. Was it not conceivable, in fact, that Cristobel had taken it on the very night of the murder? She had talked that first time about coming down to get aspirin because she couldn't sleep. She had hesitated when she said it. It was possible that the reason she couldn't sleep was connected with her pregnancy, and hence the hesitation. But it was surely equally possible that she had lain in bed, meditating some decisive action in the matter of the letter; that she had come down to the first floor, got the letter from Butler, and then—what? Destroyed it? But how? There had certainly been no fires in the Gothic wing on the day of the murder. The police had moved in on the same night, and since then nothing had been altered. The grates were perfectly clean. If paper had been burned with matches or a lighter, the police would have picked up traces of it, in ashtray or dustbin. And if she was desperate to destroy it, Chris would certainly not regard tearing up as final enough.

She *must*, surely, have hidden it again—if only as a prelude to a more final destruction. And then she had heard, from downstairs, the sound of the machine going . . . On top of the tension involved in the stealing of the letter, it was no wonder the finding of our father had led Chris to her monumental bout of hysterics. The wonder is she didn't miscarry on the spot.

There was only one speck of light in the situation as I saw it: this was that *since* those hysterics, Chris had not set foot in the wing, and could be prevented from doing so now. If necessary we could draft a whole posse of constables from the army currently infesting the house and get them to take the Gothic wing apart. I didn't want that. There was nothing much here I would grieve for, except the books of my childhood, but since the place was now Chris's I did hope it could be prevented. I know what a thorough police search can do to a place.

It was difficult to know what to do next, but as a precaution I went down to warn PC Smith, on the door, that he was to enforce the strictest of bans on *anybody* unauthorized coming into the Gothic wing, and that the main door was to be guarded twenty-four hours a day. No doubt this was in any case supposed to be the rule, but Lawrence's gardeners had got in, no doubt during one of PC Smith's trips to the loo, or to get a bite to eat, and it would do no harm to underline the orders as heavily as I knew how. It was odd, giving orders to PC Smith, who had chased me out of orchards in my youth. I reflected that if I'd tried to join the police at the time I'd left home, and if they'd contacted him, he would probably have told them that I was a young tearaway and not at all the type they were after. PC Smith was not of the brightest, and would probably never have understood my need to break out after my dreary childhood at and around my mother's death-bed.

'What's going on in there?' I said, to break the ice a bit after I'd laid down the law, and jerking my head in the direction of the Torture Chamber.

'Him as made that there Indian rope trick arrangement,' said

PC Smith. 'The Superintendent phoned him, and he turned up half an hour ago, bold as brass and twice as cocky.'

'*Really?*' I said. 'He wasn't a furtive little man in a mac, then?'

'No, sir,' said Smith, bewildered. 'Sun's shining today, sir.'

'So it is. Well, I'd better go in and have a look at him. After all, he's the one who made all this possible.'

'Quite an *ordinary*-looking chap,' said PC Smith, as if deeply disappointed.

And he was right. Mr Ramsay Percival was a sharp, jolly little man, running to fat and to baldness, but with a chirpy manner that even his presence in the same room as his ropey contraption could not dampen.

'Well, well, you must be Mr Peregrine, the poor old fellow's son,' he said, getting up from his chair on the wrong side of Tim Hamnet's improvised desk and coming over with his hand out-stretched. I took it. It's not often you get the chance of shaking hands with the man who's indirectly killed your father.

'How did you know?'

'Your name? It's in all the papers,' he said. 'Big Perry. Picture in the *Northerner*. Your aunt says you have a razor sharp mind like all the Trethowans. She's a genius, that old bird. Marvellous story this is making. Shouldn't wonder if it doesn't prove a real gold-mine for me.'

'I shouldn't wonder either,' I said. 'Do you have a wide circle of clients, or were you living off my father?'

'By no means. I do very nicely—keep myself busy, which is as much as anybody wants, isn't it? Of course, I could expand, but at my time of life who wants to become a tycoon?'

'Tell me,' I said, gesturing him back into the chair and coming over to stand by Tim, 'how you came to go into this line of busi-ness.'

'Just what I was about to tell the Super here,' he said cheerily, deciding to sit on the corner of the desk. 'Well, three or four years ago, I got the sack. Made redundant, they called it, but it didn't take the sting out of it. Getting the sack is pretty much of a facer when you're pushing fifty, I can tell you. Doesn't give you much to look forward to in the years before you start to pick up your

pension. Now, I've always been a handy, inventive sort of chap, all
my life. Now and then I'd knocked up a few little things for my
friends. Ingenious little devices of one sort or another, you know.
Well, I started picking up the odd bit of extra like that, supple-
menting the dole, like. Now, one day I was in the local—the Earl
Grey in Edward Short Street—and I was telling some blokes about
this sprinkler thing I'd made for my mate's garden—smart little
thing, it was, that moved itself round automatically and watered
the whole garden while he was at work. Well now, the next time I
goes to the bar for a refill, this chap comes up to me—'

'Leo Trethowan?' asked Hamnet.

'No, no. Not in the Earl Grey in Edward Short Street. No, well,
this chap—I won't tell you his name—came up to me, asked if he
could buy me a drink. He took me away into a corner and asked if
I was interested in doing a job for him. The fact was, it was a little
pain-giving thing called Pain Forty Dure, if you'll pardon my
French. Don't know if you've heard of it, you gents?' He looked
round at us cheerily. We looked noncommittal, and he seemed
disappointed in us.

'Well, he was a nice bloke, kink apart, and when I'd made the
thing, and given every satisfaction, he said, why didn't I try it for a
living? He suggested I put an ad in one or two of the S-and-M and
fladge publications. Well, I wasn't too sure what he meant—
thought it might be some kind of trade publication. But I got him
to do it for me, and quite frankly, I've never looked back. Always
something new to test my ingenuity, some little quirk or oddity to
be catered for, and that's what makes it such a satisfying profession.'

He looked round at us again, with an expression of enormous
self-approbation.

'Now, I don't know about you gents, but I regard that as a
success story. Just the sort of enterprise and initiative that Old
Mother Thatcher is always recommending: the small, independent bloke finding where the trade is, and going out and getting
it. As she said in Parliament the other day, the work is there, if
people are only willing to seek it out. I should get a Queen's
Award to Industry, by rights.'

'So Mr Trethowan got in touch with you as a consequence of the advertisement, did he?' asked Tim.

'That's it. Talked it over on the phone, I dropped over and had a peep at the room, and Bob's your uncle. When he died, I was working on a rack for him—nice little job, it's over there, you see. He had it on appro, to see how it worked. I was expecting a nice little succession of jobs from Mr Trethowan. Still, the great thing about this trade is, the market never dries up. You're not going to get people's kinks suddenly ironed out, are you? Soon as you lose one, there's another anxious and waiting to take his place. I'd go into exporting if I had the time. I believe Japan's got a marvellous market for things of this kind.'

'You got a fair whack out of Mr Trethowan for this, I see,' said Tim.

'Naturally I did. I always do. They're paying me for my inventive skills, remember. And it's not the kind of thing you can patent and protect yourself on. I must say, in all fairness, the gentlemen with this sort of interest, they're very generous gentlemen. They're a good class, that's what it is: public school, often as not. Very seldom a quibble, which is nice when you're in trade. Keeps it on a genteel sort of basis. The fact is, they appreciate craftsmanship, and they're willing to pay for it.'

'You're not worried by any moral scruples about what you're doing?'

'Good Lord, no. Why would I be? The market's there, and all I do is move in and supply it.'

'Pretty much like a pornographer, eh?'

'That's it. You've hit the nail on the head. In principle it is very much the same sort of thing, and pornography, as you gentlemen know, is perfectly legal these days, especially when published and marketed with the full knowledge and co-operation of the police.'

'Trethowan was pushing seventy,' said Tim. 'You realize you could easily kill yourself with one of these devices?'

' ''Course you could,' said Mr Percival. 'Same as you can on top of a Mayfair tart. If that's the way you choose to go, what business is it of anybody else's? That's what freedom is all about—we're trying to stop the State prying into every aspect of people's lives,

aren't we? And the fact is, as you very well know, Mr Leo—God
rest his soul in peace, if that's what he wants—would be here today
if someone hadn't slipped in and snipped that cord. He was a
gentleman who knew how to enjoy his pleasures *and* take care of
himself at the same time. He knew exactly when he'd gone far
enough. Enjoyed life, Mr Leo did, without endangering himself.'

'You talk,' I said, 'as if we ought to thank you for making the
last years of my father's life full and happy ones.'

'Exactly,' said Mr Percival. 'Very nicely put, and I appreciate
the thought.'

Nothing, clearly, was going to discompose Ramsay Percival.

'I've been wondering,' I said, looking up at the deployment of
ropes and pulleys stretching up to the ceiling, 'where this machine
would be best heard from upstairs, when it was going.' Tim looked
at me sharply, so he had obviously had the same thought. 'Do you
think we could set it going?'

'Nothing easier!' said Mr Percival, with professional pride.

'What we really need,' I said, 'is someone strapped into it. Otherwise the machine won't strain as it ought to do, and we won't
hear anything. You wouldn't like to oblige yourself, Mr Percival?'

'Here! Come off it! I'm normal! I'm old-fashioned—I go for
girls. I never try out my own inventions. It'd be like a bespoke
tailor trying his suits on himself.'

'What a pity. I was looking forward to that. Do you think you
could try your circus act again, Tim?'

'Oh—been trying it out for yourselves, have you, gentlemen?'
said the irrepressible Mr Percival. 'Now, if ever you wanted anything special made for the Yard, I'd be happy to oblige.'

'No chance, I'm afraid,' I said. 'We use the electrodes plugged
into the genitals at headquarters. The march of progress, you
know. Tim, give me two minutes, will you, and then start it up.
Twice will be enough.'

'It will bloody well have to be,' said Tim.

I ran up the stairs again, and went first to the little kitchen
where Chris had said she had gone to get the aspirin. It was on the
wrong side of the wing, and, as I had suspected, nothing could be
heard of the working of the machine from there. So she'd lied

about that. Neither could it from the little sitting-room, which had once been my mother's room. When I moved to the library, a dull sound as of distant jets could be heard if one was exceptionally attentive. It was only when I moved into the study that the noise could be heard at all well. So far so good. I moved around the room, trying to find the point of maximum audibility. It was, in fact, a yard or so from the fireplace. This, presumably, was the point just over the upper pulley, up to which my father (or currently Tim) was being hauled. It was a fair bet that it was around here somewhere that Chris first noticed the noise.

I stood there, looking around me. Had Chris been standing here on Thursday night, looking for a place of concealment? Was she then suddenly struck by the gruesome noise below, forced into the realization that her father was not in bed, but was still being hauled up and down on his appalling machine? But whatever happened, she must have hidden it. Must have made a sudden decision what to do with it, then hurried down to see what was up in the Torture Chamber. Because she certainly didn't take the letter with her on her raving hysterics over the house, wearing only her nightdress. Where, then?

And as I stood there, looking at the fireplace and the Dali over it, I remembered telling Chris about Lawrence sending the outdoors men to take it away. She had said 'The Dali!', with a catch in her voice. Then it came back to me that the night before, when Lawrence had gone on and on about retrieving 'his' property, Chris had immediately chimed in with the claim that Father had assured her that the Dali was his, that he had bought it himself. Now the claim was patently absurd. The Dali had been bought in the late 'twenties, was a product of his Paris period. At that time my father was a student at the Guildhall School, had inherited nothing from his father, and was certainly in no position to purchase young but fashionable painters. I had assumed that the lying claim was Leo's, which Chris had not seen through. But what if it was Chris's—and prompted not by a desire to assert her claims on portable property, but because she had hidden the letter there?

I went over and took it down from the wall. At least it was the sort of picture you *could* lift from the wall, unlike the John Martin

in my bedroom. I laid it on the floor and inspected the back. Yes—
a narrow slit had been made there, and inside . . . I eased my
fingers into the slit, and caught a glimpse of blue paper. I enlarged
the slit, and drew out a long envelope. It was ladies' notepaper,
'fifties style—a blue, padded envelope such as I remembered my
mother using. I turned it over. It was addressed: 'To my dear son
Peregrine Trethowan.'

I got out of that hated study, my father's own room, and went
through to the library, where I had spent so many childhood
hours to be within call of my mother. I sat down on the sofa, and
took out of the envelope four small sheets covered with my
mother's thin, angular handwriting—the writing I remembered so
well from her letters to me when she travelled abroad for her
health. For a moment I could hardly bear to unfold the sheets:
they seemed addressed to another person—a quiet, lonely child,
haunting a gloomy house.

Finally I took my courage into my hands and opened it. It was
dated March 21st, 1958—about two months before my mother's
death. I read:

My darling Perry,
  When you read this, I shall be dead—and so long dead, I
suppose, that you will have forgotten me, have only dim
memories of what I looked like, what I sounded like.

No Mother. I remember. I remember very well. I can hear you
now.

I know that I was a poor mother to you, Perry, and to Cristobel. And especially that I could do so little for a strong,
healthy boy like you. But something in me hopes that you
will have some remembrances of me, and retain a little from
our talks together. Above all, I know that you will always
have done your duty as a brother, and looked after little
Cristobel, as you faithfully promised.

That really got me, and I broke down, bawling unashamedly, feeling more feeble and inadequate than I had felt, perhaps, since the day my mother died. A fine one I had been, to have been entrusted with the care of Cristobel. A fine job I had made of it.

I don't think [my mother wrote] that there is any last message I can give you that will help you in any way in life. It is not for the dying and the failed to try to do this. I feel confident, Perry, that you, who are a determined little boy, will make your way in life creditably and successfully.

It is because I know that you will grow up steel-straight and with a heart full of honour—

And I cried again, at the G. A. Henty sentiments and the Freudian imagery, and the absurdity of imagining anyone of my generation growing up with a heart full of honour.

—that I entrust to you the following facts, to act on as you see fit. You see, I believe I know you, and I believe that when you are a man you will know the *right*, and the *upright*, thing to do. I wish I did myself—wish I did not have to rely on you to make a decision I am unable to make myself, but I feel totally incapable of action. You see, I am depending entirely on your judgment of what a gentleman's duty is.

Last year I went, you will remember, on a cruise in search of the health that has eluded me for many years. Alas, it was of no avail, but that is not the point now. I went, you may remember, around the world, on the *Stratheden*. When the ship docked at Sydney and began the return voyage via the Panama Canal, there came to the next table from my own a Mrs Trethowan. She was very vulgar, and jolly, and familiar, and tried to scrape up an acquaintance on the basis of our names. No, on re-reading this I think I am being unfair. I have no reason to think she was not what people call a 'good-sort', but you know how tongue-tied I am, and how difficult it is for me to talk easily to those who are not of our own sort.

She was Irish by birth, an East Londoner by upbringing, and had lived in Sydney for more than twenty years. She kept a hat shop there. I confess, I tried to avoid her, to freeze her off. However, one day, when the boat was in the South Seas, she sat herself down beside me on deck, and insisted on confiding her life-story to me. And to my horror it became clear that she was Florence Trethowan—'Flo' as he always called her, when he spoke of her at all—the first wife of your Uncle Lawrence, who according to him had died long ago, before the Second War. I couldn't believe my ears at first, but there could be no doubt about it: she had been to Harpenden, briefly; had lived with Lawrence in London for a few years in the early 'twenties; had brought up his son Wallace who died at Arnhem. The frightful thing was, that when she talked of Lawrence—in a sadly bold and indiscreet way—she always referred to him as 'my husband', and announced more than once: 'I'm a Catholic. I don't believe in divorce. He wanted one, but I refused point-blank. He'll have to wait till I'm pushing up the daisies before he gets spliced again, and I'm not going to pop off in a hurry.' She talked like that. It was quite frightful. So frightful that when she asked me about my family, I told a lie—the first one that came into my head: that we came from Cornwall. After a time, thank Heaven, she gave me up, and found friends more to her own taste and of her own class.

Perry, my darling, I have worried and worried over this, and have come to no conclusion about what is right. Of course you will see at once how this affects you. It affects your father too, as you must realize, but for various reasons, and because it could probably only be of consequence to him *very late in his life,* I prefer to confide the matter to you, leaving it to your judgment as a *man,* and as a Christian, as well as a member of a family which, to be fair, one must say has made its mark in the world. It is you who must decide whether this matter should be brought out into the light, with all the consequences that must flow from this. I am happy to die in the serene knowledge that you will take the *honourable* as well as the gentlemanly course.

And now, Perry, it is time to say goodbye.

Your very loving
Mother.

And I sat there in the library, and cried and cried. And laughed too, now and then, through my tears. Did my mother think she was presenting me with a delicate test of my honour, a nicely balanced ethical problem? Did she think of Harpenden House and the headship of the Trethowan family as an inducement? A prize to be won? A shimmering gold light at the end of the tunnel? How little she foresaw! I should have no qualm about renouncing the throne of the Trethowans. The problem was, how was it to be done.

15

A Concentration of Nightmares

I calmed down after a bit. I took out a handkerchief, blew my nose and wiped my eyes, and sat on in the library, wondering what the hell I was going to do.

Not about Harpenden and the heirship of the Trethowans, of course. That was a poisoned chalice I had no difficulty in repulsing. Even my mother, underneath, had wanted me to reject it. That much, on looking the letter over again, it was possible to read between the lines. I wished my motives were as pure and upright as my mother would have desired. Still, I had the feeling that she too did not think the Trethowans much of a family to be head of.

But the question remained: how was I to do it? How was the information in my mother's letter to be kept secret? Because the news that I was the 'rightful heir' (Oh God! How that brought back Jan's and my laughing over whether I or Peter was the Young Master!) was a vital piece, the last vital piece, in the case against the murderer of my father. And as soon as I revealed it to the police—to the *other* police, that is: I must never forget that I was part of them—the information was open, public, never more to be concealed. To tell the family was one thing. I could see that that would probably have to be done. But to tell the police was to licence them to bring it out in court. And if that happened, I was lost. Loaded on my back would be the burden of Harpenden and the assorted dreadfuls that made up the Trethowan family.

Amateur weightlifter I may be, but not even Rakhmanov could bear such a load as that.

One solution, it occurred to me, would be to conceal the letter and let the murderer go unpunished. It was not as though I felt a Hamletish compulsion to avenge the death of my father. The Prince of Denmark could perhaps not take the line that his old man was well out of the way—an awfully long-winded old chap he must have been, though, to judge by his post-mortem incursions —but I suffered from no such inhibitions. Nevertheless, there is in a policeman (the old-fashioned policeman, a dying species, like the sperm whale) an instinct that tells him that crime, and of all crimes murder, must not go unpunished. That it, above all, is something that threatens the social fabric, and must be seen to incur society's wrath. Awfully dated stuff, that, but somewhere at the back of my mind it clung. And, quite apart from anything else, who could tell where it might not end? If my father could be killed for the knowledge he acquired from my mother's letter, might not Chris in the course of time likewise fall victim, having the same knowledge? I was not going to compound my ineffectiveness as Chris's protector by virtually conniving at her murder.

It came to me gradually, as I sat there in the mounting gloom, that the only way I might conceivably be safe, safe from the burden of Harpenden, was by staging a confrontation. Even then, a lot would depend on the murderer's reaction. But I was a Trethowan—with disgust and self-loathing I admitted it; at any rate I was Trethowan enough to be fairly confident that I could get inside this murderer's mind, that I could know what his reaction would be. And if I was right, then I would be safe: Tim could do the carting away, and I could in total secrecy tell the family the whole background, make it clear to them that the information was entirely confidential, that I had no intention of acting on it. Then I could bow out of Harpenden. Hey presto, Perry Trethowan, the fabulous escape artist, leaps out of his chains and is a free man again. Curtain and general applause. As long as the information was shared, Chris would be safe, and the atmosphere in the house would not be poisoned by uncertainty and mutual suspicion. Not more than usual, anyway.

I wondered how I would put the matter to Tim. For a start I did not want him in on the confrontation: that would be a lot more effective if it at least *began* as a family powwow, however much the screw might have to be turned later on. Tim could be out there in the hall, but no closer. A bobby in the room always turns any occasion into something as natural and informal as the Sun King's *levée*. And how much should I tell Tim? That answered itself: as much as need be, and no more. On the real motive I would hold back till the bitter end. Not unless the poor chap actually had to prepare a case would I come clean. Tim would surely go along with that if I put a bit of pressure on him. After all, there was other evidence, circumstantial though that might be, to justify a trial confrontation.

I decided to give it a try. But in spite of that it was slowly, and with dragging feet, that I made my way down again to Tim. This was going to be very painful and tricky. It could also prove the decisive few hours of my life.

I had been up there in the library so long, lost in thought, that when I came down Mr Percival had gone about his business, back to his vocation of bringing pain and pleasure to his select little clientele. It was obvious when I opened the door to the Torture Chamber that Tim was pretty pleased with himself. Nothing of interest had been got from Mr Percival, not surprisingly, but one of Tim's underlings had finally got on to the member of the New-stead Board of Trustees who had been mainly involved in the buying of the William Allan.

'Offered for sale by Mr Peter Trethowan,' said Tim triumphantly. 'Fat Pete himself. Sorry, old chap: forgot he was a cousin. All negotiations conducted by him. Naturally they knew his father was still alive, and they asked for his authorization to sell. Which Little Lord Fauntleroy brought them, signed and sealed.'

'Which means—?'

'Either forged, I take it, or obtained when he was having one of his "off days".'

I had my own ideas about that, but I held my peace. I just said: 'Very satisfactory. That's one little loose end neatly tied up.'

'Precisely,' said Tim. 'And it lets your late father off that particular hook, if you'll pardon the expression.'

'Yes,' I said. 'He wasn't in on that little game.'

I wondered whether we ought to go further into the question of Peter, whether I ought to inform Tim that, in addition to his other delinquencies, he was also the seducer of my sister. But Chris's pregnancy had not come up, and if she was to be kept out of it, as I fervently hoped would be possible, there was no real need to confide it to Tim at all. So instead I said:

'Tim, do you think we could go over the case as a whole? I've got something to suggest.'

And so we chewed it over, threw it back and forth, and it soon became clear that Tim was on the same road as I was, and pretty much as far along it. Bright boy, Tim. I liked him. So far, so good. I then made my confession that there was one piece of evidence that I was loath to bring forward, for family reasons. I felt a bit of a heel doing it: morally I bamboozled Tim with the old aristocratic family notion (which frankly I don't give a pin for). And I'm afraid he was impressed by it. The great families of this country *did* have their secrets, he seemed to feel. He metaphorically touched his forelock to me. I (mentally) shuffled with embarrassment, and hastened to say that if it became clear that nothing could be done without the evidence I was withholding, I would place it at his disposal like a shot.

I went on, becoming quite eloquent, to put to him the various reasons why I did not think it would be necessary. I began to sell him the idea of a confrontation, a private one, between me and my family, in which the evidence we both had was put before the murderer, fairly, squarely and brutally. I frankly admitted I did not know how it would work out: there might be a confession, there might be blank denial, there might be some other catastrophe. But I didn't see how anything could be lost by it, from our point of view.

Tim was reluctant, at first. He is a cautious chap, as most really good policemen are. There was something flamboyant, a touch of the Dame Agatha, about the whole procedure that he didn't quite take to. But finally, after a burst of my rhetoric and an appeal to

him as a comrade, he fell in with the idea. We arranged that I
would go down to sherry as usual, and he and a couple of men
would station themselves in the hall, outside the drawing-room
door.

'But it's such a hell of a big room, Perry,' said Tim. 'How am I
going to hear?'

'Strain your ears,' I said. 'Just strain your bloody ears.'

He shook his head dubiously, and I could see he did not really
like it. As I was going out of the door, he said:

'Sure you won't tell me, Perry, what it is you've got hold of?'

And I replied, oozing an agonized sincerity: 'It's a terribly delicate family matter, Tim.'

You bastard, Perry Trethowan. This case was bringing out the
lowest I was capable of. Still, I was glad it was Tim that Joe had
sent on the case. Glad, too, as it turned out, that Joe had drafted
me as well. Think what could have happened if he hadn't. Tim
might have come breezing back to the Yard and presented me
with the heirship of the Trethowans as if it was the season's biggest
win on the Treble Chance.

All this took time. When I got out of the Gothic wing, wiping
my forehead with the strain of it, it was already nearly seven. On
an impulse I ran upstairs, had a shower, and packed some of my
things into my little case. No harm in hoping, after all. With a little
bit of luck I could be out of here in a couple of hours. I could
spend the night with Jan at the Danby, and drive her back to
Newcastle next day. You've no idea how attractive a Sunday in
Newcastle can sound when you've been lodged for a few days in a
madhouse like Harpenden.

That made it nearly half past. Sherry-time, and hour of decision. I squared my shoulders, told my heart to stop thumping, and
marched out of the bedroom. As I walked down the stairs I realized that—clean and showered though I was—the sweat was starting to run. This was it: the decisive coin was spinning in the air,
and somehow or other I was going to have to will it to come down
heads.

I saw Tim and other dark shapes lurking down one of the
corridors. We had arranged that they would not take up their

positions until everyone was assembled in the drawing-room. I made no sign to them, but turned at the bottom of the stairs and pushed open the door to the drawing-room.

And there they all were, or most of them, tucking into the sherry. Aunt Sybilla, in one of her most awful drapes, long and magenta, with a heavy amethyst necklace round her scrawny throat. Aunt Kate, in some female equivalent to battle dress. Chris in something frilly and unsuitable. Uncle Lawrence, tucked round with a rug, feeble but assertive. Mordred looking as if drink never passed his lips, but drinking. And there too was Jan, with a self-satisfied, now-I'm-part-of-the-family look on her face. Not for long, my girl, I said to myself grimly. Daniel was standing by her chair, clutching a soft drink, and looking as if this was a very fair substitute for children's television.

A policeman is used to situations where he has, willy-nilly, to take command. But I wanted to start this coolly, so when Uncle Lawrence said in his grand way: 'Sherry, m'boy? Fetch him one, Kate,' I accepted, but coming down to the fireplace (marble, quarried in Carrara or some such place and brought by donkey and steam-train across Europe, to be carved into something infinitely hideous in the North of England) I put my glass down on its absurdly assertive top and turned to them all.

'I wonder,' I said, 'if I might ask something. I thought I ought to have a few words with you all tonight about how the case is going, just to put your minds at rest a bit. If you agree, it might be a good idea if just for this once the Squealies didn't come along.'

'Excellent notion,' said Sybilla.

'Pity to disappoint the little darlings,' said Lawrence.

'Mordred, go along and fetch Peter and Maria-Luisa *alone*,' said Sybilla, flapping a drape.

'Damned woman,' said Lawrence.

'What about Daniel?' asked Mordred, as he made for the door.

'Oh,' I said. 'Perhaps he could go in with the Squealies.'

'No!' said Daniel, with more firmness than I've ever known him muster. So I left him, convincing myself, as adults do, that he would understand very little of what was going on.

I stood there awkwardly, waiting for Peter and Maria-Luisa. I felt Jan's eyes on me: she knew I was up to something. I would very much have preferred her not to be there. Sybilla was sitting snug, pursing her lips with anticipation, wafting her drapes around as if she were part of some ghastly infants' school play. Chris, I noted, was looking mulish. At last the door opened.

'Oh—Pete, Maria-Luisa—' I began.

'What's this? Taken over the family, Perry?' muttered Pete unpleasantly, as they marched in, two mountainous bulges of hostile flesh. And though I hadn't intended it, I suppose it did look a bit as if I'd taken charge.

'I wonder,' I began, now disconcerted, 'if we could put our drinks aside for a moment. This won't take long, but it'll need a bit of concentration.'

Pete, on his way to the drinks tray, glared at me in outraged, puffy dignity, like some Middle-European kingling who has been told by his Prime Minister to give up his favourite mistress.

'Who the bloody hell do you think you are?' he asked, and poured doubles for himself and his wife.

Well, eventually they would have to know the answer to that question. For the moment I was just a policeman. I could not restrain myself from throwing him a glance of distaste, but then I drew myself up, saw that the rest had put their glasses by (even, charmingly, Daniel) and were looking at me slightly agape. No doubt about it, they were interested! Time to take the plunge.

'I thought you should know—Uncle Lawrence, Aunt Sybilla, er, all of you—a little about how the case is going. These things take time, and it must seem an eternity to you all already. But we have at least come some way. We seem, for example, to have cleared up one or two side issues, such as the missing pictures—'

'I fail to see,' said Sybilla, looking like a hen who has had her favourite nest-egg snatched from under her, 'how the pictures can be described as a side issue.'

'Nevertheless, they are,' I said. 'Let's ignore them for the moment and concentrate on the main issue: the fact that my father was murdered.'

'Poor old Leo,' said Uncle Lawrence. 'Awful little squirt, but nobody here wished him any harm.'

'No?' I said. 'And yet it's always been difficult for us—us of the police, I mean—to see this as the work of an outsider. It seemed so much more likely that the murderer was someone who knew my father's habits, knew how the machine worked, knew him well enough to break in on him while he was, so to speak, at it. In fact, the first thing that struck me,' I went on, looking around the half-moon of attentive faces, 'almost as soon as I heard of the murder method, was the boldness of it. The aplomb. The theatricality.'

'As a family we are famous for our panache,' said Sybilla, purring.

'Precisely,' I said. 'I think I went a little wrong here, but that *was* one of the things that seemed to me to bring it home here, to Harpenden House. Of course, another way of looking at it might be to say that it was childish. To snip the cord while my father was playing his little sado-masochistic games might in itself seem, to a child, something of a game.' Daniel was about to put in some devastating question, but fortunately he was interrupted by a savage imprecation of a spectacularly southern kind from Maria-Luisa. Uncle Lawrence, too, looked very distressed and muttered: 'Lot of damnable nonsense.'

'Quite,' I said. 'I'm inclined to agree with you. The idea that it was done by the Squealies didn't originate with me. But I noticed that once it was in the air, it spread like wildfire through the house. With the honourable exception of their mother, everyone seems to have thought it a frightfully good idea. It fitted so well. Nobody seems to have reflected that in a sense the Squealies were not the only children in the house.'

'He means me!' said Kate, clapping her hands with glee.

'It was rather the same with the idea of the McWatterses as the thieves of the pictures,' I carried on. 'And I have to admit that the idea occurred to me when I heard he spoke Italian.'

'Well, it did seem *frightfully* suspicious, Perry dear,' said Sybilla, wafting delicately.

'An attractive idea: the art-connoisseur thief, who takes up butling and purloins the family collection. But if that was the case, why did he reveal he spoke Italian after the murder, when he knew the police were on to the question of the missing pictures?

He'd always kept quiet about it, and could have gone on doing so. No . . . it didn't add up. It looked to me as if you were all—forgive me—trying to shift the blame from one of the family, or from any member of it likely to be arrested and tried. Perhaps because you knew who had done it. Perhaps because you merely *suspected*.'

'Being a bit long-winded, aren't you, Perry?' said Peter, going back for a refill.

'Yes,' I said. 'But we'll be getting down to brass tacks in a moment. Now, I mentioned the theatricality of the thing. It seemed, as I say, childish. Perhaps, also, it could have been revengeful. I wondered whether some victim of my father's little kink might not be taking a spectacular revenge—a revenge that would certainly be clear enough to his victim in his last minutes. Uncle Lawrence didn't think there was anybody here that fitted the bill . . .'

'Not *here*,' emphasized Lawrence. 'Could have been someone from London. God knows what he got up to in London.' He licked his lips reminiscently, as of one who has got up to many things in London in his time.

'Once again, an outsider,' I commented.

'Well, why *shouldn't* it be?' burst out Cristobel, with that stupid-obstinate look which irritated me no end still on her face. 'It's perfectly possible. The insurance people have complained about the security here.'

'I think I've made it clear why that's unlikely,' I said. 'In fact, one of the things that really made me rethink my preconceptions about the murder was that, though you're all trying to put the thing on to an outsider, *almost any other* method of murdering my father would have been easier to attribute to an intruder from outside the house. That made me think. Right you are—now we'll get down to the brass tacks, as Peter demanded. When I first came here and started on the case, three things struck me at once.' I looked at them hard, and counted the things off on my fingers. 'One: almost any other method of killing would have been *safer*. Two: granted that it had to be done this way, why was the cord *snipped*, and at that height? Three: why were the lights not switched off? And to these questions I later added a fourth: why

were the scissors, which brought the murder unquestionably
home to Harpenden, hidden where they were?'

God, I was being corny. Colombo didn't come within an ace of
me! But, corny as it was, it got their attention. They goggled at me,
in painful thought.

'Just like the party games we used to play when I was a gel,' said
Sybilla. 'I used to love brain-teasers.'

'I give up,' said Kate. 'Tell us the answers!'

'Right. Take the second of the questions first. Now, if I was
going to kill my father while he was at his damned strappado, I
think I'd try to give at least the appearance that the cord was worn
away naturally. That was not done. Again, if I was going to cut the
cord, I think I'd have used a sharp kitchen knife. That was not
done either. Scissors were used. And consider at what height they
were used. Where, if I was standing watching my father playing
his silly and dangerous games, *where* would it be natural to snip
the cord?'

I pantomimed a pair of scissors in my hand, and holding them
at a natural height I snipped the air with them.

'How high was that? Over three feet from the ground, definitely. Very well, I'm tall. You, Mordred: you're about five feet
nine. Where does it come natural to you to cut? . . . Well above
two and a half feet from the ground, if I'm any judge.'

'Damned mathematics,' said Pete.

'But there's a point to it. The cord was snipped at little more
than *two* feet from the floor.'

'For Christ's sake, he could have bloody bent down,' said Pete.

'Why should he? But that's what most of us here would have to
have done.'

Maria-Luisa once again started up one of her train-whistle im-
precations, and began going on about *bambini*. I held up my copper's hand for silence.

'You're getting the wrong end of the stick. Now, remember my
third point: the light wasn't switched off. But surely it would have
been natural for the murderer to try to cover up what was happening in some way: here was my father being slowly strappadoed
to death, and yet his shadow could surely have been seen, through

the curtains, from the grounds. Anyone might have come in and cut him down. And yet the light wasn't switched off.'

I heard Aunt Sybilla, under her breath, mutter 'A Squealy', and Maria-Luisa shot a look like a stiletto in her direction.

'A Squealy, you say, Aunt Sybilla? But if it was a Squealy, wouldn't he (or she) either have just dropped the scissors on the floor and run? Or—if he was cunning—taken them back to the bathroom cupboard they came from? Hiding them argues *first* a knowledge of the enormity of the act, which I don't think any of the Squealies would have had; and *second* some knowledge that forensic science could have connected those scissors to the murder —and that they certainly wouldn't have had. Again, why did the murderer not get rid of the scissors outside the house? *Somewhere* in those enormous grounds. To slip out and chuck them in the lake would have been a natural impulse, even if we might eventually have found them, by dragging. And yet, they were hidden in the house, on the very floor the murder was committed on.'

Someone shifted uneasily. I thought it was Mordred. I was getting through. I went on quickly.

'It was when I put all those four things together that I realized that there was an alternative reading of the things that puzzled me. One that could be equally valid. I had concentrated on the theatricality of the whole set-up, the blatant self-advertisement. I had thought it—if you'll pardon me—typical of the family. But what if it was quite fortuitous? What if the murder was done like that because *there was no other way for the murderer to do it?*'

The silence was total. I had them in my hand, and as I looked at them I thought I saw dawning, reluctant understanding in one or two faces.

'Or to put it like this,' I went on, my voice rising with a touch of melodrama, of the old Trethowan theatricality: 'who *could* not have shot, knifed, poisoned, smothered anyone in what we may call the normal way, nor arranged a deceptive-looking accident? Who *could* not switch off the light, nor get out of the house to hide the scissors? Who would *naturally* have cut the cord of the machine at about two feet from the ground?'

I let my voice ring into silence. And in that silence Mordred looked at Uncle Lawrence. And Sybilla looked at Mordred, and then at Uncle Lawrence. And then the rest took their eyes off me, and looked at Uncle Lawrence. Lawrence himself seemed to have shrunk down into his rug. Suddenly the silence was broken.

'Oh, Lawrence,' giggled Kate. 'You didn't, did you? You are *naughty!*'

Lawrence—all eyes on him, thirsty for sensation—suddenly seemed to lose his passivity. He forced himself out of his rug and forward in his chair; he fixed me with a malevolent eye and began to raise his right arm. His quivering finger pointed at me, and he bellowed:

'You—you damned—' but his arm refused to go higher, and he looked at it in horror—'liar! Aaaaahhhh.'

The shriek was hideous, like a stuck pig, and the arm, which had seemed paralysed, clutched his heart as he let out breathless, agonized yelps, choking, spluttering, going hideously purple, like *The Death of Chatterton.*

'Oh, Perry,' howled Kate, genuinely concerned. 'Look what you've done. He's had a stroke.'

But before she could get to him, Tim was through the oak door, his men following, and he had Lawrence down on the floor, applying artificial respiration. Providentially—or rather, at my suggestion—they had a stretcher ready, and an ambulance outside. Within minutes, and still hard at the first aid, they were trundling him out of the room and pushing him head first into the ambulance at the door. I had stood aside while all this was going on, as if in unconcern. In fact, I (at least) was breathing normally, for the first time for half an hour. The plan had worked. I was going to be safe.

I was conscious, as the sound of the ambulance faded down the drive and along the road to Thornwick, that everybody was looking at me, and hardly in a spirit of friendship.

'That,' said Pete, 'was too bloody thick for words.'

'Was it?' I said. 'When we had come to that conclusion, he would have had to be faced with it. If it had been done tête-à-tête, him and Hamnet, I imagine the result would have been the same.'

'You mean that he would have had a stroke?' asked Sybilla.

'I mean there would have been an appearance of that,' I said.

There was a long, long silence, as everybody tried to take in the significance of that. As for Lawrence as murderer, they all accepted it without difficulty: I suspected, with no evidence for my suspicion, that for many of them it was not too great a surprise. Who could tell what these odd people knew about each other, but preferred to conceal? Perhaps some of them were glad it was not someone nearer and dearer. Lawrence was hardly adept at making himself loved. But then, which of them was? Sybilla seemed to take the first word by some order of precedence.

'Poor, poor dear Lawrence,' she breathed, in a spirit of benediction. 'So it was Lawrence after all.'

'I'm afraid so,' I said. 'Lawrence couldn't switch off the light, because, as you all know, he could barely raise his hands as far as his mouth. He could manoeuvre his chair around the ground floor of the house, and around Kate's wing, which had the lift, but he couldn't go upstairs to the rest of the house, or into the garden. Scissors were much easier for a half-paralysed man to manage than a knife—he would have had to hold the cord in one hand and cut with the other: I doubt if he had the coordination, and it would have taken too much time. I said earlier there were perhaps other children in the house, besides the Squealies. Let's be charitable and assume that Lawrence did this when he was not in full control of his faculties. As far as the outside world is concerned, he did it in a fit of senile malice.'

'He wasn't so jolly senile,' said Aunt Kate.

'Don't be foolish, Kate,' said Sybilla sharply.

'As I say, we have to take the line that he was, whatever our suspicions, and whatever we feel about the supposed stroke we have just witnessed. Uncle Lawrence will by now be in hospital. After that he will no doubt be put into some kind of institution, and the police doctors and psychiatrists will get on to him. I suspect that nobody will actually *want* to put him on trial. Who knows? Perhaps he *will* retreat into that other, shadow world of his.'

'Poor old man,' said Jan.

'Is that the end of the story, Daddy?' piped up an unregarded Daniel.

'Well, no,' I said. 'Not quite.'

'The *motive*,' said Mordred. 'If it wasn't a senile fit—and of course I don't believe that for a moment—then *why* did he do it?'

'Look here, Perry,' said Peter, stirring his flabby bulk uneasily. 'I get your point. My old dad did it, and I'm not denying it. Had half a suspicion that might be the case. Can't we leave it at that?'

'Not quite,' I said. 'You're trying to avoid *why* he did it. I think I know why you're trying to avoid it—I think it's because, by means we need not go into, you actually know. But if we leave it at that, you're all going to be asking questions for the rest of your lives. Was it some senile grudge of no importance, or was there something behind it? And if there was something behind it, are the rest of us safe? So I think you ought to know that there *was* something behind it: whether or not the killing was done when he was in his right mind, he had a motive. And at this point I'm going to have to ask you, *all* of you, to swear to keep what I'm about to tell you to yourselves. It's to be regarded as absolutely and permanently secret. Do you all swear to that?'

They all nodded their heads enthusiastically, greedily. Peter, I thought, nodded more enthusiastically and greedily than the rest. He realized I had no desire to rob him of his little kingdom.

'Then, if you all agree that what is coming goes no further than this room, I'll tell you. My mother, in the last years of her life, was on a cruise—'

'Oh, Perry,' howled Chris. 'You've found out. Do you have to tell everyone?'

'My sister,' I said, in my most elder-brotherly kind of way, 'who has not been as frank and open with me during this case as I should have liked, already knows what I'm about to tell you. Yes, Chris, I do have to tell them. This is murder, and if I don't, suspicion and distrust will go on festering for the rest of your lives. And apart from that, telling them is a form of protection for *you*. Right, then. My mother, on the round-the-world cruise she took in nineteen fifty seven, met a woman who claimed to be, and undoubtedly was, the first Mrs Lawrence Trethowan.'

'Peregrine!' shrilled Sybilla. 'You don't mean it! Not the appalling Florrie! The Gibson girl!'

She looked around her in theatrical amazement. Pete looked furious; the rest were still taking it in.

'Jolly pretty little thing, wasn't she?' said Kate.

'I think she had worked in the theatre,' I said diplomatically. 'When my mother met her she owned or ran a hat shop in Sydney. The vital point, as you must all see, is that she was still alive in the 'fifties, not dead in the 'thirties as Lawrence had given out. And he had given it out, of course, because he was unable to divorce her. As perhaps you know, she was a Catholic. If she gave him no cause, and if she refused to divorce *him,* the marriage was virtually indissoluble. He was still legally married to her, as my mother realized, and for all I know he still may be. His second marriage was bigamous.'

'Oh, I say,' said Morrie, 'but that means—'

'You don't have to spell it out, for Christ's sake,' said Peter.

'No, let's not spell it out. But that's the reason why we all must keep it secret. Anyway, the rest can be told fairly quickly. My mother communicated this to me in a letter, to be sent to me on my twenty-first birthday. It was no doubt sent here by her lawyers, and appropriated by my father. I have no doubt it put him in a terrible quandary. On the one hand it made him Lawrence's legal heir, under the terms of Great-Grandfather's entail. On the other hand, he could not reasonably expect to enjoy the exalted position of head of the Trethowan family for long. Then it would inevitably descend to me. That he could not bear the thought of. He hated, absolutely hated me. I realize that now. So he compromised by screwing money out of Lawrence. He had been doing this, I imagine, since nineteen sixty-nine, the year I became twenty-one.'

'Ah—hence the stinginess!' said Kate.

'Precisely. Lawrence wanted to leave the estate as intact as possible to Peter, and via Peter to the eldest of the Squealies, whom he loved.'

'They have names!' said Maria-Luisa, suddenly, in English.

'Quite right. I beg your pardon. To . . . Pietro, is it? Mario? Pietro, yes. Lawrence did not dare to make over the estate to Peter in his lifetime, in case it aroused questions about the death of his first wife. That's why he'd gone to great lengths to keep his second divorce quiet and scandal-free. And all the time my father was slowly—not outrageously, but surely—milking him of money. And Lawrence knew that after he died, Peter would be milked in the same way. That wasn't the only drain on the estate: over the past few years his son had been filching pictures from the house and selling them off.'

'Come off it, Perry,' said Peter, with a cunning expression on his face. 'That was done with his consent. To keep paying off *your* damned father.'

'It's possible,' I said. 'Plausible. Perhaps we can leave it at that. We could prove it one way or the other by getting an expert to look at the signature on the authorization to sell which you gave to the Newstead Abbey people. Shall we do that? No? Well, personally I suspect that he did not authorize that or any other sale, but he did consent to cover up for you afterwards. That, as I said, is a minor matter. What does seem to be clear is that my father, in the last few weeks, began to make his demands more pressing. Why? Well, I don't know, but I wonder whether it wasn't just for fun. Just as the tortures got more and more extreme, so Lawrence had to wriggle more, otherwise my papa didn't get his kick. And Lawrence took the necessary steps and killed him in the only way he could think of. He simulated an "off-day"—'

'I said he was often spoofing,' said Kate.

'—got out from Kate's wing in the lift, got easily over to the Gothic wing, used the scissors he had secreted earlier, hid them *also* on the ground floor, near the wing which had no connection with him or his, and went back to Kate's.'

'Doesn't sound as if he was having a senile fit to me,' said Kate.

'As far as we are concerned, that is the explanation we must press,' I said patiently. 'Ultimately it will be up to the police doctors, and the psychiatrists. If Uncle Lawrence is the man I take him for, he will make mincemeat of the psychiatrists. I would think it in the highest degree unlikely that he will ever come to trial. What is important is that we all, now we have heard the truth, put it *absolutely* out of our minds. I need hardly say I have no intention of acting on this information. Everything will remain as it was, and Pete will take over when Lawrence dies—or, as I suspect, rather before.' I looked round at him. Peter was expressing no great gratitude, but he did look relieved. 'Well, that's all I have to say. I'm sorry it took so long. Now I need a drink, and I expect you do too.'

I drew my fist across my forehead. It was wet as hell, and my clean shirt was nastily damp. But all that mattered was that I had got through it. I had managed it. Lawrence was on his way to some kind of clink, and I was out of the wood. Soon Jan and Daniel and I would be out of the snake-pit and on our way to Newcastle.

But then suddenly things took a terrible turn. So far, I had been in control, immaculately in control. Now the situation developed an impetus, took a direction, which was none of my choosing. The end of the nightmare had been in sight: suddenly the scenario changed and a totally new nightmare took over, of terrifying dimensions.

'Hold!' said Sybilla.

Sybilla must be the only person in the world today who can say 'Hold!' and not mean to get a laugh. I was on my way to the drinks tray, but I stopped in my tracks. Was she begrudging me a glass of their lousy sherry?

'Perry, my dear boy,' said Sybilla, fluttering a bit of magenta drape in my direction. 'I know I speak for all of us when I say we understand and appreciate the *nobility* of your gesture of renunciation. The generosity and selflessness of it staggers one, simply takes away the breath! It is a gesture in the true Trethowan tradition. But it will not do, dear boy!'

'Aunt Sybilla, it is not a selfless—'

'It simply will not do! I know that in what I am about to say I speak for Kate—'

'Oh, rather!' said Kate. 'For once!'

'—and naturally Mordred will agree with me too. I know I speak for them when I say that right must be done. Grandfather Josiah's intentions were made perfectly plain: the house and the associated properties, shares and money went to the *legitimate* heir in the *male* line. (His view of women was regrettable, but of its time.) His feelings, were he to find out that the house and the *large* sums of money and land that go with it had descended to someone born on the wrong side of the blanket, are not to be thought of. He was brought up a Presbyterian! The moral standards required of his domestic servants were strict even for those times. I can only say that for all of us, you, Perry—on Lawrence's demise, or incapacity, which, as you say, seems only too likely—will be, *must* be, head of the family.'

'You're pretty quick to give away my property,' said Peter resentfully.

'I should have thought it would be clear even to one of your intellectual capacity that one thing the property is not, is yours,' said Sybilla, with more than her usual asperity.

'Aunt Sybilla!' cried Cristobel. 'Peter has *always* been brought up to regard himself as heir.' She was rewarded by a look of venomous suspicion from Maria-Luisa.

'Then he should have *acted* as such,' said Sybilla. 'Peter has *never* been committed to the family, as a family. I fear that Peter has never been committed to anyone but himself. Hard words, especially of a Trethowan, but how true! I know that Kate and I and Mordred have been *fearful* of our future, when Lawrence should pass on. Our very living here might have been threatened! He might have demanded rent! It is quite clear that we owe no loyalty to Peter.'

'Pete's a robber,' said Kate.

'Indeed, if I understand you right, Peregrine, Peter has in fact *known* of this for some time, and kept it quiet.'

'Yes,' I said. 'I think so. But—'

'How unworthy!' pronounced Sybilla, with dire finality. 'Now you, Perry—I can only say that as soon as you came into this room the other day, I marked you down as a man of real sensitivity. Of truly refined feeling. And of deep *family* feeling.'

I almost laughed out loud at the blatant mendacity of the woman. 'Aunt Sybilla,' I said. 'I think this conversation should be nipped in the bud straight away. I simply could never agree to take on the responsibilities that owning Harpenden would entail. I

have no desire to. You forget that my commitment to the family is
even less than Peter's. I have had nothing whatever to do with it
for fourteen years.'

'That is quite irrelevant, my dear boy! The result of an unfortunate misunderstanding. One has only to look at you, standing
here now, to sense in you the qualities of a Trethowan. I'm sure
you, Jan dear, will bear me out that Peregrine is, and thinks of
himself as, a true Trethowan, and is proud of it!'

'Perry's always been very taken up with his family,' said Jan.
'He thinks of you a lot.'

The treachery of it! The blank treachery! I threw Jan a glance
of impending thunder.

'There!' said Sybilla triumphantly. 'Nor, Peregrine, can you
think only of yourself in this. There are the interests of your dear
little boy to consider. It's unthinkable that he be deprived of what
is undoubtedly his by right.' (At this point a squawk came from
Maria-Luisa.) 'By right!' repeated Sybilla magisterially. 'You must
think what is best for Daniel.'

'I do not think that inheriting large wads of money is necessarily the best thing that can happen to a man,' I said. 'Quite the
reverse. Nor do I think I want Daniel saddled with a ridiculous
white elephant of a house.'

It was the wrong thing to say altogether. 'I like it here,' said
Daniel stoutly. 'I think it's scrumptious here!'

'Precisely,' said Sybilla. 'You would confine the poor child to a
tiny little flat in—where is it?'

'Maida Vale.'

'Maida Vale. Goodness me. I remember it being built. It was
where London businessmen kept their fancy women! And very
suitable it was too, no doubt, for such a purpose. But it is hardly
an ideal place for a growing child. When one thinks too of Jan, it is
surely obvious what an eminently gracious *châtelaine* of
Harpenden she would make. Your father, my dear, you said
was—?'

'A house-painter,' said Jan.

Aunt Sybilla was unperturbed. 'I have always maintained that what the Trethowans needed was an infusion of working-class blood.'

'Uncle Lawrence did his best,' I said, 'but you didn't seem exactly delighted.'

Sybilla ignored me. 'Then surely we can regard it all as settled. We cannot allow you, as a result of a truly *Quixotic* whim, of some *absurd* notion of chivalry, to rob yourself and your lovely little boy of your rightful heritage.'

I drew my fingers round my shirt collar, and felt them wet from the sweat. This was coming altogether too close. 'This is truly nonsensical, Aunt Syb,' I said. 'I'm a working man, I love my job. I have no intention of giving it up to take over a useless fortune I haven't earned, and a monstrous house I've always loathed. I hope to do something a little more useful with my life.'

'Maintaining the heritage of the Trethowans is hardly useless,' said Sybilla. 'And it is a job you are eminently suited for. It has been clear to us, Perry, since you arrived, clear to Mordred, and to Kate, and to me—'

'You'd make a lovely head of the family,' said Kate. 'And fancy Jan's father being a house-painter!'

'As I was saying, Kate dear, we have watched you, Perry, since your return among us. We have seen you . . . *expand*! It is clear that your job, admirable and useful in its rather prosaic way, does not *stretch* your capacities.'

'I always understood you found my *size* horribly unspiritual,' I said.

'Let us not take amiss words spoken in the heat of the moment. I have in fact always had a *penchant* for large men. We must remember that Grandfather Josiah was himself a fine, large man.'

'I will not be compared to Great-Grandfather Josiah!' I shouted.

'It's true, Perry, you know,' said Jan, compounding her treachery. 'You have grown into the place. Just looking at you walking around the grounds, it seemed you belonged here.'

'He's certainly been acting as if he owned the place since he came, if that's what you mean,' said Pete resentfully.

'*And so he will*!' said Aunt Sybilla. 'Come, Peregrine, do tell us that my poor, feeble words have made you see sense.'

'No, Aunt Sybilla,' I said. 'Quite the reverse. Nothing on earth would induce me to take on the burden of Harpenden. I shall return after the weekend to my poky little flat in Maida Vale, and when I bump my head on the low ceilings and bang my elbows into inconvenient cupboards I shall not for one moment regret not being the owner of Harpenden. Of course I shall hope to see you all often in the future—' (lies! lies!) '—but I fear I shall never under any circumstances become head of the family. The secret will remain a secret.'

But then the slippery Sybilla suddenly changed her tack. 'That, I'm afraid, is hardly possible.'

'You swore—'

'Oh, certainly. If one takes note of such things. The law certainly takes no cognizance of them. But what precisely have I sworn? Not to reveal that your mother, by coincidence, discovered the existence of the first Mrs Trethowan. No doubt I shall hold to my oath. But there are many more ways than one of coming at a fact such as that.'

'Clever old Syb!' said Kate.

'The date of Florence Trethowan's death can certainly be established by enquiry at Somerset House, or wherever they keep the records these days. No doubt Australia has an equivalent if that fails—I believe they have kept excellent records there since convict times. I shall write off tomorrow if you are obdurate. It may be, of course, that she is not dead, even now. Conceivably there is a Lady Trethowan in some Old People's establishment in Bondi, or Manley, the sleeping partner in a hat shop. That would be the best evidence of all. So you see, your mother is not the only possible witness to the irregularity of Peter's birth.'

'Why the hell do you go on about that?' Peter burst out. 'I thought the Trethowans were supposed to be so bloody unorthodox.'

'Unorthodox, maybe, but *never* illegitimate.' Chris looked at the floor, her face burning. 'Come, Perry, be sensible about this.

Accept gracefully your *true* position! Do not have greatness *thrust* upon you!'

'Come on, Perry,' said Kate. 'I bet you've got a *lovely* seat on a horse! And you'd make a topping magistrate!'

'I do think you ought to give it a try, Perry,' said Jan. 'You've got to remember, it was only your father you disagreed with, not the whole family.'

'I do like it here,' said Dan, with the obstinate monotony of childhood. 'Would it all be mine?'

I stood there in anguished thought. The twisters, they'd got me. An oath meant nothing to an elderly snake like Sybilla who has a privileged position to defend. Even my own wife and son had crossed the picket lines to the other side. They had trapped me, beaten me on to the ropes. I thought of living here, day after day, month after month, year after year; thought of sitting nightly at the head of the table, listening to Sybilla's vinegarish asininities, enduring Kate's boisterous puppyishness, being the butt of Peter's sniping. I thought of Dan growing up with the Squealies. I thought of sitting on the bench, going to rural shows, mixing with the Northern gentry, who would remark behind my back that I was the son of that Trethowan who had been murdered while— had you heard?—guffaw . . .

But were their guffaws any worse than the manly guffaws of my colleagues at the Yard, their assertions of healthy normality? At least I wouldn't have to work every day with the Northumberland squirearchy. I thought of walking the grounds with Jan and Daniel; I thought of Daniel growing up with room to be free in, to wander and to explore at will; I thought of being rid of the slog and paperwork of life in the CID, of washing my hands of the petty crooks, wheedling for one more chance, of the big, sleek crooks trying to slip me a bribe, I thought of getting shot of all the sleaziness, the stench of evil, the vileness . . .

My agonized meditation was interrupted by McWatters. Entering hurriedly, he walked straight over to me (showing that he had been listening at the door). He looked unaccustomedly confused and worried.

'Mr Peregrine, sir. There's someone arrived. A . . . gentleman . . .'

'Well?'

'He says he's Mr Wallace Trethowan.'

'Who?'

'Mr Wallace, sir. Elder son of Sir Lawrence.'

And there entered unannounced into the drawing-room a large brown man of around sixty, with a broad-brimmed hat, cavalry-twill trousers and chukka-boots, followed by an encouraging-sized family.

'Greetings, all,' he said, in broad Australian. 'Thought we'd drop in as we were passing. Old place looks smaller than it used to. Jeez, it's nice to be back, though. Anyone going to offer me a nice cool beer?'

16

EPILOGUE

You lot were expecting that all along, I suppose. For you this has just been a book, and in books people who are 'missing, presumed dead' always turn up by the end. For me, this was all for real, and I'd been used all my life to looking on Cousin Wallace as dead. If Wallace was not dead, indeed, I owed my very existence to a bureaucratic error.

We got the whole story, at boozy length, over the next few days. Wallace had gone with his mother to Australia in 1933. His father had never shown any great interest in him, beyond inviting him a couple of times to Harpenden, where he had been rather grandly neglected (this, remember, was the time when the Trethowans' artistic pretensions were at their height). When they left these shores, all contact between them and the English Trethowans had ceased. On the outbreak of war, Wallace (or Wally as he insisted we call him) had come back to Europe, enlisted, and found himself in a Guards regiment. It did not take him long to be 'really pissed off, if you'll pardon the expression' with the bull, the snobbery, the grind and the danger. And so in 1944, during the Arnhem action, he just 'took off', which was his nice way of saying he deserted. He made his way, somehow, through the chaos of Central Europe at that time, through countries emerging out of one ghastly tyranny, and about to fall victim to another. In the end he made it to Greece, where he got a job on a cargo boat which finally took him back to Australia.

He seems never to have joined up with his mother again ('she lived her own life, and between you and I she was a bit of an embarrassment'), but eventually he worked his way up to owning an enormous property in outback Queensland: thousands of square miles, thousands of head of cattle, and hardly enough water to bathe a baby in. Only a man with a property like that could conceivably find Harpenden smaller than he remembered it. This was the family's first trip back to the Old Country.

I don't for a moment believe that their turning up at Harpenden was entirely coincidental. They said they were on their way to Scotland in the Land-Rover, which was no doubt true enough. But I suspect they had read about our little troubles in one of the sensational rags Sybilla had been feeding information to, had been intrigued, and had started wondering about poor old Lawrence, and what pickings there might be for them when he died.

They certainly got more than they bargained for. Uncle Lawrence, as I foresaw, totally deceived the examining psychiatrists (there is no one, but no one, more gullible than a psychiatrist), very much as I believe he had been deceiving the family in the year since his stroke: I think most of his 'off-days' were assumed, were a preparation for the murder which he finally so ingeniously accomplished. But three months later he died of a second stroke, while declaiming his poetry to the other inmates of the institution he had been confined to. He died as he lived, a grandiose old phoney, and the Wallace Trethowans were now masters of Harpenden.

It didn't go well. It was an exceptionally cold winter, Harpenden is impossible to heat at the best of times, Aunt Sybilla got on their nerves, and the McWatterses, finding that the tone of the place had gone down, left for more prestigious employ. I met Wally in London for lunch one day, and when I'd listened (with the most genuine sympathy) to his beefing for half an hour, I suggested he made the house over to the county, or to the National Trust, and hotfoot it back to Australia with what remained of the loot. It wasn't easy to manage, the financial climate of the country being what it is, but finally it went through. Harpenden House became a museum of nineteenth- and twentieth-century arts, subject to the present residents having the right to remain in their living quarters.

It works very nicely. Aunt Syb shows people round, descants on the Friths and the Holman Hunts and the Luke Fildeses, and most people imagine she dates from the same era as the pictures. When she comes to the Elizabeth Trethowan Gallery, which is housed in the Elizabethan wing, she draws attention to what she calls the 'tiny little faults' in the work of her sister, which she says 'only the eye of a fellow artist' can detect. There has even been a slight revival of interest in Aunt Kate: little parties of National Front supporters come to see her Collection, and though after the first such visit she remarked wistfully that they were not quite the superb specimens of Aryan youth she had been expecting, by now her romantic mind has managed to create a halo of the heroic even around them.

Pete vacated the Elizabethan wing very shortly after Wally took over. He had developed a close working relationship with the director of the Museum of Women's Art in Philadelphia, and he decamped to the States to make it still closer. He took three of Eliza's pictures, to ensure a warm welcome. Maria-Luisa and the Squealies took themselves back to Naples, where Maria-Luisa assumed a position of some power and influence in a branch of the Mafia her family was involved with. The Squealies are considered fine children in the Italian South, but Aunt Sybilla has been heard to remark, almost hopefully, on the high incidence of fatal childish diseases in the Naples area. Cristobel had her baby, and is the better for it, and I hope it is having a happier childhood in the Gothic wing than ever Chris and I had. Jan and I had a postcard, all lakes and scrubland, from Mordred the other day. He is with the British Council in Finland, where no doubt he is learning more enchanting things to do with herrings.

As you can imagine, Jan and I had a few bad days after the spectacular treachery of her joining Sybilla's eleven to play against me. I roughed her up a bit, verbally, and she pretended it had all been a joke, to see how I took it. After a time I said that I believed her. On the scaffold of such mutual deceptions is the stability of married life built. She has just done well in her second-year exams at Newcastle, and is beginning to wonder what to do with a degree in Arabic.

Well, so now you've heard the story of how I shopped my uncle for murdering my dad, caught my bastard cousin pinching the family pictures, discovered my sister was pregnant by the same bastard cousin, and all the rest of the little oddities and secrets of one of the grand old families that make this country what it is today. The whole thing was sheer torture from beginning to end, and if I confess that I enjoyed it now and then, you will say, I suppose, that that, at least, I got from my father. Now it's all out in the open, though, couldn't we call it a day? You can put it out of your mind, and I can go on with my life. I do have a job of work to do.

DEATH OF A
PERFECT MOTHER

CONTENTS

1

MOTHER AND SONS

Clip-clop down Carnation Road on her way to the shops went Lillian Hodsden, in the last week of her mortal life.

'Hello, Mr Davies. How's the lumbago? Better? Bet you're glad Spring is here, eh? That'll buck you up.'

Mr Davies, tottering home in the opposite direction, let out an ambiguous grunt intended to signify that, thank you for asking, it was no better, and in his opinion Spring was not here, nor even on its way. But he needn't have bothered even with that minimal response. Lillian Hodsden had clomped past him, oblivious, her eye fixed on the next recipient of her early morning cheeriness.

'Hello, Mrs Wharton. Lovely day. Saw you'd got your daughter down. That's nice. And the kiddies? Oh, lovely. Give them a kiss from me, won't you?'

At the mention of the grandchildren Mrs Wharton had shown signs of wanting to stop, but Lillian Hodsden would have nothing of it: having no grandchildren herself, thank God, she was unable to bore back in kind, so she shrilled: 'Can't stop. Got all the week-end shopping to do. Can't think where the weekdays go to, can you?' and she cantered ahead, leaving Mrs Wharton with vague feelings of rebellious irritation, for she was a widow lady who found her time, minute by minute of it, all too easy to account for. She looked round, eyes narrowed, at the diminishing form of Lillian Hodsden.

It wasn't a form you'd mistake easily. Lill was forty-eight but it needed no more than a dash of generosity to suggest forty-two. Buttoned tight round her chunky, bullet-breasted body was a leopard-skin coat, skimpy in proportions but flagrant in falsity. On her feet were a pair of cheap sandals, shiny black edged with gold braid, with heavy wooden heels that made rhythmic patterns on the stony tarmac, announcing her coming as surely as if she were Carmen practising with her castanets in the wings. Crowning the whole effect—and no one could deny that she did make an effect —was a mop of copper-red hair, blatantly untrue to nature, and looking as if she had just dipped her head in a sink full of bull's blood.

You noticed Lill Hodsden, people said in Todmarsh.

Lill was not a native of the undistinguished little southwestern seaside town where she had made her home. She had come here from Leicester in the early 'fifties, the years when Tory freedom was giving people vague yearnings: sniffing the air they smelt money, undreamed-of comforts, the chance of a quick financial kill. It was a time for mobility, geographical and social. Lill Hodsden had her eyes on both. We weren't good enough for her, her neighbours in the Midlands said when she left, and once she'd gone back to tell them they were right.

So she—and incidentally a husband, and incidentally a baby boy—had migrated to the South in search of richer pastures: a classier-sounding address; a nicer type of neighbour; schools with better names and more impressive uniforms. She never asked whether she would be accepted, any more than she listened to the replies to her casually flung cheerinesses. She was Lill, and good as the next woman. Over the years she had acquired two more children, and brought her mother down to live next door, but otherwise than that she did not change. Her neighbours it was who finally had to swallow the outrageously sugared pill. She had settled in this dull little town like a bird of exotic (albeit artificial) colouring alighting on a hen-coop. Finally the hens had had to treat her as one of themselves, though they never ceased to look bewilderedly at the plumage.

Her early morning shopping, today and every day, was a royal progress from butcher's to grocer's, from grocer's to greengrocer's. Everywhere she was known. Everywhere she had her standard little jokes and greetings. Everywhere, she was sure, she was loved. For Lill Hodsden was quite unconscious of the possibility that she made any impression other than the one she intended. 'Quite a character, our Lill,' she'd once heard the greengrocer say. She had taken it as a seventy per cent-proof compliment. She *was* quite a character. She had a cheery wave for everyone, knew everybody's history, opinions and little ways, and had the appropriate words of greeting for each one of them.

'They all say I'm a marvel,' she would tell her family. 'They don't know how I do it.'

So today she clattered from establishment to establishment, exchanging ear-singeing salutations with the other customers, chatting along in her high-speed-drill voice as she waited her turn, chaffing the butcher's boy or the grocer's wife with her age-old jokes and meaningless saws when at last she got to the counter.

'Mind you give us a good bit, Bert,' she shrilled to the butcher, gazing with ignorant vagueness down at the offered choice (for she could no more tell a good piece of meat from a bad one than she could tell a sparrow from a chaffinch). 'It's my Gordon's birthday Sunday, and he does like a good joint. None of your fatty bits, now.'

'Not on your life, Lill,' said Bert, with the forced grin that many faces assumed when confronted by Lillian Hodsden. 'More than my life's worth. I wouldn't dare.'

'Nor I don't believe you would,' said Lill, with a cackle of self-approbation. 'I've got *him* where I want him, eh?' and she turned to her audience to exact homage.

The newsagent was the recipient of her lengthiest confidences. She dropped in at the end of her tour, her shopping baskets laden with meat and groceries, vegetables and out-of-season fruit, plonked them down on the floor, picked up *Weekend* and *TV News*, and proceeded to take over the shop.

'Isn't it a lovely day? They laid it on just for me, you know. They like me up there. It's my Gordon's birthday tomorrow. I'm going to do him proud. Here, have you got a big box of chocks? Something real swank? Let's have a look, then.'

She grabbed the proffered boxes—large and plush, large and garish—in her pudgy hands and carefully picked the most expensive. (Where does she get the money from? thought the newsagent —a rhetorical thought if ever there was one, for he had a very good idea.)

'Nothing but the best, eh?' resumed Lill, slapping down the money. 'You're not twenty-six every day of the week!'

'What's your Gordon doing now?' asked the newsagent, without any great curiosity.

'At this moment I'd guess he's lying in bed,' said Lill, with her parrotty laugh. 'That's where they were when I come out, both the boys. I shouted up to them, I said: "You be out of there before I come back, or you'll feel my hand on your b.t.m's!" Oh, we do have a laugh, me and the boys. They're lovely lads, both of them.' She opened the door into the watery sunshine, a South of England apology for a fine day. 'We think the world of each other,' she said. 'They'd do anything for me.'

'She'll have to be got rid of,' said Gordon Hodsden, lying on his frowsty bed, puffing at a cigarillo and looking up at the ceiling. 'Some way or other, she's got to be put down.'

His brother Brian, lying on the bed by the opposite wall, turned his book on to its face on the bedside table and said: 'What do you think she's saying at this moment?' His voice took on the authentic parakeet shrillness: ' "Have you got a nice plump chicken for Sunday dinner, Bert? Mind it's a good one, because—" '

Here Gordon joined in the chorus: ' "—my Gordon he does like a nice bit o' breast!" '

The bedroom rocked as they both shrilled a motherly squawk of laughter.

' "You've gotta laugh, haven't you?" ' resumed Brian, unable to give up the routine. ' "Makes the world go round, a bit of laughter, I always say. We have some good laughs, me and the boys." ' He lowered his voice to a confidential pitch that was somehow just as false and unpleasant: ' "But they're lovely boys, both of them. They think the world of me. Worship the ground I walk on. They'd do anything for me, they would, my Gordon and Brian." '

'The question is, *what* shall we do for her, or rather to her?' said Gordon, lying back on the bed, his brown cigarillo pointing upwards to the ceiling, wreathing himself in smoke. 'Or, to put it bluntly, how are we going to do her in?'

Brian too lay back on his bed in rapt, companionable contemplation, though the close observer might have noticed the tiny furrow on his young forehead, the trouble in his blue eyes. Physically there was no great likeness between Lill's two boys. Gordon was tall and chunky, with a mop of dark hair, and working-man's shoulders and hands. His face was good-looking enough, but restless and instinct with a half-understood aggression. He had had five years in the army, had bought himself out with Lill's help, and was now working at the local shipyard—and the fact that she felt this was not 'good' enough for him was one reason why his mother had not answered the newsagent's enquiry as to what he was doing now.

His brother Brian was nineteen, so his half-formed look was more understandable. He was slight, fair, and in his pyjamas looked no more than a boy. He too was restless, with the restlessness of feared failure, of chafing against something he knew he was not strong enough to fight. He was aiming, uncertainly, at university. What Gordon and Brian had in common was their manacle and chain. Physically they were as different as chalk and cheese, and Lill would certainly have made jokes about their paternity if she could have done so without impugning their legitimacy. Nothing like that was to be said about either of her boys! On the subject of her daughter she had no such inhibitions.

'The great thing about Mum,' said Brian eventually, 'about Lill, sweet songbird of the Midlands, our beloved giver of life—the great thing about her is her regularity.'

'Oh Christ, don't mention her bowels,' said Gordon, turning over in his bed in disgust, and cursing as his cigarillo stubbed itself out in the pillow.

'Not her bowels, you clot, her habits. Her beastly habits. She generally does everything she does at the same time. Especially of an evening.'

Gordon, engaged in brushing the ash off his bed, and turning over the pillow, on which a tiny burnhole had appeared, paused. 'You're right,' he said. 'Regular as clockwork. Everything according to plan. Down the pub at seven-fifteen, back from the pub at nine-thirty. It's all part of her shattering predictability. It's one of the things that make her—'

'So utterly loathsome to live with. Agreed. The fact that even when she's out and you've got a bit of rest from her, you keep looking at the clock, knowing that on the dot she'll breeze in and say: "Yoo-hoo. I'm home! How's my boys? Had a lovely evening, have you?" Right you are. Still, it has its uses.'

'When you are planning to do her in,' said Gordon.

'Right. When you are planning to put an end to an existence that brings joy to none, and irritation, nausea, fear, loathing, and actual physical vomiting to thousands.' Brian rolled the words round his mouth lovingly. Words were his refuge, his secret, solitary defence. The only way he could tolerate Lill being Lill and being his mother was to form the words that described her. He lay on the bed forming more phrases, a thesaurus of hate, while Gordon began his morning liturgy of exercises—press-ups, running on the spot, lithe swoops of the trunk from side to side and violent feints at this and that. Gordon's regular exercises were a relic of his army days, something he clung to as desperate men do cling to sure things as they sink in oceans of uncertainty. Besides, as he often said, you never knew when training might come in useful.

'Bloody Tarzan,' said Brian, tired with all the activity. 'Give over and think.'

'I am thinking,' said Gordon, back on the floor and pressing himself up and down at double speed with an expert judgment that just stopped him bashing his chin against the floor. 'This is when I do think.'

'Funny brain you must have,' said Brian. 'What's the result of your thinking?'

Gordon stopped, swivelled himself round on to his haunches,

and sat looking at his brother's bed, his square shoulders hunched forward urgently.

'Saturday. That's the result of my thinking. Saturday. One week from today. As she's coming home from the pub. A sharp blow on the back of the head as she comes through Snoggers Alley. Or maybe a rope round her throat. Are you with me?'

' 'Course I'm with you.' Brian lay back against his pillow, his weaker, less intense face wreathed in smiles. 'What an idea! They'll think it's some casual mugger, eh? We'll take her handbag and keep the small change.' He drowned in ecstatic anticipation. 'Wouldn't it be marvellous?'

Gordon threw himself forward on to his brother's bed and shook him by the shoulders: 'Stupid bastard! It's not a case of "wouldn't it!" I'm serious!'

Brian looked at him, half wondering, half afraid. 'Serious? You mean you . . . you mean we could?'

'I mean we've got to. I mean it's our only chance. What else is there? I tried, didn't I—tried to get away. I went into the army, got away for five years. Only it wasn't away at all. Everywhere I went I had this ball and chain attached, labelled "Lill". It'll be the same with you. Why did you fail your Scholarship levels? Because deep down you wanted to. And she wanted you to too. Now there's no question of Oxford or Cambridge. That would have taken you away from Lill, from old Dracula curls. Now the best you can hope for is South Wessex—twelve miles of good motorway and back home for tea with Lill at five o'clock. Just what she planned for all along.'

' "They say it's very good for Socialology," ' quoted Brian with a bitter smile.

'You'll have the ball and chain on, boyo, same as I felt in the army. And it'll be there as long as she's alive, and when she dies there'll be no life left in us because we'll have been sucked dry. To get rid of that chain we've got to snap it off.'

'If only . . .' said Brian, faltering.

'What?'

'If only there were some other way.'

'There isn't!' Gordon towered over him, pumping him full of

his own energy. 'If a getaway was possible I'd have made it. But I came back, and you'll be stuck here for life. I got the job at the shipyard—and we all know how I got that—and you'll go to our little neighbourhood university and land a job as a teacher in some local dump. And that's our lives. *All* our lives. Lill in the centre of her web, entertaining her flies.'

'You might get married . . . I might too.'

Gordon's face darkened. 'Do you think I haven't thought about that? In fact that's . . . But it couldn't happen while Lill's alive. Oh, I've got girl-friends all right, plenty of them, but anything more than that? I couldn't. As long as she's there I couldn't . . .'

'There's a book about that—*Sons and Lo*—'

'This isn't a fucking book! Sod your books! It's my life! And if I went to . . . her, if I made her want me, what would happen? We set up home in this town, and I'm still mother's boy. We go away, and I'm on a longer lead, same as in the army. She's got us, body and soul. She's owned us, every minute of our lives since the day we were born. If we ever get free, it'll be violently—it'll be by doing her in.' He stared down at his brother. 'Are you with me?'

Brian didn't look up. 'Who is she?'

'What the hell are you talking about? Answer me.'

'Who is it you want to marry?'

'Ann Watson up the road, if you must know. She hasn't so much as looked at me. Why should she? Poor old Gordon Hodsden, the big milksop: still tied to his mother's apron-strings at his age. Before she'll ever look at me I've got to be free. Come on, give me an answer. Are you with me?'

Brian's heart seemed to stop still, then to leap exultantly in his slight body. 'Yes!' he said. Then he turned to his brother and said 'Yes, yes, yes!'

'All right then,' said Gordon. 'Now we can get down to business.'

'The trouble is,' muttered Brian, suddenly abstracted again, and pushing a lock of fair hair back from his forehead in worried frustration, 'that the family's always suspected first.'

'The *husband's* always suspected first,' said Gordon. 'Old Fred. Can you see old Fred doing our Lill in? Can you visualize it? He'd have to ask permission first. Anyway, Saturday night's his night on the town. His night out on parole. Darts at the Yachtsman's Arms. He's bound to have twenty people to swear he was down there being the life and soul of the party every minute from eight to ten-thirty.'

'In which case,' said Brian, 'they'll look at us.'

'Why should they? Us? Her beloved boys? We're one big happy family. The whole town knows that. Lill and her lads. We worship the ground she walks on.' Gordon came up and sat on Brian's bed, looking at him closely. 'You ever told anybody, Bri?'

'What do you mean?'

'Told anybody what we feel? About Lill? How she makes goose pimples go up and down our spine every time she opens her bloody mouth? How we'd like to put her guts through a mincer? Shut her in a slow oven and listen to the howls? Have you told anyone?'

There was silence for a minute. 'No. I never have,' said Brian, swallowing hard. 'It's not—the kind of thing you say, is it? I mean, nobody at school talks much about their mothers. And anyway—I mean, when she goes around, saying what she does—'

'Spreading the gospel of light—the Hodsdens, mother and sons, as the apostles of cheery family togetherness. Exactly. Every-one knows we're devoted. Lill has told them so. She thinks so herself. She's given us our let-out. She's dug her own grave.'

Brian smiled, slowly. 'That's nice. It seems—appropriate.'

'Too bloody right it is. Now all we've got to do is think through the details.'

Downstairs a door banged. 'You lads still up there, wasting a lovely day like this?' carolled the crow voice from downstairs. 'You shift yourselves or I'll be up there with a broomhandle.' And she burst into affectionate laughter.

'Coming, Mum, just getting dressed,' came the duet from the bedroom. But as they scrambled into their clothes Brian took Gordon by the arm and whispered: 'I've just remembered. That book. *Sons and Lovers*. He did his mother in there, too.'

'Bully for him,' muttered Gordon. 'I didn't think we'd be the first. How did he do it?'

'Drugs. She was ill already.'

'That's no good. Lill's got the constitution of a horse. It's got to be some other way. Think about it.' He suddenly took Brian by the shoulders and pushed him against the wall. 'You do agree, don't you?' he hissed, looking into his eyes. 'It's the only way. She's got to be killed.' Brian, wondering, nodded. 'All right then. Now we've got to decide on the way.'

As they pushed in the tails of their shirts and pulled on their shoes they both were turning over in their minds various delicious possibilities.

2

FAMILY NIGHT OUT

It's a rehearsal. That's what it is, a rehearsal, thought Brian. This is how it's going to be, one week from today. And one week from today Lill will get her chips, hand in her cards, bite the dust, go to meet her (much to be pitied) Maker. This is a trial run for her murder. I've got to keep my wits about me; observe everything; notice possibilities—things we could take advantage of, pitfalls that could arise. I can't just switch off like I usually do. I'll have to keep on the *qui vive*.

It was very much a family night out. They were celebrating Gordon's birthday a day early—because, as Lill said, Sunday night in a pub's dead as a doornail. So as usual they had gone down to the Rose and Crown (even the pub names in Todmarsh were un-imaginative) as they did every Saturday. They had as always taken the side way, through the little cutting known popularly as 'Snog-gers Alley', and then down Balaclava Road. Their whole route was vilely ill-lit—providentially, wonderfully ill-lit, Brian had whis-pered to Gordon. Six and a half minutes ordinary walking time, Gordon had said as they opened the door to the Saloon Bar. Gordon was very consciously the technician of the enterprise.

Now they were all seated round a table, and beyond the fact that Lill had flaunted up to the bar and announced 'It's my Gordon's birthday, so we'll expect a free round later on,' and then had turned to the sparse collection of early evening drinkers and shrilled, 'Get yourselves in good voice for "Happy Birthday To You" later on'—apart from that, it was a normal Saturday night out for the Hodsdens.

Well, almost. Because tonight Fred was with them, just for a first pint, and just to be friendly, like. Fred invariably played darts at the Yachtsman's Arms on Saturday nights, but tonight he raised his glass to his elder son and looked with satisfaction around his little table. Fred was thin, decidedly wizened, and very quiet. Almost humble, you might say. He was like a plant that had never quite flourished after transplanting. Here he was, still pottering round the town's parks as a basic wage gardener twenty-odd years after they had moved to Todmarsh. Happy enough, in fact, but hardly prosperous, and looking all of twenty years older than his wife. It was not quite what Lill had envisaged when she'd made the move. She told him often enough that he ought to consider himself bloody lucky she'd married him, and indeed that was exactly what in his own mind he did feel. He agreed with his wife absolutely.

She's a real winner, my Lill, he thought, raising his mug to his lips. Regular life and soul of the party. And she's brought up a wonderful family. I'm a lucky man.

Lill Hodsden's daughter was also out with the family tonight and drinking a gin and lime. She was an occasional rather than a regular addition, and as a matter of fact she was still well under eighteen. But what landlord would argue the toss with Lill? Come to that, what policeman? So tonight Deborah tagged along with Mum and the boys because until later she had nothing better to do.

Deborah she had been christened (C. of E., what else?), Debbie she had become. She hated the name in both forms. It symbolized Lill's classy aspirations, and their shoddy outcomes. Mary, Eileen, Dorothy would have been better. Or even, come to that, Petula or Cilla. But she was Deborah, become Debbie. She heard her mother speaking:

'Look at old sourpuss over there. Come on, give us a smile, Debbie. It doesn't cost you anything. It's Gordon's birthday, what do you think we brought you out for? Get a smile on your dial, fer Chrissake.'

Lill disliked her daughter. For a start she wasn't a boy, and Lill preferred boys—well, didn't everyone? Then, in the last year, she had grown up, so on family outings there they were together, mother and grownup daughter, thirty-odd years all too evidently between them. They were like two pages in a family snap-album, wide apart. Only Deborah had all the looks that Lill had had as a girl, without any of the coarseness. She hasn't got a *bit* of my go! said Lill to herself, consolingly.

If I can only get away from her, thought Debbie to herself, nothing in my life can ever be as bad again. If I can only get shot of Lill . . .

'Well, we won't let old sauerkraut cast a blight over the proceedings,' said Lill, turning back to her boys. 'This place seems to need a bit of pepping up tonight. I can see I'll have to brighten things up with a few verses of "Lily the Pink" later on. That'll put a firework up them.'

Oh God, thought Gordon, not 'Lily the Pink'. I don't think I could stand it. It's *my* birthday. Why should *my* birthday be celebrated with 'Lily the Pink'?

For even Gordon didn't quite realize that it was *his* birthday, but Lill's celebration.

Luckily Lill's attention was distracted for the moment by the arrival of Mr Achituko.

'Archie!' she trilled. 'It's my pal! Yoo-hoo, Archie!' For Lill, never very good on words of over three syllables, had been totally defeated by Achituko and had picked on Archie as friendly-sounding. Mr Achituko, his smile fixed and imperturbable, wished he had gone into the public bar, or to the King's Head, or back to the Coponawi Islands. But as always happened with Lill, he gave in to his fate and brought his glass over to the table by the Hodsdens. He was greeted by Lill as manna from Heaven. He was something to enliven her evening.

'It's my boy-friend. Isn't he lovely? I could eat him.' Instead of which she kissed him loudly, for the benefit of the whole bar.

Then, as she always did, she regarded his blackness comically, and said: 'Does it rub off?'

Mr Achituko smiled—fixedly, imperturbably. Debbie flushed and looked at the table. Fred, watching out of his washed-out blue eyes like aged overalls, said to himself: My Lill's in great form. Always gets a bit of fun going. Just what this place needs.

Darts were Fred's treat of the week, but when he drained his glass and stood up, it was almost with reluctance.

'Well, I'd better be off,' he said. 'Enjoy yourselves.'

'Okee-doke,' said Lill, off-hand. Fred threaded his way apologetically through the drinkers, and as she heard the door-latch click after him, Lill beamed round at her brood and said: 'Well, he doesn't leave much of a hole, does he?'

And it was true. That was the trouble with so many of Lill's brutalities. They were true, or horribly close to target at worst. When Fred had left the room you couldn't remember whether he had a moustache or not, whether he wore glasses or not. He left behind himself nothing much more than a vaguely snuffed-out atmosphere and a smell of old clothes.

And now, thought Brian, this really is a rehearsal. This is how it will be next Saturday. Just Gordon and me, Debbie perhaps, and Lill. Debbie will go before long, because she can't stand being out with Lill for more than an hour or so. She'll drift off to see one of her friends. She'll be sure to be somewhere where there are people to swear to her presence. Just as there'll be people here, in this pub, to swear to us.

' 'Ere, look,' said Lill in a stentorian whisper, 'look who's over there. It's that little Mrs Watson from along the road. Isn't that good? She's such a lovely girl. Sort of distant . . . aristocratic, know what I mean? She shouldn't shut herself away like she has been. She must be getting over it at last.'

In the far corner of the bar, sitting with a girl-friend, was a woman in her mid-twenties. She had long fair hair, an unmade-up face with classically perfect features, and eyes full of pain. Distant she may have been, but she registered Lill: a twitch of the mouth, a fleeting expression of annoyance, showed she was aware of Lill's interest. She leaned forward over a bag of potato crisps, talking with desperate concentration to her friend.

'Do you know,' said Lill, still in that same ear-shattering whisper, and leaning across to Mr Achituko in hideous intimacy, 'her husband was killed in Northern Ireland. Shot in the back. On duty. Isn't it awful?'

'Yes, I know,' said Mr Achituko, his fixed smile disappearing for a moment. 'I have talked with her.'

'Oh, have you?' said Lill, withdrawing in displeasure. 'Well, don't you go trying to cut out our Gordon. I've got her marked down for him.'

'Stow it, Mum,' said Gordon, who had flinched when the name' was first mentioned but now responded with great geniality: 'I can choose my own girl-friends.'

'Well, you've never chose half such a smasher as that yet,' said Lill. 'She's just what you need. She's just coming out of her shell too—it's taken her quite a time.' A thought struck her. 'Crikey, if old Fred snuffed it I'd be on the look-out for my next on the trip back from the cemetery.'

She had forgotten to whisper, and bellowed it round the whole bar, looking complacently at the people at the surrounding tables. One of them said: 'I bet you would, too, Lill,' and she chuckled in self-approbation.

Getting serious again, she turned to Gordon and said: 'Why don't you go and chat her up a bit, Gord? She's a lovely girl, just your style. You ought to get to know her better, it's only neigh-bourly.' And she winked suggestively. Lill prided herself on not keeping her boys tied to her apron-strings. She was always telling them to go out and get themselves girls. Mrs Watson would make a lovely wife for her Gordon. She'd be a better housewife than most, having been married before. And he'd be living just up the road.

'Come off it, Mum,' said Gordon, with that unabated good-humour that now, more than ever, it was essential to preserve. 'What would I say to her? "My Mum says I was to come over and chat you up a bit"?'

'Oh, go on with you. You've got more nous than that. You can do it casual, like.'

Gordon smiled enigmatically, but when five minutes later he went to the bar, he exchanged a few cheery words with little Mrs Watson from along the road. And Lill, pointy ears aquiver, caught them, purred, and smiled at Brian a smile of (she thought) great subtlety, full of hidden meaning.

Don't smirk at me, you old crow, thought Brian. You've got us all on a puppet-string, haven't you, or so you think? Just a little twitch from those pudgy, purple-painted fingernails and we jerk up and do your bidding. In one week's time, oh horrendous Lill, you are going to feel a jerk from your Muppets that you haven't been expecting at all.

With her second, and then her third, drink, Lill—as usual— began to get rowdy. Her advances to Mr Achituko became more brazen than ever, and before long he downed his drink with un-characteristic zeal and managed to get caught up in conversation by the bar. This gave Lill an opportunity to engage in raucous conversation with all the tables around her about the sexual prow-ess of 'darkies'. Even the Todmarshians got a mite embarrassed at this (though it was a subject they greatly enjoyed speculating on in hushed tones). Deborah thought her mother might conceivably take it as a reproof if she took herself off, so without a word she got up and went out.

Lill's reaction, however, was no different from her reaction to Fred's departure: she took care to say to Debbie's departing back: 'She's getting stuck up, that one. She's too proud for her own family.' Deborah, reaching the outside air and the darkness, leaned for a moment by the wall, laid her forehead against the coolness of it, and breathed deep. Then, with the resilience of youth, she shook herself and went off to play records with one of her friends.

Inside things were working up inexorably towards 'Lily the Pink'. Lill could sing other songs: her tastes tended towards the music-hall—to the blowsier numbers that she thought of as 'a bit of fun', where she could bring out all the innuendoes and add a few of her own. But 'Lily the Pink' was to her what 'My Way' is to

Frank Sinatra: an irresistible mixture of Credo and blatant self-advertisement. She had been in her seventh heaven when the song was rediscovered. It beat 'Lily of Laguna' into a cocked hat. So now it came out on all feasts and high days, and the whole bar, after five or six hints, recognized its inevitability.

'All right,' said Lill at last, as if giving in to overwhelming popular demand. 'Stand back and give me a bit of room.' And pushing back the chairs in her vicinity she slipped off her apple green plasticated shoes and stood on the chintzy seats built solidly into the saloon bar wall. 'Come along, all,' she shrieked, 'help me with the chorus!'

And only half-reluctantly the bar turned in her direction, paid homage to the buxom bright figure standing there, bursting out of her electric blue dress and grinning encouragingly from under her outrageous mop of red hair.

'Go it, Lill,' someone said. 'We'll back you up.'

And as someone, from long training, began simulating the hurdy-gurdy accompaniment, Lill steadied herself on the bouncy cushions, opened up her healthy pink throat and let them have it.

> *'We'll drink-a-drink-a-drink to*
> *Lily the Pink-the-Pink-the-Pink,*
> *The saviour of the human ra-a-ace . . .'*

She was in her element. This, she thought, should have been her life. Doing the Halls. Doing the Clubs up North. No class there, of course, but lots of life. She waved her hands for the chorus and a ragged sound emanated from the saloon bar regulars. 'Course everyone had life in them, Lill thought, but with some you had to work to get it out. She grinned encouragingly at them, and the sound grew louder and more in unison. She purred. She might have been God listening to the Hallelujah Chorus. She looked at little Mrs Watson, sitting with her back to her in the far corner. Funny: she hadn't had her back to her before. She looked at Mr Achituko over by the bar. Dear old Archie. What memories he'd take back with him to—wherever it was! Well, he can't say anyone was prejudiced here! Then her eyes rested on her boys, chairs pushed back, looking up at her smiling. That's what she liked—just her and the boys. That was how it should be. They were lovely boys. Good-looking too, though she said it herself and shouldn't. And they adored her. You couldn't put it any other way. Look at them now—you could see it in their eyes. They simply adored her.

Gordon glanced at his watch surreptitiously as he raised his mug to drink. Twenty past. A bit of applause, a quenching of the thirst, and Lill would go. Half past on the dot on Saturday night. He'd join in the applause, then he'd make himself scarce. That should be easy enough. After one of Lill's performances everything became somehow more . . . flexible.

And indeed, when Lill bleated the song to its conclusion the bar, led by her sons, burst into proprietorial applause—she was *our* Lill, after all, and quite a character when all was said and done—and then the groups began loosening up, talking, laughing, and trotting to the bar for orders. And at the centre of it, as always, Lill, standing flushed and happy, accepting the compliments and finishing her drink.

'That's the stuff to give the troops,' she said. 'That Olivia Newton-John's got nothing on me, eh?'

Gordon, with an athlete's grace and quietness, sauntered through the various shifting and coalescing groups and out through the door marked 'Toilets'. The door led into a corridor with, at the far end, two doors marked with diagrams supposedly indicative of gender, which you had to peer at closely before pushing the one of your choice. But immediately to the left was a door leading out to the Rose and Crown's back yard, and close by it was a gate out to the street. Gordon was through it in a flash, and then walking coolly up the street towards home. No point in hurrying it. Might attract attention. Anyway, he only had to be sufficiently ahead of Lill for her not to recognize his back. His watch glowed phosphorescent in the darkness. Nine-twenty-eight. He was going to time this operation like a miler making an attempt on the record.

Back in the Rose and Crown Lill was collecting up her belongings—handbag, best coat, assorted make-up gear she had scattered over the table after a 'patching-up' operation. Once gath-

ered together, she smiled her fearsome smile of maternal love at
Brian.

'What you fancy for supper, love? Nice hamburger with a fried
egg on it?'

'Lovely, Mum.'

'Where's Gordon?' Lill looked around the bar in the direction
of Mrs Watson, and her eyes registered disappointment.

Brian swallowed. 'Gone for a leak, Mum.'

'Oh, you are common. Why can't you say "Gone to the toilet"?'
Lill thought for a moment. 'Well, I suppose it being your birthday
doesn't stop you having to go for a leak. I must be off. Tell him I'm
doing hamburgers.'

'OK, Mum, I'll tell him.'

And Lill, trolled through the Saloon Bar, gave a goodnight to
practically everyone there, and pushed the door out into the
street. Someone at the bar looked at his watch and said: 'Good old
Lill. You could set your watch by her.'

Too right, thought Brian, draining his glass. Good old Lill.

The Saloon Bar settled down to be what in Lill's absence it
always was: a dull little bar in a dull little town. They'll miss Lill
when she's gone, thought Brian.

That night after hamburger (under-) and egg (over-cooked)
Gordon and Brian undressed in their room and conversed in a
whisper—unnecessarily, since nothing they said could have been
heard over Fred's snores and Lill's noisy undressing in the next
bedroom.

'I left at nine-twenty-seven,' hissed Gordon, 'and I was in position this end of Snoggers Alley at nine-thirty exactly. Actually I
nipped into old mother Mitchell's garden in case she saw me, but
in fact I'll stand under the telegraph post, where the lane widens
out. Lill came by at nine-thirty-four, so I could have left a minute
or two later, but I don't want to hurry—people might notice. And
the four minutes' rest means I'll be in tip-top condition. Two minutes to do it, and I can be back in the Rose and Crown by nine-
thirty-nine. Twelve minutes away in all. Plenty of people spend
longer than that in the bog.'

'Old Fred in the mornings, for a start,' said Brian. They both giggled childishly, from nerves.

'Anyway, it won't matter if I'm a minute or two over time,' said Gordon. 'No one will notice I'm gone.'

Brian's face fell. 'Don't bank on it,' he said. 'Lill noticed, for a start.'

'What?' Gordon's voice suddenly assumed its normal baritone, and they both jumped nervously. But they needn't have bothered. Lill was in the bathroom, simultaneously cleaning her teeth and gargling her signature tune, and Fred was snoring away in the sleep of the just and stupid.

'What did she say?' hissed Gordon.

'She noticed you weren't there. When she went out. She asked where you were.'

'Oh Christ. Drawing the attention of everyone in the bar to the fact that I wasn't there.' Brian nodded. 'What did you say?'

'Well, I didn't say you were up in Snoggers timing an attempt to murder her this time next week . . .' They both sat on their beds, hunched forward in thought. 'What could I say? I said you'd gone to the bog.'

Gordon thought and thought, but came up with no very comforting solution. 'That's the trouble with Lill,' he said. 'You think she's absolutely predictable, then she springs a nasty surprise on you. We're going to have to think about this. If we're not careful we're going to be shopped, by Lill herself.'

3

GINGERING THINGS UP

Sunday was a somnolent day at the Hodsdens'. It always was. Lill didn't like it, but she recognized there was nothing she could do against the collective lethargies of the other four. Saturday night was always Fred's big night of the week: darts at the Yachtsman's took it out of him, and Sundays he crept blearily about the house, all passions spent and considerably in overdraft. Brian and Gordon, as a rule, followed suit, if Gordon had nothing sporting on: they sprawled in armchairs reading the papers, they played cards or they watched television. 'It's natural,' Lill would explain to people, 'they work and play hard the rest of the week in their different ways—Gordon the physical, Brian more the—' she shied away from the word mental—'more the *psychological*!' Debbie just took herself off, quite inconspicuously. As usual, thought Lill bitterly, though she would certainly have gone on at her ceaselessly if she for once had been around.

So Sunday they slept, ate well of Gordon's birthday dinner of beef, Yorkshire pudding and three veg, followed by tinned peaches, then reread the *Sunday Mirror* and the *Express* and watched Bruce Forsyth on the enormous colour television that Lill said (and Fred believed her) she had picked up for practically nothing from a family going to live abroad. The chocolates, which they opened after tea, turned out to be all soft centres, which Gordon did not like. Still, Lill did, and the evening was punctuated by the sound of Lill's pudgy hand reaching down into the box and scuffling around in the paper that crackled like money.

'Come on, Gordon,' she would say, 'tuck in. They cost the earth.'

'I've had enough for the moment, Mum.'

' "He has a proud stomach, that boy",' murmured Brian.

'There's nothing wrong with his stomach,' protested Lill. 'He's got a lovely body. Not an ounce of surplus anywhere.' And she leered at her eldest and reached down again into the chocolate box.

But the consequence was that Monday morning Lill felt in need of some sort of reviver, a tonic, something to put pep back into the system and get zing coursing through her veins. Which meant, though she was largely unconscious of this herself, that she was in need of a good stand-up row. All her best rows occurred on Mondays, as all the family but herself realized—it was a day that might well have been observed by family, neighbours and circle of acquaintance as a day of lamentation, fasting, and general breast-beating.

At breakfast Lill was in high good humour, and, quite unaware that she was working up to a row or two, she planned them. She scrambled some eggs to a leathery consistency and then found she'd forgotten the salt. She toasted the thin sliced loaf into wavy North Sea shapes and slapped them in a pile down on the kitchen table.

'Eat it while it's warm,' she said.

'Here, Mum,' said Gordon, poking a spoon sceptically at the marmalade dish, 'what's this?'

'Mother's special,' replied Lill cheerily. 'Had a lot of jam jars with just a bit left in them, and I put 'em all together. I think I'll patent the idea. Call it plumberry marmalade or something.'

Gordon groaned.

'Tasty!' said Fred, chewing meditatively.

When Brian and Debbie had run off at the last minute to catch the bus to school, and when Gordon and Fred had cycled off in opposite directions to work (Christ, thought Lill to herself, we must be the only family in the whole bloody town without a car.

Just my luck), Lill washed up and made the beds—all but Debbie's, because a girl of that age ought to make her own—and while
she did it she meditated ways of giving a lift to the day, gingering
things up in her vicinity, giving life a spot of zip. So round about
half past ten, when she knew she'd be having coffee, she stuffed a
fag in her mouth and went in next door to see her mother.

'Do you want a cup?' her mother asked, having that moment
sat down with hers at the kitchen table.

'Just to be friendly,' said Lill. 'Make it milky.' Her mother, without a word, got up and put a saucepan of milk on the gas-ring.

About the only thing Lill had inherited from her mother had
been her regularity—that was how she knew she'd be settling
down to a quiet cup at half past ten. In other ways they were as
different as camembert and gorgonzola. Old Mrs Casey, widow
long since of a plumber in a small way, was short, fat and formidable more from her grim silence than her tongue. Wherever she
went she was a Presence, steel-eyed, incorruptible, disapproving.
She had her Standards, unspoken, unwritten, unanswerable, and
she was openly contemptuous of anyone who wittingly or unwittingly sinned against them. She cut no figure in Todmarsh at large
but she attended Methodist Chapel morning and evening, rain or
shine, of a Sunday. In fact, the image of nonconformity she presented was of so rigid and regrettable a kind that one trendy
minister had offered to bring the service to her if she would only
stay home. She had stared him out of countenance, and finally
said: 'I'm not gone that soft yet.' In all her life she had had only
one failure, and made only one mistake. The failure was Lill, the
mistake was consenting to come and live next door to her.

'I've been thinking,' said Lill, starting straight in.

'Oh yes . . . ?' Grimly, very grimly.

'About Debbie moving in here with you . . .'

Mrs Casey removed the milk from the ring and poured it with
rock-steady hand into the cup which had been a wedding present
back in the days when a tea-service was a possession for life.

'As far as I'm concerned there's never been any question of it,'
she said. 'The question doesn't arise. And don't drop cigarette ash
in your cup, for goodness sake. Milk costs the earth these days.'

But such diversionary tactics had less than no chance of success. Why had Lill put a cigarette in other than to annoy her mother, who hated above all to see her with it hanging loosely from her mouth?

'That's where you're so daft, Mum,' said Lill, deftly aiming ash in the direction of the stove. 'You're not as young as you were. You need someone here all the time, to see you're all right.'

'Hmm,' said Mrs Casey, settling down into her chair again and taking up her coffee cup, 'you needn't pretend it's concern for me that's behind it.'

'Well, there's Gordon and Bri too, of course. They need a bedroom to themselves each. Stands to reason at their age. Debbie's would just suit Bri down to the ground. Give him room for all them books of his.'

'Not to mention the fact that you'd be pleased to get Debbie out of your hair. Well, I've told you before, it's not on. I'm too old to go looking after a girl of her age. My notions are not her notions, and it's silly to pretend she'd put up with it. After the sort of life she's had in your house. I'm seventy-five. That's no time of life to start bringing up a teenager.'

'It's because you're so bloody old you need somebody here,' said Lill, sucking in her coffee noisily. 'Someone around all the time to see that you're still living and breathing.'

This appeal to the perennial fear of the old cut no ice with Mrs Casey. 'It's not me has to be afraid of dying. I'm ready. And it's not as though I'm *alone*, with all you lot living next door. The boys are very good. They pop in.'

Lill's voice took on a harsh edge: 'I'm not having my boys running in and out here every five minutes to see if you're stretched out. They've got better things to do. You've gotter have your fun while you're young.'

'Of course,' said Mrs Casey cunningly, 'if you want the boys to have a room of their own, then Gordon could move in here with me.'

' 'Ere, you're not having my Gordon! What a cheek! That's disgusting, an old woman like you!'

'He's older,' continued Mrs Casey, paying no attention, 'so

there wouldn't be the same problems. He could go his own way. And it's always easier with a boy, as you know.'

The conversation had taken a turn that Lill Hodsden had not at all anticipated, and she tried to change tack. 'The boys are staying together, and that's flat. You only suggested it because you knew they wouldn't—'

'I knew *you* wouldn't have it, more like.'

'You're just a selfish old woman. You haven't changed a bit all the years I've known you. Think about nothing but yourself. All my childhood you kept me down, stopped me having my bit of fun—'

Mrs Casey sniffed expressively. 'I tried to stop you leading a life of sin and depravity—'

'No need to chuck the ruddy Bible at me. Nobody gives a damn about that sort of thing these days. You were jealous, that was all, under all that religious talk. Jealous. That's why you forced me to marry Fred—'

'Forced you! Ha!' Mrs Casey let out a bitter, reminiscent laugh. 'You'd have married Jack the Ripper only to get away from home. When you went off and married Fred I was just pleased it was no worse.'

'How would you know how worse it was? You know nothing about it. You never understood me. You've made trouble in the family all the time you've been here. You've never fitted in—I should never have let you come here.'

'Went down on your bended knees,' amended Mrs Casey, who never let swervings from the literal truth pass uncorrected. 'So you'd have a home help and someone to dump the kids on to when it suited you.'

'And a fat lot of dumping I've been able to do on you!' said Lill bitterly.

Mrs Casey smiled a hard, complacent smile. 'Not much, I grant you. I wasn't having any of that. Why should I? I'm not so green as I'm cabbage-looking. You met your match wi' me, Lill. You and I'll never get on, because you're not as smart as you think you are, and I'm a deal smarter!'

Stung perhaps by the truth of it, Lill clattered her coffee cup back on the saucer and stood up. But before she could frame a sufficiently annihilating parting shot, her mother said:

'Perhaps that's the trouble with Debbie, too, eh? She's a mite smarter than you already.'

Lill banged out the back door, barged past the milkman, who had been idly listening, and bounced through the back garden home. Mrs Casey went about her morning dusting and sweeping with a sprightliness she hadn't felt in her when she got up.

It had given a bit of excitement, thought Lill, but still, it wasn't much of a row. Which meant, of course, that its outcome was not at all the one she had been banking on. It certainly hadn't given the day the central focus she had unconsciously planned for it. Every day, for Lill, had to have some kind of focal point she could remember as she lay in bed—some moment when she stood in the spotlight in one or other kind of triumph. Through the rest of the morning, and over dinner with Fred and Gordon—shepherd's pie and tinned pears and cream, rushed and scamped as always—she wondered how to give it that focus. When she had washed up she seemed to make a quick decision: she emptied the contents of the sugar bowl back into the packet, and she cantered up the road to little Mrs Watson:

'Coo-ee,' she shouted at the door, which stood open: 'anyone at home?'

Mrs Watson flinched, being just around the door trying to get her stove to light. But then, she flinched automatically at Lill. Todmarsh was a small town, though, and open warfares were best avoided, so she hid her dislike and irritation behind a brave social face and said: 'Hello, Mrs Hodsden.'

'Oh hel*lo*,' said Lill, steaming in and assuming a dreadfully refined manner, like a parody of one of the more uppitty Archers. 'I didn't see you round there. *Could* you help me? I clean forgot sugar down the shops today. *Could* you lend me a spot, save me going down before tomorrow?'

'Of course,' said Ann Watson. She refrained from wondering why Lill had not gone borrowing at any of the nine or ten houses that separated them in Windsor Avenue. She merely took the bowl

and went to the kitchen cupboard, her thick, long hair shielding
her face from Lill's hungry gaze. But when she brought it back
and handed it over she could not avoid looking at her and paying
the social price of a polite smile. She received in return a smile of
combined sympathy and good cheer that oozed over her and
dripped down, as if she'd been crowned with a plate of cold por-
ridge.

'I *was* pleased to see you out on Saturday night,' said Lill, her
voice throbbing with personal concern. 'I thought to myself:
"She's coming round," I thought.'

'I beg your pardon?' said Ann Watson, sheet ice in her voice.

'Getting over it,' pursued Lill, blithely unconscious. 'Coming
back to life, and getting about a bit again. Because it doesn't do,
you know.'

'What doesn't?' said Ann unwisely, still frozen hard.

'Giving yourself up to grief,' said Lill luxuriantly.

But for once Lill had hit the nail on the head. Ann Watson had
been married less than two years when her husband had been shot
in the back while on patrol in Northern Ireland. He had died the
next day and become two lines in the national newspapers. The
War Office had flown her to his funeral. Her life, it seemed to her,
was like a snapped twig, and she was living the broken end now. It
is not fashionable to talk of being grief-stricken, any more than it is
fashionable to talk of happy marriages, but Ann Watson had been
grief-stricken because her marriage had been happy. And she
didn't fool herself that happy marriages happen twice. Even now,
more than two years later, all the social gestures seemed difficult
and meaningless—even the social gesture of looking after her little
girl. She constructed a daily round, and followed it like a somnam-
bulant nun. At moments of stress she had visions of her husband
falling in the street, and the pointlessness of it, the futility, en-
raged her to the breaking point. Hardest to bear was the feeling
that people she met could not face her pain, tried to butter it over
with clichés. Time was not, she had found, the great healer.

'I've been back teaching part-time for eighteen months,' she
said. 'It doesn't exactly look as if I'd given myself up to grief.' As

she said it she kicked herself: why should she justify herself to this woman? Someone she didn't even like?

'Oh, *that's* not what I meant,' said Lill, happily unconscious of opposition or offence. 'I meant going out and enjoying yourself, getting a kick out of life again. That's what I want to see.'

'It's none of your business,' said Ann, back to the stove and feeling pressed into a corner by her ignorant goodwill.

' 'Course it's our business. We've all been concerned about you, everyone along the road. It's just that old Lill's the only one to speak out honest about it. It's not nice to see someone moping for so long. I know my Gordon's been very concerned.'

'I'm sure it's kindly meant,' said Ann, aware that Lill was pushing her into the stalest of conversational clichés, and fearful that she would soon be reduced to the purest fishwife abuse. 'I just wish you all wouldn't bother.'

'He's a very kind-hearted chap, my Gordon. He feels things, know what I mean? 'Course, he was in the army like your hubby— five years he was in. Did his bit in Northern Ireland too, like they all have to. I expect him and your chap are very alike, really.'

'They're nothing like,' said Ann shortly.

'Oh, I don't mean in the face, or anything, just in their natures. Though I will say this, though I shouldn't as his mum, but you wouldn't find a better-looking, better setup chap than my Gordon.' The voice became more insistent. *'Would you?'*

'I really can't say I've thought about it.'

'Go on. Don't tell me. You've thought about it all right. I know what it's like when you're young. What are you? Twenty-four? Twenty-five?' Lill's leer split her face in two, a great cracked doll's face, surmounted by a shrieking red mop. 'I know what it's like being twenty-five, widow or no widow. Now, your David was a nice-looking chap, I'm sure, and one in a million, but he wasn't the only fish in the sea and why should you pretend he was? He's been gone two years and more now. And there's things that a girl like you needs at your age—'

'Do you mind—?'

'And there's my Gordon, he's really got an eye for you. You'd go lovely together, I know it. I can just see you, together. You might be made for each other. Go on—admit it: you wouldn't say no to a bit of you-know-what now and again, would you? No girl ought to be ashamed of that. Wouldn't my Gordon just suit you down to the ground, eh?'

Ann Watson faced her across the kitchen table, and Lill's evil old face suddenly touched a nerve which made her control snap as it never had since the day her husband had died: 'You disgusting old bag,' she shrieked, red in the face. 'You're pimping for your own son.'

'Words!' said Lill, momentarily disconcerted and retreating towards the door, clutching her sugar bowl. 'I wouldn't have expected words like that from a girl of your education. That's what comes of trying to do a bit of good in the world. I only wanted to help you, because I saw you needed it. All I want's for you both to be comfortable.'

'Get out of my house, you old harridan,' yelled Ann, and as Lill turned tail and started down the step she marched over and slammed the door brutally on her retreating ankle. Then she tottered over to the kitchen table and sat down, clutching the legs of it until her knuckles were white, racked by violent, silent sobs that would not come out in tears.

Limping down the road, having enjoyed herself hugely, Lill nevertheless thought to herself: I don't think she'd do for my Gordon, after all. He'd never want to get hitched to a girl with a temper like that.

4

A BIT ON THE SIDE

Lill Hodsden's colour television—a large, poor-quality model, out of which salmon-pink announcers gaped at her as from a fish-bowl, dressed in shiny turquoise suits unbecoming their age and dignity—was in fact a present from a friend, though for form's sake, and because she liked lying when it could give her a delicious sense of romantic intrigue, she had invented the family emigrating to foreign parts. It was a present she had been grateful for at the time. ('Oh, it's *ever* so much prettier,' she had said, and indeed she had sat for hour after hour gazing at washy-blue hills alive with the sound of music), but the first fine bloom of gratitude had by now worn off, hardly at all prolonged by the occasional gift of cash. She was beginning to wonder whether the time wasn't ripe for another more substantial tribute. She'd have to start hinting, very delicately, to Mr Corby.

It was a Corby evening tonight, Monday. Lill always gave her boys—and inevitably her family—a cooked tea. She prided herself on it. When Brian and Debbie had got back from school by bus about five, and when Gordon and Fred had separately cycled home from work, she served them all toasted cheese and Beefomite, an invention of her own she was very proud of, though *Woman's Home* had surprisingly failed to print the recipe when she submitted it for their Tastisnax page. Debbie ate only one little triangle, then went out and got a lump of cheese from the 'fridge and ostentatiously nibbled it, heedless of Lill's cold, hard stares. The rest of them had got used to it, and managed to get it down.

'Champion,' said Fred, licking his lips.

By seven-fifteen Lill had smoked two fags cadged from Gordon, washed up the tea things ('By rights I ought to have a machine, with a family this size') and listened to *The Archers* ('That Shula's a right little madam, just like my Debbie'). At twenty past seven she took down her leopard-skin coat from the hook in the hall, fixed a perky green hat on her scarlet mop, and poked her head round the front-room door:

'I'm just going round to sit with Mrs Corby for an hour or two,' she called.

'Right you are,' said Fred, breaking out of a doze.

Debbie was upstairs in the much-discussed bedroom, Brian was in the back room doing a history essay for the morning on Benthamism and nineteenth-century industrial legislation, and Gordon was upstairs changing into his track suit preparatory to going jogging. To all of them Lill shrilled blithely, 'Won't be gone long!', and then clip-clopped out into Windsor Avenue with a silly complacent smile on her face which gave her away to the merest cat, sunning itself on the garden wall.

Mrs Corby was an invalid who for five years now had kept to her room, laid low by an indefinable illness that doctors in the last century would probably have labelled 'nervous prostration'. Now and again in summer her husband, with the help of a neighbour, bundled her into the car, wrapped up like an oversized and querulous baby, and took her for a drive to Portsea along the coast, or inland to some of the beauty spots and picturesque villages of South-West England, at all of which Mrs Corby glared malevolently, as if this was what she was glad to have got away from. This was her only contact with civilization at large. She had a nature illadapted to friendship, being a thoroughly nasty woman with a vinegar-soaked tongue and a need to cut everybody within sight down to half her own size, so she had no visitors. She saw her husband, the doctor, and the twice-weekly char. She had never in her life, certainly, spoken to Lill Hodsden, for in Todmarsh, as elsewhere, there were circles within circles, and Drusilla Corby was on the inner, and Lill Hodsden the outer line. By now this was irrelevant. For Lill she was just an excuse, a convenience, a lie that could not be checked up on. W. Hamilton Corby had once described her to Lill as a legal fiction, and Lill, thinking he'd said friction, had snarled: 'Christ, she's that all right.'

She let herself into the large, weather-mellowed, red-brick house, with the feeble pretence of battlements and turret windows, and went straight through the hall to the study at the back. Finding nobody there, she opened the bar-cupboard in the far corner (rosewood lined with pink silk—Corby had had it made specially) and mixed herself a gin and tonic. Holding her glass in a sophisticated manner, imagining herself to be Princess Grace at a diplomatic reception in Monaco, she went over to the desk and casually went through the correspondence there. Then she remembered to take off her parody leopard-skin, threw it over the desk chair, and settled herself on the leather-covered sofa, fingering it meditatively and pricing it in her mind. It wouldn't have been *her* choice, but the cost of it excited her. When finally Hamilton Corby came into the room, muttering 'She's a bit troublesome tonight,' Lill drained her glass, waited till he had safely closed the door, then cackled and said: 'When isn't she?'

W. Hamilton Corby (born Wilf Corby, he had taken in his wife's surname when she had made him the happiest man in Todmarsh, and one of the wealthier) was not a romantic figure, looked at objectively. The impression one took away was of sagging tummy, baggy trousers, and watery, shifty eyes. He was the sort of man one sees in droves at the better sort of main-road pubs, boasting about their deals by the bar with their sagging, baggy, shifty fellows, or sitting silent at tables with their wives. No, beyond his income he scored few points as a lover, and more often than not all he wanted on Lill's visits was a befuddled fumble. More's the pity, as Lill often said to herself.

'She's a poor creature,' said Corby, settling himself on the sofa and putting his hand absent-mindedly on Lill's knee, apparently because it was there. He went through, as if by rote, the litany of phrases he always used about his wife. 'She's her own worst enemy. She makes no one unhappy but herself. I don't know what she'd do without me. Because I can tell you this: she'd never get anyone else to stop with her, pay them what she might. She's the sort nobody can help because she won't help herself.'

Lill sat complacently through this, the terms of which were as well known to her as a weather forecast. When he came to a stop the hand went further up her thigh. Lill would have liked another gin and tonic, but she thought he might as well do whatever he wanted to do or was capable of doing, and then they could be comfy. Five minutes later she got her gin.

'Business booming?' she asked, sipping. It was one of her four conversational openings.

Hamilton Corby grunted. 'Not bad. Could be worse. Thank God we're a small firm, making small boats people can still afford. If we'd built liners or tankers we'd have been in the hands of the receiver long ago. Or taken over by Wedgie Benn.'

'How's my Gordon doing? All right?'

Corby grunted again. 'All right. He's a good worker. Not that there's much for him to do. I only took him on to oblige, as you know. But he pulls his weight . . . Shouldn't have thought it was really his line, though.'

Lill preened herself and put on her Lady Muck face. 'Well of *course* he should really be doing something *far* better, something with *lots* more class. He's a boy with *tremendous* potential.' She relaxed a little, and immediately collapsed into bathos: 'I've always thought my Gordon ought to be in films.'

Hamilton Corby said nothing. The last time he'd been to the cinema had been in the Anna Neagle-Michael Wilding era. Gordon didn't remind him all that much of Michael Wilding.

'He's got the looks,' continued Lill, looking dreamily ahead over her glass of gin. 'That nobody could deny. A real smasher. And he's got something else . . . A sort of dangerous quality.'

Corby did not consider that last statement as seriously as he might. 'Can he act?' he asked nastily.

'He used to do marvellous imitations as a child,' rejoined Lill, unperturbed. 'Killing he was, had us all in stitches. They're both very talented, my boys.'

'He strikes me more as the sporty type,' said Corby, who genuinely liked Gordon. 'Should have gone to college, become a P.E. teacher or something.'

'Well, of course that's what I *wanted*,' said Lill, hearing the notion for the first time. 'It would have suited him down to the ground. But no, it had to be the army. He *would* go. Christ, when I think of that Mrs Watson's hubby, dead at twenty-four, I get the cold shivers. Thank God my Gordon got out.' She suddenly thought of something and cackled. 'They both got out in a way, eh?'

She quietened down after a bit, when Hamilton Corby merely contemplated his whisky glass mournfully. 'Oh dear, aren't I awful? Anyway, as I was saying, Gordon's *not* really got as far as he ought to have done. That's why I want him to have a car.'

The remarkable logical leap from vocational heights to physical distances did not escape Hamilton Corby. He declined to leap at once in the required direction. He said: 'Plenty of cars around.'

'Of course, I meant a sort of family car,' said Lill. 'Only Gordon could drive it. Brian too when he's a bit older, because there's nothing unmechanical about him, for all his brains . . .' She paused for a little, and then added meaningfully: 'You've got more money than you know what to do with.'

'*Nobody's* got more money than they know what to do with,' replied Corby, with intense conviction.

'Oh, go on. You wouldn't even notice a sum like that,' said Lill, nudging him encouragingly. Hamilton Corby was not stupid: he may have got where he was (and paid for it) by marriage, but he had kept there by a modicum of sharpness. He had several ways of not getting caught by the likes of Lill.

'My brother-in-law's got an old Mini,' he said eventually; 'belongs to his wife, but she never uses it. He's thinking of selling it.'

'That wasn't the kind of car I was thinking about,' said Lill.

'I'm sure it wasn't.' And Hamilton Corby smiled a sly, aqueous smile and held his peace. Lill thought she'd let the subject drop for a moment, and the two turned to other things.

'Hey, I had the chance of a lifetime last week,' she said eventually, as the hands of the clock neared nine-thirty. Her fat, coarse face had brightened at the very thought.

'What was that?'

'Guy Fawcett next door. Made what you might call an indecent suggestion.'

'Oh? What was that?'

'What do you mean what was that? What do you think it was? Wanted to go to bed with me, that's what. He's often home during the day, and his wife's out at work. And of course, none of my lot's home during the day.'

'What did you say?'

'Called him a dirty old man and said he ought to be ashamed. Doesn't do to jump at it first time.' She cast a sideways glance at Hamilton Corby, sagging apathetically on the sofa beside her, and said: 'Not that he is old, not by a long chalk. About forty-five, I'd say. Not much older than me . . . Got a good job, too . . . He's a car salesman.'

'Perhaps you'd better go to him for your car,' said Corby, with unexpected quickness of mind. As a ploy for arousing jealousy, Guy Fawcett's indecent proposal seemed less than a total success. She began collecting herself together.

'Of course, he's a very attractive man,' she said, persistent. 'Tremendous shoulders. And what I'd call a really sensitive face. You never know when you'll get that sort of proposition again . . .' She shook her head meaningfully.

'See you Thursday, Lill?'

'Shouldn't wonder. Same time.' At the study door she gave him a tremendous passionate kiss five seconds long, and after tiptoeing through the hall another at the front door.

'Don't you worry about Fawcett,' she whispered, as if he had; 'I can put him in his place any time.'

'Don't take any nonsense from him, Lill,' said Corby, playing along.

'Not more than I want to. Keep your pecker up. It can't last for ever, you know. If she was gone, I'd marry you like a shot.'

Hamilton Corby, who knew he could do very much better if marriage were in question, said: 'What about Fred?'

'Oh, I'd soon get rid of *Fred*,' returned Lill, her whisper more urgent. 'Never you mind how. Ta-ta for now.'

Above them on the first floor a door closed. On the step, taking a last genteel peck, they heard nothing. Then Lill set off at her usual brisk pace down Balaclava Road and turned into the enveloping shadows of Snoggers Alley. She was not altogether satisfied with her evening, but still, a seed had been planted. And if the worst came to the worst, a Mini would be better than nothing. So when she got home, at nine-forty prompt, she was quite her normal cheery self.

'That's my good turn for the day done!'

'How was she?' asked Fred, who was in the same half-asleep state he had been in when she went out, this time in front of a TV Western.

Lill shook her head gloomily. 'It's a terrible disease. She's in purgery the whole time. The doctors can't even put a name to it.'

Fred nodded. He never showed any greater curiosity than this about her twice-weekly visits. His store of curiosity was tiny at the best of times. The rest of the family, sprawled around the television in various attitudes of inattention, kept tactfully silent.

'Do you know,' said Lill, who could never keep quiet about anything that was on her mind. 'I think it's time we bought a car.' Gordon looked at Brian and Brian looked at Gordon, but neither of them said anything. Debbie sniffed and left the room. 'We'd've had one years ago if it hadn't been for buying Gordon out of the army. I think I know where we could pick one up dirt cheap. I've always said, it's what you boys need. Get you out so's you can have a good time. Meet a few girls.'

'I thought I was supposed to be marked down for Mrs Watson,' said Gordon. 'I don't need a car to go courting her—she just lives up the road.'

'Mrs Watson! That stuck-up little tailor's dummy! Christ! Whatever gave you that idea? You're a sight too good to take up with other men's leavings.'

Lill always let her family know when she changed her mind.

'She's screwing a car out of him now,' said Gordon to Brian, when at last they had escaped from rusks and Ovalmix and had reached the womblike safety of their bedroom. 'God, what a cheek she's got!'

'Would you have the nerve to drive round in a car that was the price of your mother's shame?' demanded Brian with a melodramatic gesture of the arms.

'Frankly, I wouldn't give it a second thought. Only I don't think I'll be getting the chance. Lill's next ride is going to be in the back of a hearse.'

Brian shivered when it was put that bluntly. 'Funny to think about it. Free, after all these years of . . . of being her doormats. I wish I felt better.'

Gordon looked at him keenly. 'What do you mean, better? What's the matter?'

'Just this ruddy cough. It's the climate. "Bronchial isle, all isles excelling", as the poet said. They shouldn't have put people down in this climate.'

'It's not the climate does things to you. It's Lill. It's just some nervous thing. Remember last year—you weren't any better in Tunisia.'

Brian, lying on his bed with an unread book, shifted uneasily at the mention of Tunisia, as he always did. 'Christ, no wonder I didn't feel up to much,' he muttered. 'What with Lill and all. Remember Lill on the plane?'

The two heads on their pillows—Gordon's dark and purposeful, Brian's fair and distressed—lay for a moment in silence as last year's holiday in Tunisia came back to them. It had been explained to Lill that the firm they were traveling with was 'up market', and, when she expressed bewilderment, the term had been spelled out in words of one syllable. But she never quite understood that the people on this trip were a different sort from the mob they had been with to Benidorm three years before. Just in those early moments, when everyone was settling into their seats, swapping with each other at most a murmured comment on the rate of exchange or the price of Glenfiddich, Lill showed she misjudged the prevailing mood by shrieking across the plane to Gordon, six rows in front: 'Soon be there now, Gord! How long will it be, d'you think, before some sheikh snatches me up in his passionate arms and takes me off to his harem, eh?' And as soon as the 'Fasten Seat Belts' sign was switched off she was swaying along the aisle to the loo singing 'The Sheikh of Arabee-ee' with special smiles at all the more desirably distinguished men on the trip. One frozen air hostess at the back of the plane raised a plucked eyebrow at the other frozen air hostess at the front; the up-market travellers glanced sideways at each other and coughed in the backs of their throats. Still, over the Channel, and everyone had got Lill's number. None of them exchanged a word with Lill for the rest of the fortnight. 'They're a stuffy lot,' Lill kept saying. 'I prefer the wogs. Don't understand what they're going on about, but at least they're friendly.'

At last Brian, deep in memories, said: 'No it's not the climate. It's Lill.'

'And it's Lill,' said Gordon, 'makes us the laughing-stocks of the town. Disgraces us every time we try to climb out of the mud. You know what people say about you and me?'

'Yes,' said Brian. 'I know. Still, when all's said and done—'

'Anyway,' said Gordon quickly, 'your role is to be my alibi. Your health doesn't matter. You haven't got to do anything.'

'It sounds a bit feeble,' complained Brian.

'What's the point of all this training I do if I can't even kill off my own mother? It's got to be one of us, not both, and obviously I'm the fit one.' He stubbed out his cigarette in the ashtray. 'I'm even giving up smoking tomorrow—for the duration. Yours is the brainy bit. You've got to convince the police I was in the pub the whole evening, except for the odd minute in the bog. You've got to have it off, pat, the whole story.'

'What about if Lill opens her big mouth and draws attention to it, like she did on Saturday?'

'We've got to make damn sure she doesn't.' Gordon lay on his back, looking darkly at the ceiling. 'I've been thinking about it. I think we could work it like this: if I slip off a couple of minutes before Lill's due to go, and say "I'm just nipping over to have a word with John" or Chris or whoever happens to be in the pub that night—"see you at supper", then she won't comment on my not being there. And I'll make sure I do have a word with them some time in the evening, in case anyone asks. Either just before or just after.'

'You've got to be careful just after,' said Brian. 'I've read about the physical effects of murdering someone. It makes you want to—'

'I know it makes you want to—well, that's what Lill's done to me all her life.'

'Just be careful. Even if you're only a bit jittery, people notice things. You'd better just come back to the table and talk to me . . . What are you going to do it with? Not your hands?'

'No,' said Gordon. 'Though I could. But it's too risky. I'll use rope. I can get a short bit from work.'

'They'd be able to trace the type.'

'It's common stuff. You can buy it anywhere.'

'Why not just hit her on the head?'

'It might not kill her, not with that thick skull. If I hit her several times, there'd probably be blood. That's one thing I can't risk, blood . . . Anyway,' he added slowly, 'I don't think it would give me the same pleasure.' A smile was on his full lips.

'You're really looking forward to this, aren't you?'

'Yeah, baby brother, I'm looking forward to it.' He looked mockingly at Brian across the bare length of their room. 'Aren't you? Touch of the cold feet?'

'No,' said Brian carefully. 'No. But if I was actually *doing* it . . . The alibi business, that's a piece of cake. I'll enjoy that. The other, the . . . strangling, I don't know if I could. She's our mother.' He swallowed. 'When it comes down to it, I don't suppose she's meant any harm.'

'Christ, you bloody intellectuals,' hissed Gordon through his teeth. 'You never go straight at a thing, do you? Never meant any harm? What else has she ever meant? In twenty years you'll be toasting her on the anniversary of all this with tears in your eyes: "To the finest Mum a man ever had!" '

'Don't be daft . . .'

'And in twenty years, I'll join you.'

5

TUESDAY

Lill's life changed course somewhat on Tuesday, though by no means as drastically as it was to later in the week. The day began in the usual way, with the family crawling reluctantly out of their beds, quarrelling over the bathroom and loo, slouching down to breakfast half asleep (a good job, really, because the poached eggs were hard as stones), and gradually dispersing themselves in their various directions. Once that was over, the day opened up with manifold possibilities for Lill. Now she could dispose of her hours as she would, captain of her fate, mistress of her soul; meaning, in fact, that she could plan any manner of mischief she set her heart on.

Lill wondered whether Guy Fawcett would be home next door during the day.

The thought stayed with her as she performed in her slapdash way her various early morning chores. The cat—black with white paws and whiskers, and knowing eyes that saw through Lill all right—demanded breakfast, and Lill reached down a tin. As she opened it she noticed a By Appointment sign on the label, and said to herself: Blimey, you'd have thought she could afford something better than this! She washed up the breakfast things, and slapped a greasy cloth over the kitchen table. Then she put some coke on the kitchen stove and emptied the ashes from underneath. Throughout she kept half an eye on the kitchen window and the gardens outside.

At nine-fifteen Guy Fawcett appeared beyond the next-door fence, large and visible, and carrying a spade which he showed no inclination to use.

Didn't do to seem too eager. Lill knew the moves in the game as well as anyone alive. She went upstairs to make the beds, opened the bedroom windows wide and carolled in her crow-scaring singing voice the first two lines or so of 'Oh, What a Beautiful Morning', over and over. She knew the ropes. It gave him an opening. 'You sound happy today,' he could say when she finally emerged into the back garden. As she made Brian and Gordon's beds her eyes strayed to the figure of Guy Fawcett, wandering around his back lawn in the pallid April sunshine. His heart doesn't seem to be in it, she thought. Better give him something to keep his pecker up. So when she went downstairs, she took out the sink-tidy, with the rubbish from breakfast, and slapped the contents into the dust-bin, humming cheerily the while a healthy Cliff Richard number.

'You sound happy this fine morning,' said Guy Fawcett from over the garden fence. 'Come into a fortune?'

'That's right,' said Lill, not pausing in her trot back to the kitchen. 'I come into the pools. Just like that woman said, it's going to be "Spend, Spend, Spend" with me.'

'It would be too with you, Lill,' said Fawcett, his bass baritone throbbing with admiration. Lill laughed all the way down the scale, threw him a sideways look that could mean whatever he chose it to, and charged through the back door. The first move had been made. The gunfighters were circling warily round the dusty town square, waiting for the moment when they would come out into the open, all cylinders blazing.

Lill hurried through the rest of her chores. After all, though it doesn't do to seem too anxious, still—Fred and Gordon would be back at five past one. Another little bout of teasing would be strictly within the rules of the game, but it would take time. She finished her scanty Hoovering, decided not to dust the bits of brass, china dogs, cheap African pots and other ornaments dotted around her mantelpiece and window ledges, then fetched her handbag and put on a bit of make-up lovingly in front of the mirror: not too much—didn't want to make it too obvious; not too little—have to give him an excuse for mentioning it. She smirked at herself when she had finished: she could still show the young 'uns a thing or two! This done, she armed herself with a fearsome pair of secateurs from Fred's gardening drawer, and sallied out into the fresh air.

The garden was Fred's responsibility. When not tending the parish parks he came back to dig his own potato patch, and it would never have occurred to him to complain at this. Now and then Lill acted in a supervisory capacity, told him what she wanted, where, and so on; but basically she took no interest in it. Flowers, like cats, were too involved in their own intricate magnificence to minister to her self-love. So beyond demanding great clumps of gladioli, peonies, or any other slightly monstrous bloom that caught her eye in other gardens, she left it to Fred. And it looked like it. Fred had his successes, mainly turnips and chrysanthemums, but he could not be said to run to a green finger. The Hodsdens' back garden was a dull little patch of earth.

Still, spring flowers there were, and the odd bush she could make feints at, in pretence of pruning. Which is more than could be said for Guy Fawcett's garden, which was a weedy lawn, and beyond that a wilderness: tall straggly bits of weeds, grasses and flowers that had been planted and forgotten. Any less blatant person would have been embarrassed at the pretence of ever working in it or caring what happened to it.

'Hot work this,' said Guy, unbending from doing nothing very much by a border and drawing a fleshy arm across his brow.

'Got to be done,' said Lill, flashing a head-on smile while snapping away at a depressed and dusty rosebush that looked more in need of pep-pills than pruning. 'You don't get anything in this world you don't work for.'

'True,' said Guy, though neither of them believed a word of it: neither of them had got where they were, or enjoyed the pleasures they did enjoy, as a result of the sweat of their brows. Guy weighed straight in, as was his custom. 'God, you look a million dollars today, Lill. I don't know how you do it. Time doesn't just stand still with you. It walks backwards, like leaving the Queen's presence.'

This flowery compliment was typical of Guy in the early stages, but it was wasted on Lill, who knew nothing of the mysteries of locomotion before royalty. 'Go on,' she said, which was a good all-purpose remark she made a lot of use of. 'Few more years and I'll be past my prime!'

'I shan't live to see that,' returned Guy. As though drawn by invisible plastic gardening twine they both approached the waist-high fence. Lill threw up her arms in a gesture of girlish ecstasy and exclaimed. 'Oh, I love Spring!'

They looked at the scratchy earth, poked through by the dusty leaves of newly-sprouting bulbs and sighed sentimentally. 'Yes, it makes you think, Spring,' said Guy. His thick, sensual self-admiring lips slid into a meaningful grin: 'Eh Lill? Doesn't Spring make you think of a lot of things you could be doing?'

'Maybe,' said Lill. 'And I don't suppose you mean digging the potato patch either.'

'Not exactly,' agreed Guy, the grin still fixed but mobile on his lips, and his eyes resting on her powdery face. 'But when you get to our age—say thirty-five—'

'Say twenty-five if you like,' said Lill agreeably.

'—You realize there's some things—things you want to do—and that time's not on your side any longer—that you'd be silly *not* to do them if that's what you fancy—because in a few years it'll be too late, if you follow me.'

'Just about,' said Lill. 'It's difficult, but I'm doing my best.'

'Specially,' concluded Guy with a leer, 'when they hurt nobody. Not, of course, that anybody'd know anyway.'

'My Fred's a terror when he's roused,' said Lill. 'You wouldn't think it to look at him, but by golly he is!'

Guy repressed a chortle of disbelief, and tensed his shoulders and arms to show off his biceps. I'd fight for you, Lill, he was saying as clearly as if he'd spoken. Lill was thrilled. She said: 'Naturally whatever I did I'd always be careful, because of Fred . . .'

The half-concession was obvious, but Guy played his game for one more move. He put on an expression of great tenderness. 'You're lucky to have someone who really cares. I don't think my wife would care at all, whatever I did. Ours is a funny marriage. My wife doesn't understand me at all.'

'Blimey, she ought to,' cackled Lill, breaking the mood. 'I understand you all right.'

'Why are we wasting time, then, eh Lill?' And Guy Fawcett bent his heavy body urgently forward to hers over the fence. 'Let's get on with it. Have a bit of fun before your lot comes back for their lunch.'

Lill retreated flirtatiously to the depressing rosebush. 'Well, I don't say that if you come round the back door in ten minutes with a book you'd promised to lend me I wouldn't let you in.'

'Oh, come off it, Lill. Since when have you taken up with literature? Nobody'd buy that even if they heard me. I'll just hop over the fence—'

'Hey, give over you saucy bastard—' But by then Guy Fawcett had done a one-hand spring over the rickety fence and was approaching her with looks of cinematic lust in his eyes. 'Hey, give over, Guy, someone might see us. Me mother—'

And at that moment Lill, in giggling mock-flight, did turn her head round in the direction of her mother's garden, and saw through the gap in the straggling hedge her mother, square and aproned on a kitchen chair, peeling potatoes in the watery sun and regarding them with an air of malevolent disapproval, lips pursed, old black eyes flashing.

Lill's reaction was instantaneous and sincere: she turned back towards the gap in the hedge and whipped her fingers into a vicious V-sign. Then she put her arm around Guy Fawcett's substantial waist, let him paw over her shoulders and round to her triumphal breasts, and so the pair went off towards the kitchen door in an ecstasy of simulated amusement. The back door was shut with tremendous emphasis, and strain as her old ears might, Mrs Casey heard no more. Lill and Fred's bedroom was at the front of the house. Shaking her head, and with a tear of shame or rage at the corners of her eyes, she put a cloth over her bowl of potatoes and slowly, arthritically, made her way back to her own kitchen.

'Penny for 'em, Fred. What are you thinking about?'

It was one of Fred's mates in the parks department who asked, coming up behind him as he filled in time before the dinner-hour in the garden around the war memorial. It was a question they often felt impelled to ask him, as he poked aimlessly around with hoe or rake, doing no good to anyone and positive harm to the newly bedded plants that before many weeks were out would spell 'Welcome to Todmarsh' in pink, yellow and blue under the names of the fallen. And when he was challenged, Fred usually replied: 'Wondering what'll win the two-thirty at Newmarket,' or 'Remembering that goal in the second half of the cuptie last Saturday,' and then went back a little more purposefully to his work. A more honest reply would have been 'Nothing.' For in fact Fred had a tremendous capacity for letting his mind go completely blank and stay that way for hours at a time. But even Fred realized that reply would lay him open to ridicule, so he always concocted something. Today he said: 'Just thinking that if I'd got that double seven in the darts Saturday night we'd've won.'

'Oh aye,' said his mate. 'Thought you were down the Rose and Crown Saturday night with your family.'

'Only early on,' said Fred, perking up a little, and excavating energetically around a petunia which would very much rather have been left alone. 'Only early on. Couldn't let the team down.'

'Celebration, wasn't it? Birthday or summat?'

'My Gordon's twenty-sixth,' said Fred, his skinny frame swelling with pride.

'Glad he's out the army and doing well for himself. Looks a fine lad. Twenty-six, eh? Wouldn't have thought it possible, looking at your Lill.'

'No, you're right. She's a fine woman. O' course I married her young.'

'You must have, at that. Bit of a handful for you, eh Fred? Beautiful woman like that?' His mate nudged him in the ribs.

'Better keep her on a short leash, eh, or there'll be others wanting to poke your grate.' And he snickered.

Fred remained for a minute in contemplation, and then he said with the shadow of a spark: 'Hold on, Bill. I don't like you making suggestions like that.'

But by this time his mate had gone back to his work, and after looking blearily at his back for a minute or two, Fred went on with his picking and poking around the flower-beds that never came to anything very much. It would be difficult to tell whether he was deep in thought.

'Oh lumme, what are you doing?' shouted Lill, dying with laughter. 'Blimey, I never thought of that one!'

'Learn a lot when you're with me, Lill,' said Guy Fawcett, continuing what he was doing.

Mrs Casey went around her house, meticulously dusting and wiping over her relics of Leicester in the 'thirties. Then she finished the preparation for her lunch. She had been so long alone that cooking for one presented no problems for her. Today she had a little bit of cod, which she was fond of and which had become quite a treat in recent years. But now her heart wasn't in her preparations. She read her paper, but it was one that had recently been shaved down into a tabloid, and it gave her no pleasure. There are no newspapers now for the Mrs Caseys of this world. She took up her library book, but she had lost the thread of the story and failed to pick it up again. In the end she gave in, and sat before the electric fire in her front room, just staring ahead of her.

Finally, she said to herself aloud—that aloudness giving it the seal of a conclusion or a decision: 'It's a right shame. In his house too. Someone ought to tell Fred about it.'

She drew her thin lips even tighter around her old teeth, nodded her head and went out in better heart to fry her cod.

'Oh, you are a devil,' said Lill at last. 'I'd never have thought you had it in you. Quite an education, really. Just like one of those manuals you read about.'

'Quite good, eh?' agreed Guy Fawcett, relaxing on his back with an expression of sublime conceit on his face. 'Expect I could teach old Fred a thing or two.'

Lill sniggered disloyally. 'Gawd, don't mention him. I'd better go down and boil his potatoes.' For some reason Guy sniggered in his turn. 'Here,' said Lill, as she struggled out of bed. 'We ought to do this more often.'

'Come back when you've put the spuds on, and we'll see,' said Guy in a seigneurial way.

'Didn't mean that, you clot,' said Lill. And when she returned and snuggled back against his fleshy frame in bed she said: 'We could make this a regular thing.'

'Tuesdays and Fridays?' said Guy. 'Regular servicing with a stamped receipt? That's not my line, Lill, not my line at all. I'm not the sort to get fenced in.'

'Why not?' protested Lill. 'If you enjoyed yourself . . . ?'

'Oh, I enjoyed it. But I like to play it by ear. Take it as it comes. I'm not a boy that can work regular hours.'

'Well, you're damned lucky your wife does,' said Lill with spirit. 'Wonder what she'd say if I told her.'

'Don't push your luck, Lill,' said Guy Fawcett, pressing her shoulders brutally down against the pillows. 'Or you'll be riding for a fall.'

'Hey, Brian,' said one of his classmates as they came out of a period on Palmerston's foreign policy and headed towards the long huts where dinner was served. 'Some of us are going over to Puddlesham to a disco on Saturday night. Are you coming?'

'Saturday night?' said Brian, pushing back that troublesome lock of hair from over his eyes. 'No, Saturday night I've got something on.'

6

COLOUR SENSE

The Coponawi Islands, which Mr Achituko had left for the drizzle and wheeze of an English winter, were dots on the map—courtesy dots at that—in the middle of the Pacific Ocean, thousands of miles from civilization, and not much nearer to Queensland. The islanders had undoubtedly been cannibal until the early eighteen-seventies, when they were Christianized by a gaunt, determined missionary, inevitably a Scot, a graduate of Edinburgh and Exeter Hall, a man so feared and respected that at his death—four years after his arrival, and before his flock could readily distinguish between Elijah and Elisha—his body was subjected to no more than the odd reverent nibble.

His flock's understanding of their new faith was at that point still wavering and nebulous, but some few could read, and when they discovered among his books (most of them too long and heavy for intellectual comfort) a little volume entitled *The Wise and Witty Sayings of George Eliot* they modelled their religion around her precepts and (in direct defiance of the good man's commands, which they easily in their minds reversed) set up wooden idols of the Sage which visiting anthropologists from Scandinavia later mistook for some form of horse worship imported by boat people from prehistoric North Africa.

Things had progressed rapidly in the Coponawi Islands since the Second World War. Nuclear tests had taken place in the vicin-

ity and had put them on the map. Hippy colonies from California
and Sydney had waxed there in the 'sixties and waned there in the
'seventies. Tourism had burgeoned, concrete blocks had risen
among the coconut palms, and only the occasional disappearance
of a well-fed mid-Westerner, and the subsequent discovery of
sneakers or orange-feathered alpine hat had led people to wonder
whether old habits didn't die hard. Mr Achituko's mind had been
formed by Peace Corps volunteers, very nearly deformed at the
University of Hawaii, and now he was studying cultic offshoots of
the major religions at the University of South Wessex, where a
group of atheists and defrocked priests ran a very high-powered
Comparative Religion Department. His was now a well-honed,
highly sophisticated mind, though when he had recently visited
the George Eliot Museum at Nuneaton the curator had been astonished to see him at various points during the guided tour performing the fourteen Stations of the Cross.

Thinking it over in bed on Saturday night, after the encounter
with Lill in the Rose and Crown, Mr Achituko had been highly
amused that Lill should suspect him of having designs on little
Mrs Watson up the road. For in fact he was sleeping, on and off,
with little Debbie Hodsden down the road, and he wouldn't have
minded betting that, had she known, Lill would have been livid,
not with moral outrage, but with jealousy.

Of course, it was hardly a settled thing with Debbie and could
not be yet, even if Achituko decided to stay in Britain beyond the
end of the academic year. His landlady was a woman of comparatively liberal mind (he had been accepted by her as a lodger after a
long succession of Todmarshians had suddenly and unaccountably
decided not to let rooms to students that academic year), but she
had made it clear that she drew the line at miscegenational sex.
'It's not so much me,' she had explained, in fear of attracting to
herself that most hated of modern labels, being called narrow-
minded, 'it's what the neighbours might say. You know what people are.'

Still, Wednesday night was bingo night for her, and now and
again as Spring had approached things had been possible under
the inky grey skies. In the Coponawi Islands Debbie would already

be a mother, and about to take on those extra rolls of flesh that were the signs of status and prosperity in those latitudes. Mr Achituko certainly did not think of himself as debauching a minor, but neither did he think of taking her with him when he returned home: he had no very high opinion of the chastity or housekeeping of English women, and it might have caused trouble with his wife and three children on the islands.

This Wednesday he was staying home to rough out a chapter of his thesis, dealing with various exciting Coptic heresies, but he had managed to exchange a couple of words with Debbie as she flew for her school bus, and he felt the day was likely to be a satisfying mixture of the sacred and the profane. However, his sally to the gate had been observed, and when his landlady came to clear away his breakfast things she lingered meaningfully, and finally said: 'Quite friendly with the Hodsdens, aren't you?'

'So-so,' said Mr Achituko, flashing his irresistible black and white smile. 'I see them sometimes in the Rose and Crown.'

'So I heard,' said Mrs Evangeline Carstairs (Eve to her friends), a considerable, opinionated and not unattractive woman whose husband worked in Bristol and was generally only to be seen at weekends, exhausted by work, Mrs Carstairs and British Rail. 'Of course, it's just a matter of taste, isn't it?'

'You dislike them, do you?' asked Achituko, who preferred to come out into the open with her, since her opinions were pithier when there were no polite manoeuverings.

'Oh, the children are all right,' said Eve Carstairs, crashing plates and saucers around on the tray. 'Though if you ask me, the boys are a poor-spirited lot to put up with it the way they do . . .' She ostentatiously said no more.

'But the parents—?'

'Well, you couldn't say anything against Fred, I suppose, because there's really nothing there, is there? More like a tadpole than what I'd call a man. But her—if you ask me she lets the road down and has since the day she came here. She's common as dirt, and if you believe half of what you hear around town, she's got the morals of an alley cat with it!'

'Really?' said Mr Achituko, who in fact knew infinitely more about Lill's activities than Mrs Carstairs. 'I must admit that at times I find her a little—embarrassing.'

'Don't we all? 'Course, you've got the colour thing with it, which makes it worse. Still, it's that daughter of hers I feel really sorry for: you feel it at that age. I expect Debbie does, doesn't she?'

She looked at him with a knowing air.

'Very likely,' said Achituko noncommittally. He wondered for a moment if—were things to come out into the open—Mrs Carstairs would be persuaded to give her blessing to his activities with Debbie. But, wisely, he remembered her age and refrained. And in fact Mrs Carstairs had quite other things on her mind, for as she took the tray out she said:

'If I was the girl I'd leave town as soon as I could. Get a job somewhere—she's not stupid. But nobody around here who knew the mother would want anything to do with the daughter. Whatever they say, there's such a thing as bad blood!'

For Eve Carstairs did not look with favour on Mr Achituko's choice. After all, she was herself a woman in the prime of life, magnificently fleshed, and in all the time he had been there Achituko had come no closer to the personal than to praise her Yorkshire puddings.

'What were you and Achituko talking about?' asked Brian as he and Debbie climbed breathless on to the school bus.

'Just passing the time of day,' said Debbie. 'Get off my back, will you?' And she went up front and sat with her friends, where they talked about various spotty and loud-mouthed youths whom her friends fancied and Debbie felt she was now infinitely too experienced to contemplate seriously. But she hugged her secret to herself, and gave bored attention to the discussion of the finer points of these adolescents.

Brian sat in the back seat of the upper deck, surrounded by his fellow sixth-formers touching up their last night's prep. But after a minute or two Brian, remembering that encounter between Debbie and Achituko at the Carstairs' gate, went off into a dream. Was there something between those two? No—couldn't possibly be. Debbie was much too young. Still, there *were* girls who . . . he knew there were girls that age at the High School who . . . But Debbie wasn't the type. She was just an ordinary schoolgirl. He'd seen her grow up. Now Lill at that age! . . . She'd once told a story about herself at sixteen, an encounter with the shop-floor manager of the cuddly-toy factory in Leicester where she had worked . . . 'Oh, he *was* a saucy one!' Lill had ended, having got herself and him into the works canteen after the rest had knocked off. Brian had laughed with the rest, and later he had gone up and been sick in the bathroom.

He remembered Lill in Tunisia . . . Why was it always Tunisia? . . . He remembered Lill and the middle-aged German with the bulbous body like a potter's discard . . . the way he lingered heavily round them by the swimming-pool in the first days, the way he started buying Lill expensive drinks, pawing her when Fred was not around, uttering guttural endearments and giggling obscenities when the younger ones went off into the pool . . .

He remembered Lill on the beach, surrounded by the sellers of bangles and pots and rugs and sunhats—swarthy men and boys, haphazardly clad, men the other English declared were terrible pests and waved away, fearful of being swindled. But Lill had welcomed them, and chattered away to them in pidgin Midlands, admiring their wares, trying them on, exacting their homage, now and then fetching out her purse and buying one of the pots that now sat unsteadily on the mantelpieces and coffee-tables around the house (the pot-seller had been young, younger than her sons, and doe-eyed, and wicked). Lill had lapped it up. 'They think I'm marvelous,' she would announce at dinner. 'Nobody else will talk to them, stuck-up lot. I could fancy one or two of them too, even if they are wogs! I wish they'd come selling things round my back door at home!'

And he remembered the boys that day he and Gordon had walked alone into Hammamet, the boys who ran after them as they lounged around the medina, laughing, prancing, joking and shouting—shouting *'Voulez-vous coucher avec ma soeur?'* and then . . .

'Here wake up, dreamy,' said the boy next to him. 'I want to read your answer to the question on *Lord of the Flies*.'

As luck would have it, Lill and Mrs Carstairs found themselves alone behind the butcher's counter that morning, Lill waiting to buy a pound and a half of snags, while Eve Carstairs bought some nice kidney chops.

'That's right,' yelled Lill, with that unconsciousness of her effect on others that was her hallmark and her death-warrant, 'you feed up my Archie. Don't want my lover-boy wasting away.'

Mrs Carstairs compressed her lips, looked straight across the counter at the butcher with an expression of conspiratorial long-suffering, and said: 'Nobody can say I don't give my lodgers good value.'

'Hope you get good value in exchange, then,' said Lill with a squawk of laughter. 'Lucky old you, that's what I say. I got a taste for darkies in Tunisia.'

Perhaps she touched a raw emotional nerve in Eve Carstairs, perhaps it was the butcher's presence, so obviously enjoying himself, that made Eve take her up on something she ordinarily would have contemptuously passed over. At any rate, she wheeled round with whiplash suddenness and said: 'And what is that supposed to imply?'

Lill laughed on cheerily, regardless of anger or opposition: 'Oh, no offence. I'd give a quid for your luck. If my hubby was away all week like yours I'd have a couple of darkies—one for my bed and a reserve in the spare room!'

Eve Carstairs exploded. 'If you want to know who is sleeping with Achituko, you'd best go and ask your own daughter,' she spat, and flounced from the shop.

Gordon Hodsden, cycling home from the shipyard that Wednesday at five, saw Ann Watson walking with her little girl towards the recreation ground. He rode up beside the kerb in front of her and stood waiting till she came up, straddled across his bike.

'I say, I'm sorry if my mum's been round your place saying

things, and that. She gets ideas in her head, you know, but she doesn't mean any harm.'

Ann Watson, looking at him—his appealing smile, his obvious good-will, his chunky presentability—nevertheless felt her anger at Lill spurting up anew. 'Well, she ought to be careful,' she said. 'People like her do a lot of harm, even if they don't intend to.'

'But you can't tell my mum that,' said Gordon, widening that disingenuous smile. 'If she thinks a thing she goes ahead and says it. It's not her fault, really, it's what she's like. All she wants is to help people.'

'Sometimes it's best not to interfere,' said Ann Watson, almost rudely indicating she wanted to be off. 'People are better off left to themselves.'

'Oh, Mum has to do her little bit—wouldn't be happy otherwise,' said Gordon gaily. 'Well, just thought I'd say something. Hope there's no hard feelings.'

And he rode off, apparently unconscious of the fact that there was no reply. But as he rode, his face darkened into an expression as unlike that open, smiling boyishness as it could possibly be, and, lowering and heavily thoughtful, he pedalled furiously the last stretch of the way home. Well, that's cooked my goose with *her,* he thought. She wouldn't give a second thought to someone as stupid as I made myself out to be. All in a good cause, though. There'll be time to bring her round—afterwards.

'What do you think about when my mother goes on like she did on Saturday night?' asked Debbie of Mr Achituko as they lay, close and cosy, in his single bed at No. 38 at nine o'clock that evening.

'Think about? As little as possible. I just let it wash over me,' said Achituko, shrugging his fleshy shoulders.

'Yes, but when she goes on about your colour and whether it washes off and all that sort of stuff, like she does all the time. It had me cringing. I mean you must react to that, surely. It's about your skin—about *you.*'

Achituko leaned over her lean, adolescent body and drew his brown finger down her cheek. 'Does yours come off? Do I get white chalk marks all over my finger? No, it doesn't. And you don't get annoyed, do you?'

Debbie giggled. 'That's different. You're not Lill. Anyway, I'm white. Nobody . . . nobody despises whites.'

I do, I do, thought Achituko. But he merely smiled his wide, open smile at her naivety.

'I'd love to have seen you give her a tremendous slosh round the chops,' said Debbie, with relish. 'I was sitting there hoping for it. That's what I'm going to do before very long, one day when she really gets my goat.'

'You'd better wait, little fire-cracker,' said Achituko. 'She's a tough customer, your mother. Better wait till you're a little older. Or leave it to me to do, when she finds out about us.'

'Just so long as I'm there,' said Debbie, with a childish anticipatory smile. 'But I wish you'd done it on Saturday. That'd have stopped her going on about how she loves wogs.'

'You've got a violent nature, you know that, girl?' And Achituko lay there chuckling happily, cuddling her to him, his eyes dark and thoughtful in the shadowy bedroom.

Outside in the darkness, as far as possible from the streetlamps and sheltered by an overhanging apple tree, Lill waited silently, puffing on a rolled cigarette which she hid in the palm of her cupped hand. There were no lights in Eve Carstairs's house, and not a sound emerging. She had loitered past earlier, twice, but had not heard a whisper. And yet, surely, if they made love there at any time, it must be Wednesday nights. When Eve Carstairs invariably went to bingo. Lill's lip curled. Normally she herself would be at bingo tonight. Very convenient for the little slut, she thought: both mother and landlady out. She only kicked herself that she had let Debbie disappear after tea without following her. No doubt she had gone off to a friend's, then come back here later. It hadn't been practicable to keep a constant watch until night had fallen. In half an hour Mrs Carstairs would be on her way home. Debbie would be well out of the house by then, if she had any sense. Twenty minutes more and she'd give up.

She stiffened. A light went on momentarily in the hall of 38, then off again, but in those two seconds she had seen two shapes through the lead-lighted window in the front door. Now the door was opening silently, now there were muttered intimacies—Lill ground her cigarette under her heel savagely—now a dark shape was through the tiny front garden, out through the gate, and off down the road in the other direction. Lill left the shadow of the Cox's Orange and hared off after it. Sure enough, the shadow turned into No. 10, and she heard her own back door open and shut.

Now she threw off all disguise or stealth. Charging forward, she flung open the gate and crashed through the front door, nearly bowling over Debbie, taking off her coat by the clothes-peg in the hall.

'Oh, hello, Mum—' her daughter began.

Lill seized her by the arm, her purpled fingernails biting into the flesh, and pushed her bodily through to the kitchen. Once there she threw her across the room with such passionate force that she landed crying over the sink. Lill banged the kitchen door and stood against it, arms on her hips, her face blotched with jealousy and hate.

'Now, my girl,' she said. 'I'm going to make you regret what you've just been doing.'

7

THURSDAY

Thursday breakfast was a meal on tenterhooks. Lill stood tight-lipped over the stove and boiled eggs on principles of guess-work. The family scurried down one after the other, gobbled their under- or over-done free-ranges, and then dived out of the kitchen and went about their business. Debbie came down defiantly, the whiteness of her face emphasizing the blue bruise around her left eye and the cut on the side of her mouth. When she said disgustedly, 'This egg's hardly done at all,' the rest of the family shushed her agitatedly, as if she were tempting the wrath of the Almighty. Unconcerned, she pushed the egg aside and helped herself to toast and marmalade. She did not try to conceal the fact that she was eating with difficulty. Lill could hardly bear to look at her. But when she got up from the table Lill rounded on her and snapped:

'You're not going to school. Not like that.'

Debbie gave her a long, cool, impertinent look, but then said: 'All right.'

Ten minutes later, though, she hared down from her bedroom, whipped her coat off the peg in the hall, and was out the front door in a flash meticulously timing it so as to catch the bus by a hairsbreadth and avoid pursuit and capture. All Lill could do was stand by the front gate and glower at her retreating figure.

'Forget something, did she?' said Mrs Forsdyke from No. 18,

passing in the other direction. 'These teenagers are all alike, aren't they?'

'You can say that again,' snarled Lill. 'Bloody little slut, I'll teach her.'

Not quite sure she had heard, Mrs Forsdyke smiled vaguely and went on her way, but the conviction gradually came over her that Mrs Hodsden had called her daughter a bloody little slut, and the expression on Lill's face convinced her that All Was Not Well with the Hodsdens. Since she served in the best greengrocer's in Todmarsh she had plenty of chances to communicate this conviction to half the town, including many of her neighbours in Windsor Avenue and the surrounding streets, before the morning was out. Her news, conveyed in a hushed whisper, like a royal scandal, met with a series of raised eyebrows. 'Really's,' 'I don't wonder's,' and 'How that family puts up with her I don't know's'. Uniquely, nobody sympathized with the parent. Because Lill was not loved in her neighbourhood.

Nor did she do anything to make herself loved that morning. Lill spoiling for a row was one thing: that was a variety of good mood. Lill in a black, destructive temper was quite another thing, and infinitely more frightening. Her plans were in ruin, her self-love had received a blow, the arrangement of her world, that elegant construction of castles in the air peopled by admiring dummies, had been flattened by a brutal kick. Lill was livid. She felt within her a dull, throbbing, continuous rage—or, as she put it, she felt all churned up. And it was clear that someone, several people, had to get hurt. That was only right.

She began the day as she meant to go on. In the garden that backed on to her own children were playing hide-and-seek with squeals of excitement. Seeing the mother at the door, Lill marched down to her back fence and bellowed: 'Can't you keep those bloody kids quiet? I can't hear myself think in there. They're a public menace.' Ten minutes later she swaggered round next door to 'have it out' with her mother. Only in her most brutal moods could Lill hope to win such a contest, but by the end of half an hour the redoubtable Mrs Casey was close to tears. Finally Lill banged out of the back door with an expression of grim triumph on her face, and turning back, she shouted:

'And if you're thinking of sneaking to Fred, you can give up the idea. I've told him about it myself, so put that in your pipe. There's going to be some changes around here before long, I'm telling you, and you're not going to like them.'

It wasn't the last brush of the day with one or other of her natural enemies. Meeting Guy Fawcett's wife slipping home from work at mid-morning, she roared: 'Christ, some people have it lucky. Get paid for doing nothing. But I suppose you've got to check up on that randy husband of yours.'

Mrs Fawcett looked at her with open contempt before slipping in through her front gate. Once safely inside she said: 'I've given up worrying what Guy was up to long ago.'

'Haven't got much choice, I shouldn't think,' said Lill, with ferocious directness. 'Need a red-hot poker to put him out of action.'

'I expect you'd know,' said Jane Fawcett, going into the house and banging the front door.

News of Lill's mood spread along Windsor Avenue like a thick, stinking cloud from a burning chemical plant. As she went by people watched from well within the shadows of their front rooms, and decided not to go down the street until she was safely back home. Poor old Miss Gaitskell, retired post-mistress, bulky and all too aware of it, had not sensed the cloud and was unwittingly weeding her front garden as Lill strode past. She did not entirely register the relevance of the remark 'Blimey, if I had an arse like that, I wouldn't bend over' until Lill was well past her, but when she did she straightened, flushed, and looked indignantly at the retreating leopard-skin coat. In the course of Lill's daily round the butcher was flayed, the newsagent was flattened. It wasn't that Lill's remarks were acute, but if the aim is to annihilate, the meat-axe is more effective than the scalpel.

Dinner with Fred and Gordon was not a happy meal. Even Gordon, the beloved son, felt the rough side of her tongue. They shovelled the food in, swilled down a mug of tea each, and then mumbled excuses to get out of the house.

Tea was worse. Debbie came home from school exhilarated by the support of her friends, self-congratulatory about the air of sad mystery she had assumed when commiserated with by her teachers. Her defiance was by now almost perky. It rubbed up Lill the wrong way like a pen-nib on the bottom of an ink bottle. Instinct told her that—as with her mother—brutality was the only sure weapon now. 'I'll teach you to defy me, you little cow,' she shrieked, and grabbing her by the arms she dragged her upstairs —'Gordon!' screamed Debbie, but Gordon didn't come—and threw her into her room. Grabbing at the key, she banged the door and locked it noisily. 'And there you stay,' she yelled. 'And not a bite of food do you get till I give the say-so.' She marched downstairs.

'It's about time that girl had a bit of discipline,' she said with something approaching self-satisfaction. 'She'll feel the weight of my hand tomorrow if I have a squeak out of her. She's been let run wild.' She looked daggers at Fred, as if it were all his fault, and threw him the key. 'It's your job to see she stays there all evening. Keep your wits about you. Don't go dozing in front of the telly like you usually do.'

'If the girl's locked in—' began Fred.

'She's sharper than a wagon-load of monkeys,' snapped Lill. 'She'll be out of that window or I don't know what if you don't keep a sharp watch-out. So STAY AWAKE—I'm warning you!'

And she went off to get the tea. Something during that scene had clicked in the back of Brian's head, and it refused to come forward. It worried him. Or was he just worried by his failure to stand up for his sister? Fred also looked unhappy, and slipped out of the front door to prod futilely at the rambling rose climbing feebly up a trellis, perhaps with the vague idea of seeing if Debbie could climb down that way. When he had wandered wraithlike from the front room Gordon, on his way upstairs to wash and change, hissed to Brian: 'Garry Prior's having a bachelor party at the Rose and Crown tonight. Registry Office do in the morning, hurried. I said we'd go. It'll be the last dry run before the killing.'

Something still tugged obstinately at the back of Brian's mind.

He said: 'I hardly know Garry Prior. You go, he's your age. He won't want me there.'

'Without you it won't be a rehearsal, you idiot. I said you'd be there.' He winked. 'He's a bit down. Caught, like. The more the merrier.' And he bounded up the stairs to get out of his overalls and to soap away the rasp of work from his hands.

Downstairs, languidly flicking through the pages of a dated history book, Brian was suddenly struck by the revelation which had been struggling to come out all day. Was it revelation, or self-deception? Debbie's black eye, seen and discussed in Todmarsh and at school, had surely ditched their whole scheme. They'd been relying on the happy-family Hodsden image, and now—for the moment, anyway—that had been shattered. Kill Lill now and you only landed Debbie in it. Kill Lill now, and the whole family was in it. The first people the police would be looking at. The more he examined the idea, the more the impossibility of their plan struck him. They could not kill Lill! Not on Saturday. Not ever. A great wave of nauseous relief washed over him. They were stuck with her, but they were not going to be her killers. He'd have to hammer it into Gordon's thick skull somehow. He'd discuss it with him in bed tonight. He felt elated with a sense of—of what? Freedom? No, not that. Then could it be relief at the continuance of his bondage?

Lill was full of grim triumph at tea-time, and read the riot act to her men.

'That little slut's not to have a bite of food until she's come round, right? I'll give you what for, Fred, if you slip up with anything while I'm out tonight. Same goes for you two—and I don't want you talking to her at the door either. Silence and starvation—that'll bring her round. I'll have her crawling for forgiveness by Saturday.'

'Better not keep her away from school too long, Mum,' said Brian. 'You'll have the authorities on to you. They must have noticed the bruise.'

Lill looked at him in outrage. 'Cheeky bugger. I'd like to see the school inspector that would interfere between me and my daughter. I'd soon settle his hash if he tried.'

Brian kept quiet, because Lill spoke no less than the truth. And Gordon snarled inwardly at the whole episode, but told himself he'd soon be doing Debbie more good than ever he could by standing up for her now. And, after all, she had asked for it.

At the usual time Lill gathered herself together, slapped on make-up more crudely even than usual, and announced her departure.

'I'm just off to see Mrs Corby. Now mind what I said, Fred. You're to have nothing to do with that girl whatsoever. And you drop off in front of that set and I'll skin you alive.'

'No, Lill, I'll remember.'

Lill banged out of the front door and out through the front gate. But she did not get far along Windsor Avenue, since as ill-luck would have it she nearly ran into Mr Achituko, strolling amiably past. Alone of Windsor Avenue he knew nothing about 'something being up' at the Hodsdens'. Only Eve Carstairs would be likely to tell him, and she as it happened had felt a twinge of guilt when she heard of the nebulous 'trouble', and wondered whether she might not be herself responsible. So Mr Achituko was surprised (though not entirely bewildered about the cause) when he found himself grabbed by the lapels of his immaculately cut suit and found Lill's eyes—bulbous, black outraged—two inches from his own, part of a general expression of murderous malevolence.

'Listen to me, you bloody black stud. Now don't pretend you don't know what I mean. I know what you and Debbie have been up to. And I tell you this: I'll have the law on you if you so much as touch her again—do you hear? I'm not having a nigger son-in-law and coffee-coloured grandchildren. You say one word to my daughter, ever in the future, and I'll get your license revoked?'

And she let go his lapels and marched off down the road in triumph. Mr Achituko, patting his suit back into its pristine smartness, restrained his desire to run after her and do her some modest violence. Mentally he translated Lill's last phrase into a threat to have his temporary residence permit withdrawn. Ludicrous as the threat was, he knew enough about the police and immigration officials to know that people—blacks—had been expelled for infinitely more trivial or idiotic reasons. He stood in the street, dignity outraged and unrevenged, and felt very far from happy. Then, setting his face back into its usual amiable grin in case he was watched, he wheeled round and marched dignifiedly in the opposite direction.

On the way down to the Rose and Crown, Gordon was obsessed, as he had been since Saturday, with his plan of campaign. So bright, intent, absorbed was he that Brian hadn't the heart to argue the case with him, to throw in doubt the whole plan. Gordon was a boy again, fighting global battles with toy soldiers. It was all a matter of tactics, strategy, logistics, reduced to a tiny scale.

'Then sometime in the evening,' he finished up, 'I'll disappear. I'll be doing it tonight—so notice. Strictly twelve minutes, or perhaps a minute or two over, to be on the safe side. I'll just stay in the bog this time. Just go on as usual, talk, notice whether I'm missed. But I won't be—no chance. There's a whole crowd coming tonight, and it'll be just like a Saturday.'

'When it comes down to it, it's not much of an alibi,' remarked Brian.

'It's good enough. There's nobody can prove I wasn't there at the crucial time. Nobody remembers a blind thing on a Saturday evening, when things have got going. It'll be the same tonight.'

And certainly Garry Prior and his mates seemed determined to make quite a do of it. The cynicism behind the gaiety added an extra note of frenzy to the occasion. Half the shipyard seemed to be there, and a whole group that ten years ago had been a loud-mouthed motor-cycle gang, terrorizing roadside pubs and rendering respectable neighbourhoods hideous with their din, now sunk into a world of nappies, baked bean suppers and querulous wives.

Gordon fitted naturally into this mob, knew the indecent songs that ought to be sung on such occasions, had the inevitable follow-up remarks to the inevitable jokes at his tongue's end. Brian was at first diffident, with that feeling of apartness which is the great achievement of the English grammar school. He watched the clumsy, jolly men pretending to be boys and wondered what he could find to say to them. But little by little the barriers of ice were melted by the warm beer, and Brian found he could join in the

choruses of the songs, swing his mug joyously at the crucial obscenities, and throw back his head and roar at jokes that he had
trained himself to find crude or sexist. He was feeling, through his
whole body, not fellow-feeling, but the lifting of a weight, the
lightening of his future, a great sense of freedom-in-captivity.

We can't do it now, he periodically told himself. Now it would
come straight back on the family. Gordon's got to see that.

So happy was he that he failed to notice when or whether
Gordon left the bar, how long he was away, or whether anyone
noticed. But he was light-headed with relief: it didn't matter now.
They would never do it. Lill had won through again, he thought,
and wondered how long he would be happy that she had.

Fred sat bolt upright in his chair at No. 10, Windsor Avenue,
consciously on guard like a meticulous sheep-dog. One thing he
was not going to do tonight was go to sleep. He wondered
whether he might take a bite to eat up to Debbie in her room. His
consideration of this topic was a mere matter of form, something
to think about: he knew he would not dare. Lill had said he wasn't
to, and he wouldn't. He watched the beginning of an episode of a
Francis Durbridge serial, and tried to make head or tail of the
mysterious phone calls, the multiple identities, the inexplicable
goings-on in the stockbroker belt. It took his mind off Debbie for
the moment, but he came back to her. No doubt Lill was right. She
always was. And what the girl had done was shocking—real disgusting. He played with the idea of sexual licence, and felt a vague
pang of unease somewhere at the back of his head. No—he
wouldn't take a bite up to Debbie. He'd do as Lill had told him.
Naturally he would. He settled down into his usual rut of non-
thought . . .

Suddenly he shook himself. The Francis Durbridge was over,
and he hardly remembered a thing that had happened in it. Must
watch out. He'd nearly dropped off then.

The evening at the Rose and Crown developed as such evenings do. By ten o'clock the bridegroom-to-be was in a state that
could only be described as off-putting, but of course the bride was

not there to be put off. Red, sweaty, distended and bulbous of eye, he was alternately raucous and maudlin, and resisted all attempts by his more responsible mates to get him home to bed. 'It's my last night,' he kept saying, as though the hangman were coming for him in the cold quiet early hours.

As far as Brian could tell—and he was pretty high now, with drink and relief—Gordon was mixing with dazzling virtuosity among the various groups: a word here, a joke there, hands on shoulders for a rugby song elsewhere. It was a marvel: he was everywhere, and yet nowhere in particular. He's keyed up, thought Brian, exhilarated by the thought of Saturday, just as I'm relieved we won't be doing anything. The thought suddenly depressed him again. How long before the project came up for discussion once more, even if they did shelve it for the present? And Brian had a sudden stab of fear that Gordon never would consent to shelve it. He was emotionally committed, and for all his apparently cool tactical planning, Gordon ran on his emotions. What if the thing went ahead after all? Fear now was back with him, back with that iron grip on his stomach it had had all week, making ominous rollings among the beer. But even if Gordon got caught and jailed, he told himself through a haze of drink and uncertainty, they could never pin anything on him, Brian. That was what was so humiliating in a way: his part in the whole thing amounted to nothing plus, and that was why nothing could be pinned on him. And then, if Gordon went to jail, for a long, long sentence . . . The thought of life without Lill or Gordon sent that strange pang of longing and fear through him again. It would be freedom. But could he cope with freedom?

On one of his bee-like hops from group to group Gordon found Brian temporarily alone, and stopped.

'How did it go? Anyone notice I was gone?'

'No. Nobody would, not in this shambles. Gord, there's something I want to say—'

'Not here, you fool. The mugs have ears.' And with a smile in which only Brian could detect signs of strain Gordon sailed into his next all-boys-together encounter.

And now it was all songs. You had to end the evening with a

song, didn't you? And then another. The plasticated imitation oak rafters rang, and Methodist households streets away shut their windows and doors. The beer-loosened voices rose in ecstatically scatological songs of praise, and in the unholy din Brian did not hear the phone ring in the landlord's little den behind the bar, or see him disappear into it. But minutes later he registered with bleary surprise the figure of the landlord coming round the bar with an odd, unaccustomed expression of worry and uncertainty in his face and bearing—not like Jack Perkins, life and soul of the party except with his wife and kids. And Brian saw him enquiring something of one or two of the less drunk, saw him move towards Gordon, saw him bring him over, heard him say through the haze of beer and song and smoky bonhomie:

'Look, I'm sorry, you boys, I've just had a message—you'd bet-ter—well, you'd better cut off home—it's rather serious—it's your mum—she's—'

'Ill?'

'Well, sort of, but worse. I'm sorry, lads. They say she's dead. I couldn't hear right well, you know, not through all this. But they said she'd been killed.'

Brian felt Gordon keel over towards him, crumpling at the knees and up the strong trunk of his body. Then with a powerful effort he righted himself, clutched on to the table uttering great racking sobs. Suddenly he cried 'Killed!' and then shoved his way bodily through the crowd and out of the bar door. Brian ran in his wake and followed him in his first fast sprint up Balaclava Road. Two hundred yards from the pub Gordon stopped by the lamp-post and heaved mountainously and noisily. And as Brian caught him up and stood over him, helpless, Gordon gazed at him through his heaving and retching, his face blotched hideously red, his eyes wet with grief and disappointment, and said:

'Some bastard's gone and done it instead o' me. She was mine. I had it all worked out, you know that, down to the last detail. Some bastard's got there first. Now I'll never be able to throttle the life out of her.'

'Come on,' hissed Brian, shaking himself into taking control.

'He said she'd been killed. He probably meant an accident. Don't crack up.'

And with a last mountainous heave and a shake Gordon did seem to get a grip, stood up, took out a handkerchief and wiped his eyes. Then he took off like a professional sprinter up the dark road. He faltered a little as they ploughed their way through the blackness of Snoggers Alley, and Brian caught him up so that together they could run the last stretch home.

Home. Lill's nest for her boys. But now transformed with lights, with two large police cars outside, and with a little knot of shameless neighbours and their children, watching the comings and goings. They made way for Gordon and Brian, gazed at them with ravenous, awkwardly respectful curiosity, stayed silent as they pushed their way through the front gate.

And Brian's most abiding memory of the day was the open front door, the hall blazing with light, and Fred meeting them, his skinny frame racked with sobs, his face red with rage and grief, tears running down his wrinkled cheeks, his voice cracked with shock and outrage.

'Somebody's done her in,' he shouted. 'Some bugger's been and killed our Lill.'

8

THE MORNING AFTER

Morning. Waking. A dull sense of activity around the house. A sense of policemen in the house. Heavy feet and low, muffled voices. The aftermath of a murder.

Brian struggled to consciousness through a thick blanket of reluctance, hangover, and sense of impending disaster. It was seven o'clock. He had had, perhaps, five hours' sleep. He and Gordon, long, long after midnight, and after questions dimly understood and haltingly answered, after cups of thick black instant coffee, had staggered up the stairs and—silent, almost, uncertain where they stood—had thrown themselves on to their beds and sunk into welcome, immediate oblivion.

Or not quite oblivion. Brian had had terrifying dreams of Lill, blue, strangulated, hideous, dead but still active, stalking the house where once she had reigned intent on revenge. He knew too that Gordon had cried out in the night without knowing how he knew. A sharp cry of pain or triumph. Lill was there in his sleep too. Of course she was. What else could one expect? Demons are not to be exorcized so easily.

In the next bedroom Fred, similarly wafting towards consciousness, turned his meagre, flannel-pyjamaed frame over in the bed and felt the space where Lill always slept. It was empty. Good old Lill, he thought: she's making the tea. Then he struggled upright, his thin body racked by coughs till tears came to his eyes.

Next door Mrs Casey lay wakeful in bed. Now that she was old she found she needed very little sleep. She lay in bed most nights thinking about her life, about what the Lord had given her and what He had withheld, about the lives and doings of her family and neighbours, about sin and retribution and kindred subjects. She was never bored. Last night after she had heard, she had thought about her daughter, about her life and death, so perfectly in accord with each other, and no doubt ordained that way by a Higher Power. She imagined Lill's face blue with strangulation, then remembered it thick with pancake make-up, mascara and lipstick. There was a rightness about the comparison that pleased her and brought a thin smile to her face. Lill had lived vilely and died violently. Mrs Casey stolidly turned back the bedclothes and began the process of getting up. Now no doubt there would be interviews and questions. The police would be round. That was only right. They had their jobs to do. But she did not expect them to discover the murderer of Lill. She had an odd idea that the murderer of Lill enjoyed the protection of the Lord.

The Hodsdens gathered downstairs, haggard, pale grey around the eyes. Debbie's right eye had something more than mere greyness round it, and she felt the flick of an eye as one of the policemen noticed it. That was the new policeman, the one from Cumbledon, come to take over the investigation.

They all looked at him, the one who had not been there in the horrible, frenzied session late the previous night. He's very good-looking, Debbie thought. And he was too, in a self-conscious way. Very fair hair, damped down close around his head. Blue eyes—so much more policeman-like than brown. A rounded, regular sort of face on a sturdy neck. He looks a capable sort of chap, thought Fred. He coughed portentously and came forward to shake him by the hand.

'We're all hoping you're goin' to find the rotten bastard that killed our Lill,' he said.

The policeman nodded, rather superior. Of course he was going to find the bastard that killed their Lill, seemed to be his message. Brian suddenly thought: he looks *stupid*. He hides it well, but really he's rather dim. Brian analysed his feelings, not quite sure whether to be glad or sorry. One thing he was certain of: he did want to know who it was had killed Lill. That didn't mean he wanted them punished.

The policeman cleared his throat and looked around him, using his clear, blue, frank eyes in a way he often practised in front of the bathroom mirror. Female shoplifters often went weak at the knees and confessed in the face of that gaze. The Hodsdens looked suitably impressed, which gratified him.

'My name is McHale,' he said, in a voice resonant with official-dom. 'I've been called in to take charge of this case. Believe me, I realize what a distressing time this must be for you. But I expect you'd like to know how far we've got.'

'Aye, we would that,' said Fred, who seemed anxious to make an impression on McHale as head of the family, something he never had been.

'Well, as you know, your wife—your mother—was strangled along Balaclava Road, just up from the little cutting that takes you through to Windsor Avenue here.'

'Snoggers Alley, that's what we calls it,' said Fred.

'Really . . . ?' (The pause suggested he found the Hodsdens rather common.) 'Where she was strangled there's a garden wall jutting out on to the pavement, making a dark little corner. It's very likely the murderer hid himself there—if he aimed to surprise her, that is, which seems likely. The killing took place, we would imagine, somewhere between eight-thirty and ten past ten, when the body was found. Any questions?'

'Can't they be more exact than that, these doctors?' asked Fred. 'It's so vague, anyone could have done it.'

'No, it's only in books the doctors are willing to be so exact about the time of death. But no doubt as time goes by we'll narrow it down by other methods.' Chief Inspector McHale oozed self-confidence. 'Now, just one or two more details: Mrs Hodsden's handbag was open and her purse had been ransacked—it was empty, in fact. Was there likely to have been much in it?'

'We're not rich folks,' said Fred.

We are poor, but we are honest, thought Brian, victims of old

Lily's whims . . . What's Fred up to, answering all these questions as if he was somebody? He's a changed man. Lill's death has gone to his head.

Perhaps Gordon thought the same, for he spoke for the first time: 'Mum never had much on her, and she wouldn't have had last night, not on a Thursday. She'd have got the housekeeping on Friday . . . today.'

'Makes you think,' said Fred, gazing ahead.

An expression of irritation crossed McHale's bland, handsome face, as if he were used to a better class of murder victim. 'At any rate,' he said, 'what there was in the purse is gone. We'll also have to ask you to look at the contents of Mrs Hodsden's handbag to see if anything else is missing.'

'What sort of things?' asked Fred.

'Oh . . . valuables . . . you know . . .'

Fred shook his head, bewilderedly. 'We're ordinary folks,' he said.

Christ, thought Brian. Somebody ought to offer us starring roles in *The Diary of a Nobody*. Fred Pooter and all the junior Pooters. Aloud he said:

'Mum was very careful: she wouldn't have carried anything valuable around with her.' Like the latest tray of diamond trinkets sent on approval from Cartier's, the Farbergé Easter eggs she had purchased from an impoverished survivor of the Russian Imperial family. My God, I can't stand it. If Fred's going to go through this investigation waggling the banner of our ordinariness I'll have to put him down. At least before we were Lill's brood, objects of pity mingled with contempt. By the time the murder fuss has died down we'll be nothing minus, if Fred has his way.

It seemed as if Fred couldn't keep himself quiet. He said greedily: 'What did the bugger strangle her with?'

'Probably wire,' said McHale with reluctance and some distaste. 'A length of wire. There may have been some sort of makeshift handle on the ends, so he could grip it better.'

Brian felt sick. In fact, all but Debbie looked green. Lill had been garrotted. They shifted uneasily in their chairs and gazed at the floor.

'Well,' said McHale, putting on an expression of deep sympathy and beginning to collect his things together. 'There's nothing much I can say, is there? You have my deepest sympathy, but the best service I can do for you is to get the chap who did it, as you say. I'm afraid I'll have to talk to you all later, at the Station. I don't think at the moment there's anything more I can do here.'

'Will we be able to get the funeral over soon?' said Debbie suddenly.

McHale shot a quick, surprised look at her, then smoothed over his features into their habitual officially bland expression. 'I'm afraid that won't be possible until after the inquest. I hope that won't be too long hence.'

'Awful to think of her lying there—like that—in that morgue,' said Fred mournfully, wiping away a feeble tear. 'That's what's worrying our Debbie—isn't it, Debbie?'

After a pause Debbie nodded. It was half the truth. Until Lill was buried, burned, disposed of away from mortal sight, she still had a horrible marginal existence. She was still *here.* Debbie wanted her underground. Then her liberation would be complete, and she could begin the business of life, unshackled . . .

'I'll call you in, then, when I want you,' said McHale, 'and I hope you'll all be thinking about this, trying to put your finger on something that might be of use to us.' He once more indulged in his sweeping look around the assembled Hodsdens and their ineradicably lower-middle-class front room, then took himself self-importantly out. Left on their own, they looked at each other, feeling somehow truncated, and found they had nothing to say. Finally Fred cleared his throat and said: 'Well, we'd better all lend a hand with the breakfast, and then I'll be off to work.'

'Oh, for God's sake, Fred,' exploded Gordon. 'You don't go to *work* on the day your wife dies!'

Fred looked bewildered. It was Friday. A working day. What was one to do if one didn't go to work? 'I suppose I could prick out those petunias out the back,' he said.

Where were they to talk? Over breakfast—interrupted by policemen coming in and out of the back door and marching all over the house on odd errands—the problem exerted both Brian and Gordon, and they threw significant glances in each other's direction over Debbie's scrambled eggs. A strange fear gripped the two of them: they felt watched, spied on, overheard; they felt like Embassy officials in Moscow, walking in the parks to escape ubiquitous bugs in their offices. Where could they go? In the house the police were everywhere. They could hardly go for a walk without attracting comment. If they went into the garden, even, what would people think—that slimy bastard Fawcett from next door, for example—at the sight of the two of them strolling up and down the path in low, urgent conversation?

In the end it was eleven o'clock, when the police infestation of the house had somewhat abated, before the pair of them, obeying a silent signal from Gordon, could disappear to the bedroom and begin to thrash the matter out.

'If you could talk French,' said Brian, 'we wouldn't have this difficulty.'

'Cut it out. If I could talk French so could your common-or-garden policeman. And what the hell would he think if we started jabbering away in Frog? Come to that, I didn't notice you were so bloody fluent when we were in Tunisia. You never wanted to translate, I remember.'

Tunisia.

'Anyway,' continued Gordon, 'there's no problem now. Any copper comes up those stairs and they'll creak to high heaven. This house was jerry-built before we were born and it's housed Lill for twenty-five years or more. That would wreck the Tower of London. You can hear every goddam thing everybody does.'

'We don't want it to look as if we were conspiring, getting our stories right,' said Brian obstinately.

Gordon sat forward in the little bedroom chair, shoulders hunched, intense, blazing: 'For God's sake, what is this? We're not guilty, remember? Why the hell should we get our stories right? All we have to do is to say to the police what we were going to say . . . tell the truth.'

'Which?' said Brian, still with a mulish expression on his face. He stood by the little fireplace in the bedroom, boarded, up, and with a pathetic little electric fire set in the boards, a useless crusader against the mists and damps of winter. He looked down at it, the long straight lock of hair coming forward as usual over his eyes and making him look even younger and more defenceless than he was.

'Look,' he said: 'we plotted. We intended to do it. We wouldn't want that known. Right?'

'Of course we wouldn't want that known. Why the hell should it be? There's only you and me know.'

'All I'm saying is, we've something to hide. For example, you must have been in the bog in that pub timing yourself for hours, I'd imagine.'

'Didn't you notice I'd gone, then?'

'No. To tell you the truth I forgot all about it.'

'My God, what a partner you make,' groaned Gordon in disgust. 'Well, I was there thirteen minutes. You don't say anything about that, natch.'

'All right, then. But you see what I mean. I *feel* guilty. It doesn't matter that we didn't do it. Morally it's the same.'

'You've got too much bloody imagination. And what's all this about morality? If I plan a murder again I'll get a partner who's all solid muscle and a head six inches thick. You do bugger all, and then you get eaten up with guilt. Forget it, for Chrissake. For all we've done to the contrary, Lill would still be alive now.'

'Just,' said Brian.

'Well, don't you forget it. That policeman's going to be giving you the once-over. I don't want you blubbering and saying "we planned it, Mr Grouser, sir; we're morally guilty." Remember: we've done *nothing*, boyo.'

'OK. But somebody did. Somebody got in first. Don't you even want to know who it was?'

'Some day I might. As of now I just want to get through the next few days. Devoted son mourning his much-loved Mum. After that, I might like to find out. If it was some mugger I'd like to bash his face in. Doing me out of my fun.'

Brian flinched, then left the mantelpiece and came over to him.

'Some mugger—OK, that will be all very convenient. But what if it was our Debbie? Or old Fred?'

Gordon let out the beginnings of a raucous laugh, then arched his body forward and choked it in his lap.

'Our Fred! He couldn't chop a worm in half with his spade without botching the job.'

'Debbie, then. She hated Lill's guts. More than us.'

'If she did it, she's acting in a damnfool way this morning. Asking about the funeral, and all that!'

'Debbie's like that. She can't hide anything.'

'Well, she'd better start learning, if she's going to go around knocking people off. She'll find herself in some bloody reformatory with a matron the spit image of Lill.'

'Look, face up to it, Gord. What are we going to say? Are we going to put on the grief-stricken act, or are we going to be honest about her?'

'Oh, for God's sake, of course we're not going to be honest about her. Do you think people ever are when there's been a murder? Do they all troop along to the Station and say "I hated her guts, I admit, but I didn't do it"? We're the devoted sons. Everybody thinks so. Lill thought so. We're broken-hearted, like old Fred: all we want is for them to catch the bastard who did it.'

'OK. All I'm saying is there's some pretence.'

'The _same_ pretence we've been going on with for years.'

'Debbie knows we hated her.'

'Telepathy, that's all. She couldn't swear to it. Why would she want to? If she knew who'd done it, she'd be all over him like a rash in pure gratitude.'

'If she didn't do it herself.'

'Well, if she did she'll have to look after herself. We've got enough to do worrying about us.'

'You see? It's not that simple. You're starting to act guilty yourself.'

Gordon glowered at him, and banged out of the room. As he ran down the stairs a policeman in the hall looked up at him, curious, speculating.

* * *

Down at the Todmarsh Station, Chief Inspector McHale—sleek and complacent in his recent promotion, a new honour which, like most other things that had ever happened to him, had gone straight to his head—unbent sufficiently to talk over the case with the local man. Haggart was older, wiser, but unused to cases of murder and inclined for that reason to defer without cause. Mc-Hale had wandered distantly among the local men drinking their coffee and stuffing thick sandwiches, but now he had come to rest by the window, gazing contemptuously at the little patch of garden worked by the Todmarsh force in their spare time, with its neatly marshalled beds and paths, lawful and orderly. He pursed his lips at the dirty window, and paid little attention to the lower ranks.

'How did the family impress you?' Haggart asked.

'Pretty ordinary collection,' returned McHale, without pausing for thought. 'Cut up, as you'd expect, and saying some silly things, just like everybody does at this sort of time. Perfectly run-of-the-mill lot. Nothing out of the way there.'

'The second boy's at Grammar School, going on to the University, they say,' said Haggart. McHale merely raised his eyebrows and continued staring out of the window. 'You're not inclined to suspect one of them, then?'

'Not unless I get any evidence that points in that direction,' said McHale confidently. 'You told me this morning they were thought of as a pretty devoted little family. Why should I suspect them?'

Haggart shook his head. 'No obvious reason. Still, I had the impression there was *something*. The mother—the dead woman—had a bit of a reputation.'

'Really? Well, no doubt I'll be learning plenty about *that* in the next few days. What sort of reputation?'

'She was rough. The loud, vulgar type—irritated most people . . .'

'Shouldn't have thought the family were sensitive plants,' said McHale with a superior smile.

'I think she'd slept around a bit in her time—without the husband being aware.'

'I suppose that sort of thing makes a bit of a stir in a small town,' said McHale, still oozing city complacency. 'Well, I'll keep it in mind. No doubt this *could* be a straightforward family killing. On the other hand, it could be a simple robbery with the killing thrown in for kicks. You've no idea how much of that there is these days—and the devil's own job it is to pin it on anyone. Then again, as you yourself said, she wasn't liked.'

'Most folk around here couldn't stand her guts. She touched a nerve, you might say.'

'I know the type, believe me. I expect the family will be able to help us there—who particularly disliked her, and so on.'

'If they know. In a way they'd be the last to hear. I don't suppose Lill—Mrs Hodsden—realized herself. She sort of sailed through life, if you know what I mean. Full of herself, she was, and never gave a damn about what anyone else said or thought. If anyone gave her a piece of their mind, it would be like water off a duck's back.'

'It would get through to the family, though,' said McHale, with his usual congenital confidence. 'Children at school, and all that. I've no doubt they know just who had reason to loathe the mother. I expect when I come to talk to them I'll get a great deal out of that family.'

A sergeant spoke up from the back of the room, undaunted by McHale's air of remote authority, like royalty visiting the other ranks' canteen:

'Those two boys were up to something, up in their bedroom. Chattering away like magpies. One of them started to laugh, and then choked it down. I heard them from the hall.'

Chief Inspector McHale turned and looked at him for a moment, and then said: 'When you're a little older, Sergeant, you'll know that people behave in a funny way when there's a death. They don't tiptoe round and talk in hushed whispers as they're supposed to. And a murder's no different—worse, in fact. There's a lot of tension there, waiting to be released.'

The sergeant's mouth had set firm at the snub. Haggart rushed in to cover over: 'So you don't think of the Hodsdens as murderers, then?'

'In my experience,' said McHale, 'the first things a murderer needs are brains and guts. I wouldn't have said any of the Hodsdens had either in sufficient quantities.'

And nodding in a positively lordly manner, he left the recreation room to take up the threads of the investigation. No one in the room was to know that this was his first proper murder investigation, and indeed he himself had managed to put that fact totally out of his mind.

9

OLD FRED

When all is said and done, thought Fred, painstakingly buttoning the cuffs of his shirt, being interviewed by the police was a bit of excitement. The whole thing was terribly upsetting, quite horrible, and yet—a sensation of heat in his bowels made him aware that he was thrilled at being at the centre of a real-life sensation. He put on his shabby old grey suit and looked out at the police car by the side of the road outside. It was there to take him to the Station. He caught sight of himself in the bedroom mirror and was shocked to see something like a smile on his lips. He composed his face into an expression of extreme depression. Grief was beyond him, outside his emotional range. He thought: Poor old Lill; she'd have enjoyed all the fuss. She always liked a bit of life.

Thought is perhaps too definite a word for what went on in Fred's head: impressions, feelings, vague impulses and desires floated through his brain like skeletal autumn leaves, driven by the vaguest breeze, slow, wanton, uncatchable. Fred could never have verbalized one of these thoughts, still less could he have argued for any of his opinions. Still, there was this low heat in his belly, this smouldering excitement, that made him, today, more than usually self-conscious, awake to everything going on around him. In the road outside a police constable got out of the car and leaned heavily over the top of it, looking towards the house.

They're waiting for me, thought Fred. He straightened his tie, dusted a speck of dirt from a sleeve, then walked round the double bed and left the front bedroom he had shared for nearly thirty years with Lill.

In the car Fred was silent. What was appropriate conversation for a man whose wife had just been garrotted in a public thoroughfare to make with the policeman who is driving him to the police station for questioning? Fred's was not an inventive mind. As he got into the car he hazarded a 'Looks like rain, don't it?' but thenceforth he held his peace; blew, in fact, on those little coals of excitement in his guts. He was head of the household, going—the *first* to go—to talk to the man investigating the murder of his wife. Made you think.

Awkwardness made him shuffle when he was led into the presence of McHale, but then he told himself that that was stupid, and took his eyes from the brown lino on the floor. The sight of McHale, poised elegantly and impressively over an unnaturally tidy desk, confirmed Fred's impressions of earlier in the day. Good-looking chap. Good class of chap, too. Well spoken, clean, a natural leader. Ambitious, capable. Fred respected that kind of chap. Voted for them—the Conservatives—in local elections. You could trust a chap like that to get things done.

He said: 'You've got to get him, that bastard. Must have been some kind of crazy mugger, eh? Christ, you wonder what the country's coming to in this day and age, don't you? Bombs, assassinations, and now this.'

McHale, though he was not inclined to see Lill's murder in a national context, did in general terms agree with Fred: the murderer was probably some stray maniac. Last year there had been, in the Cumbledon area, that nasty business of the gay ripper. He had not, as it happened, got very far—being so unlucky as to choose for his second rip a fair-haired, angelic-looking judo black belt. But the case had impressed McHale (who had not been on it) with a sense of meaningless, perverse horror. It had confirmed, for no very obvious reasons, some odd feelings he had about the moral health of the nation. The garrotting of Lill Hodsden seemed to him to bear the same hallmarks. But of course, as he told himself, his mind was very much open.

He said: 'You may well be right. And believe me, I've got a whole troop of people working on those lines—' As if to confirm what he said the telephone now rang. He snapped a couple of 'yes's and a 'no' into the mouthpiece and then slammed it down. 'But of course,' he went on, 'until we can be sure we've got to fill in the picture as far as your wife is concerned—just as a matter of routine. I'm sure you understand that.'

'Oh aye,' said Fred.

I hope you do, thought McHale. He took hold of a handbag that was lying on his desk, a plastic affair that made only the most half-hearted attempt to imagine itself leather. Its red-brown colour was clearly designed to tone in with Lill's hair. At the sight of it in McHale's hands, two little tears squeezed themselves out of the corners of Fred's eyes, and ambled down his cheeks. He wiped them off with an earthy handkerchief.

'Sorry,' he said: 'brought her back to me, like.'

'Quite natural,' said McHale briskly.

Fred—hesitantly, as if expecting to hear the upbraiding voice of Lill asking him what he thought he was doing—took the bag in his work-rasped hands and began to rummage inexpertly around in it.

'Can you spot anything missing?' asked McHale unhopefully.

'There's nowt as far as I can see,' said Fred. 'But then I wouldn't really know. I've never been one to go poking around in my wife's things.'

'No, of course not,' said McHale. 'But you would know if she'd been accustomed to carry anything valuable around with her?'

'Can't say she had anything valuable,' said Fred. 'We're plain folks, like I said. 'Course, there was the engagement ring . . .' Thirty-five bob, he remembered, back in Festival of Britain year, bought with a modest treble-chance win that had also run to a plaice and chips lunch at the Odeon cafeteria. He'd been happy that day. He did not see the sneer on the face of McHale. McHale had seen the ring too.

'No—the ring was still on the—she was still wearing it,' he said.

'And your son said she wouldn't have been carrying much money . . .'

'Don't know what *he'd* know about it,' grumbled Fred, as if loath to share the limelight. 'We wouldn't know, would we? She might have had money from anywhere.'

'Really?' McHale jumped in, leaned imposingly forward and looked Fred in the eyes. 'You think she could have had money you know nothing about?'

Fred jumped. That was coming it rather fast.

'I didn't question her about money,' he said, his mouth set in an obstinate line. 'Just gave her the housekeeping and let her get on with it.' (The housekeeping, be it said, was all but a quid or so of Fred's weekly wage.)

'But you think she could have got money from somewhere else?'

'Could have,' said Fred, still mulish.

'Where, for example?'

'How would I know? I tell you, I didn't ask questions.'

'But it was you who made the suggestion, Mr Hodsden.'

'I didn't make any suggestions at all. All I'm saying is, with Lill you never knew. She was a smart one, was Lill.'

McHale was bewildered. He was not sure how carefully he needed to tread. How besottedly stupid was Fred Hodsden? Or was he a complaisant husband? He dipped a toe in the water.

'Your wife had been out visiting, hadn't she? At a Mr . . . Hamilton Corby's.'

Fred, it seemed, regarded this as a change of subject, and shifted in his chair so he did not have to see the red-brown hand-bag. 'That's right. Well, Mrs Corby really, of course. She's an invalid. She'd been very good to her, my Lill had. Visited her twice a week, regular as clockwork. She'll miss Lill will Mrs Corby, poor soul.'

McHale raised, fractionally, a silver-blond eyebrow at the cretinous obtuseness of mankind. From a glance at Lill's dead body he could have told that she was no devoted sick-room visitor. 'Would there be any reason' he asked, treading warily over Fred's stupidity like a super-power edging its way into a Third World country, 'why Mr Corby should have paid her a sum of money last night?'

Fred looked at him blankly: 'No, not as I know of . . . Mind you, he was a generous man: found a place for our Gordon when he came out of the army, even though work's scarce in the yards. But what would he give her money for?'

'Or jewellery, perhaps? A present of jewellery?'

At last the idea got through to Fred. He struggled forward in his chair, spluttering and coughing. 'Here, what do you mean? What are you trying to say? Ruddy cheek! There's no one can say my Lill was one of that sort!'

'You misunderstand me,' said McHale with a patient smile. 'I merely meant he might have given her something, some token, as a thank-you . . . for her care of his wife . . . Perhaps some trinket of his wife's that she had no more use for—after all, I gather that she's bedridden.'

Fred sank back into his chair, apparently somewhat mollified. 'Oh well, if that was all you were implying, that's all right. I suppose he might have. But it hadn't happened before not to my knowledge.'

'You took me up very sharp there, Mr Hodsden,' said McHale, super-smooth, in a way that made Fred sweat. 'Is there something you're keeping back? About your wife's relationships with other men, for example? Did she have—friendships?'

Fred, having once exploded, seemed now to be working on a longer fuse. 'She was a real character, my Lill. Everybody knew her in this town. She was everyone's friend. Brightened up the place as soon as she came here. Ask anyone. Ask 'em at the Rose and Crown. 'Course she had friendships.'

'With men?'

'Men and women. And I expect there's dirty-minded people round the town who might have talked about it. I don't mean you —you're paid to snoop. But people do talk. Any road, they'd've been wrong. Lill wasn't like that. She was just—outgoing. But at heart she was a family person . . . She was a wonderful mother.'

A memory of the Hodsden daughter, her eye bruised, wafted

through McHale's mind. He lowered his head and made a little note on his writing-pad.

'Of course, I'll be talking to your family,' he said. 'And then there are the friends you mention. Who would you say were your wife's greatest friends?'

Fred drew a finger round the collar that loosely spanned his scraggy, contracting neck. 'Well,' he said, 'there's Mrs Fawcett next door, but I wouldn't say she was a particular . . . And then there's Mrs Corby, of course; they were devoted . . . But I'm out all day, so I . . .'

'I see,' said McHale. 'Well, I'll ask your daughter. I expect she's more likely to know.'

He preened himself on his sharpness when he saw Fred's reaction. His concrete-grey face went rose-pink, and again he bent forward, choking: 'Well, Debbie's away all day too, you know, at school,' he said and then it seemed to strike him that anything he said might make things worse and he trailed off into silence.

'Still, women talk to their daughters, don't they?' said McHale, in his most molasses voice. 'Or is it more your sons your wife was close to? I seem to have heard . . .'

'Oh aye,' said Fred, leaning back in his chair with relief and now seeming to have no jealousy of sharing the spotlight with his sons: 'Gordon and Brian worshipped the ground she walked on. Couldn't do enough for her. Yes, you talk to Gordon and Brian.'

'Mr Hodsden,' said McHale, again leaning forward and looking impressive, 'there is one thing I have to ask you: where were you and the rest of the family last night?'

' 'Course you have to ask it: I understand. It's easy, anyway. Debbie and I were both home, and Brian and Gordon were down the Rose and Crown.'

'I see. So you and—Debbie, is it?—can vouch for each other, can you?'

'Oh aye. She was in her room and I was watching telly.'

'Well, that's not quite vouching for each other, as we understand it. Did you see much of each other during the evening—she came down now and then, I suppose?'

'No, no—she didn't come down.'

'Not once?'

'No—but I know she was up there . . .' Fred pulled himself together, backing away from the brink of telling how he knew Debbie was up in her room, and finished lamely: 'I'd've heard if she'd come down or gone out.'

'But you might have nodded off. People do.'

'Oh no. No. Lill was very . . .' Again he pulled himself up and shook himself, as if bewildered by the web of deception he was entangling himself in. 'Lill didn't like me falling asleep. Said it was dangerous, 'specially if I had my pipe in. No, I definitely didn't fall asleep.'

'I see. But that means nobody can vouch for you, I suppose. Nobody came to the door, or anything?'

'No—not as I mind. It's all become a bit of a blur, like, after hearing about . . . it. Still, it doesn't do to give way, does it? Life's got to go on, and there's the family to see to.' Fred seemed suddenly to become conscious that he was rambling into matters irrelevant to the police investigation, and asked: 'Was there anything more?'

'No, nothing for the moment, I think. Of course, the police will be around your place quite a lot in the future, I'm afraid. So if there's anything else crops up I want to ask about, I can contact you there.'

'Yes, I see,' said Fred. 'Well, we all want to help you, you can bank on that. The main thing is, you catch the bugger who done it.' He got up and shambled to the door, but once he hesitated, as if thinking hard. Then he turned and said: 'Still, you want to be careful what you say about my Lill and other men. That's libel, that is. You ought to watch your tongue!'

'Mr Hodsden, I was implying nothing—'

'Well, you ought to watch it. I nearly fetched you one then, I did!'

As Fred Hodsden fumbled his way out of the room, McHale smiled a thin smile like winter sunshine on Northern waters. He did not see Fred Hodsden as a murderer. In fact, he held to his opinion that none of the Hodsdens looked like murderers. Still, there might be some amusement to be got out of them on the way.

Dominic McHale was born and brought up near Bristol. His family was doubtless Scottish from way back, but there was nothing of the border ruffian or the highland savage left in their blood. They had obviously been respectable for centuries. His father was a tax official, and one who brought a good deal of cold enthusiasm to his job. His mother was local president of the Mothers' Union, and wonderful at organizing bazaars. Dominic had been a superior child: at school he was good at games and held his own in academic subjects, but he was aloof, and less than popular. The High School girls went with boys who were less good-looking but more forthcoming. He was sure he would get into Oxford, and he very nearly did: he was on the borderline, but in the end the commoner's place went to a boy from a Northern comprehensive, to make the intake tables look more respectable. 'If my father had been a bloody miner I'd have got in,' he remarked bitterly to his contemporaries. A tax-inspector father was neither fish nor fowl as far as admissions committees were concerned, and could never swing a vote in his favour.

He did not settle for red-brick, or white tile, or plate glass. People so sure of themselves never settle for anything less than their deserts. The only thing that could salve his pride was a complete change of course. He went into the police force. When all was said and done, people in general always felt at a disadvantage when dealing with a policeman. Even a little afraid . . .

He thought, too, that his (as he saw it) cool, rational mind would make him a cinch for promotion in the Detective branch— even for mild local fame. At last—distinctly more slowly than he had expected—the promotion had come. He was now a Chief Inspector. He had also a cool wife with two well-drilled children in a tasteful home in a nice suburb of Cumbledon. He had arrived. Until the next move upwards.

He strolled confidently into the outer office, a hive of activity, with junior personnel rushing hither and thither in the excitement of the first murder in Todmarsh's living memory. McHale said to Inspector Haggart, who was standing by the desk, 'Send someone up for the elder Hodsden boy, would you?' and then seemed inclined to linger.

'Didn't get much out of Fred Hodsden, I reckon,' said Inspector Haggart, when he had made all the necessary arrangements.

'Hmmm–so-so,' said McHale. 'Not the brightest of intellects. Not the strongest of bodies either: can't see him strangling a fit, hulking woman like that one in there.' He jerked his thumb in the direction of the morgue and Lill's body (white topped with claret red, like some hideous Andy Warhol woman).

The Inspector looked dubious: 'You can't tell with these skinny, wiry types. I've known farm labourers you'd think the first March winds'd blow away, but you get in their way in a pub brawl and you wonder what hit you.'

'Hmmm,' said McHale.

'Was he at home last night?'

'So he says. Him and the daughter.'

'They certainly were when the police arrived. But it's funny—'

'What is?' McHale raised those bored, superior eyebrows.

'Jim—that's Partridge, the constable that got there first. He— oh, there he is: he can tell you himself. Jim! Tell the Inspector what you told me—about what happened when you got to the Hodsdens' last night.'

Jim Partridge had ambled over, a big, slow Devonshire man. 'Aye, that were odd,' he said. 'I told him—gentle, like—what had happened and he were, well, you'd say he were overcome. I'd swear it were genuine. And then, he pulled himself together like, and instead of calling to his daughter upstairs, he went up to her. And it's funny, but I thought I heard a key turn in the lock. Then he told her, and she came down.'

'Ah!' said McHale. And then, with that condescending smile that robbed his compliments of any warmth, he said: 'Good observation, Partridge!'

10
HALF TRUTHS

Fred arrived back home in an uncertain mood. He was unsure whether the interview had been a success or not, whether he had imposed his importance, as husband of the deceased, on the mind of the rather distant young Chief Inspector from Cumbledon. It was a question, as even Fred realized, whether he had been impressive or ridiculous. And then there were those questions about Debbie . . . He did not feel he had shone there. If only Lill were still around to tell him what to do.

He came through the kitchen and hall and into the front room, and immediately blinked in bewilderment. Something was different; something was wrong. He sensed it immediately. Gordon and Brian were there: Brian reading in the easy chair by the window, Gordon standing by the fireplace exuding caged energy. He was smoking—he'd taken it up again. But still, something else was different. Fred blinked again, and looked around.

'How did it go?' asked Gordon. 'What's the bloke like? What did he ask you?'

'Here,' said Fred, his voice rising in pitch to a tone of feeble bluster. 'What've you been doing? There's something wrong here. Where are them ornaments of Lill's?'

He'd got it. The room was different: it had been denuded. Lill had prided herself on her bits and pieces. The little brass knick-knacks on the mantelpiece—a bell, a yacht, a tiny candlestick of vaguely Jewish design. The flower stand, silvered plastic, depicting a reclining Venus, which always sat on the television. The souvenir novelties from Blackpool, Southsea and Torquay. All the vases from Tunisia, bought from the beach vendors around Hammamet. They had festered over every surface, becoming more huddled together as their numbers had grown. Once a week Lill had flipped a duster lovingly in their direction. They were her pride, and each one had a story attached to it, to be told to the occasional visitor to the front room. Now many were missing: hardly more than half were there, newly distributed around. The room had indefinably become less Lill. That's what was annoying Fred.

'What've you done with her bits and pieces?' he repeated.

'We sort of sorted them out,' said Brian.

'Well, what do you mean by it? What've you done with them?'

'We put them away—just some of them. None of us would want to dust that lot.'

'Putting her things away the day after she dies! I never heard the like.'

'We had to,' said Gordon, his voice deep with emotion. 'They reminded us of Mum. It was too—poignant.'

Fred looked at him. That was a funny word for Gordon to use. Fred wasn't sure what to make of it. Anyone might think Gordon wasn't serious. He felt uncertain, frustrated. Now it was the boys who were bewildering him; yesterday it had been Debbie.

'Well, put 'em out and put 'em back where they should be,' he muttered. 'You don't know what people might think . . . Any road, Lill'd hate to think of them mouldering away in some drawer.'

He bumbled along querulously to his chair, fished out his tin of tobacco and began rolling himself a scraggy cigarette, dropping strands of tobacco into his lap from his shaking hands.

'Well, how did it go?' repeated Gordon, apparently unperturbed. 'What did you tell him?'

'Told him everything I know, of course,' said Fred, still dimly bellicose. 'We've got to help the police as much as we can . . . naturally.'

'Did you tell him about Mum and Debbie?' asked Brian.

' 'Course I didn't. What business is it of theirs? It's got nowt to do with it. Just a little family squabble. So don't you two go telling him neither.'

'So you didn't tell him all you know,' said Brian.

'None of your smartyboots remarks. I told him everything he needed to know. Just because for once in their lives your mum and Debbie fell out . . .'

For once in their lives! Brian put aside his book and looked at Fred in wonder. Talk about pity my simplicity! Was Fred completely stupid, or did he just genuinely fail to notice things? Debbie and Lill had disliked each other, it seemed, all Debbie's short life: open warfare had been declared when Debbie was twelve. That was the occasion when Lill, in one superbly timed swoop of her brawny arms, had shoved her daughter's head into the plate of cornflakes she was supposed to be eating. Since then life at the Hodsdens had been punctuated by such incidents: Debbie's first fashionable shoes thrown into the kitchen stove; her first lipstick ground under Lill's heel into the rose-bed; Debbie herself pulled upstairs by her hair after some piece of cheek. Culminating in that fight in the kitchen and the damaging bruise seen by everybody on the school bus, by all the girls and mistresses at school.

As if reading his brother's thoughts, Gordon turned to Fred and said: 'It's not us you have to tell to keep quiet. It's Debbie. We're not ones to wash the family's dirty linen in public, but she wouldn't care tuppence who she told.'

'She's not that daft,' said Fred, totally without conviction. 'Why should she go blabbing?'

'To get attention. She's that age.'

'And have them on her back, thinking she done it?'

'She's got a perfect alibi, remember. She was locked in upstairs and you were down here on guard. She's only got to tell them that and they'll see she couldn't have done it.'

'I might have dropped off,' said Fred reluctantly, looking down at his knees in embarrassment. 'I don't say I did, mind.'

'There's still the locked door. I bet you didn't tell the Chief Inspector about that, either.'

'Well, how could I, when I didn't tell him about the other?'
Fred grumbled his way into silence and digested the points that
had been made. He said at last: 'Well, one of you'd better talk to
our Debbie. Make her see sense. Keep her mouth shut. We don't
want to get ourselves talked about.'

It seemed a curious hope after a murder in the family. But
Brian's attention was focused on something else he'd said.

'Why one of us? Why not you?'

'Eh,' said Fred uneasily. 'I've never had that much to say to
Debbie. You two are more her own age. She'll take it better coming from you.'

Gordon and Brian looked at each other. But at that moment a
constable appeared at the sitting-room door and asked Gordon to
come with him to the Station. As he straightened up and walked
lightly from the room with his impressive athlete's walk, Fred
turned to Brian with a new access of confidence and said: 'It'll
have to be you then, as talks to her.' He got up and marched from
the room, turning at the door to say:

'And put them ornaments back, double quick!'

Gordon, squatting on the hard kitchen chair opposite McHale's
desk, his dark wavy head in his large workingman's hands, said:
'She was a wonderful person. We loved her. There was nobody
like her. 'Course, old Fred—Dad—does his best, but she was head
of the family. She had so much personality.' He straightened up,
and swallowed. 'Everything's so different, now she's gone. The
world's a different place.'

(Am I overdoing it? I've got to get the message across, but
enough is enough. He'll think I'm a right softie. Brian thought he
wasn't too bright. Hope he's right about that. Don't like the type
myself. We had officers like that in the army. One of them damn
near led us into an IRA boobytrap. Perhaps that's what Brian
means.)

'Sorry about that,' he said more normally. 'Haven't really got
over the shock yet. Somehow it all seemed to happen in such a
rush.'

McHale showed standard sympathy. 'Perfectly natural. You and your brother were at the pub, is that right? You heard down there?'

'That's it. That made it worse. All that singing, all those people. And we were a bit high: there was a celebration on—bachelor party, you know what they're like. What a time to hear your mother's been done in!'

'Yes, I can understand that. I suppose you were there all evening, were you?'

'That's right. From about eight till . . . till Jack Perkins came over and brought it out.'

'Then there'll be no difficulty in getting people to vouch for you, I imagine. You didn't leave the party at all?'

'No. I went to the . . . toilet, I expect. Yes, I must have. I was drinking beer. Otherwise I was around all the time. Having a great time. Makes you think.'

'Now, before yesterday evening, in the last few days, for example, was there anything—in the family, say, or in your mother's relationships with . . . friends—that had stood out, been in any way unusual?'

Gordon seemed to have a big think. 'Not that I can remember. She did all the things she usually did. She had a pretty fixed programme: had to, because she was a busy woman. Like she always went to the Corbys' on Mondays and Thursdays.'

(I can see it all: middle-aged body to middle-aged body in unlovely huddles on the sofa, bulges bouncing for a few minutes, and then Lill screwing out of him what she wanted: the odd quid here, the second-hand car there. I can just picture it.)

'Ah yes. That was to see—to visit the sick lady, Mrs Corby, was it not?'

Gordon made a quick decision.

'Well, six of one and half a dozen of the other, I expect. Old Hamilton C. admired her, I can tell you that. He's got an eye for a good-looking woman. Men who marry for money usually have. No harm in it, of course. For Mum it was just a bit of excitement. We're not living in the nineteenth century, after all.' He looked at Inspector McHale with a roguish glance of male conspiracy. 'You're a man of the world.'

McHale responded with a similar glance, the small change of pub and police canteen, and sank back in his chair. 'Very sensible of you to tell me. And what about your father?'

'Old Fr—Dad? He didn't know, naturally not. He's not that bright, as you may have noticed.' Gordon was now relaxed in his chair, sure he had done the right thing. 'But don't get me wrong. I'm not saying there was anything—anything really going on.'

'I see . . .'

'Not anything serious. It just gave a bit of spice to Mum's life. After all, you've seen Dad. He's no big pools win. He looks years older than Mum did, and sort of feeble, to put it bluntly. And Mum was still a woman in her prime.'

(How does it look, that corpse in its prime, now lying probably in some police morgue here or in Cumbledon? The red hair with the line of brown roots, the flesh—white, waxy and transparent now, like when I identified that soldier in Londonderry, when they wouldn't let me see more than his head and shoulders. She's as lifeless as him now, more lifeless than a Tussaud waxwork, Lill who made me what I am.)

'So you think, anyway, there was more to your mother's visits to the Corbys' than holding the invalid's hands?' said McHale with a pale smile.

'Natch. I expect she gave Hamilton C. a bit of womanly sympathy after she'd been up with Mrs Corby. Poisonous woman that, everyone says. She's hardly been seen by mortal eye for five years or more, other than poor old Hamilton's. He doesn't have much of a life when you think about it, poor old bugger. He's been good to me too, in his way—got me a job at the shipyard, and that.'

'Do you think your mother had other—friendships like that?'

'Oh, I expect so. I've been away, in the army, so I wouldn't know any of the details. But a woman like that's bound to attract men friends, I'd say.'

'I expect you're right,' said McHale smoothly. 'Now, you don't think there'd been anything else of interest—anything unusual happening in your mother's life in the last few days? For example, in the family . . . ?'

Gordon took another quick decision. 'Oh no. We jog along

pretty much as usual most of the time. I mean, nothing out of the ordinary happens. Fred—Dad—goes to work in the park, or the Memorial Gardens. Bri goes to school—he'll be going to university next year. I work in the shipyard, do a bit of training some evenings. Debbie's still at school. We go to the pub of an evening now and then, mostly Saturdays. That's the usual pattern.'

'So there hadn't been any disturbances in the past week or so? Any . . . rows, for example?'

'No,' said Gordon. 'We're not much of a family for rows. Mum kept things on an even keel, mostly. And if anything else unusual had happened, we'd all have heard of it, that's for sure. Mum wasn't one to keep things back.'

(It can't do any harm, not telling him. No good Brian priming Debbie to hold her tongue and me blabbing it out. Stick to one plan. Then if it comes out, as it probably will, it will just look like the devoted family sticking together. It won't look *suspicious*. Christ! The idea of Lill the Peacemaker, though!)

'I'm wondering—' said McHale cautiously—'I'm trying to get an idea of what sort of woman your mother was. Do you think you could try to sum her up for me?'

(Careful: those cold blue eyes, watching me. Don't make the mistake of overdoing it. None of the ham stuff. Only pull out some of the stops.)

'I suppose everyone thinks their Mum is something special, don't they?' said Gordon slowly. 'Anyway, all I can say is, ours was to us. She was a very warm person, very vital. She was so outgoing you always felt it when she was around. The rest of us don't amount to much. But everybody in Todmarsh knew Mum. She'll really be missed around here!'

(A slut, a loud-mouthed, vulgar slut who ruined my life.)

When Gordon had been thanked, and the wintry eyes had simulated understanding and sympathy, he was shown out. In the outer office he told the constable who had driven him down that he preferred to walk home. As he made his way along, very slow, hunched over (with grief, for all anybody knew), he went over in his mind the interview with McHale. On the whole he felt he had got things right. Fred had been established as feeble and foolish, he himself—and the rest of the children—as besottedly devoted. Any suspicion there might be about people in Lill's personal life had been directed outwards: at Wilf Hamilton Corby. Even at his wife. And they were rich bastards who could look after themselves. Any road, he'd done his best. The only possible problem was Debbie. Well, if she wanted to muck things up, that was her affair. She wasn't a girl to listen to reason, and she'd have to bear the consequences. In any case, nobody could seriously suspect a sixteen-year-old girl of killing her own mother. Could they?

Brian, heavy-handed, heavy-hearted, took Lill's knick-knacks one by one from the back of the sideboard and began to restore them to their rightful, Lill-ordained places. The little brass windmill, the plaster duck with the cheeky expression, the model of Anne Hathaway's cottage. And all the pots and plates from Tunisia, with their sharp, pressing associations—the sun, the leafy gardens around the hotel, with their orange and lemon trees, and the loose-bowelled birds overhead; the endless beach, with Lill in her two-piece holding court, surrounded by sellers of rugs and sun-hats, toy camels and earthenware pots, sitting at her feet, dark, doe-eyed and teasing, delighting in the polyglot sparring before bounding off to more profitable prey: the German couples, pumped full of heavy food and deutschmarks. And Lill, lying back on the beach, holding her nasty little vase or plate and announcing which of the vendors she fancied.

Brian looked around the room. Now everything was back, down to the dreariest little pot, the price Lill willingly paid for five more minutes' attention. The room had returned to normal, Lill had resumed her sway. Brian felt he had been appointed keeper of the Lill Hodsden Memorial Museum. To put the thought out of his mind he went up to talk to Debbie.

Debbie had mostly kept to her room since Lill's death—almost as if she were still locked in. As if to emphasize, in fact, that she *had* been locked in, and no one had lifted a finger to help her. Or perhaps she did not care to mingle with the family and join in their grief, real or pretended. At any rate, she was not going to be hypocritical: she was not grief-stricken and she was not ashamed.

She kept insisting on this to herself. She lay on her bed, exaggeratedly casual, reading a Harold Robbins.

'Hello, Debbie.'

'Hello.' Debbie went on leafing through her block-buster from double-cross to rape, exaggeratedly calm, taking no notice of her brother. Her dark brown hair fell down untidily over her sharp, passionate face. One day Debbie would be a beauty; even now she was the sort of schoolgirl one noticed, wondered about. She turned another page, and cupped her chin in her hands. Brian knew perfectly well she was not reading.

'About the police . . .' he began.

She looked up. 'Dishy, wasn't he?' she said.

'I thought he looked rather stupid,' said Brian, allowing himself to be sidetracked.

'That too,' said Debbie.

'But about when he talks to you: we thought—'

'Oh yes? Have you been concerning yourselves with me down there? That's nice. That's heart-warming.'

'—we thought it would be best if you didn't mention that little trouble between you and Mum.'

'Little trouble? You mean when she half knocked my block off?'

'Well, all the more reason for not mentioning it.'

'I don't know what it's got to do with you lot, but if the copper doesn't bring it up, I won't.'

'But if he does—'

'Well, I'll tell him, of course. Why not? I've got nothing to lose.'

'I wouldn't be too sure of that. The Inspector seems to think it was some kind of mugger, but if he hears there'd been trouble in the family it'll direct his attention here. And after all, you wouldn't want that.'

'Wouldn't I? Why wouldn't I? Is he supposed to think we were all devoted to her? Well, *I* wasn't.'

'Now, Debbie—'

'Were *you*, Brian? Were *you*?'

Brian swallowed. 'Of course I was. We all were. And all we want is to find out who did it. That's why we don't want to give a false impression.'

'That's what you *do* want to give. If you go round spreading the idea that Lill was loved by all who knew her, they're never going to find out who did it. Perhaps that's what you want, at heart. Well, I'm not going along. If he asks me, I'm going to tell him the truth.'

'You'd be a fool to.'

'Why? I was locked in this room all evening, with Fred on guard downstairs. I couldn't have been more out of it if I'd been in Australia. I'm one person he's not going to suspect.'

Brian went to the window. 'You could have climbed out.'

'Through those bloody roses? I'd've been cut to bits. Look at my hands—see any scratches?' She held out her hands, which were inky rather than bloody. 'I thought of it, actually, and decided against it. If I'd managed to get down, I could never have got back up. Look out: there'd be lots of broken stems and crushed leaves if I'd climbed out and in.'

Brian looked out. The climbing rose clearly hadn't been disturbed. He turned back into the room, disappointed, but as his eye lighted on the door he was struck by a flash of inspiration:

'Of course,' he said. 'The key.' He saw Debbie's eyelids flicker briefly.

'There was no key. Mum locked me in and took it, remember?'

Brian went out on to the landing and grabbed the key to the next room, the double bedroom shared by Lill and Fred. 'This house was jerry-built in the 'thirties. I bet any key turns the lock of any of the doors.' He jiggled it about and then turned it triumphantly. 'See! It does. This place is no Broadmoor.'

'Well, so what? I was in here: I couldn't dart out and get one of the other keys.'

'You had one in here in readiness, I bet. None of us ever locks the bedroom door, so it wouldn't be missed. The last time one of these was locked was—what? two years ago, and then it was you being locked in, just like last night. Mum locked you in because you'd been at her make-up. I bet you've had one of the other keys in here all that time, in case it happened again.'

'Prove it.'

'I bet the police could. By examining the locks and keys. Scratches and that.'

'Are you going along to them to suggest it? You're the one who's promoting the idea of the idyllically happy Hodsden family, remember. Anyway, if the subject comes up in future, I'll be able to say that if the key of Lill's bedroom has been used in my lock, it's because you just tried it out.' Brian looked down at the key in his hands in dismay. 'You really are the lousiest detective. Now go away and leave me alone.'

'Look, Debbie,' said Brian, coming to sit down on the side of the bed, 'all I'm trying to say is this: your alibi's not foolproof by a long chalk. You'd be a fool to dub yourself in by broadcasting all the family dirt. If you do that you'll do none of us any good. Nor Achituko either, for that matter.'

Debbie blinked again. It was clear she had not thought of Achituko. She thought for a while. 'Well, I suppose I won't say anything. But you needn't think I'm going through with all this disgusting pretence—'

'What pretence?'

'That we were all devoted to Lill. One big happy family, with her the light of all our lives. I bet Gordon's plugging that line down at the Station now. I think it's disgusting.'

'Just so long as you keep quiet about the fight. And about how you didn't get on with her.'

'Didn't get on! What a lovely expression! She made me puke. I loathed the sight of her. And so did you and Gordon. Didn't you, Brian?'

Brian jumped off the bed and headed for the door. But even as he escaped through it she threw out the query to him yet once more: 'Didn't you, Brian?'

And she burst out laughing at his pale, anxious face. Then she put aside her book and lay back to think things through.

11

BRIAN AND DEBBIE

The two younger Hodsdens, McHale thought to himself later in the day, exhausted by his excursion into the proletariat, were clearly a cut or two above Fred and Gordon in the mental-agility stakes, but he would hardly call them intelligent.

McHale set great store by intelligence in his thinking about the murderer. On the one hand, this killing might be a totally random piece of brutality, in which case the culprit would be difficult to spot because the field was impossibly wide. On the other, it might be a personal thing, a premeditated crime in which Lill Hodsden and Lill alone was the intended victim, and in that case he was convinced that the murderer was a deep one indeed. These two solutions had one thing in common: they demanded great intelligence and insight on the part of the investigating officer. McHale was convinced that he had them; therefore he was convinced this was a crime that demanded them. He was not a man to be content with apprehending common or garden criminals, not he.

So, without the thought consciously surfacing, he was on the look-out for a suitable partner in a duel of brains, and he did not feel he found him in the Hodsden family.

Brian, no doubt, was bright enough as schoolboys went, but he was hardly Oxford material, McHale decided. In addition, there was the undoubted fact that, by any standard of everyday life, Brian was 'wet'. The word belonged to McHale's generation and his attitude of mind, and he stuck it on Brian like a price-tag. The boy looked years younger than he was, had a confident manner which highlighted rather than concealed the fact that he was a bundle of nerves, and seemed to know no more of the world than a day-old chick. Add to that a slight frame and an air of frailness (he somehow did not seem to fit into his jeans and check shirt, and what kind of clothes were they, anyway, for someone who'd just lost their mother?) and McHale felt quite safe in marking him down in his mind as 'feeble', and ruling a line through him on his list of suspects.

Brian's account of the evening before largely confirmed that of his brother.

'Well, it was pretty drunken,' he said, pushing back a lank lock of hair with a gesture that McHale found irritating and pathetic. 'I'm not all that used to these do's, and I was just thinking we ought to be making it home when . . . when . . .' He swallowed. 'Gordon's more the type for that sort of thing: he was the life and soul of the party—had a joke with everyone there.'

'He was in the Rose and Crown the whole evening?'

'Oh yes. I was watching him, because of course I felt a bit strange. They were his friends: he knew everybody and I didn't. He probably had the odd quick trip to the loo, but that was all. Ask anyone.'

'And you?'

'Well, the same, really. I suppose I went to the loo—yes, I did, once. Otherwise I was there in the Saloon Bar, either talking to someone, or just watching. I expect some of the people there will remember—the more sober ones.'

Like his brother, Brian was sure there had been no ructions in the Hodsden family in the days before the murder. They were not that sort of family. Like his brother, he was willing to admit (not surprisingly, since they had had a hushed, hurried consultation before he was called down to the Station) that his mother might have had the occasional flirtation, with one or other of the men on the fringes of her life, though he justified this in different terms.

'People's life-styles have changed,' he said, with that horribly unconvincing man-of-the-world air. 'Nobody thinks twice about that sort of thing these days.'

Not in Todmarsh? said McHale to himself sceptically. He knew his small-town England and its inhabitants. Permissiveness had not reached them, and if it did they would not know what to do with it. He also noticed Brian's use of the phrase 'life-styles' and thought: pretentious little prig!

Brian's estimate of his mother was less breathlessly admiring than Gordon's (they had agreed that too much of that sort of thing might arouse rather than avert suspicion), but it was equally wholehearted.

'Of course, she wasn't an educated woman at all,' he said. 'Probably you would have called her common.' (It was a shrewd shot. McHale would certainly have called her common, and preened himself on that impeccable, inland revenue background that allowed him to do so. He hardly even bothered to gesture a dissent.) 'But she had more life than a hundred more intelligent people, and she had a wonderful human understanding. Nobody could ever be dull when she was around.' (Thank God, he thought, now I have the right to be dull.) Then he pulled himself up for a suitable summing up of Lill's life and works. 'She was the sort of mother who influences your whole life. She'll always be with me.'

He never spoke a truer word.

Debbie Hodsden was another kettle of fish entirely. In some ways even less mature than Brian, still she seemed to nurse some kind of inner confidence which nourished and protected her. At any rate, it was only rarely that the Chief Inspector dented her breezy front. Unlike Brian, who seemed to have shrunk into his jeans and gone too far, Debbie bloomed out of her school uniform, not so much physically, like a younger version of overblown Lill, but emotionally, as if proclaiming that it represented a stage in her life that in reality was past for ever.

She made no elaborate show of grief for Lill. She appeared serious, sober even, but there was no question (as there had been with Gordon) of her being about to burst into tears. Her notion of the proper behaviour was to be sensible and calm, and leave it at that.

'Mum? What kind of a person? Well, she was very extroverted —big voice, big personality, you know the type. I expect you can guess just by looking at her. I suppose you'd call her common.' (McHale blinked at the repetition. On reflection he decided to feel flattered at being the type of man who inevitably would call Lill Hodsden common.) 'Well—that's what she was, all right. But a lot of people like that.'

'You got on with her all right?'

'Oh yes, we jogged along. Of course, most girls have problems with their mothers—'

'Oh yes?'

'Well, they get jealous of their growing up. It sort of dates them, you know. Makes people think they're past it. So we had a few argie-bargies about my wearing makeup, modern clothes, and that sort of thing.'

'I see. Nothing worse than that?'

'Oh no. Just the normal.'

'You say she resented your growing up. Do you mean she liked to think she was still attractive to men?'

'Well, of course. Naturally. Everyone wants to think they're still attractive to the other sex. I expect you like women to notice you, don't you?' She launched a provocative smile at him.

'We weren't talking—'

'I was. Obviously you wouldn't like women to think you were past it.' McHale choked with annoyance. He had no wish to be compared with Lill, either in age or in inclinations. 'Anyway, the answer is *yes*. She liked men. She could attract them too—a certain type. No harm in that, so long as Dad was happy.'

'And was he?'

'So far as I know. I don't think he even noticed . . .'

'Was there much to notice?'

'Well, I'm not saying she was Cleopatra or anything. Still, he could have asked questions about all those visits to the Corbys. And I'd have kept my eye on that Guy Fawcett next door. He's been pinching my bottom since they moved here, and making some pretty direct propositions. Still, what the eye doesn't see . . .'

'You're quite sure he suspected nothing?'

Debbie shrugged. She felt no inclination to fight for any member of her family. None of them had fought for her. 'Never gave any sign, that's all I'm saying. Not a great one at registering emotions, my dad.'

McHale decided on the direct approach.

'You seem to have a sort of mark . . . a little bruise, by your left eye.'

Debbie rubbed it unconcernedly. 'Yes?'

'It wasn't the result of some . . . quarrel?'

'Good Lord no. What makes you think that? I was bending down in the bathroom to pick up the toothpaste, and when I straightened up I caught my head on the edge of the bathroom cabinet. It hurt like hell.' She laughed. 'I told them at school I'd been fighting with Mum. It made a good story.'

McHale felt a spasm of frustration pass through him. The cunning little minx! Covering herself in advance in every direction! But he'd pin her down soon enough.

'Ah, I see,' he said easily. 'You were upstairs, weren't you, when the news of your mother's death was brought to your dad. Had you been there all evening?'

'That's right. I was doing my homework. I had a French essay to write.'

'And it took you all the evening? You didn't go down for a snack? Or to watch something on the telly—there was a Francis Durbridge on.'

'The television?' Debbie queried, as though she were rebuking him. 'No. I don't watch much television. That's mostly for old people.'

'Ah! That puts me in my place, doesn't it? So you stayed in your bedroom all evening. And then your dad came *up*, didn't he, and told you about your mum. He didn't call you down. That seems a little odd, doesn't it?'

'Well, naturally, he wouldn't want me to hear in front of all those coppers, would he? What's odd about that? Did you think my dad wouldn't have that much delicacy?'

She had neatly checkmated him. There was no possible follow-up to that put-down. In spite of which, clenching his teeth, Mc-Hale told himself that Debbie was not a girl of any great intelligence.

McHale had made a home-life for himself that was hygienic and orderly. His house—'sixties neo-Queen Anne—on the outskirts of Cumbledon was rather more pretentious than his income at the time of acquiring it had warranted: it had been bought in the expectation of that promotion which, in its unduly laggardly way, had eventually arrived. By now its garden was stocked with evenly trimmed box hedges, like plump guardsmen; its paths were as if drawn with a schoolboy's geometry set; its flowers flourished and faded in the appropriate seasons—or else.

His wife was an admirable helpmate. She admired him very much. She entertained the right people when he suggested it, and served better wine than they were used to with conventional dishes she knew they liked. The children were well disciplined, and taught to be demonstrably affectionate to their father when he came home. If they said cute things during the day, Sheila McHale taught them to say them again in the evening to their father, so that he felt he was the first to hear them, and could repeat them next day on duty. As a housewife she fulfilled all the expectations he had had when, after due consideration, he had asked her to marry him. The house was always spotlessly clean and seemed to run itself, and she had a wonderful repertory of meals suitable for a man who came in at all hours and needed to feel cherished.

When he arrived home that night he went upstairs to kiss the kids goodnight (they woke up specially), and then he settled down to a good casserole which somehow was not overdone. Afterwards he expanded on the sofa, a brandy on the table by his right hand, his wife snuggled temperately up beside him.

'How's this new case?'

'Oh—' he paused for due consideration—'not over-exciting, perhaps. But interesting in its way. Ordinary housewife, cheap as dirt; middle-aged, but still something of a looker. Lively—something of a hotpants too.' He smiled apologetically to emphasize that he was using the language of her world, not of theirs. 'The question is: was it someone who knew her, or was it just plain murder in the course of robbery?'

'Did she have much on her?'

'Don't know yet. That's one of the interesting points. In any case, if it was a sort of mugging, it's not likely the murderer would know. She made a bit of a show, in a cheap and nasty kind of way. He may have been taken in by appearances and expected more than he actually got.'

'Not enough for murder, though, you'd have thought?'

'You just can't say these days. They're kinky, these young people: they start in on someone, then they go the whole hog. Not like the old days, when they had the fear of the rope in front of them.'

McHale always talked of 'the fear of the rope' rather than 'hanging'. It had a poetic ring.

'Is that what you think happened?'

'Well, on the whole, yes. And if that's the case, there's not much we can do but wait till he tries it again—apart from chasing up all the possibles on our books and keeping an eye on them.' His good-looking face crinkled in thought, and he took a sip of brandy. 'But it would be fatal to rule out the other possibilities. You've only got to look at the body—' his hands sketched vulgar curves, and his wife smiled sympathetically. 'There's no mistaking the type. Something of a handful: dyed scarlet hair, bags of make-up, slapped on, dirt under the nail varnish.' Sheila McHale shivered dutifully. 'Exactly. I wouldn't employ her as a char. But she'd be attractive to some. And she'd know how to work on them, get what she wanted. I'm on to one of them already—though the poor bloody fish of a husband seems not to have caught on, and it's been going on for years. There may have been others.'

'Sounds a nice type.'

'Mmm. By the look of her she'd be something of a trouble-maker, to boot: I'd be very surprised if she wasn't cordially loathed by the neighbours.'

'What about the family? What you'd expect?'

'Pretty much. Hubby works in the parks, eldest son works at the shipyard. Not a good class of murder at all.' He smiled as if he had made a joke. 'And they were all well and truly under her thumb.'

'You don't see them as suspects?' She was very good at knowing the track of his thoughts and following them; she was accessory after the fact to all his wrongful arrests, and there had been one or two. McHale screwed up his mouth.

'Hardly. Dim as hell, frankly, and spineless into the bargain. And mostly they've got alibis of a sort—not watertight ones, but the sort of natural, normal ones that are better in a way.' He suddenly had a thought. He should have asked Fred details of the television programmes he said he had watched between eight-thirty and ten. Before he had a chance to talk to anyone else. He put the thought from him.

'Well,' said his wife. 'It sounds rather a sordid little murder.'

'Oh, it is,' said McHale. 'Still, it is my first, apart from the odd manslaughter where there was no reasonable doubt. I should be able to get some mileage out of it. I'm looking forward to getting in with the neighbourhood. I bet there were some suppressed hatreds at work there. Lill Hodsden would have put some backs up that I'm sure of.'

He smiled in anticipation. His wife, looking at him, thought how handsome he looked. She did not see that touch of heaviness in the face that had made Brian Hodsden pronounce McHale a stupid man. She would never see it.

'Yes,' her husband repeated. 'I think I'll enjoy talking to the neighbours.'

12

FRIENDS AND NEIGHBOURS

A murder in one's immediate vicinity is a sort of test: a test of the
dead person; a test of the family of the corpse; a test of the
neighbourhood. Suddenly, dormant characteristics are highlighted, rugs are snatched away to reveal the dust that has been
shovelled beneath them over the years.

In Windsor Avenue and the surrounding streets, in the houses
of plywood tudor and the bungalows of superbeachhut design,
first reactions were to whisper about it over back-garden fences.
'Isn't it terrible?' or 'I couldn't believe my ears when I heard.' The
last of these was true enough: no one expects murder in the vicinity, unless they live in the hinterlands of savagery, in Kampala or
New York. But 'terrible' was to be interpreted loosely: 'shocking',
or 'stunning'—not anything implying grief, or that Lill's end was
undeserved.

That was the immediate reaction. It was quite soon superseded
by the question of what one said about the family, or—more vitally
—how one behaved to them. At first people said: 'It must be awful
for *them*,' rather as if it hadn't been awful for Lill. But when they
thought about things, weighed up all the circumstances, they
rather wondered about the Hodsdens. It wasn't a *nice* thing to
have a murder in the family—'nice' to be interpreted as respectable, or socially acceptable. And then—of course Lill must have
been killed by one of these muggers you're always reading about,

and why wasn't something done about them? . . . On the other hand, if she hadn't . . .

After the first couple of days, people who met one or other of the Hodsdens in the street tended to gabble quick condolences, and hurry on.

This tendency was increased when Chief Inspector McHale and his subordinates came among them, probing, prying, asking about Lill, about the Hodsdens, and about their own relationships with the afflicted family. It was exciting, everyone would have been affronted to be left out, but there again, it wasn't really respectable. You had to pretend you'd found it unpleasant. After a while opinion on the point definitely hardened: they remembered that the Hodsdens, after all, were foreigners. And one and all they had always said that they were a funny family . . .

Gordon Hodsden met Ann Watson in Todmarsh High Street on Saturday morning, before the first wash of generalized sympathy had totally receded. Not that Ann Watson was affected by tides of sentiment in Windsor Avenue: aloof, remote, she wandered through her daily round never letting herself become part of any community, neither at home nor at the school where she taught. But even she was not quite sure how to behave to Gordon Hodsden. There is nothing for it on these occasions but to take refuge in cliché.

'I was awfully sorry to hear—' she said, not feeling it necessary to specify. 'It must have been a terrible shock to you all.'

'It was,' said Gordon. Hypocrite! he said to himself. Liar! 'Somehow Mum was the last person you'd expect that to happen to.'

'Yes, she was,' said Ann Watson. Hypocrite! she said to herself. Liar!

'Of course I know you had your disagreements with her—'

'Oh—nothing. A silly little thing. Best forgotten.'

'—but what I really meant was not that everyone loved her, because I know they didn't, but that she was so bursting with life and energy. And suddenly, just like that, it's all gone.'

Gordon, in his cautious way, was trying to soften down the

picture of himself as a fatuous admirer of his mother's talents and charms. Ann Watson did not help him very much.

'It's particularly bad for you, because you were such a close sort of family,' she said.

Gordon felt he had to take another tentative step towards self-liberation. 'Oh, I don't know about that. Pretty much like most, I suppose. We had our ups and downs. Still, give Mum her due: she didn't interfere much. Let us go our own ways.'

'Oh?' said Ann Watson, with just a trace of upward intonation.

'I mean in our personal lives and that . . . We went our own ways, got our own girl-friends . . .' Ann Watson blinked twice at that, and confirmed Gordon's suspicions of what the row with Lill had been about. Christ, he thought, if I ever make it with her, it'll be against all the odds. 'At any rate,' he said, 'one way or another the neighbourhood's going to miss her.'

'She certainly made an impression,' agreed Ann. Gordon grinned cryptically, to tell her they really shared the same opinion on his late departed mother.

'She didn't give the place tone,' he said, 'but she did give it a bit of life. And Todmarsh could do with all the life it can get.'

'What will you do now?'

'Do?'

'Now she's gone. Will you leave the place?'

With a sudden shock of panic Gordon realized that he had not begun to think in those terms. He had to face it: Lill's death was a beginning, not an end. He felt bewildered, adrift. But he squared his shoulders and made an instant decision.

'No, I don't plan to move on, not yet awhile,' he said. 'My roots are here. I expect for a bit we'll go on as we always have. Only we'll have to get used to Mum not being around. It'll take time.'

'Oh yes,' said Ann. 'It'll take all the time in the world.'

Somehow that was not the way Gordon had hoped the interview would end. He did not want Ann Watson to compare in her mind his loss of a mother with her loss of a husband.

Along Windsor Avenue Miss Gaitskell—she whose arse had been so rudely assaulted in words by Lill Hodsden on her last trip down to the shops of Todmarsh—had a satisfying posthumous revenge by inviting Inspector McHale in to have 'just a *small* glass of sherry' and telling him just about everything she knew about the Hodsdens. The sherry was South African, but the gossip was the real McCoy.

She fussed over him, massive in shape but birdlike in manner, sometimes putting her head on one side as the insidious suggestions flowed out, sometimes bending forward over their glasses and letting fly with the brutal truth.

'Of course, everyone was always sorry for Old Fred—it's funny, he's always called that, even by his own children I believe—but when it comes down to it, he's a poor fish. I like a man to be a man, I must say. Underneath I think everyone does, don't you agree?' McHale assented confidently. 'And of course, that's what's intriguing everyone.'

'Oh?'

'The *difference*.'

'Difference?'

'In Old Fred. He's a new man since she died. Well, half a man. He's like an extra who's suddenly been given a line to speak. Why? Do you think that underneath he's relieved?'

'I've known it like that before with devoted husbands,' said McHale. 'Though it doesn't usually last.'

'No. Very wisely put. He'll be as dim and lost as ever within six weeks. Or married again to the same type. Still—intriguing. Then there's the Other Man in her life.'

'Ah yes—'

'You know already, I see. How, I wonder? The family told you, perhaps? Who? The boys? Gordon knew it couldn't be kept under cover, I suppose. Well, Corby's been looking like death warmed up since Thursday. He's talking of closing the yard and retiring to a cottage. A cottage not too far from a pub, I imagine. You've talked to him already, I expect?'

'Just on the 'phone—about when she left the house that night. I'll be going back to him, inevitably, when I've pinned down exactly what sort of relationship there was between him and Mrs Hodsden.'

'You could ask him about the colour TV the Hodsdens have—
and probably lots of other things she'd screwed out of him that we
haven't heard about. She told someone she was thinking of getting
a car, and you can be sure it wasn't Hodsden money was going to
buy it. There is no Hodsden money, I know that for a fact. They
blew what little they had buying that lump of a son out of the
army.'

'Were there any other boy-friends, would you say?'

'Hmmm. Probably. But I've no evidence. If a guess is any use to
you I'd say try Achituko and that Guy Fawcett.'

'Akki—?'

'Achituko. From the Coponawi Islands—Pacific, you know.'
Her big body softened, as if she became sentimental at the thought
of Todmarsh's token black. 'He's a nice boy; exceptionally polite.
Still, you wouldn't expect good taste from someone like that, not
our taste, would you? And I'm sure there's *some*thing with him and
the Hodsdens. Fawcett's only moved into the road in the last year.
The sort of man who makes respectable women itch to have a
good wash. Put that type next door to a Lill Hodsden and the
result is as predictable as strikes next winter.'

'I'll certainly keep them in mind,' said McHale, fixing her with
his gaze of professional appreciation. 'Is there anyone who had
cause to hate Lill Hodsden, would you say, around here?'

'Well, we none of us liked her. None of us had cause to.' Miss
Gaitskell blushed slightly as the insult to her posterior came back
to her mind. 'When she was in a good mood she was tolerable for
five minutes. When she wasn't—we scattered! I know for sure she
had a row with Mrs Carstairs.'

'Oh yes?'

'Because she was muttering to me about it next day. We were
comparing notes. She'd had Lill Hodsden up to the ears. But she
wouldn't make it clear what the row was about.'

'Anyone else who hated her?'

Miss Gaitskell's eyes sharpened, as she hazarded a guess that
had nagged at her mind all day: 'You could try the family,' she
said.

But McHale did not bite. 'I've seen the family,' he said. 'At the moment I'm more interested in the neighbours.'

So Miss Gaitskell filled his glass, and resuming her bird-like stance told him more and more about the neighbours, though she would dearly have liked to wonder aloud about the Hodsdens. But at the end McHale was well satisfied with his morning's work. He could not have picked his informant better. Obviously an ex-post-mistress had ways peculiar to herself of finding things out.

Guy Fawcett, home at midday and looking for all his burly frame oddly gaunt, turned out of his front gate and walked along Windsor Avenue to the brown painted house two doors down. Uncertainly, for him, he trailed down the stone-dashed side path and knocked tentatively on the back door. He wasn't looking forward to this. Mrs Casey, square, black and off-putting, opened the door and eyed him sourly.

'Yes?'

'Oh, er, Mrs Casey, we haven't actually met, but I'm Guy Fawcett from number eight.'

'I know,' muttered Mrs Casey sepulchrally, as if the lack of formal introduction had not stopped her marking him down for damnation in her little black book.

'I wondered if we could just have a little talk about a certain matter . . .'

'Yes?'

'Could we go inside, do you think?'

'I've nothing to say that can't be said on my own doorstep.'

'Yes, well, I have. Please . . .' She gazed at him with the flame of hell lividly present behind the arctic grey of her eyes. Then she stood silently aside. Guy scuttled past her into the kitchen, and wedged himself gracelessly into a kitchen chair. Mrs Casey stood by her back door and waited.

'It's this business of what went on . . . what you saw the other day . . . Tuesday . . . in the garden,' said Guy Fawcett, stumbling over his words and becoming even sweatier and nastier than usual. He hadn't behaved or felt like this since his headmaster had been more than usually insistent on hearing precisely what he had been doing with little Sally Foster in the boys' lavatories after schooltime. Mrs Casey, like his headmaster, had an impressive line in silence, and gave him not an inch of leeway.

'Of course it didn't mean anything . . . what you saw. Just a bit of silly fun. Meant nothing at all. But I'd be glad if you didn't mention it to the police.'

'Oh?'

'You see, people misinterpret that sort of thing.' Something like a malevolent laugh escaped Mrs Casey. 'And I'm a married man— a good husband too, very fond of my wife. You understand, I wouldn't want her to get hurt. And she'd take it very hard if it got round to her that . . . that . . .'

Mrs Casey sniffed, which seemed to mean that she very much doubted whether Mrs Fawcett would care a jot.

'And then there's your daughter—that was. I don't suppose you'd want to blacken the reputation of your own daughter—'

'She blackened her own.'

'Well, even if that were true, which I don't own, you'd have to be a funny mother to want to blacken it further.'

'I can't compromise with the truth.'

Guy's voice rose. 'I'm not asking you to compromise with the truth. I'm asking you to keep your trap shut when the police question you.' He was getting both irritated and querulous, as he always did when things went against him. It was one of his least attractive moods. 'We all know this thing was done by a mugger. But that won't stop them raking around in your daughter's private life if they feel like it. And if they do that they might find more dirty linen than even *you* would like to see hung out in public.'

'Oh? You think so?'

'I know so. You take it from me.' He slowed up, and began to alter his tone. 'And you'd better remember that if you say anything about me and her to the cops, I'll be the first to spill the beans.' Mrs Casey seemed for the first time to falter in her adamantine stance by the door, like a guardsman about to crumble at the knees. Guy sensed his advantage and weighed in. 'Like the details about Debbie and that Achituko, for a start. There's more dirt in that family than just Lill's dirt.'

Mrs Casey flinched, and looked as if she would demand what he meant. But that would have been stooping to his level, and Mrs Casey never stooped. Her mouth was working, with an expression of distaste: she seemed to find his presence in her kitchen repellent, demeaning. Miss Gaitskell was right about Fawcett's effect upon respectable women. Mrs Casey closed her eyes, thought hard and long, and then said:

'If they asked me a question, I'd have to tell them. Being police. It wouldn't be right otherwise. But if they don't ask, I'll let the matter be.'

Guy Fawcett breathed out, summoned up a greasy smile, and made straight for the door. 'That's all I wanted,' he said. Unable to leave without reasserting his masculine advantage he added with an attempt at satire: 'Just so long as you don't regard it as compromising with the truth, of course.'

Passing briefly in Snoggers Alley in the early afternoon sun, Debbie and Achituko paused, just momentarily, as if for condolences.

'Wednesday?' muttered Debbie.

'If Mrs Carstairs goes out,' muttered Achituko. 'I think she suspects. Will they let you?'

'Who's to stop me now?' said Debbie with a smile of new-minted triumph, and went on her way.

'I hear my *friend* Mrs Hodsden has been murdered.'

His wife's words from the bed caused Wilf Hamilton Corby to give a start worthy of a sneak villain in a silent film, and almost to drop his wife's lunch tray, which he was carrying downstairs.

He had, after all, made sure that Friday's *South Wessex Chronicle* held no word of Thursday night's event. His wife never listened to the radio, so she could have heard it on no local bulletin. The cleaning lady had not been in since Thursday morning. He himself had said, and intended to say, nothing.

But Drusilla Corby spoke the literal truth. Todmarsh—boring, moribund Todmarsh—was speaking of nothing else. And lying on her bed, reading her never ending supply of books from Cumbledon Public Library ('I can read *any*thing,' she would declare, 'except love stories,' and she would look viciously at her husband as she said it) she had had the gossip of two shrill-voiced neighbours wafted in by the breeze through the open window.

'You never told me,' she pursued, dangerously feline, 'about the death of my good friend.'

'Didn't want to upset you,' muttered Wilf, looking as if he wanted to make a dash for it.

'Why should it upset me, though, I wonder?' she asked, her mouth twisted and ugly as she looked towards the ceiling for inspiration. 'I've never to my knowledge set eyes on the woman.'

Wilf Corby cleared his throat. 'Murder's always upsetting,' he hazarded. 'Didn't want you to hear—'

'But you know I *dote* on murder! Murder's my greatest stimulant!' She flapped a pudgy paw at the pile of books on her dressing-table. 'In fiction, as second best to fact.'

'You wouldn't like murder as close as this.'

'Close?'

'Just down the road here. Hardly any distance—'

'Really? Now isn't that odd? My best friend killed within a few hundred yards of my own house.' A spasm of genuine irritation crossed her perpetually discontented face. 'Thursday night. How annoying. I took one of my draughts. Otherwise I would have heard all the fun . . . Did you hear all the fun, Wilf?'

'I watched telly. Then I turned in early.'

'Not much of an alibi. Still, you hardly need one . . . or do you? And how was she killed?'

'Strangled, they say.'

'They say strangled, do they?' The voice caressed the word oddly. 'Would any great strength be required, do they say?'

'Average. Moderate.'

'You're hardly in condition, are you, these days, Wilf? Not even average. Not even moderate. But your hands are carpenter's hands—I remember them so well.' She shivered ostentatiously. 'Rough. Calloused. That was before they started to shake.'

'Is there anything you want?'

'Want? Oh no. I shall enjoy myself now. Just lying here and

thinking. In the course of time, perhaps, I shall want to talk to the police.'

'Police be buggered,' Corby shouted. 'You'll do no such thing.'

'Coarse as always. And still imagining you rule the roost. Really, Wilf, you never do have the last word—you should know that by now.'

The voice died away to show she was content to leave it at that. Wilf Hamilton Corby fussed off downstairs, fuming impotently. Drusilla Corby lay back, her pink filmy nightdress emphasizing the bony fragility of her body, the odd pudgy hands clutching the turned-over top of her sheets. She gazed at the ceiling, the day-long screen of her own thoughts and plans, with a smile on her wide, unlikeable mouth and a sparkle in her black-rimmed eyes.

13

FRED AND FAMILY

'Everyone's been very good,' said Fred, looking meditatively at the knife which had just carved its way through an underboiled potato.

'What makes you say that?' said Gordon aggressively. Everything Fred said these days became the subject for scrutiny or contradiction. As though they were competing in some way—over a woman, or a patch of land.

'All the sympathy. Everyone's had a word to say.'

'And hurried on double quick when they've said it.'

'That's natural,' said Brian, desperately fed up with this petty bickering and anxious to avoid another futile uprush of temper. 'People do find death—well, sort of embarrassing.'

'More especially murder,' said Debbie flatly.

It was the first time the word had been used in the family. Killed, after all, is an expression that clutches a few shreds of ambiguity around its bareness. Murder says it all. Trust Debbie to be the one to use it.

Sunday dinner, even before that, had not been going well. Debbie, who took after her mother in so little, walked doggedly in her footsteps as a cook. But they had had to accept gratefully from Lill; Debbie aroused no such instincts of cowardly acquiescence. In fact they all felt vaguely hostile towards her, even before the blushing pink pork chops and the cricket-ball potatoes: it was almost as if they thought her delinquencies had led to Lill's death, though consciously they knew this was not so. And anyway two of them, at least, had no objection to Lill's death.

'The fact is,' said Gordon, 'we're an embarrassment to people. They don't know how to behave. I expect it'll be like that for months. Or until the police nail someone.'

'Shouldn't be long now,' said Fred, chewing, as well he might, a nasty piece of underdone pork. 'That McHale isn't one to let the grass grow under his feet, I'll be bound. Looked a capable chappie.'

'He could probably spot a parking offence at twenty feet,' said Brian.

Fred blinked. 'No call to be sarky. You young people are so sharp these days you cut yourselves. Remember it's your mother's death he's investigating. And I say he'll get him.'

'Well, let's hope he gets him double quick,' said Gordon. 'I don't like the way people are looking at us.'

'I was wondering,' said Fred, the old uncertainty taking over from the new, almost confident self, 'if I might just slip out and have a drink tonight. Of course, it wouldn't have done last night, not a Saturday, but Sundays is always a quiet night . . . it's very *quiet* always, of a Sunday . . . I don't know. What do you think?'

'Providing you choose a very *quiet* pub,' said Brian satirically.

'Oh, I would,' said Fred, missing the satire in his haste to clutch the straw. 'I know it sounds downright heartless, but I missed my pint last night.'

'Anybody'd think we were in the nineteenth century,' complained Debbie. 'Life doesn't stop, just because . . . she's gone. I'm going out tonight, anyway.'

'Where?' Gordon's voice rapped out, sharp and loud.

'Mind your own business, nosey.'

'None of your lip,' cut in Fred. 'I'm your father and I've a right to know.'

'Well, he's my brother, and he can mind his own business. If you want to know I'm going round to Karen Dawson's like I always do on Sundays. Any more questions?'

'Just you mind your tongue, my girl,' said Fred, getting up and beginning to stump off to the living-room to doze in front of the television. 'Now your mum's gone it's me 'as got to keep an eye on you. It's plain as the nose on your face that you need it.'

As he closed the kitchen door, Debbie put her finger to her nose in a gesture of derision.

'Look, my girl,' said Gordon, turning the whole force of his personality on her and fixing her with an angry, smouldering stare, 'let's get this straight. There's nothing changed by Mum's death as far as you're concerned. You've been disgracing us, and you're going to take the consequences now. You've got to account for all your movements, and be in by ten o'clock every night. We want to know where you are and who you're with. And if you so much as exchange a word with that black bastard, you'll be locked up in your room like you were on Thursday.'

'Gordon—' warned Brian.

'Oh, don't worry, Bri. I'm not bothered by Gordon,' said Debbie, unconcernedly inspecting her nails. 'I know him too well: he's muscle-covered cotton-wool. He's all bluster and no guts.'

'You little bitch!' Gordon grabbed her by the wrists and twisted her hands down on to the table. 'Look at me, damn you! Someone's got to get you in hand, and if it's not old Fred then it's going to be me—'

'You can shout and bully as much as you like,' said Debbie, returning his gaze with equal intensity. 'But I know you. Did any of you protect me from Mum when she was alive? You all saw her picking on me, and you did bugger all. I respect Brian more than you because he doesn't pretend to be anything else but a mother's boy. You're both milksops at heart. Why should I take any notice of a gutless pair like you? The only person who rules my life now is me.'

She got up from the table and took herself over to the door. ' 'Bye, Brian. Enjoy the washing-up.'

'Little bitch,' said Gordon under his breath. 'I'll show her who's boss. She's been running wild. If we don't rein her in she'll be the talk of the town.'

'Well, Mum's methods never did much good,' said Brian.

'Who's going to use Mum's methods? I'll come down on her a

damn sight harder than Mum ever did if I catch her with that Achituko.'

Brian, pensively clearing away, said nothing for a bit. Obviously Gordon in this sort of a mood was past reasoning with. But when he did speak, what he said was not to Gordon's liking: 'In the long run I don't suppose we can do much about it. She'll soon be seventeen. And it's probably not all that important.'

'Not important! A girl of that age sleeping with a bloody black!'

'What age did you have your first girl, Gordon?'

'You know bloody well that's different.'

'What bothers you is that he's black.'

'Too right it bothers me, and it would you too if you hadn't got all those namby-pamby notions you educated buggers get. But that's not the only thing. If she goes on the way she's going now, she'll be the town bike before she's twenty. She'll be dropping 'em so fast there'll be scorch marks on her thighs. She'll make us the laughing-stock of the town. What this family needs is a bit of discipline.'

Brian thought sadly to himself: I don't think that's what I need. He said: 'What do you think the police are doing? Have you heard any rumours?'

'Talking to the neighbours as far as I know.'

'Do you think they'll get anywhere?'

Gordon shrugged, still hunched over the table and puffing at a cigarillo. 'Maybe I'd have thought it was pretty sure to be one of them, if it's not a mugger. Or Corby. Or—God knows, there were enough who hated her.'

'If it wasn't one of the family,' said Brian quietly, scrubbing at a plate with his mop.

'Oh, for Christ's sake!' said Gordon, stubbing out his fag. 'We've been over this already. Who've you got in mind now? Fred again? He hasn't got the strength.'

'You think strength's just a matter of being big, and being in training. It's not. Fred may be small, but he's been a gardener for thirty years and more.'

'Look, Bri,' said Gordon, getting up and coming at Brian from behind, turning him round to get his words across, 'you know and

I know that Fred never made a decision in the whole of his married life. He's bloody feebleminded. Then all of a sudden he makes a decision to murder Lill. Don't be bloody potty.'

'Debbie could have done it.'

'Debbie was locked in.'

'Debbie had a duplicate key in the room. She's practically admitted it. She could have sneaked out any time if Fred was dozing. Come to that, Grandma Casey could have done it.'

Gordon let out a great hoot of laughter. 'Oh my Lord! That really takes the cake, that does! Poor old Gran at seventy-five strangling her own daughter!'

'She's as strong as an ox.'

'She wields a hefty rolling-pin, that's about the extent of her strength. You don't seem to realize, baby brother, that strangling someone isn't like tying a knot in a bit of string. And what the hell *is* this, anyway? Why this sudden urge to prove one of us is a murderer?'

Brian swallowed and turned back to the sink. 'We were going to do it,' he said. 'Or we said we were going to do it.'

'We *were* going to.'

'Perhaps it runs in the family.'

'Oh my God,' muttered Gordon. 'This is like some . . . some ruddy superstition. "Keep away from that family—there's bad blood there." Give over. That's just melodramatic.'

'Well,' said Brian, 'I tell you I won't be happy until they've got him. As it is, I just look around, at us, and I think—'

'You think too bleeding much. It's none of us. I can think of three or four who're more likely than us.'

'Who then?'

'That black. Old Corby. Fawcett next door.'

'I hope you're right, that's all.'

'Of course I'm right. Meanwhile we've got to present a front . . . as a family. Keep up our public image. Give them the idea we're one big happy family, temporarily desolated by the loss of our beloved mum. And I tell you I'm not having Debbie destroying that by playing hotpants with a wog. I'm not having *anybody* stepping out of line—get me?'

He walked to the door, then turned and insistently repeated: 'See?' Brian nodded miserably, seeing Gordon's point but hating his way of putting it. Then, desolately, he trailed through after him towards the sitting-room, through the door of which they could hear the television going.

'Forget it,' hissed Gordon. 'You're just getting the willies. Come on—there's athletics on the telly.'

He opened the door. The set was going full blast, and in the armchair Fred was snoozing, mouth open, with the Sunday paper over his face.

'Look!' said Gordon. 'The head of the family.'

By the time McHale came to interview Mrs Casey she was so upset by her apprehensions of scandal in the Hodsden family and uncertainties about the morally correct course to take that he found something very different from her usual rocklike self. In fact, she was butter in his hands.

Of course he had the advantage of knowing the type. Every policeman knew the type. After a mugging, or a bank raid, the only totally reliable source of information would generally be a Mrs Casey—someone whose sharp eye was undimmed, whose brain was unfuddled by excess, who took in better than any camera the colour of the attacker's shoes, whether he wore a moustache or glasses, his approximate height. The Mrs Caseys of this world see, register, collate and disapprove.

So, after trailing through the details of her activities on Thursday night—all irreproachable and quite uncheckable—McHale leaned forward in his armchair, in the specially opened front room, redolent of pre-war Leicester and enshrining relics of Alfred Casey, plumber, departed, and said in a solemn voice:

'I think you and I have something in common, ma'am. I think we both have standards!'

He really believed it. He would never have understood that, though their opinions might sometimes overlap, his standards were a mere assemblage of conventionalities that happened to boost his self-love and his vision of his own place in the universal scheme of things; whereas in her there remained, however perverted by the straitjacket of nonconformity, some sense of a Deity who had to be served, irrespective of personal inclination.

Mrs Casey nodded grimly and said: 'Aye. There's not so many has standards these days.'

'That was what I was meaning,' said McHale. He paused.

'I don't know where I went wrong,' said Mrs Casey, ruminating as she caught his line of thought. 'But go wrong I did.'

'You shouldn't blame yourself,' said McHale.

'Who else is there to blame? Alf—that was my husband—was hardly ever home, not during t'war and after. And you can't blame the father for how a daughter turns out.'

'You must have seen a lot of things, things that went on next door, that pained you?'

Mrs Casey nodded—but with a hint of wariness.

'I should tell you that we have a pretty good idea that your daughter had—shall we say boy-friends? The name of Wilf Hamilton Corby has come up.'

She seemed to breathe out. 'There's plenty could have told you that. That's no great discovery.'

'Precisely. But then there are the other names. This Mr Achituko, for example.'

'Not *her*,' said Mrs Casey, then pulled herself up. 'I've no evidence Lill ever went outside her own colour.'

McHale registered the moment, but imperceptibly. 'And then some people have mentioned the next-door neighbour, Mr Fawcett.'

Mrs Casey looked straight ahead of her.

'What would you say to that?'

'You haven't asked me anything.'

'Do you think your daughter was—carrying on with Mr Fawcett?'

Mrs Casey choked. 'I can't tell a lie,' she muttered. And really she almost couldn't. 'I—I think she was.'

'What makes you think so? Did you see anything?'

And suddenly a great tear welled up at the sides of Mrs Casey's eyes, and she gulped back a sob. 'I don't know what's for the best,' she cried. 'He's *wicked*. Coming to me like that.'

'Don't you think,' said McHale, leaning forward with a gentleness whose genuineness she was not in a position to examine, 'that it's always best to tell the whole truth?'

The tawdry truism went straight to Mrs Casey's methodistical heart, with its impulse for open public confession. Since Guy Fawcett's visit she had been unhappy about covering the family shame with lies and concealments. She was not even sure what she was concealing. McHale's simplistic appeal went straight to her heart.

'She was a dreadful woman, my daughter!' she wailed. 'A scandal and a shame! To think that any woman could *throw* herself like that at a man—practically *asking* to be . . . to be made wicked! And a man like him, too! And Fred thinking her the perfect wife!'

And then it all came out. The scene in the garden, the retreat to the house, and what she imagined went on in the house. And then Guy Fawcett's visit to her, and his threats. And then, under McHale's gentle probing, the implications about Debbie and Mr Achituko.

'But there can't be anything there, can there?' she cried. 'Debbie's just a little girl. It must be something in his horrible mind!'

'I'm sure it is,' said McHale soothingly. 'Just don't worry your head about it. You feel better now you've had a good cry, don't you?'

And certainly she did. He could see she did. When he went to his car he felt much like a parish priest who has just shriven a particularly tough sinner in his flock. And his mind was buzzing with the names of Corby and Fawcett, of Achituko and Debbie Hodsden.

Brian, at the sitting-room window, watched McHale leaving his gran's, and felt a dull sense of being inside a net, a net contracting with every day that passed.

The family was in danger of breaking up. He could see it coming, all the time. Not on the surface. Everything was normal on the surface. Debbie was out at her friend's—going off half an hour since, turning ostentatiously in the opposite direction from Achituko's lodging and walking down the road with indecent

perkiness. Gordon had put on his track suit and gone on a training run. Fred had more or less woken up—how much sleep he
seemed to need these days!—and was attempting the *Sunday Grub*
crossword. He had filled in the answers to three clues, probably
wrongly.

But underneath everything was cracking up. Debbie and
Gordon were at war, just as Debbie and Lill had always been. Fred
was making foredoomed attempts to assert himself, and would
soon retire, defeated and resentful, before Gordon's greater force
of personality. He, Brian—he, Brian . . .

He, Brian, was wondering if things hadn't been better on the
whole with Lill alive. He was scanning the past to see whether
there hadn't been happy times then as well. Lill and her boys at
the Fair, twice a year regular, when the fair came to Todmarsh.
Lill and her boys at Torquay, walking up the beach and scandal-
izing the residents.

Had it been so bad? Hadn't it been *something,* some stable centre, which was now missing, leaving him lost and bewildered? Was
it so dreadful, Lill's ghastly vulgarity, which raked the beaches of
Tunisia with its screeching laughter and drew forth the shivering
distaste of the other British holidaymakers?

Brian remembered Tunisia, and stirred uneasily in his chair.
Remembered the sun, the camel rides, the endless sands. Remembered the tightness in his chest, like an intimation of mortality.
Remembered Fred wandering lost around the grounds of the hotel, grateful for a casual word thrown in his direction. Remembered Gordon making up to a gross German Frau, bathing topless
under stony Moslem gazes. Remembered the lemons and the figs,
the little Arab cakes, the Berber women in town . . .

Remembered the boys who danced around them as they
walked past the medina—their handstands, their importunities,
their mocking imitations, and their haunting, inviting cries:
'*Voulez-vous coucher avec ma soeur?*'

And then: '*Êtes-vous anglais? Voulez-vous coucher avec mon frère?*'

14

THE TWA CORBIES

Wilf Hamilton Corby did all he knew how to stop his wife getting in touch with the police. The cleaning lady came on Mondays, and, purchasing her loyalty with a five-pound note. Wilf impressed upon her that on no account was she to ring them if his wife asked her to. He also told her to stick around the house till he got home. 'Sick fancies,' he said: 'that's what she's got—sick fancies.'

But he was no match for his wife. Drusilla Corby sent the char down to the shop with another five-pound note for a box of tissues: 'Keep the change—you've been so good to me,' she said, with a smile that would have made the Albert Memorial blanch. The char found she might have multiple loyalties, and trotted off obediently. Then Drusilla Corby simply rose from her bed and tottered interestingly downstairs to the telephone. Wilf Hamilton Corby, had he seen, might have regarded it as a miracle of nearly New Testament proportions, but then he knew almost as little about his wife's condition as we know about the gentleman who took up his bed in that interesting volume. Within ten minutes of the phone call Chief Inspector McHale was ensconced in an uncomfortable reproduction Chippendale chair, prepared for the goods.

Mrs Corby regarded him speculatively from her bed. Not as a man, or as any kind of sexual object. She had never greatly liked men, and her marriage had by now contributed to a positive aversion. She regarded McHale solely from the point of view of the degree of discomfort, fear and sheer panic he might induce in her husband. And she thought that—properly worked on—he would do very well. She saw an element of the bully, the respectable moral thug in McHale, and she liked what she saw.

'I suppose you're wondering what made me call you,' she said, her voice soft with physical weakness.

'People do still call us, even in this day and age, when they have information,' said McHale.

'I mean what I suppose you'd call my *motive*,' said Drusilla Corby. 'I'm sure there *are* still public-spirited people in the world, but I'm quite sure I couldn't claim to be one of them. I'm not even a good wife, or perhaps I would have held back. I'm afraid all my motives would seem to you intolerably vengeful. I have to tell you, Inspector, that the reason I am—like this—is that my husband . . . But I won't go into details. Much better not. I merely give you the hint so that you won't think me mentally sick, as well as physically—destroyed!'

'There's no question of that, Mrs Corby,' said McHale, whose sympathy was marginally more genuine than her story. 'I can see that you've suffered.'

'So much! But that's enough of that subject. I wanted to see you, and talk to you, because I knew you would have heard by now about my connection with this—this creature that has been murdered.'

'I had heard,' said McHale cautiously, 'that Mrs Hodsden was a friend of yours.'

'False!' said Mrs Corby, with whiplash scorn. 'I never set eyes on the woman in my life.' She paused. 'And do you have the impression, Inspector, that Lill Hodsden was the *kind* of woman likely to be *my* friend?'

'The point had struck me as odd,' admitted McHale.

'Ah, you have realized, have you, that she was a creature of quite stupendous vulgarity? Very perceptive of you. And whatever else may be said of me, I am not that. I am comforted that you understand—but now I have seen you I realize you were bound to. I think Mrs Hodsden's connection with this house will be quite plain to you when you meet my husband. Like clings to like, they say, don't they? And those two certainly did cling.'

'What you are saying, then, ma'am, is that Mrs Hodsden came to this house solely to see your husband, never to visit you.'

'Precisely. She came to minister to his sexual needs—needs of a minimal and totally ridiculous nature, I would conjecture. She came on Monday and Thursday nights, regular as clockwork, and —doubly insulting—she had her own key, and went straight through to the study, where these acts of passion took place.'

Mrs Corby leaned back against her pillow and cultivated her fragile invalid look. In fact she was bewildered by her impulse to swing between two roles, that of bitch (which came naturally) and that of pathetic victim of a brutal man's aggression (which was a rarer assumption). Like most people shut away from society at large, she was not in the habit of preparing faces to meet the people that she met. But McHale barely noticed her amateur dramatic assumptions. He was too interested in what she was saying.

'So in fact,' he said, 'these visits on Mondays and Thursdays were exclusively to your husband, were they?'

'Certainly. How monotonously regular they were, weren't they? Even Shakespeare couldn't have made much out of two hours on Mondays and Thursdays.'

'Do you know anything more about the visits?'

'Certainly. First of all, she exacted her price. Gifts at first. Money now and then, on an irregular basis. She was also starting to mention marriage.'

'What!'

'Precisely. Bizarre in the circumstances, isn't it? But that is exactly what she did on Monday night.'

'And did your husband seem of the same mind?'

'I have nothing but contempt for Wilf Corby,' enunciated his wife, gazing ahead like a dyspeptic Jane Austen as she made the judgment; 'In general he has the brains of a lemming. But even I will admit that were he to divorce me or encompass my death (which he will not, because he hasn't got the nerve) he would not be foolish enough to do it in order to marry Lill Hodsden.'

'Still,' said McHale, 'that's a bit of a stunner.'

'Quite. And that,' said Drusilla Corby, 'is why he tried to buy her off, I wouldn't mind betting.'

'Buy her off?'

'My other piece of information. My last, I'm afraid. Shut away up here one is so . . . out of things. But this I do know. It was on Thursday night . . .'

'The night of the murder?'

'As I now know. She arrived, I suspect, in a temper. She slammed the door of the study, a thing she'd never done before. Wilf was up here with me, fussing around the bedroom as usual. When the door slammed he muttered "wind"—just the sort of idiotic lie he would jump into, since it was a perfectly still night. Anyway, he went down, and I heard nothing for a bit. But half an hour before she was due to go—she *always* went at half past nine— I heard the study door open and Wilf walk through to the lounge. The lounge is little used these days, as you can imagine, and I wondered what he could be doing. There's a fine old cabinet there, wonderful craftsmanship and solid as rock. It holds a lot of china and glass—stuff I inherited, wasted on *him*. In the bottom section my jewels are kept. I have no use for them now, a worn-out old invalid woman—no, no, don't protest. Anyway, I *know* he opened the cabinet: I can't mistake that sound. I *think* I heard him get out my jewel case and rummage in my jewellery. And that seems the most likely reason he'd go to the cabinet: that painted creature would have had no use for fine china.'

'I see.'

'Now do you understand why I called you? Rifling *my* jewel-box for something to placate his ill-tempered whore?'

'I can understand very well. But there is one thing: there was no jewellery of any consequence on the body.'

'Was there not? Certainly if there was cheap stuff he didn't get it from *my* jewel-box. I'd like to think he fobbed her off with some-thing cheap, because it would be so easy to do, but that doesn't seem to fit the facts . . .' She meditated eagerly and came up with the most damaging of all possible explanations. 'Do you think he could have killed her to get it back?'

'Hmm,' said McHale, who wasn't happy with a murder for that sort of motive a bare ten minutes after the jewel had been given. 'I wouldn't want to commit myself. You've certainly provided me with food for thought—and a possible motive for *someone*.'

'I'm glad you think so. You know my husband has been sweating *blood* these last few days.'

'Really? Well, he won't have to do that much longer. You're sure there's nothing else you have to tell me?'

Mrs Corby squirmed restlessly in her bed, greedy for the attention and excitement McHale provided her with. 'I wish there was. But there's nothing. I'm so cut off up here. Day after day, nothing but silence.' She sighed, an April breeze through a willow tree.

'I should have thought it was remarkable how much you managed to . . . be aware of,' said McHale.

'Sometimes,' said Drusilla Corby, switching roles, 'I manage to *totter* to the top of the stairs.'

A quick trip to the Station put McHale in touch with the forensic people in Cumbledon. He had thought it all out in the car: it was possible Corby had loaded Lill with necklaces or rings but on the whole McHale doubted it. Necklaces were difficult to explain away, and rings were nastily ambiguous. Natural parsimony would tempt him to get away with less if he could, and on the whole a brooch seemed more the ticket.

It proved a lucky hit. The lab people confirmed that on Lill's pre-Raphaelite green dress, under her leopard-skin coat, were two minute holes that probably were the marks of a brooch pin. It might be worth checking the position of the holes against Lill's existing jewellery.

But all things considered, McHale thought he could go for bust without checking. He chuckled with joy and self-love, sure he was on to something. The constable driving him to the Corby shipyard could feel the self-approbation oozing out of him, and gazed darkly ahead: McHale had not made himself loved in the Todmarsh Station. There was something else too: the anticipation of pleasure, the Achilles heel of a policeman about to grill a suspect. McHale's lips twitched as they pulled up at the yard, for he

could see, watching them from the office, the terrified eyes of Wilf
Corby. But as he got out of the car the first person who came into
his line of vision was Gordon Hodsden. And Gordon—overalled,
dirty from sawdust and oil—was obviously wanting to waylay him.

'Do you think I could have a word, sir?' he asked. The 'sir' was
deliberate and premeditated. McHale responded: he looked towards the office, and smiled at the thought of Wilf Corby waiting
inside.

'Certainly,' he said. He glanced in the direction of a deserted
wharf, and together they strolled away from the massive shed
where the boats were built. McHale remained courteous but remote, and Gordon placatory rather than worried.

'I've got to come clean,' he began. 'I wasn't altogether open
with you on Friday.'

'No,' said McHale. 'I know you weren't.'

'It's not easy when it's your own sister.'

'It's foolish, whoever it concerns.'

'Anyway, I want to give it to you straight now—'

McHale was not going to let anyone claim virtue on such flimsy
grounds. 'You want to give it to me straight now because you know
your grandmother has already told me all she knows.'

'Fair enough,' said Gordon, looking him straight in the eye.
'But that's not the whole truth. I couldn't get out of Gran exactly
what she said. She was too upset.' He stopped at the end of the
wharf and looked sombrely out to sea. 'No, it's not just that; it's
something else . . . I suppose you know the basic facts.'

'I've guessed. But you tell me.'

'Mum and Debbie had a row. Debbie got a bit bashed about
(not serious—you saw the bruise). She disobeyed Mum, though,
and went off to school the next day. Mum was furious with her
when she got home, and locked her in her room. We didn't tell
you that because we . . . we felt it would give a wrong impression
about Mum.'

McHale kept silence. He had a half-sense that Gordon's explanation of their motives for concealment was inadequate.

'The point is this: the row was about Achituko. The bloody
black who lives along the road. She'd been sleeping with him.'

McHale sighed. That was better. That was coming cleaner. 'That was what I suspected.'

Gordon whirled round to face him and spoke with a low, controlled intensity: 'The point is, can't you do something about it?'

'Do?'

'Get him out of here. Deported or something. Away from her. Have you talked to him yet?'

'Not yet—all in good time.'

'You should. He and Mum had a row in the street, couple of hours before she died. He could easily have done her in for revenge. But what I really want is to get the bugger deported. You could manage that. How long have they been sleeping together? We just don't know. She could easily have been under the age of consent when they started. You could get him on that.'

The idea appealed to McHale. In matters of race he had all the innate liberalism of his middle-middle-class, tax-inspecting background. He hated the bastards, and behaved to them with impeccable courtesy. Cutting short Achituko's so-called study at this local so-called university was a notion of delicious appeal to him.

'Bit early to speak of deportation,' he said cautiously. 'Though it's something we could keep in mind. In fact, we could take him in for questioning and on this angle we could definitely give him the works. But I'm not sure what your interest in this is.'

'What do you think? We're going through a difficult time, but we're a decent-enough family.' Gordon turned his dark eyes broodingly out to sea again. 'Now Lill's gone most of the responsibility comes back on me. You've seen Fred. I've got to find some way to keep that little—Debbie in order. She's not going round disgracing us by sleeping with blacks, or anyone else at her age. Christ, you must understand: don't you have a sister?'

'No—but I understand,' said McHale. Gordon Hodsden was articulating attitudes which lay very close to his conformist heart. You didn't hear them so much from the younger generation. In fact, he was beginning to feel a much greater respect for Gordon Hodsden, though he failed to realize this was because Gordon had changed his performance since the earlier interview. 'I'll do what I can.'

'Thanks. I'm very grateful,' said Gordon. And together they trudged up the wharf, watched by supplicating, terrified eyes from the windows of the shipyard offices. As they turned into the yard the eyes disappeared.

When it became clear that McHale was not going away in his nice big car but was coming into the yard proper, Corby oozed out of his office to usher the Inspector in. He was a pathetic sight, but he tickled some little instinct in McHale which made him overlook the pathos: he never disliked the thought of an inquisition, but now he looked forward to this one with positive relish. It was the bonhomous cheeriness of Corby, trying to cover over the beginnings of a piglike sweatiness, that aroused the relish. McHale rationalized it by characterizing Corby in his mind as a savage husband and an adulterer, but he hardly believed the first, and didn't greatly care about the second. It was Corby's craven fear that tickled his inborn relish. He decided to play with him for a bit, catlike.

'I'm sure you understand why it is I'm here,' he said, sitting down opposite the boss's desk.

'Oh yes—perfectly.' Corby puffed and glistened as he sat uneasily in his position of authority. 'You have to follow everything up. I realized you'd want a bit more than just the time Mrs Hodsden left us that evening.'

'Precisely. Now, you told me on the 'phone that she'd been visiting at your house.'

'That's right.' Eagerly, with pathetic, transparent mendacity, he added, 'Visiting the wife.'

'Who is I believe an invalid.'

'That's it. Sees no one as a general rule. Not up to it. Any excitement and—whoof—she might go. That's what the doctor says.'

'Really? But Mrs Hodsden was a regular visitor, wasn't she?'

'Aye, that's right.' With that same fatal eagerness. 'Devoted. Twice weekly. Regular as clockwork.'

'No excitement from her, then.'

Corby squirmed. 'No. She was a marvellous sick visitor. Knew just the right tone to adopt. Soothing, like.'

'Really? Odd, I haven't had the impression of Mrs Hodsden as an exactly soothing figure.'

'Adaptable. Surprisingly adaptable,' said Corby, oozing another layer of sweat.

McHale sat back in his chair, a dangerous half-smile lurking in the corners of his thin mouth. 'Tell me, Mr Corby, is your wife's illness a mental one?'

'Mental? Good Lord no. Well, of course, it involves a lot of mental *suffering* . . .'

'It's just that your wife tells me that she never in her life set eyes on Mrs Hodsden.'

Corby exploded into a weak man's rage and shambled to his feet clutching his collar. 'Tells you? When—? How—?' He sank back in his chair, as if exhausted by all the tension. 'The bitch. How did she—?'

'Never mind that, Mr Corby. I think I'll do all the asking of questions. Perhaps you'd better decide to answer them truthfully this time, eh?'

Corby settled muttering in his chair, and looked at the inkwell, a picture on the wall, anywhere but into McHale's face. 'You'd no call to go behind my back and talk to her first,' he muttered, as if there were some obscure cricketing rules attached to police investigations.

'I'm very glad I did,' said McHale, that half-smile now more openly decorating his handsome, heavy face. 'Though frankly it doesn't seem as if your relations with Lill Hodsden were any great secret. Half the town seems to have known.'

'Oh, if you listen to the gossips—'

'Are you denying there were sexual relations between you?'

'Denying? 'Course I'm denying it. You've seen my wife: she's no companion to a man. Lill Hodsden came round to see me to chat —give me a bit of womanly sympathy.'

'Frankly, my impression is that womanly sympathy was no more Lill Hodsden's line than soothing invalids. You're not ringing true, Mr Corby.' McHale leaned forward and started raising his voice. 'You certainly paid well for this womanly sympathy, didn't you?'

'Paid? Who said anything about paying?'

'I did. I don't just mean money, either. That we might have difficulty tracing. But that colour TV—that'll be child's play to track back to you. And then there was talk of a car—'

'I bought her no bloody car.' Corby looked at his inquisitor with anguished indignation. 'If you ask me, a second-hand colour TV wasn't much to pay for all her kindness.'

'And if you ask me I'd say that brooch you gave her was a good deal too much.'

Corby jumped six inches out of his seat. 'Brooch? Who said anything about a brooch?'

McHale sighed, as if Corby were an antagonist unworthy of him. 'Mr Corby, I know you gave Lill Hodsden a brooch from your wife's jewel-case not an hour before she died.'

Wilf Hamilton Corby's pudgy, heavy face was brilliant with sweat by now, and he seemed on the verge of crying. He began twisting his shoulders in anguish as if trying to find a physical answer to the question of which way to turn. 'Well—what if I did? It was just a trinket—nearly worthless. *She's* never in a condition to wear them now.'

'How do I know it was worthless? Since it's disappeared we can't check that.'

'Disappeared?' Wilf Corby seemed outraged. McHale kicked himself. He should have tested Corby to see if he knew it was not on the body. As always with lost opportunities in his investigations, he smoothed it over, hid it even from himself.

'No doubt we can check that with your wife. She—I suspect— will know exactly what was in the jewelbox, and how much the missing piece was worth.'

'You'd believe her? Any old cracked bit of china's a family heirloom if you listen to her. And she'd say it was worth a fortune if she thought it'd land me further in the shit.'

'She's been very helpful so far, at any rate. It would save all of us a lot of trouble if you described the brooch yourself.'

'Hardly noticed, tell you the truth. Just grabbed something to calm her down. Sort of peacocky design—bird, silver I think, glass in the eyes and the tail. Dressy sort of stuff, if you know what I mean.'

'And you gave her this to—to calm her down.' McHale leaned forward with a nasty sneer on his face. 'Had you been getting her unnaturally excited, then?'

'Nothing to do with me.' Corby went scarlet, and for once in the interview McHale believed him. 'She arrived all het up. She'd had an argy-bargy with her daughter. Been sleeping with that black student or something. Makes your hair curl what girls will do these days, doesn't it? Then she'd met the bloke himself in the street, and had a showdown. He's the chap you ought to be grilling, you know. Anyway she was really put out when she arrived. Started going on about this and that—'

'Like getting you to marry her, for example?'

Corby let out a mystified yelp of anguish. 'Are you joking? With both of us married already?'

'It's easy enough these days. If you wanted to, it could have been arranged.'

'Who wanted to? I certainly didn't.'

'She wouldn't have been blackmailing you to make you more keen, would she?'

'Blackmail? What the hell would she have on me?'

'That,' said McHale, 'is something I shall be trying to find out.' He got up. 'Well, Mr Corby, I'm sorry to have to leave you dangling like this—'

'Wha'd'ye mean—dangling?'

'Uncertain, so to speak. Of course, if you were to act sensibly and come *completely* clean—'

'Wha'd'ye mean—completely clean? You've screwed my whole private life out of me—'

'Oh, I don't think so, Mr Corby. I really don't. I'm afraid we're going to have to follow this up very completely indeed if you don't come over with the complete story. You were, after all, the last man to see Mrs Hodsden alive. Your wife says your affair with her had lasted two years or more—'

'My wife! My God! What have I done to deserve a woman like that? What did I do, marrying a treacherous cow like her?'

McHale paused at the door and waved a hand at the shipbuild-ing yard beyond. 'She brought you—all this, didn't she, sir?'

He left Corby staring after him vindictively, with a sense of having said something rather neat.

15

TROUBLE AT THE HODSDENS'

McHale acted swiftly in the matter of Achituko, but in the event matters did not sort themselves out as quickly as he had hoped. Fetched from his lodgings at Mrs Carstairs's on Monday night by a peremptory pair of police constables (McHale chose the largest and thickest in Todmarsh), Achituko displayed admirable self-restraint and forbearance during the inquisition about his row with Lill Hodsden and his activities thereafter (by ten o'clock on the night of the murder he was sharing a chaste cup of Maltino with Eve Carstairs, but before that his doings were difficult to check). It was when the talk turned to his relationship with Debbie Hodsden, and in particular when the word 'deportation' was airily slotted into the conversation by McHale, that Achituko showed his metaphorical teeth and made it clear that he was no illiterate wog picked up on the streets without an entry permit and easy to bully into damaging admissions. He knew his rights, and stood on them; he knew English law, and he invoked it; he knew the techniques of opposition, and he used them. The thing developed into a duel between two obstinate personalities, and of the two Achituko was much the more subtle.

By Wednesday morning a stalemate had been reached. Achituko had mobilized on his side the Comparative Religions Department of the University of South Wessex, and McHale was having to face the prospect of figuring in a national civil rights

314

scandal, with articles in the *New Statesman* and questions to the Home Secretary in Parliament. This was not how he had imagined achieving prominence in the larger national context. With a sigh he released Achituko into the custody of one of the defrocked clergymen on the staff of the Comparative Religions Department, on the understanding that he would not return to Todmarsh or attempt to make contact with Debbie Hodsden. Achituko enjoyed the duel and felt flattered by the friendly interest of his teachers at South Wessex. By the end of the week, though, he was finding the interest of the defrocked clergyman a good deal friendlier than he liked.

This was the news that McHale was able to give Gordon Hodsden when by chance he drove past him early on Tuesday evening, McHale on his way to talk to Guy Fawcett, Gordon out on his training run. Gordon bent over attentively at the window of the car, and when he got the details his saturnine face lit up with pleasure.

'Thanks,' he said, 'I appreciate what you've done.' And then he continued on his run.

As he jogged efficiently along the drab sea-front of Todmarsh he felt a warm, satisfying feeling in his bowels at a difficult job well done. Now Mum was gone, thank God, someone had to keep the family together. Fred's attempts to step into her shoes were ludicrous, as they all could see; and if it wasn't to be Fred, then who else could it be but he himself? There wouldn't be any problem about that, aside from Debbie. Fred had always done as he was told, and would do so again, when he got used to the new regime. Brian was pretty docile, and might be expected to get a place at South Wessex in autumn, and do well. It was Debbie who was the green, useless sucker shooting from the Hodsden bush. She had gained an unruly independence during her years of fighting with Lill which was going to have to be knocked out of her. She complained she'd had to fight her own battles. Didn't everyone? Life didn't present you with your victories on a plate. Now that Achituko was gone, there could be a new start for Debbie: firm discipline, hard work, and something worthwhile and respectable when she left school. Something in an office, with good prospects. It would all work out all right if she was treated with a firm hand.

Gordon smiled. He was a young man who lived for the moment. Everything was beginning to look rosy for the future. His whole body felt suddenly relaxed from tension. He broke his training rules and turned, track-suited and sweating, into the Rose and Crown for a drink. His luck was in. Ann Watson was in there, for a casual hour's drink with a friend. Clutching his pint in his big carpenter's hands, he went over and sat down with them. They both welcomed him with smiles. Yes, the future was beginning to look brighter.

'OK, so I went into her house,' said Guy Fawcett, walking around his own front room, red-faced and blustering. 'So what? We were neighbours. Neighbours do drop in on each other. I know who told you about it, and you can take it from me, she's an evil-minded old woman.'

'She struck me, in fact, as an exceptionally truthful and observant person,' said McHale coolly.

'She'll be sorry she squealed to you, I can tell you that,' burst out Guy Fawcett, unwise in his agitation, and letting the bully show through.

'Are you threatening a witness?' asked McHale, raising his voice to an authoritative roar. 'I can assure you if you do that, it's *you* that will be sorry.'

'Just a joke,' muttered Fawcett, cringing. 'I can't stand these nosey-parkers.'

'The fact is, the pair of you were leading each other on, and then you went off into the house, with your arms round each other, and you doing God knows what with your hands. I suppose you'll say you were going to borrow a gardening book.'

Which put Guy Fawcett into a quandry, because that was precisely what he had been going to say, and he couldn't for the life of him think of anything better.

When Ann Watson's friend had gone, Gordon began to feel for the first time that they were really getting on well together. No mystery about why. Now there was no reason why the subject of Lill should embarrass them. There was no reason why it should come up at all. Instead they sat at their little table, companionably, talking about the army, about being an army wife, about Northern Ireland.

'It's the women I'm sorry for,' said Gordon. 'Always was. I'd never have got married if I'd stayed in the army. No sort of life for them at all.'

'Oh, I quite liked it,' said Ann Watson, talking freely with him because with his background he was one of the few people she knew who might understand. 'Of course there was the loneliness, and the separations, and you saw some of the wives going off the rails—but at least there wasn't any question of getting *stale*.'

'Most women would hate it,' said Gordon.

'Well, the army was his life, so it had to be part of mine. Some of my friends seemed to think I ought to be mildly ashamed of that, but I never was. The army's a job like any other . . . Of course, when he had a tour of duty in Northern Ireland, that was different . . . terrible.'

'Aye, it was that,' said Gordon, remembering. 'Still it wasn't so bad for us on duty. It made a man of you.'

'Oh?'

'You've no idea how quickly you grow up when you know the boy down the end of the alley may have a gun in his pocket. It makes you think—about yourself, about life. In the end, you're on your own in Northern Ireland: your mates can't help you much and you can't help them—all you can do is get a bit of your own back afterwards. When you've seen your mates blown up, you don't give a f—, you don't give a damn about the rules and the bloody procedures anymore. It's you against the rest, and you've just got your fists and your rifle.'

'Yes' said Ann sadly. 'I suppose that's how it gets you.'

Later, when he walked her home, Gordon tried to slip his arm around her, but she put it aside quite coolly: 'Don't.' But she talked away quite naturally, and listened when he told her about himself, about how rootless he felt, how uncertain about the future, lonely. Wasn't she lonely too?

'Yes, sometimes. But it's not really an unhappy feeling. Sometimes I almost like it.'

'But it must be difficult for you—just yourself and the child. And having a job too.'

'In a way. I wish I could care more about Beth. I wish I could give more of myself to her. She needs it, but I can't.'

They stopped by her gate, and Gordon put his hand on the post, loomed over her and kept her with him. 'You need to come out of yourself more. Get around a bit. You'd find it helped.'

'Everyone says that. But I don't think it would.'

'We could go out next weekend. There's a disco in Cumbledon. Would you come?'

'Oh, I don't think so. I used to love them, but that was years ago, and I was a different person.'

'Come on. It'd do us both good . . .' Gordon put his arms around her and very quickly drew her close to him. 'You know it's what we both need.'

'No—don't.'

'Come on. Relax. All I want's a kiss.'

'No no.' She pushed his chest and stooped from under to fumble with the latch of the gate. 'I'm sorry, Gordon.'

'Come on. Why won't you? You like me.' He caught her hands in his strong grip and pulled her back to face him. 'Admit it: you want me, don't you?'

'I like you,' she said gently. 'I don't want you.'

'*Why*? Tell me why?'

Ann Watson seemed to make a decision. 'It's funny. Sometimes . . . even at times like now . . . you just don't seem to be *there*.' She escaped into her front garden, and then seemed overcome with remorse. 'I expect it's something in me.'

Gordon swore loudly and charged off down the road.

'All right,' said Guy Fawcett at last, sweating—McHale thought he had been here before—but with a wry, lopsided grin on his face which was the prelude to an all-chaps-together act, 'I'll admit it: we had a bit of the old one-two. Heavens above, you're a man of the world. You can see what kind of a weed old Fred Hodsden is.

Old Lill could eat up ten of him before breakfast and still be ready for more. She needed someone who knew what it was all about. And this wasn't the first time she'd marked down something she fancied and grabbed it with both hands, I can tell you.'

'I'm sure it wasn't,' said McHale with distaste written all over his face, side by side with the enjoyment. 'Unfortunate that in your case it happened to be only a couple of days before she was murdered, wasn't it?'

'Well, so what? Just a coincidence. We'd been eyeing each other off for weeks.'

'You're implying this was the first time, are you?'

' 'Course it was the first time. Ask old Mother Casey. We wouldn't have been going through the whole fandangle if it wasn't. Even that old battle-axe must have realized that.'

'Possibly. Or you could both have been putting on an act for her benefit.'

'We didn't know she was *there,* fer Chrissake. If we had it'd have been different, I can tell you. We'd have been round the front garden for a start. It was the first time—and the last.'

'Ah—so that was the kind of affair this was, was it? Just a once-off?'

'God, yes. I'd have seen to that.'

'Oh? You mean she'd have liked something more permanent?'

'Given half a chance.' Guy Fawcett swelled like an athletic bull-frog. 'I've got what it takes.'

'How interesting. Well now, let's recap on the situation: she was trying to nail you down, and you wanted out. Does that about sum things up?'

'No, no!' An expression of panic came over his face. 'I didn't mean that at all. I'm being misrepresented!'

'It sounded like that to me, sir. Perhaps we'd better go into this a little more closely.'

'Oh Christ,' muttered Guy Fawcett, regretting—not for the first time in his life—the too indiscriminate employment of his one great talent.

* * *

Gordon arrived back home in a foul mood. He felt the bile rising in him, and the urge for a fight—not a fight to liven up the day, such as Lill had enjoyed after a dull Sunday, but a fight to the kill, such as Lill had engaged in when she'd been thwarted.

Only Brian and Debbie were in—Fred having been emboldened to go out for the odd half pint for the third night running. Debbie, as usual, was crouched over a blockbuster, while Brian was watching some trendy media man condescending to the arts on BBC 2.

Inevitably it was Debbie who caught the full force of Gordon's mood. There had been only one thing in his day to give him any satisfaction, and he brought it out with a snarl of grim triumph.

'Well, I've settled your black stud's hash,' he said.

The unfamiliar word took a moment to get through to Debbie, but when it did, she flinched, and, raising her dark, dangerous eyes from her book said: 'What do you mean?'

'I say I've settled his hash. You won't be seeing him again.'

'I'm seeing him tomor—' She put her hands to her mouth.

'Oh, that was what you were planning, was it? Just as well I stepped in. Well, get this into your crazy skull: your little black Sambo's gone from Todmarsh for good. Before the end of the week he should be on his way back to Baboon land or where the hell he comes from. If he's not up on a charge of murder.'

'They can't send him back home. They've no right—he's studying here.'

'They've every right. There's immigration laws in this country, thank God, and they apply to students and all. There's other laws too—like about seducing a minor, for instance.'

'Oh, don't talk rot, Gordon. He didn't seduce me.'

'According to the law he did, or it'll be the same as if he did. I've been into all that. When they've finished going over him they'll put him on the first plane home. Got that? They'll deport him.'

As the idea got through to Debbie she let out suddenly a howl of rage and pain. 'They can't. Who's doing this? Is it that damned policeman?'

'Yes, it is. After I tipped him the wink.'

Screaming with anger and frustration, Debbie suddenly threw her book at his head and sprang at him herself in its wake. 'You beast! You bastard! I'll get you for this! I'll kill you!'

Sobbing and screaming she grabbed his hair and started clawing his face. Glad the thing had become a full-scale fight, fully confident at last, Gordon grabbed hold of her arms and started bending them back behind her. 'You bitch. You vile little bitch. You've met your match, little sister . . .' As her arms started to go limp and her face twisted in physical pain, Gordon relaxed, and still bending them back and up towards her shoulderblades, he started talking more softly: 'You're going to be grateful to me for this, you know. Later. When you know a bit more about life. You're going to see I was right . . .'

Now Debbie was sobbing with pain, and Brian said: 'Give over, Gordon. That's enough.' Slowly Gordon relaxed the pressure and Debbie collapsed on the floor in a racked, snuffling heap.

'You can't do this to me,' she gasped. 'I'm going to see that policeman.'

'Don't you try it, kid,' said Gordon, standing over her in gladiatorial triumph. Quick as a flash Debbie seized one of his ankles and half-toppled him over one of the easy chairs. Then, on her feet in an instant, she made for the door. Gordon, righting himself, caught her just as she was going out of the front door, dragged her back into the hall and banged her head against the wall.

'Oh, little sister,' he shouted, 'you've got so much to learn. Do you want to learn it the hard way?'

Next door, with Guy Fawcett squirming and twisting on the end of his inquisitorial line, Inspector McHale heard the shouting and the banging on the wall from the Hodsden house. He raised his eyebrows imperceptibly. The happy Hodsden family . . . He hadn't expected them to break out like this. Perhaps he ought to go and investigate.

But that very moment there came through from the Station the 'phone call that was to change the whole course of the investigation.

16

CONFESSION

It was what McHale had half expected all along. In fact it was what he had hoped for. He had alerted his colleagues in the Cumbledon police, and they had contacted him immediately it had come up.

The boy sat in the charge-room, a heavy lad of nineteen or so, his manner poised between bluster and terror. If his body—incipiently mountainous and ugly—might arouse fear, his face could only arouse contempt: large-headed, dim, inarticulate, his mouth always in danger of falling open, he was the typical rural lout who in this urban age finds himself a place among the dregs of the towns. His face was spotty and pockmarked, his eyes shifty and wet; he wore a cheap plasticated leather jerkin, zipped to the throat and sewn over with incomprehensible badges, and filthy jeans. He smelt. Even as McHale entered the room he involuntarily wrinkled his nostrils. A sensitive policeman, McHale.

'Well, you've landed yourself right in it,' he said.

'I ain't done nothing,' muttered the boy feebly.

But what he had done was all-too-well attested to. Earlier that evening, at dusk—he had not even had the wit to wait until it was completely dark, so keen was he to pick up a few pounds and buy himself a drink, and perhaps a piece of skirt—he had attacked an old lady limping home along one of the back alleys of Cumbledon. Watched from behind the curtains of one of the little cottages that lined the alley, he had grabbed the woman's handbag and hit her efficiently with a homemade cosh. But the old lady was fragile, and when she was found two minutes later she was dead. And when this boy was picked up ten minutes later he was scrabbling in her purse, which he threw away under the eyes of the police patrol that took him. Crumpled in his hand was £1.75. When told that the old lady was dead, he said: 'She can't be. I didn't hit her hard.' He was a boy who seemed destined from birth to a lifetime of shorter or longer jail sentences. By bad luck he was likely to start with a stiff one.

McHale settled himself, comfortably yet intimidatingly, on another upright chair on the boy's side of the desk.

'What's your name?'

'Jack Cobbett. I told the other one.'

'It's me you're dealing with now. Where do you live?'

'Furmety Lane.' It was a tatty, slummy district in East Cumbledon that even the coming of university people to the town (which had transformed many undesirable areas into estate agents' dreams) had failed to make habitable except by those who couldn't help it.

'What does your father do?'

'He's with the Council. On the roads.'

'Mother?'

'Yer.'

'Does your mother work?'

'On and off. Cleaning and that. When she can't get anything better. She won't care.'

'So I gather. She's been informed.'

'Coulder told you she wouldn't care. She never has. Ran off with a bloke when I was thirteen.'

'Ah. You hold it against her?'

'Wish she'd never bloody come back.'

'You've got a grudge against your mother?'

'No . . . Just can't stand the sight of her.'

'Interesting. Well, what she actually said when she was told was: "I seen it coming. He can stew in his own juice." '

The boy was silent, his face impassive. 'What am I supposed to do? Cry?'

'I'm interested. Why do you attack women? Are you getting your own back for being deserted?'

'Don't be bloody daft,' muttered Jack Cobbett.

'There must be some reason why you choose women . . .'

'Women are bloody weaker—' burst out Jack. 'Don't be f— daft.'

'Older women too, not younger. There was the one tonight, and then the one in Todmarsh: she was nearly fifty. About your mother's age.'

'What the bleeding hell do you mean? Todmarsh.'

'Nearly fifty. Not unlike your mother too, I'd guess.'

'I never been near Todmarsh.'

'Never been there? Are you really telling me that? Todmarsh on the coast, and Cumbledon being inland?'

'Well, I been there . . . in my time.'

'Of course you have. Silly to tell unnecessary lies. You were there last Thursday, for example.'

'The hell I was.'

'Where were you last Thursday then? Thursday night.'

'Thursday night? How would I know? One night's like any other.'

'Not this night. You'd better think carefully.'

The boy, sweating now, cradled his big head in his hands. The long, thick, strong fingers picked convulsively at his dirty, lifeless hair. McHale looked at him, looked at the hands. Strangler's hands, he thought.

'I was at the flicks with a bird,' said Jack Cobbett at last. 'One I picked up. Casual.'

'What did you see?'

'Don't remember . . . *The Stud*.'

'*The Stud* was on the week before last. You were in Todmarsh Thursday evening, weren't you?'

'Sod off. I told you. I haven't been there for years.'

'You were there last week. And you wanted the odd pound for a drink, didn't you? Just like tonight.'

'I didn't do nothing tonight.'

'You were caught with the money on you so don't try giving me that stuff. You were seen to throw away the dead woman's purse. You had a receipt with her name on when we picked you up.'

The boy was near to blubbering. 'It's a bloody frame-up. I didn't have no receipt.'

'What's more, you were seen from the house when you attacked the poor old creature. By someone who knew you. It's an open-and-shut case. Hardly worth the bother of a trial. They're just getting the details of the charge ready out there.'

Jack Cobbett choked and spluttered. 'It's a frame-up. I never . . .' His big shoulders began to heave with fear and nausea. 'I didn't know . . .'

'You didn't know your own bloody strength, is that it? I'm not so sure about that. You'd enough practice. Did you go for an OAP this time because you wanted an easy victim? You had more of a struggle last time, eh?'

'There wasn't no last time, I tell you.'

'She wasn't so weak, that one, was she? A real tough bird I should think.'

'You're bloody making this up. You'll be saying I did the Great Train Robbery next.'

'No, just another mugging, like this one. You had us fooled for a bit there, Jack. Quite a neat job. How much did you get out of that one?'

'You're talking a load of balls.'

'More than one seventy-five, I bet. And then there was the brooch.'

'What brooch? What are you talking about?'

'The brooch you took off her dress. What did you do with it, eh? Get anybody to take it off you? Did you give it to a bird? Or did you throw it away? Pity if you did that. It was a valuable little piece.'

He looked for signs of disappointment, but saw nothing but bullish vacancy.

'Either way,' he said flatteringly, 'You managed that little job better than the one tonight, didn't you? Nice dark little patch you found. No one to see you. And Mrs Hodsden trotting down the road. Did she remind you of your mum? She's got bright red hair. What colour's your mum's hair?'

'She's a bleeding blonde.'

'Dyed, I suppose. Out of a bottle?'

'What do you think? She's no bleeding Swede.'

'Just like Lill Hodsden. Bit of the tart there, eh? And you'd got your bit of wire there, hadn't you? Nice little instrument, I'd guess . . . with handles all prepared, eh? Just wanted to frighten her, didn't you?'

'I don't know what you're talking about,' said the boy, still half way between a snarl and a whimper.

'But when you got it round her neck you found you wanted to go on, didn't you? You found you liked it, that was it, wasn't it? Enjoyed it. Did you have an erection while you were doing it, eh, Jack?'

'Here—'

'And before you knew where you were she was on the ground dead, wasn't she? What did you do with the wire, Jack?'

Jack was breathing hard, and sweating, and snivelling on and off. 'You're talking in bloody riddles,' he whined.

'Oh, I'm not. You know what I mean, don't you? You took her purse, didn't you? And the brooch. And then you made off. What did you do with the wire? Did you go and throw it in the sea? Or have you still got it at home? Ready for the next time?'

'You go and look. I ain't got nothing there.'

'Because there would have been a next time, wouldn't there? You got such a kick out of that little job. It felt as if it was someone else's neck in that wire, didn't it?'

'Give over—'

'Someone you wanted very much to do in, and didn't dare, eh?' McHale leant his face very close to the boy's crouching figure and his panting, distorted face: 'Why don't you admit it? Come clean. It'll help you in the long run.'

The boy whimpered miserably. 'Oh, all right. I did it. That job tonight. I didn't mean her to snuff it. God's truth.'

'Oh, we all know about that business tonight. No mystery about that. What I'm interested in is the Todmarsh one.'

'There wasn't one. I didn't—'

'Oh yes you did. Last Thursday. What did you think when you saw her, walking down the road? There was you in this dark little recess, and there was this woman, walking down the road. Big, sexy woman she was, wasn't she? Reminded you of your mother . . .'

'What's my bleeding mother got to do with it?'

'Quite a lot, Jack. Quite a lot. I don't suppose you intended much harm when you put the wire round her neck, did you? That's what you can say at the trial, anyway, and we won't go against that, not if you cooperate. We're not against you, Jack. We just want to clear this thing up.'

Jack was whining noisily all the time now. 'You've got it in for me . . .'

'We haven't, Jack. We just want to know how it happened. You tightened the wire, didn't you? You're a strong lad, Jack. Tighter and tighter—'

'No!'

'And she was gasping, and choking, wasn't she?—'

'No! No!'

'Tighter, and tighter. And you could feel her body under you go limp. And still you kept pulling it, tighter and tighter—'

'No! Yes! No! Yes . . . yes . . . yes . . .'

17

HAPPY ENDING

And that was the end of the Hodsden case. As a case. And it had all worked out as McHale had prophesied—and publicly prophesied at that. He drew Inspector Haggart's attention to the fact when he cleared up his things at the Todmarsh Police Station.

'You remember I said as much at the time,' he said, congratulating himself with the air of pinning a medal on to someone else. 'It's often the way: these casual muggings lead to killings, and they're the very devil to clear up. Can't do much more than wait for the bastard to do it again.'

'The boy confessed, didn't he?'

'Oh yes,' said McHale, stacking his papers into a neat pile and sliding them into his brief-case. 'Of course, now he's got himself a lawyer—at your and my expense—and he's taken it all back. Just to make things difficult. But he confessed all right, and signed on the dotted line.'

'Did you trace the money, or the brooch?'

'Not yet. We'll have to, if we're going to make any sort of a case. But luckily that's not vital. We've got a cast-iron case on him with this poor old thing he did in Cumbledon last night. Vicious little bugger. Makes me livid.'

Inspector Haggart, standing there in the evening sunlight, thought for a bit. 'Funny the two different weapons,' he said. 'That garrotte thing, and then the cosh. Suggests two different kinds of crime. Two different personalities.'

'Well, naturally he wouldn't use the wire again, not the next time,' said McHale impatiently. 'He's dim, but he's not defective.'

'Do you see any pattern in these things, then?' asked Haggart, with an appearance of deferring, since this seemed the best strategy with McHale.

'Oh yes, I think so. I thought so the moment I heard from one of the sergeants over there what kind of woman his mother was. Same type as Lill Hodsden, that was clear. Ran off with a truck-driver when the boy was thirteen. Came back, but there it is—the damage was done. These killings are a sort of revenge on his mother. These women are surrogate victims, killed because of his love/hate for his mother. He's revenging himself for his feelings of desertion and neglect.'

McHale was not an unintelligent man. If he had thought a little he might have come up with something better than this Freud-and-pap. But McHale did not cultivate his intelligence. He cultivated his career. And of course he'd seen how this case would end all along.

'Interesting case,' said Inspector Haggart, noncommittally. He was a genuinely intelligent man, though it had never got him very far. He seemed to be the kind of man who always said things his superior officers did not want to hear. Now he said: 'I misunderstood. I thought you said the woman in Cumbledon was a "poor old thing".'

McHale shot him a look. 'Well?'

'Hardly the same type as Lill Hodsden. Or as the mother, by the sound of it.'

McHale drew his already thin lips still more closely around his teeth. 'It was nearly dark. Late evening. That's a minor detail. I tell you, if we can trace the brooch back to him, we've got a case. If we don't find it, we'll come down on him heavy as we know how on the Cumbledon killing. He's in for a long stretch, that thug. As far as we're concerned, the case is closed.'

The case was closed. Everybody satisfied. Happy ending.

Well, McHale was happy anyway. He did not see the look on

Inspector Haggart's face that followed him as he stalked out of the room. It was a look that was to be reproduced quite often in his later career, on the faces of both his superiors and his inferiors in the police force. But McHale did not see it, and felt happy. The case was closed.

He used almost the identical phrase again when talking to Fred Hodsden about the outcome of the investigation, a little later in the day.

'You can rest assured, Mr Hodsden,' he said, speaking earnestly to cover the contempt he felt, standing in the Hodsden living-room (now so bare of ornament) but poised for flight as soon as the decent civilities were over, 'that this young thug is the man who did it. That'll be a weight off your mind, I'm sure. And if we can't bring your wife's murderer home to him, then we'll throw the book at him over the Cumbledon one. It's good to be able to tell you at last that the case is all sewn up.'

Fred breathed a sigh of relief. 'You've done a grand job, Inspector. A right down grand job. The kids and I can rest in peace now.'

And that evening, down at the Yachtsman (for Fred went out much more often of a night, now) Fred said to his mates: 'They're a grand body of men, the police. Brains like razors. You don't want to believe what you read in them Sunday newspapers. You wouldn't hope to meet anyone sharper or straighter than that McHale.'

And everyone round the table nodded, because isn't that what everyone wants to believe?

So the case was closed. Everyone in Todmarsh accepted that, though one or two (such as Miss Gaitskell, who had poured sherry and information into the Chief Inspector, and had her own ideas on the matter) were a mite surprised at the outcome. It was now no longer a matter of uncertainty how to treat the Hodsdens—they fell neatly back into place: they were a brave, bereaved little family, not quite up to par socially. Everyone behaved accordingly.

So everything was quite satisfactory. A happy ending. Well, happyish. Happy endings only occur in books, and then only in books written long ago. But certainly the Hodsden family settled down into a peaceful enough routine. Brian got his scholarship levels, not brilliantly, and got a holiday job in a bookshop over the summer. He and Gordon sometimes went out together in the long warm evenings. They acquired a taste for good food, and sampled the three or four better restaurants in Cumbledon, turn and turn about. They talked about a holiday in Italy next year.

I should feel free, thought Brian often. Eventually I will feel free.

So they were both busy, especially as Gordon was running an intricate love-life at the same time. Brian wondered at the number of the girls he had, and speculated that the murder had rendered him even more attractive. But he never went out with Ann Watson, never. In spite of the bustle of their lives, both the boys were good to Gran next door. Mrs Casey was at the same time vigorous and failing. She gave her opinions as unsparingly as ever, but sometimes now those opinions did not seem to make sense. Her mind seemed more lurid than ever with hell-fire and burning rocks, though she still enjoyed her creature comforts.

At home Gordon was able to rule with an easier rein. Fred was off out most evenings, and that was all right by Gordon. If he would never do them any credit, equally he would never disgrace them. Everyone would have said it was a happy ending for Fred— though Fred himself would have denied it, and said that he missed Lill painfully. Debbie too was quiet enough. The strong-arm tyranny of Gordon's early days in command seemed to have paid off. She rarely disobeyed him, perhaps thinking him, in comparison with Lill, the lesser of two evils.

Debbie then was happy? Perhaps. And broken in? Hmm. Did Debbie Hodsden give you the impression of being easily broken in?

A busy, sunny, active (especially for Gordon) summer shaded gracefully into autumn. Brian started at the University of South Wessex, doing History. The History Department was not a very good one: it was staffed by trendy publicists who spent their time reviewing unread books for *Kaleidoscope,* with a sprinkling of incompetent youngsters engaged because they were cheap. Still,

Brian began to make new friends, to get himself into a circle. Not a fast set, but a quiet, cosy circle. All in all he was not unhappy though he was now and then listless, now and then restless.

So that's how things worked themselves out for the Hodsdens. And things were just as predictable for all the other men and women who crossed Lill Hodsden's path in the last week of her mortal life. Perhaps we could take the sphere of their lives and slice it through at one day, just to see how they are getting on. Let's say, at random, Saturday October 18th.

On Saturday October 18th, nearly six months after Lill's death, most of the people who knew her best were by coincidence, in Cumbledon. There was a disco-dance at the University Union, the biggest event so far in the student term. A group called Scarlett O'Hara was coming over from Bristol. Brian hadn't intended going along, but Gordon had urged him, and it had ended with his taking Gordon along as his guest. Oddly enough, he felt decidedly proud of Gordon. Gordon had force, even a sort of magnetism— which his student friends certainly did not have, though they recognized it in him. He had lived, where they were merely peering cautiously over the tops of their nests. What was more, he knew how to behave with them: if the conversation went above his head, he had the sense not to try and join in it, and was equally impressive silent.

He went down well with the girls, that was for sure. Practically the whole of the student population was there, as well as a sprinkling of staff, and the clothes ranged from sequins to sackcloth just as the behaviour ranged from courtly to rural. As the evening wore on and the boys of Scarlett O'Hara played wilder and wilder (going periodically behind the scenes for something or other) Gordon spread himself around (his big, looming body tastefully, almost conventionally dressed, with a stupendous splash of colour in the tie) first among the three or four rather dim little girls that had come along with Brian and his group, then with some who had caught his eye, then—it seemed—making joyous efforts to dance with the entire female part of the university. He even danced with a Professor of Microbiology, *and* took her off to a dark corner afterwards.

* * *

Back in Todmarsh three of the circle who had known, or known of, Lill Hodsden and perhaps would have liked to murder her were at home. Ann Watson put her daughter to bed, marked some exercise books, made herself cocoa, all in a dream, from which she would not wake for years yet. Drusilla Corby, alone, sat before the television in her living-room having got up as soon as her husband left the house. Made up to the nines, in a sequined evening gown from the late 'fifties, she hugged a whisky bottle to herself. This was the life! She should have done this before! One of these days she might actually go out. Lill Hodsden's death, somehow, seemed to have liberated her.

She took another swig. And though it was only an old movie, and an old Bob Hope movie at that, she sat there on the sofa, giggling helplessly, perfectly happy.

Not half a mile away, at home and in her own bed, Mrs Casey lay—as so often nowadays—not wakeful, but hideously torn between consciousness and sleep, racked with dreams that seemed not so much dreams as visions of hideous prophecy. She went to bed early these days, but her nights were always thus, and her mornings hag-ridden. Once she had been near to asking her doctor for a prescription for sleeping tablets, but she had finally put aside any such display of human weakness. So she tossed, and turned, and moaned, and sometimes there would ring out from the sleeping form some phrase or other, some fragment drawn from her reading. She cried one now:

'And the dogs shall eat Jezebel . . . all but the skull and the feet and the palms of her hands.'

Her forehead wrinkled in puzzlement in her sleep.

In a tiny, nasty cinema in Cumbledown, once a section of a large, nasty cinema, part of a chain, Guy Fawcett went through the usual motions with a seventeen-year-old dolly bird he'd bought for a whisky and ginger ale and the price of admission. He grunted and she giggled and the ten or twelve other people in the cinema shifted uneasily in their seats.

'I think you're wonderful,' the witless creature said breathlessly. 'So *virile*. Will you buy me a vodka and Coke afterwards?'

Guy's life seemed to have reverted to normal. Guy was happy.

About quarter to eleven, still tirelessly dancing, it occurred to Gordon to wonder about Debbie. And being Gordon he had to do something about it. When the music ended for a moment he excused himself and went over to the table where Brian was sitting alone with Eric, one of his new university friends. Gordon said: 'I think I'll ring Mrs Dawson, see Debbie's all right.'

Mrs Dawson was mother of Debbie's friend Karen, with whom she was spending the night.

Brian felt a bit embarrassed at this display of old-time patriarchy on the part of his brother and in front of his friend. 'Oh don't, Gordon. You'll make her ashamed. It'll look as if you're checking up on her.'

'Well, I am. No reason to be ashamed if she's not doing anything.'

And Gordon swung off confidently in the direction of the telephones. Brian turned to Eric in renewed intimacy.

'It's since Mother died,' he said. 'Gordon feels he's responsible for the family. He's a good chap.'

'Great,' agreed Eric, a fair, stocky lad from Torquay. 'Still, you don't want to let him overdo it.'

'Overdo it?'

'This head of the household business. After all, you've got to lead your own life, haven't you?'

'Oh yes, of course,' agreed Brian readily. But a sudden wave of depression came over him. Would he ever lead his own life? *Could* he? After a while Gordon came back, happy again.

'Did you talk to her?'

'No, she was out with the dog for a last walk. But Mrs Dawson said it was all right.'

In a little coppice on the farthest extreme of the University's grounds (sold to the fledgling body in 1960 by a squireling at a sum so exorbitant that he was still busy squandering the money at casinos in the South of France) Debbie Hodsden lay ecstatically happy under a body much larger than her own, enjoying pleasures all the sweeter for having been in abeyance for some months.

'Aren't you afraid of your brother finding out?' the body said.

'He won't,' giggled Debbie. 'I've got Mrs Dawson squared. She thinks he's a tyrant, and she said she'd lie for me. He'll never find out, not Gordon. Give Mum her due: she was a good deal brighter than our Gordon.'

The other body muttered with satisfaction, and pressed himself closer in his pleasure. The leg of his trousers, protruding from the coppice, slid up over his sock. The skin underneath it was smooth, gleaming, and black.

Wilf Hamilton Corby, in a cosy little semi-detached on the outskirts of Cumbledon, was enjoying a companionable glass of something strong with a widow he had met by answering an advertisement. 'Companionship,' it had said, was the end in view. And certainly he seemed to find her soothing. She listened very well indeed, and rarely tried to tell him about herself.

'Of course, I'm the last one to complain,' he was saying, 'but being tied to an invalid wife all these years has been no joke.'

'I'm sure it hasn't,' said his widow.

'Particularly one of her disposition,' said Wilf resentfully.

'Tell me about her,' said the widow.

And Wilf got down to doing just that. Odd that he hadn't noticed the determined set of the widow's jaw, or the glint of contempt for him in her eyes. Had he done so, might he not have thought of frying pans and fires?

Watching Gordon out on the dance floor again, still smart and precise in his dress, yet spreading his vitality around him like shock treatment, Brian found himself unable to throw off that slight cloud of depression. All that energy, that zest, that animal enjoyment of life.

'I wish—' he said.

'What?' said his friend Eric, bending close.

'I wish . . . looking at Gordon, out there, dancing . . . He's so alive, so . . . electric. He's got something I haven't got. I wish . . . I wish I could give pleasure like that . . . or feel it.'

'I expect you will one day,' said Eric, looking at him.

'When I go out there . . . and dance with a girl . . . I can't do it, not with my whole body, not like Gordon. It doesn't do anything to me. Look at him now. That girl, she's quite an ordinary girl, but Gordon's all bright, like she was plugging him into the mains . . . I never feel like that.'

'That's because you're different, made different,' said Eric.

And with a strange, secret shock of pleasure Brian felt Eric's hand, under the table, reach out for his, and take it in his own warm one, comfortingly.

Eve Carstairs, at a business dinner-dance with her husband, danced the last waltz, holding him closely to her. He was pot-bellied, tired, resentful of her energy, but she closed her eyes and transformed him in her mind into something else again—taller, stronger, younger, and of quite another colour.

Fred Hodsden, drinking his last half pint after the darts tournament he had helped to win (his game was much improved these days, by practice) sank into a sea of well-being and became quite loquacious, for Fred. He talked about Lill, what a wonderful mother she'd been, how he'd like to flay alive the young bastard who did it, and what a wonderful little family he'd got, thanks to Lill.

'I'd best be getting back, soon as you're ready,' he said, looking around the team. 'The boys are at a dance, but I reckon they'll be home and wanting their suppers before long.' He sighed contentedly. 'It's a big responsibility, bringing up a family on your own.'

'You should be looking about you now, Fred,' said one of his mates. 'You're the marrying type.'

'Aye,' said Fred. 'I'd thought of that.'

'I need the loo,' said Brian, after he and Eric had sat at the table, silent amid the din, for a very long time. It had seemed there was no group, no amplifiers, no dancers. Only a still world, suddenly remade.

'So do I,' said Eric. 'I'll join you.'

They made for the door, but Brian said nervously: 'I expect Gordon will be back soon.'

'What if he is?' said Eric. Brian, as though treading on uncertain ground, cast his eyes back nervously at the dance floor, at the bright clothes and the drab, at the sweaty faces red from drink, the matt faces glazed from drugs, those vile bodies. He could see no Gordon among them.

'Come on,' said Eric softly, and he pulled himself through the door.

Out in the corridor they avoided by silent consent the big lavatory nearest the Student Union hall, by now probably vile with spew or worse. They walked along corridors, up stairways, into alcoves, until the music receded to nothing and there seemed to be only themselves suspended over nothing, with something drawing them together they hardly understood and could not talk about. Finally they found a little gents in the corner of the Russian department, totally deserted, quiet as the grave. They went in. They had reached the ultimate bourne of so many predecessors of their kind, the little-frequented public loo.

They pissed, looking everywhere but down or at each other, and then they went over to the washbasin. They looked, not at each other but at each other in the mirrors: they looked overbright in the harsh fluorescent glare, tensed up for something to happen. As Brian put his hand down to turn on the tap Eric took it again, openly, tenderly, and drew Brian around to face him. After a moment he drew him closer, closer . . .

The door opened and they shot apart.

'Oh Gordon—'

Gordon walked over to the latrines with a false casualness.

'Oh hello, Brian. Just the chap I wanted to talk to. Been looking all over.' Eric and Brian stood awkward in the over-bright light, unable to do anything but watch. Gordon finished and zipped himself up. 'I said I wanted to talk to my brother,' he repeated.

'Can't you—?'

'GET!'

Eric looked at Brian, and then at Gordon. Then as Gordon took two menacing steps forward he scooted through the door. They heard his footsteps echoing down the corridor. Gordon continued his walk forward, and when he got to the basins, with a sudden lithe movement he caught his brother under the collar and jerked his head back against the mirror.

'You bloody little fool!'

'Gordon—'

'You bloody little fool! You need cooling off! I've a good mind to put your head under this tap.'

'Stop it, Gordon. You're choking me.'

'I would too. Christ, you make me sick. I never thought I'd see my brother playing monkey tricks like that. Handy-pandy under the table with another adolescent queer.'

'It was the first time!'

'And the fucking last!'

'Nobody saw us.'

'I saw you!'

'Nobody would care. What's it to them? People's private lives are their own these days. Nobody thinks about it like that anymore.'

'I THINK ABOUT IT LIKE THAT! Get that message, boy. Do you think I want a pansy for a brother?'

'You're just old-fashioned.'

'Thank Christ I am. Do you think I don't know about your sort? We had them in the army all right, don't you worry. Officers. Offer you a drink all friendly, and the next thing you know they're feeling your crotch. Oh no, little brother. I'm not having anyone in our family joining the fairy-queen set.'

'Give over, Gordon. Let me go. We'll talk about it in the morning.'

But Gordon was not going to be temporized with, and kept his large hand firmly on the neck of Brian's shirt.

'We're talking about it now. Are you getting the message? You'd better be. Because you're going to swear to me that this is the last time you try any of those grubby little tricks.'

'Oh, don't talk rot, Gordon. I'm nineteen. I'm not under your thumb. I'm at university. Soon I'll be out working. I'm not going to swear away my life just because you're so bloody medieval.'

'You're going to do just what I tell you to. I can see I was wrong just to worry about Debbie. All the time there was you, itching to play arse bandits with your little palsy-walsy. Well, get the message, boy: I'm in charge of the Hodsden family now. And if I find you playing these little games again, I'll take you apart, I'll half murder you.'

'Don't be so bloody melodramatic, Gordon.'

'You think it's just wind, do you? Well, it wouldn't be the first time. There was a boy in Northern Ireland. I suspected him of shopping one of my mates to the Provos.' Gordon forced Brian down on to the washbasin and stood over him, twisting his tie, and looking at him intently with a glowering, remembering gaze. 'I got hold of that boy, and I took him, in my army truck, way way out of town and when I'd finished with him his own mother couldn't bear to look at him . . . I worked on him for three hours, slowly . . . He'll never walk again . . . So don't think this is just big talk, baby brother. I'd do it to you if I thought you were disgracing us.'

'You're making this up. You'd've told me . . .'

'There are some things you flabby intellectuals are too soft to hear. You think you know about life, don't you, but you know *nothing*.'

'I know I'm nineteen. I know I can leave home and come into residence here whenever I want. I know you've got no legal hold over me.'

'That's typical. That's your sort of knowledge. Legal knowledge. Book knowledge. Well, this is my gut knowledge: I've got all the hold I need. In fact I've got you by the short hairs.'

'Oh yes? How?'

'I've got the hold that you and me, together, planned the murder of our late departed mum, Lill Hodsden, who was duly murdered on April 24, 19—'

Brian laughed with relief and almost forgot the hard hand at his throat! 'Some hold! Who's going to care about that? That boy in Cumbledon's been tried.'

'Not for Lill's murder. It wouldn't matter even if he had. Cases can be reopened. They'd still be interested if I went along.'

'Went along and what? Said that, lying in our bedroom, we talked about the murder of our mother—? Don't talk rot.'

'Which murder duly took place in the manner we had planned it, strangulation, by a piece of wire, strong, thick wire now lying buried in the War Memorial Gardens—'

'They never found the wire—'

'Where one day next Spring, perhaps, old Fred will turn it over with his rake and throw it on the rubbish heap—'

'Old Fred?'

'—without thinking it's the wire that sent his better half to judgment, because the handles aren't there, the handles were twisted off it, and thrown on the fire of the Rose and Crown, in the Saloon Bar, at ten to ten on the night of the murder, where they burned away to nothing.'

'Gordon! You're lying!' Brian struggled free and looked at his brother. The vital body that had seemed so full of energy on the dance floor now seemed to crackle with violent force as Gordon remembered back to the night in April. When the full realization of what he was saying struck Brian, he keeled over towards the washbasins and retched.

'Oh, you throw up at the thought, don't you? I knew you were too weak to go through with it. Do you think I didn't feel like throwing up? I held it back. All the way back to the pub I held it back. I drank beer with the rest—poured it down while I was churning up inside. It was only after we'd heard, on the way up—'

'Stop it, Gordon, for God's sake! I don't believe you. You're just saying it because that's what you *wanted* to do.'

'Wanted to do and did. I could see you were chickening out. You were never really on in the first place, were you? And as soon as Mum and Debbie had that fight you were going to use it, weren't you, as your little get-out? You're a gutless little weed. So I had to take it all on myself. I just changed the day, changed the venue, then went ahead and did it. I enjoyed it, too.'

'You didn't—'

'I did. I enjoyed feeling her body under me. I enjoyed seeing her looking at me. I put my head out into the light, just for a second so she could see, and know. She knew it was me. She knew I was murdering her. That's what I enjoyed most of all.'

'You're lying, Gordon. Romancing. Just to make yourself feel big.'

Quick as a flash Gordon dived into the inside pocket of his suit and came out with something cradled in the palm of his hand. 'Remember that brooch? The one the Inspector was after, to get a lead on that boy? The one Corby had given her? What do you think this is?'

He opened his palm and shoved his hand under Brian's eyes. Sparkling in the over-bright light was a little silver peacock, with diamonds studding its head and tail—a worthless, expensive trinket, Lill's last love-offering.

'Lovely, isn't it? Real class. It's been hidden at work. If they'd found it they'd have suspected old Corby. I'm going to keep it on me always. To remind me of my finest hour. Tell me I'm alive.'

Brian's eyes, glazed and disbelieving, stared at the jewel, winking hypnotically in the white light. The brooch from Lill's dress, the brooch that had been ripped off the body. Suddenly he felt stunned, crushed: there was no more room for doubt. Again he keeled over, and sobbed and retched into the washbasin till he felt empty of everything except fear.

'So you see,' said Gordon, silky of voice, when at last Brian forced himself upright and cooled his forehead against the icy mirror, 'here we are, both in this together. Just as we planned. You—at the very least—as accessory before the fact. So get this straight: if I go and confess, you're in it with me.'

'You wouldn't confess. Why would you?'

'I don't know,' said Gordon, suddenly thoughtful, almost sad. 'Sometimes I feel like it. Sometimes I feel there . . . there isn't any point to things. Any meaning anymore. Do you know what . . . she . . . what Ann said to me? She said: "When I'm with you, it's as though, somehow, you're not *there*." ' He swallowed, as if he had crunched a nasty pill. 'I know what she meant, now. Mum did that to us. To you too. She sucked us dry, and spat out the pips. These girls I've been fucking all summer. Do you know why there've been so many? Because they're not interested after they've been with me two or three times. I expect they feel the same. That's how she left us, our Lill. Really all I've got is the family . . .'

Brian did not speak, a terrible fear on him.

'You. And Debbie. Even old Fred. It's something. Something I've got to do. My responsibility. And I'm going to make a job of it. We're not going to be the town laughing-stocks, like we were. You're none of you going to disgrace us.'

Brian could stand it no more. 'I've got my life to live, Gordon,' he wailed. 'My life!'

His tone of desperation seemed to wake Gordon out of his depression. He shook off his mood like a dog reaching dry land.

'No, *we*'ve got *our* lives to live. We're all together in this, even more so since she died. I'm never going to get Ann. Perhaps I never expected to. Perhaps what I did it for was so the family would have a future. So I could knock it into shape. And I will too. This mood of mine, it'll pass. Things will get better. All we need is a bit of discipline. You'll be a credit to us. Debbie will come to something. I'll keep you on the right lines.'

'Gordon, I don't want to be kept on your lines. I don't want you to take responsibility for me.'

'You've no choice. That's what I did it for. I've got to make it worthwhile in the long run.'

'Gordon, I didn't want that. I didn't want her dead.'

Gordon squared his shoulders and took his brother by the arm.

'I know. That's why I did it alone. I had to set you free. I did it for you, baby brother. I did it for you.'

Brian looked bleakly ahead, in the bright white light of the washroom, and saw nothing but the shadow of another tyranny looming before him.

DEATH IN A
COLD CLIMATE

CONTENTS

AUTHOR'S NOTE

Setting a book in a real town always involves the danger that the reader will assume that the characters as well as the topography are based on reality. I should like to insist, therefore, with even more force than usual, that though I have remained fairly faithful to the geographical facts in depicting Tromsø, the characters are entirely fictitious: the policemen are not Tromsø students, and above all the Professor of English is not Tromsø's Professor of English.

1

TWILIGHT AT NOON

Seen from the windows of the café, the main street assumed an aspect less than solid, though more than shadow. The light, such as it was, had a temporary, unwilling feeling to it. The sky had earlier been faintly tinged with a pallid blue, but haze and cloud had robbed it by now of any suggestion of daylight. The wooden cathedral looked large, a solid, comfortable mass, but its features and those of the main street of wooden shops were as if under mufflers, to be seen only indistinctly. The people, hurrying over the gritty snow and ice, were interested solely in getting where they were going. The day, such as it was, would last no more than an hour or so, and then everything would be wrapped up in fitting, natural darkness.

It was midday on December 21 in the city of Tromsø, three degrees north of the Arctic Circle.

The boy standing by a table and stripping off his anorak and scarf seemed to be deciding that he'd had enough of the city for the moment. He looked at the faint glow of light outlining the shops and offices, like a faded halo around a grimy saint, and then looked down at his newspaper. Something caught his eye on page one, and he took it with him to the counter. Absently he took a tray from the pile, collected on a plate a ham smørbrød and a cheese roll, and then made himself a sort of cup of tea, with a bag and some near-boiling water.

'To-og-tyve nitti,' said the woman at the cash desk, pressing the keys. The boy looked at her for a moment, before fumbling in the back pocket of his jeans. 'Twenty-two, ninety,' the woman said in careful English. The boy counted out the money slowly, then carried the tray over to his table.

Half an hour later he had digested his paper and his meal and drunk his tea, but he did not seem inclined to go. He fetched another cup of tea and sat over it, looking yet not looking out at the twilit town. There were things going round in his head, but too many things: sometimes he frowned, as if trying to work something out, or trying to dismiss from his mind something he did not want to think about. As his tea got cooler and cooler, he sat there, staring, unseeing.

He was about twenty-two. His hair was fair, but with a rich, golden fairness that was not Norwegian. His face was lean, old for his years, and his eyes—when they were registering anything— looked slightly calculating. His hands were rough as sandpaper, with stubby fingers, and his nails cut close and dirty. He sat in his jeans and his bulky, shapeless sweater, gazing at the ashtray, in which his teabag was mingling to a disgusting mush with the ash and butts.

In fact, he was hardly even thinking. Impressions, memories of the last few days, swam sharply to the front of his mind, then retreated to become part of the great wash of recollection. The woman, blonde, desperate, and the nerve in her cheek that twitched as she asked him round for coffee . . . The American girl, horribly earnest, confiding her emotional problems, as she confided them, he guessed, to friend and total stranger, indiscriminately . . . The cellar pub, with the alcove where everyone spoke English and tried to make in that corner of a foreign field that fuzz of togetherness which is an English country pub . . . The dreadful Professor of whatever it was, with the Dracula teeth and the watchful eyes.

His mind turned to the business in hand, and his eyes contracted from infinity to the here and now. He looked at his watch. Twenty past one. The appointment was for half past two. He had no desire to walk and re-walk the main street of Tromsø until it was time to get a bus or a taxi. But perhaps he could walk to the place. He looked out of the window; it had not started to snow, though it threatened. It would pass the time. And on the way he could think the matter through. He had a feeling he had been too casual—had started something that could get out of hand.

He took out his map and spread it over the table. It was across the bridge, he knew that. A fair distance then, but easy enough to manage if the roads were all right.

'Can I help you? Anywhere you want to go?' asked a voice.

The boy looked up. A middle-aged man with a tray—kindly-faced, probably not trying to pick him up. Still . . . He replied coldly: 'No, I'm just looking.'

The man went on to another table, discomfited.

The boy drew his finger over the bridge. Here things were less built-up, it seemed. His finger followed the main roads on the other side of the bridge until suddenly it lighted on his destination: Isbjørnvei. If he were outside, he thought, he could probably see the house across the water. He judged the distance with expert appraisal. He could walk slowly and still do it easily. He stood up, tallish, slight, but tough-looking, and began swathing himself in his anorak and long woollen scarf—multi-coloured in stripes, the product, perhaps, of some unstoppable girlfriend or mother.

Out in the street, in a world of bright shop windows and street lights surrounded by looming shadows, he set his face towards Storgate, and walked along it for the last time, he hoped, that day. He idled, noting the decorations for Christmas in the shops and the Christmas trees oddly decorated with the Norwegian flag, as if Christ had been born in a stable near Oslo. He bought a hot dog, and stood for some time munching it and staring ahead of him at the shoppers, streaming this way and that. When he had finished eating, he patted his anorak, heard the crinkle of paper from his inside pocket, and went on his way again, reassured.

Now he was nearing the bridge. Underfoot the snow and ice were grimy and gritty, but he wore heavy boots, the soles deeply rutted, and there was no danger of sliding or falling. The footpath over the bridge was very narrow, and the traffic passed unpleasantly close, but he paused when he reached its highest point, the wind biting through his too light trousers, and looked back to the island on which Tromsø is built, and then out to the other islands, mere sleeping monsters in the distance, guarding the deep. The fjord sent back dull twinklings from the dying day and the lights of the city. Impassively he turned on his way.

Once he reached the mainland he lingered around the Arctic Cathedral, two great white triangles, and peered in the windows. The place held no memories for him, and he dawdled on. Up the road, with the traffic grazing his ankles, then to his right and a long, quiet, straight walk to his destination.

It was a quarter past two when he neared the end of Anton Jakobsensvei and began to turn down to Isbjørnvei. There were a couple of people walking and the occasional car, but by now the light was all but gone. The moon had come up, round the mountain behind him. 'Darkness at Noon'—the phrase went round in his head. He stopped and considered. The walk had not sorted out his thoughts and he was aware he needed to decide what to do —not knowing how little use there was in his meditation.

Then, finally, in the gathering dark, he walked down and found Isbjørnvei. The name was dimly lit on the side of a house, and he walked along the road, peering at the numbers. The snow was rather roughly cleared here, and many of the paths to the houses not swept at all. He trudged rather than walked. Finally he came to No. 18, made his way through heavy snow up the path to the door, and rang the bell. He turned on the doorstep while he waited, and looked once more over the fjord to the white and coloured lights of the town.

Nobody had seen him come. Nobody saw him again alive, except for the person whose footsteps in the house he now heard, and whom, turning, he saw as the door opened.

2

DOMESTIC AND FOREIGN

Sidsel Korvald was—all her friends agreed—a model Norwegian wife. Her house was always spotless: the windows, upstairs and down, were cleaned (with some publicity) once a month, and the curtains washed nearly as often; the dishes were never allowed to stand over from one meal to the next, and if the children played in the living-room, their mother made clear to them the difference between a pleasant sort of disorder and a mess. Her husband's meals were invariably ready for the table the moment he came home from work, and were never more than mildly experimental, ringing the changes from sausage, to meat-balls, to cod, and pork chops, invariably served with boiled potatoes. Her mother had impressed on Sidsel that one thing the menfolk could not stand was novelty in their diet. The children were kept quiet while her husband slept off his meal, and coffee was waiting for him when he woke. At weekends she made herself genteelly desirable for bedtime, and was sweetly co-operative on any other day of the week.

Her husband hated her very much indeed.

Affection had declined into boredom almost before the honeymoon was over; pity succeeded boredom, irritation pity, and hatred had come after eight or nine years of marriage. Then Bjørn Korvald knew the time had come to move out.

On that day, December 22, he had been alone in his tiny flat off

Kirkegårdsveien for three months, and the magic of separation had still not worn off. Everything he did seemed to be invested with a new significance. When he came home from work the pleasure of cooking for himself renewed itself every day, and unpacking the things he had bought for the meal gave him a piercing, unnatural delight. Deciding how to cook it was an intellectual treat and an adventure—especially as he avoided sausage, meat-balls, cod and pork chops, from instincts very close to superstition. When he had eaten, he piled up the dishes on the tiny draining-board, and finished off his beer. Sometimes he listened to a record, and as he did so he walked around the flat and looked at everything, sometimes even touching the cheap or second-hand furniture as if it were the concrete evidence of his liberation. Sometimes he laughed out loud for no reason.

Today he did things with the same relish as ever, but he did not laugh. He had decided to take his Christmas presents to his children, and he did not expect the visit to go easily. His wife had greeted his decision to leave her with a stunned bewilderment, like a puppy left for the first time in kennels during the family holiday. Before he left it seemed as if a smouldering anger was succeeding the bewilderment. Since then his contacts with her had been limited to formal greetings when he went to collect the children every Saturday for his ration of their time. All the financial arrangements were done through the bank, with computerized impersonality. He did not know how Sidsel was standing up to the separation, and in his heart of hearts he did not want to know. Sometimes, in the middle of the night, he was terrified at the way he had hardened his heart. But he did not think that she, any more than he, wanted any extended contact, and in fact when he stood on the doorstep, gaudy boxes in hand, and she opened the door to him, her words were:

'Oh. Do you want to come in?'

'Just for a moment,' he said diffidently.

He shook the light dusting of snow off his overcoat, and took off his shoes by the front door. He caught his wife looking at his stockinged feet, and remembered that she always did like guests to bring slippers with them. He weathered the excited rush of his little girls and bore them upstairs to the living-room, his wife following behind.

The house was as it always had been: every little piece of brass was shining, every surface immaculately dusted, the carpet clean, glossy, its pile unnaturally erect. Everything was as usual, but Bjørn Korvald, perhaps oversensitive, thought he detected now in his wife's cleanliness a note of desperation, of fanaticism. Was it boredom, was it a visible piece of bravado, was she defiantly asserting that she was not abandoning her standards, was it done especially in anticipation of his visit, to remind him that she had always made him a very good wife?

He wished he could care. Sidsel had seated herself neatly in the other armchair, and when the little girls had borne off their parcels to their bedroom, to be gazed at and gloated over as part of their pile of bright paper packages, Bjørn took up the last parcel and (feeling the deadly fungus of hypocrisy clutching round his heart) said: 'For you.'

'Oh. Thank you very much,' she said, glancing at it, and putting it neatly on the side table. It was, Bjørn thought, about as much as it deserved.

'Are you managing all right?' he asked.

'Oh yes, perfectly well, thank you,' she said, with an impersonal polite smile, as if he were a welfare visitor.

'Is there anything I can do for you before Christmas?' he asked, battering against her blandness without quite knowing why. 'Anything you want fetched, any wood chopped?'

'No, I don't think so,' she said, as before.

'Of course, I could come round on Christmas Eve . . .' he said, his heart in his mouth in case she accepted.

'No,' she said calmly. 'It would only disturb the children. They're just getting used to the situation. It will be better for you to have them on Boxing Day, as we arranged.'

He said to himself: she hopes I will be lonely. 'Well, if you're sure you can cope—' he said.

'Oh yes, I can manage quite well.' Her blonde, china impassivity never faltered, and her mouth was firmly set in an expression of sweet resignation. Her husband edged himself forward in his chair.

'Have you thought of taking a part-time job?' he asked. He had not intended to ask it—it was one of those things that flash into the mind and are out before they can be considered.

'Certainly not,' said his wife, her tone immediately edgy with opposition. 'I suppose you're thinking of the money. You forget that Karen isn't five yet. I've never had any time for these women who go out and leave their children all day with just anyone. My business is here, making a home for them.' She looked him coldly in the eye. 'Especially now,' she added.

'Of course, if you feel like that about it . . . It wasn't the money—I thought you might find time hanging heavy. Thought you might be better for an outside interest.'

She looked at him with the old, painful bewilderment on her face, genuinely not understanding. 'But I have the home,' she said. Suddenly he saw in her left cheek that involuntary nerve twitching, as it had in the few crises of their marriage. It gave her a cruelly lop-sided look. 'I have friends,' she said; the pitch of her voice suggested carefully controlled hysteria. 'I'm not lonely. I'm as free as you are, remember.'

But Bjørn Korvald knew she was desperately lonely. Had she had a man round, invited him round, scared him off, perhaps, by that strange new desperation? The thought did nothing to him, but he thought it was time to go, before antipathy reverted to pity. Luckily his wife made the move.

'I think you'd better go now,' she said, seeming unhappy that the beautiful china mask had slipped a fraction.

'Yes. It is getting on. Perhaps if I can tiptoe out I needn't disturb the children.' He saw his wife looking down at his stockinged feet, as if he could do nothing else. She was always wonderfully good at making one apologetic. He slipped on his overcoat and shoes, and his wife opened the door for him. Standing there in the doorway, having regained all her blonde impersonality, she had as much individuality for him as an air hostess on a short-hop flight, and he had as much difficulty as any passenger in framing words of good-bye.

'Well—Happy Christmas,' he said.

Sidsel Korvald smiled, a yuletide frosting over the face, and closed the door. As he walked down the path, meticulously cleared of snow, a great wave of relief that the visit was over swept through him. He decided to celebrate by catching the bus into town and going to the Foreigners' Club.

Tromsø, properly considered, is the Norwegian equivalent of an outback town. To the east stretch the great open spaces of Finnmark, and the Russian border—the country of Lapps, mosquitoes, and the hardier breed of tourist. To the north, west and south are fjord and islands and fishing grounds. It is the gateway to the Arctic, but that is not a portal many have cared to go through. Its history is of fishing and whaling and subsistence agriculture, and it is only in the last decades that it has expanded, with pockets of industry, a university, and the threat of oil. Its expansion has made it a city of exiles, vaguely nostalgic for the sun of East Norway, or the rain of Bergen. It has also acquired a rich sprinkling of foreigners.

The Foreigners' Club as such met once a month, for talks and musical evenings and little plays. The lonelier foreigners came there to meet, drink beer and coffee, and talk over with the others the iniquities of the Norwegian immigration laws and all the things one couldn't buy in Tromsø. But the club proper had an illegitimate offspring which met informally most evenings in the Cardinal's Hat, a Dickensian, cellar-like restaurant, where members ate snacks, drank beer and talked English, in a corner which by tradition had come to be reserved for them. Here the foreigners were often joined by Norwegians who liked to practise their English, or who had nostalgic memories from the war. Bjørn Korvald, who worked with a shipping company that ran one of the daily coastal steamers up the west coast of Norway, had plenty to do with tourists in the summer, and liked to stop himself from getting rusty in winter. An occasional visit to the Cardinal's Hat had become an agreeable variation on the pleasures of newly-won solitude.

Tonight the crop of English speakers was not very promising.

Coming with his beer and hamburger over to the dark, wood-walled corner, with cushioned benches round the wall and two or three tables, he found only four people, and these included two young Americans deep in the sort of conversation only young Americans can ever get into.

'I have this problem relating to people,' said the girl—shabbily dressed as if by conviction, with a thin, peaky, worried face and hair all anyhow—desperately earnest and (Bjørn suspected) hideously boring. She paused to throw a 'Hi!' in his direction, as if marking him down for future use, and then went back to her subject, speaking low and devoutly, as if at confession. 'I do think the socialization aspect is vital, don't you, Steve?'

'Right,' said Steve, without conviction. He was a boy in his early twenties, beanpole-thin, and gazing dejectedly down the expanse of dirty sweat-shirt covering his upper half.

'I just flunk out, somehow. I just never make the grade. I mean —well, how do I affect you? What sort of person do I strike you as, frankly, Steve?'

'Sort of average.'

'Yeah, well, you see. It's always like that. I don't reciprocate easily. I have such a restricted social set-up. I try to get in contact with people, and I just bomb . . .'

The possibilities for breast-beating on the topic seemed endless and infinitely dreary, and Bjørn, sinking down on to the bench by the girl, turned to his other neighbours.

Helge Ottesen was a local businessman, with a men's outfitters just off the main street. He was small, plump, balding, genial, hand-rubbing, and moderately trustworthy. His wife Gladys, acquired from Essex during the war, was matronly, jolly, and had a sort of English High-Street smartness about her, which showed she had kept contact with home. Bjørn knew the pair well. Helge had gone into local politics a few years ago, and now—in his fifties —was a leading light of the Tromsø Conservative Party, and constantly active to keep that light shining bright. Gladys revelled in the activity, and strove with all her jovial energy to play the part of Mary Ann to his Disraeli.

'Nice to see you, Bjørn,' said Helge, speaking in English, as was the custom of the place. 'How are you keeping? What have you been doing with yourself?' His bald head glistened reflections from the wall lamp, and his teeth flashed tradesman's sincerity.

'Well, actually, I've just been taking Christmas presents round to the family,' said Bjørn Korvald. Helge Ottesen's face collapsed in several directions. He was a man who liked situations where one could be jolly, optimistic and encouraging, and he shunned death, disease and financial collapse as things unsuited to his personal philosophy of life. Separation was one of those nastily ambiguous things that upset him most: did one commiserate, or did one dig roguishly in the ribs? Anyway, Sidsel Korvald's father was a good customer of his. He tried to put his face into neutral.

'It's awful for the kiddies,' said his wife comfortably. 'But there, it might be worse if you stayed together, that's what I always say. How's the tourist trade?'

Helge Ottesen brightened up immediately. His wife was a jewel like that, and always knew how to steer the conversation round from the emotional uncertainties that he hated to subjects where his own particular brand of bonhomie could operate.

'Yes—how about it?' he said. 'I hear it's likely to be a good year, eh?'

'I expect so,' said Bjørn. 'Bookings are very good. Of course they always are. But the season seems to be lengthening. The boats are filling up from Easter on, and the bookings go on into late September. It makes up for the off-season.'

'Yes, pity about the off-season,' said Helge, consoling himself with a sip of whiskey. 'Nothing much came of the attempt to attract a Christmas trade, did it?'

'You mean "Spend Christmas in the Land of the Midnight Sun"? No. It wasn't really honest, and most people saw through it too easily.'

'Pity, that. I'd have thought Americans might have gone for it.'

'Once perhaps. That sort of trade's no good.'

Helge Ottesen looked uncertain again. 'Anyway, as businessmen, we've got to admit that things aren't all that bad. Lots more trade than there was ten years ago, and if the oil comes, things will get better and better.'

'In one way, perhaps,' said Bjørn dubiously.

Helge Ottesen did not like doubt to be cast on the great god oil, and became almost polemical. 'You mark my words,' he said. 'In spite of what people say, it'll transform the whole of North Norway!'

'That is precisely what people do say,' said Bjørn. 'That's what they're afraid of.'

'That's just the carpers, the professional troublemakers. They said the same about the university, but it's done wonders for this town. The people there have money to spend.' He looked at the scraggy American boy with the dirty sweat-shirt and the jeans genuinely rather than artificially aged. 'Not that they always do spend it,' he added sadly.

The exploration of personality problems at the next table was still in full swing, and involuntarily they paused to listen.

'Some people like they just walk into a room and pow! everyone smiles, they feel better, they really do. When I go in, they just kinda wilt. Know what I mean, Steve?'

'Errgh.'

'Somehow I'm just not self-actualized. I mean, what do people say about me? What kind of social reciprocation do you think I set up?'

'You piss people off,' said Steve. He looked up momentarily from his gloomy contemplation of his beer, as if he half hoped the girl would burst into tears and dash out into the night. But in fact there was an expression on her face of the deepest masochistic satisfaction.

'Exactly,' she said. 'Now I need to analyse those reactions, you see, and . . .'

Helge Ottesen had listened to this conversation as if he could not believe his ears. He shook his head, and looked uncertainly from Bjørn to his wife and back again. 'I don't think I understand young people any more,' he whispered plaintively.

'They're not all like that,' said his wife comfortably, sucking the lemon from her drink. 'You meet lots of nice young people around.'

'That's true,' said her husband, brightening. 'You meet lots at the Club, and we've had some of them home, haven't we, Gladys? That's where the Club is so useful.' Helge Ottesen was a vice-president of the Foreigners' Club, and was used to defending it to his fellow townsmen who didn't particularly like the influx from abroad or want them to feel at home in Tromsø. 'We bring them together, and make sure they're welcome. Then there's this place, too.'

'That's right,' said his wife. 'There was that English boy came in here the other night—two or three nights ago. Quite by accident, and heard us talking English. He seemed a nice type.'

'That's right,' said her husband, subsiding into contentment. 'He was a pleasant chap, fitted in very nicely. I think he enjoyed himself. He didn't say what he was doing here, but at least Tromsø gave him a great welcome.'

He smiled happily into his glass at the thought of Tromsø's great welcome.

3

FIRST LIGHT

On January 20 the sky over Tromsø was clear at midday, and the sun showed gloriously but briefly on the horizon and splashed orange gold over the fjord. All over town little ladies had coffee with each other in celebration, and men in shops and offices who had missed it because they forgot to look up from their desks nevertheless said that they had seen it, and how nice it was to have it back. Life, everybody felt, was returning.

For the men on duty at the Tromsø police station it was a day like any other. The only ones who glimpsed the returning sun were those out in twos patrolling the streets—and that was very few, for the police in Norway prefer that crime should come to them, rather than that they should go out looking for it. Most of the men in the large square building down from the Cathedral laboured over paperwork in quadruplicate, lounged over coffee with their mates, or typed with their two index fingers lengthy and impressionistically-spelt reports. In the office near the main door where the general public was received Sergeant Ekland, square and dark, and Sergeant Hyland, square and dark, stood fingering their square, dark, droopy moustaches, modelled on a television policeman, and thinking what a fine pair of fellows they were.

It was shortly after twelve-fifteen, as the sun disappeared in a final liquid flicker and Tromsø re-entered its familiar twilight

state, that the office door opened and a little old man entered with
an odd walk, half cocky and half defensive—the walk of a man
who is trying to say he has nothing to fear from the police, and is
saying it none too convincingly. He was not particularly clean and
not at all well shaven—the whitish stubble bristling defiantly
round his sunken mouth and his nicotine-stained teeth. He was
half carrying and half dragging a large knapsack attached to a
metal frame—a type of burden much used by Norwegian hikers
and campers, who like to carry their life history round with them.

'I can't stop, I'm busy,' he said, dragging his burden over to the
centre of the office.

'Nobody asked you to stop, grandad,' said Sergeant Ekland,
magnificently bored.

'I've got *middag* to prepare,' went on the old man, as if he
hadn't heard.

'Crowded out with guests, are you, Mr Botilsrud?' asked Sergeant Hyland, sardonically as he thought. Old Botilsrud was pro-
prietor of the *pensjonat* up near the swimming pool, a rather dirty,
musty affair that did well enough in summer when all the other
hotels and boarding-houses were packed out. Botilsrud was suspected (and more) of selling bottles of spirits to his guests at laugh-
ably high prices without the licence that made that sort of robbery
legal, and though the suspicion had never actually led to charges
being brought against him, the two sergeants felt they could dis-
pense with their usual thin veneer of respect.

'I've got guests,' said the old man defiantly. 'Casual workers,'
he went on, his face falling. 'Scum. Anyway, what I've come
about's this knapsack.'

'So we see,' said Sergeant Ekland. 'What's it all about? What's in
it? Empty bottles?'

'There's not much in it,' said Botilsrud, once more cultivating
deafness to insinuation. 'I looked, just to check, but there was
nothing worth—nothing much in it. It was left by this lad who
stayed up there at my place. Just left it behind, he did.'

'When was this, grandad?'

'Matter of a month or so ago. Just before Christmas, it was. I'm not sure of the exact dates, because my books got in a bit of a muddle about then.'

'I'll bet,' said Sergeant Hyland. 'Festive season and all.'

'Anyway,' said Botilsrud, preparing to leave, 'I thought I should bring it in, because he disappeared.'

'Here, hold on, grandad—your guests will have to wait for their princely meal. You can't just dump this here and go off. We have to get something down on paper. Now—what exactly do you mean, disappeared?'

'Well,' said Botilsrud impatiently, 'as far as I recollect, he said he was staying three nights. Then after the second I saw nothing more of him, not sight nor sound. He took the room key, too, and I never had it back.'

'Had he paid?'

'Oh yes,' said the old man, with a look of feeble cunning. 'I made sure he paid in advance. I always do—have to, with some of the types you get coming to this town.'

'OK, then, what was he like?' said Sergeant Ekland, taking a pencil and paper, and only pausing to smooth lovingly his splendid black moustache with the back of his hand, as a prelude to composition.

'Well, sort of ordinary, really. About your height or a bit taller, but not so bulky. Very slender, really, I'd describe him as. Then his hair: well, it was fair—yellow fair, you know what I mean? Not white fair. What was he wearing, now? Oh yes—jeans and a check shirt, same as they all do—they've no imagination, young people today. That's about all, really. Oh yes, and of course he was foreign.'

'Foreign?' Sergeant Ekland perked up. Foreigners were always of some interest in Tromsø, due to its closeness to the Russian border, and the politically sensitive area of Svalbard. And Christmas was not a time one would expect many foreign visitors in North Norway. 'What kind of foreign?' he asked.

'How would I know? English, perhaps, or German.'

'You should have details of his passport.'

'I told you, my records got jumbled,' said the old man. Sergeant

Ekland sighed a great big theatrical sigh. To placate him, Botilsrud said: 'Anyway, he wasn't American.'

'That's very helpful,' chipped in Sergeant Hyland. 'How do you know that?'

'Anyone can tell an American,' said the old man contemptuously. 'You can hear.'

'But he spoke Norwegian?'

'He had a bit. Enough to hire a room. Otherwise,' said the old man grandly, 'I'd have known what nationality he was.'

'Hmm,' said Sergeant Hyland. Coming round to the front of the counter, he humped the knapsack up, and vaguely began to turn over its contents. They were not very interesting. 'Just clothes,' he said. 'Change of shirt, vest and underpants, a pair of boots. Not much.' He peered closely at the shirt. 'No identification marks or name tags. You're not giving us much to go on, grandad. I suppose you nicked all the diamond rings and the stolen Rembrandts, eh?'

'He-he,' said Botilsrud unenthusiastically. 'Look, I've got to get back.'

'O.K., O.K., get back to your beef stroganoff,' said Sergeant Ekland. 'I expect the boy just did a bunk, or got a girl or something. But we can put a bit in the paper, and see if anything turns up.'

And as old Botilsrud edged out, crabwise, to the street, Sergeant Hyland heaved the knapsack into the corner and went back to contemplating his image in the plate glass door, while Sergeant Ekland tucked his tongue between his lips and began composing for the newspapers a three-line paragraph about a missing person.

It had made a break in the monotony of the morning.

Sidsel Korvald had got up heavily, given the children breakfast, got the elder off to school, put several layers of clothing on the younger and sent it out to play in the snow, and then began brewing her second cup of coffee of the morning. She trudged through the dusting of new snow to the letter-box and fetched the morning paper, then she poured the thick black liquid into a large breakfast cup, took three lumps of sugar from the packet in the cupboard, and settled down on the sofa to read the paper.

Or rather, she did not settle down, and did not read. She had not settled down—ever, she felt—since her husband moved out; since the humiliating, inexplicable day when he left her. She had gone about the house doing the usual things, behaving as if nothing had happened. But she knew that everything had happened, nothing was the same. Her body felt stiff, as if poised to receive another blow. It was so unfair, so *wrong*. It was the sort of thing that happened to women who had been bad wives. It had happened to people she knew, and she had often sympathized with the husband. But she had been a good wife, none better. She looked around her house now, and suddenly it wore a completely new air. Suddenly it was a desert of labour-saving appliances—and for what? She did not want to be saved labour. She had all the time in the world. Her very shopping had suffered: she had bought in bulk before the price went *down;* she had fallen for several crazy non-bargains. She told herself that things would get back to normal before long. But she could not imagine what was 'normal' for a single woman with children. She felt reality slipping through her fingers, day by day.

She tried to concentrate on *Nordlys*. Sport she skipped over, the foreign page she did not so much as glance at. She tried to read the leader on North Sea oil, but lost the thread; then she tried to take in all the little items of local interest which were the staple of the newspaper, and which had always roused what interest she could take in things outside herself, her family and her home. The grievances of fishermen, the lack of doctors in North Norway, the doings of the radical students—she read them, and did not read them, her mind elsewhere, anywhere. She registered a heading, 'Missing person', and was about to move on to something else, when her eye caught the description:

Foreign, possibly German or British. Was in the Tromsø area 19th–21st December. Height—about 1m 80. Slender build, fair hair . . .

She paused. The dates had caught her attention, and the nationalities. She uncrossed her legs suddenly, and jolted the coffee table. Coffee spilt from the cup on to the polished wood surface, but she did not, as normally she would, rush for a cloth to mop it up. She got up, tenser than ever, and went towards the window. Outside her youngest was fighting with the boy next door, but she did nothing, merely looked unseeing. But over her face there had spread a vivid crimson blush.

Helge Ottesen was late into the shop that morning. He had to go to a Town Council meeting in the evening, and was expecting a hard day. He prided himself on being able to delegate authority, though he took all the important decisions himself. The shop would run itself, while he enjoyed a late breakfast. He and his wife divided the paper in two, and retreated into companionable silence, he at the same time spreading a piece of bread with marmalade, and stirring the thick coffee which was the first of his daily necessities.

'Helge,' said Gladys Ottesen from the other side of the table. 'Listen to this.' And in her slightly cockney Norwegian she read out the heading 'Missing person', and the description of the boy.

'Could be anybody,' said her husband, hardly looking up from the sports page.

'But don't you remember that boy who came into the Cardinal's Hat, just before Christmas? He joined us in the foreigners' corner, and we had a bit of a yarn—you can't have forgotten.'

'Why should it be him?'

'Well, the description: English—then the height, I'm good at heights—' (Gladys worked now and then in her husband's menswear shop)—'and the fair hair. The date's about right too, because I remember that when we met him I'd just been Christmas shopping, getting in the last-minute things. So it all fits, really. Do you think we should go along to the police?'

Her husband looked at her with those wonderfully frank businessman's eyes of his.

'Why should we get mixed up in it, Gladys? It doesn't do any good, politically or any other way. And after all, we only met him for a couple of hours, if that. What information could we give the police that would be any use?'

His wife sipped her coffee and nodded her head. 'Yes, I suppose you're right. Even if it *was* him, there's nothing much we could tell them, is there?'

Helge Ottesen returned to his newspaper with a grunt of assent. He'd said it before, and he said it now: his wife was an invaluable woman, absolutely invaluable.

Steve Cooling was eating dinner out for a change. The Pepper Pot was the best restaurant in town, and eating there was something of an extravagance, but Steve had had a largish cheque from home that day, and the cheque had coincided with his finishing the penultimate chapter of his thesis. It seemed worth a minor celebration, so he sat eating reindeer, drinking a half-bottle of red wine, and vaguely peering now and then at the local paper.

Steve was from the State of Iowa, and was working for a year in the History Department at Tromsø, completing a Ph.D. on emigration from North Norway to the States. He liked the University of Tromsø. It was small, like the one he had come from, and one could put up with a lot, weather-wise, to be in a place where everyone knew everyone else. Looking around the Pepper Pot he found he knew nearly half the people there: there were students who had just received their loans and were blowing a hundred kroner as a good start to the term; there were people from the University Administration, ordering North Norwegian specialities for a sceptical-looking distinguished guest; and there were members of the academic staff, some single, some presumably escaping for a night from Norwegian Home Cooking (a curse called down upon good food to rob it of all taste and texture), and all of them scanning the menu earnestly, as though it were *Middlemarch*. Among the academics, in fact, was the Professor of English Literature, sitting at the table next to Steve, talking and eating an enormous meal, and not properly separating the two activities. He was watched with a degree of ascetic disgust by a youngish lecturer in French.

Professor Halvard Nicolaisen was thin, gaunt, unattractive: his face was like a face in a spoon, sunken, cratered, an area of dark corners and uninviting crannies. His manner, when he was most natural, was gloomy and intense, which he tried to cover with dreadful jokes, jokes which lasted minutes because he embellished them with Victorian convolutions of plot and syntax. His laugh was high and unamused. When he ate, he showed two brown Dracula fangs on either side of his mouth, for he did not close it properly and breathed fragments of food over his companion. He was now—as he usually was—deep in the minutiae of university politics.

'This matter of starting Finnish,' he was saying, in a lowered voice thick with food and conspiracy. 'I wanted to get your opinion, since you're on University Council.'

'I haven't really—'

'It's a mistake. It'll never catch on. It's the sort of thing the radical students cry up, but none of them will think of taking it.' He waved a meaty fork at his companion and leaned forward, fixing his despondent eyes on him. 'It's not in your interest, either. Too many small languages competing for not enough students.'

'Of course that is one thing I—'

'Right. Now, if we can come to some agreement, work together, make some plan of campaign . . .'

The two of them sank without trace into the mire of university intrigue, and Steve savoured the last scraps of his meal. With one half of his mind he read his paper, while with the other half he planned the broad outlines of his last chapter, with its magisterial summing-up of economic factors and regional trends. It was when he was thinking his way into his final paragraph—misty and grand —that his eye caught the tiny item about the missing person. He read it through, then read it again. It pulled him up with such a start that, without thinking or considering whether it was the right thing to do, he drained his glass, pushed back his chair, and made his way over to the next table.

'Excuse me—' he said.

The two academics surfaced, blinking. The French lecturer looked as grateful as Wimsey being hauled out of a bog. Professor

Nicolaisen, on the other hand, fixed Steve with a cold eye, pursed his thin lips with irritation, and simply said: 'Well?'

Professor Nicolaisen spoke in English, but it was his only concession. Steve could see he had made a mistake. At the Cardinal's Hat Professor Nicolaisen affected good fellowship, attempted a meagre heartiness. It was, clearly, a role which was for there alone, and not part of the serious business of his life.

'I don't want to butt in, Professor,' said Steve, hesitating, 'but I just saw this in the paper.' He was committed now. Professor Nicolaisen, twitching his long thin nose with irritation, accepted the paper, took with great show his glasses from his pocket, polished them, and put them magisterially on. Then he read wearily through the item. When he had finished, showing no vestige of emotion, he folded the paper and handed it back.

'Well?' he said again. The word was not an invitation to explain, but a rebuke. Steve plunged further in.

'You remember that boy who came into the Cardinal's Hat just before Christmas. An English boy—he said he was just in Tromsø for a couple of days.'

'I can't say I do.' The voice was high and precise.

'You were there, I remember. And your wife came in.' Professor Nicolaisen blinked his eyes in extreme irritation, as if Steve had somehow committed a *faux pas.* 'He was a fair-haired boy, in his early twenties, and about that height.'

'Fair-haired young men are not uncommon in this country,' said Professor Nicolaisen with a weary sigh.

'He was foreign,' said Steve, his face flushing slightly. 'How many foreign fair-haired boys of that height do you think were in Tromsø on exactly that date?'

'I wouldn't like to guess. Perhaps you could try the Mathematics Department.' Professor Nicolaisen looked at his guest and attempted one of his counter-tenor laughs. Then he turned his glacial eyes back on Steve. 'Really, I can't see why you should interrupt me with this. I understand young people are very—' intake of breath, indicative of distaste—'mobile these days. It is part, is it not, of their—' another quick intake—'*life-style.* No doubt the young man just—moved on.'

Steve repressed a desire to say: 'In the middle of December?' Instead he just murmured: 'Possibly. If so, he left his luggage behind.'

'Oh, no doubt there was some—*girl* or other,' said Professor Nicolaisen.

'So you don't think I should go to the police?'

'You must do as you think best, of course. I shouldn't think it would be anything to get involved in, not as a *guest* in this country. But you must use your own judgement about that, naturally. As I was saying—'

Professor Nicolaisen turned back to his companion, with a gesture of dismissal.

Steve Cooling went back to his table, dissatisfied, and settled his bill. He had hardly been helped by the conversation. But he got the same sort of answer half an hour later, when he went along to the Cardinal's Hat for his coffee. He was hoping (for once) to meet Nan Bryson, the American girl with the problem of relating, and there she was alone, stewing over a long-drawn-out litre of beer, and scanning the horizon for acquaintances as if they were ships passing her desert island.

'Steve!' she cried in a pitiable wail, as if she had just killed the thing she loved. 'You've been avoiding me, and I know why. I deserve it, I know it. I can't *tell* you how sorry I am I bored the *pants* off you last time you were here. Going on and on about *myself*. Just *stop* me, Steve, when I do that, because I *tell* myself not to, and then I go and do it every *time*. So just *stop* me—'

'Oh, that's all right,' mumbled Steve.

'I'm not going to say one word tonight, Steve, not a word. Now —what about you? How do you tick over? Tell me about yourself, just for a change.'

Steve Cooling tried to begin to tell her that he would find that conversation almost as boring as he had found the last, but he gave up. Nan Bryson was too irredeemably personal to understand what he meant. Instead he pushed the paper in her direction, tapping the paragraph with his finger.

'Hey,' she said when she had read it. 'Isn't that the guy that was in here?'

'Right,' said Steve, relieved at her promptness.

'Just before Christmas, I remember it well. Dates are right, and everything.'

'You and he had something going, didn't you?'

'We *did*.' Her face lit up for a moment, then slipped back to its usual doubtful misery. 'Or I *thought* we did. Actually, to tell it to you straight, we made a date. Right here, we made a date. He was coming round to my flat.'

'And—?'

'Well—' Nan Bryson turned down the corners of her mouth in an expression of despair, half real, half play-acting. 'He broke it, tell you the truth. It cut me up, because I liked him, I really did.'

'He seems to have disappeared about the twenty-first,' said Steve, looking down at the paragraph in *Nordlys*. 'Was that about when you had the date?'

The girl's grubby, thin little face puckered in thought, then she swooped down into a great big untidy shoulder bag by her feet, fished in it for some minutes (dumping some rather embarrassing personal items on the table in the process) and finally surfaced with a pocket diary.

'Still got last year's,' she explained. 'This year hasn't done much for me yet.' She flicked through the pages. 'Hey, yeah. It was the twenty-first he was supposed to come. That evening. Reckon that's why he didn't show up?'

'Could be. Maybe we should go to the police.'

The girl's face fell again.

'Oh hell, Steve, I wouldn't want to do that.'

'Why not? They're asking for information.'

'Well—I'm kinda ashamed.' She pulled herself up. The young will never admit to shame. 'Not ashamed, sort of embarrassed. I made a bit of a set at him—like you saw. I guess you knew what was going on. Then he didn't show up, and I felt kinda cheap.'

'What if he didn't show up because he disappeared?'

'Well, even so, I don't feel that much better about it. I wouldn't want to talk about it. Then there's my job, you see.' She looked meaningfully at Steve. Light dawned. Nan Bryson had a part-time job with the United States Information Office in the town, generally considered a far-flung outpost of the CIA. 'We're supposed to keep a very low profile. There's enough talk about us at the moment—you know how it is.'

'But hell—if you just went along with information—'

'That's getting involved. And if I'm put out on my ear, what then? No job, no work, no work permit. It's back to the States for me. No, Steve, I'd like to help, honestly I would, but just keep my name out of it, can't you?'

And so in the end Steve Cooling, like the rest, did nothing. The paragraph in *Nordlys* caused a little trickle of comment and speculation, especially in the foreign community, but it seeped gradually down into the fjord, and was buffeted by the currents till it finally sank. Quite soon it was replaced by other topics of interest. The year wore on, the weather grew milder, and the sun gained confidence enough to stay in the sky for several hours a day.

4

DEEP FROZEN

In the late afternoon sun, a man and his dog walked up past the Arctic Cathedral towards Anton Jakobsensvei. It was the second week of March. There had been an unexpected early thaw the week before, and the black of the road stood out against the prevailing white—as, too, did the bright daffodil-yellow patches on the snowy verges, part of the great dog postal network. There was hardly a soul about. The Norwegians had mostly had their Sunday constitutional, and had retreated home for their Sunday *middag*. As the man walked along, the extractor fans of various houses flung out to the cold afternoon air odours of meatballs in tomato sauce, fried cod and roast pork in gluttonous profusion.

The man was medium height, slight but running to tummy, with fat red cheeks and a splendid furry hat. He had skis on his shoulder, carried somewhat inexpertly. The dog was brown and nondescript—a sort of basic dog, but perky and interested. They proceeded spasmodically, from daffodil patch to daffodil patch. The sun shone on them, watery but welcome.

They turned into Anton Jakobsensvei—past the supermarket, past the Ebenezer chapel with the long icicles hanging from its guttering, cold as nonconformist charity, past the road up to the cable car. A few stragglers were stepping it out manfully from the bottom station back home to eat. These were not going up the mountain to ski, however: that was for experts. They went on, past the houses for naval officers, and then, just before the turn-off down to Isbjørnvei (where the man had lived for a time, when he came here from the Middle East), up towards the mountain. Here there were open spaces and gentle slopes. Now was the time of little light; now was the time when the younger members of the family finally dragged themselves in for television children's hour; now was the time when the novice skier could get in a little practice on the easier slopes, unembarrassed by kindly adults or frankly contemptuous children.

The brown dog, already excited at the recognition of old haunts, became delirious as they turned off the road into the snow and he was let off his lead. The snow here was not too thick, after a mild winter and the recent thaw. Along the best paths it had been nicely packed down by skiers. The man walked a bit, away from the lights of the road, and turned towards the increasing gloom. The dog went around inconsequently, on and off the ski tracks, sniffing, giving little yelps of recognition, and sometimes bounding off at nothing. Eventually the man unloaded his skis from his shoulder, and began inexpertly the business of getting them on his feet.

It's just a bloody clumsy way of walking, he said to himself.

While he fumbled with the straps his eye caught a moving black shape to his right. There was a man some hundreds of yards away, skiing down the mountain. Damn. He'd expected to be alone. He fussed over the straps once more, determined to take his time. The skier would soon be past him and on to the road, and then he could begin an exploratory practice.

A sharp bark. Another—questioning, uncertain, summoning. Come and tell me what to do about this, you. The man looked up, one ski on, one still half off. The dog was now just a dark shape against the snow. He was barking, whining, approaching, looking round, digging furiously, looking round again, wagging his tail experimentally. The man, his skis now on, stood up and cautiously moved forward. As he did so, the skier from the mountain also neared the dog and swerved to make a classy halt. The dog now was more confident, and had begun tugging at something.

The two men came together, and the owner called 'Jingle',

without much confidence, clearly not expecting to be obeyed. The dog looked at him, then went on tugging, backing away, then going back to tug again. In the gathering gloom the two men went forward, to get a closer look at what he had got hold of.

It was a human ear.

5

MORTUARY MATTERS

No body looks its best in a morgue. There is something abstract, wholesale, impersonal about the setting which robs the corpse of individuality or pathos. It requires an effort of the imagination to summon up the sympathetic responses that would have come unbidden if the body had been seen resting its last rest on a bed or in a coffin.

The body that had been found on the snowy slopes behind Anton Jakobsensvei lay in the long, cold room in the university's Medical Department, which served as the morgue of the Tromsø Police Force. It was naked, as it had been found. No scrap of clothing or possible identifying object had been left on it. Some damage had been done to the right ear, but it was nothing to the damage done to the back of the skull, which had been smashed in by a single blow from a heavy implement. It was the body of a young man, just under six feet in height, fair-haired, slim. In other circumstances one might have felt he was 'carrying back bright to the coiner the mintage of man'. Now he was just a body on a slab in a police morgue.

Standing by the body and looking at it with the police surgeon was Inspector Fagermo of the Tromsø police. He had one of those fair, unlined, ageless Norwegian heads. How old was he? Perhaps somewhere between thirty-five and forty-five. But if he had said twenty-eight or fifty-five one would hardly have been surprised. It was a good face, deceptively sleepy but regular, intelligent, blue-eyed; only the occasional crinkling at the edges of the mouth signified the presence of a sense of humour that was unNorwegian in its irony and blackness.

The mouth crinkled now. 'Would you care to hazard an opinion as to the cause of death?' he asked.

The police surgeon, who liked his humour cosy, folksy and conventional, merely pursed his lips and fixed his eyes on the smash at the back of the skull. Jokes were of his life a thing apart—they were Fagermo's whole existence.

'There's something about that body,' Fagermo went on. 'The shape. Look at those thighs and calves. Thin, aren't they? The chest too, though he looks a healthy young chap. He doesn't look like a skier, does he?'

'Is there any reason why he should be one?'

'People don't usually go skiing naked, agreed—not at this time of year anyway. Still, most of the young people around here do ski . . .'

'Are there any young people missing from around here?'

'There are always missing young people. You find they've gone to sea, or to the university, or something . . . That fair hair, now —it's almost yellow, isn't it? Very unusual. Have you had a look at his teeth?'

'I've had the body no more than a few minutes,' said the surgeon, rather snappily. He went to the head and peered into the jaws. The body was still half frozen, and he was careful not to disturb the gaping wound at the back of the skull. He took a torch and shone it into the slightly open mouth.

'You could be right,' he said at last. 'There's dental work there that doesn't look Norwegian. I'll be able to tell you more when I've had a more thorough look.'

Fagermo went on looking, his lips pursed as he considered the boy's way of death. 'Whoever did it,' he said at last, 'clearly didn't want it identified. He stripped off everything before he took it out and buried it in the snow. Including a ring, you notice. It could have been a fairly messy business.'

'He could have been naked when it was done,' objected the police surgeon.

'It's a possibility, but I fancy not,' said Fagermo. 'Look at the neck. There seems a definite line to the blood from the wound—as if it's been stopped by something: a shirt, a jacket, something fairly tight that's later been removed.'

'If so, it could certainly have been messy,' said the surgeon.

'So the longer the body is unidentified, the better our friend will like it,' mused Fagermo. 'I think this calls for a bit of inspired guesswork . . . Wasn't there a missing persons ad from us in the paper five or six weeks ago? Some tourist or other, I seem to remember—a young lad.'

'Search me,' said the police surgeon. 'I wait for trouble to come to me.'

Fagermo looked at him with his characteristic look of somnolent humour, and went outside to his car. He put it in gear, and did the two-minute drive back to the station. There he went through to the inner office, a large but windowless room, rather smoky and smelly. Here was where most of the policemen in Tromsø spent much of their time during their spells of weekday duty (it was the weekends that were rich in hooliganism and drunkenness, and then they could sometimes be seen on the streets). And here they mostly were now, shirt-sleeved and feet up.

'Who's missing?' said Fagermo casually as he went in, looking around from under his heavy lids.

'That's what we were just discussing,' said one young constable, with some traces of eagerness still in him. 'There was that young Fagertun boy—'

'He ran away because his father knocked him around,' said Fagermo. 'Don't blame him either—we should have locked the man up years ago if we'd had any gumption. We'll find he's got a job on a boat I wouldn't mind betting. In any case he's much too young—only fifteen or sixteen, and I seem to remember the description said dark. What about foreigners?'

'Foreigners?' There was a general vacant look.

'You know, Germans, Englishmen, Americans, people who

come from overseas,' said Fagermo in a deceptively helpful manner.

There was a general pause for heavy cogitation.

'There was that boy,' finally said Sergeant Hyland, stroking his superb dark moustache and looking wise. 'That boy we put out a notice about.'

'Yes?'

'Old Botilsrud at the Alfheim Pensjonat came in about him. Don't think there was anything in it myself. Boy had obviously cut off with some girl. He'd left behind a knapsack, but that didn't mean much, because there was very little in it. We put out the notice just in case, but nobody's come along.'

'But he was foreign?'

'So Botilsrud said. Couldn't put a nationality to it, though. Of course his records were all to pot.'

'Get Botilsrud,' said Fagermo. And as Sergeant Hyland casually finished off his cup of coffee and started looking for his cap he added in a whiplash voice: 'Fast!'

As Sergeant Hyland went through the door in as near as he liked to get to a hurry, Fagermo said: 'I'll be next door. I'd better have a chat to the chappies who found him, though I don't suppose they can know anything of much interest.'

In the waiting-room next door the rather weedy man with the fat red cheeks and incipient tummy was sitting with his brown dog at his feet—the dog crouched forward, his head between his paws, suspicious and melancholy, painfully convinced that kennels were in the offing, or an injection, or some other dimly remembered canine disaster. By them sat the other witness to the discovery of the body—a well-set-up man of thirty-five or so, sporty, and half in, half out of ski gear. They were talking a weird mixture of Norwegian and English, in which they were misunderstanding each other very amiably.

'Ah,' said Fagermo to the Englishman, and sticking to English for safety's sake, 'now it was you who found the body, wasn't it?'

'Well—him really,' said the man, pointing to his dog, who brushed the dusty floor with a tentative wag of the tail. 'He was making such a fuss I had to go over and look. Then Captain—

what was it?—Horten came down, and we both more or less found it together.'

'I see. And you are—?'

'My name's Mackenzie. Dougal Mackenzie. I'm a Reader in Marine Geology at the university.'

'And I'm with the navy, of course,' said Captain Horten.

'Good,' said Fagermo. 'Well, when you'd seen it was a body, what did you do next?'

'Well, we didn't disturb anything—that's very important, isn't it?'

'Oh yes. Though it would be more important if we thought he was lured naked under some pretence or other and killed there on the spot, but that seems unlikely. Still, at that stage you could hardly know.'

'No—we didn't realize.' The Englishman's face had fallen. 'We only waited to see that the ear was joined to a head, if you see what I mean. Not just a stray ear. Anyway, we put Jingle on his lead—I hope he didn't damage the body—and then one of us had to ring for the police. Captain Horten lives in Anton Jakobsensvei, only a minute or so away, so he went and I stayed on guard. Then the police came and took over.'

'I see. Well, I don't suppose there's any more help you can give. Have you seen the body?'

'Yes,' said Horten. 'We both cut off home for a bite to eat, then came along here. They took us over to see—it—soon after they brought it in. I'm afraid I can't help: I've never seen him before.'

'And you?' said Fagermo, turning hopefully to the Englishman.

'No, never,' said Dougal Mackenzie. 'It's not one of my students.'

'You thought it looked like a student, did you?'

'Well, he looked about the right age, that's all. And I'd heard there'd been several student suicides recently, though you seem to hush them up in this country.'

'Hmm,' said Fagermo, not too pleased with the expression 'hush up'. 'Well, if that wound on the back of his head was caused by the lad himself, he'd have made his fortune in a circus. I won't keep you, but we'll certainly be needing you for the inquest. If you'll both just leave your addresses in the outer office . . .'

In the outer office, and making a superb fuss about it, was old Botilsrud from the Alfheim Pensjonat. He had not changed his manner since January (any more than he appeared to have changed his clothes), but behind the shrill cantankerousness and crankiness Fagermo detected a degree of human relish which he recognized as all too familiar: it was the feeling that he might be in on something important, something sensational even, and the anticipation that it would provide material to bore his guests with as he served them meals and illegal drinks in the months to come. Such emotions Fagermo had come to recognize as among the less pleasant side-dishes to murder.

'This'll be a lesson to me,' he was saying in his high, thickly accented voice. 'Never give information to the police. Keep my mouth shut in future. I brought it on myself, and I'll take care not to do it again.'

'I hadn't noticed you made a habit of trotting along to us with gen about the criminal activities of your guests in the past,' said Sergeant Hyland in his world-weary voice. 'Quite the reverse seems to be the usual pattern, I'd say.'

'Dragged away in the middle of serving dessert—what does it look like, eh? Driven away in a police car. Most of my guests will have paid up and left by now.'

'What a refined type of clientele you must have,' said Hyland. 'You must have gone up in the world since I was last there.'

'Nonsense, Botilsrud, they'll be sitting up waiting for details,' said Fagermo, genially breaking in on the double act. 'Your guests aren't fazed by the word "police", if I know them. And I could even slip a word to the reporters about how helpful you've been.'

'Then everyone will assume I've done it, whatever it is,' grumbled Botilsrud.

'Come into my office, will you?' said Fagermo. 'No, wait: better come over to the morgue first.'

Botilsrud did not seem to have caught the last bit, for he muttered all the way out the main entrance: 'If you was to tell the reporters you was deeply indebted to me for promptly coming forward as soon as I noticed the disappearance and the invaluable assistance I've rendered since . . .'

'It doesn't sound like anything anyone would believe,' said Fagermo. 'We usually like to assume the public wants to be helpful.'

'Here, where are you taking me?' said Botilsrud, as he was hustled back into the police car.

'The morgue,' said Fagermo, and kept quiet until they got there, though Botilsrud kept up his aggrieved whine. Fagermo opened the door to the morgue and signalled to the police surgeon to cover the body to the neck.

'Oh,' said Botilsrud, looking through the door; 'it's a body, is it? I thought it might be.' The idea did not seem to upset him.

'Yes, that's what morgues are for,' said Fagermo. 'Nothing too unpleasant, though.'

'Oh, I've seen bodies enough in my time,' said Botilsrud. 'In the war, you know. I was in the Resistance.'

'And never left it since,' said Fagermo. 'Now—do you recognize him?'

Botilsrud came close to the dead face and squinted at it for some seconds. It looked almost as if he were trying to smell his breath. Then he straightened and said: 'Yes, that's him. As far as I can say for sure. My eyesight's not so good as it was.'

'That'll do to be going on with,' said Fagermo. 'We might be able to get some more definite identification later on, when we have put a name to him. Let's go back to my office.'

They drove back again, and trailed up the cold stairs of the police station to Fagermo's office, this time Botilsrud making the journey in silence.

'Now,' said Fagermo as he closed the door, 'let me hear all you know about this boy.'

'I told Ekland and Hyland everything I know,' said Botilsrud. 'Why do you all want to waste my time? You could just go and look up their reports.'

'We didn't know then what we know now,' said Fagermo, mentally adding the rider: and Ekland and Hyland haven't got the brains of a pair of pea-hens. 'I gather since there was no name on the missing persons notice that you don't know his name. How come?'

'It was near Christmas. My lists were in a muddle.'

'Ah yes. Either through drink, or you're doing an income-tax fiddle. Not that that's anything I'm interested in. So this boy didn't book in advance, then?'

'He rang, as far as I remember,' said Botilsrud sullenly. 'I think he rang up from town, then turned up at my place half an hour later.'

'Ah ha—then he probably tried the hotels in town, found them full, and then went to the telephone directory. Might be worth making enquiries to see. Was this in the morning?'

'It's a long time ago now,' grumbled Botilsrud. 'It was a busy period. If you'd asked me in January, now . . .'

'What were you doing when he turned up?'

'Beds,' said Botilsrud, after a pause for concentration. 'Came down from doing the beds, and showed him straight to his room. So it must have been morning.'

'There, you see. If he'd arrived by coastal steamer he wouldn't get here till three. So if he came from any distance, he probably arrived by plane. Now—did you have any sort of conversation with him?'

'No. Why should I? I was busy. Anyway, the lad was foreign.'

'You don't know what nationality?'

'No—I told the sergeant. He spoke Norwegian, but he didn't have enough to have a conversation in.'

'Now that's interesting: just how much Norwegian did he have? Just a couple of phrases, for example—*takk* and *god dag*—a few things like that?'

'More than that,' said Botilsrud. 'He asked on the phone if I had a room—very slow, like, but it was in Norwegian. And he seemed to understand what I said to him—when I told him the cost of the room, and said he had to pay in advance.'

'So perhaps a foreign student of Norwegian, or someone who'd been living here for a bit? Or would you expect a student to have a bit more than he had?'

'How would I know? I don't mix with students. Don't hold with them. Filth.'

Fagermo sighed. He looked down to the little clipping of the missing persons advertisement, which he had had sent up from records and which was now lying on his desk. 'O.K., then, let's just make sure of the details. He came on the nineteenth, is that right? And he paid you for three nights, meaning he intended to leave on the twenty-second, just before Christmas. But in fact he only slept in his room two nights.'

'That's right. Well—only one and a half, really. I heard him come in on the second night. I give them keys to the outside door, save me getting up. He didn't come in till three or half past.'

'How do you know? Were you still up?'

'Well, as it happened, I was. Some of the boys were making a night of it.'

'And you were making a packet out of them I suppose? O.K., O.K., ignore that. I don't care a damn what goes on at Christmas at the Alfheim Pensjonat—you can stage the Second Coming for all I care. But this night—the night of the twentieth it must have been—you were sober enough to remember the time he came in, were you?'

' 'Course I was. Doesn't do to get drunk with that type. I heard the front door open—we were in the kitchen to be more private, like—I opened the door just a crack, just to see who it was, and there he was, creeping in.'

'I presume you'd gone all quiet in case it was the police, eh, so he was afraid of waking anybody. Did you invite him in?'

'Not on your life.'

'Well, that's all very clear, very helpful. Now, what about the next day?'

'He got up late, as you'd expect. He was still in bed when I went up to make it, and I hadn't been early up. He must have gone out about half past eleven.'

'And that was the last time you saw him?'

'That's right.'

'Nothing to make you suspect he'd gone for good?'

'Nothing. Didn't take anything with him. Left his knapsack behind and just went off.'

'Only he probably *didn't*,' said Fagermo. 'I think we can take it that he was killed that day—the twenty-first.'

'Poor young bugger. Just before Christmas too.'

'Yes, well, let's hope he wasn't a practising Christian, shall we? Now, as far as you were concerned, that was it, was it? You talked to him on the phone, and when he arrived, and other than that you never exchanged a word?'

'That's right.'

'And on those two occasions the talk was only about practicalities—the room, the price, and so on?'

'That's right.'

'So he didn't eat with you?'

'No, no: he just had the single room. By the night.'

'And when he left, he left behind just what you brought in in the knapsack—nothing more?'

'What are you suggesting? There was just what there was in it when I brought it in.'

'Did the boy smoke?'

'Oh yes, he smoked.'

'Ah—you remember that. How?'

'He left one behind in a packet.'

'So he *did* leave something else behind?'

'Well, you couldn't count that, could you? I mean, not just a measly fag. And of course, I smoked it, so I couldn't bring it in, could I? You're not going to charge me for stealing one butt now, are you?'

'Do you remember the brand?'

'It was untipped, I remember that. Because I prefer the filters myself these days. One of those foreign brands.'

'Pall Mall?'

'No—one of those tight-packed kind. Don't see so many of them here these days, but there were lots who used to smoke them after the war.'

'Senior Service? Player's?'

'That's it. Player's. It was a good smoke.'

'I'm glad you enjoyed it. So the balance of probability is, he was British. Or perhaps from one of the colonies or whatever they call themselves these days?'

'Search me. Your job to find out things like that.'

'Quite right. And I'm most grateful to you for being so co-operative and forthcoming, Herr Botilsrud.'

Botilsrud looked at Fagermo closely, and saw only the bland, fair blankness which served him so well as a shield of his thoughts.

'Oh well,' said Botilsrud, cracking a smile across his own grimy face: 'Don't mention it. Any time. Here—tell your boys to lay off me for a bit, then, will you?'

And he shambled out.

6

RELUCTANT WITNESSES

The morning began for Bjørn Korvald with five minutes of luxurious drowsing in his small, hard bed in the boxlike bedroom of his tiny flat. Reluctantly he heaved himself on to the cold vinyl and pattered into the kitchen to put on the coffee-pot. Then he blundered into the living-room and switched on the radio. The Norwegian Broadcasting Company was providing its usual morning blend of weather forecasts, news headlines, accordion music and religious indoctrination. Bjørn sliced bread, and fetched cheese and sardines from the fridge. Then he threw on a few clothes and slid down to the front gate to fetch *Nordlys* from the letter-box. He spread it on the table and began to read: the state of the fishing industry; oil exploration north of the sixty-second parallel; letters from crazy teetotalists; letters from dogmatic radicals; foreign news two days old. He browsed contentedly through the usual mixture, ate his sandwiches and then poured himself a second cup of coffee.

There were few items in the paper that could strictly be called news, and these were mostly of the cyclical, almost ritual kind which punctuated the passing year in Tromsø: someone had thrown himself off the bridge; there had been drunken disturbances on Saturday night—windows had been broken in the centre of town and charges had been brought; the local theatre company was threatening to wind itself up. But there was one item, huddled down on the lower corner of the third page, that was something out of the ordinary. It had clearly been written in a hurry as the paper went to press: a body had been found buried in the snow out in Hungeren . . . murder was suspected . . . a man in his early twenties . . . fairhaired, 1.80 metres high. There were several misprints in the report, but the gist was clear.

As Bjørn walked down the street to his office in Grønnegate, sliding expertly over the icy patches as if his shoes were skis, his mind was active. Of course it was none of his business. And the body could be anybody's—though it was fairly clear from the report that the police did not know the identity. He'd heard of Steve Cooling's conjectures when that boy had been reported missing some weeks ago. He knew Steve hadn't gone to the police then. So far as he knew nobody else had either. Would anyone go along now?

Of course the police would probably make the connection between the two—but would they be able to find out who had spoken to him while he was in Tromsø? Not unless one of those who met him in the Cardinal's Hat went along to them. And since they seemed so disinclined, it might be worth while doing it for them.

When he arrived at his office he settled the morning paper down on his desk, open at page three, and pondered for a few minutes. Then he took up the phone and rang the police station. Jøstein Fagermo was one of his friends from schooldays—someone he met now and again around town, when they said 'long time no see' and how they ought to get together some time, but never got around to it, not from lack of liking but from laziness. On an inspiration Bjørn asked the switchboard operator for him.

'Hello, Bjørn, what can I do for you?'

'You're busy I can hear.'

'One hell of a case just landed in my lap.'

'Is it the body they found out in Hungeren?'

'Yes, it is. Know anything about it?'

'Well, no, only indirectly, but that's what I've rung about. Tell me, is it the same boy you advertised for some weeks ago? Fairhaired foreigner in his twenties, who disappeared round about Christmas?'

'Yes, it is. Or almost definitely it is. What do you know about him?'

'Not much. I never met him. But I did hear one or two things after the advertisement came out.'

'What sort of things?'

'Well, there's this American student called Cooling. He read the ad, and of course he couldn't be definite but it reminded him of a boy who'd come into the Cardinal's Hat just before Christmas and spent the evening there. I don't know if you know, but there's a table there where the foreigners collect and talk English—and a lot of Norwegians join them. I do myself sometimes. That's how I came to talk to this American boy. He'd been asking around the people who had spoken to this boy the night he came in, the ones who'd been sitting at the foreigners' table—asking whether they thought it could be the same boy, and whether he ought to go to the police.'

'And?'

'They all said no.'

'God damn people!' exploded Fagermo. 'What makes them treat us like lepers? Do we have some kind of collective bad breath, Bjørn? They run to us soon enough when the least little thing happens, wanting help and protection, but as soon as we ask for a little co-operation—'

'Keep your hair on, Jøstein, this isn't a press-conference. These were mostly foreigners, remember. Things haven't been so pleasant for them since the Immigration Ban. Several have been thrown out of the country.'

'Only if they were working without a permit . . . Well, let it pass for the moment. Did this American student know the boy's name?'

'No, I'm pretty sure he didn't.'

'Damn. Yanks are usually so good about names. They seem to have some sort of mental card-index for them. Did you hear who else was in the Cardinal's Hat that night?'

'Well, I know he went over and asked a couple of university people at the Pepper Pot—that was where he was eating when he read the ad. I don't know who they were, but he said they had both been at the foreigners' table when the boy came in. Then he mentioned a rather pathetic American girl—I think she works at the US Information Office. Quite likely she got the boy's name. I think there were some others, but you could ask him. Oh yes—he mentioned Ottesen the outfitter—you know, the chap on the Council.'

'What would he be there for?'

'He has an English wife. Anyway, a lot of Norwegians do join the table. I do myself.'

'Why?'

'Practise my English. And it's one of the few places you can go where people don't get into long arguments about the Norwegian language.'

'Point taken. You must invite me along.'

'Any time. But you must have better ways of making contact with these people. Sounds to me as if they may need a spot of intimidation.'

'You know we don't go in for that sort of thing, Bjørn. You've been listening to those people in the Sociology Department.'

'Anyway, I thought I'd let you know. It may save you a bit of time.'

'It will. I'm tied up with the medics most of the morning, and the scientific boys, and then I'm going to get on to Interpol and Scotland Yard. But when I'm through I'll have to follow up those names . . . Though, actually, I'm quite glad I can't do it right away.'

'Why?'

'Last time it was just a missing person. This time it's murder, and people will notice it and talk about it. It will be interesting to see how many of the people who met him contact *me* first . . . Bjørn?'

'Yes?'

'Could you go along to the Cardinal's Hat tonight?'

In the event, the only one of all those whom the dead man had met at the Cardinal's Hat to come to the police station of his own accord was Steve Cooling. Shambling into the outer office, his

bean-stalk body clad in dirty jeans and tee-shirt, an anorak, and a
long woollen scarf, he looked sheepish and uncertain. Hyland and
Ekland, officiating in the outer office, when they heard what he
had come about took him down for a quick visit to the morgue
(where Steve only nodded his head and swallowed ominously),
and then passed him through to Fagermo. Steve sat down on the
edge of a wooden chair on the other side of Fagermo's desk, looking intensely uncomfortable.

'I guess I should've come earlier,' he drawled.

'I *know* you should,' said Fagermo, without overdoing the heavy
hand. 'You knew the ad was about the boy you'd met, you went
around saying someone ought to go to the police, and in the end
you never came.'

'Hell,' said Steve. 'How d'you know that?'

'Why didn't you come?'

'You know how it is . . . Everyone said they didn't want to get
mixed up in it . . . In the end, I got scared, and sort of wondered
whether I did.'

'You're not working here illegally?'

'Hell no. I'm not working at all. I'm writing a thesis. Would it
have made any difference if I *had* come?'

'Probably not,' admitted Fagermo. 'I suppose we'd just have
asked a few people who were there that night about him, then let
it go. There was no body at that stage. We'd just have assumed
he'd taken off somewhere, or gone home.'

'Yeah, well, that's what everybody said.'

'Everybody?'

'Well—people I talked to. The foreigners, and the Norwegians
who come to the Foreigners' Club.'

'Is that a close little group?'

'Not specially. 'Course some of them stick together thick as flies
on a bull's tail. But mostly we just meet when we meet.'

'Can you tell me who was there—at the Cardinal's Hat, I mean
—on the night the boy came in?'

'I can, I reckon. Because I've been thinking it over, and talking
with the others like I said. Right, here's the list, and this is just for

the time I was there: the one he was talking to most was Nan
Bryson—'

'Who's she? What does she do?'

'Nan—hell—she's American, she does odd things. She's typist
at the US Information Office part of the time, then she does the
odd private typing jobs and a bit of translation. She's not too hot at
the translation. Her Norwegian's all right, but they complain
about her English spelling and punctuation. She's kind of pathetic. She just about makes out, and that's all.'

'O.K., who else?'

'There were a couple of university guys. I know one of them's
called Nicolaisen, but I don't know about the other. I think they're
in languages. Pretty cold pair—look through you, know what I
mean? One of them may come in when he reads the papers today.'

'They may. No sign of it so far.'

'They're kind of respectable, that's what I mean. Then there's
this chap has a business in town, always smiling and rubbing his
hands. Ottesen his name is. Some kind of men's shop—men's
clothes. Has a plump English wife—quite friendly.'

'Yes, I know him.'

'Oh yeah—he's on the Council or something, isn't he? I suppose you would.'

'Anyone else?'

'Well, I think the Mormons dropped in briefly.'

'The Mormons?'

'Yeah, well, they didn't stay or sit down, and of course it's not
their scene really, not being able to drink, and all, not even coffee.
They were looking for someone, and they just stopped at our table
and talked for a bit, just to be friendly. They don't give us the
religion spiel—I think they're just lonely.'

'Too much competition in the way-out religions field up here,
perhaps,' commented Fagermo.

'Right. Screwballs all over the place. Well, I think that's all,
while I was there.'

'So the boy was still there when you left. Do you know whether
he stayed long?'

'I guess so. Someone said he was still there pretty late on.'

'Now—what did you talk about? Did he say who he was?'

'No, I didn't hear him give a name, or any personal stuff. He just heard us talking English and came and joined us, but he didn't seem to know anyone there.'

'Hmmm. So he didn't even say where he'd come from, or why he was there?'

Steve creased his forehead. 'I've been trying to remember that. I know Trondheim was mentioned. And Bodø came up, and he said, "We've put in there." Or it might have been "We put in there"—like they'd called in on the way up on the coastal steamer.'

'Could be. But I rather think he came by plane. Would you say the boy had probably been working in Trondheim?'

'Hell,' said Steve, 'I just can't remember. I don't think he actually said that.'

'You think he was actually *working* in Norway, rather than just here on a visit, though?'

'Yeah, I guess so. We went up to the serving counter together one time, and the way he ordered and had his money ready—yeah, I guess he knew what he was doing.'

'Well, I suppose the Trondheim Aliens Office is a line of enquiry . . . Well, if you didn't talk about him, what did you talk about while he was there?'

'That's what I can't remember. I mean, we were talking when he arrived—you know, English Christmases, American Christmases, Norwegian Christmases—and he was mostly listening for a bit. People asked him how long he was in town, whether he liked it, where he was staying, but he was pretty quiet. You know how it is, when the others all know each other and you don't know anyone. Anyway, after a bit we sort of got into groups and then I didn't notice him any more.'

'And what group was he in?'

'Well, he was talking to Nan Bryson mostly.'

'You didn't hear what about?'

'There is only one subject with her—herself.'

'I can't wait to meet her. So you don't think he would have done much talking?'

'Just sat there paralysed like the rest of us, I guess.'

'Well, I suppose I'd best talk to her next, if I can get a word in edgeways.'

'I'll give you a tip: she had a date with him a night or two later, only he didn't turn up.'

'I think I can guess why,' said Fagermo.

The speed with which Nan Bryson appeared at the police station after he had rung her at the US Information Office gave Fagermo delusions of grandeur: he felt like a Senate Investigating Committee putting salt on the tail of the CIA. Did she feel guilty about not having come voluntarily, or was she booted down at high speed by her superior, who wanted the Office to remain as co-operative and inconspicuous as possible?

Fagermo felt less good twenty minutes later when, with less than no prompting towards autobiography, Nan Bryson had only come to the point in her life when she experienced feelings of rejection at play group. Fagermo felt that the case would be stale long before she had got through the more vividly remembered trials of her adolescence.

'That's fascinating,' he said, with his warmest smile. 'But I wonder if you could give me a bit more about what *he* said to you?'

'I was just trying to give you the atmosphere,' said Nan Bryson plaintively, the great ghostly brown eyes looking up at him like a spurned spaniel's. 'I thought it would be helpful—like how we came to be talking together, and the sort of thing we had going. But I guess you think it's just me droning on as usual. Stop me if I do it again.'

'Well, now—while you were telling him . . . all this, what was he saying?'

'I guess he was just saying "Yes?" and "Really?" and that sort of thing. You know how the English can say "Really?"—all cold and snooty.'

'You're quite sure he was English.'

'Oh yeah. He had that sort of glaze, like they have.'

'What exactly do you mean?'

'Well, I don't mean he was really snooty, not like upper-crust snooty. He was friendly enough on the surface. But he was a pretty cold guy. He didn't give any.'

'I see. Then what happened when you . . . exhausted that topic?'

'Well, I guess I said "Now tell me about yourself". I usually do —like I feel guilty. But by then they've had enough.'

'Was that what happened that night?'

Nan Bryson tried to remember. Clearly she had not thought over the encounter as Steve Cooling had—having in all probability had fresh fields and pastures new to occupy her mind. Finally she said: 'I think it was. By that stage it was getting fairly late, and things sort of tailed off.'

'Had he told you his name, by the way?'

'I think so . . . Hold it . . . What was it? Brown, that's it.'

Fagermo had seized his pencil eagerly, and now made a note in his book. 'And his Christian name?'

'Er—let me see. Charles . . . That's right, Charles.'

Fagermo put down his pen, and Nan Bryson fixed her great eyes upon him like a puppy who has tried to lick its master and been spurned. 'Is anything wrong?'

'The boy said Brown because if you say Smith people are immediately suspicious, and Brown and Jones are the next most common after that. Once he'd committed himself to Brown, he inevitably became Charlie Brown, but he disguised it a bit. If you'd woken up to it, he'd have pretended it was a joke.'

'Hey, that's real neat,' said Nan Bryson. 'But I thought I was telling you something really useful.'

'You were in a way. You told me that the boy wanted to hide his real name.'

'He *could* really have been Charlie Brown,' said Nan Bryson, as if unwilling to give up the idea of perfect honesty between them.

'And I could be Queen of Sweden,' said Fagermo. 'The boy wanted to keep his identity quiet—which suggests he was here for something crooked, or at any rate secret. He didn't give any indication?'

'No, none. He wasn't stupid.'

'I just thought,' said Fagermo carefully, 'that it might have had something to do with this US Information place you work at.'

Nan looked horrified. 'No—I'm *sure* it didn't. I mean I *told* him I worked there, and he didn't register at all. Gosh, you won't be pursuing that line, will you? I mean, I could get into trouble, and it's the only regular job I have. I mean they like to keep such a low profile, like practically *invisible,* you know . . . ?'

'I'll only pursue it if it seems likely to lead anywhere. I just thought you had contacts with some pretty odd characters, up and down the country, one way and another . . .'

'Oh, that's just what people *say,*' said Nan pleadingly.

Everyone knows it's a spy-ring, Fagermo felt like saying; the least secret one in the world. But he held his peace. There was no point in getting at an underdog on a matter like that. He said: 'Was the boy still there when you left the Cardinal's Hat?'

'Yes, he was. I've looked in my diary. I went to the ten o'clock movies with a girl-friend. I remember he said he'd have another small one—so he was still around.'

'And the others were still there—the academics, the Ottesens, the Mormons?'

'Not the Mormons. They only dropped by for five minutes—I hardly noticed them, because I was talking. And Steve had gone. But the others were still there, I guess.'

'And you made a date with him, didn't you?'

Nan Bryson's face fell. 'Who told you that? Hell—it must have been Steve. Will I bitch into him about that.'

'We want to know *everything,* Miss Bryson.' What did they think this was? A spooky children's party game?

'Yeah,' conceded Nan, unconvinced, 'but it didn't come to anything, so it's kinda embarrassing.'

'What sort of date was this that you had? Was he coming to your flat?'

'Room really. Yes, he was. He was coming for coffee, we said, the evening of the twenty-first, about eight. That's why I feel sorta cheap. And then, when he didn't turn up, that made it worse. It's humiliating.'

'I doubt whether he could turn up, you know,' said Fagermo. 'I should think he was under two feet of snow.'

'Yeah,' said Nan Bryson. 'That's the best excuse anyone's ever had for standing me up.'

7

HUSBAND AND WIFE

The rest of that day was a whirl of activity for Fagermo. Activity for him was not in itself unusual—though for many of his fellows in the Tromsø force it was—but the kind of activity was right out of the ordinary. Murder and manslaughter were certainly not unknown in the town, but they usually took very different forms from this: teen-agers now and then went too far in their weekend jollifications and did each other in in a playful manner; murderous lunatics were given temporary passes to the outside world from the local mental hospital and had a glorious time carving their families up, after which they were taken back, and the psychiatrists rubbed their hands together and said, 'We seem to have been a little premature,' smiling sad, gentle smiles. But murders mysterious, murders involving unknown assailants—more, unknown victims—these were very much outside the general run. Even Fagermo was not entirely sure how to proceed.

One of the things he did was to get an artist's impression of the dead boy's face, and get it sent hot foot to the local newspapers. The next thing he did was to send a detailed description to Interpol. Then he got on the phone to the Trondheim police station and dictated to them a series of detailed questions about aliens—aliens with police records, and above all aliens who had gone missing. An hour later they rang him back with a negative report.

'There's nobody missing that would fit the bill. Nobody that we *know* is missing, that is. All we have on our files are a middle-aged Italian musician and a pregnant German waitress. Both of them presumably have just gone home. Or possibly gone off together.'

'I see.'

'The point is, if his work permit wasn't up for renewal between Christmas and now, we wouldn't necessarily know he was missing. And even if he is on our books, he could easily have wound things up here, settled up with his landlord for his flat or whatever, and simply moved elsewhere.'

'He's supposed to notify change of address.'

'Yes, but the bastards seldom do—you know that.'

'The point is, this boy didn't just move: he got killed. I'd have expected some landlord or girl-friend to have been on to you with questions.'

'Well, nobody's come in here. Perhaps he wasn't intending to come back here after Tromsø anyway. What do you want us to do now? I suppose we could go through our records, start picking out likely names and checking up on them.'

'Yes—that's what I'd like.'

'It'll take time, as you know. And of course they'll all scream "victimization"!'

'You could confine yourself to men from the English-speaking countries, and I think you can cut out the States and Canada. They are usually recognizable when they try to speak Norwegian, and two of the people who spoke to him are quite positive that he wasn't American. Check on anyone between, say, eighteen and late twenties. Those are the outside limits. I'd have said early twenties myself.'

'That narrows it a bit. But we've got hundreds of the buggers here, remember.'

'I know. But make it top priority, will you?'

'Sure, sure,' said the voice at the other end, in an intonation Norwegians take on when wishing to convey that they wouldn't be hurried by the last trump itself.

This casualness on the part of the Trondheim police, this re- fusal to be unduly put out by other people's problems, was all the more aggravating the more Fagermo thought about the case, since he did not see how he could make a real start on essentials or make any significant progress before he had got for his corpse a name, a history, a personality. Here the boy was, murdered in a town in which he had just arrived—murdered, no doubt, by someone he met here, either by arrangement or by accident. But surely the *reason* for the killing must lie behind, lie elsewhere, in the boy's past. This was no casual knock on the head from a drunken teenager. The concealment of the body surely proved that. The investigation therefore had to be two-pronged: establishing precisely what the boy did during his two days in Tromsø; establishing his past and his personality, with a view to finding connecting links with Tromsø. Until he could get some lead on the second strand of the investigation—and surely the vital information must lie in Trondheim, or Britain, or at any rate elsewhere—then he would merely be marking time.

He looked down at the list of names of the people the boy had met at the Cardinal's Hat. The Ottesens would have to be approached cautiously: the kid-glove, would-you-be-so-gracious-as-to-spare-us-a-minute-of-your-valuable-time approach, as befitted a local Conservative councillor and a possible future Mayor. The Professor could be approached a little more freely, a man of title without power. He took from his bookshelf the University Catalogue and looked under Nicolaisen. There were three, under the various possible spellings, but two of them were women. The other was Professor of English Literature, and his address was in Isbjørnvei. Not more than two or three hundred yards from where the body was found. Interesting. Fagermo looked at his watch. Five-fifteen. Not the ideal time for a visit in Norway, but it looked as if today the gentleman was going to have his after-dinner nap interrupted.

As he was driven over the bridge in the direction of Hungeren where Professor Nicolaisen lived (and where the boy had found his long home) Fagermo noted walking down towards the bridge the two local Mormons, instantly recognizable figures. Always in twos, like Norwegian policemen, they wore dark grey suits in all weathers, with white shirts and neckties, and generally were impeccably turned out, as if their religion were an off-shoot of Wall

Street, or at the lowest Savile Row. Fagermo looked curiously at the current representatives: both were healthy, prepossessing specimens as they all tended to be (what did they do with the unhealthy ones? Expose them on the Salt Lake?). These were clearly walking advertisements for their non-alcoholic and decaffeinated life-style. One was thick, chunky and serious, rather like a mortuary attendant in his dark suit and overcoat; the other was slim and fair, more carefree-looking, and with a tiny note of the careless in his dress: his tie was less than impeccably straight. He was looking around him with genial interest, while the other was looking directly ahead, his eyes on salvation, or the main chance, or something.

They can keep, thought Fagermo to himself. The Mormons are always with us. They can only have seen the chap for five minutes or so. Anyway it sounds as though he was talking to (or suffering conversation from) Nan Bryson at the time they came in.

Isbjørnvei was a new area of Tromsø, part of the opening-out that had taken place over the last ten years or so, and changed Tromsø from a large frontier outpost to a medium-sized country town. Little blocks of terraced houses had been built by various local interests around a small ring road, which thus divided itself into thirds: one third for navy personnel, one third for the university and one third for employees of the local council. These three groups existed apart, occasionally holding out the hand of sceptical friendship—rather like the Western and Eastern power blocs, and the Third World.

When Fagermo rang the door-bell at number twelve there was a longish pause. However, he was conscious of the pattering of socked feet upstairs, and sensed a face at the kitchen window looking down at the police car parked by the side of the road. Eventually the front door was opened by a long, gaunt, unattractive man with brown teeth and a manner which uneasily combined arrogance and uncertainty. The uncertainty was in this case probably aggravated by the nature of the visit: the man's expression, Fagermo felt, would have been positively hostile, if only he dared.

'Well?' he asked.

'Professor Nicolaisen?'

'Yes—' opening the door an inch further.

'I wonder if I might talk to you?'

'What about?'

Fagermo smiled in the friendliest possible manner, and said in a stentorian, neighbour-reaching voice: 'About the murder of the boy whose body was found up the back here yesterday.'

It was an infallible way of dealing with that sort of witness. The door was pulled hurriedly open, and he was ushered into the hall by a very flushed and flustered academic.

'What an extraordinary thing to do,' said Professor Nicolaisen.

Fagermo looked at him blandly, as if his words might refer to the murder, or anything else under the sun but his own actions. Professor Nicolaisen, further fussed by this lack of reaction or apology, led the way up the stairs which ended in his sitting-room. All the main rooms of the house were on this floor, and there hung around the room a faint smell of cooking—unpleasant, as if the food had not been very good, or well-cooked, or the meal not very sociable.

'You'd better sit down,' said Nicolaisen. He stood for a moment towering over him like a crumbling crag, seeming uncertain whether or not to offer him coffee. Then, deciding against it, he collapsed into a chair, like a block of flats in an earthquake, looking at him all the while gloomily, and glowering with some obscure resentment.

'Well?' he said again. The word was obviously one of *his* words, an off-putting ploy to put students at a disadvantage, socially and intellectually. His face was cratered with the scars of many battles —of easy victories over cocksure students, of sterile trench-warfare with colleagues over matters of principle. There was in his manner a nervous intensity which contained the odd mixture of aggression and defensiveness which rodents have, and those who engage in university politics.

Fagermo remained genially sociable. 'I don't know if you've seen the paper today?' he said.

'I've read *Aftenposten*.'

'Less exalted than that. The local papers both had a report of the body which was found up the back here yesterday.'

'Yes?'

'Perhaps you've heard of it?'

Professor Nicolaisen made a grudging admission. 'I did hear some talk of it yesterday. People saw the police cars around, I believe. But I was busy with a guest lecture I've been invited to give in Gøteborg. And in any case I would not have gone up to gawp.'

'That's a pity, now. You might have recognized the corpse.'

'Really? Hmm. A student, I suppose. Strange how the universities attract all the unstable types.'

'No, not a student. Or not one from here, at any rate. No, this is the boy that's been missing for some time. I believe the American student Steve Cooling came and spoke to you about him in the Pepper Pot some weeks ago.'

'Oh yes? . . . I think I do have some vague recollection. But it was nothing to do with me.'

'But you had in fact met him?'

There was a pause, and then the same grudging assent, as if anything but contradiction came awkwardly to the man: 'I think we may have sat at the same table.'

'Exactly.' Fagermo smiled ingratiatingly. 'But you didn't come forward in answer to our advertisement.'

Professor Nicolaisen bristled. 'My God, I've had my office burgled three times in the last six months. On the last occasion they scattered my lecture notes out through the open window and defecated on the floor—and your men couldn't even be bothered to cross the road and give it a look. Why do you expect me to come running to do your work for you in those circumstances?'

Fagermo was unpleasantly conscious that—nasty though his manner was—the man had made a palpable hit. He decided he'd better not try to browbeat him, and became still more ingratiating.

'Well, well, I do take your point. Yes, indeed. Well, perhaps I could tell *you* when you met the boy. In fact, you were both of you in the Cardinal's Hat on the evening of December the nineteenth, and as you say, you both sat at the same table. You were with another member of the university, I think—?'

'Botner. Lecturer in French literature.'

'Ah, good. Now, I think you in particular should be able to help me. I've talked only to Americans so far—and you are something of an expert on English speech, so I've heard.'

Fagermo went thus far with the soft soap rather dubiously, since he thought the man might be too intelligent to respond, but he was gratified to see a faint relaxation of the cheek muscles—a near-smile of gratified vanity.

'Oh. You heard that . . . ?'

'Now, you must have some memory of how this boy spoke. Would you say he was English?'

Professor Nicolaisen sat back in a pose of contemplation, as if sitting for a bust of Milton. 'Ye-e-es,' he said finally, with lawyer-like deliberation. 'Ye-es, almost definitely, I'd say. I couldn't detect any trace of the colonial there—it almost always shows through.' It was as if he were talking of a stain on the tablecloth.

'*English,* you would say—rather than Scottish or Welsh?'

'Ye-e-es, yes, I'd say so.'

'Anything more precise? A Northerner, for example?'

The intellectual pose was intensified: *Paradise Lost* was in gestation. 'A Southerner, I'd say. And perhaps there was a trace of West Country there.'

Fagermo took this with a pinch of salt, as so much flim-flam, but he was glad his witness was mellowing into a better humour. He rubbed his hands with delight. 'Ah, now we're getting somewhere. Now—what sort of impression did the boy make on you?'

The response was very ready this time, and the good humour vanished. Professor Nicolaisen never spoke other than dismissively of the young: 'No particular impression at all,' he said. 'He was just a young man—someone who happened to drop in and join us. No great *force* of personality—' he smiled satirically—'that I can remember.'

'What did you talk about?'

'Good heavens, Inspector, this is months ago. I couldn't possibly remember. And I fancy I spoke to him very little. I was in conversation with Ottesen, I remember—sound man, not unintelligent. If I remember rightly, this boy was talking to some American girl: the young stick to the young, you know.'

It was unfortunate that at this moment the door from the hallway opened and a young woman walked in, clearly straight from
the bedroom. She could hardly have been more than twenty-
three, was blonde, sleepy and well-fleshed, with a jumper pulled
over bra-less breasts, and tight jeans. Fagermo might have fallen
into the unlucky assumption that this was Nicolaisen's daughter,
had he not caught a glimpse of the man watching her with a
greedy, untrustful look.

'A visitor, darling?' said the young woman in a bored voice, but
looking at Fagermo appraisingly.

'Inspector—Fagermo?—yes—my wife Lise.'

She sat on the sofa opposite them, picked an apple from a bowl
on the coffee table beside her, and bit into it, all the time watching
Fagermo intently from under a Lauren Bacall lock of fair hair. He
felt he was being added up like a column of figures. If she desired
to make an effect, she certainly succeeded with Fagermo, for when
Nicolaisen said rather testily: 'Where were we?' he couldn't for the
life of him think, and for a moment there was an awkward pause.

'I suppose you were talking about the boy,' drawled Lise.

Fagermo turned to her quickly, and she added: 'The one they
found up there,' jerking her head back towards the big window
behind her as if she were talking of a lost cat or an elk strayed
from the herd.

'You know about him?'

'Ye-es.' Her word was drawled with no sort of emotion, but no
hesitation either. 'He's the one we met in the Cardinal's Hat.'

'I didn't know that you'd met him too. We've been enquiring
about him for some time. I wish you'd come forward.'

'Didn't think about it,' she said, bored. In the silence her husband filled in nervously.

'My wife came to fetch me at the Cardinal's Hat. She'd been to a
meeting, hadn't you, dear?'

'That's right,' said Lise Nicolaisen, and her gaze fixed itself on
Fagermo with great intensity. 'Amnesty International.'

The gaze was unblinking, yet if anyone could be said to wink
without moving an eyelid Fagermo would have said she had done
it. How wonderful, he thought, to marry a young wife and be

made a fool of by somebody half your age. Nicolaisen was plainly confused and uneasy.

'She just came in, and we—went, didn't we, dear?'

The girl chewed steadily on her apple.

'And you left him there, did you, still talking to—who?—the Ottesens by then, I suppose?'

'That's right. The girl had gone a bit earlier. He was talking to the Ottesens.'

'Actually,' said Fru Nicolaisen, in that distant, languorous voice, 'actually, he wasn't talking.' Fagermo turned towards her, to find her still gazing at him, apple at her mouth. 'I had to go back, didn't I, Halvard? I left my—'

'Your gloves, you said, dear—'

'That's right, my gloves . . . and he was still there, and the Ottesens were talking with this lecturer in French—what's his name?—and the boy was just sitting there on the other side of the table, looking into his beer.'

'I see,' said Fagermo. 'Did you talk to him at all?'

She looked him straight in the eyes with her deep blue, untrustworthy gaze. 'I said: "Do you happen to have seen a pair of gloves?" ' she said.

That evening Bjørn Korvald, after he had watched the news on his little portable television (the new bankruptcies in Norwegian industry, the terrible plight of Norwegian ship-owners, the allocation of new blocks in the exploitation of North Sea oil) and after he had looked at the list of the evening's programmes (old age pensioners singing age-old songs, and a two-hour programme on the role of women in the emerging Bulgarian trade-union movement of the nineteen-twenties) Bjørn Korvald decided to act on Fagermo's request and drop into the Cardinal's Hat. It seemed the sort of evening when there was nothing much to keep people at home.

It wasn't often that the table where the foreigners usually gathered was empty of an evening. But tonight it was. Quite empty.

8

TWO GIRLS

In the event, the next day the Trondheim police, through no exertions of their own, came up trumps.

The artist's impression of the dead boy's face had appeared in the Trondheim newspaper that morning, and before ten o'clock a girl had rung up to say she knew who it was.

'She says he's English, and he left Trondheim in the middle of December,' Fagermo's contact in Trondheim said with unjustifiable pride in his voice. 'She hasn't heard from him since. So it looks as if it's the chap you've got there.'

Leaving Tromsø entailed leaving Ekland (who had been assigned to him on the case) in sole charge for a day or more. As a rule, Fagermo contrived to send him out slogging away at some side-issue. Ekland was very adept at sitting in on an interrogation and laboriously taking notes of all the inessentials, but beyond that, and a certain country humour Fagermo liked, he had few talents. It was a wrench to leave things to him, but as Fagermo saw it, the first priority was to fill in the boy's background, and whatever Ekland did while he was away, he could do over again when he came back.

He got to Trondheim in the late afternoon, and drove the endless drive from the airport to the city in gathering twilight. They had found him a spare office in the police station, and the girl was sitting there when he arrived. She was perhaps twenty-one or twenty-two—blonde, good-looking, self-assured, with a hint of sharpness in her features. She looked like a girl who saw her first duty as taking care of herself. There was no great grief in her bearing—nor any ghoulish relish either. She was business-like, contained, moderately concerned. The sort of girlfriend for a man who didn't want to get too involved. Her name, she told him, was Sølvi Martens, and she was twenty-one.

'Well, let's get straight down to business. You think you know this man?'

'I think so. It all seems to fit, doesn't it? I mean the dates and so on.'

'Do you happen to have a picture of him?'

'Yes, I do. I found one back at the flat and brought it along.' She dug in her handbag and came up with a coloured snapshot. It had been taken by flash at a party, no doubt by the kind of social menace who hands round the results with a chuckle weeks later. These two, however, did not look particularly resentful, or particularly drunk. They were smiling at the photographer, he with his arm round her shoulders, she looking as self-possessed as she looked now, sitting opposite Fagermo. The boy looked young, lively and carefree—dressed in a heavy fawn and black Norwegian sweater and jeans. Only when one looked at the eyes did one see an aspect that was not young and carefree: there was something withdrawn, ungiving, calculating about their expression that contradicted the wide, smiling mouth and the relaxed pose.

'That's him,' said Fagermo.

'I really am sorry,' said Sølvi. 'I wouldn't want him dead.'

'Well, somebody certainly did,' said Fagermo, 'and went the right way about it, too. Would you have any idea who it could be?'

'No, of course not,' said Sølvi. 'It's so—melodramatic. Everyone that I knew liked him all right.'

'What was his name?'

'Martin Forsyth. Some people called him Marty, after Marty Feldman.'

'Do you know anything more about him?'

'He came from somewhere called Mersea. I remember he sent a card once to his parents.'

'Did you know him well?'

'We lived together for several months. But I wouldn't say I knew him well.'

Fagermo looked at her hard, but she didn't seem to be joking. In fact, he wouldn't have set a high price on her sense of humour. 'Were you waiting for someone to introduce you?' he asked. She gave him a hard stare.

'I mean, he didn't give away much. For example, when I'd known him for a long time he'd come out with something that would be a complete surprise—somewhere he'd been, you know, or some job he'd done—and I'd never heard of them. It wasn't exactly that he was secretive: he'd discuss these things with you quite openly. But he didn't give much away casually.'

'What sort of things did you learn?'

'Well, he'd knocked around the world a bit. As I say, some place-name would be mentioned, or come up on television news, and he'd say: "I've been there." Italy, Turkey, North Africa, even Asia. I think he worked at home for a bit after he left school, and then he more or less took off. Since then he'd been wandering, with spells back home with the family. You know how it is.'

'Yes, I know how it is,' said Fagermo. 'It worries an old family man who pays his taxes and watches the price of fish-pudding. I wonder how people like that manage to eat.'

'Well, they pinch things, of course,' said Sølvi unconcernedly. 'And if they're on drugs they don't need much.'

'Was he on drugs?'

'Not while he was with me. But I think he was once, like most of them, fairly mildly. You know how it is.'

Fagermo sighed his knowing-how-it-is sigh. Then an idea struck him: 'He wasn't pushing drugs here, was he?'

'Oh no, definitely not. I wouldn't have stopped with him if he'd been mixed up with anything like that . . . But he knew a lot about how to get hold of them.'

'He talked about it?'

'If he was asked. People—young people in our group—knew he'd knocked about a bit, and they'd angle for information now and then, casually, you know.'

'But what did he actually do—for a living—while he was in Trondheim?'

'Worked on boats. That's what he mostly did, if he could, as far as I could gather. I think he'd been with some boat-building firm after he left school, so he knew a lot about them. He'd been on some Greek millionaire's yacht too—not one of the well-known ones, one of the second-rate lot. But it was a pretty big yacht, he said. He worked for the Continental Shelf Research Institute here.'

'Are they attached to the university?'

'I don't think so. I think they're more or less government, or something. They chart the shelf, and do a lot of the scientific side of oil exploration. Anyway, they have several research ships. Sometimes Marty would be off for several weeks, sometimes he'd be in port for a long stretch and only put out on short trips. It meant I didn't see all that much of him, even though we lived together for a fair while.'

'How exactly did you meet?'

'It was more or less his first night in Trondheim. We met at a disco—he'd just dropped in there, and still had his haversack in the left luggage place at the station. Anyway, he came home to my flat, and then—he more or less settled in with me.'

Fagermo sighed. He felt he knew the type. 'He paid his way?' he asked.

'Of course. I wasn't a complete fool, even then.'

'But you don't seem to feel particularly warmly for him, even though he's apparently been murdered?'

Sølvi Martens sat thinking for a little. 'Well, no,' she said; 'I suppose I don't.'

'Why? A row?'

'No, no, nothing like that. It's just that he wasn't a warm sort of person, I suppose. He never did anything without thinking things out carefully. Well, that suited me all right too. We were two of a type. I don't like anything messy. It was really a sort of convenient arrangement, our living together. Nothing much more than that.'

'And when it stopped being convenient—?'

'We split up, and that was that. No hard feelings, but no particular regrets either.'

'Why exactly did you split up?'

'He just said he'd be away for a bit and wouldn't be coming
back to the flat. He may have left his job—I don't know. He'd
always been a bit unsure what he was doing for Christmas, then
around the middle of December he said he'd be moving out, and I
said: "Please yourself." '

'No indication where he was going?'

'He just said north. He didn't give much away as a rule, as I
told you. So I just said it seemed a funny time to go north, and left
it at that.'

'And since then, nothing?'

'No. I wasn't expecting anything really, though he could have
run to a postcard. But then he was dead, wasn't he? But there was
something came to the flat for him—at Christmas.'

'Cards?'

'Just one. I kept it for a bit. It was one of those cards with a
snapshot of the sender. It was from Ålesund, and there was an
address on the back—Kirkegårdsveien, I think the street was
called. He'd had letters from there before, but he'd never said
anything about them. This was a girl, with a baby. A kid of a few
months, I'd imagine. It just said: "Hope to see you soon. All our
love, Anne-Marie and Tor." I didn't keep it.'

'What did you make of it?'

'Well—I thought the kid was probably his.'

Thinking over the interview on the plane to Ålesund, Fagermo
found himself most struck by the coolness of the girl. It frightened
him, perhaps as all signs of our own ageing frighten us. Even in a
small, provincial city like Trondheim the young people had that
null sophistication, that terrible chill that reduces all passions and
tragedies to a shrug of the shoulders, a muttered remark about
'Just one of those things'. She had lived with the boy and now he
was dead, and the experience was hardly more than a flicker of
the eyelashes to her. By now she was no doubt living with another
man, and soon he would pass out of her life without causing any

great flutter of emotion; one day she would contract a marriage as sterile as a hospital operating theatre, and she and her husband would build their own house as soon as possible, aim for a Volvo before they were forty, and bring up two children by the currently accredited text-books.

At Ålesund police station he was given the number of the house in Kirkegårdsveien which seemed to be the one he wanted. He told them he would walk, though they looked at him strangely. Ålesund always affected him badly, and he wanted to get the atmosphere. After Trondheim it was like taking a couple of steps back towards the nineteenth century. A hardfaced city, which only ten years ago had enjoyed the benefits of near-total prohibition, and whose joyless, life-sapping religion seemed to have moulded not just the faces of the older inhabitants, but the stance, the tone of voice, the choice of clothes and colours as well.

At No. 24 the door was opened by a true native daughter: hardly more than fifty, her hair was dragged back from a pear-shaped, unmade-up face, her mouth pursed into a perpetual line of disapproval and distaste. She was like a heavy autumn mist over the fjord.

'They told me about you,' she said, pulling around her thin body a hideous, coke-grey cardigan. 'You'd better come in.'

She ushered him quickly through the door, held open no more than a fraction, and then shut it quickly. 'It's coming to something,' she said bitterly. 'Police twice in one day.'

Fagermo stood awkwardly in the hallway, enduring her hard stare. 'Did the local man tell you what the business was?' he asked, hoping for a nominal softening.

'Something about a death,' said the woman, tossing her head. 'We've no cause to regret him, if it's true, I can tell you. As you can see for yourself.'

She led the way along the hall to the sitting-room—an airless, lightless room, furnished with hard, highbacked, styleless chairs and a heavy, stained table with dropsical legs, covered with a thick olive-brown cloth.

On one of the chairs, playing disconsolately with a little boy of about a year, was as sad a girl as Fagermo had seen. She was small, but with a fine face—quite unmade up, but regular of feature and with superb, honest eyes. Her hair was cut close, but was of a beautiful shade of auburn which defeated the unflattering attentions it had received, perhaps from her mother. She had clearly been crying, but Fagermo felt that this was only a climax to months of hopelessness—to a weight of misery which was part of her family inheritance.

As she stopped playing with it to greet him, the baby let out a howl of outrage.

'*That's* what *he* left behind,' said the woman.

'Mother!' The girl showed signs of bursting into tears again. The woman sat down at the table, contemplating her daughter with a gloomy relish, as if she were personally allocating the wages of sin. It was clear that nothing could be done as long as she was in the room.

'I would like to see your daughter alone,' said Fagermo.

'No, better I'm here too,' said the woman with finality.

'That would be quite impossible,' said Fagermo, with all the firmness he was capable of. He added, untruthfully but convincingly: 'It would be totally against the regulations. We have very strict procedures, you know.'

Like most Norwegians, the woman was cowed by talk of regulations. She got up heavily and moved towards the door.

'You want to watch what she says,' was her parting shot. 'She's a deceitful little hussy.'

She shut the door firmly, but as he was sitting down Fagermo noticed the girl throw an apprehensive glance in its direction.

'Can you carry your little boy?' he asked. 'We could go over by the window and talk.'

A sad half-smile crossed the girl's face. Humping her baby on her arm she went over with Fagermo to the window. He opened it; the air blew chill from the fjord, but the noise from the traffic would defeat any twitching ears on the other side of the door. The baby gazed rapt on the procession of little boats.

'You're Anne-Marie Lausund—is that right?' Fagermo began.

'Yes.'

'You know that Martin Forsyth is dead?'

'Yes.' The girl's tone was dead, but deliberately damped to stop tears. 'It makes it better in a way. I mean for me. I thought he'd deserted us. Tor and me. Gone on to someone else and just forgotten. I couldn't bear that. Now at least I know that wasn't true—that he would have come back.'

'You wrote to him at Christmas, didn't you?'

'Yes—I sent a card. We didn't write all that often. He rang me up a fair bit—about once a fortnight. And he came down a couple of times from Trondheim.'

'Didn't you do anything when you didn't hear from him?'

'He told me not to. The last time he spoke to me. He rang and said he was taking a holiday from Trondheim. He wouldn't say where, but he said he had something big on. He said he'd contact me as soon as he could—and we'd get married soon. I was so happy—it was the happiest Christmas I've ever had. I expected to hear again so soon—he said we could be married some time in the New Year.'

Two tears forced their way out from the corners of her eyes, and Fagermo imagined the hours of hope deferred, ticking by in this dismal house, making the heart sick.

'How long had you known him?' he asked quickly.

'Oh, we met in England, just over two years ago. I was there as an *au pair*.'

'Where did he live?'

'He was living at home. At Mersea, in Essex. It's a small seaside place with a lot of yachting. He'd been around the world a lot, all sorts of places—he seemed to know so much!—and now he was home for a bit. He wasn't happy there, but he liked the work he was doing. It was to do with boats. He loved anything to do with the sea. I was living with some people who worked at Essex University—sociologists. They rather used me, and I wasn't very happy either. So when it was time for me to come home, he came back with me and he got work in Stavanger for one of the North Sea oil companies. They're not so fussy about work permits you know, and he hadn't got one then. He didn't like the work much, but then the permit came through—they let him have one because he was engaged to me, or so we said. So then he left Stavanger, came up to Ålesund for a few weeks, and then got this job in Trondheim.'

'Why didn't he look for work around here?'

Anne-Marie looked at him pityingly. 'We didn't want to stay *here*. Would you? With that sort of atmosphere in the house? And anyway, he wanted to get on, get ahead. He always knew he could get money if he wanted it—he had brains. But to do that you've got to be in a city.'

'So he moved to Trondheim.'

'That's right. And of course by then I was pregnant, so I couldn't go, or he didn't feel I should. He didn't want us to get married until we'd got something to live on and somewhere permanent to live. He said it would be starting off wrong. Of course my parents created merry hell, but he pretended he didn't understand what they were talking about. He was wonderful at letting things just flow over him. He found a flat in Trondheim quite quickly, I don't know how, but he can't have liked the job, I suppose, or else it didn't have the sort of prospects he'd hoped. Because when he phoned at Christmas I assumed he'd decided to move on. I'm sure he had something definite in view this time, and that he intended to call me.'

She said it defiantly, as if this was a bone of contention with her parents.

'I'm sure he did,' Fagermo said.

'He didn't realize, you see, the sort of atmosphere in this house. He had the idea people didn't worry much about illegitimate children in this country. He'd met my mother and father, of course, but he hadn't actually lived in the house. They wouldn't have allowed that, even if we'd wanted it. At that time he didn't know any Norwegian much, and he didn't realize how—how bad they could be. He didn't want us to be married until we could afford it and be really comfortable, and I said I agreed.'

'Did he send you money?'

'I told him not to,' said the girl quickly. 'So we could save. *They* told me I had to get maintenance for Tor from him—they went on and on. Money and the Lord, that's all they think about. Finally I told them I couldn't be sure he was the father . . . That made them worse, of course, but it kept them off that tack.'

'It wasn't true?'

'Oh, of course it wasn't. A great big lie. There's never been anybody else, not since we met.'

'Can you think of anything—' Fagermo paused—'anything unusual in his past? Perhaps something suspicious, even. Or anything that happened while he was here—perhaps a quarrel, or a fight with somebody, or something odd? Or could there have been anything connected with his family?'

'I only met his family two or three times. We went to pubs on Saturday nights . . . Oh, it's nice, looking back on it. Before I met him he'd been all over the place, as I said, and I don't know much about that part of his life. I used to make him tell me about it—Greece, Italy, Libya—all the places he'd seen. We used to sit down near the boats at Mersea, talking about it. He'd never been in trouble in those years, I'm sure. He'd have told me. And he never made any enemies while he was here—except *them*, of course. And no one can stand *them*. I don't think he even realized —I mean we'd be talking, or kissing, and they'd be looking at us with hell-fire and damnation in their eyes, and I just don't think he understood. They don't have religion much in England.'

'So there's nothing you remember about him that might suggest any sort of motive for murdering him?'

'Nothing. He was just a nice, ordinary boy. Not ordinary to me, of course. But he wasn't the type to get murdered, that I'm sure about.'

'But he wanted money. You said that yourself. It's dangerous to want to make money fast. Do you think he would have—gone along with anything shady to get it?'

'He wasn't a crook! He would have earned it! He had real talent. He always knew he'd do well, but he didn't need to cheat or steal it.' She paused. 'You're always hearing these days of people who just take off into nothing. Nothing's heard of them for months, years, and then they come back. They're not crooks— they just live simply.' Fagermo didn't tell her how expensive living simply was these days. 'He was like that. He'd been all over, but he hadn't done anything crooked. He was the type people liked, and he'd always come off well. He was wonderful: so cool and uninvolved. He was the most wonderful thing that will ever happen in my life.'

Fagermo watched for a moment the traffic under the window, and avoided looking at the enthusiastic face beside him. He had his suspicions about Martin Forsyth and his two women. He thought he took the opportunity of the trip to Tromsø to cast himself off from both of them. But of that, nothing could be said. 'What will you do now?' he asked finally, turning back into the room.

'Get out of here. I've been waiting—for him, you know. I always hoped he might ring. And I couldn't trust *them*. I didn't know what they would do if he came, or rang, while I wasn't here. Now I can go, get a job, perhaps study. *Something*, away from here.' She humped her little boy up higher on her arm and turned to see Fagermo to the door. He chucked the baby under the chin.

'I hope he'll grow up like his father,' said Anne-Marie.

9

No Place

The police at West Mersea regarded Fagermo—emanating, they had been told, from Norway—as a strange bird blown from its accustomed nesting places to land inexplicably on their unlovely marshes. When he told them, in addition, that he was from the far North of the country, from above the Arctic Circle, the information, as it sank in, led them to look at him with the slow country equivalent of curiosity. Even in this age of unaccountable and undesirable migrations, they seemed to feel, nothing like this had been seen there before.

'Cold up there, is it?' said the local police inspector at last, as they sat in the cheerless little station.

'Cold—and hot sometimes, too,' said Fagermo.

'Oh yes? . . . Get a lot of snow, though, I suppose, don't you?'

'Quite a lot,' said Fagermo, refraining from adding that it had buried one of the inspector's fellow townsmen. He had given them no details of the case, and they had showed no curiosity about it.

'We had a Norwegian girl living round here, couple of years ago,' said the inspector, after the obligatory pause. 'One of these *au pairs*' (how he leered), 'name of Anne-Marie.'

'I was talking to her yesterday,' said Fagermo.

'Oh yes?' said the inspector, without surprise, as if Norway to his imagining were about the size of Mersea, and folk could be

416

expected to run into each other almost daily. 'A bit of all right, she was.'

'She wasn't looking too happy yesterday,' said Fagermo. 'How did you meet her?'

'Can't recall now . . . That's right, she used to go with your lad, with that young Forsyth. Met 'em in a pub, with his family. He likes his pint, does Jack Forsyth.' The inspector drew his own hand across his lip, as if in anticipation.

'Is that the father?'

'Aye. He likes his pint, does Jack.' The inspector thought for a bit, as if trying to find something else to say about Jack Forsyth, but he was unsuccessful. 'If you're ready, I'll drive you there,' he said, getting up and feeling for his keys.

They drove the few hundred yards from the station to the Forsyths' house along the boat-strewn quay, then off it towards a collection of depressingly similar houses—a junk-yard of residences put up by a speculative builder, which looked all too likely to have cleared him a packet. Very soon they would have all of the symptoms of age, with none of the dignity.

'It's that one,' said the inspector, pointing. 'Number seventeen. Nice little places, aren't they? Mostly they're retired Londoners live there—we get quite a good type, on the whole. But the Forsyths are local.'

'I see,' said Fagermo, mentally shutting out the hideous estate. 'Did you ever have any trouble with the Forsyth boy?'

'No—there wasn't any trouble from him, that I remember. Wish I could say the same for all the young 'uns round here. All these university students . . . bloody young thugs, most of them. But the Forsyth boy never settled down here, as I remember. He'd be away for a period, then back again for a bit, then suddenly he'd take off. Other than that, we never had any trouble with him.'

'Do the parents know?'

'Oh yes, they know.'

'Did they seem surprised?'

The inspector looked at him in his slow, country way, and scratched his head. 'Can't rightly say,' he drawled meditatively. 'You better talk to them yourself.'

As Fagermo went up the path, through a weedy failure of a garden, he was aware by some sixth sense of inspection from behind the lace curtains of the living-room. Mersea was not so different, after all, from any small Norwegian town, he thought. The curtains fell back into position, and a decorous interval passed between his ring and the opening of the door.

Standing in the opening was a fleshy woman of fifty or so, with tinted auburn hair, carefully made-up face, and hard, gimlet-sharp eyes. She wore a navy Crimplene costume, which seemed odd wear for half past five in the evening. Fagermo wondered if she was going out, if this was in anticipation of his visit, or if it was put on as an attempt at half mourning. It must have been some vague mental image of the last, he decided, because the woman was clearly very unsure how to behave: most notably, she was not sure what she ought to do with her face, though finally she decided she might smile.

'Oh hello-o-o,' she said, in a voice with a sharp country edge like a jagged scythe. 'They told me you'd be coming. Would you like to come in?'

She stood aside, and Fagermo stepped into the hall. She looked up and down the street, and then closed the door and led the way toward the living-room. 'You're from Norway, aren't you?' she said. 'That's nice. I've heard it's very nice there.'

'Yes,' said Fagermo. 'It's very nice.'

'I've heard the countryside is lovely. Mrs Nethercoat down the road went there before it got so dear going abroad, and she said Bergen was lovely.'

'Yes,' said Fagermo. 'It's very lovely.'

They had got themselves to the living-room, and Mrs Forsyth's uncertainty seemed to increase. Some show of emotion seemed to be called for, but she seemed to have no idea of what was appropriate. Her notion of tragedy seemed to date back to Joan Crawford in a forties melodrama, and she gave a convulsive gulp, her hand on her bosom. Then, even she finding this unconvincing, she gave up and contented herself with a careful dab at her eyes.

'Well,' she said, looking at the black-stained handkerchief, 'doesn't do to give way, does it? Will you sit down, Mr—?'

'Fagermo.'

'Oh . . .'

They sat down on two soft, unsteady-looking easy chairs. Tentatively the two of them looked at each other appraisingly. Mrs Forsyth seemed to like what she saw. Fagermo, covertly, did not.

'This must have been a great shock to you,' he said, giving her a cue to display what feelings she had.

'Oh, it *has*,' she said, stretching down toward her heart for an emotion she did not feel. '*Aw*ful. When they came and told me this morning, I just didn't know what to say!'

Fagermo could believe it. He said: "It was a complete surprise to you?'

'Well, it *was*. Of course it was.' She blinked a dry eye. 'I mean we *heard* from him only—well, let's see, I suppose it would be about last autumn, or not later than summer, anyway. We had a card from him, ever so pretty, one of your towns over there. So of course we didn't think for a moment there was anything wrong . . .'

'He hadn't written to you more recently than that, I suppose—at Christmas, for example?'

'Well, no. But of course Christmas is so *busy* we didn't think anything of it, you know. We've got the other little girl, you see, and it's all *go* then. He wasn't a great writer—we none of us are in this family. Awful when you think of the amount of money they spend on education, isn't it?'

'So usually when he was away, you just got the odd card, is that right?'

'Yes, that's right. Sometimes—you know, when he was away before, and went all over the place—we'd get cards and *I* wouldn't know where they were from. I kept meaning to look them up, but we haven't got an up-to-date atlas.'

She spoke as if towns made a habit of moving restlessly about the world, and she looked at Fagermo as if to establish a sort of intimacy of self-satisfied ignorance. He found her still, as he had from the beginning, oddly repellent.

'You don't have any of the cards, do you?' he asked.

'I don't. I expect I threw away, or gave them to some kiddy or other. They're always doing these *pro*jects in school these days, aren't they? My little girl or one of her friends is always on at me for this, that, or the other.'

'Do you remember any of the places they came from?'

'Well—' it was clearly a major effort—'I *think* one of them was from Italy. Tripoli or some such town . . . Then there was a town with a funny name—like Aberfan or something, but that's where the kiddies died, isn't it, wasn't it awful? and this one was foreign, I knew from the stamp . . . Anyway, there weren't many cards, no more than two or three to the best of my recollection. And then suddenly he'd turn up on the doorstep, large as life.'

'So you'd say he was a restless boy?'

'Well, they are, aren't they? Young people. I mean, it wasn't like that when *we* were young, was it? 'Course, there was the war, so people had to stay put, but I don't think we *wanted* to go traipsing off to these places the way they do now. I know *I* didn't.'

'But he did?'

'Well, he must have, mustn't he?'

Fagermo was beginning to find this a very strange conversation indeed. As soon as he asked a question about her son, Mrs Forsyth seemed to want to generalize out, to say what 'they' did these days, or to talk about herself—anything, in fact, except talk about her son and his habits. Could it be, Fagermo wondered, that she knew practically nothing about her own son, and had a faint sense of embarrassment at her own blankness?

'You never tried to stop him, though, going off to these "foreign parts"?' he asked.

'Fat lot of use it would have been if I had,' she said shortly. Then, thinking she might have offended him, she added: 'Not that I've anything against foreign countries, of course, and anyway Norway's not really foreign, is it?'

'Not for me,' said Fagermo, and put on a charming smile he usually reserved for worthier recipients. He decided to take the conversation back to an earlier period, when it might be thought she would have been more aware of her son and his doings. He said: 'Had your son been unsettled earlier—when he was at school, for example?'

'Well . . . I wouldn't say that, no. We gave him a very good education . . .'

'You mean he went to private school?'

'Oh no, no. He went to the Grammar School at Colchester. We've still got one, you know.' Her bosom swelled with inexplicable pride.

'Does that mean he won a scholarship?'

'Well, sort of: he got through his eleven-plus. He was never one of the *really* bright ones: they put him in Science. But he always did quite well, really. We let him stay on till he was sixteen, and he got his GCE.'

Fagermo had heard the expression 'Big Deal,' and thought it might be an appropriate reaction to that 'let him stay on'. He asked: 'Was he ever in trouble—girls, for example?'

'Not that I know of. Of course they know so much these days, don't they? Makes you wonder sometimes—the things they come out with. It must be the telly, or some of these sex books they read in school. My father would have walloped me, I know that, if he thought I knew half what these youngsters know today. But I don't think Martin was ever in what you'd call trouble.'

'Did he get on with his father?'

'Well . . . I don't know what to say, really. They never *didn't* get on, if you know what I mean . . .'

'No rows?'

'Oh, rows . . . Well, Jack would shout at him now and then, as is only natural, and he'd swear back, but there was nothing . . . nothing *nasty* about it. There wasn't much between them at all, really, if you know what I mean. They both went their own ways.'

Fagermo had a sudden vision of this home as a bare prison, full of self-contained cells—or as a frozen waste of non feeling. Somehow it seemed pointless to continue the conversation, so little did the woman seem to know of what her son was, or thought, or did. He stirred in his chair, preparatory to leaving.

'Did you know your son's Norwegian girl-friend, Anne-Marie Lausund?' he asked.

'Oh *yes*. Ever so nice. So quiet-spoken and that. I *do* think Norwegians are *nice*.' She looked at him invitingly, and was disappointed in his clear blue gaze in return. She chattered on, apparently quite happy to get off the subject of her son. 'Oh yes, we knew her quite well. She came out with us a couple of times, perhaps three. We used to drive over to the Bull at Thaxted, I remember, ever such a nice pub, lots of university people use it, and professional people, and there's ever such a nice atmosphere on Saturday nights. Yes, we had some lovely evenings there. She was such a nice little thing, and spoke lovely English—ever so attractive.'

'She has a baby now.' She looked at him blankly, and Fagermo added: 'Your son's.'

At the thought of grandmotherhood an unconcealable spasm of distaste crossed her face.

'I hope she's not expecting us to do anything about it. We're not well off, and we've got more than enough on our plate as it is. And I mean, you can't *prove* that sort of thing, can you?'

'She's not expecting anything from anybody. I just thought you might be interested.'

'Oh, I see. Well, it's not something anyone'd be proud of, is it? . . . I don't know as I'd want it known.'

'There's no reason why it should be.' They reached the front door, and Fagermo asked: 'Will your husband be in later in the evening?'

'Well, I don't know. He's on the boats, you know. He'll probably be down at the Yachtsman at seven or half past.'

And at half past seven he was, indeed, in the Yachtsman. He was sitting at a table with a group of his pals, engaged in an intense discussion over a newspaper, folded over to the racing results. The landlord pointed him out, and Fagermo took a pint of (he thought) typically weak English beer over to the table, and made himself known. The table fell silent at his name, and he realized that Jack Forsyth had certainly heard the news, and so had his pals.

Forsyth cleared his throat with embarrassment, and then got up and shuffled off with Fagermo to another table, where he sat down and contemplated his beer. His eyes were wetter than his wife's, but not with grief. He searched his mind for something to say, and then finally came out with: 'Rotten thing, this.'

And for the rest of the ten minutes Fagermo stayed, he got out of him nothing more meaningful than that. As he left, he saw him scuttling back to his mates, eager to resume the business of living.

10

WORK AND PLAY

On the way back from England Fagermo stopped off again in Trondheim, and took a taxi to the Continental Shelf Research Institute, where Forsyth had worked. It was a tubular building on the outskirts of the town, like a hideous white worm, curiously involuted. Nobody much seemed to be around, or to know where anybody else was, but finally he found himself talking to Gunnar Meisal, a large man with a genial, chinny face that seemed to have been carved out of sandstone by an inexpert hand. He at least had known Forsyth—remembered him from several North Sea expeditions.

'Perfectly capable lad,' he said, sitting Fagermo down by his desk, piled high with crazy graphs and endless lines of computer figures. 'Unusually so. A real find, because they're not so easy to come by these days. He was experienced, and knew what he was doing. The great thing was, you didn't have to keep your eye on him the whole time.'

'He was crew, was he?'

'That's right. The Institute has a couple of boats, with full time crew, because one or other lot of us here is out at sea for one reason or another much of the time.'

'Doing what? Or is that top secret?'

'No, no, *what* we're doing isn't top secret, though the details of what we *find* sometimes are.'

'Why?'

'Oil. A lot of what we're doing these days goes straight to the Department of Oil and Energy, or else to the State Oil Company. It's the sort of information that all sorts of foreign oil companies—especially the American and British—would like to get their hands on. The Russians show a lot of interest as well—that's partly why there's been so much Russian activity up in the Northern waters recently: curiously well-equipped fishing-boats—you must know all about that sort of thing, coming from Tromsø.'

Fagermo nodded. It was a common joke how advanced fishing technology had become in Russia. 'Could you give me some idea of what Forsyth was involved in, in his work for you?' he asked.

'Basically it's a question of collecting scientific data: what everyone is interested in is which areas of the North Sea and the Barents Sea are most likely to be profitable. Let me put it very simply —' and Gunnar Meisal crouched forward in an expository pose and gave a little lecture involving gas chromatographs, spectrometers, hydraulic content, multi-channel folds and subsamples. At the end (Fagermo had fixed his eyes on him in desperate attentiveness, and tried to stop them glazing over) Meisal leaned back again in his desk chair, a benevolent expression on his face, conscious of having rendered the subject simple almost beyond the limits of scholarly responsibility. Fagermo trod his way carefully forward with his next question, conscious of the danger of revealing his still near-complete ignorance.

'I see,' he said, sounding unconvincing to himself. 'The long and the short of it is, you're getting information, doing research, that a lot of people—foreign companies, and governments as well —would like to get their hands on.' Meisal nodded. 'Would that be relatively simple information—the sort of thing that can be carried in the head?'

'No, no—certainly not. Highly technical. It's the sort of stuff that we would have to analyse in depth. Or often the Oil and Energy Department uses consultants—highly qualified people in universities, technical colleges, and so forth.'

'So it's difficult to imagine Forsyth being able to make use of the sort of information you might be getting on these trips.'

'Very difficult. Because he'd have to know what he was doing. Much of what we're up to would be quite meaningless to the average crew member; he wouldn't know what was of value, what wasn't. Of course Forsyth was a bright boy, and experienced. It's just *possible,* if he was really clued up, he could get hold of the stuff people are willing to pay good money for. But if it's a question of leaks to foreign concerns, it's much more likely to happen at the consultant level—they would really know what's wanted.'

'And the companies would really pay good money for this information?'

'I wouldn't mind betting. It would have to be good money, to be worth anybody's while. The oil companies have got their fingers in all sorts of pies in this country, since the various North Sea blocks proved workable and profitable. They use some of the same people as the Americans and Russians use—spies, information agents, whatever you like to call them. And they've usually got someone or other on the relevant local councils in their pay: they get a retainer to keep the oil company's interests in mind.'

'*Really*? That could be interesting. Mostly the rightwing people, I suppose?'

Meisal shrugged. 'Not necessarily. The other lot don't go much on oil, but they're pretty fond of money. You know how easy they find it to square things with their consciences. Suddenly you start hearing them say that if there's one thing they think they can justify spending money on it's a bit of extra room for the kiddies to play in, and before you can blink your eyes they've got five-bedroom houses and ten-acre gardens.'

'You could be right,' said Fagermo. 'And of course the oil companies are probably interested in Tromsø.'

'They're interested in all the bigger towns in the North—for when the bonanza starts north of the sixty-second parallel. It'll be this year, or next year—but whenever it is they want to have their lines open well in advance. They say there's even more money to be made from the Northern blocks than there has been from the Southern ones. And they're damn right!'

Fagermo sat for a moment in thought. 'Well, well,' he said finally. 'The modern gold rush. It seems to have some funny side-effects . . . Now, this boy, Forsyth, did he strike you as trustworthy?'

Meisal pondered. 'It's not something we think about: security is something that usually only matters higher up, and anyway the cloak-and-dagger aspects are not really our affair, only the research . . . I was just with him on a couple of trips. He was certainly a pleasant chap: not talkative, but you could talk *to* him. He fitted in well, even though he didn't talk much Norwegian. He liked earning money—from overtime, that sort of thing—but most of the crew-men do. And I knew we wouldn't keep him for long, because he was too bright. There are lots of jobs waiting for a chap like that. I imagine he was biding his time, saving up, and he just moved on when he was ready.'

'So you weren't surprised when he left? Did he actually give in his notice?'

'I imagine so, though you never know with crew: they can be pretty casual. Would you like me to find out?'

'Can you?'

Meisal took up the phone and dialed a number: 'Kjell—you remember that Forsyth boy, on the boat? Did he give in his notice before he left? . . . Just took off . . . No hint at all? . . . When was this? . . . I see, thanks . . . Not the immigration people, the police . . . He's dead.'

He put down the phone.

'He left without giving notice just before Christmas, and never came back.'

'The last part I know already,' said Fagermo. 'Well, I'm grateful to you for your help.' He got up to go, but paused at the door. 'You've not given me much idea of the boy's personality. Did you know him well enough to get one? Did he make any impression on you at all?'

Meisal thought, his Grand Canyon face resting on his cupped hands: 'Self-contained . . . self-reliant . . . ruthless . . .'

'Why ruthless?'

'You asked for impressions. That was mine. You don't get much opportunity to be ruthless in the middle of the North Sea on a

geological research expedition. But that's how he struck me.
Someone who knew what he wanted, and went after it.'

Back in Tromsø, Fagermo went straight to the station in the
setting sun of early evening and caught up with developments.
Sergeant Ekland was off duty, and even now (no doubt) was snoring in front of his television set with a beer-glass in his hand. He
had left behind a report of very much the kind which Fagermo
had anticipated: written in a Norwegian which (even granted the
chaotic free-for-all which is the current state of the language)
could only be described as semi-literate, it detailed the various
approaches by members of the public to the police following publication of the artist's impression of the dead boy in the local paper
two days before. Reading through the details as mistyped by Ekland, Fagermo could only feel that there was more to be said for
literacy than was usually allowed these days—and for typing les-
sons for policemen as well.

Among the disorganized mass of details and names and addresses there was one item that caught his eye. Among others who
said they had seen him (but, as far as could be judged from Ekland's notes, had had nothing whatsoever more to say about him)
was a Fru Barstad who manned a kiosk up in Biskopsgate as it
wound up from the main street towards the top of the island.
Ekland had noted down the date she gave—December 20—but
beyond that his notes consisted entirely of irrelevancies: her marital status (widow); her age (sixty-five); the number of years she
had worked at the kiosk (twenty-five). But Fagermo did not need
to be told how long Fru Barstad had worked at the kiosk. He had
known Fru Barstad from her first days there. On an impulse he
put on his coat and went out into the street.

When Elin Barstad had begun to work at the kiosk in Biskopsgate she was a capable woman of forty whose husband had begun
to take the easy way out of marriage to her and was graduating to
full-time alcoholism. Fagermo had not yet even begun at *gumnas*.
She had sold him chocolates, mild pornography and his first cigarettes. Over the years the pornography on offer had got less mild,
but Fagermo had lost the need for it. For old times' sake, though,

he still bought chocolates or cigarettes there, if he was in the vicinity. And as he had grown into a young-looking middle-aged policeman with an amused mouth and sharp eyes, Fru Barstad had aged into the kind of old lady Norway alone can produce—the kind of old lady who is convinced she is the backbone of Norway. Bulky, upright, tougher than any man, she was a heavyweight opponent, and took on all comers. At sales or crushes of any kind her umbrella, wielded vigorously, felled all bystanders and brought her to the front of the queue, where her voice, first cousin to Kirsten Flagstad's without the musicality, summoned the shop assistant to her immediate service. She was tough, pushing, opinionated, aggravating and totally irresistible, a force of nature that the most foul-mouthed teenager or drunken tramp could never hope to best. She sat in her kiosk like Pius IX in the Vatican, ruling her roost and the streets around, utterly secure in her own infallibility. She made no concessions to manners, good-nature or old acquaintanceship. She simply *was*.

'Yes?' she enunciated sourly, when Fagermo had stood patiently before her counter for something approaching a minute.

'I'll have a bar of chocolate,' he said. She handed it to him silently, took his money, and slapped it into the till.

'I hear you've been giving us some valuable information,' said Fagermo conversationally. Fru Barstad sniffed virtuously, as if to say: I did my duty.

'Mind if I ask you a few more questions?'

A smile of triumph wafted over Fru Barstad's face. 'I knew that chap didn't know his job! I said to myself: those are stupid questions you're asking, and you're forgetting to ask the right ones! But it wasn't *my* business to teach him his job!' She sniffed again. She took great pleasure in the inferiority and moral frailness of the world in general. Fagermo saw no reason to take up the cudgels for Sergeant Ekland's intelligence. No policeman likes lost causes.

'How can you be sure it's the same boy?' he asked.

'Well, of course I can't, and I'm not. I said so to him. These artist's impressions—they're very clever, but they're not like a photo, are they?'

'We could show you the body,' said Fagermo. A definite flicker of interest passed over Fru Barstad's face.

'That's as you please. Anyway, as I told your little I-should-be-on-TV sergeant, I know most of the customers at this kiosk by this time. Most of them live around here—or they wander up after the pictures.' She surveyed gloomily the white road shading into darkness as it wound down to the town. 'And there's not much I don't know about *some* of them that come here, I can tell you! Don't give me you're police, because police don't know half of it! So anyway, when there *is* someone completely new, and in the middle of winter to boot, you notice them.'

'I suppose you do,' said Fagermo, who believed her. 'But the date—I don't see how you can be so sure of *that*.'

'Ah, but I can!' said Fru Barstad, with gloomy triumph. 'Because it was my last night on before Christmas. I'd ordered a taxi to take me to the airport, because my sister was coming up on the night plane from Bodø to stay with me for Christmas—and a right foolish idea *that* turned out to be! Anyway, I was just thinking of locking up for the night when he came along and demanded a hot dog or something, I forget what. I muttered a bit, but I could hear he was English—'

'You're sure about that?'

'You think I could have been here twenty-five years without being able to hear whether someone's English or not? We used to have hundreds and hundreds here every summer, before they got their Troubles.'

'That makes it pretty certain it was Forsyth you saw, then.'

'Anyway, I got it for him, whatever it was, and then I locked up. Then, when the taxi came, we drove to the airport, and I saw him again, just up the road here—' she nodded her head up the road, along the way that led over the crown of the island to the airport— 'there he was finishing his hot dog and standing talking to someone, and I thought to myself: Well, you are a fast one, and no mistake.'

'What do you mean? Was it a woman?'

'Of course it was a woman. He was talking to her by the roadside as if he'd just picked her up—or her him, you can't tell these days.' She sniffed vigorously, a testimony that she was brought up in the days when men were men and women were women, and the ritual dance was danced with quite other steps.

'This is interesting,' said Fagermo. 'If you're right about the date this was only his second night here.'

'This town,' said Fru Barstad darkly.

'Was it someone you knew, this woman? One of the usual?'

'Oh no—though I think I've seen her before. Definitely from Tromsø or around, I'd say. *Looked* quite respectable. Smart, permed hair, took care of herself. Oh no, definitely not one of the regulars.'

'Could you describe her, or recognize her again?'

'Not to swear to—I only saw her in the headlights. She was a blonde: twenty-five, thirty, thirty-five—these days you can't tell, not like you could thirty years ago. Good-looking, well-dressed—there's nothing that stands out about her that I remember.'

'Just thinking back to how they looked,' said Fagermo carefully, 'would you say they were meeting by appointment, or just casually?'

Fru Barstad considered the question carefully, gazing up into the darkness. 'Well, as I said, my impression was that one had picked the other up, and I dare say there was something that made me think that—I'm not one for jumping to conclusions without I have my reasons. It's the way people stand, isn't it? I mean, not too close, trying to look casual, sizing each other up. It's like dogs, isn't it? And it usually ends up pretty much the same way, too!'

Fagermo sighed. 'It's a pity. If it was just something casual, like asking the way, it probably led to nothing. But the boy did get in late that night, and it would have been interesting if he'd met this woman by appointment.'

'Well, he wouldn't have been just asking her the way somewhere, you can bank on that,' said Fru Barstad. 'If he'd wanted to know that, he'd have asked me. People do all the time—it's more likely I'd know than someone you stop casually in the street.'

'She may have stopped him.'

'But I *think* she's local. And he didn't look in the least Norwegian, in spite of being fair.'

'Do you think she lives around here?'

'No—I'd have seen her more often. But there are people you just see occasionally—walking home after the last bus has gone, or out for their Sunday stroll. She's one of them.'

'She may have just asked him the time,' said Fagermo despondently. But Fru Barstad was not willing to have her information disregarded as easily as that.

'Very likely she did ask him the time,' she said, with her lips pursed. 'It's been done before! But it didn't stop at that. The lights were on them as we drove up the hill, and when we passed them they were *talking*. You don't talk when somebody asks you the time, unless you're hoping it will lead to something else.'

'You could be right,' said Fagermo.

'There's no "could be" about it,' she returned sharply. 'No doubt you smart boys in the police think you know better than the rest of us, but you parade around in your uniforms and people make themselves scarce when they see you coming. You don't see half of what's going on. Do you know what this job has made me?'

A cantankerous old battle-axe, thought Fagermo to himself, but he merely raised his eyebrows.

'A student of human nature. You look at the way people walk, the way they hold their hats, the way they get into their cars, and you can tell what they're up to, or what's about to happen to *them*.'

'You didn't by any chance guess the young man was about to be murdered, I suppose?' murmured Fagermo.

'Not that. Of course not. But I'll tell you this. When I saw him in the headlights, he was thinking of bed. And it wasn't his own!'

11

MARITAL RELATIONS

'That's funny,' said Sergeant Ekland, with an expression of sub-lime complacency on his face. 'Aren't women funny. She never said anything about that to me.'

'No,' said Fagermo, with equal complacency.

It was the next morning, and Ekland was sitting in Fagermo's office—massive, self-congratulatory and elegantly lethargic. He had the happy knack of never being able to see that he had done wrong, or done too little, or might have done better. He had the equally happy knack of giving to everything he did an equal amount of attention or inattention: knocking up a shelf in the garage or investigating a murder case occupied in his mind places of equal importance or unimportance, and were accordingly done in much the same take-it-or-leave-it manner. Such men live to a ripe and inconvenient old age.

'Well anyway, now we have a woman in the case,' said Fagermo. 'Which would at least have the effect of brightening it up, except that it's a totally unknown woman.'

'What about that Professor's wife you were talking about?' asked Ekland. 'The one you said was the nymphet type? Couldn't it be her? You said she was blonde.'

'Oh she was, along with fifty percent of this town. I suppose she's about twenty-five, though she looks a lot younger. There's no reason to think it's her rather than anybody else, though. She'd be a long way from home—she lives on the mainland.'

'Some things are best done a long way from home,' said Sergeant Ekland sagely. 'I'd follow it up if I were you. As a matter of fact, I think I've heard of her before.'

'Really?'

'The boys did a raid at the students' place a few months ago—drugs—and I have an idea she was one of the people there. Wife of one of the professors, but more of an age to be a student. Can't be many of them.'

'I don't know about that. I have the impression that's a bit of an occupational hazard. Did you say drugs? That could be interesting. Was she brought in?'

'Well, actually it wasn't drugs. They went through the place with a toothcomb, but there wasn't a trace. It must have been some kind of hoax—they had a tip-off by telephone, and that evening the students did something else: had a demonstration about something, or blew something up, I forget what. All they found was a nice sexy party with nothing worse than alcohol. They were all students there except her.'

'So she sort of stood out, did she? Was it really a sexy party, or are you making that up?'

'Would I?' asked Ekland, injured. 'There were ten or twelve there, mostly men, nobody had a stitch on, all the furniture had been moved out and there were mattresses all over the floor. By the time our boys had finished the investigation they were down to their underpants themselves. Just my luck I wasn't on duty! But there were no drugs.'

'Well, well, just an ordinary student party, eh? I wonder if she goes in for that sort of thing often. When I saw her she certainly seemed—well, never mind. Where she met the boy—if it was her—is only five or ten minutes from Prestvann Student Hostel. She could have been entertaining herself for the evening.'

'She's probably not important,' said Ekland lazily, the flicker of interest, or lust, he had shown now being replaced by his habitual lethargy. 'I mean, the guy probably just slept with her. We've no evidence she goes around killing the blokes she sleeps with—otherwise the student hostel would have been littered with corpses that night.'

Fagermo spread out his hands in a gesture of helplessness.

'What can we do but follow up all the contacts he had while he was in Tromsø? We have precious little else, though of course I'm thinking what I can do about tracking him further in the past. Meanwhile, we're bound to probe his connection with the people he met here, like this woman. Did he know her from before? Did they meet by arrangement? Did he tell her anything about what he was doing here? That sort of thing.'

'Doesn't sound particularly hopeful to me,' said Ekland with a big sigh.

'It's not. But they're possibilities, and they're about all we've got at the moment . . .' He paused, and looked down again at the jungle of Ekland's notes. 'I suppose one of the things we could begin to do would be to draw up a timetable of his activities while he was in Tromsø.'

He took up a clean sheet of paper.

'Let's see. He arrives some time during the morning of the nineteenth, probably tries various hotels, and then lands up at Tromsø's Little Hilton—Botilsrud's Pensjonat. We don't know what he did for the rest of the day, but in the evening—almost the entire evening—he was in the Cardinal's Hat. Slept at the Pensjonat. Next day is pretty blank, but we have a reliable sighting around ten o'clock at night, an encounter with a woman, and then a late arrival back at the Pensjonat—around three o'clock or so.'

Fagermo paused: 'Question: if he was sleeping with the woman, why go back to the Pensjonat at all? It can't have been just to get his money's worth.'

'Husband?' hazarded Ekland, with a lazy, experienced air.

'Not many jobs where you knock off around two or three in the morning.' Fagermo pulled the paper towards him again. 'Next day, it seems probable, he was killed. Where? Possibly over there on the mainland, though he could just as easily have been taken there by car. The doctors say he *was* moved after death. When was he killed? Any time after dark, if it was outside—in any case, it was dark practically all day . . . I see you've got a sighting for him around midday, day unspecified.' He peered down at Ekland's notes trying to find something more concrete, and Ekland leaned forward too with an apparently quite disinterested curiosity. 'Seems to be someone called Solheim. Is that right? Who was he? Reliable?'

'Oh yeah,' said Ekland, with false confidence. 'Some fairly high-up bod in the Post Office. Said he saw him in the Viking Café a bit after midday.'

'Anything else?'

Ekland scratched his head. 'Not that I remember.'

Fagermo, getting that haloed feeling one does get when keeping one's good humour in circumstances guaranteed to enrage the average Archangel, pulled the phone towards him and got on to the central switchboard at the Post Office.

Solheim, he learned, was a fairly big wig with a ridiculously long title that could mean anything. When he came on the line he sounded competent and decided. He often went to the Viking Café, just by the Post Office, when he forgot to bring his lunch sandwiches. He remembered the boy because it was just before Christmas, and you didn't see many tourists around that time. He couldn't remember the exact date, but there were lots of people with Christmas packages. He had picked out the boy as English from his clothes. He said a few words to him because he liked talking English now and then—having been there in the war.

'What sort of thing did you say?'

'Well, I think I asked him if he needed any help—he was por-ing over a map.'

'Did he accept the offer?' asked Fagermo, his hopes rising.

'No, he didn't. He seemed sort of—reserved. He wasn't exactly rude, but he didn't seem to want to talk, you know how it is. So I just went on to another table.'

'You say he was poring over a map. Do you remember what sort it was? A motorist's map?'

'No, no: it was a map of the town—you know the one: it's the only big one available, with all the streets on.'

'Did you by any chance notice where he was looking? Some-where on the island?'

There was a pause. 'Now you come to mention it, I think I do remember. He'd had to fold it—it was too big for the table. He was looking at the bottom section, the mainland—bottom lefthand corner, in fact. That's where his finger was.'

'Good, that's very useful. Did you notice him again?'

'I think he went out not long after that.'

'And you can't swear to the day—that's a pity.'

'No, I wouldn't swear to a date, because you just don't remember things like that. But it was certainly just before Christmas . . . and it was probably a Friday.'

'Probably Friday?' said Fagermo, flicking through the last year's desk calendar he still had in his drawer.

'Yes: it's mostly Friday I forget my sandwiches. That's the day my wife goes to work early, and she's not there to remind me to take them.'

'I'm very, very grateful to you,' said Fagermo, putting down the phone. He pulled towards him the sheet on which he had detailed the boy's movements, and entered: '12.00 Viking Café? About to go over to the mainland?' He sat back.

'I wouldn't mind betting,' he said, 'that he was killed not far from where he was found. Anton Jakobsensvei, Isbjørnvei—one of those around there. They're on the bottom lefthand end of the map . . .' He looked again at his little timetable of the boy's movements. 'There's still an awful lot of blank spaces. A lot of time unaccounted for.'

'Isbjørnvei,' said Sergeant Ekland, who throughout the telephone conversation had been picking his teeth with an intentness and concentration he rarely exhibited in his day-to-day work, and had now reached an excavation of particular delicacy and interest. 'Isn't that where the Prof lives—the one with the dishy wife?'

'Yes,' said Fagermo with a sigh. Trust Ekland to notice the blindingly obvious. Still, when there were so few promising lines of investigation, the obvious could certainly not be ignored. Sergeant Ekland, having finished the hideous probings, was grinning like a manic model.

'Oh, stop posing, man—drive me there,' snapped Fagermo.

* * *

Outside the station, as they got into their car, Fagermo said: 'Wait a sec. Drive me over to Brennbygget first—that's where the Prof works. There's no point in talking to the girl if the husband's there. I've done that already.'

They drove past the Amundsen statue and the little customs shed, and came to the office block which temporarily housed the library and various other parts of the university. Fagermo pottered up the stairs, looking into the library and the canteen, outside which the various left-wing student groups fought out their ideological battles in shrill red wall posters dotted with exclamation marks. On the fourth floor he found the Department of Languages and Literature, and here he met a snag: he was just about to enquire at the office whether Professor Nicolaisen was teaching today when he saw him stalking along the corridor towards the dark, smelly little seminar room, set windowless in the middle of the building. Nicolaisen saw him, stopped, and regarded him with a commendably frank dislike. Since he made no opening to start even the most casual of conversations, Fagermo was forced to accept that the onus was on him.

'Oh, Professor Nicolaisen—I wondered if you were teaching at this hour.'

'I am. My students are waiting,' said Nicolaisen, nodding towards the seminar room where one or two students were sprawled in attitudes not notably expressive of anticipation.

'Oh, then I won't keep you,' said Fagermo. 'I just wanted—' he nearly dried up for a moment, but invention seldom failed him entirely and he seized gratefully on the first thought that happened to come into his head: 'I just wanted to know if you remembered whether Martin Forsyth was wearing a ring of any sort when you met him in the Cardinal's Hat.'

Nicolaisen's face, creviced like a relief map of his native country, expressed as clearly as words: what a foolish question! He said: 'Good heavens, how could I be expected to remember that! It's not the sort of thing one notices.'

'Well, well,' said Fagermo, glad to make his getaway so easily, 'that's all I wanted to ask. Perhaps somebody else will have noticed.'

'Not many Englishmen do wear wedding-rings,' said Nicolaisen, to his departing form. He loved imparting useless information, and now went on to do more of it to his seminar group, in the sort of mood that guaranteed that withering and crushing would be the order of the day.

On the drive out to Isbjørnvei and the Nicolaisens' residence Fagermo remembered why the question of the ring had flashed into his mind. The boy had been wearing one, presumably, when he died: the rounded indentation was there on the fourth finger of his right hand. Nicolaisen's reaction had been interesting . . . A possibility of further questioning suggested itself.

When they got to Isbjørnvei Fagermo tossed up in his mind the advantages of leaving Ekland outside and taking him in with him. Finally he decided on the latter: he had a certain dreadful appeal which might go straight to the heart, or something, of Fru Nicolaisen. Together they clambered over unswept snow, watched by an unashamedly interested face from the kitchen window. The response to the ring on the doorbell was immediate—even, one might have fancied, enthusiastic. Fru Nicolaisen came tripping downstairs and pulled open the door invitingly.

'I knew you'd come back,' she said. 'Oh—you've brought a friend with you.'

It was one way of putting it. Ekland brightened up visibly and took a vital interest in his official duties for the first time since the case began. Fru Nicolaisen was wearing something between a brunch coat and a brunch jacket—a short, frizzy, nylon-gauzy creation that led one to wonder if she was wearing anything underneath and kept one within an ace of finding out. Fagermo generously allowed Ekland to follow her upstairs. She sat them down on the sofa and then, without asking, went into the kitchen, opened a bottle of beer, and poured three glasses.

'Isn't this cosy?' she said, looking from one to the other with experienced naivety.

'We actually came to ask you some more questions, Fru Nicolaisen,' said Fagermo.

'Lise, call me Lise,' said Fru Nicolaisen; and then, with a pretty pout: 'But why shouldn't we be comfortable? So much nicer to relax. Especially as I suppose these are the questions you didn't like to ask while my husband was around . . .'

'Well, that's pretty much the truth,' admitted Fagermo. Then, chancing his arm, he added: 'Or anyway, ones we thought you might not have been quite honest in answering.'

She put on an enigmatic smile, then let it fade slowly, fascinatingly from her face.

'Did you notice whether Martin Forsyth was wearing a ring when you met him at the Cardinal's Hat?' Fagermo asked experimentally.

Lise Nicolaisen raised her pretty blonde-grey eyebrows and stared at him: 'What an odd question. I was hoping for something more . . . personal. Yes, he wore a ring—do you mean specifically when he was in the Cardinal's Hat that night, or just generally?'

'Well—'

'Though actually I did notice when I met him the first time, because it's one of the things one *does* notice, or I do, anyway. Not that it makes much difference to the way they behave, sometimes.'

'So you met Martin Forsyth more than once?'

'I *always* meet attractive men more than once,' said Lise Nicolaisen, with a baby-doll wriggle of her shoulder, and that wicked pout. 'That's why I knew you'd come back!' She curled her legs up under her on the chair opposite them and looked even more like something out of a 'fifties film. Sergeant Ekland's note-taking ceased entirely as he took in the augmented expanses of thigh.

'So you met him again—at around ten o'clock the next night?' hazarded Fagermo. She opened her adorable eyes still wider.

'At ten o'clock the next *morning*, actually,' she said with a little giggle. 'Still, it was a good try.'

'Ten o'clock next *morning*?' said Fagermo, disconcerted. 'Then you didn't meet him on the evening of the twentieth up Biskopsvei?'

'No. Why? Did someone? He *does* seem to have got around, doesn't he? I'm sure I got the best out of him.'

Fagermo tried to readjust his ideas. Was she telling the truth?

Why should she admit to the morning but deny the evening? He said: 'So you met him in the morning. Here?'

'No, actually not here. I don't often—unless it's one of my husband's students. It—excites them, you know, sometimes. It doesn't bother me particularly. There are some who like to keep things within the Department, but I'm not one of them. It seems silly to me. I like to range around!'

'Where did you meet?'

'Up in the student hostel in Prestvannet. It's a friend's room. He got me a duplicate key, and I use it in daytime now and then, when he's at lectures. Do you know, none of the hotels in this town will let rooms by the hour!'

'How did you manage to arrange all this? You didn't have much time.'

She giggled cosily and sipped her beer. 'Who needs time? I don't. I have talking eyes.' She looked at Sergeant Ekland and blinked invitingly. 'Did you notice I had talking eyes? . . . So had he. We agreed to it when I was collecting my husband, actually, though we didn't say a word. Then, when I went back for my gloves I just whispered the place and time, and he nodded. It's awfully simple to do, Inspector, if you've got my experience.'

'I'm sure,' said Fagermo. 'And when you met you—?'

'That's right. Do you want details, Inspector, or have you read the little manuals?'

'Hgghh-hmmm. Er, did you talk as well?'

She considered. 'I can't remember. I expect I made coffee. We may have talked a bit while we drank it. Yes—that's right. He said he'd been on some sort of boat in Trondheim, mentioned some of the expeditions they'd been on. Sounded deadly boring, all male and all that, but I think it was scientific or something.'

'Anything else?'

She threw back her head. 'Let's see. What's the usual? I expect I asked how long he would be in Tromsø—that's right, I did—and he said he didn't know for sure, but he hoped to finish his business the next day, and if he did he'd probably take the plane the day after.'

'Back to Trondheim?'

'I suppose so. I don't remember.'

'Anything else?'

'I don't think so. There wasn't much time . . . I don't go in for too much talking. That's the trouble with half the university people: it's all jabber and no—'

'And you parted—when?'

'Parted! Sounds like a novelette! I suppose we left the flat about half past eleven. When we walked down to town it was light. We "parted" in the main street.'

'Did he say where he was going, or anything?'

'No. I think he just said "Thanks".' She looked at him wonderingly. 'He was a man of few words.'

'I see,' said Fagermo. 'Well—at least that fills in one of my blank spots in the timetable I'm making of his movements. I suppose there's nothing else you'd like to tell me about him?'

She giggled sexily and said in a Joan Greenwood voice: 'No . . .'

Fagermo sighed, drained his beer and got up. 'Well, I'm very grateful to you—'

'Funny to think of him buried up there . . . all stiff,' said Lise Nicolaisen, who seemed to feel no compulsion to hide her more appalling thoughts. 'When I slept with him just a day or two before. Sort of—exciting, somehow!'

'If you should think of anything else—'

'I'll come along to the police station,' she said, unwinding herself from her chair and putting on a pretty pout of anticipation. 'I've always wanted to.'

Fagermo let Ekland go first down the stairs, but at the bottom he turned, received a very full view of what Fru Nicolaisen was not wearing under her brunch coat, and—swallowing his embarrassment, which she seemed to find charmingly old-fashioned—he said: 'You are quite sure you didn't meet him again in the evening?'

'Absolutely sure,' said Lise Nicolaisen. 'Have I hidden anything from you?' Fagermo spluttered. 'I had another date, as far as I remember. It wasn't with Amnesty International, so it may have been the Warm Clothes For the Elderly Committee, or Reclaiming the Alcoholics. I'm chock-a-block full of good works, Inspector!'

Fagermo gained the front door and slipped and slithered down to the car. Ekland already had his hand on the driver's door, but as Fagermo climbed in he said: 'Oh, I've forgotten my gloves,' and made his way nippily back to the front door.

Christ, thought Fagermo, settling grumpily into the passenger seat. How bloody uninventive. Gloves.

12

One Day

As March shaded into April, the elements played coy games with the North Norwegians. Some days they flattered them with hopes of an early spring: the roads were clear, and there was the pleasure of walking on nature's own tarmac again; sometimes the temperatures rose above zero, and on some evenings, as the sun set in a clear sky, the surrounding hills seemed draped with pink snow, like enormous cheap cakes. These were the days of delusion. Next day the skies would be angry grey and lowering, the snow would fall, and by nightfall nature white in tooth and claw had reasserted its accustomed iron rule.

It was on one of the flirtatious days, when the town and the surrounding fjords and mountains were bathed in blinding sunlight reflected from the snow, that the people who had briefly met Martin Forsyth back in December had cause to remember him again. It was nearly two weeks since the body had been found, and already the newspapers had gone on to other things—contenting themselves with brief remarks about the Inspector in charge being in touch with Interpol, and vague suggestions that the body being found in Tromsø was totally fortuitous.

Fagermo was content to leave that suggestion in the air. The apparent dearth of interest in the case, however, did not reassure all the people who had crossed Forsyth's path during that fatal visit. More than one wondered exactly what the wider implications of the murder were, and whether there would be any fall-out that might involve others. And one of those persons was still very worried.

So as they went about their daily business, many of them thought about Martin Forsyth.

Professor Nicolaisen travelled to work by car on those days when his wife did not require it for her private purposes. He parked it behind the Post Office, getting tetchy if there was a lack of space. The morning was, for Professor Nicolaisen, a process of gathering tetchiness. He would have been disappointed if there had been nothing to thwart or aggravate him, but fortunately there always was. Today, as usual, the lift was out of order. He sighed theatrically at nobody in particular, and trudged up the bleak coal-grey stairs, telling himself how bad it was for his heart—though physically that organ was in perfect working order.

He pushed open the main door on the fourth floor and went into the bright orange, blue and white corridors of the Department of Languages and Literature. It seemed to please him no better than the dreary stairs. His nose twitched. The air was redolent of aborted research and stale feminism. He went to the common-room to collect his mail, throwing grunts in the direction of the newspaper readers there. In his pigeonhole was a pay-slip for external examining: four-fifths to the government, one-fifth to himself. His lip curled, and he emitted a sound like an outraged cockerel.

So far the morning was going well.

Those who knew Professor Nicolaisen well—and really, in a small university, there was not much option—contended that it was best to get hold of him early on. Something got into him as the day wore on—'home thoughts', said some wit who knew how his wife spent her time. Or perhaps it was just the cumulative effect of contact with his kind. Certainly the coffee-break at twelve seemed to do nothing for his humour, perhaps because most of the others in the coffee rooms were so much younger than himself, perhaps because of the radical orthodoxies they spouted. Whatever the cause, he was best left alone after the sun had started its long, lingering decline.

Which was bad luck for the student who sat in his room at two-fifteen presenting to his professor the plan for his forthcoming thesis on Crime as Social Protest in the Works of Arthur Morrison. It could not be the chosen author that was niggling Nicolaisen, because he had never heard of him. It could not be the proposed organization of the thesis, because he was not listening. He sat in his poky room, surrounded by cheap reproductions of Gainsborough and Stubbs, and looked witheringly at the boy as he sat reading painstakingly from his disquisition.

Jeans. Check shirt covering grubby sweat-shirt. Fair hair, and the lightest of stubbles on his chin and cheeks. Halvard Nicolaisen's eyes were odd, neither attentive nor abstracted, clearly not listening, and yet *noticing*. Thoughts of some kind were clearly going through his brain, for he sometimes swallowed in a meaningful way that ended up in a little whinny. The student would half look up, then return hastily to his notes.

Jeans. Long thin body. Fair hair. Nicolaisen snuffled. It was that that reminded him . . . reminded him of . . . He pulled himself together. Silly to give way. Nothing to do with *this* boy. Incredibly silly to give way . . .

'Then I thought to give a whole chapter to *The Hole in the Wall*, concentrating on the East End background and taking up the whole subject of the derivation from *Our Mutual Friend*—'

He reminds me . . . There's a look there . . . Fair hair. Check shirt. Professor Nicolaisen emitted a choking sound that threatened explosion:

'Oh Christ in hell, get out of my office, you incompetent driveller,' he said, to one of his more promising honours students.

Nan Bryson sat in a dusty corner of the little US Information Office, copy-typing busily and thinking—for she was competent enough to do both, though any demand for original endeavour found her faintly lacking. She always worked enthusiastically, because her job with the Office was important to her: it was her lifeline, her means of staying put in Tromsø. Here she had put down some feeble roots, got herself into some kind of circle. Nowhere in the States did she have either. If she nursed feelings of having been rejected at an early age she did so for the excellent reason that she had been rejected at an early age.

What Nan was typing was not of any great interest, to her or very probably to anyone else. She was producing paperwork for the bureaucratic machine that in its turn could be expected to beget more such. If the Information Office was indeed part of the ludicrously ineffective CIA network, it kept its secrets from her. She was always telling people that, and never being believed. Perhaps she didn't entirely want to be believed. Perhaps something did go on here that was vital to the security of the Free World. Perhaps her boss, dark and bulky, hunched over something behind his desk, was reading some sort of secret report. But it looked more like a paperback.

She wondered why spying was on her mind. Was she afraid she was being investigated herself? Fat lot they'd find. No—that's right: they'd been talking about it in the SAS pub the other night, all the local drunks and near-drunks. They'd got hold of a rumour that the dead boy was a spy. Charlie Brown she thought of him as, Martin Forsyth she now knew his name was. The gossip was that he was a spy. She'd sat for a couple of hours over her beer just to listen to the talk. As usual in that kind of place it got progressively wilder and wilder. From being frankly and openly gossip, it became by the minute more and more bogusly 'inside'.

And yet—what if he had been? What if he'd scraped acquaintance with her because he had found out she worked at the Information Office? She did not stop to examine whether he had scraped acquaintance with her, or she with him. Nor even whether the thought was flattering. It was a story, a dream, a web of possibility in which she sat at the centre. Bunched over her typewriter, tapping out a long and heavily reasoned memorandum about the proposed closing down of the Information Office's unused library, she set up an image of herself being courted by glamorous male spies in the pay of foreign leftist governments, and her pale, uninteresting little face lit up.

She preened herself.

* * *

In his room in the Faculty of Science, Dougal Mackenzie stood looking out over the fjord. The water sparkled, small fishing boats chugged up and down, there was much activity. He could see over to where his own little boat, new and almost unused, was moored. Turning his head he could see towards Hungeren, the rows of houses, the mountains . . .

He had his dog with him today. Scenting restlessness, and scenting some possible advantage to himself, Jingle had got up from the rig by the door and tentatively come over, looking up pleadingly, wagging his tail, and panting slightly. Looking down at him, Dougal Mackenzie remembered him barking in the snow, tugging at the ear, remembered the gradual uncovering of that young human face.

Quite suddenly, he retched.

Business was slack in Ottesen's men's outfitters when Fru Ottesen dropped in on her husband in the course of the morning's shopping. Two assistants were draped over a rail of sports jackets discussing the English FA Cup match on Saturday's television. Helge Ottesen was sitting in his little office at the back, working on sums that never seemed to come right.

'Not much doing today,' said Gladys Ottesen cheerily.

Her husband grunted. 'Not much doing any day these days. It's these damned package tours to Britain. They ought to be banned. Three hours in Oxford Street and they buy up clothes to last them for years. It's ruining the Norwegian clothing industry.'

'Well, it won't last,' said his wife, with her usual optimism. 'Prices are going up in Britain too. There's not the saving there was, everybody's saying it. And you don't get the quality.'

'If only people *did* realize it,' said Helge Ottesen dubiously.

'Oh, they will, they will,' said his wife. 'I've got a lovely bit of cod for your *middag* . . .'

But after his wife had gone Helge Ottesen went back to his figures and sank further and further into despondency. If Gladys did but know, things were pretty grim. Or would be if it weren't for that little extra, that delicious untaxed little undercover income that kept things precariously afloat. It had been the saving of him—and if all went well it would go on, and on. If all went well . . .

His mind unaccountably turned to the boy who had died in the snow of Hungeren, the boy he had met so briefly. There were rumours going round, talk—but then there was always talk, and half of it contradicted the other half, or was the purest nonsense. There was no reason to believe any one thing people were saying rather than another. No reason to fear the end of his little bonus. And he had always found the police very amenable.

Idling along Storgate in a day full of frustrations and unproductive leads, Inspector Fagermo happened to see, by the open space in front of the Cathedral, two of the people on the fringes of the case whom he had not yet spoken to. On the pavement were planted the two local mormons, with a hortatory placard, a hail-fellow manner and a promise of salvation available through the combination of Jesus Christ and Joseph Smith. They seemed to have plenty of well-wishers and casual acquaintances, but not many takers. On one of them the Arctic spring seemed to have laid an icy finger: the fair-haired, open-faced one had his tie riotously askew, his jacket and overcoat open, and he was getting as near to chatting up the girls as a street-corner evangelist could reasonably be expected to go. Fagermo stopped by them.

'I've been meaning to look you up,' he said. 'I suppose you can guess what I want to talk about.'

'We told the police we'd be here,' said the heavy one, aggrieved. 'It's our usual time and place.' His Norwegian was very grammatical and highly accented. As old Bostilsrud had said, one never had much doubt with an American.

'Not that,' said Fagermo. 'It's about this murder.' The two faces at once looked mystified and concerned.

'We haven't heard about any murder,' said the fair one. 'Why should we have expected that you'd want to talk to us about a murder?'

'We don't read the papers much,' said the other one. 'We can, but we can't really afford to.'

'I thought it was the main topic of conversation among the foreign community, that's all,' said Fagermo.

'We're more religious,' said the heavy, obstinate one, obscurely.

'Anyway, it's about a boy you met, way back before Christmas, in the Cardinal's Hat. I don't know if you remember?'

'The Cardinal's Hat? Were we there?'

'So all the available testimony agrees. I'm sorry if you're not supposed to be.'

'Oh, it's not that so much. But we can't afford eating out or anything, and there's not much we can drink, so I can't quite see why we were there.' The fair boy thought for a bit. 'Wait a minute! I remember now: we did go in one time, just before Christmas.' He turned to his fellow. 'After Steinar, you remember.' He explained to Fagermo: 'It's a boy we've been talking to a lot. He was really getting the message, but he sort of relapses now and then. We've been trying to be good influences, and if we hear of him like going off the rails, we try and get hold of him and talk him out of it, see what I mean?'

Fagermo nodded. It figured: drink and religion were the great weaknesses of a certain type of Norwegian, and some veered enthusiastically from one to the other. He said: 'You went and talked to the foreigners' table there, if you remember.'

'That's right, we did. I suppose we must have known somebody sitting there.'

'Can you recall who?'

The two Mormons thought for a bit. 'There was that man who's an outfitter—has a shop along here somewhere,' said the heavy one. 'He was interested in our suits, said we always looked so smart.'

'We had to tell him they were issued from headquarters,' said the fair one. 'No sale. Then there was an American boy—often see him around—fairly quiet type. Student. And the girl from the USIO: we keep in well with them. They're a lot of help sometimes.'

'Anyone else?'

'There *were* others. I can't recall exactly—'

Fagermo prompted him. 'There was a fair-haired boy, a stranger. You wouldn't have seen him before.'

The two of them thought. 'That's right. Didn't say much. Looked—you know—sort of contemptuous. There's some like that: they look at us like we were some kinda freaks. Yeah, I remember him.' It was the fair-haired one speaking, and Fagermo felt fairly confident he really did remember.

'You didn't talk to him?'

'No, sir. We don't push in where we're not wanted, whatever some people may say. And we were just in looking for Steinar. But I remember seeing that boy again—'

'The boy in the Cardinal's Hat? Where?'

The fair Mormon thought. 'I know I did . . . Not long afterwards, too.'

'It would have been the next day, or the one after.'

'Was it him who got his number?'

'Yes—we found him in the snow above Hungeren.'

The Mormon thought. 'I can't get it. Give me a bit of time, though, and it should come. I'll get on to you as soon as it does. I usually do remember—'

'If you do,' said Fagermo, 'you'll be one of the few to admit remembering anything definite.'

'Part of the training,' said the fair boy, grinning wide and tugging at his crazily askew tie. 'Healthy mind in a healthy body, you know.' He sounded infinitely cynical.

Back in his office Fagermo sat at his desk and looked over the fjord, glimmering blue and gold like a vulgar evening gown. Things were beginning, just beginning, to make some sort of pattern in his mind. Always he had believed that one of the keys to the case lay in the character of the boy himself. What sort of person was Martin Forsyth? There was still a lot of work to be done there, but he thought the blank outline, symbolized by that anonymous frozen corpse, was beginning to be filled in. But then there was that other vital question: what had Martin Forsyth *been*, what had he *done*? Here there were some pieces in place—pieces from Ålesund, from Trondheim, even from Mersea—but also great gaping blank spaces.

He turned back to his desk and began formulating his second set of questions for Interpol. Precious little he'd got from the first lot: no trace of a criminal record anywhere, not even of any minor involvement in questionable activities, or immigration troubles. But *something* of the boy's past must be recoverable, must be relevant. In fact, he felt sure that something would be crucial, that this was not a murder that could be explained by some sudden burst of passion that sprang up during his three days in Tromsø. He sighed. It was just his luck that Iran was currently in a state of turmoil—a jungle of conflicting forces so complex that none of the great powers seemed to know who to kowtow to. And yet, it was very possible that there some part of the solution might be lying. Aberfan, Mrs Forsyth had said, vaguely. Aberfan, Abadan . . .

He would have to trust to time and returning normality. Meanwhile the only thing to do was to formulate a series of clear, concise, to-the-point questions. He drew his pad towards him and wrote and thought for half an hour, concentratedly.

When he had finished he picked up his phone and got through to Bjørn Korvald.

'Bjørn? Fagermo here. Do you remember you offered to take me along one night to the Cardinal's Hat? Nothing like being introduced by a friend if you want to break down barriers, is there? Well, what say we make it tonight?'

13

THE CARDINAL'S HAT

At eight o'clock that evening the Cardinal's Hat was comfortably full, with the usual mixture of students and shop assistants, stray bachelors and stray spinsters, drunken sailors and drunken lecturers. The air was thick with the fumes of beer and frying steak and the smoke of self-rolled cigarettes, but luckily for Fagermo this was not one of the evenings with live jazz. Then you had to bellow your lightest inanities, and take your companion's reply on trust. So up and down the narrow L-shaped room conversation was rife, insults passed from table to table, girls passed from hand to hand, and lonely men on shore leave lurched around in search of confidants for their boozy, lying tales. It was not a smart place: jeans predominated, and heavy jerseys like dead, matted jungle undergrowth. The smart people went to the clubs and the hotel bars, where their sense of importance burgeoned in proportion to the grossness of the overcharging. The clientele of the Cardinal's Hat went there because it was cheap and good; they ranged only from the middling well-off down to the middling hard-up.

Bjørn Korvald and Fagermo collected their litres of beer at the bar counter and pushed their way through the dark-panelled room round to the foreigners' table. For a moment they were not noticed, and Fagermo, gently stopping Bjørn's progress with his hand, had a chance to observe the table and decide that he seemed to have struck it lucky. Crouched over their beers and red wines and Cokes, and deep in a variety of conversations or solitary musings were seven or eight people, and among them were at least two people he was happy to have a chance to speak to away from the inquisitorial atmosphere of the police station. There in the centre, chairman-like, was Helge Ottesen, plump, condescendingly matey, prosperous; and not far away was a young man—flushed, verbose, indignant—whom Fagermo strongly suspected to be the lecturer in French who had been here on the night of Martin Forsyth's visit. For the rest there was a Hong Kong Chinese boy whom he recognized as working at one of the local restaurants, an Algerian student-cum-street-vendor, Dougal Mackenzie, who had found the body, and Steve Cooling, draped enervatedly over a half-bottle of red wine, some of which had streaked a vivid flash across his grubby tee-shirt.

Not a bad haul. But now Bjørn Korvald made a move forward, and the table registered their presence. A sudden hush fell, silencing even the lecturer in French who had been in full self-justifying spate about something or other. The hush was uneasy rather than respectful. Feeling as welcome as the returned Magwitch, they drew back chairs and sat themselves down at the table.

It was Helge Ottesen who broke the silence and did the honours of this informal branch of the Foreigners' Club. With a gesture both nervous and expansive—the behaviour of the fledgling politician in a tight spot—he half rose, shook hands with Fagermo with an unconvincing smile on his face, and gesturing to left and right made embryonic introductions around the table.

'Mr . . . er . . . Cooling you know, don't you? Yes? This is . . . Dr?—no—Herr Botner who teaches . . . er . . . French at the university, and Dr Mackenzie . . . oh, you've met . . . and, er, Monsieur . . . and . . . er . . .'

These last introductions were to the Algerian and the Chinese sitting at the end of the table, quiet and self-contained, regarding the scene with a genial fascination that showed they knew exactly who Fagermo was and why his appearance was received roughly like that of the spectre at the feast. Ottesen fussed further to cover up the coldness of the welcome.

'It's a pity there are no ladies here tonight. Gives you the wrong impression. My wife is at a Church ladies meeting, bazaars and things, you know. And there's usually someone or other here: Miss Bryson who I think you interv—er, met, didn't you? And we have the odd librarian and nurse who often drop in. Really we are not such a—what's the phrase?—such a male-dominated group as we might seem tonight.'

The tawdry cliché seemed to trigger something in the French lecturer, who was clearly on the way to being very nicely drunk indeed.

'Male dominated? Male dominated? Fat chance these days. *Fat* chance. Have I told you—?'

'Yes,' said Steve Cooling, with that lazy American tolerance-with-limits. 'Over and over. Put a stopper in it, can't you?' He turned to Fagermo. 'He's just been refused a grant for leave, and he's convinced it's because he's a man.'

Botner looked about to explode, and then just as suddenly subsided into his glass. Fagermo took the chance to study him. He was tall, well-fleshed and good-looking in a rather academic, rim-less-spectacled way. The type to wear a suit to work, though at the moment his bachelor smartness was looking a little crumpled. He guessed he was the type who might as a rule be reserved, distantly charming, congenitally buttoned-up, but who occasionally broke out. Tonight seemed to be one of the occasions when he broke out.

'Well, of course, we all know who you are,' said Helge Ottesen, unable to conceal that nervous apprehension beneath a gummy smile, but making heroic efforts. 'Is it allowable to ask whether you are on duty now, or is this a visit of pleasure?'

'Oh, pleasure, pleasure,' beamed Fagermo, raising his glass merrily to all and sundry, the ironic glint in his eye telling them that if they believed that, they'd believe anything. 'We policemen have to have time off, you know, when we're not terrorizing the poor motorist, or doing violence to the delinquents by our mere presence on Storgate on Saturday nights. We're human, you know: we like to go out and have a drink, just like anybody else.'

'And is it permitted to ask how the case is going?' asked the slightly Scottish voice of Dougal Mackenzie, the irony in his eye answering that in Fagermo's, and showing that he for one wasn't taken in by Fagermo's night off.

'Oh yes, quite permitted. But I'm not sure I can tell you a great deal at the moment. It's progressing—progressing in the way cases do. I'm learning more and more, stacking up a little heap of pieces of information. Eventually I'll have to look at them all, discard quite a number of them, and then try to fit the rest together to make up a picture. It's a long process, and very intricate.'

'What you're saying is, the case has wide repercussions, is that it?' asked Steve Cooling.

'If you mean: was it something more than his being slugged by a drunken teenager in a Saturday night brawl, then I'd say *yes*. It's been clear from the beginning that there is more to it than that. Just how much more I can't really decide at this stage.'

'And yet he seemed such a very ordinary young man,' said Helge Ottesen, in an almost pleading voice. 'One really wonders if the sort of thing people are saying—'

'Saying?'

Ottesen was confused and declined to come out into the open. 'Oh, you know, just gossip, gossip.'

'Are they talking about spying? Or oil, perhaps?' Fagermo asked the question casually, but when he put forward the second suggestion he saw Helge Ottesen blink so violently that it almost amounted to a flinch. He could have sworn too that somewhere on the table—where?—there was a flicker of movement from someone else too.

Bjørn Korvald said: 'Whenever anything odd happens in this town people always have explanations like that: Russian activity, American activity, one of the multi-nationals, one of the big oil companies—the more fantastic it is, the more important it makes people up here feel.'

'Absolutely, absolutely,' said Helge Ottesen, with such obvious eagerness that Fagermo marvelled at a politician being so transparent. He raised his eyebrows.

'And yet spying *isn't* unknown around here, is it?' he said. 'All very tin-pot and amateur, no doubt, with one side knowing exactly what the other is up to, and Norway winking at the antics of both because we're a little country and don't want to offend our big friends and neighbours. But it *does* go on, and it could suddenly get serious—like the U2 incident. Then again, we know from Stavanger what sort of effects an oil bonanza would have. It's perfectly obvious that some very big interests do get involved, and some decidedly murky happenings take place. One sometimes finds the fantastic explanation is the only one that makes complete sense.'

There was an uneasy silence. 'So what do you think?' drawled Steve Cooling. 'Was he some kind of small-time spy doing dirty work for one of the oil companies, or what?'

'Oh,' said Fagermo, holding up his hand in protest, 'now we're getting too near the bone. I'm just offering a few conjectures, and I'm not going to tell you what I might or might not *think*. What I've got to do is reconstruct what this boy's life has been like these last few years, since he left school. Reconstruct what *he* was like, come to that. One or other of you that I haven't talked to yet might help me with that. You saw him. What sort of impression did he make on you?' He looked around at the politely hostile faces around the table.

'Cold little sod,' said Botner, looking up from his near-empty glass. He had been drinking steadily and morosely. 'You take . . . you take my word for it—cold little sod.'

Helge Ottesen looked pityingly at Botner and raised a significant eyebrow in Fagermo's direction: 'He was a perfectly well-spoken young chap,' he said. 'Not a great talker, but I'm not sure I like that in young people. All too much of it among the students, I'm sure you'd agree. No, I'd say he was a very responsible young chap, as far as I spoke to him.'

'How far was that? Did you have much conversation?'

'Let me see: not a great deal. But Gladys—that's my wife—Gladys and I tried to make him welcome, since he was a visitor. Told him about the town, what there was going on, what there was to do: the Museum, the churches and so on.'

'You thought he was here for tourism?'

Ottesen blinked. 'Well, not exactly. Not at that time of year. But it was just a sort of introduction to the place.'

'And you didn't talk about anything more personal? Such as his work, for instance?'

Helge Ottesen thought very carefully, with an appearance of trying to remember. 'Let me see. He said he'd worked on boats, which surprised me rather, because he wasn't what I'd call the type. How can I put it, not to seem snobbish? He wasn't at all *rough*.'

Botner threw back his head and roared a drunken laugh. 'Splendidly democratic! Why don't you say he wasn't an obvious yob or an obvious lout and have done with it?'

'Now you're putting words into my mouth. All I meant was that he was rather a—'

'A smooth customer?' suggested Steve Cooling.

'Was he wearing a ring when he came in?' put in Fagermo quickly.

'A ring?' said Ottesen, startled. 'I really couldn't say. Does anyone remember?' He looked round the table. All faces were studiously blank. But this time there *had* been a reaction, a flicker, Fagermo was sure of it.

He said: 'Well, never mind. Just a detail. Are you all agreed then, he was a smooth customer?'

'Well certainly he was nobody's fool,' said Ottesen. 'That's really what I meant. You wouldn't easily put one over him. And though he'd knocked around the world he really seemed to have got something out of it.'

'Ah!' said Fagermo. 'He talked about his travels?'

Ottesen was on his guard at once. 'Er . . . he talked, yes.'

'Where exactly did you gather he'd been?'

'Well, let me see, I'm not sure I remember that he specified . . .'

'If you talked about travel, *some*where must have been specified,' pressured Fagermo.

'Wasn't there some talk about Greece?' suggested Steve Cooling.

'Yes,' said Ottesen quickly. 'I think you're right. Gladys and I went there last year, you know, so I think we talked a bit with him about Rhodes.'

'North Africa? The Gulf States? Iran?' hazarded Fagermo.

'Not that I remember,' said Ottesen uneasily. 'Gladys and I have never been there.'

'No package tours to watch the adulterers being stoned? . . . Sorry, just my sense of humour. Well, this has all been very helpful. All the more so since we seem to have two very distinct impressions of young Mr Forsyth. On the one hand, he was respectable, well-spoken, responsible. On the other, he was—I hope I'm not overstating it—cold, calculating, ruthless.'

'The two sides don't entirely rule each other out,' put in Bjørn Korvald.

'By no means. I realize that. And I've met both views before tonight. Two of his girl-friends, for example, would seem to have lived with two entirely different men. But I'd like to hear more about the second view,' said Fagermo, turning in the direction of Botner. 'Because that's more the type that gets murdered, isn't it?'

Botner was clearly not quite with them, but sitting back on his bench gazing vacantly at the ceiling with a petulant expression on his face.

'Don't mind him,' said Dougal Mackenzie. 'He's drinking to forget.'

'I've got a grievance,' said Botner distinctly. 'I've got a bloody grievance. Did I tell you? I was—'

'Yes, you told us,' said Mackenzie.

'Well, I haven't told *him*. I was turned down for leave because I was a man. Of the male sex. Masculine in gender.'

'Oh, don't talk crap,' pleaded Steve Cooling.

'Let him have his say,' said Fagermo. 'Then we can talk about something else.'

This seemed to sting Botner. 'Oh, uppity, aren't we? Well, I tell you it's true. There's not a penny piece for anyone these days unless they're studying *women's* literature, or *women's* history, or women's bloody grammar for all I know. If you're not studying role stereotypes for women in the negro novel or some goddam thing like that, you haven't got a *hope*. It's discrimination, that's what it is! We've become the bloody underdogs!'

'Well, now you've had your say,' said Steve Cooling, 'and it's a pity you couldn't do it a bit softer because there's such a thing as lynch law where that subject is concerned, perhaps you could tell the gentleman what he wants to know?'

'What gentleman?' asked Botner, pulling himself to an upright position and looking round the table.

'I was wondering,' said Fagermo, 'now you've told us your grievance, which was very interesting, if you could say why you thought Martin Forsyth was—what was your expression?—such a cold little sod.'

'Because I remember watching him.' Now he had got away from his sorrows he was speaking more naturally. 'He was just here by chance, you know, just dropped in—or so he said—but there were certain things he did instinctively. Like right from the moment he sat down at this table he was alert to find out who was the most important person at the table. He just did it instinctively.' He looked round triumphantly at the rest of the table to see if they were impressed by his perceptiveness, but he met studious blankness. 'Well, he decided that self-important twit Nicolaisen was the most important—which is a bit of a joke, and shows he wasn't as bright as you lot have been trying to make out. Anyway, he tried talking to him first, but he didn't get anywhere, because our Halvard doesn't like the young, and more especially young men, for reasons we all know and needn't go into, so he saw he wasn't getting through and he switched round and let old Ottesen prose on at him—oops, sorry! Forgot you were here!'

'Oh now, I say—' said Helge Ottesen, but whether in protest at being allotted only secondary importance or at this interpretation of Martin Forsyth's behaviour was not quite clear.

'And then, he was good at getting beer bought for him. I don't think he bought one after his first. Both that poor little Bryson girl, who has to count every penny, and that streak of nothing Cooling—there I go again!—bought him drinks just before they left: he knew he wouldn't have to buy them one in return.'

'I've known other people at this table do the same,' said Mackenzie, with Scottish wisdom.

'And then he let that girl pour out her boring little life story to him, just because he knew she was an easy lay. I was sitting opposite him and I could see he wasn't listening to a single word, just thinking about his own concerns.'

'Hell—if you go by that we must all be cold little sods, because we've all done the same,' said Steve Cooling.

'Wait, wait. He let her give him her address before she left, and he made some sort of a date with her, but after she'd gone he looked at me and said: "In case nothing better turns up." Just like that. Do you see? He was a right bastard. He was ashamed, not because he'd led her on, but because she's so boring and ordinary. He wanted me to know he was used to a better class of girl than that. For Christ sake get me a drink, someone. I've talked myself dry as a bone.'

Bjørn Korvald obligingly got up, collected glasses and set off for the bar. Satisfied, Botner continued: 'So I doubt if he ever turned up in *her* bed.'

'He couldn't,' said Fagermo. 'He was dead.'

'Well, he wouldn't have anyway,' said Botner, 'because he went on to something better.'

'Oh? How do you know?'

'I saw him! The next night, with a woman.'

'Oh, you did, did you? A blonde, I presume, is that right?'

'Oh, you know.' Botner looked deflated. 'I thought I was telling you something new. I might have known there were plenty of others who saw them.'

'Was this on Biskopsvei, above the kiosk there?'

'Oh no, no.' Botner seemed to be trying to concentrate. 'Not there. If I'd seen them there I'd have been in my car. And I wasn't in my car. Was I?' He looked around appealingly.

'Let's take it as read that he wasn't in his car,' said Dougal Mackenzie.

'Well, then, if I wasn't in my car, where would I be?'

'Going to see Marit?' suggested Steve Cooling.

'Got it! Got it! I was going to see Marit. She's one of the girls around the place, you know. I go there sometimes. So does Steve. Sometimes we meet in the street and toss up. That's it. I was on foot, somewhere between my flat and Marit's house. There you are. Now you know.'

'If you could tell me where your flat is, and Marit's house.'

'Oh yes—on the edges of Håpet. That's where we both live. A bit of a university slum. And this boy—what was his name?—Forsyth, and this girl, this woman rather, blonde, thirtyish, thirty-five maybe, they were walking along, he with his arm around her, casual, and she talking very high and fast. That's it. And I know where it was. I've got it. It was the corner of Elgveien. They were turning in. He saw me over his shoulder—saw me and grinned. That's how I know. That's how I know he was a cool, slimy bastard.'

'Elgveien,' said Helge Ottesen. 'Elgveien.' He looked up at Bjørn Korvald returning with two glasses of beer. 'Isn't that where you . . . where you used to live, Bjørn?'

Half-way through the question he had faltered, and an air of profound embarrassment came over him.

14

WIFE OF A FRIEND

The goodbyes as Fagermo and Bjørn Korvald left the Cardinal's Hat were genial but edged with unease, like a schoolboy's to his teachers on the last day, uncertain of what relationship each might have with the other in the future. Fagermo was urged to come back often, but like the schoolboy he felt he would not. A policeman does not mingle casually like other men: how many of the normal topics of conversation in the Cardinal's Hat would be discussed with equal freedom with a policeman there? He ánd Bjørn fought their way through the fug to the cold, clear darkness outside, and stood together uncertainly on the icy pavement.

'I think we'd better talk,' said Fagermo abruptly. 'Where shall we go? My office?'

Bjørn nodded unhappily, and they trudged the two minutes' walk past the SAS Hotel and round to the station. As soon as he swung open the door to his office Fagermo realized his mistake. The room was dominated by his desk, and the only natural place for him to sit was behind it. It was no place for a heart-to-heart with a friend about the friend's wife. With a sigh he accepted the inevitable, took off his coat, and sat himself on the swivel chair.

'I'm sorry about this,' he said to Korvald. 'Not exactly cosy, but the only people I usually entertain here are suspects or witnesses. Still, at least we're not likely to be interrupted. Pull up a chair and make yourself comfortable.'

Bjørn Korvald pulled up a chair, but could hardly make himself comfortable: seated opposite that intimidating desk he seemed immediately to fit into that slot marked 'suspect'—or, worse, that slot marked 'informer'. It seemed to affect him adversely. He sat there grimly, waiting for Fagermo to begin.

'Well, let's get it over with,' said Fagermo. 'You realize as well as I do what everyone there tonight was thinking.' Bjørn nodded. 'It's a small road, Elgveien, isn't it? How many houses would you say were in it altogether?'

Bjørn thought: 'Not more than seven, I suppose. And most of them single-family houses.'

'Yes. And this Botner saw a blonde woman going into it with Martin Forsyth, the night before the murder, in all probability. I'm putting it bluntly, you see. Is there anyone else in the street the description might fit?'

Bjørn sat with his head in his hands. 'Most of the families are older than us. I practically ruined myself building there. There are two couples in their sixties. Three I suppose in their fifties. One of them has a teenage daughter . . .'

'It didn't sound like a teenager.'

'No, it didn't. I suppose my—my *wife* is the obvious one.'

'That's what I was thinking. Do you mind if we talk about her a bit?'

Bjørn Korvald looked as if he minded a lot. Suddenly he had lost all that air of youth regained that Fagermo had noticed in him since he had left his wife. His shoulders sagged, his face-muscles were relaxed like a gassed soldier's. He seemed to want nothing so much as solitude to think. But Fagermo decided he had better talk now, and be done with it.

'I'd better tell you what I know about this blonde. Tonight wasn't the first time I'd heard of her. As far as we know they met some way up Biskopsvei on the night after Forsyth was in the Cardinal's Hat—probably the day before he was murdered, as I say. Whether they'd met before we don't know. Perhaps—but our witness thought, and our witness is a sharp old body I wouldn't like to contradict. She thought, in fact—sorry to have to say this, Bjørn, she thought that one picked up the other.'

Korvald looked up, great thick lines along his forehead, but he flapped a hand dismissively: 'No, no—it's nothing to me. Would to God she had someone. But not *him*.'

'Exactly. Not him, and not him *then*. But we've got to take the facts as we find them, as we always do in my job. Let's take it as a hypothesis, nothing more, that she was walking down Biskopsvei, and stopped him and talked to him on one pretext or other. Now —does that surprise you? She was twenty minutes or so's walk from home.'

Bjørn Korvald straightened. 'Well, not entirely, to tell you the truth. Once or twice people have mentioned that they've seen her, on her own. Don't know why they tell me. Busybodies, I suppose. And one evening, coming home, I thought I caught a glimpse of her—near where I have my flat.'

'Spying on you, do you think?'

'Something of the sort is what I thought. Perhaps wanting to know if there's any other woman. There isn't, by the way.'

'What about the children? What have you got?'

'Two little girls. Five and seven. That's what's been worrying me, of course. But I've no evidence that she's often out at night. They're very good sleepers, and in fact she may well get a baby-sitter in. What occurred to me was . . .'

'Yes?'

'It's just an idea, but I thought she might want to *prove* some-thing—to the neighbours, and so on. She always worried about the neighbours.'

'What sort of thing?'

'That she wasn't lonely, went out a lot, had heaps of friends, that sort of thing.'

'I get you. And it wouldn't be true?'

'No, it wouldn't. It was always just the home with her, and the children of course. And me, I suppose, in a way. So I just thought that, having got a baby-sitter in, she might have to go out. And she'd have nowhere to go.'

'It's pretty pathetic.'

'Don't I know it. I've tried—but anyway, we're not talking about my domestic problems. The point is, I think she'd like to know what I've been doing. Perhaps she's been around more often than I've seen. Or perhaps she's made a habit of picking men up. I'm afraid I'm pretty remote from her now, so I really wouldn't know.'

'How often do you see her?'

'Once a week, when I go for the kids. Not always then. Often they're watching for me, and they run out. And sometimes they come to me by bus.'

'What sort of state would you say she was in? Mental state?'

Bjørn said reluctantly: 'Not too good, I'd say.' He was clearly a battle-ground of conflicting emotions that told him that he *was* responsible and was *not* responsible, *was* involved and was well out of it. He said: 'It's difficult to know what to do. I couldn't go back to her and stay sane, not after I've had my freedom. But there's nothing else would satisfy her. No—not even that would. It just *shouldn't have happened*. She simply can't face up to the fact that it did, it has happened. She has no idea *why*. She's as bewildered now as the day I said I was getting out. The only thing that would really put her little world together would be to wake up and find it was all a dream. So really there's nothing I can do.'

'The question is,' said Fagermo, 'what should I do? I'll have to go and talk to her. How should I approach her? Do you think she'll deny it?'

'I think she may well,' said Bjørn. 'She doesn't have any beautiful abstract passion for truth, certainly. I suppose nobody much does, these days. And you've got to remember that there's no proof it was her.'

'No, no. Still, we've got Botner. If necessary we could have him identify her. I shouldn't think she'd want things to go so far—that is, if she's nothing worse to hide than a night with a stranger. Do you think there's any way of getting her on my side—palling up with her? It would make it easier.'

Bjørn thought. 'I'll tell you how I see her. I think she has always lived in a fairy-tale world in which she is the perfect woman, the perfect wife, the perfect mother. Her mother coached her in what she had to do and be when she married, and she fulfilled her instructions to the letter, and lived in a kind of dream in which she was sanctified by virtue of her clean windows and aired sheets. Do you get me? She's self-righteous without being religious. If you're going to say anything that smashes that image she has of herself, I think she's going to deny it, I'm afraid, however you approach her.'

'So—no chink in the armour?'

'If there is one, I never found it.'

'Try around eleven-thirty,' Bjørn Korvald had said to Fagermo before he left. 'Åse should be at school, and with a bit of luck Karen will be playing with the neighbours' little boy.'

So at eleven-thirty, with the sun shining in a postcard blue sky and the temperature edging over zero, Fagermo trudged up the snow-lined path to the house Bjørn and Sidsel Korvald had built for themselves in their less than blissful married years. It was a moderate-sized wooden house, with a built-in garage and large plate-glass windows, unnaturally clean, on the first floor. He rang the bell—electronic, two notes with an interval—and looked at the lead-lighted coloured windows around the heavy wooden front door.

Sidsel Korvald was prompt in answering, opening the door with an automatic smile switched on simultaneously with the turning of the doorknob: 'Yes?'

She was doing a very good performance of an ordinary Norwegian housewife on an ordinary day of the week, going about her ordinary business. That it *was* a performance Fagermo realized by that sixth policeman's sense, which is a combination of sad experience and common-sense psychology. There was strain in the lines of the forehead, a haunted, inward-looking anxiety in the eyes. But the mouth put up a show of confidence and welcome, and she was boringly neat as a pin.

'Fru Korvald? I wonder if I could talk to you for a few minutes? My name is Fagermo—I'm from the police.'

She showed no sign of stepping aside to let him in, and the smile was extinguished. 'My husband doesn't live here at the moment,' she said.

'It was you I wanted to speak to,' said Fagermo. Then, lowering his voice considerably, a thing he wouldn't have done for Professor Nicolaisen, he said: 'It's a matter of some importance. I think it would be better if we could go inside.'

She looked at him with a wild glint of fear, the mouth now set in a resentful straight line. But finally she stood aside, and Fagermo went determinedly through the hall and upstairs to the living-room. She followed him with every appearance of feeling deeply injured by his call. As if to make something or other plain to him she looked at his shoes and did not ask him to sit down. He sat down.

'I'm sorry to barge in like this, Fru Korvald,' he said, 'but believe me, it's going to be easier if we try to talk things over in a friendly way.'

She pursed her lips together, said nothing, but finally sat down on the sofa, her knees close together, her hands clasped in her lap. As he was trying to think up a way of approaching her, she suddenly blurted out, as if clutching at a straw that had already proved its fragility: 'If it's anything to do with money, I think you ought to see my husband. He sees to all the bills and things.'

'It's nothing to do with money,' said Fagermo gently. 'It concerns a boy—a young man—you may have read about him. He was found dead, murdered, over in Hungeren.'

'Oh yes?'

Her clamlike stance was more revealing than a more gushing response would have been. Of course she must have read about the murder. Fagermo said: 'No doubt you will have read about it in *Nordlys*.'

'I may have,' she said, as though the words were being prised out of her. 'I don't have much time . . .'

'Did it occur to you when you read about it, that you might have known the young man?'

'Certainly not!' The words shot out bitterly, shocked but without surprise. 'Why should I have known him? He was a foreigner, wasn't he?'

'That's right. English.'

'Well, then.' She subsided into silence, as if she had proved a point.

'And yet, I think you did know him. I think you met him one night just before Christmas, up on Biskopsvei. Or perhaps you had met him before?'

'No!'

'No, you hadn't met him before?'

'No—I don't know what you're talking about! Biskopsvei is miles from here. What would I be doing there at night?'

'That I don't know. I don't suppose it's of any importance. What is important is that you met this boy—Martin Forsyth his name was, by the way—up in Biskopsvei, just above the kiosk.'

'I deny it. You're talking nonsense.'

'I see. There could, of course, have been some mistake. But we have several witnesses. I'm afraid I shall have to arrange an identity parade . . .'

Sidsel Korvald's mouth was working convulsively. 'I don't understand what you're saying. Why should I go through an identity parade? What are you accusing me of?'

'Nothing. Nothing whatsoever.'

'Then this is just—persecution!'

'Fru Korvald, the only reason I have to get you to confirm that you met Martin Forsyth that night is because I have to trace *all* his movements in the two days before he was murdered. Can you see that? It would have been much easier for you if you had come forward yourself when the case first came into the papers. Now I can see that you find it hard, and embarrassing. I'm sorry about that. But as far as we can gather he was seen alive after you met him. We have no suspicions of you. You need have no hesitations about speaking. Only please tell the truth—and tell *all* the truth.'

He leaned back in his chair. What he had said was not perhaps as impeccably truthful as he had enjoined her to be, but he had the satisfaction of watching it sink into the pretty, empty, self-absorbed face of the woman opposite. He let the ball settle down in her side of the court, and waited long minutes for her to say something.

'What do you want to know, then?' The words came very low, reluctant.

'How did you come to meet Martin Forsyth?'

'I . . . I met him on Biskopsvei, as you said, one night. I, well, I asked him the time.'

'You were doing—what?'

'Walking. Just walking.' She saw him watching her, waiting for more, and she burst out: 'I've had a lot of troubles. You don't know. I've been shamefully treated. I need to walk sometimes. To think.' A nerve in her cheek began to twitch uncontrollably, making her left eye blink grotesquely.

'Yes, I had heard that,' said Fagermo.

She cast a suspicious look, as if to enquire who he had been talking to, but getting no response, her grievance took hold of her again, and she spat out: 'Can you understand how—how a man who has a lovely home, and lovely children, and everything made easy for him, just as he likes it, can just get up and go off? Not go off with anyone, but just go off? Off to some nasty little room, and live on his own? Can you explain it?'

The voice was like a wailing saxophone, full of humiliation and despair. Fagermo felt no compulsion to answer honestly, and he said gently: 'It must be difficult to understand.'

'I can explain it. He's mad. That's the answer. There must be madness in his family somewhere. He's taken leave of his senses.'

She subsided a little. This was clearly an answer her walking had evolved, the only possible solution to her personal conundrum.

'So you were just walking, and thinking. That's very understandable. But you talked to Forsyth for a little while, didn't you? What about?'

'I suppose about—about his being a foreigner, and what he was doing in Tromsø at that time of year. Things like that.'

'And then you asked him back here?'

For a moment all rage and shame seemed to have left her, and she answered dully: 'Yes,' adding, as if not expecting to be believed: 'For coffee.' Then, with some of the old defiance she said: 'You don't know what it's like, only having children to talk to all day long. I get *sick* for a grown-up voice.'

'I can imagine,' said Fagermo. He could, too. 'What did you talk about? Yourself? Him?'

'Oh, we talked about him. A man doesn't want to be burdened with a woman's problems, does he? I—I asked him to tell me about himself.'

It sounded like a whore's ploy, but Fagermo blessed her for it. 'That's what I was hoping. What did he tell you?'

'Well, we came home and in fact we—we had a drink. I had some in, for Christmas. I have a lot of friends who might call.' No friends, no calls, thought Fagermo. 'So we walked back, and it was nice to have someone to—to lean on, and we sat down and I got drinks, and he told me about his travels. It was fascinating. Such interesting things, wonderful places.'

'What sort of things, places?'

She drew her hand over her forehead distractedly. The strain was telling. She had to think, hard. She hadn't listened, thought Fagermo; she hadn't been interested. 'I remember a lot about Greece,' she said finally. 'About a shipping millionaire's yacht. He'd been a crew member. Not one of the millionaires you read about . . . And then there were a lot of Arab places, I don't re- member their names, but it was . . . fascinating. And then Iran. I remember that because it was in the news, and of course I'd seen pictures of the Shah and his wife. Isn't it awful about them? Yes, I remember he talked about Iran.'

'What sort of things did he tell you about? Was it mostly about his work?'

'Yes, I think so. He had worked there, definitely. Something to do with oil, I think. I remember the names you see in garages. Yes —I'm sure he had worked a lot with oil.'

'Can you be more specific?'

The hand went over her forehead again. 'No. I mean I didn't really understand . . . And of course we talked about other things as well—'

'I suppose things got more—personal, did they?' Fagermo hated doing it, but he had to know the sort of terms the two ended on.

She flushed up, and the twitch on the side of her face, which had stopped working and distorting her china good looks, began again with redoubled intensity. 'I know what you mean. I know what you're implying. Well, why not? I'm not ashamed.'

'I'm not trying to suggest that you should be.'

'What is a woman to do when her husband—goes off his head? Just settle down calmly and forget all about—that sort of thing? Nobody does these days!'

'I know,' said Fagermo. 'Please put it out of your head that I'm trying to put you on trial. It's not even something I'm particularly interested in.'

Her face was crimson now, and her eyes were full. 'So long as it's understood that I'm not ashamed.'

'Absolutely. But before things got more . . . down to earth, did he tell you anything about his personal life?'

'Not much. He was quite reserved, in a way, at that stage. He said he'd been living with a girl in Trondheim.'

'That's true. Did he say anything about his life before that?'

'No—we didn't go that far back. As a matter of fact, that wasn't what he wanted to talk about. Not about his personal life.'

'Oh?'

'Well, you don't, do you? Not when you're with another woman.'

Fagermo took her point. 'But you must have got some impression, through all this talk, of what sort of a boy—man—he was. What he was like.'

She pondered, the flush hardly diminished, and her face seemed to be suppressing memories of some bitterness. She said in a low voice: 'Very self-contained. Very confident. Not very . . . giving.' Then suddenly she looked at him straight, her eyes full of tears, and almost cried out: 'You know the sort of person! Who doesn't give a damn about anyone but themselves! I've had enough of people like that!'

Fagermo looked unhappily at his knees, she seemed so utterly to fit the category she described. 'You think that's the sort of person he was, do you?'

She almost wailed: 'I know it! I know it! All I wanted was a little tenderness!'

'And you didn't get it?'

'Get it? He wasn't capable of it! It wasn't in him! He just used me!' Now she was working herself up with remembered rage, the nerve in her face going double time at the thought of her humiliation. 'Do you know what I was to him? I was a pick-up. An easy lay. He did what he wanted, and that was an end to it. The only difference was he didn't have to pay, and that was the sort of thing he thought about, believe me. He had saved money. There wasn't an *ounce* of feeling in it. He didn't know I was a person. I'll tell you what he was: he was a machine! A beautifully maintained machine!'

'Is that why you . . . got rid of him? That *is* what happened, isn't it?'

She nodded. 'Yes. I got rid of him. I don't know if I can make you understand. After all, I know how men think. I expect you're saying "Well, she picked him up, didn't she? That's what she wanted. What's she complaining about?" Oh, you can't tell me anything about men!' But suddenly she seemed to forget her grievance and speak honestly. 'He made me feel *dirty*. Filthy. It was the way he talked . . .'

'Talked?'

'All the time in here. And then in bed, after . . . The way he talked. It sort of built up. He was so . . . full of himself. How smart he was. How he was up to everybody's tricks, and knew tricks worth two of theirs. Silly jargon like that. Then he kept talking about the ways he had of "making a quick buck". He had some other expression, what was it? "An easy kill".' She stopped in her tracks. 'Funny when you think about it, isn't it? But what I hated . . . what was so insulting that I couldn't stand it any longer was *why* he spoke to me like that—'

'Why? What do you mean?'

'Well, I don't suppose he talked like that to everyone. In fact, early on he was quite—as I said—quite self-contained. But then he decided I was nobody. Something he'd picked up off the streets. He found out who my parents were—nobody important—he knew I had no connections any longer with my husband. So I didn't matter, I couldn't harm him. After we—in bed, it got worse. It was like I was his whore, and he paid me to listen to him talking, as well . . . He just *swelled* with his own cleverness. He was going places. The world was still open to a smart operator, it was still possible to "do an Onassis" as he called it—get rich quick. He knew a thing or two that nobody else knew. He just lay there, talking on and on. About how damned smart he was. About his plans. His big plans. He'd made me feel dirty before. Now I felt like some rotten accomplice.'

'What sort of plans was this he was talking about? Did he go into any details?'

'I didn't listen very much. I was getting—worked up, I suppose. Angry, I mean. Just lying there, feeling ignored. I'd served my purpose, and now he could get back to thinking about himself and his great prospects. His shining future. How he was going to do down this person, double-cross that.'

'Do down? Double-cross? Can't you remember any details? It's very important! Think!'

'Oh, does it matter, does it matter?' She drew her hand across her wet eyes. She felt nothing about the boy's murder, that was clear. If anything, glad. Seeing Fagermo watching her, she seemed to pull herself together and try to think. 'It was to do with information. Facts. Data. I don't know what you'd call it. I remember he lay there, with his hands behind his head looking so . . . complacent. And he said something like: "So many people want it. Everyone's interested. That's why I went into this business. It's a sure-fire thing. If you play your cards right you can sell the same info over and over again." Those aren't his exact words. Does it make sense?'

'Yes, it could.'

'And he said: "And then, you see, if you channel the info cleverly, that gives you a hold on the middleman. Once you've done shady business with someone, he's yours—if he's respectable and you've nothing to lose. If you play your cards right, you can squeeze him, too." I didn't understand what he meant.'

'I think I do. Anything else?'

'Oh, I expect so. Plenty more. I just lay there, feeling ignored, and it just washed over me. And it was all very vague—he wanted me to admire his cleverness, but he wouldn't give too much away.

He just went on and on, and I lay there, listening to him, and getting sicker and sicker—with him.' She stopped and added emphatically: 'With *him*, not with myself.'

'And then what happened? He didn't just go.'

She smiled, a smile of strange self-satisfaction, giving Fagermo the idea that what had happened that night was a clash of two overweening egotisms. 'I threw him out. I listened and listened, and finally I couldn't stand it any more, and I got up and threw his clothes at him, and screamed and screamed: "Get out, get out, get out." '

'And he did?'

'Yes, he did. He just got up and dressed, with me screaming at him, and him looking at me . . . sort of, not understanding . . . supercilious. As if he was saying "Stupid woman".' For a moment she looked uncertain, but then she put a confident front on it: 'Then he slunk from the house.' She smiled complacently. 'I don't think he really understood.'

That, Fagermo thought, was probably the problem with Martin Forsyth. He never really understood.

15

BLOOD IN THE *VINDFANG*

In the course of the next morning Fagermo began to feel the mist imperceptibly rising. That it did so was not the result of any of the international enquiries he had set in motion. Very little had come out of the series of questions he had sent to Interpol. The situation in Iran was such that Westerners were fleeing the country like migrating birds, so concerned to escape the firing-squad, the whip or the bastinado that they even tactfully refrained from enquiring about duty-free grog at the airport. In such circumstances of chaos and panic, little was to be expected from officials of the major oil companies. Feeling helpless, Fagermo decided it was time to turn his attentions to those companies' head offices in Britain and the States, and made contacts with Scotland Yard and the FBI with this in view.

But the first really valuable piece of jigsaw to turn itself up in the box that morning came in the shape of the fair-haired Mormon who enquired for him in the outer office, and was shuffled by Hyland straight up to Fagermo.

'Good morning,' said Fagermo. 'Where's Tweedledee?'

'I've just seen him off at the airport,' said the young man. His going seemed to have made a difference to his companion: he still wore his suit, probably his only gear, but underneath his tie was discarded, and his hair was in a ruffled state and generally far from Madison Avenue. The boy seemed to feel the need to explain his state of liberation. 'He'll be back in Salt Lake City by tomorrow, turning in his suit. Gee, I envy him. I've got six months to do. But his replacement doesn't arrive until tonight.'

'You must feel lost on your own,' said Fagermo. 'Tell me, do you always go around in twos?'

'Well, mostly. It prevents unfortunate happenings. There was a young Mormon chap in Britain recently—'

'Ah yes, I remember,' said Fagermo, who sometimes bought an English Sunday paper when the seamy side of Tromsø life was beginning to seem uninventive. 'I can see that you have to take care. Well, what can I do for you?'

'I've remembered where I saw this chap—the boy who was murdered. Is that any help?'

'Could well be. Depends on how definite you can be.'

'Pretty definite, as it happens. You see, the fact is, we have a pretty set routine: we do certain areas at certain times—I mean the going round and knocking on doors and giving our spiel, you know. We have it all planned out well in advance and written down: on such and such a day we do these streets in Håpet; on such and such one we do those in Kroken, and so on.'

'Just like salesmen.'

'I reckon. So the fact is, if I can remember *where* I saw him, that also tells me *when* I saw him. Right?'

'I see. Sounds just what we need.'

'That's what I thought. Now, I'll tell you where I saw him: we were coming down from Nordselvei into Anton Jakobsensvei. It's mostly naval wives around there, and they're often lonely and ask us in just for a chat, especially those that've been to the States. I've had—well, never mind. Anyway, we tend to knock off round about two, because people start cooking their *middags* then. So it was *around* that time—couldn't be more definite than that. Anyway, he was coming along Anton Jakobsensvei from the town end, as if he'd walked over the bridge. I just about recognized him through the gloom, and I was going to stop and talk to him.'

'Why were you going to do that? I thought he hadn't expressed any great interest in your line.'

'Hell, no, but nobody much is interested, except students writing papers on us and things like that. But we like to keep tabs on the English-speakers in town, just for someone to talk to.'

'And did you talk to him?'

'No, we didn't, because he turned off: before we got down to where the road forks he'd turned off down into Isbjørnvei.'

'And kept on going down there?'

'I guess so. We didn't follow him, because we were on our way home. But in any case, you can't really *go* anywhere down that road—only Isbjørnvei and Binnavei just above. Binnavei's full of university people, and so's the first part of Isbjørnvei: they shut the door on us like we were the curse of Dracula. Must have something to hide, I guess. Then along Isbjørnvei there are some more naval people—they're O.K. Then round the loop in the road there are some people employed in the Town Council offices. Real snooty, some of that lot. But anyways, I guess this guy must have had a date with someone or other in those three groups down there.'

'That,' said Fagermo, 'is what I'd guess too. Now—when was this? Can you be absolutely exact?'

'Yes, I can,' said the Mormon boy, taking out his diary for the previous year. 'Every month we enter up the area to be canvassed each day, and we only depart from it if something *very* special or unexpected turns up. In other words, virtually never. Right?'

'Right,' said Fagermo, impressed in spite of himself by the Big Company efficiency of the whole futile operation.

'In my eighteen months here I only remember us changing schedule once—about a year ago, because of Easter: the holiday was longer than we'd calculated. Right? So this is a regular record—' tapping the diary—'of where we were, and when. And it says we did the far end of Anton Jakobsensvei and up to Nordselvei on December twenty-first. So it was coming down from there, some time I'd guess between one-thirty and two-fifteen, that we saw this boy.'

He leaned back in his chair with a self-congratulatory smile on his fair, open face.

'I'm impressed,' said Fagermo. 'Tell me one thing, though. You've told me how you can be sure *when* it was you saw him, but how come you're so sure *where* it was? People don't remember so exactly as a rule.'

For a moment the young man looked embarrassed. 'Well, hell, we're trained in that kind of thing—cultivating the memory—it goes with the job . . . But, well, if you want to know, something had just happened that made everything stand out in my mind that day. I'd—well, I'd just met a girl—'

'Really? I thought Tweedledee was there to protect you against things of that kind.'

'Yes, well, that's the idea. And he did his best, by Chr—George he did. But sometimes it happens you can—sort of—get a message across without talking. Right?'

Mindful of Fru Nicolaisen, Fagermo began to wonder why the human race had ever taken to speech. 'So I believe.'

'And well, I let him talk to the parents, and let him get all bogged down with his diagrams—we have a lot of diagrams, but Joseph, he wasn't too hot with them—and, well, while all that was going on I sort of—well, I suppose you could say I made eyes at the daughter. Or we made them at each other. And I managed a date before we got out of the door. So you see, I was all keyed up when I saw this boy, and I suppose that's why I remember exactly where.'

'Well, well,' said Fagermo, 'it all sounds practically Shakespearean. I didn't know such things happened these days. I trust the course of true love has run smooth?'

'Pretty much so, but it's getting time alone that's the problem. Joseph was pretty hot on the rules.' He got up. 'So I'll be getting along, O.K.? She's got the day off *gymnas* today. Sick. We've got till eleven-fifteen tonight, when I have to meet the plane. See you around, O.K.?'

'I expect so,' said Fagermo. 'Oh, just one more question: do you ever actually make any converts?'

The boy paused in the doorway and scratched his chin: 'Well, no. Not what you'd call converts. Lots of people are interested, but they don't actually—come over. We're really just sort of showing the flag. What you might call maintaining a presence in the area!'

And he breezed out. So that was it. They were the spiritual

equivalent of a NATO base. Fagermo meditated on this idea for some time, then shrugged it from him, regretfully.

Moving house is always a business, and Norwegians like to do things thoroughly. No good Norwegian housewife would want to move into a house that was not, from the beginning, spotlessly clean. Fru Dagny Andersen was a very good Norwegian house-wife, and she had made it clear to the removers, her husband, her friends back in Bergen and anyone else who would listen (for she was a thoroughly tedious woman) that she needed three solid days' cleaning in this new house before the family could be moved from Bergen to Tromsø, where her husband was taking up a Pro-fessorship in Reindeer Husbandry.

So there she was, with a sleeping-bag and lots of plastic buckets, with a rigidly classified collection of cloths and mops, giving the house a thorough going over from ceiling to basement before the removal men could be permitted to unload their household effects into it. She scrubbed, scoured, washed and polished, her whole body sweating in the spring sunshine, her mind almost blank but for the topics of rival cleaning fluids, and washing powders, and a dreadful generalized feeling of self-righteousness.

'They *said* it was done,' she said with a smug smile to Fru Vibe, her neighbour, as she passed on her way to the shop, 'but it never is, is it? Not *properly*. I wouldn't have wanted to bring my family into *this*. Not the state this place was in. I like to know a place is really *clean*.'

And Fru Vibe kept her end up by agreeing wholeheartedly, and with lots of housewifely detail about corners and bottom cup-boards, though in her heart of hearts she did have a slight sense that cleanliness could be carried too far.

But now Fru Andersen was coming to the end of her tasks. The hall had been done, and the downstairs bedroom and the store cupboards, and now, with the front door open to let in the after-noon sun she was beginning on the *vindfang*, the little square place just inside the front door, designed to keep draughts out and protect the blessed greenhouse quality of the Norwegian home.

Even a *vindfang* should be clean, and be *seen* to be clean, she said to herself complacently.

But when Fru Vibe came home from the shop an hour or so later she found Fru Andersen still on the floor, still at it, and in far from happy mood.

'They said it had been done,' she said, stopping her scrubbing and poising herself on her haunches. 'But look at that.' She pointed to a brown mark on the skirting-board near the floor. 'It's not mud, I know that. I've been at it for nearly half an hour, and I can't get it out. I think it must be blood.'

Something stirred, uncomfortably, in Fru Vibe. Of course, it couldn't be, it was impossible, and yet . . . It was as well to be sure. Something close to fear seized her stomach. Her solution, in all matters of doubt or complaint, was to dump the topic in the lap of Lindestad, the housing officer of the university. After all, they were the landlords.

'I should give up scrubbing,' said Fru Vibe. 'I'll ring up Lindestad and tell him to have a look.'

As luck would have it, Fagermo was sitting in Lindestad's office in the University Administration building when the call came through. Lindestad, a tough little man with a gnome face, was a rare specimen of omnicompetence, with an elephant's memory and the ability to fix anything that went wrong in his domain— which was what he usually did do, rather than undergo the frustrations of trying to get outside men to do it. But it was his memory that Fagermo was interested in at the moment.

'The girl next door said it would take time to get the information,' he said. 'She had to go through her files, I suppose. She said it would be quicker to talk to you.'

Lindestad grinned with amiable modesty. 'What do you want to know?'

'Well, basically this: who was in the university houses in Isbjørnvei in December of last year—that for a start. I gather there are flats in them as well, and I'd like to know who was in those as well.'

Lindestad thought and drew towards him a piece of paper. He

wrote down the numbers of the university houses, and after some thought put down by them a list of names. 'These are the main tenants,' he said, 'of the houses that were occupied. The flats are a bit more difficult.'

He pushed the list towards Fagermo, and it was at this moment that the phone rang. As Lindestad answered a patient and monotonous yes to the upbraiding voice on the other end of the line, Fagermo studied the list. But when Lindestad said 'Blood?' he looked up with a definite flicker of interest. As Lindestad put the phone down with a promise to come out and see, Fagermo said: 'Blood? Where was that?'

'Isbjørnvei. Are you interested?'

'Too right I'm interested. What number?'

'Let's see. Must be eighteen. New people moving in today.'

Fagermo looked down his list and with a pang of disappointment saw by the number eighteen the one word 'vacant'.

'Was there no one at all there in December?' he asked.

'No one in the main part of the house, anyway,' said Lindestad, getting up. 'These houses are kept for Professors and the like: really it's a sort of ghetto for upper-rank academics. They're often vacant for a fair while, being kept for someone or other. This one has been vacant from last summer right up to now.'

'What about the flat?'

'Let's see . . . I think it's someone in the library . . . Yes, that's right. Don't remember her name—rather a pathetic-looking creature.'

Fagermo shook his head. That hardly sounded promising. 'Let's go and have a look, anyway.'

When they got there they left the car below the road, down by the garages that served the houses, and as they climbed through the snow to Isbjørnvei Fagermo was aware of a face watching them from No. 12. Fru Nicolaisen, no doubt, perhaps hoping for a visit from her policeman lover. Shielding their eyes from the golden glare of sun on snow, Fagermo and Lindestad trudged up to No. 18. Fru Andersen and Fru Vibe were ensconced in the doorway, deep in the only topic Bergen people do talk about when they get together, a nostalgic ramble through their rainy home city. They gave it up for business, however, on the approach of the two men.

'Look at that,' said Fru Vibe to Lindestad, whose tolerant expression told of years of dealing with complaining tenants. 'And you said it had been properly cleaned.'

'It was cleaned after the last tenants left,' said Lindestad, edging his way into the *vindfang*. 'That was last summer. You must expect a bit of dust.'

'That,' said Fru Andersen triumphantly, 'is not dust.'

Nor was it. It was a smallish, obstinate brown stain, clinging to wall and wooden skirting-board, just above floor level, and the lighter colour of the wall around told of Fru Andersen's Trojan endeavours to scrub it out.

'Let me see,' said Fagermo, and squatted down on his haunches in the tiny space. He needed little time to make up his mind. 'This mustn't be touched any further,' he said, getting up.

'Not touched?' howled Fru Andersen, outraged. 'But you can't expect—'

'Police,' said Fagermo, showing his card. 'This *must* not be touched. I'll have a man out to look at it in an hour or so. He'll have to take some sort of sample. Luckily there's still enough there to make tests on.'

'Tests?' said Fru Vibe, agog with interest. 'Then it *is* blood?'

'I think so.'

'I wondered,' she said. 'That's why I rang. Do you think it's that boy?' She nodded her head in the direction of the mountains.

Fagermo looked at her with interest: a handsome, intelligent-looking woman. 'Perhaps. It's what I'm working on. Had you any reasons for thinking it might be?'

'Oh no. It's just that since he was found, so close to here, we've all had rather a creepy feeling. And then when there was this blood . . .'

'But this house was empty, wasn't it, in December?' Fru Vibe nodded. 'Did you hear anything from next door?'

'Not a thing,' said Fru Vibe. 'It was winter, Christmas. You sort of shut yourself away at that time of year.' And as the reality of the thing struck her, she shivered. 'I don't understand.'

'Nor do I,' said Fagermo. And as he turned to go towards the car, leaving Lindestad to cope with the protests of Fru Andersen at being moved into a blood-stained house which seemed likely to be infested by policemen, he stood in the street, looking down the road at the other blocks and muttered: 'I think I'm going to have to do some research into these houses.'

16

ILLUMINATION

The University Library, two floors down from Department of Languages and Literature, where Professor Nicolaisen had his office, presented next morning a fairly somnolent appearance. There were no students around: perhaps they were at lectures, or perhaps they never came. A few hen-like women scuttled around from shelves to catalogue clutching cards, books and periodicals, and having a frail, burdened look, as if the world were too much for them. An enquiry to the two pregnant ladies on the desk resulted in Fagermo being shown into the back room where Elisabeth Leithe worked. One glance at her was enough to dispel any idea of her as a conceivable murderess. She was barely five foot four, thin and pathetic, wearing a dreary nondescript cardigan over a nondescript dress, and having a dreary, washed-out face over a nondescript body. Fagermo tried to imagine a murder in which she took an active role: imagined Martin Forsyth obligingly kneeling on the floor of the *vindfang* while she swung a blunt instrument and bashed the back of his skull. The idea was absurd. Even as he turned into the doorway she was sitting at her desk, seeming merely to peer over it, and contemplating several piles of books waiting to have something done to them. Her eyes were great wet globes, as if somehow too much was being expected of her by someone or other. Fagermo introduced himself, sat down, and weighed straight in.

'I understand you live in the flat downstairs in Isbjørnvei 18, is that right?'

The creature looked at him fearfully, her wet, bulbous eyes almost obsessively fixed on his face. She nodded.

'Were you there on December the twenty-first?'

The girl thought, and then shook her head with a little high grunt that Fagermo took to be a negative.

'Where were you?'

'I went home. I had back holidays due to me. I had permission.' The words came out in a terrified squeak. Fagermo had the idea that she thought the university had put him on to her for taking unauthorized holidays.

'I see. So the house has been unoccupied since—when? When did you leave?'

'The fourteenth. I had permission. I had—'

'Yes, yes. I understand. When did you come back?'

'January the fourth.'

'Was everything all right in the house? You didn't notice anything changed?'

The terrified, rabbity face shook in wonderment.

'Nothing in your flat, anyway. I suppose you didn't go into the main part of the house?'

The girl swallowed and hesitated. 'I did. Because . . . I'm alone, alone in the house, I have been for months. I get . . . frightened. I went through the house when I came back, to make sure . . .'

'That you were still alone. Very sensible. Quite understandable. And there wasn't anything odd that you noticed?'

The head shook again.

'There was a brown stain in the *vindfang* when I was there yesterday. Have you noticed it?' She nodded. 'When was it, precisely, that you first saw it?'

'I noticed it soon after I came back. In January.'

'You didn't think anything of it?'

'No. I thought Lindestad must have been showing somebody over the house. He does sometimes. Or I thought I must have spilt something there, but I couldn't think what.'

Fagermo looked at the great dim eyes and got up to go. There was nothing to be got out of her. As he thanked her and began to slip unobtrusively through the door, her squeaky voice shrilled out: 'What was it?'

'Eh?'

'What was it? The brown stain?'

'Blood,' said Fagermo, and was thus directly responsible for a long, hag-ridden night of hideous dreams filled with vampires and rapists and fiendish torturers—dreams which led to another phone call to the harassed Lindestad, with a hysterical demand for a change of flat.

But Lindestad's obligingness and omnicompetence were put to a further test before that. Fagermo rang him up when he got back to the office with the fruits of his meditations overnight.

'Those houses in Isbjørnvei,' he said. 'I suppose all the keys are different?'

'Well, of course.'

'But each of the houses will have had a fair number of tenants in its time?'

'Depends. Some of the people stay a long time, others are only short-term—either because they're not permanent in Tromsø or because they want to buy themselves a house here. So some of the houses have the same tenants they've had since they were built four or five years ago, but others have had a long line of them.'

'Including number eighteen, perhaps?'

'Yes—there've been a fair few there.'

'And what happens to their keys when they leave?'

'They deliver them back to us, of course.'

'Only sometimes they've lost one, perhaps?'

'Oh yes, it happens. People are careless. It doesn't matter much to us: we can get more made.'

'And so can they, of course: get further keys made while they are tenants, and keep one.'

'They could,' said Lindestad, sounding bewildered. 'It's not something we've ever thought of. There wouldn't be much point unless they intended to rob the people who came in afterwards. As far as I know, not many of our professors have burglary as a sideline, though I'd be willing to believe anything about some of them.'

'Not burglary, no. Still, it's an interesting thought. Now—could you give me a list of all the people who've lived in number eighteen since it was built?'

'I could try. We've got the records, of course, but I could probably do it in my head. Could you give me half an hour?'

'All the time in the world. Think about it and get it right. I'm just collecting information.'

And collecting information was what Fagermo did most of over the next few days. Dribs from here, drabs from there. Phone calls here, tentative letters of enquiry there, resulting in little piles of paper on his desk, notes in a grubby notebook he had kept in his trouser pocket throughout the case and had made scrawls in, decipherable only by himself. And in the end they really did begin to make a pattern: Lindestad's lists: the reports from Interpol; the lists of people employed by British Petroleum and other major oil firms; the information from the Continental Shelf Research Institute. And then there was that very interesting conversation on the telephone with the man in State Oil, the Norwegian national oil company. He had been very cagey, of course: had displayed all the caution of the natural bureaucrat, one of the worst species of *homo sapiens* a policeman has to deal with. Nothing must go down on paper, that had to be made clear. Everything he said was off the record—right? And so on, and so on. But in the end he had unbuttoned at least one little corner of his mouth, and Fagermo and he had had a very interesting conversation.

There were still many, many minor aspects of the case to be attended to. It was going to take time, lots of time. Fagermo was a Norwegian. He liked taking his time. Before the real grind of routine investigation set in, though, there was one more brick to be placed in position, one very important thing to be attended to.

Dr Dougal Mackenzie lived in a handsome white wooden house towards the top of the island. Spacious, attractive, often old farms, some of them built by profiteers from the First World War, these houses were prized by some for their style, despised by others for their draughts, their inconveniences, the expense of their upkeep. Like most of the old wooden houses in Tromsø, they were in daily risk of burning down, either through faulty wiring or at the hands of the Town Council's official pyromaniac. But they were stylish, satisfying places to live in for people with the means to maintain them. Fagermo noted as he walked up the drive a man odd-job-bing around the well-shrubbed garden who was not Dougal Mackenzie. The snow lay now, in this first week of May, only in odd, obstinate patches in shady corners. Spring was beginning its long, flirtatious love-affair with the people of Tromsø.

Fagermo's ring on the door-bell was the signal for excited little whines and yelps on the other side, and—when the door was opened—for a doggy onrush, indiscriminate shows of friendliness, jumpings up and attempts to lick his face. After this, Jingle departed down the path to inspect the course of Fagermo's footprints and do a routine check around the murkier parts of the garden—for all the world as if he were a police constable.

Dougal Mackenzie seemed used to taking second place to his dog at the moment of opening the door. He appeared to take Fagermo's visit equably, but his eyebrows were raised quizzically when he spoke.

'Well, Inspector, what can I do for you?' He held the door as if uncertain whether to invite him in or not.

'Could we have a chat for a little, do you think?'

'By all means.' Mackenzie—smiling and friendly, and quite un-like Sidsel Korvald in his reception of a police visit—opened the door wide and ushered him into the house, pausing only to call Jingle in from a distant lilac bush, and then make futile attempts to persuade him on to his chair.

The sitting-room was pleasantly furnished in a modern style of comfort which did not clash too obtrusively with the traditional air of the house. English newspapers littered the side tables, and dotted around other spaces in the room were files, open books, and what looked like drafts of examination papers. It was the house of a busy, untidy academic.

'Sorry about this,' said Dougal Mackenzie. 'Bit of a mess, I'm afraid. My wife is sick.'

'Oh dear—anything serious?'

'Not really. Finds it difficult to adapt, you know. Had to have a spell in hospital in February. I've packed her off to Scotland for a month or two. Should set her up.'

Fagermo had been in Scotland, and had his own opinions of what a couple of months in that country in springtime would do to a person, but he held his peace. He knew that some foreigners, and many Norwegians too, did find it difficult to adapt to the darkness of a Northern winter, particularly in their second or third year.

'That's sad,' he said. 'I hope she perks up.'

'Oh, these things—' said Mackenzie, flapping his hand vaguely towards an armchair unencumbered with papers or files. 'Luckily I'm used to looking after myself.'

'Oh yes—when you've been living abroad, I suppose.'

'That's right,' said Mackenzie. He said it with an American intonation: That's *right*. 'What was it you wanted to see me about? It's a long time now since I found the body. I don't suppose there's anything new I can add.'

'No, no—probably not. No, I'm really consulting you in your official capacity.'

'What do you mean? As an academic?'

'Exactly. You see, I'm a pretty unscientific person. A bit of a disadvantage these days for a policeman: mostly when we solve a crime it's the boffins who do the lion's share of the detection. So I trail along with the good old human factor. And when you said you were a marine geologist I didn't immediately connect you with oil.'

'Really?' said Mackenzie, an open smile spreading over his plump, pink face. 'Lots of other things as well, of course, but to be sure oil is among them—especially up here. I'm sorry. I didn't realize the name didn't mean anything to you, otherwise I'd have said something when we talked about oil in the Cardinal's Hat the other week. You know how it is: I just didn't want—'

'To teach your grandmother to suck eggs, isn't that the English expression? No, I quite see. My own fault entirely. But it might mean that you can help me a lot: fill me in on the background. I've had a lot of help from the Continental Shelf people down in Trondheim, as a matter of fact.'

'Oh, yes—some first-rate people down there. And of course he'd worked there—hadn't he?'

'Yes, he had, actually. But there are some other things I thought you were probably the best person to come to for. For example, he'd worked, as you say, on boats with the Continental Shelf research people. Collecting data, and so on—most of it done electronically, with pretty sophisticated equipment. How much do you think all that data they collected would have meant to a chap like that—a chap with a respectable but fairly ordinary education?'

'Little or nothing, as a general rule.'

'Even if he'd worked in oil before?'

'Oh yes, even then. You need a real grounding in the subject— from a university or polytechnic in fact—before the sort of info they're getting would mean a thing. It's the sort of education we're aiming to provide here. And of course, even then the data by itself is nothing: you'd need time to work on it, even if you were an expert. You'd have to sit on all the stuff for a while before you could really assess its significance.'

'So normally all the data they collected would go straight to, say, State Oil, and even then they'd often call in expert advice, from the universities or wherever.'

'That's about it. It's a long job.'

'The end result being a better idea of the most profitable areas for drilling?'

'Yes—put very simply, that is one of the things they're interested in.'

'And not just State Oil.'

'Well, no. You know the way of the world, Inspector. There's a pretty cut-throat competition among the oil companies, and the gentlemanly rules sometimes get passed by. Don't they always? And particularly now, with the Middle-East supply getting more and more uncertain, everyone's interested in the North Sea fields. Particularly the Northern ones.'

'Why particularly the Northern ones?'

'Because they're so rich. That's one of the things we're pretty sure about. Enormously rich—much more so than the fields further south, the ones between Norway and Britain. And then, they represent the future—they will probably be the next big ones to be opened up. But there are so many imponderables: the cost of getting at it is one big one; then the technical difficulties due to the rugged weather; the political opposition to it from people up here; the opposition of the ecology people. It's all very exciting, just because it is so uncertain. So naturally all the various companies are interested in just about every aspect of what's going on, and what's being found out.'

'I see. That's roughly what I thought. But now, where do the universities come in?'

'Well, not as directly as the Continental Shelf people. But the fact is, this discovery of the North Sea oil found Norway pretty unprepared in a lot of ways. It was like a big pools win, you know. It wasn't something anyone could predict, or that you could do anything about in advance. So suddenly there was this big need for experts—in all the related fields. What's happened has been enormous expansion in the relevant university departments, with lots of money from the government to push it along. In the early years Norway has had to rely on a lot of foreign advice—Americans, Britons, Dutch, and so on. But Norway's in the grip of the same sort of petty nationalism as everyone else is these days: foreign help isn't good for national pride: she wants to breed her own experts and run her own show.'

'But meanwhile?'

'Meanwhile she still often has to call in experts from abroad to train the Norwegian experts of the future.'

'Hence you?'

Dr Mackenzie smiled broadly and leaned back on the sofa, stroking the head of his dog, who had given up all idea of going on his own chair and had finally jumped on the sofa and settled down with a sigh of boredom by the side of his master. 'Hence me, as you say. There are lots like me in Norwegian universities—in geology departments and elsewhere.'

'People with foreign experience?'

'Yes—people with foreign degrees, people with lectureships at foreign universities who can get a step up by coming to Norway. We've got in while the going's good, of course. In a few years they'll very likely be restricting jobs to Norwegian applicants.'

'I see. And you teach, supervise—you also act as consultants for State Oil now and then, I suppose.'

'Yes, now and then.'

'So in many ways you're key people in this whole business of North Sea oil?'

'Oh, I wouldn't say that. The key men are all down in Oslo, within State Oil. They're the ones who make the decisions. They've multiplied like rabbits down there in recent years, and I must say—well, perhaps I'd better not. One learns to be tactful after a time.'

'You think they're inefficient?'

Dr Mackenzie smiled and held his peace.

'Still,' said Fagermo, 'if you're not the key figures, here in the universities, still you have a lot of sensitive information going through your hands.'

'Yes, I suppose so, now and then.'

'Information that a lot of people outside the system would give a packet to get their hands on?'

'I think you're being a little melodramatic there, Inspector. There are various ways of getting this information. Companies can mount research operations of their own, for example.'

'Illegally, surely, if they were within the Norwegian sphere of interest?'

'Yes, surely. But it happens. You've just got to look at the Russian fishing fleet . . .'

'Yes—that's the local joke, of course. Still, the big oil companies at least would prefer not to do anything so flagrantly illegal as mount their own operations, if it could be avoided. If there were other ways of getting hold of the sort of information they're after—'

'Well, yes, I suppose they'd take it, if there was no great risk involved.'

'Yes,' said Fagermo. 'So I would have thought. And a large wad of money to one or two people is in any case cheaper than an elaborate and clandestine scientific expedition.'

'No doubt. Though as I say, I don't think you should dramatize this too much. The State Oil people do a lot of sharing of information, when it suits them, and most of the data from these geological surveys gets around eventually.'

'Eventually. That may be the crucial point. Where there's a lot of money to be made, the various parties will want all the information they can get, and they'll want it fast. Hence the Russian fishing-boats, I suppose. But really, what I'm trying to do now is what I've been doing all along: fill in on Martin Forsyth. The boy and his background. See what possibilities he had for getting into trouble. Because one of the few things we know about him is that he certainly did get into trouble. One possibility was—still is—sex. But the difficulty with that is: he was here for such a short time. Another possibility is money. But then the question arises: what from? As far as I'm concerned the two most likely answers are spying—political spying—and oil.'

Dougal Mackenzie looked thoughtful. 'There have been some pretty odd deaths in the area, haven't there? Those Japanese or Chinese or whatever down near Bodø: they were never identified. People talked about spying, I remember.'

'They certainly did. It's the sort of thing people say when they don't know anything definite but think there's something mysterious going on. But nobody ever identified those foreigners. With Martin Forsyth we had the advantage of identifying him pretty easily. And then we found—amid lots of uncertainties—some background in oil. Here in Norway, both in the Stavanger set-up, and in Trondheim. And also in the Middle East. I soon found out that he'd probably worked in Abadan.'

'Really?'

'Yes. And as far as I'm concerned that seems to mean one thing: if there was anyone working on that boat doing geological surveys who was likely to know what he was doing, it was Forsyth. He was intelligent, he had a moderately good educational background— and above all he was sharp: he had a keen eye for the main chance, and he seemed to want to use it to make money quick.'

'Yes, I see,' said Mackenzie. 'That does seem to add up to a fair conclusion.'

'Doesn't get me far enough, though,' said Fagermo. 'If Forsyth was feeding information direct to—say—an American oil company, why should they kill the goose that was laying the golden eggs, or why should anyone else? It seemed to me that the situation was a bit more complex than that.'

He sat back, took out a cigarette, and lit it. 'Now, Dr Mackenzie, these foreigners who come and work in oil in this country, or in the universities, what is their background as a rule?'

'Well, as I say, they come here mostly for promotion. Norway needs people in a variety of fields connected in one way or another with oil: geologists of various kinds, geographers, economists with rather special interests—and plenty of others. Where you get a sudden demand like that you'll always get people applying from outside who think they'll get ahead faster abroad than they will in their own countries. Nobody likes being stuck on the lower rungs of the academic ladder when the only chance of rising is by stepping into dead men's shoes.'

'You're implying that most of them come direct from foreign universities, aren't you? But that's not always true, is it? Some have come here whose main experience is with overseas oil companies, isn't that right?'

'Oh, yes, certainly.'

'As in your own case, Dr Mackenzie.'

Dougal Mackenzie sat back in his sofa, his hand once more on his dog's head, his whole body lazily drooping over the arm in a way designed to suggest relaxation. He smiled faintly. 'Yes, that's quite right. I had a period with one of the big British oil companies and another short spell with an American one. Most of us have, as you say, been with them at one time or another.'

'So I gather,' said Fagermo. 'It must make you very useful when it comes to all this consultation work.'

Mackenzie shrugged. 'Perhaps. They come to me—the State Oil people—now and then. All of us in geology departments who have this sort of special knowledge are used from time to time. Most of us have done our stint with the big oil people.'

'Again, so I gather,' said Fagermo. 'You, I believe, were working in Abadan for about five years before you came here.'

'That's right. Something like five, I suppose. In a way I expect you could say it was that experience got me this job. Naturally if they start drilling up here, someone with first-hand experience on the spot will be worth his weight.'

'Very nice,' said Fagermo, keeping his eye on that carefully relaxed body. 'Well—you can understand my interest. Martin Forsyth's mother says he worked at "Aberfan" or some such place as that. You've worked at Abadan—'

Dougal Mackenzie laughed and spread out his hands. 'Have you any *idea*, Inspector, of the size of the place, of how many foreigners work in or around Abadan?'

'A good many, I've no doubt. I presume you would deny that you ever met Martin Forsyth there?'

'Certainly I would—there or anywhere else as far as I remember. But one met a great number of people out there—many of them British. And remember that I only saw him dead here. But as far as I know, certainly I never met him. You've got to remember these oil companies are pretty stratified little societies. I don't want to sound snobbish, but Marty Forsyth and I would have moved in very different circles.'

'I notice you call him Marty. And yet I've never used that form in talking about him with you.'

'Martin—Marty. It's a common abbreviation.'

'*Is* it, sir? I'd like to check up on that. I had an idea that it was fairly unusual—more of a pet name, or a joke name based on a television star than a common abbreviation. Well, well—interesting. Now, one more little thing. Our medics are agreed that Forsyth was not killed where he was found—he was taken there later, after the blood on the wound had already congealed. Now, by pure luck—and it's about the only piece of luck we've had in this case—Forsyth had an unusual blood-group: he was AB positive. And the other day we were put on to a nasty bloodstain in the *vindfang* of Isbjørnvei 18. It was the same blood-group. And when I looked up the names of the people who had been tenants of number 18, I found your name, sir.'

'My dear Inspector, you're on to a loser there. That was all of three years ago. The first couple of months I spent here, before I bought this house.'

'Exactly, sir. I know the dates. But the idea I'm playing with is this: if you *should* have planned to kill this boy, you would hardly have wanted to use your own house, would you? Quite apart from the obvious danger of his being traced here, your wife was with you at the time, wasn't she? And yet you would want an address to give him, somewhere to meet him: he would have been highly suspicious of an outdoor tryst at that time of year. Now if it *should* happen that you had still got a key to the house in Isbjørnvei—one you thought you'd lost, and which therefore hadn't been returned to the University Administration—what better place to appoint to meet him than a house you knew was empty, and which you could get into. Around Christmas there's very few in those houses: a lot of tenants have gone to their families in other parts of Norway. It's dark by two, and most people huddle inside. Really, a very good place to kill.'

Dougal Mackenzie's smile had not relaxed, and if there seemed a new tenseness in the body he nevertheless gave an impression of relief that things had come into the open, a readiness to accept a challenge and enjoy a duel.

'Well, well, at last you've said it out,' he said. 'Fantastic as it all is, I know now exactly what you're thinking and suggesting. Let's take it from there: I know what I'm being accused of, and you know that I know. I think there's a distinct lack of anything in the way of evidence in your case so far, and the whys and wherefores are still a mystery.'

'You're right,' agreed Fagermo amiably. 'Quite right. Very little evidence. Only very tenuous indications. Little connections like spiders' webs. Now, here's another little dribble of information. As you say, the people at State Oil often use the high-ups at the universities as consultants to evaluate the data collected on these various research expeditions in the North Sea. But well over a year ago, they stopped using you.'

'But, Inspector, this isn't a regular thing. There are several of us. This sort of work goes in fits and starts.'

'Quite possibly. But they *deliberately* stopped using you. There are several Professors and Readers in your field previously employed by one or other of the big oil companies. For various reasons—mainly, of course, the suspicion that some companies were acting on information which they shouldn't have had—they began to have doubts about the reliability of some of the people they were using. Because this stuff was definitely confidential. So they began making little tests. And as a result, a couple of people were dropped as consultants. One of them was you.'

'I see. Well, this is news to me. It seems rather like condemnation without trial. And, with all due respect, I still don't entirely see the significance.'

'End of useful extra income,' said Fagermo, with his most urbane smile. 'And I don't mean the payment from State Oil for your consultancy work: eighty per cent of that would go back in income tax at your salary level. But why else would you have been passing on information except for money? What was threatened was that extra whack you have been getting, tax free, from whichever company, or compan*ies*, you were passing on the information to. I don't know the rate for the game, but I'd have thought these must have been tidy sums, to make it worth your while.'

'You have, I suppose, Inspector, some shreds of *evidence* that this is what I've been doing?'

'Quite frankly, no, sir,' said Fagermo, with undiminished amiability. 'As you will be aware, this is an area where we can't get information by our normal channels. Nothing short of a Congressional Committee or a Royal Commission or something of that sort could get details of the sort of payment I'm thinking of: under-cover payment by one of the big multi-nationals. So you're quite right: here we are definitely moving into the realms of conjecture.'

'Have we ever been out of it? Still, go on and entertain me further.'

'Well, I'm quite willing to acknowledge that what I'm suggesting here is sheer guesswork. We'll keep it on that level. I think that somewhere around this time, when you stopped being used by the State Oil people, you met up again with Martin Forsyth—if in fact you'd ever lost touch. For all I know you could have got him his first job in this country with the oil people down in Stavanger, but that's not a vital part of the story. I think it occurred to you, when you met up with him, that there were other ways of getting the gen the oil companies wanted than by having it referred to you as consultant. If you had somebody bright, sharp, somebody with experience and a bit of grounding in the subject, and if he got a job with one or other of the bodies doing the geological surveying, then you could go on with your little sideline. Splitting the proceeds, of course, with your partner, doubtless in some such proportion as eighty per cent to you and twenty to him. That was your downfall.'

'You've given me precious little reason to think I've fallen down so far.'

'In the first instance *his* downfall, of course. But eventually yours. I'll see to that. For some while I'd guess the scheme worked very well: Forsyth got the job with the Continental Shelf Research people. They were very happy to have him: he was significantly better than the men they usually recruited as hands on their boats. Suspicious in itself, I think. I've found out they were paying him decidedly *less* than he was getting in Stavanger, and my impressions of the sort of chap Forsyth was suggest that he wasn't one to take a pay cut just for the joy of working on boats. Everyone says he was a loner, a reserved sort of boy, but one who knew what he was doing. I feel pretty sure that what he was doing was feeding all the information he could get hold of to you. And that you were doing what he wasn't qualified to do: interpreting it, and feeding it forward to one or other—perhaps more than one—of the big oil companies. Conceivably even to the Russians as well, who have oil interests of their own in the Barents Sea, and are very interested in everything Norway is doing in the way of oil exploration.'

'Quite a lucrative little side-line. You make it sound as if the whole of the world's oil industry was knocking at my door and stuffing money through my letter-box.'

'Not quite—but I should think you did very well. The big companies have a pretty good network of contacts, covering any area where they have an interest, or hope to have an interest: local politicos (I think they have one here); academics; journalists; any sort of leader of local opinion. They're interested in information, and they're also interested in shaping local feeling towards the coming of oil, and towards their own claims. I think they pay well.'

'But from your point of view it's frustrating that it's so difficult to get proof, I should think?'

'Very frustrating. But I'll go on with those little cobwebs of suggestions. When we look at you and your life-style, we can't help but wonder, sir. It's not many academics can afford these old wooden houses, particularly one as large and handsome as this. It's one of the best specimens in Tromsø. Then, you've got a large Swedish car, and more recently you've acquired a boat. Somehow all this takes you just that bit out of the academic rut as far as life-style is concerned—it's more the very prosperous doctors and lawyers, or the really successful businessmen who run to houses like this, to boats the size of yours.'

'Of course, you know nothing about my personal background, about my family, and so on.'

'I will, sir, I will. Did you inherit money? Did you make a lot when you were with oil, and did you save it? I'll be looking at all that. I'll be looking at your bank accounts—not your Norwegian ones: those are too easy, too open to inspection. But somehow or other I'll have to get a look at your British ones, possibly an American one, a continental one? It won't be easy. Perhaps it will be impossible. But I've set things in motion already, and I think in the long term I'll get results.'

There was a silence as Dougal Mackenzie contemplated, still with a slight, thin smile on his lips, the long term opening up before him. His dog, Jingle, was now resting his head on his lap, seeming pleased with the restfulness of the conversation.

'You haven't explained,' said Dr Mackenzie at last, 'why I should kill this boy. Does your little trip into fantasy not include motivation? I should have thought it was the last thing I'd want to do if I was using him to make money out of all and sundry.'

'I think that's quite easy, if you take in the human factor. I think you were two of a mind. Like you, Martin Forsyth could never get enough. You used him. I expect you despised him. You thought that because he had no academic background he was stupid, that he would be an easy tool. But Martin Forsyth was nobody's tool. And he wasn't stupid, though he was very, very unwise. You both slipped up on the human factor: if you had underestimated him, he certainly underestimated you. I think quite early on in the game he realized that he *was* being used; that provided he could make contacts higher up he could feed the information *direct* to the various potential customers, without having you as middleman, since it could be interpreted at base there. But above all he realized that now you'd entered into this arrangement with him, you'd put yourself in his power. It's something middle-class people almost always forget.'

'What is?'

'That if you *use* someone like Martin Forsyth, you're using someone who has nothing to lose—no stable job, no "respectability", no reputation. Whereas someone like you, sir, has all of those things, and doesn't want to lose them. It puts you in his power.'

'I should have thought an academic these days was one of the most generally despised members of the community,' said Dougal Mackenzie, his smile broader than ever.

'Ah—that's just your little academic joke. In fact, an academic has an almost impregnable position. Perhaps that's what attracted you, after serving with the oil companies. You're virtually impossible to sack, however incompetent. You're actually looked up to by a lot of people, at least here in Norway: it's very much a "status" job, and in a country with no aristocracy, it's the people in the status jobs who are the cream of the cream. It's something you people in the university come to take for granted. I've heard a left-wing academic complain bitterly that when he went to jail for drunken driving he was put in with common criminals. He thought he could shelter behind some impregnable bourgeois fortress. No, the fact is that you had everything to lose, and Forsyth had nothing.'

'You're saying, if I understand you right, that he blackmailed me. No doubt you hope my bank account will bear this out too.'

'Possibly it will. More probably not. Because I should think this was just the beginning. He can't have been feeding you information for many months, and he'd need a really good hold over you.

And, as for you, you'd realize as soon as the first hint of blackmail was made that this was something that could go on for ever. I think the sequence was this: Forsyth began with oblique approaches, you spotted his game from the beginning, and made an appointment in Isbjørnvei to talk things over.'

'And there killed him?'

'Yes. I think he came up here a day or two early, to spy out the land and think things over. I don't know what he'd decided on when he went to the appointment, but I guess he was hardly in the door before you killed him, quickly and quietly.'

'I see—the blood in the *vindfang*. You're building an awful lot on very little, Inspector.'

'I know, I know,' said Fagermo. 'I'm telling you my thoughts, not making out a case. I'm just at the beginning. There's going to be months of rummaging around after proofs. Now—as I say, I take it you hit him hard as he was turning to take his coat off in the hall, and that he fell backwards into the *vindfang*—hence the bloody mark. Then I think you pulled him into the hall or one of the downstairs rooms and stripped his clothes off.'

'To hinder identification, I suppose?'

'Of course. That was very important. There's one interesting thing there. You stripped off not just his clothes, but also his ring. That must have been difficult to get off: it was tight, and left a deep ridge. A nasty, sick-making process, I think, for someone who wasn't a natural murderer. I've been mentioning rings to a lot of people, on the assumption that a once-off murderer would remember that most of all. I sensed a reaction when I mentioned it in the Cardinal's Hat, and I fancy it was *you* who reacted. You hadn't banked on the ring.'

'Hadn't banked on it?'

'I mean that not many ordinary young men in Britain wear rings. You hadn't expected it. But he was engaged—sort of—to a Norwegian girl, and she did what any Norwegian girl would do: she bought him a ring. And so you had to tug and tug to get it off. And you remembered that in the Cardinal's Hat. I think you are remembering it now.'

A flicker of emotion had passed over Dougal Mackenzie's face.

He said quickly, 'And so I went and buried him in the snow, only to decide to discover him there three months later.'

'Well, oddly enough, as it turned out—yes.'

'I've heard of murderers revisiting the scene of the crime, but other than Burke and Hare I've not heard of them burying the body and then enthusiastically digging it up again. It sounds more like my dog than me.'

Jingle looked up at the mention of his kind, and tentatively wagged his tail.

'Told like that it sounds absurd,' said Fagermo confidently. 'But what you're describing is what *happened*, not what you *wanted* to happen. Things didn't pan out as you expected on that occasion. As I say, I think the murder was a hurriedly planned affair. A quick response to a dangerous threat. You stripped the body of all identifying marks, and then—at night, probably—you took it a little way up in the mountains away from the houses and there buried it. It was snowing in any case. It must have been an easy job. But later I imagine you regretted it. Especially when that paragraph appeared in the papers about the boy missing from the Alfheim Pensjonat.'

'I don't actually read Norwegian, Inspector.'

'It was a topic of common gossip, especially among the British community. And when that came up, you realized there was a real danger if the body was discovered of its being identified; and if that happened, all sorts of connections might be made. Whereas if the body had been well weighted and thrown in the fjord, the chances are it would never have been found—or if it had been, it would have been totally unidentifiable. Difficult to do without detection from dry land; difficult to do from either of the bridges, because people keep a look-out for suicides, and anything suspicious might have been noticed. But I think that about this time the question began to nag you: was it too late? And in fact it was about this time, the end of February, that you bought the boat, wasn't it?'

'How well informed you are—already, Inspector.'

'I've checked what I *can* check here, sir. That was one of the things. Anyway, you bought the boat, and then one day early in March, shortly after the first thaw, you went to look at the state of the snow. I don't think you realized how much difference even a brief thaw makes to the snow levels. You went to satisfy yourself that you could get the body up with comparative ease—it was a reconnaissance trip. But in fact he was already practically exposed.'

'I could very easily have covered him over again, though.'

'But in fact you had the most awful luck, didn't you? I've read over the accounts again, and it's clear how it happened. Your dog started tugging at the ear in the snow, and just at that moment Captain Horten skied down the mountain and came to the spot. And the aggravating fellow stopped to look. From then on, your plan was sunk. Horten realized there was a body there, and all you could do was participate in the discovery. A good, innocent-seeming role for a murderer, but much, much less safe than the one you had planned. We have an awful lot to thank your dog for.'

Dougal Mackenzie's fondling of that dog's head was by now becoming somewhat obsessive, but he slept on, head in lap, oblivious of all except the sounds of interest to dogs—birds, barks, nature outside the window. He looked, in fact, rather pleased with himself. But then, the expression on Dougal Mackenzie's face was hardly less complacent.

'Well, sir,' said Fagermo, 'that basically is my case.'

'Your *case,* Inspector?'

'You're quite right. As I said before, it's not a case at all. Just a fantasy based on a few significant connections—Abadan, geological research for oil, number eighteen Isbjørnvei, the blood in the *vindfang* . . . just a series of slight, suggestive indications.'

'Wouldn't it have been better to wait until you'd got something more substantial? At the moment what you have is hardly, I would have thought, worth mentioning.'

'Right again, sir. Normally I would have got a great deal further before I even broached the subject. But then, normally any investigating I had to do would be within Norway—plodding work, painstaking details, but easy, open, accessible stuff. Now the investigation of this case is going to be very different. Heaven knows when—if ever—it's going to be possible to do any serious work in Iran. If it proves not to be, I'm going to make contacts

with other people who were working for the same company—
people on your own level, the sort of people who are getting out
fast now. And perhaps I shall be able to find some who were
friends of Forsyth, if he had any: he kept his cards close to his
chest, that boy. Then of course there are the oil firms themselves,
their central offices. And of course the consultancy work you did
for State Oil here, and the reasons for their thinking you had been
guilty of leaking information. Then, as I said, there are your own
personal records—bank accounts, and so on.'

'What a long, tedious prospect seems to stretch in front of you,
Inspector.'

'Very long. Not tedious, I hope. I expect at the end I shall be a
lot better informed about the ways of the big world.'

'Very foolish of you to put me wise to what you are going to be
doing before you even start, isn't it? There's no knowing what I
mightn't be able to have destroyed.'

'Very unorthodox, certainly. But I had a reason. You see, I
don't at this moment know the extent of your activities. I will, but
I don't yet. This may be an isolated—lapse, shall we call it? Or you
may have a much bigger thing going than I know about. More
Martin Forsyths doing dirty work for you—picking up pocket
money while you go off with the big sums. As long as you thought
you were entirely in the clear in this case, that kind of thing could
still be going on. And that meant this thing could happen over
again.'

'You think I'm some kind of mass murderer or something?'

'Anyone who has killed *can* kill again. And in fact, *they* might be
in danger, *you* might be in danger. Things might work out very
differently a second time. I don't give a hang about the grubby
little spyings of the oil companies, or the Russians, or any other
nation on earth. But I care about murder. Martin Forsyth may
have been a contemptible little tick, but he had a right to go on
breathing beyond his twenty-third year.'

Fagermo got up, smiled at his antagonist, and began to move
towards the door.

'So what I've been saying has been in the nature of a warning.

You're being watched. All the time I'm engaged in this long, detailed investigation, you'll be watched. You can't take one step
outside the strict path of the law without it being known. As long
as you realize this, everyone will be a lot safer. I know there's no
sort of court case to be made out of a few slips of the tongue on
your part: Marty for Martin; knowing he'd worked for the Continental Shelf people in Trondheim when you shouldn't. Easy as pie
to make up a story to cover that sort of lapse. But I'll be going
round the world, looking at records, talking to people who knew
you during your days in big business. I'll be talking to your colleagues here, your bank managers. I'll be uncovering every little
thing about you, down to the last detail. I'm afraid I'll have to talk
to your wife too. She was in fact in Aasgård, wasn't she, sir, the
mental hospital? Did she have her suspicions of you, perhaps? I'll
be gentle with her, but I'm afraid I'll have to talk to her. Because
there *is* a case to be made. And I assure you, I'm going to make it.'

They arrived at the front door, and Dougal Mackenzie held it
open with theatrical politeness and stood framed in it while
Fagermo made his way down the front steps, Jingle at his feet still
looking friendly and wagging his tail in ignorant good will.

'I suppose the only thing to do is wish you a pleasant time in
your researches, Inspector,' Mackenzie said, raising his voice
above the traffic noises from the street below. 'A pleasant time, not
a successful one.' He paused and went on: 'Of course, if this were a
book, what I'd say at this point would be "All right, Fagermo, you
win", or something fatuous like that. They always give in so easily
in books, don't they?'

'Often in life too, Dr Mackenzie,' said Fagermo. 'You'd be surprised.'

'Well, I'm not going to oblige with any such cliché. So I'll just
wish you a thoroughly gruelling and frustrating next few weeks,
Inspector.'

Fagermo grinned amiably at him, and ambled off towards the
front gate. But when he got there, he turned.

'Of course, you're quite right,' he said. 'It is a cliché from books,
nothing more. But you know, it really would be better if you did

just what you say. Much better—for you, your wife, for everyone. It sounds silly, but you'd be much happier in the long run.'

He paused a moment, but his eyes met with no change in Dougal Mackenzie's arrogant smile. With a sigh he turned on his heel and made for his car.

17

MIDNIGHT SUN

Early one evening, when term was over and June well advanced, Dougal Mackenzie—having pecked uninterestedly at his evening meal, and cast an eye over the newspaper headlines—put Jingle on a lead, gathered his various bowls and sources of entertainment into a plastic bag, and took him round to his neighbour's.

'It *is* all right, isn't it?' he asked.

'Of *course*,' said his neighbour, a comfortable, fat Norwegian lady in the prime of widowhood. 'For as long as you like. Take a really good break. You've been looking tired lately, I said so to my daughter. It's a long term, isn't it, spring term? Take a good holiday. He's always welcome here.'

And Jingle, having extracted the maximum of dramatic pathos out of saying farewell at the gate, went wagtailing it around the garden, determined to establish for himself from the beginning a regime of the utmost permissiveness.

Dougal Mackenzie went back home, got one or two necessaries, then got into his gleaming Volvo station-wagon and drove towards town. It sped along, with no more noise or friction than if it had been an arrow speeding towards some half-seen target. Dougal Mackenzie almost relaxed. A good car always made him feel good, and if it was his own good car he felt doubly good. It wasn't often recently that he had felt so nearly free.

He sped over the bridge, past the Arctic Cathedral, and finally left his car at the end of Anton Jakobsensvei.

Superstitious, he said to himself.

There were plenty of points from which to begin a climb up the mountains, but somehow it had to be here. He had never thought of anywhere else but here.

As he took off from the road, up the path edged with stunted bushes and sturdy little trees, he neared the spot where the body of Martin Forsyth had been buried. He turned his head away. He had never offered so much as a mock-reproach to his dog about that finding of the body—a dog was a dog was a dog—but it was natural that as he went by the place his mind should play on what might have been, on what chance had done to him, on what might have happened.

But perhaps, he thought, it would all have come out the same in the end.

When he had managed the first stiff ascent he stopped and looked down. Parked not too far from his own car was another— anonymous, unobtrusive, but well-known to him. One man was still in the driver's seat. Another was standing by the passenger's door, smoking a cigarette and idly looking up. Dougal Mackenzie could just make out his thick, black, drooping moustache. He smiled, and turned his face upwards again.

It was odd how serene he felt, in the evening air, with the sun, bright and warm, streaming down on him. Odd how untroubled, unresentful, unregretful. His mind had somehow cleaned itself out. There were no 'if only's now; no curses against the greed of the boy; no sad backward glances at things he himself had botched. What was done was done. By now he no longer even felt he had any control over himself. He merely walked blindly ahead to an obscure destination—unclear, but safe. He patted his pocket.

Really, it wasn't the end that was unclear, but the beginning. When, where, had it all begun? Not at school, surely. He remembered himself as a thin, sickly schoolboy, inclined to priggishness and goody-goody friends. Surely that boy was not father to this man? He never remembered any fast bits of schoolboy commerce, any sharp cutting of corners. He wouldn't have dared.

University had liberated him from the priggishness, but he didn't remember dreaming of luxury, of the quick buck dubiously acquired. Perhaps it was the grinding three years afterwards, at Hull, as a research student. Prolonged penny-pinching maketh the heart sick.

But whenever it was, by the time he had come to work at Abadan it was there—gnawing, writhing inside him. A little worm of envy, of twisted ambition. Because as soon as he had met Martin Forsyth he had recognized him as a fellow, spotted the same disease in him. They had stood there one day, in the overwhelming morning heat in the dusty centre of the oil processing works—the thin, tough boy with the hard eyes and the workman's hands, and the pot-bellied executive, haltingly acquiring the manners of his middle-rank—and like had spoken to like, greed to greed. Dougal Mackenzie had not liked Martin Forsyth. He had recognized him.

After that they had never spoken often. They weren't, in the company structure, in the same class by a long chalk, and habit and convention set all sorts of barriers and gulfs between the minutely distinguishable grades. Nevertheless, he had once invited him home for a drink. He remembered him sitting there, making small-talk with off-hand confidence to him and his wife, yet all the time his eyes darting round the various objects in the room that bespoke Mackenzie's status, almost costing the furniture. His wife had said when he left that she thought him unlikeable, and he had agreed. It was true. He had not liked him. He had recognized him.

He paused half-way up the mountain. The bush and undergrowth around the path had given way momentarily to more open country, sloping green down to open fields, and presenting a vista of great glory. Below him, island, town, mainland and fjord came together to form a jigsaw more intricate and beautiful than human mind could devise, chamber music in green and white and gold. A valedictory spread.

In the very far distance he could see his own car, and the car that had been parked nearby. Now there was nobody standing beside it. Was he now inside? or had he begun to climb? Dougal Mackenzie smiled faintly, and patted his jacket pocket.

Funny, that was the last thing he remembered Forsyth doing. He was just about to take his anorak off, and patted his pocket as he did so. The papers were there—the last lot of data from the survey boat, the bone that was to be dangled before his eyes, the sweetener of the coming blackmail. He had got the papers easily enough, after he had hit him. After he had dragged him back into the hall. And before he had begun the grisly job of stripping the body—the job that had ended with his pulling, dragging like a maniac at his ring. Even now the sweat on his forehead was not from the heat of the sun.

That had been the last day of his peace. Before that the worm born in the black liquid wealth of Abadan had given him many good days. He had enjoyed his first months in Tromsø, settling into a stable, safe job, and the moderate luxury of a beautiful house, money to buy good Scandinavian furniture, a quiet, powerful car, the knowledge that his means could encompass most of what he could want, with ease. He had thought it a kindly worm. His wife, he thought, had been happy too those months.

But 'things' had turned against him. The safeness, the stability had been threatened before the first year was out. The worm had seemed less kindly, and had gone on gnawing. When the major threat came out into the open he had acted fast to preserve his safety, but he had preserved nothing. Even in those first weeks after the murder, nothing had been quite the same. His wife had suspected—suspected *something*. She had looked at him in a new way. She had known what Martin Forsyth was. Now she knew what he, her husband, had become.

One last half-hour's climb through steep terrain overgrown with bushes and growths which covered the path and he emerged at last on the uplands. He sat down for a minute on a ledge and got his breath back, but—restless—he got up almost at once and began walking again. The plateau stretched in rolling greens and browns, with the night sun streaming upon it and dancing in the occasional patch of water. He was in the open. He was free.

It was freedom, in fact, that he had lost. It was not only his conscience that the worm had eaten away, it was his freedom. Ringing him round over these last years with new fears, new unspeakable secrets, new hindrances to action. That was why, unconsciously, he had known it had to be up here—on the top of a glorious world, free of shackles and guilts. Just to have the illusion again for a few hours.

Because Fagermo had been wrong. It would not have been better to give up then, throw down the cards, admit it all. It would have been infinitely worse. Of course these last few weeks had been terrible, feeling the net tighten, every facet of his life under scrutiny. Yesterday had been the last straw, when he knew the inspector had been talking for hours about him with his own colleagues.

But there was a way of cutting the net. He knew that once his safe, respectable existence had been shattered there was no putting it together again. He had sometimes contemplated the careers of exposed civil servants, local councillors, Members of Parliament, whose financial malpractices had been revealed and prosecuted. What could they be when they emerged from jail but shifty, pathetic shells of people? Fagermo's way was no way. It led only to that. And there was something better open to him.

And as he wandered over the winding paths, around mounds and crags with occasional views, tantalizing, of distant islands looming over the fjord, he experienced again that subtle sense of freedom, that illusion of infinite possibilities.

Until suddenly, in the glare of midnight, he realized he was not alone. There in the distance, now visible, now hidden by the terrain, was a dark, bulky figure, watching him, following. His hours of freedom were over.

There was no regret. Mackenzie reached in his pocket, fondled the gun for a brief moment, then—hidden for a moment from his observer—carefully took it out. Experimentally he opened his mouth. The shot, when it came, was not loud—sounded indeed irrelevant in this natural vastness, a petty thing measured against the blaring trumpets of the sun.

DEATH OF A
MYSTERY WRITER

CONTENTS

1

The Unpleasantness at the Prince Albert

It was Saturday Night, and the saloon bar of the Prince Albert was nicely full: there was plump, jolly Mrs Corbett from the new estate, whose laugh—gurgling with gin and tonic—periodically rang through the whole pub; there was her husband, her teenage daughter looking bored and her old mother looking daggers—all on a family night out; at other tables there were would-be-smooth young men and their silly girl-friends, fat men with fishing stories and thin men with fishy handshakes, and in the corner there was the inevitable sandy-haired man on his own, with his single whisky and his evening paper.

From the public bar came the dull, horrendous thud of the juke box, concession to a civilization in decline; but on good nights the saloon bar could make enough noise to forget it, and tonight was a good night: Jim Turner, the publican, had early cottoned on to the fact that nobody cares any more about the quality of beer in a pub, and that all they are interested in is pub food. Thus, on a Friday and Saturday night he did a roaring trade in pies, plates of beef and turkey, scotch eggs and sizzling sausages—all washed down with a brew that looked like dandelion juice and tasted like poodle's urine.

'Here's a nice bit of breast for you, sir,' he would say, bustling up with a plate, 'and I can't say fairer than that, can I?'

Around the bar stood little groups of men and their wives and ladies, telling stories and waiting to tell stories. But at the end of the bar, nearly squeezed into a corner, was one solitary young man, his eyes concentrated on his pint mug. He was quite well-dressed in his way: his dark suit was new, almost sharp, his shirt good quality, though not very clean. He was good-looking in his way, too, but it was not a very well-defined way: his lips were full, but self-indulgent, without line or determination; his cheeks were unfurrowed, almost hairless, and his eyes were large and liquid—so large and liquid that he seemed as he stood there to be near to tears of self-pity.

He was, in fact, rather drunk. This was his fourth pint of best bitter, and though it was not very good he had declined Jim Turner's suggestion that he go on to stronger stuff. His trips to the lavatory had become frequent, and last time he had nearly knocked over Mrs Corbett's glass, and had been given a piece of that lady's tongue. He talked to no one, read no paper: he merely stood or sat on his stool, contemplating his glass as if it were his *curriculum vitae*. Now and then he smoked—nervously, carelessly, and always stubbing out the cigarette before he was halfway through it.

At the nearest table to him a local couple from Hadley had met up with 'foreigners' from Bracken. Bracken was a new town, thirty-five miles away. It was full of Londoners and Northerners, all of whom could be treated with friendly contempt by locals when they motored out of their brick and glass elysium and stopped for the evening at a real pub. Tonight Jack and Doris were doing the honours of the vicinity, and Ted and Vera from Bracken were being quiet and humble.

' 'Course, a lot of the old places have been bought up for cottages,' said Doris, 'places I knew when I was a girl, real run down and awful—well, they've been bought up, by outsiders, you know, and you wouldn't believe the prices!'

'Lot of well-known people, too,' said Jack, 'because we're still pretty convenient for London. There's that Penny Feather, for example, the actress—'

'I don't think I've—'

' 'Course you have. You know: "Why is your hair so soft and shiny, Mummy?" She does the mummy.'

'Oh yes, I—'

' 'Course you have. Well, she's got a cottage just down the road. Comes down at weekends. Real smasher. Comes in here sometimes, with different men. You do see life here, I can tell you. Specially on a Saturday night.'

'Then there's Arnold Silver—*Sir* Arnold, I beg his pardon.'

'The financier?'

'That's it. Got it in one. Always bringing libel actions. *He* bought the Old Manor. Wife sometimes lives there weeks on end. He's just down here now and again, of course.'

'We don't see *them*—they're never in here. Pity, really. We could ask him for a good tip for the Stock Market.' Everyone laughed jollily and drank up.

'Then,' said Doris, 'not in Hadley, but in Wycherley—that's twelve miles south on the London road—in Wycherley there's Oliver Fairleigh.'

She paused, and gazed complacently down at her navy two-piece, knowing that Ted and Vera would need no prompting over the significance of this name.

'Really?' said Ted, decidedly impressed. 'I didn't know he lived around here.'

'Just outside Wycherley,' said Jack. 'It was the old squire's house, but the family went to pieces after the war. He's lived there twenty-odd years now.'

'I like a good thriller,' said Ted.

'He's *ingenious* with it,' said Doris, not quite sure this was the right description.

'Yes, they're more detective stories, aren't they? People buy them, though, don't they?'

'He's top of the best-sellers every Christmas,' said Doris, now swelling with vicarious author's pride. She did not notice, by the bar, that Jim Turner was giving significant (and obsequious) grins at the young drunk man in the corner.

'I've heard he's a bit of a tartar,' said Ted. Jack and Doris were rather unsure whether it added more to the prestige of the neighbourhood if he was or if he wasn't a tartar.

'Can't believe all you read in the papers,' said Jack.

'Well, he *is*, that's true,' said Doris. 'But he *is* an author. It's different, somehow, isn't it?'

'I suppose so,' said Vera, not quite convinced.

'And he's had his troubles,' said Jack, lowering his voice, but only by a fraction.

'Oh?'

'From his family,' said Doris, who had never set eyes on any of them. 'You know how it is. They've not turned out well.' She shook her head enigmatically.

'Well, there's one boy,' said Jack, 'plays with a pop group.'

'There's a lot of money to be made wi' them groups,' said Ted.

'It's not *that* good. And it doesn't go well with the image: his real name is Sir Oliver Fairleigh-Stubbs, you know, with the hyphen, and he's always been very country squire. The children had nannies and all that—everything the best and no expense spared. Anyway, it's not just him—the girl's very wild they say—'

'And the eldest boy, well, he really has been a case,' said Jack, quite unconscious of the fact that behind him Jim Turner's face was creased in anguish and he was trying to get one of his other customers to dig him in the ribs.

'Drifted from job to job,' said Doris, 'never held one down more than six months.'

'Debts here there and everywhere,' said Jack, 'and not a matter of five or ten pounds either, believe you me. His father had to foot them, of course.'

'Had the police up there once,' said Doris.

'It's the mother I feel sorry for.'

'He's a hopeless case, they say—a real ne'er-do-well. Still, it's often the way, isn't it?'

'It makes you think, though, doesn't it? A young chap like that, with everything going for him.'

They were interrupted by the crash of an overturning bar-stool. The young man from the corner lunged in their direction, paused unsteadily in mid-lunge, and then came to rest with both hands on their table, gazing—red, blotchy and bleary—into their eyes.

'He had everything going for him, did he? Well, he had his

father going for him twenty-four hours a day, that's true enough.'
He gulped, his speech became still more slurred, and the lakes
that were his eyes at last overflowed. 'You don't know what . . .
You don't know what you're talking about. You never met my . . .
my famous father. If you had you'd know he was a . . . *swine*.
He's a bastard. He's the biggest goddam bastard that ever walked
this . . . bloody earth.' He turned to stand up and make a pro-
nouncement to the whole bar, but he failed to make the perpen-
dicular, and crashed back on to the table.

'My father ought to be shot,' he sobbed.

2

OLIVER FAIRLEIGH'S WEEK

Sunday

Sir Oliver Fairleigh-Stubbs sat in the back seat of his Daimler, surveying the world through bulbous, piggy eyes. Over his knees, and over those of his wife who sat beside him, was a rug, although it was June and the sun was shining. Sir Oliver, though still enough to the casual glance, was far from asleep. His eyes were noticing everything, and sometimes sparkling as if in anticipation. From time to time he pursed his mouth up, or blew out his cheeks; at others he let out little grunts, like a sow in ecstasy.

Lady Fairleigh-Stubbs knew the signs, and sighed. Oliver was intending to be difficult. Perhaps to make a scene. Against her better judgement (for she knew that nothing she said was likely to have any effect on her husband's behaviour, except to make it worse) she said:

'Such a nice couple, the Woodstocks.'

'Who?' or rather an interrogatory grunt, was the reply.

'The Woodstocks. And charming of them to invite us to lunch.'

The grunt, this time, was just a grunt.

'They're poor as church-mice,' said Lady Fairleigh-Stubbs.

'Must want something,' said her husband.

'So brave, to set out on a writing career at the moment, when things are so difficult.'

'Not brave, bloody ridiculous,' said Sir Oliver. 'Deserves to land himself in the poor-house, if by the grace of God we still had them.'

He puffed out his cheeks to give himself an expression of outrage. Lady Fairleigh-Stubbs sighed again.

'Drive slower!' barked Sir Oliver suddenly to Surtees, the chauffeur. 'I want to look at the trees.' As the car slowed down, he let his great treble chin flop on to his chest, and closed his eyes.

'Oliver, we're here,' said his wife—a thing he knew perfectly well. He opened his eyes wide, and surveyed the landscape as if he had just got off an international flight.

'Not *that*,' he said, as the Daimler pulled up at a wicket-gate. 'Good God, I thought artists' cottages went out in my youth.'

'They've knocked two together and done them up,' said Lady Fairleigh-Stubbs, as if that excused the decidedly twee effect. 'I think it's awfully pretty. I gather this is one of the few bits of property the Woodstocks have left.'

When Surtees came round to open the door, Oliver Fairleigh remained seated in the car for a full minute, his hands spanning his monstrous tummy, gazing with distaste at the orange-painted cottage, and knowing perfectly well he was being observed from inside. Then he climbed puffily out and stood by the gate. When the front door opened—the minimum acknowledgement that he was looked for—he condescended to open the gate himself.

'You've got no hollyhocks!' he bellowed to the young couple in the doorway.

'I beg your pardon . . . ?'

'You've got no hollyhocks,' he repeated, at twice the volume. 'Cottages like this have to have hollyhocks.' He gave his arm to his wife and stumped into the house—past his hosts and straight into the living-room.

'Eleanor!' said a washed-out-looking lady by the fire-place, coming forward to kiss her, 'So good of you to come. And Oliver! How well you're looking.'

Oliver Fairleigh-Stubbs surveyed the elder Mrs Woodstock. Her gentility, like the colours of her woollens, seemed not to have been fast, and to have come out in the wash. 'I have got gout, impetigo and athlete's foot,' he announced, 'but no doubt to the casual observer I look well.' He sank into the best armchair and looked ahead, as if contemplating mankind's extinction with gloomy relish.

'Harold Drayton you've met,' said Mrs Woodstock vaguely. Oliver Fairleigh grunted. Harold Drayton was a walking gentleman, a tame nobody who could be counted on to make up a lunch-party, one who valued a reasonable meal more than he disliked the company of Oliver Fairleigh (there were few such). He was worth, in the estimation of the guest of honour, no more than a faint grunt.

By this time the host and hostess were back in the room, having been exchanging glances in the tiny kitchen. Benjamin Woodstock was tall and willowy in the Rupert Brooke manner, though without the good looks. In fact, like his mother, he looked indefinably mangy. Celia his wife was, at that moment, looking frankly terrified.

However, with the offer of sherry, Oliver Fairleigh's mood changed. He sat back in his chair, beaming in his porcine way at all and sundry, and responding to conversational advances. His voice, something between a public-school sports-master's and a sergeant-major's, was not adapted to polite conversation, but nevertheless everyone in the room began to relax a little—except Eleanor his wife, who knew him too well.

'They tell me you write, eh?' boomed Sir Oliver, baring his teeth at Ben Woodstock.

'Well, yes, just a little,' said Ben. Then, thinking this did not sound too good in view of his purpose in inviting the great Oliver Fairleigh, he added: 'But I'm hoping to make a living out of it.'

Oliver Fairleigh left, for him, quite a short pause.

'Oh yes? What at? Eh?'

'Well, I've just had a detective story accepted.'

Oliver Fairleigh snorted. 'Detective stories? No money in them. You'll starve in six months. Write a thriller.'

'Oh, do you think so?'

'Write a thriller. One of those documentaries. Somebody trying to shoot the Pope—that kind of nonsense. Fill it full of technical details. Those are the things people buy these days.'

'I'm not sure about the technical details—I don't think I'd be too good on them.'

'Make 'em up, dear boy, make 'em up. Only one in a hundred knows any better, and he won't bother to write and correct you. You'll never get anywhere if you overestimate your public.'

'Trying to shoot the Pope. That does sound a good idea,' said the elder Mrs Woodstock meditatively. Oliver Fairleigh turned to her urbanely.

'Ah—you feel strongly about birth-control, I suppose?' He looked at her in a frankly appraising way, and then laughed.

This comparatively bright mood lasted Sir Oliver just into lunch, as his wife knew it would. Such a mood was never to be trusted, and was the prelude to (and was intended to contrast with) some other mood or series of moods which would be launched on his companions' lulled sensibilities.

The fish was a very uninteresting little bit of plaice, hardly able to support the circlet of lemon on top. Everyone went at it as if fish were a duty which there was no point in trying to make into a pleasure. Not so Oliver Fairleigh. He gazed at it with a beam of anticipation, then set about masticating it with an elaborate panto-mime of savouring every succulent mouthful. He devoted himself to the miserable triangle of nutriment with all the zest due to a classic French dish. Periodically he wiped his mouth and beamed with simulated enthusiasm round the table, as if to ensure that the other guests were properly appreciating the gastronomic distinc-tion of it. They looked at him in dubious acknowledgement of his sunny temper. His wife looked at her plate.

Over the crumbed cutlet that followed a new performance was enacted. Oliver Fairleigh sank into a mood of intense depression: he gazed at the cutlet as if it were a drowned friend whose remains he was trying to identify at a police morgue. He picked up a fork-ful of mashed potato, inspected it, smelt it, and finally, with ludi-crously overdone reluctance, let it drop into his mouth, where he chewed it for fully three minutes before swallowing. Conversation flagged.

It was the wine Ben Woodstock was worried about. Oliver Fair-leigh was acknowledged a connoisseur of wine: every other book he wrote was studded with some item of wine lore or some devastating judgement designed to wither the ignorant. He was consulted by experts, and had been quoted by Cyril Ray. As he took up his glass, Ben's heart sank. It wouldn't be right. In spite of all the advice he'd had, all the money he'd spent, it wouldn't be right.

Sir Oliver looked, frowned, sipped, frowned, set down his glass and stared ahead of him in gloomy silence. Once or twice he made as if to say something to his host (sitting beside him, and looking more meagre than ever) but each time he stopped himself, as if he had had second thoughts. Finally he took up his glass and downed the contents in one go.

Over the pudding—something spongy, which had gone soggy —Ben Woodstock felt the weight of the silence had become too heavy to bear, and began once to make conversation with his guest of honour.

'I suppose you find it's very important to establish some kind of routine when you're writing, don't you, sir?'

'Eh? What? What do I find important?'

'Routine.'

'Who says I find routine important?'

'I said I *suppose* you find routine important in writing.'

'Oh. You suppose, do you? Hmm.'

The silence continued until the pudding had been eaten, when Ben tried again.

'I was wondering if you could give me any advice—'

'Eh?'

'I was wondering if you could give me any advice—'

'Sack your cook,' said Oliver Fairleigh-Stubbs in a voice of thunder that silenced all the lesser voices around the table. 'Best piece of advice I can give you.'

Celia Woodstock got up and darted towards the kitchen in the fearsome silence that followed. Then they all adjourned for coffee. Having made a scene, Oliver Fairleigh was for the moment peaceful. Ben Woodstock noticed the change of mood, and knowing the reputation for brevity of his guest's good tempers, he felt he had to take advantage of it. Greatly daring, in view of the quality of the coffee, he approached the subject which the meal had been intended to lead up to.

'I was wondering about publishers, sir—'

Oliver Fairleigh fixed him with a stare. 'Thought you'd got a book accepted,' he said.

'Well yes, I have, actually. By Robinson and Heath.' The firm in question was tiny, and of no repute. Oliver Fairleigh grunted. 'Of course I'm terribly grateful to them, taking a chance on an unknown author, and all that, but naturally I'm thinking a little of the future too. I know you're a Macpherson's author yourself, and I was wondering—'

'Quite exceptionally good firm, Robinson and Heath,' interrupted Oliver Fairleigh with unusual energy. 'You're in really good hands there. Nothing like these small firms for taking care of you. Keep out of the hands of the big boys. Never know where you are with all these amalgamations. Next thing you know you're being paid in dollars or Saudi Arabian yashmaks or God knows what. No, stick to Robinson and Heath, my boy. You're in real luck if you're in with them.'

He rose, panting and snorting, to his feet. 'Come, Eleanor, we must be off.' He made for the door, and accepted gracefully the ritual gestures made to a departing guest. 'So nice to have a meal with old friends,' he boomed. 'Goodbye Mr—er—er—' and he gazed at Harold Drayton for a moment, as though trying to think of a reason for his existence, bared his teeth at the elder Mrs Woodstock, and then sailed out through the door. As he shook hands with his young host and hostess he grunted his thanks, and then fixed the luckless Ben with an eye of outrage.

'One thing I wanted to say, my boy,' he said, in his voice of thunder. 'That wine, that wine you served. It was . . .' the pause ran on, and on, and Ben Woodstock remained transfixed by that terrible eye, unable to stir a muscle . . . 'very good,' concluded Oliver Fairleigh. 'Quite exceptionally fine. Come to dinner with me next Saturday, eh? You and your wife? We'll expect you.'

And he turned and made off to his car.

As they drove home, Sir Oliver folded his hands once more over his ballooning stomach, shook now and then in delighted self-appreciation and stole glances at his wife out of the corner of his eye.

'I'm glad I told that lie about the appalling wine,' he said finally. 'It does one good, once in a way, to make simple people happy.'

Monday

Oliver Fairleigh-Stubbs sat in his study, glaring resentfully at a glass of water on the table by his side. At his feet sat his boxer dog, Cuff, grunting periodically. In this and in other respects Cuff resembled his master, and had in fact been acquired with a view to his providing a canine variation on the Oliver Fairleigh theme. So he grunted, snuffled, snapped periodically at inoffensive callers, and generally gave people to comment on the well-known idea that dogs grow like their owners. Which was unfair, for taken by and large Cuff was a harmless animal.

Oliver Fairleigh was dictating, in his over-loud voice, the last chapter of his latest detective story. It was one of his Inspector Powys ones, and it had to be with his publishers before the week was out, if they were to make the Christmas market.

' "The thing that nobody has remarked," said Inspector Powys, wagging an admonitory finger at his fascinated audience, "is the curious position of the body. Now, Mrs Edwards was cutting bread, look you—" ' Oliver Fairleigh paused. 'Have we had a "look you" in the last three pages, Miss Cozzens?'

Barbara Cozzens (whose efficiency was such that she could take perfect shorthand while her thoughts were miles away) flicked irritatedly through her notebook. 'I don't think so, Sir Oliver.'

'People get annoyed if there are too many and annoyed if there are none at all,' said Oliver Fairleigh, testily. 'Personally I've no idea whether the Welsh say it or not. Do they, Miss Cozzens?'

'All the Welsh people I know are very Anglicized,' said Barbara Cozzens distantly, adding rather acidly: 'It's a bit late in the day to start worrying about that.'

'True, true. I'm stuck with it now, just as I'm stuck with the over-sexed little Welsh idiot who says it. Where were we? "Mrs Edwards was cutting bread, look you, to take upstairs for the family supper. Now to cut bread—you perhaps would not be aware of this, Lord Fernihill, but I assure you it is so—the body must lean *forward*. Many a time I've watched my old mother doing it, God rest her soul. Now Mrs Edwards was a heavy woman, and she was stabbed from behind—and yet she fell *backwards*. Now . . ." '

For the next hour Miss Cozzens let her thoughts wander. When she had first come to work for Oliver Fairleigh she had followed his works with interest, had been eager to hear the solution, and had once pointed out a flaw in Inspector Powys's logic. But only once. Sir Oliver had fixed her with his gob-stopper eye and said: 'Any fool could see that. But my readers won't.' And he had gone on dictating, unperturbed. That was a long time ago. Then Miss Cozzens had often read detective stories for pleasure; now she shied away from them at station bookstalls, and hated the sound of the name Powys. She sat there, upright, her hand making dancing patterns over the paper, her mind full of Amalfi last summer, the widower who had made advances to her there, and the sensitive novel she was writing about the episode—a fragile, delicate story, gossamer light, every adjective chosen with loving care and Roget's Thesaurus.

' "And as Inspector Powys drove back along the stately drive to Everton Lodge, he shook his head at the pity of it, and smiled his sad, compassionate smile. THE END." That's it. Thank God I've done with that Welsh twit for another year or two. Next time it will be a Mrs Merrydale murder. Or I'll just have a common or garden policeman. A drink, I think, Miss Cozzens.'

'The doctor—'

'Damn the doctor,' roared Sir Oliver, kicking Cuff to make him growl in sympathy. 'I don't take orders from any quack. I don't get shot of Inspector Powys every day of the week. Now, unlock the bottom drawer, there's a good girl, and we'll both have a glass of sherry. You know where the glasses are.'

With a sigh Miss Cozzens complied. If Sir Oliver was going to start this sort of thing regularly, he'd be well on the way to killing himself. At least nobody could say she hadn't warned him. She found the concealed bottle, got two glasses from the cupboard, and poured two not-quite-full glasses.

'Full!' roared Oliver Fairleigh, like a baby in a paddy. Cuff got laboriously to his feet and growled at her in an ugly manner. Miss Cozzens, with another sigh, filled her employer's glass, and—after a moment's thought—her own too. Then all three of them settled down to a rather frosty celebration.

'Did you enjoy the book, Miss Cozzens?' enquired Sir Oliver Fairleigh-Stubbs, after his first sip.

'I beg your pardon?'

'The book, Miss Cozzens. The masterwork that we have been working on together.'

'I'm afraid I haven't been paying much attention, Sir Oliver. I'm sure it will do very well.'

'Of course it will do very well,' said Sir Oliver testily. 'Other people like my books, even if you do not.' He softened under the influence of the sherry. 'You're quite right, though. They're very bad. And especially the Inspector Powys ones. They are quite beneath me. Perhaps I won't write any more. Get myself a new detective. Someone who's a gentleman.'

'I believe the trend is all the other way these days,' observed Miss Cozzens.

'I SET MY OWN TRENDS!' roared Oliver Fairleigh. He impressed Cuff, but Miss Cozzens declined to jump, and went on calmly sipping her sherry. 'The best thing,' went on Sir Oliver, as if he had never raised his voice, 'would be to write just one more, and kill the little beast off in the course of it.'

Miss Cozzens nodded her approval. '*Inspector Powys's Last Case*,' she said. 'I'm sure you could think of a good way to get rid of him. Something lingering with boiling oil in it would be nice.' She found her spirits rising already at the very thought.

'Absolutely,' agreed Sir Oliver. 'There's a project we might both enjoy collaborating on. It would cause a great sensation.'

'People would be desolated. The letters would flow in.'

'Exactly,' said Sir Oliver. 'The lights would go out all over Wales.' He considered the prospect benignly for some minutes further. Then the practical sense which had gained him his present position and kept him there reasserted itself. 'And if the new man didn't catch on,' he said, 'after a few years we could somehow or other bring Powys to life again.

Miss Cozzens's spirits sank.

Tuesday

Sir Oliver Fairleigh-Stubbs was assisted into the BBC studio by the producer. He did not normally need assistance when he walked. Sixty-five years, and habits of self-indulgence, had left him less than spry, but he did manage to get around on his own, with a good deal of puffing and blowing. On the other hand, it was a common practice of his to lull his victims into a false sense of security, whether by an assumed geniality or by putting up a pretence of being but a shadow of his former self.

He's a shadow of his former self, thought the producer to himself, with relief.

A show of geniality would not have worked at the BBC. His brushes with that institution had been too many. He had disrupted innumerable talk-programmes, driven the audience of *Any Questions* to throw West Country farm produce at the stage, turned on inoffensive interviewers with accusations of communism (the more embarrassing since most of them were prospective candidates in the Conservative or Liberal interests). No. Geniality would cut no ice at the BBC.

Today Oliver Fairleigh was to broadcast for *The Sunday Appeal* and the producer congratulated himself that nothing could go radically wrong. He would be alone with his script, with no one to antagonize or be antagonized by. He led him to the table, sat him comfortably in the chair, and drew his attention to the glass of water placed at his right hand.

Oliver Fairleigh sat still as a gargoyle on a waterspout, staring beadily at the microphone while the technical preparations went on around him. Finally the producer smiled ingratiatingly.

'If we might just test for voice, Sir Oliver . . . ?'

Oliver Fairleigh cleared his throat with a bellow, and began:

'I am speaking to you today on behalf of the Crime Writers' Benevolent Association . . .'

The producer nodded his head in appreciation. It was an admirable radio voice, rich, resonant, redolent of pheasant, port wine, and good living in general.

'Right,' he said, 'I think we can go ahead.' And at a signal from him, Oliver Fairleigh began again.

'I am speaking to you today on behalf of the Crime Writers' Benevolent Association,' he said. 'I have no doubt there are few among you who have not at one time or another whiled away the tedium of your summer holidays with a detective story.' The producer smiled sycophantically. It was a good script as these things went—different, made people sit up. 'I leave it to the sociologists to explain the fascination of crime stories for the public at large—as no doubt they can do, at least to their own satisfaction. For myself I have no idea whether we incite people to crime, or deflect the impulse they feel to commit it, and it is not germane to my purpose today, which is quite different: it is, quite frankly, to ask you to put your hands in your pockets. The Crime Writers' Benevolent Association—which I might describe as a very harmless sort of trade union—has acquired a large country house in a non-violent part of rural England, and aims (if public support is forthcoming) to set up a home there for elderly and infirm writers of crime fiction.'

Still gazing intently at his script, Oliver Fairleigh went on:

'Picture to yourselves the condition of these poor hacks, whose mastery of their miserable trade is so uncertain that they have proved unable to provide for themselves a comfortable autumn to their lives.' The producer looked at the technician, and the technician looked at the producer but Oliver Fairleigh, apparently oblivious, continued gazing at his script. 'Picture to yourselves the condition of mental debility to which a lifetime of locked-room murders, rigged alibis and poisons unknown to medical science has reduced them. Imagine them in their final days quoting to each other the feeble catch-phrases of their fictional sleuths. If such a picture of mental and physical decay does not evoke from you feelings of benevolence, then you are, I fear, beyond the reach of calls upon your Christian charity. Good night to you all.'

As the technician switched off the tape, the producer got up, wringing his hands, with a wide smile on his face.

'That was most amusing, Sir Oliver. If we could record the last paragraph again, as it stands in the script—'

'Script!' bellowed Oliver Fairleigh, pushing back his chair and making for the door with an astonishing speed and agility. 'I've been reading the script. Must have sent you an early draft. Take it or leave it, my dear chap. Take it or leave it.'

And he disappeared out of the studio in the direction of the lifts.

The producer sank back into his chair, looking very depressed.

'I suppose I'd better get on to Dick Francis,' he said.

3

OLIVER FAIRLEIGH'S WEEK (TWO)

Wednesday

Oliver Fairleigh had arranged to meet his daughter at Manrico's, a restaurant on the less seedy outer fringe of Soho where he knew the food would be up to his requirements. He did not meet her at any of his more usual haunts because he was afraid she would turn up in patched denim and raucous check.

As it was, Bella turned up crisp and delectable in ravishingly close-fitting shirt and slacks which cried aloud of fashion and expense. The faces of middle-rank executives, pink from expense-account wine, swivelled at her entrance and followed her greedily and regretfully until she seated herself opposite her father. Bella, when she wanted to, could epitomize style and breeding, and use both qualities to add to her desirability. She had beauty, of a slightly pixie quality, she had a glorious mass of auburn hair, she had a body which moved confidently knowing it would be admired and that a chair would be there when she sat down. Bella was Oliver Fairleigh's favourite child. Indeed, she was the only one he liked at all.

Over the antipasti Bella looked at her father—that hoydenish look that made strong men grovel—and said: 'What's this I hear about you at the BBC?'

Oliver Fairleigh, biting on an olive, burst into a great wheezy chuckle of delight, which turned into a choke.

'How did you hear of that?' he asked.

534

'We in the newspaper world hear everything—you should know that by now,' said Bella.

'Newspaper world!' snorted Oliver Fairleigh. 'A gang of pimps and informers! A fine crowd for my daughter to mix with.' He paused, and then it was his turn to look roguish. 'Anyway I should hardly think the *Gardening Gazette* deserves to be dignified with the title of newspaper.'

'It's a start,' said Bella, shrugging with indifference. 'One makes contacts.'

'Hmmm,' said Oliver Fairleigh, looking displeased. 'I suppose that means you're sleeping around with the editors.'

'The editors, Daddy, are far too old to be interested,' said Bella. 'And anyway, they keep such peculiar hours.' Oliver Fairleigh looked far from satisfied with this answer. 'But the BBC,' said Bella, noting his mood. 'What exactly did you *do*?'

A great wicked grin spread over Oliver Fairleigh's face.

'I wrote a new script. I'll give it to you if you like. You should have seen the producer's face. He's been hearing these bromides week after week, and suddenly I pumped an enema into him!' The great wheezy chuckle emerged again, pushing itself out like reluctantly emitted wind. It stopped short when the wine waiter appeared at his elbow. Oliver Fairleigh was never frivolous about wine.

'Are you allowed to drink?' asked Bella suspiciously.

'Wine, yes. Not anything stronger, except at weekends. But a little wine, oh yes, certainly.'

'For your stomach's sake, I suppose.'

Oliver Fairleigh gazed with comic dismay at that great protuberance. 'Well, it would certainly play up if it were denied it,' he said. 'Whisky it can do without: a vulgar, provincial tipple. Even liqueurs it can deny itself. But wine—it would be the height of idiocy to deny oneself wine merely to live a little longer.'

When he had tasted the selected bottle, Oliver Fairleigh nodded his head, and settled down to enjoy his meal, muttering as he did so: 'I'm not satisfied about you and those editors!'

'How odd,' said his daughter, 'that good wine never puts you in a good mood.'

'Why should it?' growled Oliver Fairleigh. 'Good wine should be taken as a matter of course. Superlative wine might put me in a good mood. Bad wine certainly puts me in a bad one. Bad wine like that fool Woodstock's.'

'Woodstock? Do you mean Ben Woodstock?'

'Some such name.'

'I didn't know he was back in Wycherley.'

'Living in a damnfool artist's cottage. Looks as if he expects Henry James to drop by any minute and swap ambiguities with him. But he got me instead.' He pursed out his lips in delighted remembrance of the occasion.

'Poor Ben,' said Bella, watching him closely. 'I suppose you scared the living daylights out of him. You used to when he was a boy.'

'I think,' said her father, 'that they'd do a term in the prisons of President Amin rather than go through that again.'

'Oh Daddy, you *are* appalling. You're a monster. Why do you do it?'

Oliver put on a pout, looked like an overfed baby, and said: 'I get bored. I have to have things happening. Don't be hard on me, Bella. You should understand.'

'Oh, I understand only too well. I'm just sorry for poor old Ben. He never had much backbone.'

'He certainly didn't go through the fire unsinged,' said Oliver Fairleigh. He added, with a wicked anticipatory expression: 'However, I have made up for my bad behaviour. I have invited them to dinner next Saturday.'

'Saturday? But that's your birthday.'

'Precisely. I shall need the family gathering to be diluted. I shall need—how shall I put it?—diversionary targets.'

'Is everyone coming?'

'I believe so. Mark is apparently in the area—has even been home, though he made sure he didn't bump into *me*. No doubt I shall have news of his doings before long in the form of tradesmen's bills. Terence I gather has also signified that he will graciously take time off from making everybody's lives miserable with his cacophony—'

'It's quite a good group—'

Oliver Fairleigh indulged in a trumpet of elephantine disapproval. 'What nonsense! A good group! A contradiction in terms! People have gone mad! Someone will be recommending them for OBEs next!' He quietened down as the waiter poured him more wine. 'And then you'll be there, of course,' he went on.

'Oh yes, I'll be there.'

He gave her a look expressing the opinion that she would be the only thing that would save the day from disaster, and then they ate their meal in silence for a little. At last Bella said:

'Daddy—' (when she said that, with a wheedling upward intonation, Oliver Fairleigh knew there was something special coming) 'why don't you surprise everybody this birthday dinner by being nice, the whole evening?'

The babyish expression appeared once more on her father's face.

'I tried it once. I got bored. Anyway, it made everybody twice as jumpy.'

'That's because you're usually only nice when you're planning something awful. I mean, be nice the whole evening, and the whole weekend, if necessary.'

'You can hardly expect me to be nice to Mark for one whole evening. Terence I might just manage it with, but Mark . . .'

'Yes, Mark as well. And Ben too—'

'And Ben's mousey little wife?'

'Does he have a wife?' Bella raised her eyebrows. 'Yes, of course. I'd forgotten. He's the sort that someone was bound to get hold of and cling on to, so that they both sink without trace together.' She remained a moment in thought, and then said: 'Yes, her as well. You like surprising people. Well, surprise them by being genial, and pleasant, and tolerant.'

'Tolerant!' snorted Oliver Fairleigh. 'The mediocrity's virtue!'

'Daddy!' said Bella. And then, with an implied threat in her voice: 'You do want me to come, don't you?'

Oliver Fairleigh looked pleadingly at his daughter, who did not soften her gaze. He returned to his plate, and toyed with his food for a little, but when he looked up again, the same stern gaze was upon him. At length he pushed his plate away.

'Perhaps,' he said. 'Let's talk about it.'

Thursday

Oliver Fairleigh's visit to London had gone very well. He had created hell at the BBC. He had delivered the last chapters of his new book to his publisher, and received the nervous homage due to a best-selling author. He had partaken of a good meal with his favourite child. He had heaved himself into his club in St James's, where old men who had sodomized each other at school shook their heads over the younger generation. All these things he had enjoyed. It would be too much to say that they had put him into a good mood, or made him at peace with the world, but they had certainly made him feel that for the moment life was bearable.

Eleanor Fairleigh-Stubbs was rather surprised. After the euphoria had worn off, the period between books was usually especially difficult. Yet here was Miss Cozzens sitting in the study, putting her files in order and writing replies to fan letters, and here was Oliver, walking with her and Cuff in the gardens of Wycherley Court in the early summer sun, for all the world as if he were an ordinary country gentleman.

It wouldn't last. She had a sinking feeling in her stomach that it wouldn't last into Saturday. Every year the birthday dinner—the preparations, the mere thought of it—filled her with a gloom that was amply justified by the occasion itself. It was the nadir of her year, worse even than Christmas. But Lady Fairleigh was a hopeful woman. If she had not been, she would not have married Oliver Fairleigh. So she put her forebodings from her, and tried to enjoy the brief period of peace.

'The roses are coming along well,' she said tentatively, bending close and inspecting them for aphids with an expert eye.

'Don't know how,' said Oliver Fairleigh, peering at them less expertly, his gooseberry eyes popping out from under flaring eyebrows. 'With that incompetent Wiggens as gardener.'

'I see to the roses myself,' said Lady Fairleigh, with the very slightest touch of asperity in her voice. 'As you know.'

'Probably accounts for it,' said Oliver Fairleigh. 'I wouldn't trust Wiggens to water a pot-plant if I could get anyone better, but I can't.'

'He does his best,' said his wife vaguely. 'Perhaps Bella could find us someone—with her gardening contacts.'

'Bella doesn't know one end of a daffodil from the other,' said Oliver Fairleigh. 'And her only contacts would be with other young devils in a similar state of ignorance.'

'How did she look?'

'Beautiful as usual,' said Oliver Fairleigh, smiling benignly. He looked sunnily around the lawns and hedges and flower-beds that comprised his domain, and positively oozed self-satisfaction. 'We did a good job there, my dear,' he said.

Eleanor Fairleigh-Stubbs was rather surprised at the concession to her embodied in the "we". 'Such a *dangerous* name to choose,' she said. 'Lovely that it turned out right. Is she really liking the job?'

'Says she is.' Her husband's mood seemed to cloud over slightly. 'Just waiting to get on those damnfool colour supplements, I imagine. And sleeping around with that end in view.'

'Now *Oliver,* I'm sure you don't know she's been doing anything of the kind.'

'I've never known a girl that good-looking who wasn't sleeping around,' said Oliver Fairleigh, grandly general. 'That being so, I suppose she might as well do it with an end in view.' He added, as he so often did when talking about the affairs of his children: 'She can't expect anything more from me.'

Eleanor Fairleigh knew that if there was one person who could wheedle cash out of her husband, it was Bella, but she did not say so. 'She'll be coming to the birthday dinner anyway, won't she?' she asked.

'Oh yes, she's coming.'

'Perhaps we can talk about it then.'

'About what? Who she's sleeping with?'

'No—of course not. Just how she's doing, and so on—who her

friends are. Girls will tell things to their mother that they wouldn't tell anyone else.'

It struck Oliver Fairleigh that his wife had a genius for hitting on generalizations that were the exact opposite of the truth, but he was used to her combination of woolly thinking and unjustified optimism, and he seldom bit her head off more than three or four times a day, so he left her in her comfortable delusion.

'Well, I'm glad boys don't do the same to their fathers,' he grunted. 'I couldn't bear to be made the recipient of Mark's confessions.'

The name of that particular son was always a danger signal in conversations with Oliver Fairleigh. His wife, no wiser now than ever, weighed in with an appeal: 'But you will be nice to him on Saturday, won't you, Oliver?' As she said it, she felt sure she was only making things worse.

Oliver Fairleigh left an eloquent pause.

'Yes,' he said.

Eleanor Fairleigh was so surprised that she stopped in her tracks, and looked with earnest enquiry into her husband's face.

'What's the matter, woman? You asked me a question and I gave you an answer.' He continued on his way, with a sort of mock-aggrieved grumbling: 'It was a truthful answer, too. That's the trouble with women. They'll believe any amount of comfortable lies, but you tell them the truth and you haven't a hope of being believed.'

Lady Fairleigh-Stubbs put her arm through her husband's, and they continued their walk.

'Well, that *will* be nice,' she said. 'If you can. Because he's not a bad boy, and he's very good-natured.'

'He *is* a bad boy, and he is *not* good-natured,' said Oliver Fairleigh. He added, with a rare honesty: 'Not that I'd like him any better if he *was* good-natured.'

Eleanor Fairleigh was puzzled by his attitude. 'Just so long as you *try* to like him,' she said, smiling vaguely at a rhododendron bush and gripping his arm a little closer.

'I am most certainly *not* trying to like him,' said Oliver Fairleigh, irritated by the grip on his arm which seemed either proprietorial or conspiratorial. 'I said I would be nice to him on Saturday. That is the limit of my oath.'

'It's a start, anyway . . .'

'Sunday I do not vouch for. Sunday I said nothing to Bella about,' said Oliver Fairleigh with grim relish. Relieving himself of her arm he turned abruptly, and, kicking Cuff to follow him, stomped towards the house.

'Oh, Bella . . .' said his wife wistfully.

She turned and resumed her walk. The garden *was* looking lovely, though of course Oliver was the last person in the world to appreciate it. A garden to him was a sort of backdrop to his own performance; to her, since her children had grown up, it had become almost the most important thing in her life. She walked around, more briskly now that Oliver had gone, noting what was coming on well and what had not recovered from the drought last year. Finally she made for Wiggens, relaxing over his spade, and gave some directions about the flowers to be cut to decorate the house for Saturday.

'Family do, then, is it?' asked Wiggens, who had only been with them six months.

'Yes, Sir Oliver's birthday. All the family will be there—Bella, and Terence, and Mark.'

'Oh, Mr Mark too?' asked Wiggens, and it struck Lady Fairleigh that he gave her a rather odd look.

'Yes,' she said firmly. 'Mr Mark too.' And she turned and went towards the house.

When she walked into the kitchen, to see—in her vague way, for food did not interest her, except as a way of keeping her husband in equable mood—what was happening about lunch, she knew at first glance that Mrs Moxon had something to confide in her. Mrs Moxon was ample, reliable, and talented, and her only drawback was an insatiable curiosity and an unstoppable tongue. It was not just that one could not avoid hearing the affairs of everyone in Wycherley retailed at inordinate length; there was the question of what went in the other direction, from the manor to the rest of the village, and that worried Lady Fairleigh intensely. Not that it did her husband. He liked being talked about.

'I *was* sorry to hear about it, madam, I really was,' said Mrs Moxon, rubbing her doughy hands on her apron, and putting on an expression of sympathy profound enough for a family death.

'Sorry, Mrs Moxon? There's nothing to be sorry about. Nothing has happened.'

'Oh, then you've not heard about it, then, madam? Well, I'm sorry I mentioned it, I really am. Just that I thought you looked worried, so I supposed you must have heard.'

'Heard what, Mrs Moxon? Please don't be so mysterious. Come straight at it.'

'Well, it's Mr Mark, my lady. What he said at the Prince Albert in Hadley last Saturday.'

'He was drunk, was he?' said Lady Fairleigh-Stubbs, with a watery smile. 'Well, you've been with the family long enough to know that's nothing new, Mrs Moxon. And he *is* still young.'

'Oh, it's not that, ma'am. Of course I know all about that, and locking the spirits away, and all. Though never a word has crossed my lips, of course. But it's what he said—screamed through the whole pub, they say.'

'What did he say?' asked Eleanor Fairleigh, her heart thumping against her ribs.

'It was about his father,' said Mrs Moxon, now frankly enjoying herself. 'He said he ought to be shot. Straight out like that, shouted it through the whole pub. All the village is talking about it.'

Eleanor Fairleigh turned to go up the stairs. 'I expect it was just a joke,' she said. Even to herself she sounded feeble and defeated. She went to her bedroom, and sitting wanly on the bed she found that her forebodings about Saturday had returned in full measure.

Friday

It was early evening, and Oliver Fairleigh had been signing letters —the grateful yet faintly magisterial letters that were sent in reply to his fan mail, and which were generally, in fact, the work of Miss

Cozzens. The extent of his fan mail was always a matter of interest to Oliver Fairleigh, though he affected to despise the senders and made comments on their standards of literacy. Work on the last chapters of *Murder Upstairs and Downstairs* had meant that it had mounted up over the last few weeks, and signing the replies had put him in a good mood.

At present he was not alone in his study, but the interview he was conducting was not dissipating his good mood. Seen athwart the broad back of his interlocutor, his face glowed with lugubrious anticipation.

'I've no doubt I shan't like it,' he said with a genial snarl. 'Come along man, out with it.'

The broad back remained impassive, the large hands stayed respectfully at the sides, and the gentleman commenced a lengthy and circumstantial recital in a voice devoid of personality or drama. Oliver Fairleigh settled in his easy chair, and gave the narrative his attention only at those points that seemed important.

'Where?' he cut in. 'The Prince Albert? That mid-thirties monstrosity on the main road to Hadley—a pull-in for the middle-class motorist? I might have known he would drink at a place like that.' He grunted in contented gloom. 'Go on.'

His informant took some time to get into his stride again, but he regained Oliver Fairleigh's interest when he got to the conversation of the two couples in the pub.

'Talking about me, were they?' he said, as if the fact alone gave him pleasure, irrespective of what was said.

When the recital was finished, Oliver Fairleigh lit up a cigar, which only seemed to increase the geniality of his mood.

'Well, well,' he said, 'what a jolly little episode. I'm glad you picked it up, very glad. I'll be making it square with you.'

He waved his hand, which was rightly taken as a gesture of dismissal. Left alone he remained pudgily sunk in the easy chair, puffing contentedly. Twenty minutes later, when the cigar was finished, he was still smiling, though it was not a pleasant smile.

4

OLIVER FAIRLEIGH'S SATURDAY

'This egg,' roared Oliver Fairleigh, gazing bulbously into its depths, 'has most certainly not been cooked for five minutes.'

Sitting up in bed, a great Humpty-Dumpty figure, with rolls of flesh pushing the buttons on his pyjama jacket to bursting point, he looked like an eighteenth-century princeling whose subjects are unreasonably demanding bread. To Lady Fairleigh this, his morning look, was a familiar sight, but not a particularly grateful one.

'Oh dear, hasn't it?' she said vaguely.

'Sack that woman.'

'Oh Oliver, don't be foolish. You know you could never get anyone half as good. And as a matter of fact, Mrs Moxon is busy preparing the birthday dinner. I cooked your egg myself.' She looked distractedly at her wrist. 'My watch is *very* small, and it's very difficult to see the minutes.'

Oliver Fairleigh grunted. 'I'll go down and supervise the meal when I've had breakfast,' he threatened.

'Oliver, please don't. You know she doesn't like being watched. She's never yet let us down over the birthday dinner. And I do think you ought to have the morning in bed.'

'Why?' roared Oliver Fairleigh.

'Well, it is going to be a big day, and you know you're not to overstrain yourself.'

'Rubbish,' yelled Oliver Fairleigh. Then remembering, he reduced volume. 'Why should I overstrain myself? There won't be any scenes. I've told you I'm going to be good.'

'Oh Oliver,' sighed his wife. 'That of course will be the strain.'

Terence Fairleigh's room was at the back of the house, but it was a large well-proportioned bedroom with high ceilings, and there was ample room for amplifiers, loud-speakers, and the assorted junk of modern music-making. The walls were painted puce and green, both in shades of such virulence that his father had not entered the room since he first saw them. The decor was otherwise dominated by a large colour poster with the words *Witchetty Grub* in phosphorescent pink lettering across the top. It was the name of Terence Fairleigh's group. In the poster Terence (or Terry) was shown clutching a microphone as if it were the breathing tube on a crashing aeroplane. He was dressed in a skin-tight suit, every inch of which was spangled; the rest of the group were dressed, or in one case undressed, as the fancy took them.

Terence Fairleigh was not wearing spangles today. Even his mother would have drawn the line at that. He was wearing old jeans and a check shirt, and he was barefoot. His mother did rather dislike the bare feet, but she said nothing about them: today was Oliver's birthday, and she was again trying to look on the bright side and believe that for once, just once, the thing would go off without a hitch. What was more to the point than hazy optimism, she was doing all she could of a practical nature to ensure that Oliver's promise of good behaviour was not put to the test by any of the more predictable family phenomena that were the usual cause of thunderclouds.

'You will dress properly for dinner, won't you, dear?' she said, looking at her son anxiously.

'Of course, Mum. The whole hog, if necessary.'

'Well, it *is* the birthday dinner. I think your father would rather like it.'

'Then the whole hog it shall be,' said Terence, carelessly flipping through a magazine. 'And polite conversation throughout dinner—not a word of slang more recent than nineteen-twenty-five, not an obscenity, not a mention of music, and not a political opinion one centimetre to the left of Ghengis Khan.'

Terence looked at his mother, fair and open, his bright blue eyes utterly guileless.

'I know it will be a strain, dear. But it would mean such a lot to me to have a *happy* birthday for a change.'

'I doubt whether it will suit Dad. Why else have we kept up the custom but to have a satisfying occasion for fireworks in the middle of the year, to balance Christmas at the end? And of course it is *his* birthday. Still, I'll do what I can.'

'And then there's Mark—'

Terence held up his hand. 'Mum, I can exercise self-control, but I'm not a miracle-worker. Mark will have to take care of himself.'

'But that's what he never can do! If you could keep him away from the drink . . .'

'Mum, there's no way in the world of doing it. He's got a nose for it sharper than a beagle's, and ways of getting at it you and I couldn't begin to fathom. If you lock it away in this house, then he'll get it outside. Is he here yet?'

'No.'

'Then it's a near-certainty he'll arrive sloshed. The best thing you could do would be to put him to bed.'

'Oh, but I wouldn't want to do that. Your father promised to be nice to him—all day.'

'Christ! What's gotten into the old man?' As he looked at his mother enquiringly, his frank blue eyes took on an expression that was almost crudely speculative.

'He promised—he promised me—' (a disinterested observer might almost have fancied that Lady Fairleigh-Stubbs was jealous of her daughter, so deliberate was her concealment here)—'that he wouldn't let anything provoke him today.'

'Okay,' said Terence. 'Problem solved. So what are you worrying about?'

'Well, you can't always rely on your father's promises, you know. I think we should do our part too—not do things that we

know annoy him. And if we *could* get the idea through to Mark—
well, it might be a new beginning.'

Her voice had a vague wistfulness, as if even she could not
believe such a thing possible. Terence smiled at her encouragingly.
But as she left the room he lay back on the bed, stared at the
ceiling, and furrowed his brow. Fancy his father promising good
behaviour for one day. What was he up to? Or had the situation
changed? Was this the result of some rapprochement between
him and Mark? If so, what was Mark up to?

This needed watching, he said to himself, still gazing at the
ceiling with his innocent blue eyes.

'Ben, do we have to go tonight?' asked his little wife in the
kitchen of the little cottage without hollyhocks. 'It *is* really a family
affair. We'll only be in the way.'

'We'll have to, Celia. He asked us specially, and there are not
many people get asked there these days.'

'Not many who'd go, I shouldn't think,' said his wife.

'Of course he's a terrible old monster, I don't deny that. But he
could be useful to me in a hundred ways.'

'Oh Ben, I realize that,' said Celia Woodstock. 'But the point is,
will he? He hasn't exactly shown evidence of good will, has he?
And I know I shall be so nervous, and frumpish, and clumsy—I'll
annoy him every minute of the evening. I did last time, and I'm so
nervous now it will be much worse tonight.'

'We don't have to stay long after dinner,' said Ben, wiping up a
brown-veined plate that looked as if it might have been part of a
large family service, but had seen better days. 'Then we can fade
away. It's a long time since we saw the whole family together.'

'We?'

'Oh no, you don't really know them, do you? But it will be nice
to see Bella and the boys again. Our families used to be quite
close.'

'It's not a family I would want to be close to,' said his wife, quite
waspishly.

*   *   *

'Wycherley double-two five one,' said Lady Fairleigh-Stubbs cautiously, in case it was someone to whom her husband had been rude. It was. 'Oh, Mark, lovely to hear your voice. Where are you? I wondered if you'd be here by now.'

Lady Fairleigh-Stubbs smoothed her hair as she listened for signs of slurring in her son's speech. At least he couldn't see her: he got so irate if he saw her listening for it, or thought she was trying to smell his breath.

'I see,' she said, when he got to the end of a story about having to meet a man about a deal, and their having missed one another, and having had to leave messages here and phone there. By now she was almost sure there was a slur, but she smiled brightly into the receiver. 'But you're on your way now, dear, aren't you? We'll expect you in an hour or so—' And she put the receiver down on his plausible evasions.

'Still hoping for the best from Mark, Mother dear?' said a cool female voice, breaking into Eleanor Fairleigh's rather sad reverie like a March wind.

'Bella!' said her mother, and folded her in her arms. Bella was in travelling gear, but managed to show no signs of travel: how could anyone contrive to look like an ice lettuce on a hot summer's day, her mother wondered? Her make-up was bright and un-smudged, her blouse looked as if it were straight from the shop hanger, there was not a bulge in her slacks. It was almost inhuman. 'You look so lovely, my dear. I don't know how you manage it.'

'All for Papa's sake, of course,' said her daughter, with a slightly supercilious smile. 'Where is he, by the way? I'd better wish him happy birthday.'

'He's not down yet. He's been getting rather tired lately—what with finishing the new book, and the trip to London, and so on. I thought it would be best if he stayed in bed for a bit, and kept his strength up for the dinner.'

'All the better to give us hell with?' said Bella, resting her elegant case on the bottom stair.

'My dear, he's promised to be good the whole day—but of course, you know that: I gather it was your doing.'

Oh, so it was Bella's doing, thought Terence, who had been passing above on the landing on his way to the bathroom, but had stopped to listen in. Bella glanced carelessly at her mother, not quite sure of the meaning of the expression on her face.

'He's still going along with that, is he?' she asked. 'I'm flattered. Still, knowing Daddy's resolutions, he's not likely to keep it beyond the second sherry.'

'At least he's promised to make the effort,' said her mother, looking nervously upstairs in case he should descend in thunder, but seeing only the glint of light on her younger son's fair hair. 'It was really nice of you to persuade him.'

'I thought it would make a change,' said Bella, indifferently. 'And I felt sorry for Ben.'

'Ben Woodstock? Yes, poor boy. Your father was just a *tiny* bit difficult when we went round there. It will be pleasant having him tonight. It must be years and years since you saw him.'

'Oh, quite a time anyway,' said Bella, and not looking at her mother she swung herself and her suitcase upstairs to her bedroom.

'Everything seems to have blown over,' said Mrs Moxon somewhat regretfully in the kitchen, to Surtees, the chauffeur-cum-valet, who was tucking into a great meal at the kitchen table.

'Blown over?'

'That business of Master Mark—that scene he made at the Prince Albert.'

'Oh, that,' said Surtees, not letting such a triviality put him off his food. He was in his mid-thirties, stocky, and what Oliver Fairleigh would call vulgarly handsome—which meant that the observer had a suspicion he might use his looks to his own advantage. 'I reckon it's a bit late in the day to start taking notice of the things Master Mark says.'

'Sir Oliver likes a stick to beat him with,' said Mrs Moxon. 'But it seems to have been forgotten. Her Ladyship says she spoke to him on the phone, and he'll be here soon.'

'Let's hope he's sobered up, then,' said Surtees.

'How do you know he's been drinking?'

'I saw him at the Rose and Thistle, out Barclay way. And he'd had more than enough, I can tell you.'

'Oh dear,' said Mrs Moxon with relish. 'Poor Lady Fairleigh.'

Wycherley Court was an early eighteenth-century manor house, built by a gentleman who had done well out of the French wars. Like the great Marlborough (who had done even better) his instinct was to plant himself heavily on his native soil, as if daring God or the Supreme Being to uproot him. The manor he built was rectangular and solid, a matter of straight lines and angles at ninety degrees. When Oliver Fairleigh's rotund figure stood in the doorway, he looked like the circle in the square. Architecturally, the Brighton Pavilion would have suited him better.

It was five o'clock when Mark Fairleigh's Fiat drove through the gates and up the splendid circular drive to the front entrance. He was driving too fast, and his steering was too uncertain for comfort. The car skidded to a stop in front of the house, and there was an ominous pause before the driver got out. It seemed as though Mark was collecting his wits.

He got out of the car, and removed a small suitcase from the boot with a little too much care. His mother, watching nervously from the hall, was glad to see that his walk was steady enough: certainly he was not yet at the staggering stage. But he tripped slightly on the top step, and swore. By then his mother had opened the door to him, and he looked hazily embarrassed.

'Mark!' said his mother, not embracing him because he would suspect her of smelling his breath, but nevertheless distinguishing on the breeze a mixture of gin and menthol chewing-gum which she found unpleasant and ominous. 'You are looking well,' she said.

Mark certainly had a kind of bloom, though it was not the bloom of health. His cheeks and temples were flushed, and his eyes did not seem to focus properly: at the moment they were straying around the large oak-panelled hall of Wycherley Court, apparently looking for signs of his father.

But Oliver Fairleigh was never just *there*—he always appeared, always had to make an entrance. Today when he strode in at-

tended by Cuff, snuffling, there was a new effect. Today he was not
Oliver Fairleigh, but Sir Oliver Fairleigh-Stubbs: local landowner,
adored squire, a hunter and a fisher, a supporter of sound men
and sound measures, one of a class that has been the backbone of
the country from time immemorial. Odd that this impersonation
should have faint overtones that reminded one of mine host at the
local on Saturday night.

'Mark, my boy, good to see you!' he said, emerging from his
study in a lather of geniality, and baring his teeth in a fearsome
smile of welcome. 'Staying the night I see! Keeping busy, eh? I'm
glad you're here: I'd like your opinion on a new consignment of
port from Witherspoon's. Can't make up my mind about it—I'd
like a second view.'

If his father had put in his appearance in a scaly green costume,
breathing flames from his nostrils and dripping blood from his
claws Mark could not have been more disconcerted. He backed
two paces, swallowed, murmured a vague assent, and then seemed
inclined to turn to his mother and ask what was up.

'Take your suitcase up, my boy, and have a bath if you want
one. I'll have a sherry waiting for you in the lounge—or is it gin
and tonic, eh? Haven't been keeping up with your tipples recently.'

Mark murmured that a gin and tonic would be fine, took up his
suitcase again, and mounted the stairs—once more tripping on
the top step, and swearing. He seemed to have a genius for not
quite making it to the top.

'Well, well,' said Sir Oliver, not relaxing his mask even when
alone with his wife, perhaps for fear it would crumble to nothing.
'Now we're all together! Nothing like it, eh, my dear? I have just a
few more letters to sign—Miss Cozzens is really keeping me at it
today—and then we'll all meet for a drink before dinner. Eh?'

And he pottered off—even his walk was different from his normal one—to his study, leaving his wife to gaze after him in
bemusement. Oliver not flying into rages was one thing, Oliver
positively genial was quite another. She had known it but once
before: when he went to the Palace to collect his MBE, an honour
which had pleased him out of all proportion to its worth. She did

not know whether to find Oliver's behaviour today a pleasant change, or an alarming one. If only it had been she who had been able to persuade him into it, rather than her daughter . . .

Making up for the evening in her bedroom some half an hour later, and listening to the grunts from next door as her husband changed into his dinner-jacket, Eleanor Fairleigh-Stubbs looked at herself and wondered in her vague way why she bothered: why she bothered worrying, why she bothered trying to coax Oliver into good behaviour, why she bothered trying to build a normal family life. Oliver was Oliver; nothing would change him; he did not want a peaceful life, and those who were closest to him were too used to the scarifying changes of mood to value the brief cease-fires that were part of the household routine. It had never been a happy house, even when the children were young, even before the children had been born. She wondered why Terence and Mark continued to come home. Bella, of course, had a real affection for her father, or seemed to have, but the boys . . . Why return to the battlefield if one didn't have to? Apart from to see her, of course. And because of the will.

She looked closely at her face. Forty-nine, and showing it: scrawny, worried, tired hair, unsightly throat. People said she was at a difficult age. All her ages had been difficult, and they had left their mark. The only thing to be said about her face, she thought, backing away from the mirror, was that it was undoubtedly aristo-cratic. It had style. It had breeding. Which is more than can be said for Oliver's, she thought grimly.

Oliver Fairleigh playing the country squire brought out the gentlewoman in his wife.

When she finally emerged from her bedroom, Eleanor met Mark on the landing and went down with him. He was trying to be bright, but not very coherently. He had not put on a dinner-jacket, and his mother suspected he had had more to drink. He had taken trouble with his tie, but it was somehow not quite square. The degree of concentration required to take one stair after another seemed that much greater than when he had ar-rived. Presumably the suitcase had contained a bottle. Eleanor

Fairleigh-Stubbs smothered a sigh, and kept up light conversation. Mark replied, but too loudly.

Her husband was already in the lounge, and he welcomed them genially (again it was that landlord's heartiness, that grated on his wife) and sat them down. Mark tended to slump, and kept blinking his great, full, self-pitying eyes.

'Eleanor, my dear, a sherry for you? Mark—a gin and tonic?' He turned to the drinks cabinet. Eleanor noted that it was already unlocked—so as not to bring too obviously to Mark's notice the fact that because of him drink was always kept under lock and key in this house? How sensitive of Oliver, she thought, surrendering herself to unrealism. Oliver brought the drinks over with a paternal air.

'Well, Mark,' he said, sipping his own dry sherry, 'what have you been doing with yourself?'

'I've been—I've been—' Mark took a gulp at his gin and tonic— 'I've been making a lot of contacts.' He put his glass down, carelessly, with a minor crash.

'Hope they're good ones. I remember when I was your age— before your time, my dear—I was mad about making contacts. People told me the literary world was an in group, a clique, that I'd never get anywhere unless I got myself in with them. What a lot of pushing and shoving I went in for! I've never made such efforts! But they paid off, too, some of those contacts.'

He sat back after this flow of reminiscence in pop-eyed contemplation of his past, and let out a theatrical sigh of satisfaction. Mark did not seem entirely to have been following, but he said: 'You've got to have contacts.'

'One of them,' continued Sir Oliver, after giving his son what was intended as a kindly look, 'was your cousin Darcy, my dear—'

'Oh dear, Darcy—'

'Yes, well, perhaps not a happy topic of conversation, but I met you at his place, you remember. And we were engaged within the month. Ah, Terence—and Bella!'

Oliver Fairleigh's two younger children came in together, chattering happily. Both were impeccably, even stylishly dressed, and Oliver Fairleigh could not forbear a glance from Terence's dinner-jacket to the slightly bedraggled lounge suit that his elder son was still wearing, the appearance of which was not helped by Mark's slumping posture in the easy chair. Terence was smart and beautiful, with a classically regular face, distant blue eyes, and long, fair hair, cut into a sort of halo round his face. He was, Oliver Fairleigh thought, a suitable escort for the aristocracy, and he was spending his time touring the country with a band of raucous adolescents. At any other time this thought might have prompted him to an apoplectic outburst against his hair, or whatever grievance might be most conveniently to hand, but today, apparently, he was grateful for small mercies, and his surface geniality was undisturbed. He fussed over Bella and got her a drink, and the two younger children sat down on the sofa—elegant, slightly remote, handsome and well-heeled: they looked like a glossy advertisement: posed, almost too perfect.

'The Woodstocks will be here before long, I hope,' said Sir Oliver, settling back into his own chair and sipping his sherry again. 'You remember Ben Woodstock, Mark? You used to be great friends at one time.'

'Never liked him,' said Mark thickly.

'No, so often one doesn't,' said his father, popping his pudgy cheeks out. 'I hope you'll be nice to the little wife, my dear. She seemed to be a little lacking in confidence, poor child, and of course she doesn't know the young people, as Ben does.'

Eleanor bit back a reply to the effect that it was not she who was in the habit of intimidating the meek and mild, but she accepted, as always, the role allotted to her in the play Oliver was currently performing, and merely said: 'Yes—that's often very difficult when one is newly married.'

'I'll get the lad an introduction to Sir Edwin Macpherson, I think. I had a slight impression that might be why he invited us round last weekend. That should please him. Not that it will do any good, I'm afraid. No publisher is going to take on an author merely on my sayso. Still, the lad will have had his chance; and who knows, perhaps he has talent. Let's hope so.'

At that moment Surtees, who was butler for the evening, ushered in the Woodstocks, dressed in their best, which was somehow not good enough; they still seemed slightly moth-eaten, and destined for failure. As Sir Oliver overpowered them with genial hospitality, the little wife let out an audible sigh of relief.

Sir Oliver led them round, introducing Celia Woodstock to the younger members of his family. Mark was blearily friendly in a way that suggested he would not know who she was if he met her again tomorrow; Terence was cool, Bella slightly distant: she cast her eye over the large floral pattern on Celia Woodstock's dress, looked directly into her face, smiled politely, then said no more. Her father more than made up for it by seating her in the best armchair, fussing over her drink, and engaging her in conversation. Somewhat surprisingly, they found that they had friends in common.

Within half an hour, Celia Woodstock was feeling almost at home, and her only qualms occurred when she caught sight of the elegant perfection of Bella, sitting on the sofa with her husband, and talking—not about old times, as one surely ought to on such occasions, but about the world of publishing and journalism. They were very animated. Ben's thin face was lit up, as she seldom had seen it, and his hollow-chested body was alive with energy. In the pause necessitated by Sir Oliver getting up to throw a log on the (highly superfluous) fire, she noted Mark, already on his third gin, and not focusing his eyes well: she noted Terence and his mother, deep in a conversation about dates and recording schedules, and she thought how good-looking he was, but how—somehow—not really *nice*.

Then Surtees came in, and announced dinner.

5

SUDDENLY AT HIS RESIDENCE

Dinner was good. Dinner was Mrs Moxon at the peak of her form. It would not have been like her to let any inadequacies in her department disturb the equanimity of Oliver Fairleigh on his birthday dinner, though she was quite willing for it to be disturbed from any other quarter, being a woman who thrived on disorder. But when Surtees brought the plates down to the kitchen she was disappointed by his reports. There had been no explosion.

Everyone enjoyed the dinner, except Mark, who toyed nervously with it, downing a great deal of wine and seeming more interested in getting himself safely hoisted on to a cloud of oblivion than in anything going on around him.

Celia Woodstock put odious comparisons with her own performance firmly from her mind—after all, she thought, with the doggedness of the little woman, why *should* my dinners be compared with those of people who can afford to employ a cook?—and concentrated firmly on two things: her food and her host. She was seated beside Sir Oliver, and he was treating her with unending charm, asking her opinion on current events, showering her with anecdotes of the literary great, giving her fatherly advice, and even admiring her dress in a manner that seemed sincere. Celia Woodstock expanded into her dark green and orange patterned print frock, and came close to enjoying herself. It was not, unfortunately, possible entirely to relax: the dreadful shadow cast by Sir Oliver's performance last Sunday prevented her quite doing that. But she listened sensibly, she glowed now and then with pleasure, and she talked more than she usually did.

'Of course, I know people say that Ben is mad to think of becoming a writer full time,' she said confidingly. 'But he felt there was no job he could take that would leave him with the peace of mind to write, let alone the time.'

'A good point, that, very!' said Oliver Fairleigh, gazing at her with fatuous good-humour which a connoisseur of his performances might have caught as an imitation of a dim-witted Wodehousian club bore.

'After all, there are only two of us,' said Celia, looking at him appealingly, as if he were an old family friend to whom she had gone for advice. 'The cottage is ours, you know, and I'm perfectly capable of getting a job if necessary. Not—' she lowered her voice —'that it will be. As a matter of fact, we have a little more coming in than people imagine.'

Sir Oliver concealed a flinch at the vulgarity of the phrasing, and entered into the spirit of her confidences. 'I'm glad to hear it. Something tucked away, eh? A little nest egg? I wouldn't want to appear inquisitive, but I thought the family was—not to put too fine a point on it—broke.'

Celia Woodstock lowered her voice, dropped her eyes, and said: 'Not quite.'

'Good, good,' said Oliver Fairleigh, horribly avuncular. 'An independent income's the saving of a writer. Not a large one, necessarily, of course—'

'Oh, it's not large—' said Celia hurriedly.

'But enough, eh? Well, I have a little surprise for you, my dear.' He patted her hand, and she looked down at his pudgy scrivener's paw in some consternation. 'I thought it might help if I introduced your husband to Sir Edwin Macpherson. Got the idea he wanted something of the kind, don't know why. So I thought I'd take him to lunch, some time in the next week or two—just the three of us.' Forestalling her little whinnies of pleasure, he directed his glance down the table. 'Ben, my boy—'

At the roar from his host Ben Woodstock looked up hastily and apprehensively from his low and intense conversation with Bella Fairleigh.

'I'm just telling your little wife, Ben, that I'm hoping to take you to lunch with Eddie Macpherson, if you could manage it. Do you think you could, eh?'

Ben Woodstock blushed pink, stuttered his thanks, and (as Sir Oliver turned his attention back to his food) looked enquiringly at his wife. Bella looked coldly in the same direction, but found Celia Woodstock gazing back at her, perfectly straight, with something close to a smile of triumph on her face.

'Of course,' said Sir Oliver, turning to her again, and lowering his voice from a lordly bellow to a lordly whisper, 'beyond the lunch there's nothing much I can do. People think I can, but I can't. Can't force a man to publish a book if he doesn't want to. You're a sensible woman—you understand that. But we'll hope for the best.'

'This *is* kind,' said Celia sincerely. 'Ben is so pleased, I can see that. And his mother will be too.'

'Nice woman,' said Sir Oliver, licking his fat lips. 'Had a hard time of it. Sad to see the old families go down.'

'Oh, it is. The Woodstocks used to be the first family around here, so Ben says. Still, you never know: Ben always says the gentry have great staying power.'

'Does he?' said Oliver Fairleigh, gazing without any overt irony at Ben Woodstock's unimpressive form.

'I think over the years they've developed ways of holding on to what they've got,' said Celia Woodstock, conveying regretfully to her mouth the last of her boeuf bourguignon.

'Bella,' said her mother from across the table, anxious to disentangle her from the low, intense conversation with young Woodstock, which she could see was worrying his dull little wife: 'we were wondering if you could help us to get a new gardener.'

Bella raised her head and looked at her mother with something close to disdain. 'Mother dear, I suppose if you met Elizabeth David you'd ask her to find you a cook.'

'Well, I don't see why not—' said Eleanor Fairleigh vaguely.

'I'm afraid that, though I'm working on a gardening newspaper, I have no contact whatever with gardeners. In fact, no one I meet has the slightest knowledge of gardening. We just put the paper together, and we hardly see the people who write it.'

'What a shame,' said her mother. 'So impersonal, somehow . . .'

'The best way to get a good gardener, mother, is to pay well,' said Bella, and turned back to Ben Woodstock. There was nothing for it for Eleanor but to talk to her sons.

'Are you still thinking of moving, Mark?' she asked her eldest.

'Sorry? . . .' Mark had been looking dully at his plate, still well filled, and jiggling his glass to attract Surtee's attention.

'Are you still thinking of moving, dear?'

'I've moved.'

'Already, dear? Where to? You will leave me your new address before you go, won't you?'

'Islington,' said Mark, as if he hadn't quite heard. He thought for a bit, looking drearily ahead, and then he said: 'It's smaller. I didn't need all that space.'

'I'm sure it will be better, dear. After all, it will be less to keep clean.'

Mark looked at his mother as if she were crazy, but was diverted by the sight of Surtees with a full bottle in his hand.

'Mark,' said Terence, from his mother's other side, 'is not particularly interested in keeping his place clean. Nor will I be when I have somewhere permanent of my own. Cleanliness is very low on my list of priorities.'

'But you can't like living in *squalor*,' protested his mother pleadingly.

'Of course he does,' came the genial roar from the head of the table. Oliver Fairleigh was gazing in their direction with an expression of fearsome good cheer on his face, like a field-marshal visiting the Christmas Day dinner in the NCOs' mess. 'Everyone should live in squalor when they're young. Eh, Ben? I'm sure you did, before you did the sensible thing and got yourself married.'

'Well,' said Ben weakly, 'I'm not a *tidy* person . . .'

'I should hope not. Filthy, I shouldn't wonder. That's what makes people get married—being fed up with it. Don't let your mother provide you with dusters and vacuum cleaners, Mark, my boy. She cleaned me up, but she shouldn't try it on you. Squalor is part of a writer's stock-in-trade.'

'I'm not a writer,' said Mark thickly.

'I know, my boy,' said his father equably. 'I was referring to myself. Though stranger things have happened, of course . . .'

'I'd rather die than be a writer,' went on Mark, oblivious of the pressure of his mother's hand on his right sleeve. 'Bloodless, sadistic bastards. Always taking people apart, pretending to understand—God, they're the last people to understand.' His great, dark-rimmed eyes watered with self-pity, and he looked with dull resentment at his father. 'Self-satisfied oafs,' he said. 'Think themselves bloody little gods. Playing with people . . . never leaving people alone . . . I'd rather die than be . . . than be a . . . writer.'

He subsided into a comatose silence, and looked at his untasted dessert. He had effectively doused the festive atmosphere. Oliver Fairleigh's eye glinted dangerously as he looked in his direction, and there was an edge to his voice as he tried—in a parody of the tactful host's manner—to fill in the surrounding silence.

'Of course he has a point,' he said generally, looking round the table. 'Wouldn't you agree, Woodstock? We are a pretty bloodless lot, I suppose—watching people, storing it all away. Eh? All the little details that fall into place later, all the little mannerisms that give people away. It must seem a pretty inhuman sort of existence, to people outside the charmed circle.' He lowered his voice, and addressed Celia Woodstock alone: 'He's had a little bit more than is good for him, you know. Not used to it.' And then, as conversation seemed to be slow in starting up around the rest of the table, he said: 'Shall we adjourn to the library? Surtees has put out the coffee there. I've one or two things I'd like to show your husband, my dear—he'll have to humour a bibliophile's whims for a little while, I'm afraid.'

They all got up, the Woodstocks saying all the right things, and the little party trooped off towards the library. With one exception. As they reached the door they noticed that Mark had sunk back into his place, and his head was beginning to fall forward on to his chest.

Bella went back and leaned over him:

'Come on, Mark. Dinner's over. Come and have some coffee. That'll buck you up.'

There were clotted mutterings from Mark that sounded like obscenities. Bella started to lift him.

'Leave him, Bella,' said her father, his voice dangerously close to a shout. 'Best to let him come to on his own.'

'Oh no, Daddy. This is the best part of the dinner. Mark will have to be in on it.' And Bella and Terence between them stood Mark up, and—staggering slightly, for Mark was not a small man —they hoisted him across the hall and into the library. Once they had him there they let him sink into an easy chair by the door, where he promptly went to sleep, if he had ever wakened.

The study was large, luxurious and dark, lined with cupboards and bookcases, whose contents were predominantly brown and nineteenth-century-looking, though there were two shelves over the desk which contained a long line of books in gaudier dust-jackets, no doubt the host's own collected works. The desk itself was an enormous, heavy Victorian affair, and was open.

'My goodness!' said Oliver Fairleigh, looking at it. 'This is a surprise!'

It was piled high with presents, large and small, all wrapped in luxurious sorts of wrapping paper.

'My husband is a terrible child,' whispered Eleanor Fairleigh to Celia Woodstock. 'He loves presents. We put them here every year, and he always pretends to be surprised.'

Oliver Fairleigh had capered over to the presents, and was rummaging around in the pile with little porcine snuffles of glee. ' "From Bella, with love"! Goodness me! It's quite heavy. What can it be? From Terence, this one: what a nice *big* parcel. It can't be handkerchiefs, that's a blessing. Leave handkerchiefs for people who like picking their noses. This is Eleanor's—it rattles. What can *that* be? Cuff-links, perhaps? Not a lighter, anyway. I'm not sup-posed to smoke, Celia, my dear—' he drew Mrs Woodstock into the family group by the hand—'and my wife would regard a lighter as an encouragement. And here's one from Miss Cozzens. How very friendly. Perhaps I should have invited her to be with us tonight. Do you think it was remiss of me, Eleanor, my dear? Will she hold it against me?'

Oliver Fairleigh's voice trailed away, as he finished inspecting the pile of presents. There was an awkwardness as everyone real- ized that there seemed to be one lacking. Oliver Fairleigh looked towards Mark. He said nothing. Then, rubbing his hands, he flashed his teeth into a rather frightening smile—Celia Woodstock remembered last Sunday, and shivered suddenly—and said:

'Now, Eleanor, if you'll be so good as to see to the coffee, I'll pour the liqueurs.'

'Oh, Oliver, should you? Why don't you open your presents first?'

Oliver Fairleigh looked longingly at the decanters along the shelf of the open cupboard behind the desk, and longingly at the presents in their gaudy pile. The presents won.

'Well, well,' he said; 'perhaps if I just took a peep . . .'

The world is divided into those who eat their meat first, and those who eat their vegetables. Oliver Fairleigh was decidedly of the former type. Ignoring Miss Cozzens's small, square box, he dived for Bella's present, and handled it lovingly: a substantial, heavy and interesting parcel. His podgy fingers struggled with the wrapping, and when he had got it off he dived down to look at the contents, screening them from the gaze of the little knot of people round him. Little snorts of delight and appreciation were heard, and ecstatic shakings of the shoulders.

'Look!' he said. 'Look!' The others regarded this as licence to swoop down around him, only Bella standing a little aloof, smiling to herself. *'Caleb Williams,'* said Oliver Fairleigh. 'The first edition. What a find!' He straightened and turned to Celia Woodstock. 'It's the first detective story, you know, or more or less. Bella, my dear, you are a dreadful daughter. You must have spent three months' salary. I have an awful presentiment that I shall be forced to subsi- dize my own birthday present.'

He kissed her heartily, and she put her arms elegantly around his thick, publican's neck.

'You're very unfair, Daddy. I haven't asked you for a penny since I started work.'

'That,' said Oliver Fairleigh, who never lost his realism in money matters, 'is because you know how to work me up to offering it you whenever you find you need it.'

Terence's present was a substantial and handsome silk dressing-gown, beamingly received. Eleanor's was indeed cuff-links, traditional and solid, and she was given a husbandry kiss of thanks. Miss Cozzens's was handkerchiefs.

'Oh, how fortunate I *didn't* ask her tonight,' said Sir Oliver. 'It would have been very embarrassing. What could I have said? You know, one of her great advantages as a secretary is that she has no imagination, so it would be very ungrateful of me to complain.'

By now the group around the desk had dispersed around the room, and Sir Oliver surveyed them all with a cheek-popping beam on his face.

'A wonderful birthday,' he said genially. 'The best for years. So kind of you, Celia and Ben, to come and share it with us.' He turned and took a cigar from a box on top of the desk, ignoring an inarticulate protest from his wife. 'Tomorrow we must go out somewhere—for a meal, or a drink. I feel the need to spend something on my family, after all their generosity.' He lit his cigar, and puffed away at it appreciatively. 'Where shall we go? I hear the Prince Albert at Hadley is one of the places people go these days.'

There was a sudden silence in the study. Eleanor's heart seemed suddenly to suspend operations. Oliver Fairleigh was looking genially in the direction of his elder son, but if he hoped for a reaction, he was disappointed. Mark, deep in sleep and deep in his chair, gave little sign of life beyond the slight regular rise and fall of his chest. For a few seconds the host of the evening savoured the silence in the room, savoured the infinitesimal look of enquiry that passed from his daughter Bella to his son Terence, noticed that the embarrassment of the Woodstocks made it perfectly clear that the village gossip had got to them. Then he rubbed his hands and turned back to the desk.

'Now, Eleanor, perhaps you will pour the coffee. If it's cold you must blame me. Liqueurs, everybody?'

From the low cupboard just above the desk Oliver Fairleigh took a series of decanters and bottles.

'I love liqueurs,' he said happily to Celia Woodstock, as if in an attempt to restore the happy atmosphere. 'It's deplorable, but I'm afraid I have to admit to a sweet tooth. What will you have, my dear? Cointreau? Grenadine? Or what about my own special favourite—it's called lakka. You won't have heard of it. It's Finnish, and it's made from cloudberries—quite delicious.'

He took the stopper from a decanter with a small quantity of yellow liqueur in it.

'It's awfully sweet, disgustingly sweet,' said Eleanor. 'You might not like it. We have to get it specially from the Finnish Tourist place. I'm sure no one else in Britain drinks it.'

'I think you may be right,' chortled Oliver Fairleigh happily. 'Except expatriate Finns with sweet tooths, or should that be sweet teeth?' Everyone smiled nervously. It was now clear to all, even the non-family members, that it would not do to be too sure of their man. 'Now, my dear?' he enquired, smiling ingratiatingly at Celia Woodstock.

'I think I would prefer Cointreau,' she said, in the nervous voice of one who knows nothing about liqueurs, and does not expect to like them.

'Very well, Cointreau it shall be; and the same for Eleanor—' Oliver Fairleigh poured a succession of little glasses and handed them round. By now they had all managed to seat themselves around the heavy, glowering study, except for Ben Woodstock, who had been drawn to the bookshelves—or perhaps who had felt he ought to show an interest in his host's collection. After handing a glass of Drambuie to Terence, Oliver Fairleigh looked at his elder son, still comatose in his armchair at the far end of the room.

'We'll leave him, for a little,' he said, as if Mark were an underdone roast, and turned back to pour himself a little glass of thick yellow liqueur from a rather fine cut-glass decanter.

'Now,' he said—but before he could propose a toast, his wife and daughter both said, 'Happy birthday, Oliver!' and they all raised their glasses, or in some cases their coffee cups, to him. With a contented expression on his face, relishing, as always, being the centre of attention, Oliver Fairleigh drank his lakka. He drew together his formidable eyebrows. He pushed his tongue experimentally through his lips. He let out a grunt—expostulatory, bass, frightening, but finishing in an odd, questioning little whimper. He fell heavily to the floor.

'Oliver! My God! I knew this would happen.' His wife had jumped from her chair, upsetting the table beside it and the coffee cup on it. She dashed over to the bulbous, collapsed figure by the desk. 'Surtees! Someone get Surtees! Ring for an ambulance, quickly!'

She was hardly on her knees beside her husband when Surtees dashed into the room.

'What is it? I was passing—' He saw Lady Fairleigh on the floor, and ran over to where she was, finally seeing the body, moaning and feebly thrashing around. 'Water. Get some water.' He threw some flowers from a vase on a sidetable to the floor, spread the body of Oliver Fairleigh out lengthways, and dashed the water into his face.

'For heaven's sake, man, it's not a faint or a fit,' said Lady Fairleigh. 'Get him up. He's supposed to sit up.'

'This is Wycherley Court,' said Terence in an unnaturally high voice into the phone. 'Will you send an ambulance at once. It's my father—Sir Oliver Fairleigh-Stubbs. Quickly, please. He's had some sort of attack.' He pressed down the receiver rest, and immediately began dialling again.

'He doesn't seem able to breathe,' said Eleanor Fairleigh. 'What should we do?' She looked at Surtees, who was trying to prop up the immense bulk of his employer in a sitting position, and was sweating with the effort. 'Perhaps we should lay him down after all,' his wife said. 'I'm sure he would be more comfortable. Do you think we should try massaging his heart?'

'Dr. Leighton? It's Terence Fairleigh. Dad has had an attack— heart, I think. Can you come? . . . Yes, he is, but he's in a bad way. I've called for the ambulance . . . Yes, please hurry.'

Terence Fairleigh put down the phone. 'He'll be here right away,' he said. 'He said that was what he was afraid of.'

He looked at the three figures on the floor, and then turned round to look at his sister. She was standing a few feet from her father, seeming as usual to carry a quality of remoteness with her, but her eyes were awash with tears, and her mouth was twitching.

'Mummy,' she said. 'I'll go with him in the ambulance. You'll only upset yourself.'

Eleanor Fairleigh straightened her back. 'Indeed you will not, Bella,' she said directly and determinedly, looking unblinkingly at her daughter. Then she turned back to her husband.

Terence put out his hand and took Bella's in his.

Half an hour later the ambulance had been and gone, conveying swiftly and efficiently Sir Oliver and Lady Fairleigh. Dr Leighton had driven up as it was leaving, and had relieved Surtees of the task of going with them. The Woodstocks had taken the opportunity to slip off, after a few words of sympathy and hope to the ones left behind.

'I'm sure he'll be all right,' said Celia Woodstock to Bella, her face assuming a standard expression.

'Oh? Why?' said Bella. Her eyes were quite dry now, and they looked directly at Celia. She turned away, discomforted, and she and Ben were soon seen walking down the drive, he long and cadaverous, she short and homely. From a distance they seemed oddly ill-assorted. They were not talking.

At ten forty-five the phone rang. Terence Fairleigh was there in a second, and snatched it up.

'Wycherley two-two-five-one. Oh Mother . . . My God—so soon? . . . I felt sure it was going to be all right. I didn't expect . . . Shall we come? . . . Dr Leighton? All right, I'll tell Surtees to make you something. Goodbye, Mum.'

He put down the telephone. 'He's dead,' he said. He looked at Bella, whose eyes once more were overflowing. 'Mum's coming back now with Dr Leighton.'

Bella seemed about to sink down into a chair and crumple up. Terence took her hands, held them tight.

'Don't break down, old girl,' he said. 'Think of Mum. We two'll be all right.' But when she looked at him there was distrust in her face.

They were disturbed by a noise from near the door. Mark, deep in his armchair, first grunted, then rubbed his hands in his eyes, and then opened them, looking ahead blearily and uncertainly.

'What time is it?' he said. 'Why are you still up?'

He saw the decanters in the open cupboard, and focusing his eyes on them he began to struggle to his feet.

'Arise, Sir Mark,' said Terence contemptuously.

6

MOURNED BY HIS FAMILY

Barbara Cozzens really rather enjoyed the morning after her employer's death. She was a tower of strength in a crisis, she felt —without, naturally, pushing herself forward or intruding where she was unwelcome. Her unflappability and her excellence at coping were qualities which had not been called on the previous evening: indeed, if she had not slipped down to the kitchen after she heard the ambulance drive away, she might not have known that her employer was even ill. Once down there, she had allowed Mrs Moxon to administer coffee, and they had stayed on chatting in whispers (though why in whispers in that enormous kitchen with no one remotely near to overhear them she would have been at a loss to explain). Surtees, with their encouragement, went backwards and forwards periodically to the study, ostensibly to clear away the coffee cups and glasses. When he brought the news of Oliver Fairleigh's death, the two ladies had both said 'No!' Then they had all switched to brandy and begun to discuss their futures.

This morning she sat at the desk where Sir Oliver only a few hours before had opened presents and dispensed liqueurs, dealing with enquiries and setting in train arrangements for the funeral. The death had been too late for the Sunday papers, but had been broadcast on the eight o'clock news. The secretary of the Crime Writers' Association phoned her official sympathy, as did some fellow detective writers: there was little grief, but much tact.

She spoke to Gerald Simmington, Sir Oliver's editor at Macpherson's and (circling round the subject in the manner of those who are being worldly at a time when they feel they ought to be spiritual) they agreed how fortunate it was that *Murder Upstairs and Downstairs* had been finished before the tragedy of the night before.

'Because I certainly didn't know the solution myself,' Miss Cozzens confided. 'And the public wouldn't have been very interested in an unfinished detective story, would they? After all, it's not as though he was Dickens . . .'

As Miss Cozzens sat at the desk, conspicuously coping, her thoughts turned to her own future. They were helped in this direction by Cuff, who sat at her feet, but kept making sorties round the room, whining wheezily and looking bewildered. Cuff knew things were different, and Miss Cozzens faced up to the changes in her own life too. Perhaps she regretted them less than Cuff did. Of course, first she would have to stay on for a few weeks here, perhaps a few months, for she knew more about Sir Oliver's literary and business affairs than anyone in the house and she would be needed—or 'indispensable' as she put it to herself. After that—a holiday, a late holiday, a real Indian Summer, in Greece, or Southern Italy, or perhaps the West Indies. Then a new job. It would have been nice to have a change from authors, she thought wistfully, but it seemed foolhardy to waste her experience of the last few years: having worked for Oliver Fairleigh, she could pick and choose in the literary world. And after all, she could not be sure that a businessman or a politician would turn out any better.

She would be careful what *kind* of writer she engaged herself to, of course: nothing would induce her to consider employment with a romantic lady novelist, for example: candy-coated sarcasms and slavery for a pittance were the fate of those who let themselves fall into that trap. But a biographer would be nice, a sort of popular historian. Her capacity for research had never been properly exploited in her present job, especially as Sir Oliver had been so criminally careless over details. The sort of person who wrote biographies of the Romantic poets or the Queens of England would suit her down to the ground, thought Miss Cozzens, warming her feet on Cuff.

She was in the middle of constructing this particular aerial edifice when she was interrupted by the ringing of the telephone. She set her face in an expression of containable grief, and took up the receiver:

'Oh, Dr Leighton, how good of you to ring . . . No, Lady Fairleigh is already up, and taking it very well, considering . . . It's not as though it's entirely unexpected, is it? I believe they're in the sitting-room now—I'm trying to keep all the worrisome stuff from them, till they're more used to the idea, more able to cope . . . I'm sorry, Dr Leighton, could you repeat that, I don't quite understand . . . Not satisfied? But . . . an autopsy . . . *police,* but . . . Are you sure you wouldn't like to tell Lady Fairleigh about this yourself, Dr Leighton? . . . Of course, if you wish it, I'll tell her . . . Thank you Doctor, it's kind of you to say so . . . I'll tell her straight away.'

But when she put down the phone, she sat for some time, staring ahead of her, her face still wearing the mask of decorous grief, but her forehead slightly creased. Then she got up, squared her shoulders, and walked resolutely to the door.

'Of course, one keeps *saying* it's not unexpected,' said Eleanor Fairleigh, putting down a cup of strong coffee, and looking round at her children; 'I'm sure Miss Cozzens is saying that to everyone at the moment. But when it comes to the point, it *isn't* expected, and the shock is just as great, however many doctors' warnings there may have been.'

'Still, it's not as though Father was an easy person to keep in order,' said Terence, his voice on a very even keel. 'Doctors' warnings didn't mean much to him.'

'Well, but he did try, you know,' said his widow. 'He very seldom smoked, and he had cut down on his drinking an awful lot. He never took spirits at all, and only the occasional glass of lakka at weekends. Really, you know, considering your father's character, he was surprisingly good.'

'But there was the wine,' said Bella. 'Daddy said he'd rather die than give that up.'

It wasn't a fortunate expression. Bella was looking less than her perfectly groomed self, though still enormously self-controlled. Her hair was falling around her shoulders with hardly a wave, and some of her make-up looked left-over from last night.

'In any case,' said Mark, sober and suited, though somewhat bloodshot of eye, 'he kept the keys, so he could always have helped himself whenever he wanted one.'

'But I kept a very good eye on him, you know, dear,' said his mother. 'And so did Miss Cozzens. Of course there were occasions when he had one or two when he shouldn't: like finishing the last book, for example. But on the whole I think he stuck to the routine Dr Leighton prescribed, with his own little modifications. I must say I was astonished at how well he kept to it. I think in his own way he enjoyed life.'

'I'm sure he did,' said Mark inscrutably.

'Doesn't anyone feel like a drink now?' said Bella. Her mother shot her a furious glance, and attempted the hopeless task of shaking her head imperceptibly. Bella ignored her. 'Well, I do, anyway,' she said, marched to the cupboard and took out a bottle. She poured herself a neat whisky. 'No one else?'

'No thanks, Bella,' said Mark, drinking the last of his coffee and setting his cup down.

'No thanks,' said Terence after a pause.

Bella had effectively destroyed the atmosphere of discreet family mourning. They all sat there, trying not to look at Mark, wondering at his refusal, and wondering what to talk about. Eleanor felt a wave of relief wash over her, dousing the anger towards her daughter. She thanked heavens there had not been time to try and stop Mark from accepting, otherwise she surely would have driven him to doing it. The others juggled feverishly with possible topics of conversation. Money, of course, was out. It had to be something with reference to Father, but without reference to his will. It was not easy.

'I hope his last book is good,' said Bella at last, perhaps feeling a mite repentant. 'It will be so much better to go out with a bang, and so much more like him.'

As if on cue, Miss Cozzens came in with the bang.

'Lady Fairleigh, I wonder if I might talk to you for a moment,' she said.

'But is it anything the children can't hear, Barbara?'

'Well, no, I suppose they'll have to know. But it's a little difficult to explain. Dr Leighton has just rung—'

'So kind. He has been *very* good all the time.'

'—and he says they're not completely satisfied at the hospital about the cause of death.'

'The cause of death, Barbara? But it was a heart attack. I told them about Oliver's heart.'

'They're not quite satisfied about the cause of the attack, he says. They're not quite sure that it was caused naturally.' Miss Cozzens was so embarrassed that she could hardly look at them straight as she said it.

Eleanor Fairleigh-Stubbs looked at her in increasing bewilderment, and then looked round at her children. '*Naturally.* But how can a heart attack be natural? I don't understand what—'

'Mother,' said Bella in a flat, brutal voice, 'did you never read any of Daddy's books? They think someone killed him.'

'Bella!' Her mother's mouth gaped, her eyes filled with tears, and she seemed to crumple up.

'Now please, Lady Fairleigh, nothing whatsoever has been said about any such thing,' said Barbara Cozzens briskly. 'There is merely a question of an autopsy, to determine the cause of death with complete certainty. I'm sure we're all much too sensible to jump to conclusions, aren't we?' She threw a disapproving glance in Bella's direction, but Bella continued sipping her whisky and staring straight ahead. Miss Cozzens thought to herself that she seemed to have lost a lot of that quality of coolness which had always been her great weapon.

'Miss Cozzens is right, Mother,' said Mark. 'I'm sure it's just routine. It will all be cleared up in a few hours.'

'And if it's not?' said Terence significantly.

'Terence!' said Barbara Cozzens sharply, addressing him for

the first time for some years by his Christian name. 'I should have thought you'd have had more sense—'

'If it's not,' said Mark, not avoiding his gaze, 'we in this family ought to know what follows.'

Eleanor Fairleigh, who had been gazing wide-eyed at all her children, at last broke down into sobs. Her tall, strong-boned body heaved up and down, and sounds came from her that were at once heartbroken and terrified. Mark went over to her chair and sat down on the arm. 'Now, come on, Mum,' he said, putting his arm around her. 'They're just being silly. You know how we are sometimes. There's no question of anyone having killed him. Just bear up. You've had all the strain. Come on, Mum, don't break down now.'

'Really,' said Miss Cozzens (the approaching termination of whose employment seemed to have loosened her tongue), 'you two should be soundly spanked.'

'For facing facts?' said Bella. She looked challengingly at Barbara Cozzens, and then beyond her to the door. Surtees was standing there, and behind him, keeping in the shadow, was a man in uniform. They were obviously considering how to break in on the scene, and Bella wondered how long they had been there.

'Excuse me, my lady,' said Surtees, 'but this is Chief Inspector Meredith.' He seemed to want to say more, but couldn't get it out, so he retreated into the murk of the hall, where other uniformed figures seemed to be waiting.

'I'm sorry to have to trouble you, Lady Fairleigh,' said the Chief Inspector, his mouth set in an expression of grief, but his eyes dancing and sparkling as if they belonged to another play, 'but it's perhaps best to talk to you all together.'

Miss Cozzens's heart gave a strange leap, as if she had been here before. For the voice, pleasant and musical, had an unmistakable Welsh lilt.

7

SAID THE PIGGY: I WILL

Inspector Meredith was a chunky man of middle-height, who could once have been a rugby scrum-half, but had not acquired the bruiser's face that sometimes goes with the game. He was in his early forties, his hair still light brown untouched by grey, his face mobile and candid, and his eyes dancing with pleasure and mischief and joy in life. Whatever effects a policeman's lot had on other members of the force, it did not seem to have robbed Inspector Meredith of a boyish zest for experience. Even when the rest of his face was trying on other expressions for size, his eyes said he was enjoying himself hugely, rippling like a lake in a spring breeze. At the moment he looked more as if he had just solved a difficult case instead of being just about to begin one.

The eyes, darting lithely, took in Bella and Terence, both apparently relaxed in their chairs, but looking at him tensely; took in Mark, indefinably crumpled, but managing a certain dignity as he sat comforting his mother; took in Miss Cozzens and the odd mixture of respectability, disapproval, efficiency and covert enjoyment somehow mingled in her face and stance; took in Lady Fairleigh-Stubbs, struggling to wipe away the tears from her long, mobile, distinguished face. It was she in the end who reacted to his arrival. She dabbed determinedly at her face, assumed with an effort a brave front, got to her feet and advanced towards him, hand out-

stretched. It seemed like a heroic triumph of breeding over inclination.

'Good morning, Inspector.' she said, shaking him by the hand.
'I'm afraid we are a little upset here, as you can imagine. Perhaps
you had better sit down.'

'Thank you, Lady Fairleigh.' Chief Inspector Meredith, his face
set more than ever in a mask of sobriety, darted over to a chair, sat
himself neatly in it, and looked around once more at the family of
Oliver Fairleigh. Mark was standing now, and trying to coax his
mother back to her seat. Bella and Terence had not acknowledged
his presence—had, in fact, hardly moved a muscle, except to turn
their heads slightly so as to follow him with their eyes. A very chilly
pair indeed, Meredith decided.

'You won't thank me for beating about the bush, I'm sure of
that,' he said, putting his open palms squarely on his knees. 'I'm
here because we're afraid that your husband's heart attack,
ma'am, was in some way or other induced. Of course we are not
sure of anything yet, but we suspect that it may have been brought
on by some poison that acts on the heart—nicotine, for example.'

'Nicotine?' said Lady Fairleigh, who for all her efforts still
seemed to be in a state of shell-shock. 'Well, of course, Oliver had
lit up a cigar.'

'It would have to be nicotine administered in some other way,
say in a liquid solution,' explained Meredith patiently. 'Of course,
whether this was taken accidentally, or deliberately, or was administered to him by another person we have no means of knowing as
yet. That's what we are here for.'

'You mean,' said Mark, 'that his death was either suicide, or
accident, or murder.'

'That's correct, sir.'

Meredith looked round at the five faces, all trying to digest the
implications of what he had just said.

'I'm sure there's no question of suicide,' said Lady Fairleigh at
last, apparently with reluctance. 'As we were just saying, Oliver
loved life, in his own way.'

'How could a poison like that get into anything accidentally?'

asked Miss Cozzens. 'It doesn't seem possible. Especially as only Sir Oliver was affected.'

'It is rather difficult to imagine,' said Inspector Meredith. He paused, and let the third alternative hang for a moment in the room, like a bat in the rafters.

Half an hour later the sequence of events on the previous evening was becoming a little plainer to Meredith.

'So if we assume—a big assumption, I'm perfectly aware—if we assume that the cause of death was the lakka, then it seems to me that the likeliest thing is that the poison was introduced into the glass. Otherwise any number of people could have been poisoned.' The Fairleigh family considered this thoughtfully. 'And the glasses—?' continued Meredith.

'They've been washed up, Inspector,' said Barbara Cozzens, feeling less than usually irreproachable at the thought that it was she who had encouraged Surtees to be so officiously efficient the night before. The Inspector looked at her, but if he was annoyed he didn't let it show on his face. His habitual airy good-humour was undisturbed.

'Ah well, that's a pity. Never mind. My men can get the glasses that were used. There's no telling what tiny traces may still be clinging to them.'

'But you know, Inspector,' said Terence, who had dropped his passive hostility, 'I don't remember too clearly—we'd all had quite a lot to drink at dinner—but I *think* Dad poured out his lakka and took it up in his hand immediately. Then we toasted him, and he drank it down. Isn't that right?' He looked round enquiringly at his mother and sister.

'Yes, it is, dear, I remember it distinctly,' said his mother. 'He drank it almost immediately. So you see, it's quite impossible, Inspector.' She said it with an eager satisfaction, as if having proved this one hypothesis to be impossible, the whole nightmare would go away. Inspector Meredith felt that she was not doing justice to her intelligence.

'Was there an interval between his pouring the glass before his own and his pouring his own?' asked Meredith. 'If there was, the

—poison might have been introduced into the glass before the liqueur was poured into it.'

They all furrowed their brows. 'I think there may have been,' said Bella finally. 'Was it your glass he poured before his own, Terry?'

Terence shrugged. 'Search me. It's not the kind of thing you would remember, is it?'

'I think it was,' said Eleanor Fairleigh, 'But I couldn't be sure.'

'In any case,' said Meredith, 'we'll soon know, because my boys will be examining the decanter of lakka.'

'If the poison—if there *was* poison—was put in the decanter, there wouldn't have been any great risk,' said Terence. 'None of us would have touched the stuff. Only Dad drank it.'

'But you had guests,' said Meredith.

'Of course,' said Terence carelessly. 'I'd forgotten the Woodstocks. They are rather the sort of people one tends to overlook.'

Meredith noted a glance pass from Bella to Terence, of what meaning he could not guess. Lady Eleanor was thoughtfully continuing on the same track: 'Of course, I remember now, Oliver did press little Mrs Woodstock to try the lakka. How lucky she refused.'

'And of course,' said Meredith, 'if the poison was put into the decanter, it could have been put there at any time since the last occasion anybody drank the stuff. So whoever it was did it may not have known that there would be guests to dinner next time it was used. Or of course,' Meredith added, 'he may not have cared.'

'The cupboard where the decanter was was always kept locked,' said Miss Cozzens. 'And Sir Oliver kept the key himself. Whoever it was would have had to break into the cupboard.'

'Oh, he always kept the keys, did he? Why was that?'

'One of his little ways,' said his widow hurriedly. She did not look at her children. Meredith sat in thought for a few seconds.

'Let's forget that possibility for a moment,' he said at last. 'Now, while the presents were being opened, you were all crowding round the desk—is that right?'

'Except Mark,' said Eleanor, quickly again.

'Oh yes? And why was that, sir?'

'I was drunk,' said Mark, without embarrassment. 'You'll have to ask the others what I did. I don't remember anything after dinner. When I woke I was in the chair by the door, that I do recall. But by then he was dead.' Mark looked round, wide-eyed and enquiring at his brother and sister. Inspector Meredith sensed in them a certain reluctance to offer testimony on this point. Terence looked as if his thoughts were elsewhere, while Bella looked at her glass.

'We brought Mark from the dinner table to the study,' said Bella at last. 'Terence and I. We put him in the chair.'

'Did he leave it at all during the festivities?'

'I don't think so.'

'Bella, you know perfectly well he didn't,' said her mother, her voice rising.

'I didn't *see* him leave it,' said Bella, with an edge to her voice too. 'I wasn't paying any attention to him. Why should I? I was looking at Daddy and the presents.'

'He didn't get up,' said Eleanor, in a forceful, landed-gentry voice. 'I was watching him.'

'The whole time?' said Meredith suavely, not taking his eyes off her. 'Why was that?'

'Because he was drunk. Any mother would be worried.'

'I see.' It occurred to Eleanor in a flash that the Inspector knew that her son was an habitual drinker. It occurred to her too that he had heard of the incident at the Prince Albert at Hadley. She groaned inwardly. But then, he was bound to hear before long. If the servants didn't tell him, Terence or Bella would.

'Well,' said Meredith, getting up, 'I must go and see how my men are doing, and ring the hospital. I think that will be all for the moment, but I presume you will all be staying in the house?' He looked, raising his eloquent eyebrows, particularly at the three children of Oliver Fairleigh. They all nodded. 'That's all right, then. Because I shall probably need to see you later in the day.'

'If they do find poison,' said Eleanor, shakily defiant.

'If, as you say, my lady, they do find poison.'

'Excuse me, Lady Fairleigh,' said the voice of Surtees from the doorway. 'Mr Widdicomb is here.'

The family exchanged glances, then, conscious of Meredith's eyes on them, wished they had kept them to themselves.

'Will you show him in, Surtees?' said Eleanor Fairleigh.

Mr Widdicomb, it was clear to Meredith at first glance, could only be a lawyer. Meagre of form, pin-striped as if by nature, his face cautious, unemotional, non-committal. He looked like a dyspeptic bird with whom life had not on the whole agreed. He acknowledged Meredith's presence without surprise: clearly Surtees had told him of the state of affairs, or else he had heard of it before setting out, by some mysterious lawyer's channel.

'Perhaps I could see you afterwards?' murmured Meredith at the door. Mr Widdicomb assented by a sharp little bow of the head, and Meredith slipped out of the room.

All Mr Widdicomb's movements were precise and unobtrusive: he advanced towards the family group in a manner almost mechanical. 'A sad occasion, Lady Fairleigh,' he said, in a voice devoid of all passion and grief, high and desiccated. 'We shall all be the poorer for his going.'

This last remark—so patently untrue as far as the dead man's family were concerned—caused a smile of cool amusement to waft briefly over the face of Terence Fairleigh. The phrase was one Mr Widdicomb was accustomed to use of dead clergymen and other putatively indigent worthies, and his use of it now suggested that the news of the police investigation had marginally upset him, for it was very unlike him to put a foot wrong on these occasions. He compressed his lips, and looked with some annoyance at Terence Fairleigh. Lady Eleanor acknowledged his professional sympathy by a droop of the eyes, and gestured him to a seat.

'Thank you, thank you.' He perched rather than sat, clutching his briefcase to his abdomen and darting looks around him with bright, unsympathetic eyes. 'I need not say I am anxious to spare you all the worry I possibly can, Lady Fairleigh. Though as far as the police are concerned, there are, of course, limits to what one can accomplish.'

'I'm sure they will realize their mistake very quickly,' said Eleanor. 'It will all be cleared up in no time.'

'No doubt, no doubt,' said Mr Widdicomb, not bothering to put any conviction into his voice. In his experience the police did not begin investigations into cases of suspected murder without being fairly sure of their ground first.

'If you'll excuse me, Lady Fairleigh,' said Miss Cozzens, glancing tactfully towards the door.

'Oh yes, Barbara, of course,' said Lady Fairleigh distractedly. Mr Widdicomb's stainless-steel eyes registered her going and the punctilious closing of the door. Miss Cozzens was a type of which Mr Widdicomb, in his bloodless way, approved.

'Ah yes, now, as I was saying, should you need me in the next few days, regard me as absolutely at your disposal. Absolutely. The police can be unduly high-handed in such matters, though I intend no judgement on the Inspector in question, who is unknown to me. But it is as well to be prepared—upset as you already are.' He looked around him, as if to assure himself that they were upset to just the decorous degree, then opened his briefcase and began taking papers out of it. Mark quietly got up and moved a side-table to beside his chair. 'Ah, thank you, Sir Mark,' said Mr Widdicomb.

Unnoticed by him, or at least not obviously noticed by him, a glance passed between Terence and Bella at the bestowal of the title, a glance not of the most pleasant.

'Now,' said Mr Widdicomb, placing his briefcase meticulously down by the chair and laying out the abstracted papers on the side-table, 'I take it that in general terms you are all familiar with the contents of Sir Oliver's will?'

'No,' said Terence.

'My husband usually kept such things to himself,' said his mother. 'It was not the sort of thing that he felt should be discussed in the family.'

'Ah? Is that so?' said Mr Widdicomb. 'Well, well, it's a perfectly straightforward document, perfectly straightforward. Drawn up by himself, I may say. He merely sent it to me to remove ambiguities and such-like. I mention this because the phraseology is hardly as I would have liked it myself. I have noticed that in his charming books Sir Oliver was—however, *de mortuis*, eh? Let me see, the will is dated September 10th, 1976—nine months ago, in fact.'

'Nine months?' said Bella.

'Yes. Now, there are some preliminary small bequests. Two hundred and fifty pounds to Barbara Cozzens, I quote, "my secretary of several years' standing, to compensate her for the exquisite and prolonged boredom of transcribing my literary works." Very characteristic touch that! Delightful sense of humour!'

Mr Widdicomb glanced over his spectacles at Oliver Fairleigh's family, and decided they did not show the same appreciation of the dead man's humour as he professed himself. He blinked, and dropped his eyes back to the will.

' "To John Surtees, the sum of five hundred pounds, for faithful service"—very generous and proper. Sir Oliver if I may say so was a man who always knew the right thing to do.' Mr Widdicomb appended to himself the addendum 'even if he did not always do it,' for he had been the victim of several bouts of Oliver Fairleigh's persecution over the years. 'Now, "To my dear wife Eleanor, who has her own sufficient income, I bequeath all my personal chattels, and the copyright of my novel *Black Widow* for her lifetime, in testimony of my gratitude for nearly thirty years of devoted companionship." ' Mr Widdicomb bobbed his head in Lady Fairleigh's direction: 'Most moving.'

'It was what I expected,' said Eleanor, looking round at the children. 'Of course, I have more than enough for my own needs. Oh dear, *Black Widow*. I don't remember it at all. I suppose that's Oliver's sense of humour again.'

' "To my dear son Terence, I bequeath absolutely the copyright of my novel *Foul Play at the Crossroads*, to be of support to him when his musical activities should cease to entertain the British public." '

A shadow flitted across the handsome face of Terence, and he shifted position in his chair so as to be able to see Bella on the sofa.

' "To my beloved daughter Bella, I bequeath the copyright of my novel *Right Royal Murder*, not my best but my most popular work, as testimony to my great love of her, and in order to keep her over the years in the little luxuries to which I imagine she will not become the less addicted." '

As Mr Widdicomb's voice faded, Bella sat tense, as if waiting for more. 'But—' she said, flushing.

' "I devise and bequeath all the residue of my real and personal estate, whether of property, shares, money or copyright in my other works, to my son Mark, to be his absolutely, in the confident hope that he will be worthy of the family name." Dear me, not well put, not well put at all.'

But it was not the phraseology that was affecting his hearers. Terence's gaze, and that of Bella, had now shifted, and they were both gazing incredulously at Mark. Mr Widdicomb foresaw the sort of scene that he made it his business if possible to avoid. He shuffled together the papers and reached down for his briefcase.

'There are a few more remarks of no great importance that I need not trouble you with now. Needless to say, you will all be sent copies of the document. If I may say so, a most proper disposition of his property, most proper—hmm, granted, as I say, some oddities in the wording.'

He rose to his feet, and walked over to Mark, with his hand outstretched.

'Is that will legal?' broke in the harsh voice of Bella. 'Is it properly witnessed?'

Mr Widdicomb, caught with his hand outstretched in something approaching a ridiculous position, turned towards her with the nearest thing to asperity he permitted himself with the family of a client. 'My dear young lady, you could hardly imagine that I would take the trouble to read to you from an unwitnessed document.' His voice positively crackled with disapproval. 'The will is perfectly legal.'

Bella sustained his look for a second, then the corners of her mouth seemed to crease down with disappointment. 'That,' she said bitterly, 'was Daddy's last surprise ending.'

Mr Widdicomb pursed his lips, turned away from her, and fulfilled his intention of shaking hands with Sir Mark. His natural inclination to keep in well with the man in possession tied in on this occasion with his sense that Mark was the only one of the children who had behaved properly: that is, he had held his tongue. Mr Widdicomb had heard rumours on the subject of

Mark Fairleigh—had, indeed, heard his father expatiate on the subject at considerable length one day in his office—but he owned himself agreeably surprised by his conduct on this occasion. He turned to take the hand of Lady Fairleigh, dropped a few words of arid comfort on her head, nodded to the youngest children, and made for the door. Mark ushered him out, and the two exchanged some words, apparently arrangements for some future meeting.

Bella continued to sit rigid, staring straight ahead of her: her mouth had stopped working, and was now set in a straight line. Terence, on the other hand, seemed to be taking longer to gain control over himself. His eyes were round and liquid—they were, in fact, oddly reminiscent of the old Mark. Eleanor Fairleigh remained in her chair, looking at the hearth-rug. The news had not elated her. She could only think to herself: what are the police going to say about this?

Mark closed the door authoritatively. Walking back to the little group, a disinterested observer would have sized him up as a presentable, well-brought-up young man who had gone through a difficult time: his manner was good, his bearing and expression public-school, but not offensively so. The whole set of his body seemed to say that at the moment they might all be going through a tough time, but that he was now in charge, and would see them through it all right. His gaze, though still slightly bloodshot, was perfectly serene.

'Nearly lunch-time,' he said quietly. 'I'm sure you could do with a sherry, Mother. I should think we all could. Is it dry for you, Bella?'

And he walked confidently over to the drinks cabinet.

'God damn you to hell, Mark!' shouted Bella, her face crimson with fury as she flung herself from the room.

8

STRONG POISON

'It seems,' said Inspector Meredith, 'a perfectly straightforward division of the property.'

Mr Widdicomb shut the will away in his briefcase hurriedly, as if it were a rare item of Victorian pornography which he had been allowing Meredith to cast a glance over, and said: 'Quite.'

'The books, the ones left to the mother and the younger children, they will bring in a fair amount of money, I presume.'

'I imagine so,' said Mr Widdicomb, gazing around the oak, book-lined study as if it were witness enough to Oliver Fairleigh's prosperity. 'You would have to consult Sir Oliver's accountant for details, but I assume it will bring them in a little nest egg every quarter or half year.'

'The books seem popular.'

'Yes, most of them seem to be kept in print. One sees them—on railway bookstalls, and suchlike places.'

'You don't enjoy them yourself?'

'I imagine that no one who had any professional acquaintance with crime or criminals would be likely to find them very convincing.' Mr Widdicomb's expression was of the most dyspeptic, and Meredith had the impression not only that he had found his late client profoundly distasteful, but that on the present occasion he was holding back a strong inclination to say something sharp about the same gentleman's family.

'Of course,' said Meredith, at a hazard, 'younger children these days always have the idea that they should be treated on an equality with the eldest.'

'They do. Frequently,' said Mr Widdicomb, with icy warmth. 'It is not an idea with much to be said in its favour, in my opinion. Our old families have enough to contend with as it is, without that.'

'You think in this case the younger children expected more?' asked Meredith, rather disappointed by Mr Widdicomb's cautious habit of speaking in generalities.

'That I think you should ask them,' said the lawyer, rising and smoothing down the jacket of his suit. 'You must remember that the family are my clients.'

'Of course, of course. I suppose you would not wish to tell me whether you yourself were surprised at Sir Oliver's disposition of his property?'

'I presume you are alluding to the relations between him and his eldest son?'

'Precisely.'

'It is not my job to be surprised. I merely had the will made out in my office. Sir Oliver's opinions on the subject of his son were no business of mine. He did not see fit to discuss the main provisions of the will with me, nor did I expect him to.'

'But you did have direct dealings with him over the will?'

'Certainly. He signed it in my office, where it was witnessed by two of my staff. It was, in fact, substantially the same as Sir Oliver's previous will: the provisions for Miss Cozzens and Surtees were new, and the book whose copyright was given to Bella was changed—that, as I remember, was all.'

'Why was the book changed?'

'I imagine it was a more popular title than the previous choice. *Right Royal Murder* came out last year, you remember, in good time for the Queen's Jubilee. A catchpenny idea, if you want my opinion, and quite unworthy of an author of Oliver Fairleigh's standing, but the book proved very successful. No doubt that was the reason for the change. Now, if you will allow me, Inspector—'

And Mr Widdicomb made for the door.

Mr Widdicomb, thought Idwal Meredith to himself, tried to have it both ways: to be at once an oyster of the old school and to make sure that his opinions—especially his disapprovals—were known and felt. Meredith had the impression that should the need absolutely arise he could get quite a lot out of Mr Widdicomb.

Meanwhile, what he needed was someone more obviously loose-tongued, to fill him in on the sort of family background that the family themselves were unlikely to be forthcoming about. He had rather liked the look of Surtees when he had shown him in—or rather, he had liked the look of him as a potential witness. He looked at his watch. Probably he would be still occupied with lunch. On an impulse he took up the phone and dialled headquarters.

'Any results yet? . . . Oh, just come in . . . I see. The decanter and one of the glasses . . . Interesting . . . A solution—strong enough to kill a normal man? . . . I see—and with his heart condition that made it quite certain . . . Good. Keep at it, and I'll chug along at this end.'

He put down the receiver, fireworks of anticipation in his eyes. Now he had a case. Now everything could be open and direct, without the 'ifs' and 'on the other hands.' Nicotine poison. An unusual method, but easy enough to obtain, if you knew the way. It always terrified Meredith, in fact, to think how very easy poison was to obtain, if you knew the way. Luckily very few people did, or there would probably be far more murders which were cheerfully accepted as death from natural causes.

Meredith slipped out into the hall, and stopped to speak to Sergeant Trapp, massive and rural, who was stationed there to coordinate the work of the detective-constables in the various parts of the house. Trapp was being watched beadily by Cuff, who seemed to regard sergeants as a sadly deteriorated race of men.

'We have a case, Jim. It was nicotine in the decanter. I want your boys to get hold of the clothes everyone wore that night, and put the forensic chappies on to them. Oh, and you'd better send over and get them from the Woodstocks too, and all the servants.

Anyone who would have had a chance to go into the study that night.'

'Big job, sir.'

'What are the labs for, if it's not for jobs like that?' Idwal Meredith's voice had the slightest note of contempt in it. As he spoke he saw Surtees emerge from the dining-room with a tray full of dessert plates in his hands. He put the tray on to a side-table, and closed the door quietly. Then he went through into the servants' quarters.

'Tell me, Jim,' said Meredith softly, 'what's your opinion of that gentleman?'

Sergeant Trapp surreptitiously drew his hand from behind his back, and with his fingers and thumb illustrated the notion of a duck, quacking.

'That was rather my impression,' said Meredith. 'I think Surtees is my man at the moment.'

Lunch was not an easy meal for any of the three who took it. Mark and his mother tried to keep the conversation on neutral topics, but after a death and a will, there suddenly seemed to be no neutral topics left in the world. They discussed the funeral, but could come to no firm decisions in view of the uncertainties caused by the police. They broached the possibility of a memorial service, but (without their saying so) it occurred to both of them that it would turn into a gathering of people Oliver Fairleigh had insulted, congratulating themselves on having the last laugh.

Mark drank, with lunch, one and a half glasses of white wine—less, in fact, than Terence. There was a palpable effort involved, but he won a clear victory over his inclinations, and by the end of the meal seemed to be in a mood of some serenity. His mother felt that, on this score at least, her heart should have been light, but in fact her feelings were mixed: what would the police think about a young man whose alibi for his father's death was that he was drunk, who was—to all appearances—a confirmed alcoholic, yet who underwent a miraculous cure the moment his father died? Over and over Eleanor Fairleigh found her mind returning to the question: what will the police think? Which was odd, for she had so far admitted to no one that her husband's death could conceivably be a case of murder.

Terence's mind was on other things. He sat slumped through the meal, hardly bothering even to toy with his food, the picture of romantic melancholy. When he spoke it turned out that (like so many romantics) he had been thinking of himself and money.

'*Foul Play at the Crossroads,*' he said abruptly, 'which one is that?'

'It's about witchcraft,' said Mark. 'I remember it coming out, because the money paid for my twenty-first party. It was very popular—witchcraft always goes down well.'

'Yes, it's odd, isn't it?' said Eleanor brightly. 'Witchcraft and royalty, they're always popular. Whereas some of the ones that Oliver really liked himself never caught on in the same way. I'm sure he thought a great deal before he chose those two for you and Bella, Terence. He was very fond of you both.'

Terence's mouth curled unpleasantly. 'That's all very moving,' he said. 'There's a lump in my throat. But the fact is, we get one each. Mark gets—what will it be?—about twenty-eight.'

'Thirty-two,' said Mark quietly.

'Thirty-two. Always in print, sold at every damn bookstall you go to.' He looked at his brother with a look of sheer malevolence: 'I shall choke every time I see them.'

'Terence!' said his mother.

Terence brooded further through the sweet, and then, over coffee, said: 'Did you know he'd left you everything?'

'No,' said Mark. 'He never discussed the will with me.' Then, after a pause, and apparently impelled by a desire to be completely honest, he said: 'I suspected it.'

'Why?' asked Terence. And then again, louder: 'Why? He hated your guts.'

'Apparently,' said Mark, with some dignity. He sat for some moments in thought, as if trying to decide whether to say something. He seemed to decide not to, but he turned to Terence with a brotherly smile, as if he was anxious to put relations between them on a casually friendly footing, though the expression on his brother's face did not suggest he would succeed easily. 'He may have hated my guts, but I think in some ways I understood him better than you or Bella. Of course, if he'd wanted to show how much he loathed me, he could very easily have cut me out of the will. Or he needn't have gone that far: he could have left you and Bella a lot more of the copyrights to his books.'

'Well, why didn't he?'

'Because he wanted to keep this place going, keep it intact from father to son—he wanted to establish us as the squires of the place. You know he had this image of himself as squire of Wycherley. He'd been playing the part for so long, off and on, that it had become part of him. He knew whoever inherited would need as much money as he could lay hands on to keep the place going, and since I would inherit the title, it had to be me. I had to have the rest as well. That's what I think you and Bella never realized.'

'Such a ridiculous title,' murmured Eleanor. 'So ludicrous of Oliver to pay so much attention to it.' She looked dismayed at her youngest son, still sitting slouched over his coffee-cup with the expression of a petulant gigolo. 'I'm sure Mark is right, though. Your father wanted to keep everything together. It wasn't that he loved you and Bella any the less.'

'I don't care a fuck whether he loved me or not,' said Terence. 'I expected more.'

'I don't think Father would ever have cut me off, however he felt about me,' said Mark, still admirably cool and collected. 'Unless I had been involved in something really disgraceful, something criminal.' He gave his brother a long, meaningful look. 'Perhaps in your heart of hearts you did realize that, Terence.'

For a second, Terence's mouth dropped open, like a schoolboy caught out in a lie. He squirmed in his chair, and seemed about to run from the room. To fill in the awkwardness, his mother said: 'And, of course, now Mark is head of the family, he'll naturally feel an obligation towards you and Bella, if you should get into difficulties or want to branch out in any way. I'm sure he'll always be only too glad to help you.'

'Of course,' said Mark. 'Within reason.'

Later, walking in the garden, and watching Wiggens weeding the herbaceous border with highly unsteady hand (he had been selling the inside story of the Wycherley Court murder to a succession of customers at the local who were sceptical of his information but willing to pay for the privilege of being the first to hear it), Lady Fairleigh-Stubbs meditated on the new Mark: there was an almost frightening sudden maturity about him, a sense of responsibility, a calm capability that was both astonishing and welcome. There was also, it seemed to her, a cool calculation that lay quite outside her previous experience of Mark. She found it, she decided, disconcerting—almost frightening. By what quirk of genetics, she wondered, had the children of Oliver Fairleigh all turned out to be such cool customers?

Surtees was far from unwilling to talk. He was so willing, in fact, that he was reluctant to share Meredith with Mrs Moxon, and took him into the room off the kitchen which had once served as the butler's pantry, and was now apparently his own private nook. It was an untidy, unprepossessing room, with odd heaps of newspapers and weekly grub-sheets scattered around, a portable television in the corner, and photographs sellotaped to the wall—some of relatives and old girl-friends, Meredith conjectured, and some soft porn pin-ups, glossy, explicit and anonymous.

'We'll be more cosy-like in here,' said Surtees ingratiatingly, ushering him in, and throwing a threatening look behind him to Mrs Moxon, as a warning against listening in.

Meredith had not found his first impressions of Surtees very favourable. Certainly he was good-looking, in a fleshy, heavy sort of a way. His profile was classical without being in the least refined, his body capable, even powerful. The man, Meredith thought, for a g.b.h. charge, rather than a poisoner. There was too about him an air of self-satisfaction and self-seeking, as if he would do almost anything in the moral calendar if the price was right— and shop his customer to the authorities afterwards, if it suited his book. If he had been a policeman, he would probably have been in the vice squad.

'I suppose you want to hear about last night?' asked Surtees, 'all the details, and what everybody did, eh?'

'That first of all,' said Meredith.

'Well, of course, I didn't see it all, because I was in and out the whole time. But I'll tell you what I did see.'

Meredith found Surtees's narration absorbing. As far as reporting what he saw went, Surtees seemed an excellent witness. There were, Meredith thought, three salient points in his description of the previous night's birthday dinner. The first was that Oliver Fairleigh had been in an extremely, in fact an incredibly, genial mood all evening, that he had paid particular attention to Mrs Woodstock—'Normally she was the sort he kicked as he passed, and then went back to do it again,' said Surtees—and that he had not allowed his mood to be upset by any of the things that as a rule could unfailingly have been relied on to produce thunder from the deep.

'Why do you think that was?' asked Meredith.

'Search me. According to Mrs Moxon, he'd promised Bella to be nice as pie to everyone the whole day. She may be right, but she gets things arse-up fifty per cent of the time, silly old moo.' He brought out the shop-worn phrase as if it were a new-coining of his own, smiled a greasy smile and then drew his hand across his mouth in a man-among-men gesture.

The second salient point was the behaviour of Bella Fairleigh. Surtees was in no doubt whatsoever that she had been making a dead set at Ben Woodstock from the moment he arrived.

'Can you be quite sure of that? After all, beyond talking, they can't have *done* very much at the dinner table.'

'I know the signs, believe you me, Inspector. There are ways of talking, and ways of listening too. That dreary little bundle his wife saw it too, and has probably made the house too hot to hold him today, I tell you, there's no mistaking things with our Bella: if she has her eyes on someone, they show the scorch-marks pretty fast. Not that I can see what she sees in him. Straggly bit of nothing, I'd have said.' And John Surtees looked down at the fleshy bicep straining against his rolled-up shirt, and made no attempt to hide his complacency.

'When you say you know the signs,' said Meredith, himself now putting on his most deceptive air of man-to-man confidentiality, like two Welshmen Sunday-drinking, 'do you mean she'd tried out her techniques on you, eh?'

Surtees smiled his oily smile. 'Come off it, Inspector,' he said. 'I'm not the sort to kiss and tell.'

Though that, Inspector Meredith thought, is precisely the sort that you are.

The third point of interest was the condition and behaviour of Mark Fairleigh. Meredith had already learnt that he had been drunk; now he heard that he had abused his father at table. It was, Surtees asserted, very much Mark's normal way of behaving whenever he came home, though on this occasion his father had restrained himself from replying in kind.

'Restrained himself,' said Surtees, 'with difficulty. No doubt saving himself up for later.'

'Are you quite sure,' asked Meredith, 'that Mark Fairleigh was drunk? And not just pretending?'

'Sure as I'm sitting here, I know the signs,' said Surtees, once again using the phrase that seemed to sum up his pride in his worldly knowledge.

'He seems a sober enough type today.'

'Shock,' said Surtees. 'It takes some people that way. It won't last, I'll tell you that.' A smirk of anticipation spread over his face: 'Got another shock coming to him, I shouldn't wonder, that'll knock him straight back off the wagon, you see if it doesn't!'

'What's that?'

'The will. He won't be getting much out of his old dad, that's for sure. No one would blame him either, the things that boy has done over the years.'

'What sort of things?'

'Oh debts, scrapes with the police, drunk and disorderly in every pub in the area practically. Only last weekend he was broadcasting to all and sundry out at the Prince Albert, Hadley way, that his father ought to be shot.'

'Do you think his father heard about it?'

'He heard.'

'But of course they've probably learnt what's in the will already.'

' 'Course they haven't. They have to have the reading after the funeral, don't they? All sit around the table and pretend they don't care one way or the other, then the lawyer reads it out and an almighty row blows up. That's what'll happen. Seen it lots of times on the telly. We do things right in this house.'

Meredith was rather pleased to find that he was right to limit Surtees's reliability to what he had seen with his own eyes. Outside it he seemed to conform to the usual mixture of credulity and salacious speculation. Meredith merely said: 'If he hasn't left it to Mark, who do you think he will have left it to?'

'Oh, stands to reason, the lot to Bella. Something nice to little Mr Snake-in-the-Grass Terence, a tie-pin of a pair of old socks to Mr Mark, and the rest to Bella. I bet little Terry has a shrewd idea that's how it will go too. He's been like a bear with a sore head all through lunch.'

'Well,' said Meredith, once more with his secret-beer-drinker's air, 'I suppose you'd know. He confided in you, didn't he?'

'Old Lord Almighty? Confide in me? Not him. All get and no give, as far as information was concerned. No, as I say, it stands to reason: she was the apple of his eye. Made sure she was too. "Daddy this" and "Daddy that" the whole time.'

'She sucked up to him, did she?'

'Not exactly that. Not in any obvious way, anyway. She just kept him interested, kept him watching her: it was more like a boy-friend she wanted to keep on the boil if you ask me. But she had him in the palm of her hand, where the others bored him stiff.'

'You said he liked getting information. What did you mean? Information about Mark, for instance?'

'Oh yes, him and anyone else. He liked to know things. He was a conner-sewer of human nature, you might say. But particularly Mr Mark—yes, he liked to know what he was up to.'

'Did you give him information yourself?'

'If I got any. Why not? I don't owe that little sot any loyalty that I know of. I'd be out on my ear if he had anything to do with it—not that he will.' Surtees's expression was unpleasantly anticipatory, as if he foresaw for himself a special position in a Wycherley Court owned and run by Bella Fairleigh.

'What did you do last night after you served dinner? Was it you or Sir Oliver opened the cupboard with the liqueurs in?'

'Me. Why? Was it the liqueurs did for him?'

'Possibly.'

'Thought so, when I saw his glass on the floor. So someone got at the lakka, did they? Yes, it was me. After I'd served the sweets, I came down to the kitchen and hurried up old mother Moxon with the coffee. Then I took it up to the study, and opened the drinks cupboard at the same time.'

'Did you have a key to it as well?'

'Not on your life. See Sir Oliver trusting anyone else with one. No, he gave me his just before dinner, as per usual.'

'How long was the cupboard open before they came into the study from dinner?'

Surtees shrugged his heavy shoulders. 'Matter of two or three minutes, no more than that. I went into the dining-room after I'd put the coffee in the study. Mr Mark was having his little outburst about how he would rather die than be an author. Silly little shit, what does he know? Anyway, that put the damper on things, so pretty soon they went over to the study—Miss Bella and Terence dragging Mark.'

'So none of the family could have got at the lakka between your opening the cupboard and the whole party going across to the study for coffee?'

'Not a chance, mate. They were all at the table the whole time.'

'Who got to the study first—was anyone ahead of the others?'

'Sir Oliver went in first, with Mrs Woodstock, but he wasn't far ahead of the others.'

'Do you think any of the family could have had a duplicate key to the cupboard?'

Surtees thought hard. 'No, I don't. The locks on the drinks cupboards both in the study and the lounge were changed a couple of years ago, when little Lord Fauntleroy was going through a bad period—correction, when little Lord Fauntleroy was going through a *particularly* bad period, because he hasn't had a good one since he was nineteen or twenty, so far as I've heard. Anyway, Sir Oliver had the locks changed, making it a good excuse for not even giving me one of my own, and he never let those keys out of his sight, except now and again to give them to me on nights when there were guests.'

'And you—?'

'If you mean, did I get duplicates made for anyone, you can stuff the idea, matey,' said Surtees, taking advantage of Meredith's matiness because it pleased him to be able to give the police a bit of cheek. 'I'm the great incorruptible, that's what I am. Or shall we say my loyalty was to Sir Oliver, no one else. It doesn't do to sell your soul too often. Especially not when Sir Oliver had such a very good information service.'

Meredith rose to go. 'It's been very interesting,' he said. 'Just keep your eyes open in the next few days, will you?'

'Sure thing,' said Surtees ingratiatingly. 'Better not ask what it's worth to you, had I? You cops can turn funny about little things like that. Still, if I'm ever in trouble in the future, I can just quote your name, can't I?'

'Of course, of course,' said Meredith at the door, mentally adding: 'You can try.'

Back in the study Meredith tried to sort out his impressions. He had already had, before he came, a mental picture of Oliver Fairleigh, culled from local gossip. His morning in Wycherley Court had not radically altered that impression: the man seemed to have been an unpredictable and erratic tyrant, ruling a disunited and unsatisfactory family. Beyond the family circle, Meredith had no reason to doubt that Oliver Fairleigh was a man with so many enemies that a list of people who might have *vaguely* wanted him out of the way could easily run to three figures. Yet the man must have been more complex than this outline. There was, for instance, the will, the strange decision to leave everything—virtually —to a son he hated.

Inspector Meredith idly went over to the shelf behind the desk at which Oliver Fairleigh had drunk his last toast. Here were ranged, he had already noted, the English first editions of Oliver Fairleigh's works. He took out *Foul Play at the Crossroads:* a photographic cover, sky blue, depicting a finger-post decorated with a skull, and a witch's broomstick in the foreground. A work full of eye of newt and toe of frog, no doubt. He looked for *Right Royal Murder,* and took it down: a purple plush background, on which was placed the crown of England, stained with blood. An excellent cover, he thought, and a sure seller. Both Macpherson's and their star author had an eye for what would sell. He skimmed along the shelf for *Black Widow.* He missed it, and went back to read the thirty-odd titles methodically. There was none called *Black Widow.* He crossed over to an obscure corner of the room behind the door, where he had observed a serried mass of paperbacks and foreign editions. Here Sir Oliver had kept discreetly out of sight the more sensational editions of his works. Meredith went through them all, eventually having to get down on his hands and knees, there were so many. But there was no book called *Black Widow.*

Oliver Fairleigh seemed to have left his wife the copyright of a book that did not exist.

9

FATHER AND SON

Emerging from the study, with a feeling of having discovered something without having the slightest idea what, Inspector Meredith caught sight of the capable figure of Barbara Cozzens, purposefully cleaving a way from the servants' quarters to the stairs. The brief glimpse he had had of her when he had arrived had suggested to him that here was a woman with no nonsense about her—so much so, perhaps, as to be now and then an uncomfortable person to be with. She was dressed for the day after a death, in depressing dark brown skirt and severe-cut blouse. Her hair was pulled back into an exemplary bun, and her make-up was sparse and utterly unflamboyant. On the surface she looked like a shorthand-taking machine, and a totally conventional moral entity —but behind the glasses savage little glints of intelligence were to be detected.

'Oh, Miss Cozzens, I wondered if—'

'Of course, Inspector,' she said briskly, hardly even turning round; 'if you would like to come up to my office.'

The office, on the first floor, turned out to be a good-sized room—needed to be, in fact, because one wall was lined with filing cabinets, and there was an enormous old cupboard on the opposite side of the room, whose doors were hanging half open as if stuffed to the limits with manuscript, and aching to vomit some out. A quick glance from his darting eyes showed Meredith that this was indeed the case.

'I'm sorry to have to bother you, Miss Cozzens, when you must be very—'

'Oh, please don't bother with the preliminaries, Inspector,' said Barbara Cozzens, gesturing him to the second chair and sitting down herself at the desk, as if he were all in a day's work. 'I haven't been Oliver Fairleigh's secretary all these years for nothing, you know. Slapdash he may have been, but inevitably one gained a few inklings of police procedure.'

'How many years, actually?'

'Six and a half. I've been responsible for his last seven novels and the eighth to come.'

'And lived here the whole time?'

'That's right. I have a very nice self-contained flat. I'm completely independent.'

Miss Cozzens seemed to insist on this. Was it to mark herself off from the domestic who 'lived in,' or to lay emphasis on the distance between herself and the family?

'I gather you were not at dinner last night?'

'No, indeed. It was a family affair—the birthday dinner always is. It was rather unusual for outsiders like the Woodstocks to be invited to it. As for myself, I have only dined with the family two or three times in the last few years. We saw more than enough of each other in the course of the day, more than enough. If I had been invited, I should not have gone.'

'Why?'

'I believe the birthday dinner was the day in the year when Sir Oliver felt that his position as paterfamilias gave him the right to be more than usually unbearable.'

Miss Cozzens's lips slapped together at this into a kind of smile. At Meredith's involuntary raising of the eyebrows, she seemed to sense disapproval, and went on: 'I'm being disloyal, do you think? But I think I'm safe in assuming that you will know a little about Sir Oliver's character and habits—either from the newspapers, or from local gossip. You will hear all about his relations with his family from somebody or other. As far as I'm concerned, the main thing is that you understand the situation at once, since it is obviously relevant to your enquiries.'

Frankness, then, was to be the order of the day. Meredith took the opportunity to ask her at once about the drinks cabinet.

'It was kept locked, at all times—both it and the one in the lounge. Because of Sir Mark, you know—a dipsomaniac, unfortunately.'

'But Sir Mark didn't live here.'

'No—but you could never tell when he might drop in. In search of alcohol, very often, when the pubs were closed. He was here last Sunday, for instance.'

'Was he now?' Meredith's Welsh intonation was suddenly very pronounced, and Barbara Cozzens had to get a grip on herself to stop herself from flinching.

'Yes, just in the afternoon. The Fairleighs had been out to lunch with the Woodstocks, whom you'll no doubt meet. Sir Oliver was rather pleased with himself when he came home, and he went to bed to have a rest—to contemplate his own superb destructiveness, I imagine. Mark saw his mother, and stayed around for a bit, but he heard that there was someone to dinner—Mr Simmington, from Sir Oliver's publishers—so he went away again at about half past six. I imagine he drove himself straight to a pub.'

'I see. But during his visit the drinks will have been locked away, I suppose?'

'Most definitely. They were *always* locked, and Sir Oliver kept the key. The only "strong drink" around was a bottle of sherry in the desk in the study: just now and then Sir Oliver treated himself to an extra glass—extra to Doctor Leighton's orders, that is. He imagined his wife noted the levels of the bottles, and kept this as a resource in emergencies. It was a polite fiction, in fact: both I and Lady Fairleigh knew about it.'

'You know that the decanter of lakka was poisoned?'

'From what I'd heard it sounded likely.' Miss Cozzens raised her eyebrows in a gesture of refined distaste. 'Really, a very melodramatic kind of murder. Quite like one of Sir Oliver's books!' And she shook her head in disapproval.

'Yes, indeed,' said Meredith meditatively: 'the toast, the drinking, the collapse. Quite the stuff of detective stories. Was it any particular story you were thinking of?'

Miss Cozzens crinkled her brow—in thought, and perhaps in distaste. 'No, I don't think so. It's so difficult to remember: I do my best not to take much in while I take them down. But of course, when one has also to rough type them and then do the fair copy, one does inevitably get to know them. No, I don't think that any of the ones I've had to do with had any murder in them at all like that. In fact, Sir Oliver tended to avoid poison.'

'Why?'

'Dame Agatha used to do it so much better. In any case, it required too much research, and he was congenitally slothful. He preferred more direct, brutal methods.'

'I see. It's a pity. It did occur to me that someone—someone with a sense of humour—might have—'

'Used one of Sir Oliver's methods? Perfectly possible, of course. Though I have the gravest doubts whether any murderer using those books as a model would ever manage to kill anyone, let alone get away with it for any length of time.' Seeing Meredith smile appreciatively, Miss Cozzens preened herself on her sharp wit, and Meredith's quick-silver eyes saw her preening. In a second she was back to her business self. 'I'll go through all the novels at once, and see if there is anything reasonably close to what happened last night. After all, there are thirty or more, and I only know about ten or twelve at all well. What was the poison used?'

'Nicotine.'

'I see.' Miss Cozzens made a note of it. The murder, it seemed, had now been integrated into her office routine. 'I know his methods, so I should be able to skim through them quickly without actually having to read them.'

'Have you read one of his books called *Black Widow*?'

'*Black Widow*? There is no such novel.' Barbara Cozzens shook her head very definitely. 'I do all the financial side, you know— paperback rights, translations into foreign languages, all that kind of thing. So even if I haven't read them, I've got them all very clearly in my mind—how many times they've been reprinted, how much they've brought in, and so on. There is no book called *Black Widow*.'

'And yet it figures in his will.'

'Really? I don't understand?'

'He left *Foul Play at the Crossroads* to his son Terence—'

'Oh yes, a very profitable number, that.'

'*Right Royal Murder* to Bella—'

'The latest. That's going to be a goldmine—a real little goldmine.'

'And *Black Widow* to Lady Fairleigh-Stubbs.'

A flicker, Meredith could swear, went over Miss Cozzens's face, as if she was saying 'Then he must have left all the rest to Mark.' But it was immediately replaced by a furrowed brow, as she set her mind to the matter in hand. 'Well, he never used a pseudonym, so it can't be that. Wait—I know. It must be the one for publication after his death. No doubt that's it. He chose it for Lady Fairleigh because he knew it would bring in a nice little bit.'

'Do you mean the one he has just finished, or something?'

'Oh no, that's called *Murder Upstairs and Downstairs*. That was only finished last week, so it couldn't have figured in the will. No, this is one he held back. I believe he wrote it at some period when he was particularly productive—or facile, you might say. It was before my time, and I never heard what it was called. There were to be two of them—Sir Oliver's mind was very far from original— but he never got around to doing the second. People never think they're going to die, do they? And I'm sure Sir Oliver was convinced he could choose himself the time and manner of his going.'

'Where is the manuscript now?'

'At Macpherson's, I suppose. It's not here.' She waved her arms at the bulging, rickety cupboard. 'I have everything here, from first drafts to proof copies. He was always expecting some American library to offer for them, and none ever did. It may look chaotic, but I know perfectly well everything that's there.' She thought for a moment. 'Of course, it's just possible it's in the study.'

'Wouldn't you know about it?'

'Not necessarily. This room is mine—my office. The study was

Sir Oliver's. I was called in there, to be recording angel when inspiration struck, usually between eleven and one in the morning.' Her lips again slapped together in a brief, sharp smile. 'But we kept to our own areas: I found out very early that this was the only way to keep the peace. And in fact it would have been more than my life was worth to poke around in the study.'

'Well, I'll look around and make enquiries. No doubt it's a blind alley, but it seemed an oddity worth looking into. It will be interesting in any case to talk to his publishers.'

'Mr Simmington is very intelligent. Knew how to handle Sir Oliver. It's an art one had to develop over the years.'

Inspector Meredith had risen. From the window he saw the eldest son of the victim wandering down from the terrace into the gardens of the house that was now his. 'I've no doubt it was an art,' he said. 'And Sir Mark, I gather, didn't have it.'

'No, indeed. If anything he deliberately provoked him.'

'One last question,' said Meredith, turning quickly round again to Miss Cozzens and surprising a look of reluctant admiration of Mark's attitude on her face. 'Can you tell me who had the best chance of getting at the drinks cupboard in the study?'

Miss Cozzens thought: 'Surtees, of course. He was sometimes given the key. Otherwise, I suppose you'd have had to steal the key while Sir Oliver was asleep. Which wouldn't be easy, because he locked his door.' She looked with Meredith down to the gardens below. 'I'll tell you one thing. The person least likely to have been able to get hold of it was Sir Mark.'

Meredith gazed with her at the lonely strolling figure.

'That's the conclusion I've come to,' he said regretfully.

The day was warm rather than hot, and the shadows were already beginning to lengthen when Meredith slipped out of a side door and went in the direction he had seen Mark take. The grounds of Wycherley Court were extensive, and undoubtedly gentlemanly. They had never, it seemed, been allowed to go to waste. Meredith (who had been born in the county and whose Welsh accent was an inheritance from his parents, cherished zealously out of some obscure feelings of tribal loyalty) remembered when the estate had been sold by the Hattersleys—local squires from time fairly immemorial, who had been early in the emigration of their class to enjoy the benefits of birching and low taxation of the Isle of Man. That was about '50–'51, he guessed, and even then the property as a whole was in fairly good shape. Much care had gone into the grounds since then, and much love. Meredith noted a gardener leaning on a spade with an unmistakable air of waiting for knocking-off time. The love, he presumed, had come from Lady Fairleigh.

He found Mark in a little clearing on the far corner of the estate, almost surrounded by elms, which were casting long accusatory fingers of shadow towards the house. He was sitting on a seat, deep in thought, but not too deep to hear Meredith's approach.

'I am sorry, Inspector,' he said, getting up eagerly. 'I do apologize. I should have realized you would want to see me. I'd no intention of making you come to search me out.'

His manner, like his words, was apologetic, but it was oddly confident too. His apology was the apology of a man who was quite consciously in charge. Suddenly his air was that of the public-school prefect, grown up. Meredith shot one of his quick glances at the face: good-looking, rather full about the lips, the eye rather dulled. It was an oddly unformed face for a man in his mid-twenties: it was a face from which one might have expected almost anything.

'We can talk here as well as anywhere,' said Meredith, perching bird-like on the long park bench, and looking at Mark with his guileless, confidential smile. 'Until my lab boys start getting reports through I can't do much more than go around feeling my way. They're the ones who do all the work these days.'

'But still, you do know it was murder?'

'We know he was poisoned. Nicotine poison. In the decanter.'

'Poor Mother,' said Mark simply. He sat for a few moments, apparently genuinely upset. He took out a packet of cigarettes, put one in his mouth and lit it. Suddenly Meredith realized that his hand was shaking. 'Nicotine,' he said, with an obvious effort to be cool. 'I don't know anything about poisons. Is that a common one?'

'To murder someone with? Not very. But it's easy enough to obtain if you know the way.'

'Poor Mother,' said Mark again, his voice more normal. 'All those years putting up with Father, and they end like this.' He paused, and then said: 'The press is going to be absolutely foul.'

There was a note of strong feeling in his voice which intrigued Meredith, so he said: 'You have had experience of the press?'

'Some,' said Mark. His voice was very quiet. He seemed to be surveying the experiences of his last years as if they were someone else's. 'Father attracted reporters like flies to a honey jar. I was the little blob of honey on the plate that got a few stray flies. You can imagine the sort of thing they said about me: first it was "fast living," "devil-may-care," then it was "ne-er-do-well," then it was —well, you can imagine. I was never interesting enough for more than a line or two here and there, but still—yes, I've had more than enough of reporters.'

'The police are supposed to work in with the press these days,' said Meredith. 'And real little blabber-mouths some of us have become, too. But I find, personally, that the best policy is usually to say nothing at all.'

'I was not always in a condition to say nothing at all,' said Mark. His hand, though resting on the arm of the seat, was not quite still. Meredith felt that they were getting on to difficult territory, and tiptoed cautiously on.

'It was lucky for you, at any rate, that you were drunk last night,' he said. Mark looked at him, a direct, troubled look.

'Yes, wasn't it?' he said. 'It's odd to think of myself there— present in the body, absent in the mind. I've been like that often enough before, but nothing quite like that has happened while I've been out.'

'Why do you think your brother and your sister took you across to the study?'

'Considerate of them, wasn't it?' Mark's answer came quickly and bitterly. Then he paused and thought for a little. 'That's for you to decide. I suppose they'd say they wanted me to be in on the carefree jollity of a birthday dinner at Wycherley Court.'

'And you would say?'

There was a long silence now. 'Perhaps they would be quite pleased to have me there, for the finger of scorn to be pointed at,' said Mark at last.

'There is another, even less pleasant possibility,' said Meredith.

'Of course there is,' said Mark loudly, apparently genuinely agitated. 'But they are my brother and sister. You don't expect me calmly to chew over with you the possibility of their being—what's the word?—parricides, do you, nicely weighing the pros and cons? It's for you to find out.'

'Of course I don't expect you to do that,' said Meredith, very charming. 'But I have to consider the possibilities, and I've no doubt you will do the same. They (or one of them) may have wanted you there because they hoped you would come round. They may have been banking on the fact that you would be with the rest when the presents were opened, so that we could imagine you, while the rest of the party's attention was diverted, slipping the poison into the decanter. It must be obvious that in any other circumstances you would be prime suspect, in view of your performance at the Prince Albert in Hadley last weekend.'

'Ah, you know about that?'

'I suspect everyone in the area knows about it. I shall make some enquiries about when the gossip started in Wycherley, and when people in the house got to know, but I think you can assume that everyone at the birthday party had heard of it.'

'Odd, that—I don't remember much about it myself. Well, if that was Terence or Bella's little plan, it rather misfired, didn't it?'

'Yes, if it was, it did,' said Meredith non-committally. Then he turned directly to Mark and asked: 'How long have you been drinking so heavily, sir?'

'Oh years—years and years. When I was seventeen or eighteen I used to go on occasional benders. From about twenty onwards I've needed it. I need it at this moment.'

'But you're not taking it?'

'No.' There was a brief silence. 'I feel I need my wits about me.

You're implying I could have been intended as—what's the word?
—a fall guy. I had the same idea, in the back of my mind. In any
case, I don't know what's going on, and I need all the cool thinking I can manage to find out.' Suddenly his brow unfurrowed.
'And you know, coming into all this makes a difference.' He waved
his hand around the estates stretching like a *Country Life* illustra-
tion towards the house, mellow and golden in the distance.

'In what way, sir?'

'In every way. It means I own something. It means I have a
stable base, and a way of life mapped out. It means responsibilities, decisions, something solid to do. I don't know whether Father
realized it, but it does make a difference.' He paused again, as if
the interview with Meredith was part of a heavy session of self-
communion which had gone on before he came, and would go on
after he left. 'If you want to put it crudely, you could say it makes
all the difference that he is dead.'

'You drank because he was alive?'

'Oh yes, that's certainly true. Because I knew that by drinking I
would be disappointing him, ruining his plans for me, embarrassing him—in so far as that was possible. I've always been conscious
of him, in the background: he's been with me every minute of the
day, ever since I can remember.'

The brooding look in the eyes—troubled, turbulent—was that
of a man not naturally introspective, trying to come to terms with
his own situation.

'You drank because he hated you?' hazarded Meredith, opti-
mistically putting the verb in the past tense. Mark turned, and his
expression had changed, lightened, become almost one of wonder.

'Do you know, Inspector, I don't believe he did.'

10

MASTER AND MAN

At Meredith's look of surprise, Mark waved his hand deprecatingly: 'Of course, that sounded a bit silly, in view of everything that's gone on between us. And I don't even mean we had a love-hate relationship, either. It's practically impossible to explain what I *do* mean to someone who didn't know Father personally.'

'I'm getting a picture,' said Meredith.

'Yes, but is it the right one—or rather, is the emphasis right? There was the monster that the newspapers made of him, or rather that he made of himself for the newspapers' benefit. Everyone around here can tell you a story based on this monster, and quite a few of them will actually be true. But the important thing is that he was *performing* this role—and enjoying the performance, of course. And this was always true, whatever he did, whatever mood he was in. Last night he'd promised Bella to be good for the birthday dinner, and through the haze I can remember what he was like when I arrived, and when we were having drinks before dinner: he wasn't *being nice*, he was *performing* being nice—a galumphing, hearty *performance*. He was being the stage squire in a William Douglas Home play. And the point about Father was that he loved roles, all sorts of roles. And if you presented him with a possible one, he grabbed it with both hands, and hammed it up to the skies.'

Mark, as if surprised at his own eloquence and insight, suddenly came to a halt, and looked anxiously at Meredith to see if he had understood. Meredith digested the notion slowly. He was wondering whether the picture was a true one, and wondering too what had given this rather ordinary boy such an acute perception.

'So you mean,' he said, 'that you, by being—what shall we say? —unsatisfactory, presented him with a role?'

'Exactly.' Mark flung himself back in his seat, and made odd sketching motions with his hands in the air that seemed to be an outline of Oliver Fairleigh's bull-frog body. 'A plum role, handed him on a plate: heavy father; outraged Victorian parent; disappointed head of a noble family. Not just a lovely part, but tailor-made for him. And he played it up to the hilt, enjoying every minute.'

'But you think he didn't actually feel anything, any hatred or outrage?'

'That's what I've come to think.' Mark crossed his legs, and turned towards Meredith, like a salesman trying to put over a product. 'I don't think Father *felt* very much at all. He was fond of Bella, in his way. Perhaps of Mother too, though he would never have moved a muscle of his body out of consideration for *her* feelings. Beyond that, there was only himself, his comfort and convenience, fending off the boredom of life, creating fuss and kerfuffle, getting into the news, bullying and embarrassing people to *prove* himself in some way or other. But about me, I don't think he felt anything, one way or another—nothing you could analyse and say, "This is sincere." '

'You've obviously thought about it a lot.'

'I have. And I'm not sure I quite saw it like this yesterday, even. But that's how I think it was.'

'And where does this leave you, sir?'

'In what way?'

'Did *you* hate *him*?'

'Yes, oh yes.' There was no sign of reserve or hesitation as Mark stretched back in the seat and admitted this. 'I hated his selfishness, his cruelty, his ludicrous snobbery, his publicity-seeking—I hated everything about him. But in the end it may all come back to egotism on my part: I hated him because I sensed he felt nothing about me as a person. Nothing at all. Wasn't conscious of me, and couldn't care less. He made me cringe with loathing.'

The two men sat silent for a moment. Into the silence came an odd sound, like an asthmatic barrel-organ tuning up. Across the clearing, waddling, came Cuff, snuffling along with his nose obsessively to the ground, his dim eyes winking with effort. At length he arrived at the seat, smelt in a leisurely, scientific manner up Mark's trouser leg, then with a great grunt of achievement flopped his ungainly body down at his feet and went to sleep.

'The first defector to the new master,' said Mark. He did not sound displeased.

'How have you lived, since you left school?' asked Meredith, unwilling to let the subject of Mark's misspent years drop.

'I went up to Oxford when I was nineteen. Father said it had to be Balliol or Christ Church, and I just scraped into Christ Church —mainly due to Dad's giving them a collection of early eighteenth-century pamphlets for the library a year or so before I tried my luck. He liked doing deals on that sort of level: he used to say it was impossible to underestimate the power of self-interest.'

'But you didn't take your degree?'

'Good Lord, no. I didn't last more than a term and a half. I was sent down for idleness and drunkenness.' He threw a wry smile in Meredith's direction: 'You had to be *very* idle, and *very* drunken to be sent down from The House.'

'And after that?'

'Well, as I realize now, Oxford was just a period of trying my wings away from the parental shadow. After that I went on and on and down and down. The City—out. Agricultural College—out. Australia—I flew back after two and a half weeks, paying my fare with a cheque that bounced. Since then—well, whatever I felt would humiliate him most. Door-to-door salesman in ladies' underwear; chucker-out at a Soho club—only the people I had to chuck out were tougher than I was, and not so drunk. Let's see, what else? Oh, I worked behind the counter on the ground floor in Fortnum's—Dad came in and saw me, and had to be carried into the manager's office. Then odds and sods here and there:

salesman, rep, commission agent—you know the kind of thing. In fact, you name it, I've done it.'

'Was it all done as a sort of revenge against your father?'

'I think so. I've tried to pull myself together and make a go of something now and again, but the thought of his condescension or his sneers always sent me off again. If I ever make a go of anything in the future, it will be because he isn't around to coin witticisms and throw them in my direction when there are plenty of people around to hear.'

'Ever been in trouble with the police?' asked Meredith, knowing very well he had.

'Drunken driving, bad debts, disorderly behaviour,' said Mark promptly. 'As I'm sure you know only too well, Inspector.' Meredith decided it would be as well not to underestimate Mark. He was, at any rate, too intelligent to be played with. But a flicker had crossed his eyes as he recited his offences. Had there, conceivably, been something else?

'Your father had to pay the debts, I suppose?' he said.

'Frequently. Less so of late. People have been getting wise—and he put a notice in *The Times* disclaiming responsibility. So credit has been tough for the last year or so.'

'And your mother has helped you too?'

'Oh, Mother is a brick. But she's no fool, either. She's always been good for a small touch, but after the first couple of times she drew a firm line, and stuck to it. Anyway, I always thought it was more fun to get it out of Father.'

'Knowing it would come to you in the end anyway?'

Mark paused before he replied, as if it might be a trap. 'Suspecting that it would.'

'Because he would want the money and estate to go together with the title?'

'Yes, that's what I guessed. Which is pretty funny when you think of the title.' When Meredith raised his crescent eyebrows, Mark just said: 'Ask Mum about it. She's very good on the subject when Dad isn't around to hear her.' He stopped, and smiled, very naturally. 'As, of course, he isn't.'

'Well, well,' said Meredith, stretching his legs, 'I must be getting back to see what has come up. One last question: did you have a duplicate key to the drinks cabinet in the study?'

'Of course I didn't, Inspector. You'd have been questioning me in a very different tone of voice if you thought that possible.' Mark smiled confidently, got up, and the two strolled towards the house —Cuff scrambling to his feet and following cumbrously behind them, sighing noisily at the restlessness of humankind. 'As you know,' Mark went on, 'the locks were to keep me out. Though as time went on they also became a sort of symbol that Dad was to cut down himself. But if I had got hold of a duplicate—and I did sound Surtees out, believe me—the locks would have been changed. The amount I drink would have been noted, and Dad certainly wasn't the sort you could fool by watering down.'

'You weren't offered a drink last Sunday?'

'Last Sunday? Was I here then?' He puzzled a little. 'Yes, I think I remember. I dropped in while the pubs were shut, since I was in the area. Sunday's a horrible day for a man with a thirst. But Dad was asleep, and Mum couldn't have given me anything even if she'd wanted to. I stayed around for a bit, but I'd had pretty much, and I get gloomy, and it wasn't much fun for Mum. I might have stopped for dinner, but someone was coming, and I knew Dad would perform for the visitors—aim a few hob-nailed witticisms at me, and so on. So I sloped off.'

'When?'

'About six, I should think. Ask Mum.' Mark turned and looked straight at him. 'Anyway, Father hadn't come down by then. None of the drinks cabinets had been opened. And I didn't come back. Is that quite clear?'

'Do you remember where you were that evening?'

'No, I don't, frankly. But it must have been the Thistle here in Wycherley, or the Horse and Groom at Oakden. I know I didn't drive far, and those are my two usual haunts. If you check there someone should remember. I usually make myself conspicuous.'

As they approached the house (Cuff's breathing becoming ever more stentorian, a heavy performance in the Oliver Fairleigh manner, probably to indicate that he preferred a master with more sedentary habits) there emerged from the conservatory at the corner of the house the figure of Surtees. He had obviously observed their approach. There was something about the set of his shoulders, about the way he carried himself, that marked an indefinable shift from the Surtees Meredith had talked to earlier in the afternoon. There was a loss of swagger, of bounce.

'Excuse me, Sir Mark,' he said softly as he came up—whether the softness was of insinuation, or a gesture of respect to a house in mourning was not obvious—'I wondered if you would like anything special tonight in the way of wine.'

It was the sort of moment, historically sweet, when the scapegrace Prince of Wales stands to receive the crooked knees and courtly kisses of the mourners round a royal death-bed, when he sees the favourites and flunkies who have carried stories of his excesses to the parental ear suddenly acknowledge a shift in power. Instead of the sceptre and the great seal, Mark had been granted the keys to the wine-cellar and the drinks cupboard. He would have been less than human if he had not relished the situation, though only the briefest of smiles crossed his lips.

'It's hardly a day for celebration,' he said coolly. 'We can have the Médoc.'

'Of course, Sir Mark. And would you like your clothes laid out for dinner?'

'My clothes are not the sort that are laid out,' said Mark. 'No, thank you.'

Surtees turned and went back towards the conservatory, the set of his shoulders once more eloquent: he was not altogether satisfied. Mark, having watched him, resumed his walk along the path round to the front of the house, his full mouth once more indulging in a tiny smile.

'Surtees has heard about the will,' he said to Meredith. 'I wonder how.'

'These things get around,' said Meredith. 'I'm afraid I may have said something to Miss Cozzens that could have given her a clue.'

'Miss Cozzens?' said Mark. 'How odd. I wouldn't have thought she was the type who would let herself gossip with the servants. I'm not well up with the various leagues and alliances in this house.' He paused, put his hands on his hips, and surveyed the manor house, glowing in the late sun. 'Not that I will need to be. The regular staff will have to be cut more or less to nothing, and we'll rely on getting help from the village.'

'I'm surprised Surtees bothers to ingratiate himself,' said Meredith. 'It's not as though he's likely to find himself at the Labour Exchange. People in his line can practically name their price today. It seems he wants to stay on.'

'I wondered at that myself,' said Mark. 'I expect it's Bella. It usually is Bella, you know. And probably it's Bella who has told him about the will. But in any case, he's batting on a very poor wicket. Whatever happens, Surtees is going to go. I'm looking forward to giving him his notice personally.'

The two men walked up the front steps. Today Mark did not stumble on the last one. The smile was still on his face as he contemplated getting rid of Surtees. Before going in he turned and looked down the drive, curving towards the main gate. It was closed, and on either side of it stood a massive police constable. Outside, on the little country road were several cars and little knots of reporters with cameras. Most of them were in the act of photographing the new master of Wycherley Court, at the entrance to his stately home.

'The vultures are gathering,' said Mark, the smile disappearing from his face. 'I suppose it will be up to you to provide them with carrion, Inspector.'

He turned, and went quickly into the house.

Dinner was hardly a more comfortable meal than lunch, and the presence of Bella did nothing to improve matters. The passion of the morning was—to all appearances—over and had been replaced by a new ice age. Her dress, without being flashy, nevertheless made none of the usual concessions to the custom of mourning. But once more she had made herself into a beautiful object, untouchable. For much of the meal she sat in total silence.

Otherwise the pattern of lunch repeated itself. Mark drank a glass of wine. Terence drank decidedly more. His long fair hair was beginning to look heavy and lank; his face was shiny, sweaty, as if he had forgotten to wash. The conversation was carried on, when at all, by Mark and his mother. He had talked to her before dinner, telling her of Meredith's confirmation that there had been poison in the decanter. Once the suspicion that she had been fighting against was confirmed, Lady Fairleigh seemed to give a great sigh and accept the matter, though there was a sad lethargy about her, as if she could now only expect worse and worse to come. But the presence of the other children at dinner made her make some efforts to pretend normality.

'The Woodstocks rang earlier,' she said, addressing her remarks to Bella. 'They were very kind, of course. They offered us any help we might need.'

'Really?' said Bella. 'It's difficult to think what help either of those two could give.' She returned to her food, seeming hungry.

When Surtees came round with the sweet, Mark had the impression that he was trying to catch Bella's eye. If he was, he failed. Bella remained in her envelope of ice, staring contemptuously ahead of her.

'I'll put the coffee in the lounge, sir, is that all right?' said Surtees, bending by Mark's ear. Mark nodded.

'Enjoying these little marks of respect, Mark?' asked Terence in a thick, unpleasant voice.

'I am, rather,' returned Mark levelly. 'I shall have to while they last, because it won't be long. Naturally we shall be cutting down on staff here.'

'Why?' said Bella sharply. Then, as if she had revealed something, she cut her voice down to its usual drawl and said contemptuously: 'There's no reason to, is there? The royalties will be coming in as usual.'

'Except of course,' said Mark, 'that I shan't be writing a book a year to keep the flow going.' The thought didn't seem to have occurred to Bella, and he elaborated: 'One profession I do not think of entering is the mystery-writing trade.'

'I hope things won't be too hard for you,' said Bella, the cut of the voice making up for the heaviness of the irony. 'I wouldn't want you to miss the royalties from my little legacy.'

'What an appropriate word, royalties,' murmured her mother, whom family disagreements tended to send into fatuities. 'In view of the subject-matter,' she added feebly.

'I think you should be very happy with *Right Royal Murder*,' said Mark, unruffled. 'The Jubilee will soon be over, but probably every royal wedding and birth will lead to a reprint. And heaven knows, there are likely to be plenty of them.'

'Thanks,' said Bella.

'Shall we have coffee?' said Mark, rising. By now his face was a little flushed from the effort of not drinking and maintaining conversation. Not being able to think of any way of asserting themselves, Terence and Bella trailed along to the sitting-room.

Coffee was set on a side-table, and the drinks cabinet stood open. The liqueurs from the study had of course been commanded by the police, but replacements had been brought up, and several bottles of spirits had also been set out by Surtees in a tempting array. Is it a bribe, thought Mark, or an invitation?

'Will you pour, Mother?' he said.

'I'll have a whisky,' said Terence.

'Terence!' said his mother.

'Of course, Terence,' said Mark, going over and taking up the bottle in his hand. 'Anything with it?'

'Neat,' said Terence.

'Mark, please don't give it to him!'

'Terence has had a bad day, Mother,' said Mark quietly. 'I'm sure it will do him good.' He poured into the glass a good stiff measure. 'Anyway there are far worse things than whisky, aren't there, Terence?' He straightened himself, the bottle still in his hands, and looked straight at his brother. 'Drugs, for instance.'

Mark still stood, his hands automatically screwing on the cap, looking at his brother and sister. Terence's face, already fiery, seemed to grow purple and crumple. Bella's eyes opened wide, and she seemed about to say something to her younger brother. Lady Fairleigh, arrested in the act of pouring, looked from one to the other, her eyes clouded with bewilderment.

'There you are, Terence,' said Mark, going over. 'Oh dear,

Mother, is that my coffee? I think you'd better pour me another, if you don't mind.'

Lady Fairleigh looked down, and found a dark pool of coffee covering the whole tray.

11

BARABBAS

From *The Times*, obituary page. Monday 19 June 1977.

OLIVER FAIRLEIGH

The death was announced early yesterday morning of Sir Oliver Fairleigh-Stubbs, Bart, MBE, better known as Oliver Fairleigh, the mystery writer.

Oliver Fairleigh-Stubbs was born on 17 June, 1912, the only son of Frederick Fairleigh-Stubbs of Birmingham, a manufacturer of kitchenware. He was brought up in the richly independent atmosphere of a provincial industrial city, and the prosperity of the family firm was greatly augmented when it shifted to war production during the years 1914–1918. However, although his father received a baronetcy in the new year's honours list for 1922, the Fairleigh-Stubbs works did not easily weather the transition to peacetime production, and went bankrupt in 1925. It was no doubt due to the economic difficulties of the family that Oliver Fairleigh did not go to university, a loss which he never regretted.

The first years of his working life (1932–1940) were spent in journalism, initially with the *Birmingham Post*, later on Fleet Street with the *Daily Clarion*. His politics at this time were the conventional blend of idealism and socialism, and his witty and trenchant reviews in the *Clarion* won him entry into the circle surrounding Auden and Isherwood. The war, however, led to a change of direction both in his career and in his politics. He served in North Africa and Italy, proving an effective if idiosyncratic soldier. In his spare time he wrote his first detective novel, *Murder by Debrett,* and the publication of this in November 1945 marked the beginning of a series of highly entertaining stories, distinctive for their narrative pace and their mild and harmless snob appeal.

His politics, in contrast to those of many of his fellow soldiers, had moved sharply to the right. In 1947 he stood as Conservative candidate at a by-election in the Milton Grove constituency of Sheffield, but his personality proved ill-adapted to the democratic give-and-take of the hustings. In later years his pronouncements on political and social matters grew more and more extreme (a much quoted article for the *People* on the cult of the Angry Young Man was a case in point), but these were part of the elaborate public persona which Oliver Fairleigh (with the delighted co-operation of Fleet Street) built up over the years. By a series of *obiter dicta* and escapades he impressed himself on the public as a formidable upholder of Victorian attitudes, a country gentleman of the old school who had appointed himself the scourge of modernity in all its forms. The publicity he gained did no harm to the sales of the stream of works which poured from his pen, and at his death he was unquestionably the most popular writer of this kind of fiction in the English-speaking world.

Lacking the literary pretensions of a Sayers, or the ingenuity of a Christie, his stories are notable for their erratic high-spirits and unfailing readability. Among the most accomplished, perhaps, are *Murder by Degrees,* with its unkind if entertaining picture of a Cambridge College, *Skirting Death,* the first of the Mrs Merrydale books, and *Foul Play at the Crossroads,* in which to the conventional formula is added a spice of *grand guignol.*

In 1949 Sir Oliver Fairleigh-Stubbs (as he had by then become, on the death of his father in 1946) married Eleanor, daughter of the Hon. Philip Erskine Howard. There were two sons and one daughter of the marriage, of which the elder son, Mark, succeeds to the baronetcy.

The obituary of Oliver Fairleigh, spread over two columns extended nearly down to the middle of the page. Underneath (testifying to the change of values that had come over Printing House Square in the later years of Oliver Fairleigh's life) were short obituaries of a Scottish Bishop and a cabinet minister in the second Attlee government. In the centre of the obituary was a photograph of Oliver Fairleigh. He stared out on the public at large, outraged, apoplectic, incredulous. Public folly, it seemed, had driven him to the verge of insanity. He looked like a Crimean War general whose men had deserted en masse, leaving him to face alone a regiment of galloping Cossacks. Not for the first time in his career, Meredith, sitting on the early morning train from Hadley to London, felt glad that the murder victim was indeed the victim, not one of the living suspects.

Turning to page two, he found a brief and neutrally worded announcement that the police were investigating the circumstances in which the novelist Oliver Fairleigh had died.

The offices of Macpherson's the publishers were in the West End of London—an area of parks and clubs, of royal palaces and exclusive hotels, of idiosyncratic shops which remained in existence against the logic and economics of the nineteen-seventies. They were, in fact, in Oliver Fairleigh country.

The building was Queen Anne, and in spite of all the efforts of a modern construction company to halt the sinkings and slidings that Time afflicts such buildings with, it was dark, irregular and undeniably quaint. It had all the air of an old family firm, and was therefore much approved by Oliver Fairleigh; but in fact its origins (like his) were late nineteenth-century and were based on the business acumen of its Scottish founder (a small printer of great thrift, industry and intransigence). The firm had published a series of volumes of popular education which just matched the needs of the post-1870 generation of board-school products. Now they were a firm of great respectability and even greater prosperity. People in the trade laughed at their love of a best-seller—and silently ground their teeth at their skill in finding them.

Inspector Meredith arrived there by appointment at nine-thirty, and stood in the high room with the sagging ceiling which was its main office. Here a decorative young lady played with a typewriter and met the general public, while a fearsome old dragon, face to the wall, did all the real work. Meredith sent his name up to Mr Gerald Simmington, but when footsteps clattered down the sounding wooden stairway there were four feet to be distinguished. He realized as soon as the first man came into the room that he was being given the red carpet treatment. This could only be Sir Edwin Macpherson.

Sir Edwin was very large: not a fat, forceful man like Oliver Fairleigh, but a stupendously gross, flabby, hearty man, whose trousers were a great pin-striped chalice for holding paunch and buttocks in. It was miraculous how two little legs could hold up so much body. He was a man of multiple chins and bags under his eyes like chandeliers, a man of cigars and port-wine laugh, very jolly, hail-fellow, with a clear eye for the main chance and a quick profit. Gerald Simmington was a sandy-haired young man in his early thirties who kept, and seemed to belong, in the background.

Sir Edwin's demeanour on this occasion was an attempt at gravity—gravity mingled with discretion. The observer got the idea, though, that given the tiniest of openings, cheerfulness would break through.

'Sad business, Inspector, terribly sad business,' he said as he sighted the raincoated figure in the corner of the office and advanced with outstretched hand. 'A great character, you know, a wonderfully vivid personality. A national figure, you might say. One of the old school, of course—nobody like him these days. We shall feel his loss here, you know—feel it deeply.' At these words Meredith noted the typing dragon in the corner half-turn from contemplating the wall and eye disapprovingly the enormous back of her employer: her expression suggested she was calling down on him the wrath of God for his mendacity. 'Anyway, thought I should come down and see you myself, before you talk to Gerald here. Assure you we want to do everything we can to help. Just ask, and the whole staff's at your beck and call. Appalling way for a man like him to go—monstrous, almost like a bad joke. He was our most popular author you know, by a long chalk. So if we can help you, we'll pull out all the stops, eh Gerald?'

'Was Sir Oliver liked here?' asked Meredith conversationally (for it seemed that Sir Edwin's purpose in coming down was conversation, rather than making himself available for questions).

'Liked?' boomed the great voice, as if the question was so absurd as to release him from the need for gravity. 'Liked? Good heavens no. He didn't want to be liked, Oliver Fairleigh. He wanted to be feared.' The great laugh rang out, echoing against the sagging ceiling. 'And we were all scared stiff of him. I too! I most of all!' The laugh boomed out again, then stopped suddenly as Sir Edwin seemed to recollect the situation.

'He was in here last week, wasn't he?' asked Meredith.

'Yes. When was it, now?' A murmured prompt came from Simmington behind the bulwark of back. 'That's right, Tuesday. We had lunch at the Savoy. Had to go along myself this time, because I'd skipped his last few visits here. Try and avoid them if I can—too embarrassing for a quiet chap like me. Still, he was in a frightfully good mood for him, wasn't he Gerald? Didn't shout at the waiter till coffee came.'

'Do you know why he was in a good mood?'

'He'd been at the BBC during the morning, and thoroughly enjoyed himself.' Sir Edwin chuckled fruitily. 'Been a naughty boy, as usual. That was always the way with old Oliver: if you could get him just after he'd done something outrageous, he could be as nice as pie.'

'I think I heard something about this BBC episode,' said Meredith. 'There was a piece in one of the papers last week—in the gossip columns. Wasn't he insulting about other crime writers?'

'Something of the sort, I believe. Didn't specify, though: just mentioned senile hacks and so on. We've had trouble over that, I can assure you.' The great laugh rang out again. 'You know our

Golden Dagger series? Well half the people who write for that seem to have heard about it and assumed it was an insult to them personally. Rum lot, writers. Told Gerald to tell them if they were senile or were hacks, we wouldn't be publishing them. Hope they believed it. Everyone loves flattery, and when it comes to writers, you should lay it on with a trowel!'

'It's an interesting line of enquiry,' said Meredith, trying to respond in kind to Sir Edwin's merriment. 'Perhaps one of them did it, out of revenge. Or perhaps there was a whole conspiracy of crime writers.'

This set Sir Edwin off. 'A conspiracy of crime writers! You've quite a turn of phrase, Inspector! I can just imagine them all getting together to plan it! Sounds like a bad Hollywood film, eh?' He sobered down suddenly. 'Mustn't joke. They're our authors. So was poor old Oliver, with all his faults. We'll miss his books once a year. We've lots better, but none as popular, eh Gerald?' And he wagged a few chins in the direction of his shadow, and mentally contemplated his future sales figures.

'Well, I mustn't keep you,' he said finally, giving the impression he meant 'you mustn't keep me.' 'Gerald will take care of you. Come to us. Any hour of the day or night. Dreadful business, dreadful business.' At the door he paused, thoughtfully. 'Publicity isn't doing us any harm, though,' he said, and marched away up the sounding stairs.

'Perhaps you'd like to come to my office,' murmured Gerald Simmington, sounding like a harp solo after a Sousa march. He led the way along a labyrinth of narrow corridors, strategically interspersed with steps to trip or tumble. Finally they arrived at a little room, neatly stacked with books and files, with a dirty window overlooking the arid well that was the area, and a desk of exemplary tidiness.

'I find if I don't keep it in apple-pie order I'm overwhelmed with paper in a matter of hours,' said Gerald Simmington, as if some explanation were demanded. He gestured Meredith to a chair, and sat down himself. His elbows, apart, rested on the desk, but his long fingers came delicately together under his chin, as if he were trying to make himself into a neat geometrical pattern. 'As

you know,' he said in his courteous, neutral voice, 'we've published all the Oliver Fairleigh books here, so over the years we've
certainly got to know his—little ways, shall we say? I'm not sure
how else we can help you, but perhaps you'd better tell me that.'

He blinked rather formally behind his heavy spectacles. A born
second-in-command, thought Meredith.

'I wanted to ask you,' he said, 'about your dinner with Sir Oliver the Sunday before last.'

'Oh yes. It was my first real visit there, you know. He knew I
was in the area, and asked me to dinner. I was apprehensive, of
course, but it went off very nicely. I gather he'd been out to lunch
and made everybody grovel, and—as Sir Edwin suggested a moment ago—that did tend to put him in a good humour for the rest
of the day. We discussed the new book, *Murder Upstairs and Downstairs*. He was very late with it, but we here had decided to hurry it
through and get it out by early October.'

'What I was really interested in,' said Meredith, 'was the drinks:
did you have liqueurs with coffee after dinner?'

'Yes, we did. Just Sir Oliver and I—Lady Fairleigh said she was
tired. We went into the study.'

'Did Sir Oliver drink lakka?'

'Yes, he did. Was it—?'

'Yes, it was.'

Mr Simmington's colourless face lost some of its minor-civil-
servant's anonymity, and seemed to evince a spark of interest.
'Well, well,' he said, leaning back in his chair. 'I've been editing the
Golden Dagger series for four years, and this is the first time I've
encountered a real murder.' It didn't seem to upset him.

'When you went into the study, was the cabinet with the liqueurs in already unlocked?'

'No, Sir Oliver unlocked it himself.'

'And afterwards?'

'He locked it himself as I got up to leave. He was very particular
about it, and I noticed it specially.'

'Why did you notice it?'

'Well, to tell you the truth, I'd heard rumours about his son,
and I wondered whether that was the reason.'

'I see,' said Meredith. He grinned. 'You make it very difficult.'

'I'm sorry? Why is that?'

'I'm trying to establish *when* the decanter could have been tampered with. It could have been done immediately before Sir Oliver drank, in which case my list of suspects is everybody who was in the room, except one.'

'One?'

'Mark, the elder son, was too drunk. Out like a light as far as I can see, and nobody even hints he could have got up and sneaked over. On the other hand, to do it then would be extremely risky: it would need nerves of iron. The alternative is, it could have been done before—which would significantly widen our list of suspects. The problem is how anyone could have got hold of the keys.'

'You mean Sir Oliver kept them with him the whole time?'

'That seems to be the general testimony. That would make it very difficult, almost impossible, except that he sometimes gave them to Surtees, his man, which opens up certain possibilities. What I'm wondering about at the moment is whether Sir Oliver was really as careful as people make out, and I was hoping that, for example, he might have left the cabinet open while he saw you out.'

Mr Simmington blinked again, and remained sunk in anaemic thought for a few seconds. 'I'm sorry, Inspector, but it was as I said. He definitely locked up before we left the study. But of course, he drank a lot—as a general rule, I mean. Very likely some other time during the week he could have forgotten to lock it.'

Meredith shook his head. 'There again, that seems ruled out. Apparently he only drank liqueurs at weekends. Some sort of compromise with doctor's orders, I believe.'

Mr Simmington shook his sandy head dubiously. 'Well, I'm surprised to hear it. I wouldn't have thought Oliver Fairleigh had so much self-discipline. I must say he always struck me as a man who would do exactly what he wanted to do—and damn the consequences.'

'Yes,' agreed Meredith, 'that's the impression the various accounts of him have made on me. But still, people seem to agree that by and large he stuck to his regime. How many glasses of lakka did he have?'

'Just the one, I think.'

'And you didn't leave the study at any time?'

'No, we neither of us left it. I wasn't there for any length of time because frankly I didn't want to outstay my welcome. Oliver Fairleigh was the sort of man who could have found some very unpleasant way of making that clear to one. He was very quick at registering boredom. We once dined him with a Bishop who'd done a book in our popular religious series, and Sir Oliver went to sleep during the main course. So I started to make time-to-go noises quite early, and he took me to the main door and saw me off down the steps. He could well have gone back to the study and had another glass or so after I'd gone.'

'True,' said Meredith. 'But come to that, we've no evidence of Mark Fairleigh-Stubbs going back to the house between that Sunday and the succeeding Saturday. It's all so damned nebulous.' He thought for a moment. 'Oh, and there was this business of *Black Widow*.'

'Er—Lady Fairleigh?' hazarded Mr Simmington vaguely.

'No. A book called *Black Widow*.' Getting no response but a polite expression of interest, mere bank-manager's courtesy, he went on: 'It was left to Lady Fairleigh in the will. I gather there is a book for posthumous publication, and I wondered—this is probably quite irrelevant to the case—whether this could be it.'

'You could well be right. No doubt it is. Miss Cozzens would be the one to ask. I've never been told the title.'

'Miss Cozzens says it was written before her time as secretary. She also says you probably have the manuscript here at Macpherson's.'

'No, no—I'm certain we don't have the manuscript.' By now the attitude of polite interest was being replaced by a very definite expression of alarm. 'You mean it's not at Wycherley Court? But this could be very serious. I can't tell you how annoyed Sir Edwin would be. He's—well, that's neither here nor there. But an Oliver Fairleigh book represents a very considerable amount of money to us. And the posthumous one—well, we were talking about it just before you came, as a matter of fact. It would naturally do even better than usual, and in view of the murder investigation—I don't have to spell that out for you, I'm sure, Inspector. Have you searched for it at Wycherley?'

'Miss Cozzens assures me it's not in her office, with all the proof copies and carbons. She suggested the study, and I went through it pretty thoroughly last evening. There's the rest of the house: I can put my men on to taking it apart.'

'Did you say it was written before Miss Cozzens's time? Yes, that would be right, I suppose. I heard about it when I joined the firm, which is more than seven years ago now. Things would have been different if Miss Cozzens had been responsible for the manuscript. I have the highest respect for her: her work is an editor's delight.'

'Did you know his previous secretary?'

'No, I've only been in charge of the Golden Dagger books for four years. My predecessor died—suicide, melancholia, between ourselves. But it's very likely there's someone here who would remember the name. Would you like me to ask around? And we could go through our files.'

'If you would. Of course, they will remember at Wycherley Court, but for the moment I prefer to have no one on their guard.'

'I see,' said Gerald Simmington. 'The question is, if he had *one* and not a succession. As you will have realized, it's not everyone could get along with Oliver Fairleigh.'

'No, indeed,' said Meredith, getting up and looking round for his mac. 'How did you manage?'

'I agreed with him all the time,' said Gerald Simmington, without a trace of a smile. 'And I made myself very inconspicuous, hardly worth noticing as a target.'

Meredith found it easy to believe. Mr Simmington seemed effortlessly to merge in with the wallpaper of his office (post-war austerity vintage). When he had led him through the labyrinth of dark corridors, shown him the main door, and shaken hands with him, Meredith looked at his retreating back, and found it difficult to remember what his face looked like.

At the street door he looked out on the June drizzle, and drew on his raincoat. He was not used to London. He realized he was not sure of his way back to the tube, and fished into his pocket for a street map, an aggravating aid that always got itself folded up in impossible ways. As he did so, the dragon-faced secretary from the outer office came out in a drab grey street coat, and Meredith asked her instead.

'Grreen Parrk,' she said, Edinburgh in her accent and her stance. 'I'll put you on your way.'

They walked down the dreadfully genteel little side street.

'It must be an interesting job you have, there,' hazarded Meredith.

'Very interesting,' she said, with an upward intonation. 'Especially the religious side.'

'Sir Edwin seemed an exceptionally easy person to work for,' went on Meredith. 'Very good-humoured.'

'Aye, he is,' volunteered the lady, looking ahead as if she disapproved of the question. 'Sir Edwin is a very pleasant man indeed. Your way lies there.' And nodding briskly, she took herself off in the other direction.

12

SOMETHING UNSPOKEN

Chief Inspector Meredith's opinion of police boffins was that they were very clever indeed, but that criminals tended to be cleverer. Their methods sometimes seemed to border on the miraculous, and some of them clearly regarded themselves as the Cagliostros of our day, and yet the rate of crimes successfully solved by the police had not risen. This rather suggested that lots of people were one or two steps ahead of them.

By rights somebody's clothes should surely have contained traces of nicotine, if (for example) it had been carried in a phial and added to Sir Oliver's birthday lakka. But nobody's did. Meredith found that very interesting indeed, and a possible extension of the boffins' field of endeavour suggested itself to him. The trouble was, that their efforts were inevitably attended with a good deal of fuss: things had to be collected to be analysed, people were inevitably put on their guard. For the moment, he decided to keep the investigation as low key as possible: perhaps he might even be able to impress on the boffins (no, that was impossible, but to show them) how much could be achieved by the old-fashioned methods of foot-slogging, questioning and checking. He thanked his Methodist Lord however, that his rank put him beyond having to do any of this donkey-work himself.

'How are things in the house here?' he asked Sergeant Trapp, when he arrived back at Wycherley Court from London at lunchtime on Monday. 'Still one big happy family?'

'They're glowering,' said Sergeant Trapp, who had the longest ears in the business, and an insatiable relish for information gained by eavesdropping. 'One big long sulk, because Mark is very obviously in control. They're not taking it well at all. Could work to our advantage in the long run I suppose.'

'It could indeed. I propose, therefore, to leave them a little longer. You never know what tempests might brew up, and I suspect with Master Terence and Miss Bella in an acute state of disappointed expectations something or other is bound to. I think the time has come to look up the Woodstocks.'

'Fine old family,' murmured Sergeant Trapp, almost automatically, with an implied touch of the forelock.

'I've seen the boy around,' said Meredith iconoclastically. 'It looks as though the rot has set in.'

'He's got the family height, though,' said Trapp loyally. 'I remember his father, years ago it was, at the hunt meets and suchlike. He was a fine figure on a horse.'

'Do you think the Woodstocks resented the Fairleigh-Stubbs when they bought this place?'

'As interlopers? Could be, I suppose.' Trapp scratched his head. 'As far as I remember, they weren't in much of a position to resent them. By then they'd next to nothing themselves. And nobody could have resented Lady Fairleigh. She's their class, after all, or better.'

'Whereas Oliver Fairleigh—?'

'Oh, he was in a class by himself,' said Trapp.

'Well, well,' said Meredith, tearing himself away from the delusive intricacies of the English class system in decay, 'I've a job for your lot. I want this house taken apart, in the gentlest possible way. I want to be sure this manuscript isn't here.'

'*Black Widow?*' Sergeant Trapp's eyebrows rose. 'Do you think it's worth the trouble?'

'How should I know till I find it? It may be. I'm sure it's worth while to keep a lot of people busy here. I'm pretty sure something nasty is going to blow up in the family. They might overhear it, and they might even be able to prevent something really nasty happening—something that would do none of our reputations any good.'

'So they're to search the house, and keep their ears open while they're about it, sir?'

'That's about it. Meanwhile I'm asking HQ for more men—ten more.'

'Whew. You'll be lucky. What for?'

'Oh, they'll give me them. If only because of all the stink this case is making.' He gestured vaguely in the direction of the front gate. 'Have you seen that lot out there? Journalistic cannibals, hungry for a bit of gristly flesh to be thrown in their direction. Until this case is solved, they'll be on our backs, and HQ will give us anything we ask for.'

He strode off to the study, having failed signally to answer the second part of Sergeant Trapp's question. However, when the same question was put to him by the Chief Commissioner, over the phone a couple of minutes later, he replied readily enough.

'I want a complete check on Mark Fairleigh-Stubbs's movements over the week before his father's death. Where he was, when, how long he stayed, who he talked to, who else was in the bar—when it's a question of bars, which I think it very largely will be. I want saturation coverage, every possible scrap of information they can give me.'

Having received assent, however grugding, and given all the necessary orders, Meredith strolled out of the house. The midday sun, in contrast to the drizzle of London, beat down on the official dark-blue metal of a police car on the tired lawns of Wycherley Court, and on the reporters at the gate, now swelled to a sweaty, gibbering crowd, looking and sounding like a cageful of monkeys performing frenetically for a solitary visitor. The thought of driving through that crowd was distasteful, as was the thought of them following him all the way to the Woodstock cottage and infesting the ground around it. A movement under a tree in the middle-distance caught his eye. He made out, in large floppy hat and heavy shoes, Lady Fairleigh, indulging in what must have been a long-standing panacea for domestic turmoil, gardening. He walked over towards her in as casual a way as possible.

'I wonder, is there any way of getting to the Woodstocks' cottage without going through the main gate, Lady Fairleigh?' She looked startled, and he explained: 'I wanted to avoid those vampires over there.'

Her brow lost any sign of trepidation. 'Well, there is, of course,' she said, 'but it would mean a hike of twenty minutes or so.'

'Just what I need.'

'Then I'll show you the way.' They went together round to the back of the manor house. Meredith noticed what a strong, capable woman she looked, and how sturdily she walked. The nervous, fragile surface was no doubt a consequence of thirty years of marriage to Oliver Fairleigh, but the toughness that enabled her to stick it out was very visible under the surface. 'Tell me, Lady Fairleigh—' (again, that look!)—'was there something odd about your husband's title?' The handsome, beaky face cleared again, and she looked at him almost roguishly.

'Well, not odd, exactly. A bit absurd, perhaps.'

'I'd always imagined he'd been knighted for his services to literature, or something.'

'Oh dear no. His books weren't good enough for that, surely? Though perhaps they ought to have given him something nice for staying in England and paying his taxes, and not nipping off to the Channel Islands or the Algarve as most of them do. No—the title is a baronetcy, and he inherited it in 1946.'

'Yes, I saw that in *The Times*. But why absurd?'

'Well, you know, his father bought it. Paid a mint of money for it, I believe, just before the fall of Lloyd George. The business wasn't going too well, and I think he thought the title would help —would give people confidence, and so on. But of course it didn't help at all. The world is full of bankrupt baronets.'

'I see. I suppose Sir Oliver preferred not to have this known?'

'Well, he preferred people not to talk about it. What was absurd, really, was that he valued the title so highly, when he and everyone knew how it had been obtained.'

'Did the older families in the district—' they rounded a corner and made towards an overgrown corner of the estate—'did the Woodstocks for example, rather resent your husband—an interloper, so to speak?'

'Oh, that sort of thing is rather out of date now, wouldn't you say, Inspector?' Lady Fairleigh looked at him quizzically. 'Like *Punch* cartoons of the 'twenties? Nowadays the people with money stick together, whatever their background. That's your way, Inspector, through that opening in the hedge. When you get to the lane, keep to your left and it's about a mile.'

'But the Woodstocks, Lady Fairleigh,' said Meredith, putting a hand on her arm to detain her, 'have family but *no* money.'

'In that sort of case, Inspector, the people with money are . . . kind.'

'I see. Would you say it was to maintain the family position in the area that your husband left the whole of his estate, virtually intact, to his elder son?'

An expression passed over her face which he interpreted as distaste for talking about family affairs with a stranger. But her sturdy common sense soon showed her the absurdity of the feeling. She said: 'Yes, I would, on thinking about it. I genuinely never knew what Oliver had put in the will, you know—never asked. But in retrospect it seems the obvious thing, the thing he *would* do. Oliver knew that even if the first generation was a bit of an interloper, the second would be "old-established." And he would want the title and the money to go together. He never valued one without the other.'

'Hard on the younger children, perhaps?'

'Perhaps. Or perhaps better for them in the long run. A *little* money, extra pocket money so to speak, can be nice. But a little *more,* nearly enough but not quite enough to live on without working—that can be ruinous, don't you think? They'll have to get over the disappointment. And I *do* think Mark is behaving well . . . ?' She looked at him, almost appealingly, as if hoping he would agree with her. Against his better judgement he responded.

'He's being very responsible indeed.'

She breathed a sigh of thanks. 'There was never any hope of

our being a *happy* family, Inspector. I've never had any ambitions beyond keeping the peace. I still hope to be able to do that.'

This time he could not keep her, and he watched her potter off across the gardens, looking here and there at shrubs and flowers for signs that they were doing well. Gardens were so much more hopeful than families.

The Woodstock cottage affected Meredith much as it had done Oliver Fairleigh. The bright colours it had been painted, the arrangement of the newly-dug flower-beds, the looped-up curtains, all somehow seemed intolerably twee. It looked like the sort of place where one would be offered dandelion tea. Here he did Celia Woodstock an injustice. She offered him perfectly ordinary tea, with the alternative of parsnip wine.

The Woodstocks were very friendly, and terribly relaxed.

'You know, it's a bit of a thrill, this, Inspector,' said Ben, curving his etiolated length around the fireplace and stuffing his bony fingers into his pipe. 'You probably know I write detective stories too. It's an incredibly lucky thing to have experience of a real police investigation, and I feel I'm testing my powers of observation too.'

Inspector Meredith, sinking into the armchair and into the overwhelmingly cosy atmosphere, brought down the shutters across his dancing eyes, but kept them surreptitiously on Ben. A gaunt face, seemingly almost concave, with deep dark sockets for eyes and hair brought deliberately down slant-wise across his forehead. A Hamlet face, but totally without magnetism. Sitting there, Meredith felt himself bursting with life in comparison with both the Woodstocks, for somehow there hung about both of them this odd, enervated air, this feeling of predestined mediocrity and failure. And yet, Ben had had the nerve to strike out on his own, to forgo the delusive securities of regular wage-packet and pension scheme and write full time. As sometimes happened, what the man did, and the impression the man gave, simply did not come together to make a whole. He didn't gel.

'The trouble is,' said Meredith, conversationally taking up Woodstock's last point, 'that of course nobody *knows* this sort of thing is going to happen, and often they notice very little.'

'But I feel, you know, that as a writer I *should* be observant, be on the watch the whole time.'

'Ben has almost total recall,' said his wife proudly, coming in with a tray of china and a teapot, and settling herself down as the completing item in the picture of domesticity around the hearth. 'Of course, it's a terribly unnerving gift to have at times, but in a case like this it couldn't be more useful!'

'Very true!' said Meredith, unhooding his eyelids and casting in her direction a glance of dutiful gallantry. She gave a nervous little giggle as she fussed over the tea things. She was a dumpy little body, without any style but with limitless surface good-will. He had known girls who seemed to be nature's wives and mothers yet turned out on closer acquaintance to be monsters of ambition and greed, Catherine the Greats of hearth and home. He accepted his cup, and sank back in his chair, letting them dictate the atmosphere.

'I hope this will meet with your approval, Inspector,' said Ben, producing a rough manuscript. 'I've written out an account of last Saturday evening. I did it, really, as a sort of test for myself, to try to bring back absolutely everything I noticed and could remember. I hope it might be useful to you. I haven't tried to select at all, just put in everything.'

'That sounds like a policeman's ideal sort of testimony.'

'I thought that as outsiders we were in a particularly good position to see things that other people may have missed.'

'Coming quite fresh to it,' said Celia, 'and not really knowing the people concerned.'

'Exactly,' said Meredith, in his friendly way. 'A completely unbiased account is just what I need.'

'Now, I've been assuming, Inspector,' said Ben, uncurling himself from the mantelpiece and draping himself across the chair opposite, 'that his drink—the Finnish stuff, whatever it was called —was poisoned. Of course, I'm not pumping you—I just wanted to explain why I've gone into a lot of detail just at that point in the narrative, detail about positions around the desk in the study, and so on.'

'That will be particularly useful,' said Meredith, which was true, if the accuracy of the account could be confirmed.

'Of course, dinner was difficult, with lots of conversations going on at the same time. But I've written out what I remembered, and Celia has done the same.'

'It's a very *plain* account,' said Celia Woodstock, as if apologizing for her lack of the literary graces. 'I just put down what I could remember, and tried to get it in the right order. Anyway, if it's any help, there it is.' She smiled brightly. The helpfulness of the Woodstocks was overwhelming.

'You've gone to a lot of trouble,' said Meredith.

'Not at all, Inspector,' said Ben. 'As I say, I regarded it as a most interesting exercise. Also—'

'Yes?'

'Well, I have to admit, there has been an offer from one of the Sunday newspapers. I don't know, it's terrible to capitalize on the Fairleighs' troubles like this, but of course it *is* a chance to get my name known, and if I could manage to do something tasteful and inoffensive . . .'

You'll find they have ways to turn it into something tasteless and offensive, thought Meredith to himself. But he said: 'Of course, I can see you wouldn't want to offend the Fairleighs. You are old friends, aren't you?'

'Hardly that, Inspector,' said Celia briskly. 'I hadn't met any of them apart from Lady Fairleigh until ten days ago.'

'It was really one of those casual acquaintanceships on my part,' said Ben, stretching his long, runner-bean legs out from the chair with an invincibly casual air. 'I used to go and play tennis now and then during the summer. I think I once went to a birthday party, I forget whose. I had completely lost touch with them, until Sir Oliver and Lady Fairleigh came here to lunch last Sunday.'

'Did you find them changed?'

'Changed? Oh no. They never changed. I remember Sir Oliver on my visits as a boy. Terrifying. He'd join in our games, when he was in a good mood, and cheat outrageously: he'd be daring us to challenge him, staring at us with those great bulging eyes. Or he'd come and watch the tennis and start shouting things like a Liverpool hooligan at a football match—screaming crazy abuse and accusing us of fouls, and so on. Then at meal times he'd boom unanswerable questions at you, or conduct ridiculous inquisitions: "Who's your favourite author?" "George Eliot, sir." "Who's he? Never heard of him. Explain who he is." "It's a woman, sir—" And so on, until eventually he would be maintaining that she was a disguised criminal in hiding from the police, or a music hall artist specializing in drag. It's quite funny in retrospect, but it was awful at the time.'

'There are ways of doing things like that,' agreed Meredith.

'Exactly,' said Ben. 'And of course he wasn't trying to amuse us, but to amuse himself.'

'As I said on the way there, Inspector,' said Celia primly, 'it's not a family I'd want to have *much* to do with.'

'Of course, basically the poor old chap was bored,' said Ben tolerantly. 'Anything to inject a spark of life into the proceedings. I tell you, I thought he was having us on for a moment last Saturday when he collapsed. I thought he'd suddenly get up, all red and outraged, and go on with the party.'

It occurred to Meredith that Woodstock was coming to life, and that the reason was not so much that he was enjoying being a vital witness in a police investigation, but that he was rehearsing a lucrative article for the *Sunday Grub*. The picture was vivid enough for him not to want to complain, but it did make him suspect that Ben's relationship with the Fairleighs must have gone a lot deeper than he tried to pretend.

'So you and the family haven't really kept up the acquaintanceship in the years since then?' he asked.

'No,' said Ben, switching back to his casual depreciative pose. 'Of course, I've been at Cambridge, and then I did some British Council work abroad. And the three over there have been—well, all over the place. I imagine Saturday night's get-together was a pretty rare thing for the Fairleighs. No, I'm afraid we'd all drifted apart. You know how it is. My mother and Lady Fairleigh visit, and telephone now and again. Nothing more than that.'

'Isn't Bella Fairleigh a writer too, in a way—?'

'A journalist, Inspector. Quite a different kettle of fish, if that doesn't sound too snobbish.' Ben Woodstock's face creased into a smile, which wasn't much of a smile. 'Except of course that that's what I intend to be for the next few days, if I can establish a really tight contract.'

Meredith felt that Ben Woodstock had ignored the implication of his question, and slithered rather neatly towards another subject. He rather thought that Celia Woodstock (who he suspected was not quite the cabbage she looked) had also noticed, and had tensed up. She was, though, in her prim, conventional way, a rather resourceful girl, and as Meredith began to make getting-up movements, it was she who spoke.

'I *do* hope things are not too terrible over at Wycherley Court. They must be *dreadfully* worried and unhappy. Are they facing up to it well?'

'Very well,' said Meredith, all blandness. 'Sir Mark has taken over, and he's proving a tower of strength.'

He caught their reactions as he eased himself up from the chair. Ben's eyebrows shot up, and he asked involuntarily: 'Mark? Then it's Mark who—? But of course we mustn't ask.'

The implications of his remark had not been lost on Celia Woodstock either. Her face, for one moment, was a picture of triumphant spite. Then they both cosily showed him to the door.

Reading at leisure, in the cool of the early evening, the accounts by Ben and Celia Woodstock of their evening at Wycherley Court, Meredith was struck by two contrary impressions.

On the one hand Ben had, as he said, been enormously detailed. His account resembled nothing so much as one of those semi-documentary novels which piles trivial fact upon trival fact in an effort to demonstrate that fiction can (with a bit of effort) be twice as boring as life. Just as the authors of these will spare one nothing, from the position of the fillings in the hero's teeth to the name of the second housemaid's brother-in-law, so Ben threw in the kitchen sink and left him to do the selecting. His account of positions around the desk during the opening of the presents was admirable. The drinks cabinet was slightly to the left of the desk, on the wall; Ben made it clear that positions changed during the unwrapping of the various gifts, so that he, Celia, Terry and Bella had all been close to the decanter of lakka at one time or another. Lady Fairleigh had, on the other hand, remained close to the coffee table on the right. All this was excellent and (subject to checking) useful. Ben was also quite specific on the subject of Mark: he was, he felt sure, quite drunk. He did not get up, and could not have got up, from his chair at the far end of the study, the whole time the Woodstocks were there, which was until a few minutes after Oliver Fairleigh had been taken off in the ambulance.

On the other hand, the suspicious mind might well wonder if there had not been omissions in the Woodstocks' accounts. Celia mentioned Oliver Fairleigh's affability and volubility, yet apparently they had talked about nothing but some people she knew slightly from Birmingham who were also acquaintances of Sir Oliver, and of the prospect of his inviting Ben to lunch with Sir Edwin Macpherson. It seemed a meagre haul for a conversation that spanned sherry and four whole courses.

Ben, on the other hand, gave an apparently full account of his conversation with Bella—journalism, London literary life, friends in common—but his version was totally lacking in life and verve. It read like the conversation of two pensioners who had met casually on a park bench. The account given by Surtees of their behaviour at table had given a very different impression.

Meredith wondered whether, by giving a minute description of the bark and foliage of the trees, Ben Woodstock had not been trying to conceal the wood. At any rate, it seemed safer to regard his recall as selective rather than total.

13

DE MORTUIS . . .

It was Tuesday before the newspapers really got into their stride over the Oliver Fairleigh murder. Monday's edition had given him plenty of space, with zoom-lens pictures of his son at the door of his newly-inherited stately home. On Tuesday the police announcement that they were treating the case as one of murder removed all inhibitions, except the purely legal ones. It was clear that the jabbering mass of journalists at the gate of Wycherley Court was but a small portion of the sum total of industry and talent being devoted to the story. Oliver Fairleigh's death, and therefore by extension his life, was for the moment the hottest news story in the country.

Fleet Street has never set great store by the maxim that only good should be spoken of the dead. On this occasion, however, it could afford to let the deceased speak ill of himself. Oliver Fairleigh had been a prolific contributor to all but the most reputable organs of opinion: through his articles he found he could (within certain limits which he was careful to observe) attack, injure and insult people, races, institutions and habits of which he disapproved, and earn quite disproportionate sums for doing so. Now he was dead, the newspapers reprinted long extracts from the articles on which they held the copyright, and the collected crassness, wrong-headedness and spleen made the man infinitely more petty and ridiculous than any character assassination by a third party could.

His political pronouncements were perhaps oddest of all. Over the years a political event was judged solely by the criteria of whether it confirmed his dire prophecies or conformed to his deepest prejudices; if it did, it was greeted with a shriek of delight. The troubles in Ireland and the State of Emergency in India were sources of the purest pleasure for him, supporting as they did his firm conviction that both peoples were incapable of governing themselves. The Conservative Party kept a vestigial hold on his allegiance as long as it was arguably an aristocratic party, but the advent of Mr Heath was met with howls of anguish ('the apotheosis of the board-school boy'), and the reign of his successor led to a vitriolic article on the subject of women in politics, a series of savage sketches of the careers of the two Señoras Peron, Mrs Meir, Mrs Gandhi and Mrs Bandaranaike, leading up to a detailed but not too convincing comparison between Mrs Thatcher and Catherine the Great.

For the rest, his articles were hysterical swipes in all directions, particularly at every manifestation of the modern world that came under his beady-eyed notice. Teddy boys, Aldermaston-marchers, hippies, pop groups, druggies, skin-heads, all had in their turn been greeted with hymns of hate. However, while his viewpoint on his subject was very often likely to be identical with that of the readers he was aiming at, he almost always conducted his attack in such a way as to alienate most of the very people he might be supposed to be appealing to. It seemed to Meredith, reading through the depressing collection in the writer's own study, early on Tuesday morning, as if the sole purpose had been to offend as many people as possible simultaneously. A description of Scottish Nationalism which had Meredith mildly chuckling would be followed by a description of the Welsh people that brought a hot flush to his face, and set those eyes sparkling dangerously.

But it was all too random to carry conviction. 'It is sometimes suggested,' began one piece, 'that as a nation we care too much about cruelty to animals, and not enough about cruelty to children. I do not, myself, see this as an "either/or" situation: personally I care about both of them, and get quite as much pleasure from the one as from the other.' Ho-ho, thought the reader: Oliver Fairleigh trying to be clever.

The newspapers covered very fully all his more public escapades, from his attempt to enter Parliament ('Madam,' he was reported to have told a heckling housewife, 'if I allowed my opinions to be influenced by an ignorant harridan like you, I would consider myself unfit to represent this constituency at Westminster') to his relationship with his elder son (his notice in *The Times* disclaiming responsibility for his debts was one of the few occasions in his career when he enjoyed universal sympathy for his point of view, nobody in Fleet Street, apparently, having paused to wonder whether a young man brought up by Oliver Fairleigh might not have had in the course of his childhood things to put up with which could justify a modicum of wildness or irresponsibility).

What was lacking was the usual pen-portrait by a friend. The reason for this, Meredith guessed, was simple enough: for the last thirty years Oliver Fairleigh had had none. There was a reminiscence of him in the 'thirties by another member of the Auden-Isherwood group, an obscure figure long since sunk into the grooves of academe. The piece lacked impact, perhaps because Oliver Fairleigh was himself at that time a mass of unformed clay, waiting to be moulded to the protuberant shape of his maturity, and coloured with the bright red of outrage.

The nearest any piece came to intimacy was one by someone called the Hon. Darcy Howard, whom the newspapers called 'poet and man of letters,' and described as the dead man's cousin. Putting two and two together, Meredith decided the description must be wrong: he was Lady Fairleigh's uncle. Reading the article, he decided that the 'poet and man of letters' bit was beside the mark too. It was a slack, rambling piece, without style or shape. It chronicled the author's acquaintanceship with the young Oliver Fairleigh in the seedier salons of literary London both before and just after the war. It described hilarious adventures, not particularly either, in Italy in nineteen forty-three and four, when Oliver Fairleigh was with and Darcy Howard 'attached to' the Allied

Forces. It described the meeting of Fairleigh and the author's niece, and the marriage. Subsequent meetings between the author and his subject had apparently been few, or unmemorable.

The article was illustrated by two photographs. One was of Darcy Howard himself, standing at the gate of a rather run-down cottage in Wiltshire, his home. It had clearly been taken the day before, probably while he took a breather from penning his reminiscences: he was a man in his seventies, sadly seedy, with a slack mouth and watery, disreputable eyes. The other was a snapshot from Italy, depicting Darcy Howard, Oliver Fairleigh and a conventionally pretty ATS private, arms around each other's shoulders, with a Sicilian piazza in the background. Oliver Fairleigh—tubby then, rather than corpulent—was in uniform, but both men were somewhat dishevelled and were brandishing fiaschi of wine, smiling broadly. The younger, gayer Oliver Fairleigh was like a distant ancestor of the Fairleigh the world knew, a figure related but totally unlike: it was a personality which had passed without trace, trampled under by the passing years. The caption under the trio, frozen in their moment of jollity, read simply: 'Second-lieutenant Fairleigh, with friends.'

All in all, the quality of the reminiscences on that Tuesday was pretty low, but the *Daily Grub* announced that its sister Sunday paper would be running a sensational account of the last dinner by the up-and-coming young novelist Ben Woodstock, who was present at the death. Their regular readers would have to control their impatience, to give Ben time to polish his phrases.

It was nearly ten o'clock in the morning, but Eleanor Fairleigh was still in bed, asleep. She had been fretfully tossing and turning until the early hours, and then had fallen off. Now, deep in a dreamy sleep, she was living her life without Oliver Fairleigh, and without her children. She was alone, and all there was to disturb her was a nagging voice at the back of her brain that said: 'But this is Death!'

Downstairs, her children were at breakfast, quarrelling.

The quarrel had begun spasmodically, for Bella and Terence were at a disadvantage, and had been since their father's death.

Normally in such circumstances a rich store of possible grievances
has been laid by, to launch at the head of the unlucky heir: he has
fawned on the dead, he has ingratiated himself in an unprincipled
way, he has misused his position. None of these time-honoured
missiles could in the present case be used. Mark had barely spoken
to his father over the last few years other than to abuse or quarrel
with him. Yet here he sat, at the head of the breakfast table, calmly
chomping his way through a substantial meal and doubtless contemplating a future of well-heeled leisure. From being the black
sheep he had been transformed overnight into the fat cat, enjoying the cream. In the circumstances there was little to be done
except vent spite, in however random a manner.

'I envy you your appetite,' said Bella bitterly, pushing aside her
crust of toast.

'Do you, Bella?' said Mark, continuing to eat. 'I'm sorry if it
annoys you in any way. But I think it would annoy you still more if
I pretended that grief had robbed me of my appetite.'

He put a forkful of devilled kidney into his mouth. His hand
was not quite steady, and that unformed, handsome face showed
signs of strain—though not the usual strain of an acute hangover.
Perhaps if either of the others had encouraged him to take a drink
at that moment, he would have found it hard to resist. But both of
them were too self-absorbed to notice any strain in him. And, in
any case, why encourage him now to make a fool of himself? Now
it was pointless.

'You've got nothing to put you off your appetite,' said Terence,
gazing savagely at his plate.

'Nor have you, dear brother, if you thought about it,' said
Mark, annoyingly smooth. 'You've been living in a silly dream,
and you've been woken up.'

'If he'd lived,' said Bella, her voice gaining again that harsh,
harridan quality, 'he would have left it to me.'

'It's just possible,' said Mark, finishing off his plateful of food,
and leaning back in his chair with a cup of coffee. 'Though I must
say it seems to me far from probable. But I admit your case is a
little different from Terence's. He is sore at losing something he
never had a chance of getting. You can convince yourself that it

was only through bad luck and lack of time that you lost out. Quite apart from any grief you may feel at the loss of Father.'

'I *am* sorry he's dead. I *did* love him,' said Bella.

'Perhaps. I doubt whether you can sort your emotions out sufficiently to tell. I find it difficult enough.'

'The question is,' said Terence, raising his Shelleyan fair head with the bloodshot eyes, 'what are you going to do for us?'

It was the question both of them had been wanting to ask, but as he let it out, baldly, because there seemed no point in trying to wrap it up for Mark, both Terence and Bella felt the treacherousness of the ground. Mark leaned forward, took a piece of toast, and spread it with butter in an infuriatingly leisurely manner.

'I find that difficult to answer,' he said. 'Of course, you will admit that I owe you nothing.'

'You owe us plenty,' said Bella, her voice rising. 'You got everything, we got nothing.'

'Yes. In normal circumstances, I suppose I might feel some sort of moral debt,' said Mark, busy with the marmalade. 'In fact, I can imagine myself shelling out quite heroically to salve my conscience. But you know, in the actual circumstances, I don't. Not at all.'

There was silence in the room. Mark ate on contentedly, and looked round at the other two. It was they who had started the subject, he seemed to say, let them continue it if they wanted to. The silence eventually became unbearable, and Bella had to ask: 'What circumstances?'

In the pause which Mark left before replying, Surtees came in with a fresh pot of coffee, and began clearing away plates. Mark said: '*Circonstances que tu connais bien,* Bella.'

'*C'est pas nécessaire à parler français,*' hissed Bella.

'Why not?' said Mark, continuing to. 'Is he the sort of lover you have no secrets from, Bella?'

Surtees continued round the table, impassively gathering up plates and serving dishes. He gave no sign of having understood, but as he finished what he was doing, and walked carefully towards the door with his tray, he blinked twice, as if absorbing new developments, and when he went out he failed to shut the door properly behind him. Perhaps Mark, with his preparatory and public school education, did not appreciate how widely French has become taught in State schools. Surtees went down to the kitchen, and swore at Mrs Moxon when she tried to pump him about what was being said in the breakfast-room.

Meanwhile, in the hall, Sergeant Trapp, seeing the door to the breakfast-room swing very slightly open, tiptoed with surprising delicacy over to it, and stationed himself nonchalantly outside. The conversation inside had, luckily, reverted to English.

'Do you know what happens, Bella, when you suddenly stop drinking?' Mark was saying, leaning forward across the table and speaking with a low, passionate intensity. 'I'll tell you. First of all it feels like the world has fallen on top of you. Then after a bit, you blink and look around you, like a horse coming out of its stables in the morning, and you start seeing things as they are. But it's not just that, because you've got a lot of memories—very hazy ones, just wisps here and there. They start coming back, one by one—a little thing here, a little thing there—things you didn't know you'd noticed. Things other people didn't think you would notice, because you were blind drunk. And these things start falling into place.'

'And—?' asked Bella, struggling to regain her usual pose of utter coolness.

'And—you come to various conclusions about what's been going on while you've been stuck out there on your little alcoholic cloud. Just to take a little example: I realize that you've been using Surtees—the faithful servant, Crichton *de nos jours*—to go along to Father with every little bit of gossip and dirt he can pick up about me. I suspect, by the way, that you needn't have bothered, because I guess Father paid him for doing exactly the same service. But anyway, you have paid him by sleeping with him, without any particular reluctance, I should guess.'

'Evidence?' spat out Bella.

'None, sister dear. I'm not a policeman. I don't need to have everything cast-iron. The odd bit of gossip in a pub; your name and a snigger—because Surtees talks in his cups too, I suspect. Then the fact that he very much wants to stay on, and I can't quite believe it's out of loyalty to me, or the ancestral name. These things are nothing—hardly even straws in the wind. But they convince me, and really, I'm afraid, that's all that matters.'

'You're despicable, Mark,' said Bella, leaning back in her chair and lighting up a cigarette, and seeming in an odd way relieved. 'You're clutching on to fantastic excuses, so as not to do anything for us, and that's all there is to it.'

'Quite,' said Mark. 'I knew you'd say that. And that's what you can tell everybody, too, when you spread your hard-luck story. I've cultivated a very thick skin about what people say about me over the last few years, and I think it's going to stand me in very good stead.'

He poured himself a large cup of coffee from the new pot. He had relaxed since the moment of intensity earlier, but he gave the impression of being a man preparing himself for another spring.

'Actually,' he said casually, 'as far as you're concerned, Bella, I'm willing to be charitable.' Involuntarily she turned towards him. 'I'm willing to assume that you knew nothing of Brother Terence's plan.'

'Ah,' said Terence, with a Mick Jagger sneer, but his voice not quite steady, 'what are we going to bring up from the lucky dip this time? More hazy fantasies from the seven years' blind?'

'Quite recent ones, these,' said Mark. 'I think you've only recently started thinking about money and inheritances and the like. But when you start, you work quickly, don't you, Terry? It's convenient not to have any awkward, old-fashioned things like scruples or compunctions, isn't it? It enables you to go straight to the guts of the matter, doesn't it, and really get down to the job.'

'Taking up evangelical religion, Mark?' asked Terence coolly. 'Come on, skip the New Testament asides. What have you dredged up out of your dream world for me?'

Again Mark leaned forward: 'I think that you never really knew what Father was likely to do with his money, never having in your life thought about anyone but yourself for more than half a second at a time. But you had this nagging suspicion at the back of your mind, that *perhaps* Father wouldn't want to cut me off, that *perhaps* he'd want the money and the title to go together.'

'So?'

'So you thought: if he *is* in the will after all these years and everything he's done, then it's going to need something really serious to get him out. There's been debts, and drunkenness, and rudeness, so what does it take? And you thought that something not just on the windy side of the law, but something really criminal, with a big scandal and prison at the end of it, might do the trick.'

'I see,' said Terence, looking straight back into his brother's brown eyes. 'And what did I plan to do: leave you in the vaults of the Bank of England while you were dead drunk?'

'It's odd, but in the past month I've had three offers to go into the drug trade. Odd coincidence, isn't it? Tempting offers, they were. I was to be a middleman, a distributor. They knew—whoever "they" were, Terence—that I went around the country, and that no one would be surprised if I turned up in this pub or that one. They made it sound very simple and nice: it was just a question of arranging meetings with people, passing the stuff over in lavatories, and so on. Nothing dirty about the trade at all, the way they told it. And it was very tempting, in view of the sums involved. It would have been so easy to say yes.'

'I'm surprised you didn't,' said Terence. 'Which is a fair enough indication that it never happened.'

'Well, you don't want me to preach, so I won't tell you all the reasons why I didn't, but the fact is, there was also a bad bit of carelessness on your part, little brother. One of the men who made me an offer seemed just a bit familiar. I couldn't put a name to him, but I knew I'd seen him somewhere. I went into your bedroom the other day, and looked at that poster of your group. He's your bass guitarist. Some bad planning on your part there, Terry.'

'It's crap,' said Terence, looking at him viciously, his red lips pursed. 'You're living in a fantasy world.'

'So now you see,' said Mark, now quite relaxed and totally in command, 'why I feel no obligations. If you ever get anything, either of you—and it won't be much—it will be charity, pure charity, without an ounce of moral obligation on my part. And of course there is one other thing, one other possibility. I'm trying to put that from my mind, but at the moment I'm not entirely succeeding. Do you know what would happen if I went down to the Wycherley Arms tonight for a pint?' The other two frowned, not seeing what he was driving at. 'The landlord would serve me quickly, and make sure he had business in the other bar. And everyone would edge away and drink up in a hurry. And all because last Sunday I said my father ought to be shot, and a week later he was dead.'

Mark put his napkin aside and pushed his chair back. The others watched him, resentment written across their faces like a neon sign.

'Of course, people jump to conclusions,' he went on. 'But the possibility remains that someone heard about what I'd said, and tried to make a very nasty use of it. It was a very fair bet that the police would jump to the conclusion that I'd threatened my father, and then done what I threatened. It was a nice little notion, and but for the grace of alcohol it would probably have succeeded.' He got up, and leaned on the back of his chair. 'But still, it didn't succeed. And whoever had the idea has failed, and can't make it succeed now. And before long, I *shall* be able to go into the Wycherley Arms. And they'll call me "Sir Mark" there, and I'll buy drinks all round. And then I'll walk home to this house, and I'll go round from room to room—yours will have to be redecorated, Terry—and I'll sit down in the study, and have a cigar, and I'll say to myself: "This is all mine. And it came to me without my ever cringing, or flattering, or doing anybody down. I have no debts to the past." And I shall sleep—very, very well.'

He walked out of the breakfast-room, across the hall (where Sergeant Trapp was over by the front door, contemplating the June morning) and into the drawing-room, where he sat in an armchair and brooded long and gloomily over the morning papers.

At his feet, Cuff slept, noisily. It was almost like the old days again, he thought.

14

DOWNSTAIRS, UPSTAIRS

Sergeant Trapp's narration of the conversation at the breakfast table—Meredith blessed for the thousandth time that miraculous combination of sharp ears and accurate memory—was interrupted by a call from Gerald Simmington at Macpherson's.

'No news of the missing manuscript yet?' he asked, his grey voice sounding almost urgent.

'Afraid not, sir, not yet,' said Meredith. 'We've taken the whole house apart, and the only result is that we're pretty sure it's not here now. The only thing to hope for is that when the case is solved, the question of the whereabouts of *Black Widow* will become clear at the same time.'

'I fervently hope so,' said Mr Simmington. From his tone it might have been gathered that the loss of *Black Widow* was comparable to that of Byron's Memoirs or Emily Brontë's second novel, or at any rate that it would be counted so at Macpherson's. He explained. 'Sir Edwin is most put out. If it has disappeared, it will represent a considerable loss to us.'

Inspector Meredith didn't quite like the word 'loss' to describe something they had never had, but he merely said: 'To change the subject just slightly, have you had any luck with the question of the last secretary?'

'Well, a little. Not enough, perhaps. She left about seven years ago, some months before Miss Cozzens was engaged. There may have been some temporary help in between, because Sir Oliver was careful before engaging anyone permanently. There's been a period when he had five or six in a row, none of them staying more than a few weeks, so he had to make sure he got someone who could stand him.' Mr Simmington seemed to feel he had put too much emotion into the last words, and amended them to 'could put up with his little ways. Anyway, the previous one left in a cloud—or at any rate, there was some kind of row. Nobody remembers what, or probably ever knew, here.'

'And nobody knows where she went?'

'Well, the general impression seems to be that she retired. She was certainly old, and people have the idea that the row, or whatever it was, only hastened things by a few months.'

'I suppose nobody remembers her name?'

Mr Simmington's voice seemed to take on a tut-tut of disapproval at the lack of method in the ways of lesser human beings: 'Everybody does, but it's not quite the same name. Unfortunately we toothcombed our files a couple of years ago, and there's no note of hers left here. There are lots of suggestions from the older members of staff, all vaguely similar. Fennington seems the most likely, Fuddleston the least. It must be something along those lines.'

'Well then, I'll have to ask the family. I've been trying so far to keep them fairly in the dark about what I'm after, but there'll have to be some kind of confrontation before very long. Tell Sir Edwin I'm keeping the manuscript very much in mind.'

'I'll do that, Inspector.' Once more Mr Simmington's voice was that of the faithful office spaniel. 'He'll be *very* glad to hear it.'

Meredith put down the phone, and turned his mind back to Sergeant Trapp's recital. Since he had been posted outside the door, he was unable to embellish the conversation with descriptions of facial expressions, but Sergeant Trapp was useful precisely for the fact that he did not go in for embellishment. He recounted, and where possible reproduced the intonation of, the conversation over breakfast, and enjoyed himself hugely. At the end of it, as Trapp drew himself up to full height in self-satisfaction, Meredith said: 'Really one big happy family, aren't they? I suppose with a father like that, one couldn't hope for anything better.'

'I don't believe in blaming the parents always,' said Sergeant Trapp, who had a son in modelling.

'You believe in original sin, eh? Well, as a Welshman, I won't go against that. On the whole it's a much more simple and satisfying explanation, I grant you that.'

'Either way, they're a pretty nasty bunch. I thought it opened up all sorts of possibilities, what Sir Mark said.'

'Oh you're right. And it closes down some as well.' Seeing Sergeant Trapp look disappointed and bewildered, Meredith went on: 'When all the reports are in about Mark Fairleigh's activities over the past week, we'll do a bit of checking on that bass guitarist. Meanwhile, I think I'll take a look downstairs—in the servants' quarters, or whatever one calls them these days: "the domestic operatives' enclave," I suppose.'

'I don't like the look of that Surtees,' said Trapp.

'Well, if you don't, there's probably plenty that do,' said Meredith. 'Including, I'm quite sure, the man himself. I've never felt such a glow of invincible self-admiration from anyone in my life before. Keep those ears at it, my boy.'

And he trotted off, through the baize door and down the wide stone stairs to the enormous, almost luxurious kitchen: it had been extensively modernized, no doubt to keep Mrs Moxon happy, and there was about it an air both of infinite room and of comfort. Meredith had turned up most opportunely. Mid-morning coffee was in progress, and it looked as if it was serving as a sort of servants' council. Round the table were seated Surtees, Mrs Moxon, whom Meredith had briefly glimpsed some days before, Wiggens the gardener, and—somewhat apart, and sitting much more upright and angular—Miss Cozzens.

'Well,' said Mrs Moxon, slapping down her cup on her saucer as she observed his approach down the stairs, 'about time I'd say.' She folded her arms across her ballooning bosom, and prepared to be a vital witness. Miss Cozzens, on the other hand, perhaps not quite happy at being caught fraternizing, prepared to slip away.

'Oh, before you go, Miss Cozzens—'

'Yes, Inspector?' There was reluctance in the set of her hips, in the swing of her sensible navy skirt.

'Did you check on the methods of killing Sir Oliver used in his various books, as you said you would?'

'Yes, I did. He never used nicotine poisoning at all. Of the poisonings he used arsenic twice, cyanide once and strychnine once. Not very many, but as I said, it wasn't his favourite method of killing. There was one with arsenic in the toad-in-the-hole. It's one of the Mrs Merrydale ones, where she uses her domestic instincts to solve the mystery. But it's not very like, is it? In fact, none of the killings was anything like Sir Oliver's death, with the poisoned drink, the toasts and so on. I have all the various references upstairs, should you need them, Inspector.'

'That's very thorough of you, Miss Cozzens. But I don't expect to have to bother you. It looks as though, at least until we find *Black Widow,* we won't find anything very close to the way Oliver Fairleigh died.'

'You've found no trace of it, then?'

'None at all. Sir Edwin Macpherson is very concerned.'

'Well, he would be, wouldn't he?'

'For money reasons, you mean?'

'Well, it's certainly not the loss to literature that bothers him.' Miss Cozzens slapped her mouth to, in her not very humorous smile. 'He will have to make do with *Murder Upstairs and Downstairs.* The case will still be fresh in everybody's mind when it comes out in October. Sir Edwin will be coining money from it.'

'He has the manuscript to that, of course.'

'Oh yes. We were so behind with it I clean-typed most of it before it was quite finished—not a thing I would normally do, in case of changes. Sir Oliver came and got them after dinner when Mr Simmington was here, and handed them over himself. He settled down to get the last chapters done the next day, and finished them in a morning. He could always get down to work if he wanted to. He would have hated to miss the Christmas market.'

Receiving a polite nod of thanks from Meredith, Barbara Cozzens fixed her mouth into a thin, prim line, and walked purposefully away. The whole set of her body told Meredith she had not liked being questioned in front of the servants. In the elaborate dance of social do's and don't's, he seemed to have trodden on her toe.

The other three, meanwhile, had been following the conversation with eager half-comprehension, and—in the case of Mrs Moxon—with some twitches of irritation. Policemen who came down to her kitchen should concentrate their attention on her. She had twice folded her arms over her matronly bosom, in passable imitation of Mrs Bridges, and when Miss Cozzens went up the stairs, she did it again. Mrs Moxon, it seemed, was determined to be, not just Mrs Moxon, but 'Cook'.

'Right,' she pronounced finally. 'And as I said a moment ago, not before time. Now, what do you want to know?'

'Lovely to find you so co-operative, ma'am,' said Meredith, imperceptibly exaggerating his Welsh singsong. 'I've been looking forward to a little chat, like. Saving you up, you might say. We needn't trouble you, Mr Surtees,' he went on, turning towards him, 'since we've been over things, you and I.'

'No trouble,' said Surtees, sitting on massively, his face a mixture of curiosity and conceit. Meredith, his whole manner changing suddenly, fixed him with an eye of steely determination, and said nothing. Eventually Surtees grudgingly shifted his bulk, and let himself out of the door into the garden.

'Good riddance to bad rubbish,' said Mrs Moxon. 'The less you have to do with that type, the better.' This was ungrateful of Mrs Moxon, for as a matter of fact she normally had a high opinion of Surtees as a fellow news gatherer and disseminator. The animosity dated from the moment on Sunday when Surtees had led the Inspector into his private room and shut the door on her. This was not her idea of below-stairs honour. Therefore, glad to have had her revenge, she was content to have Wiggens sitting at her side, and gave the inspector to understand that with the two of them to represent servant opinion, he wouldn't go far wrong.

'I suppose you would hear a lot of what goes on in the house, here, wouldn't you now?' Meredith asked, his voice oozing celtic charm.

'Not much escapes us,' said Mrs Moxon complacently.

Wiggens nodded: 'What she doesn't hear of inside, I do out,' he said.

'That's splendid, then,' said Meredith. 'Now, I'd like to hear your opinions of the various members of the household.'

Mrs Moxon blossomed. It was just the sort of question in which she felt her own sort of informed acuteness would enable her to shine. 'Well, now,' she said. 'I suppose we should start at the top. Lady Fairleigh—she's a real lady. Had a lot to put up with—haven't we all? but her more than most—but she covers up beautifully, not that it would deceive a fly. She'd've made someone a very good wife and mother if she hadn't married Sir Oliver. Then there's Sir Mark. Well, Wiggens and me are pleased he got everything.'

'Oh? Why is that?'

'Because the alternatives was worse,' said Mrs Moxon succinctly. 'There was always this talk about Mark, but I never saw much harm in him, bar his being full as a fruitcake most of the time, and it's not as though the poor little blighter had much of a childhood.'

'Was it worse for him than for the others?'

'Oh yes, him being the first, and then Miss Bella being the favourite, and Sir Oliver having exhausted himself a bit by the time Master Terry grew up, not that he exhausted himself as much as he ought, heaven knows. Well, where was I, oh yes, then there's Bella—well, I don't quite know how I'd describe her, more a mixture really. Artful, she is. Knew how to twist her father round her little finger. It used to rile Lady Fairleigh, I know that, though she'd die if she thought she'd shown it. Miss Bella is a bit of a minx, I'd say, but she's not all bad.'

'Not like Terence?'

'Well, I didn't say that, you did, but there have been incidents, it's true—little things . . . I don't like the boy one little bit, and that's the truth. I mind once, years ago, when he can't have been more than ten or eleven, he saw me take a few scraps of food home from this very kitchen for my own tea. I didn't know he'd noticed —he's never been the wide-eyed sort of child—but he watched me for a fortnight, watched everything I did. Then he came along with everything listed neat and tidy in a notebook, and he threatened to tell his father unless I gave him a pound a week. Have you ever heard the like?'

'What did you do?'

'Laughed in his face, what else? I could afford to. Good cooks write their own contracts these days, and Sir Oliver wouldn't dare to give me notice, no more he wouldn't dare say anything to me, lest I gave mine. I spelled it out for him, young as he was. That experience taught him a thing or two about blackmail, I shouldn't wonder.'

'It may very well have done. Well, that's the family. What about Miss Cozzens and John Surtees?'

'She's all right. Keeps herself *to* herself: "I'm not one of you, but I'll be nice as pie if you know your place." She's been very matey these last few days—afraid of missing out on anything, I shouldn't wonder. Now Surtees—' she thought for a bit, obviously not having expected to be questioned about her fellow servant, and wondering how much loyalty was due to him. Not, it seemed, much. 'Well, he likes money, and he likes power, and that's a fact. No morals either.' Mrs Moxon seemed to swell, as if in consciousness of her own superiority in that respect. Her next words showed that to her (as to the Sunday papers) morals meant sexual morals. 'He likes women, that's no secret, or at any rate, he likes to have women sniffing after him. He thinks he's the cat's whiskers— the prize tom in the neighbourhood, in fact.' She cackled with laughter. 'Thinks more of himself than he thinks of any of them, if you ask me, but there's always plenty of women as will make fools of themselves for a chap like him.'

'Did he and Miss Cozzens sleep together?'

'Miss Cozzens?' Mrs Moxon looked genuinely startled, and her look made Meredith feel he should have used some such phrase as 'were intimate,' rather than his own particular circumlocution. At length she said: 'Not that I know of, no. There's others in the house I wouldn't say the same for.'

'You mean Lady Fairleigh—?'

There came over Mrs Moxon's plump face a look of the most utter outrage and rebuttal. For once she stuttered for lack of words, a rare experience for her: 'Lady Fairleigh? Why, good heavens, man, you must be out of your mind. I've never heard of such a thing. She's a lady. She'd no more sleep with John Surtees than she would with Wiggens here.'

Wiggens gave a complacent grin, as if some sort of compliment were intended. He had been sitting silent, in an old check shirt dirtied by time rather than labour, so perhaps he was pleased at last to have some real part in the conversation.

'Miss Bella, then.'

'Got it in one. Two, anyway. He talks about it when he's had a few to drink sometimes, gives hints—subtle he probably thinks them, but you'd have to be a half-wit not to understand.'

'Tell me, Mrs Moxon,' said Meredith, turning now to the things that really interested him rather than those which were designed to show off Mrs Moxon's powers as an observer, 'when was it that the rumours of what Sir Mark had said in the Prince Albert at Hadley got to Wycherley?'

Mrs Moxon, intent on being a key witness for the Crown, sat and pondered, in a real attempt to get at the right answer: 'Well, now, I'd say it was Thursday,' she said, finally. 'Because Thursday's my bread day, and my hands were sticky when I told Lady Fairleigh.'

'It was Thursday when you told me,' said Wiggens eagerly. 'Because that's one of my pub nights, and I mind we chewed it over at the Arms that same day.'

'Then I must have heard from Betty Pratt on my way to work. Her husband had been over Hadley way the night before, and heard it then. I know Surtees went along to Sir Oliver with the story the next day, must have been Friday.'

'Did he always do that?'

' 'Course he did. Sir Oliver used to slip him a fiver now and then, and a tenner if it was something he really wanted to know.'

'Then you don't think anyone in the area would have heard it earlier than Thursday morning.'

'Not they,' said Mrs Moxon confidently. 'If so, they'd have told me. I'm always the first to know. Everyone round here knows I like to hear what's going on. And I'm good about passing it on, aren't I?'

'You are,' confirmed Wiggens sagely.

'So if the poison was put in the decanter by one of the family, or conceivably by one of the servants,' went on Meredith, 'it was likely to be on Thursday or after, if the intention was to incriminate Sir Mark after what he said at Hadley. Is that right?'

Mrs Moxon looked at him with undisguised admiration: 'I call that real logistics,' she said.

The journalistic siege of Wycherley Court went on, and seemed likely to continue until either the case was solved, or some equally sensational happening displaced it from the front page. A little army of ace reporters was now camped outside the gates and along the road into the village: men with faces lobster-pink from the unaccustomed fresh air and sunshine, with beer bellies poking unattractively through shirts with buttons missing, men with an air of living in a paradoxical state of continual excitement and inbred cynicism.

Inside Wycherley Court, the inhabitants withstood the siege as best they could. Bella and Terence were already talking about getting away, but they could hardly leave with decency before a week had gone by. With luck the funeral could be fixed for Friday or Saturday, and then they could take off, to nurse their disappointed expectations in conditions of greater privacy, or solicit the sympathy of friends for their grievances. Meanwhile they sulked and skulked around Wycherley Court, watched Mark gradually assuming the reins of control, and felt their position in the home becoming more and more uncertain. Terence drank.

When Meredith came upon them on Tuesday afternoon it was tea-time, and they were all tucking into shrimp sandwiches, fruitcake and sponge fingers. The atmosphere was less tense than it had been, at least on the surface: perhaps Mark's revelation of the extent of his knowledge of their activities had had a sobering effect; or perhaps he or his mother had been pointing out to the younger children that a display of family animosities in front of the police was to nobody's benefit, least of all their own.

Meredith's arrival was a signal to Mark to do his duty as host
and head of the household. He was getting quite good at it. Meredith was ushered to a seat, and plied with offers of sandwiches and
tea. As he let himself be served by Lady Fairleigh, he eyed 'the
young master.' Mark was certainly looking better, as well as behaving better: the whites of his eyes were less like pink and red road
maps, his suit was now older but more suitable than the sharp job
he had been wearing, and his hand, when he passed the teacup,
was almost entirely steady. His performance did not please Bella
and Terence, but they had been sufficiently brought to heel to
keep quiet, and they merely gazed ahead of themselves with an
appearance of calm.

'Delicious!' said Meredith, biting a sandwich which was itself
hardly more than bite-sized. 'Now—business, I'm afraid. First of
all, I'd like you all to look at these: they're copies of an account Mr
Woodstock has prepared of the birthday party here last Saturday
night—all very detailed and precise.'

'A preparation for his article for the *Sunday Grub,* I suppose,'
said Bella. 'I think he's contemptible.'

Meredith turned to her, his attractive face open and guileless:
'You think you deserved better of him, do you?' he said. For some
reason Bella flushed and remained silent. Terence shot a sharp,
apprehensive gaze from his dulled eyes in Meredith's direction,
but the inspector had merely settled himself back more comfortably in his chair.

'I'd like you all—Sir Mark excepted, of course—to look at his
account of the positions around the desk at all stages of the pres-
ent-opening, and tell me if it agrees with your memory of events.
And, of course, his account of the conversations as well.'

They accepted their copies, and waited for him to go on.

'There was one more little thing I was thinking of asking,' he
said, still more comfortably settled, and sipping his tea, like an old
family friend. 'Could you tell me the name of the secretary Sir
Oliver had before Miss Cozzens?'

Meredith's quick, sparkling eyes caught their reactions: surprise from Lady Fairleigh, more obvious puzzlement—a creasing

of the brow—from her two eldest children, and from Terence, something more positive—alarm, or active dislike, or what?

'Goodness me,' said Eleanor Fairleigh. 'That's a figure from the past. Miss Thorrington—you remember, children?'

Terence grunted and looked down at his plate. Mark and Bella nodded neutrally.

'Could you tell me a bit more about her?' asked Meredith, helping himself to another sandwich and cosifying the atmosphere again.

'Well, let me see: her name was Victoria. I remember that, because she told me she was born on the day the old queen died—that's exactly how she put it: "the old queen." But we always called her "Miss Thorrington," because it's difficult to keep calling people Victoria the whole time, and any abbreviation sounded like *lèse majesté*. She was with us—what?—nine or ten years I should think.'

'And then?'

'Well, she retired. She was about seventy, you see. She went to live somewhere on the South Coast—Hastings, or Bournemouth or Southsea, or somewhere: flats for elderly gentlefolk—you know the kind of thing.'

'You have the address?'

'I'm sorry, I haven't. I *had,* because I sent her a card the first Christmas after she left. But there was none back, and I didn't want to embarrass her by going on sending: I thought probably she couldn't afford cards. So we've completely lost touch.'

'Was there any kind of row when she left here?'

Meredith noted that Lady Fairleigh looked troubled, and smoothed her hair distractedly. 'Oh dear—I expect so. There usually was, you know, with . . . with things as they were. I seem to remember she left rather suddenly, before we were expecting it. But what the trouble was I can't remember—if I ever knew. Sometimes I tried *not* to know, you understand, Inspector. Do you remember, children?'

She glanced round at her brood. They all shook their heads.

'Search me,' said Terence. 'I think I was at school.'

'It was some row with Father, I think,' said Mark. 'She went more or less overnight. I don't think we ever knew why.'

'Well, anyway, what you've told me should be helpful,' said Meredith, putting his plate down on a side-table, and standing up. 'If she's alive I should be able to contact her.'

'I really don't see,' said Eleanor Fairleigh, almost to herself, 'What she could possibly have to do with it.'

'I'm assuming,' said Meredith, looking at them in his sly way as he gathered his things together, 'that as the person who typed it, she's one of the few people who knows what's in *Black Widow*.'

He studied their reactions closely. They all looked at him as if he was completely off his head.

15

BLACK SHEEP

Meredith stood by the desk in the study where Oliver Fairleigh, only a few days before, had opened his last birthday presents. He was shuffling together a sheaf of reports on the activities of Mark Fairleigh in the week his father died. They represented a fortune in shoe leather, and would make interesting reading for the car trip. Meredith looked around the study, possibly, he hoped, for the last time: it was not a particularly attractive room, but it was what its owner wanted it to be: dark, substantial, smelling of wealth and social position.

He had made a discovery about the study. One of the bookcases, at the far end by the window, was not a bookcase at all, but a painted wall. He had had excited thoughts about secret passages, but it was no more than another elaborate Oliver Fairleigh joke: with Victorian meticulousness, shelves and books had been painted on the wall, making a perfect *trompe l'oeil*. The books had been lettered in gold, and given titles expressive of Oliver Fairleigh's opinions and sense of humour. They had probably, Meredith guessed, been changed here and there over the years, for the political references ranged from a heavy black book entitled *Merrie England* by Sir Stafford Cripps to a very slim volume (so slim as to be almost invisible) which was entitled *Principle in Politics* and was attributed to Harold Wilson. Elsewhere on the 'shelves' there were *The Mitford Family on Each Other* (twenty-five volumes), and a series of imaginary novels with dreadful punning titles: *From Here to Maternity, By Love Depressed,* and, obscurely, *The English Lieutenant's Woman.* The bookcase seemed to Meredith somehow an image of Sir Oliver Fairleigh-Stubbs: ponderous, outwardly impressive, actually fake, light-weight. He remembered a description of him by a police colleague who had met him in life: 'a bookie who had wangled an invitation to a Buckingham Palace garden party.'

He had made another discovery in the study, and before he went out into the early sunshine he could not resist the impulse to go back to it once more: it was an elderly dictaphone, stowed away in a cupboard, but reproducing at the flick of a switch with eerie verisimilitude the voice of Oliver Fairleigh a few days before his death—nut-brown, resonant, baritonal, a voice rich in good-living and self-satisfaction: the authentic Fairleigh sound:

' "Flanked in the doorway by two sturdy policemen, the Honourable Jane Buchanan, flushed with shame or fury, turned on her father. 'I did it for love of you,' she shouted. As she walked through the door and out to the waiting sunlight, her head held high, Lord Fernihill, standing by the superb Adam fireplace, let his head fall on his chest and wept bitterly." Do you find that rather melodramatic, Miss Cozzens?'

The reply was indistinguishable.

'No, of course you wouldn't be. And I imagine strong emotion isn't exactly your cup of tea, is it? It embarrasses you, I would imagine. Do you write novels yourself, I wonder, Miss Cozzens, in the secrecy of your boudoir?'

Again a mumbled reply.

'I suspect, you know, they must be very strong-minded novels. Something of the Ivy Compton-Burnett type, I would fancy. A touch of the Doris Lessing. God, how I hate brainy women. Where were we? "And as Inspector Powys drove back along the stately drive to Everton Lodge . . ." '

Inspector Meredith (not greatly caring for the doings of Inspector Powys) clicked the machine off. Another image of Oliver Fairleigh had surfaced in his mind: talented, perverse, intolerable —Oliver Fairleigh living up to his public image. Was such a man killed merely for his money? A man who had scattered in his wake so many hand-grenades—was none of them lobbed back at his feet?

Inspector Meredith finally closed the study door, and walked slowly out to the stately drive of Wycherley Court. The morning was still very young, and only a few greenhorn reporters—those unafflicted by fuggy hangovers or dyspepsia—were already in position at the gate. They were being rewarded by a sight of Bella Fairleigh, wafting past a laburnum tree and along the side of a superb rosegarden. She seemed to have regained every degree of her once habitual cool: with a crisp white coif over her hair, russet blouse and cream skirt nearly to her ankles, she made, in soft focus, the sort of picture Anthony Armstrong-Jones used to take of royalty. With his heart pausing a second in appreciation, Meredith stood by the police-car. By what quirk of genetics had Oliver Fairleigh been able to produce anything as gorgeous as this?

Bella continued, apparently oblivious of the photographers, apparently oblivious of everything around her. But Meredith noted that she was changing her direction, and was willing to bet she would come over to him. Without displaying any obvious signs of registering who he was or why he was there, she did so. Close up, she was very, very beautiful, and as her piquant, pixie face turned up into his, its eyebrows arched in query, Meredith's Welsh heart beat very fast indeed.

'Are you finished with us?' she asked.

'Nearly,' said Meredith. And added: 'Perhaps.'

'You've hardly spoken to me,' said Bella, stating it as a fact, not a compliment. 'Or Terry.'

'No, I haven't. Beyond getting your account of the positions in the study at the time, and your broad agreement with Mr Woodstock's picture, I haven't felt I needed to. Was I wrong? Is there anything you would like to tell me?'

Bella considered. 'No,' she said. She tilted her head to one side and looked him in the eyes. Meredith decided this must be one of her techniques. The effect was formidable. 'I just thought,' she said eventually, with a little pout, 'that you must have got the idea that I was only interested in Daddy's money.'

'Does it matter to you what I think?'

'Not at all!' She turned away, dissatisfied. But it seemed to matter. Gazing at the ground, she said: 'I loved him. I wanted his money, and I loved him.'

Meredith said: 'Unless it's relevant to the murder, it's no business of mine. It's your brother you have to make your peace with, not us.'

'Oh, Mark! He's contemptible.'

'Has he ever done anything to harm you or Terence?'

'Mark has never done anything positive whatsoever in his life.'

'Except in these last few days, perhaps,' amended Meredith. Bella looked furious. 'On the other hand you haven't been so guiltless where he is concerned, I would guess.'

'Oh? What do you think I've done to him?'

'Made sure that a good supply of stories about him reached his father.'

A not very pleasant smile crossed Bella's face. She shrugged: 'That's the name of the game.'

'There's something else I think you've done that you're not too proud of, or shouldn't be,' went on Meredith, feeling rather nonconformist. Bella raised her wonderful eyebrows and opened her eyes wide. 'I think you had an agreement with your father. About the Woodstocks.'

'They're contemptible.'

'How pleasant to have so many people beneath your contempt. Are you going to tell me about the agreement? No? Well, I guess that to get your father to be pleasant the whole evening, you volunteered to provide entertainment for him. Am I right?'

'Yes. Why not? We often had little pacts like that. They kept him interested. Poor Daddy was desperately bored.'

'And what exactly did the pact consist of?'

'Why should I tell you?' Bella began to drift off into the garden, but changed her mind and turned back. Meredith guessed that she was at all times desperate to be the centre of attention, and had missed just that sensation since her father died. 'I promised I'd do my best to reduce Ben to a condition of hopeless passion in the course of the evening, and drive that mousey little wife of his emerald with jealousy.'

'What made you think you could?'

'I *can*,' said Bella, formidably, as if her father spoke through her. Then she added: 'I'd met Ben in London, a few months ago. It was just before his wedding, and he was up arranging financial matters. I had the impression the family did some fiddling over death duties, and had more stashed away somewhere than people usually give them credit for. Anyway, he came panting after me like a bedraggled spaniel. It was quite sweet really. Actually I had other fish to fry at the time, but when Daddy told me he'd savaged him the weekend before I thought I'd try and save him from a second attack. So that's all it was. I was going to give him a nice romantic evening—'

'While your father—let me guess—was going to pump little Mrs Woodstock about the family fortunes.' Bella hesitated a moment, then nodded. 'And what was supposed to come out of this little campaign?'

Bella shrugged. 'Nothing. What could? I wasn't going to drag Ben up to my bed before his wife's outraged eyes. Father wasn't going to blackmail the Woodstocks out of their few remaining thousands. It was just something to amuse Father. It was just a game.'

'You both like dangerous games.'

'What other kind is there, worth playing?'

And this time Bella did drift away, studiedly unconscious of the clicks of cameras at the gate, the morning sun playing on her auburn hair. Meredith dived into the car, punched the back of his driver to waken him from open-mouthed contemplation of the Madison Avenue vision wafting across the lawns, and let himself be driven at top speed through the gates. For once not a camera turned in his direction, and he was grateful.

Safely away from Wycherley, with an hour and a half's drive ahead, Meredith settled himself down in his seat, and began shuffling through the voluminous reports from the men on the beat of the activities of Mark Fairleigh in the week before his father's death. It was, as he had expected, a sort of Drunk's Progress. The beginning and end of these seven days had been within a radius of 30 miles of Wycherley Court, the weekdays in and around London (where he periodically attended some kind of office, or saw people about some kind of orders). But whether in the town or the country, the lunch-times and evenings were a succession of pubs and clubs, often following in a descending curve of respectability as the night wore on. How Mark managed it financially he did not know, but it seemed clear from the reports that fairly little could send him into an agreeable haze, and then the main thing was to keep there. He was better when he had company: when he was alone he tended to drink himself into oblivion or bellicosity.

His progress from place to place in his alcoholic pilgrimage was a vivid commentary on the effectiveness of the breathalyser laws. He invariably drove himself.

The people he met were interesting: they ranged from men and boys like himself—the outcast type, black sheep, shady characters living from one shift to the next and always wanting credit on an expected loan—to petty crooks, con men, gentlemen with a minor racket, people with ways of keeping just within the law, or with manners that appealed to old ladies. In the rich tapestry of the criminal classes, Mark seemed to have stuck to the seedy fringes. Meredith felt he could pick out without too much trouble one of the occasions when Mark was solicited to come in on the drug racket. There was documented a long, agonizing and finally acrimonious conversation in the Walthamstow Three Pigeons late on Friday evening with a man in his mid-twenties—a man with a gaunt, hawkish face, sunken eyes and hook nose. The description exactly corresponded with the bass guitarist of the Wichetty Grub, whose picture on the wall of Terence's room Meredith had slipped in to check up on the day before. He had disliked the face at the time. He had also noted with interest the empty bottles scattered around the room, and the general smell of frowstiness and disappointed hopes.

The other report that Meredith studied with particular interest was that of the clientele of the Prince Albert, that Saturday night ten days before. The frequenters of the Saloon Bar had been only too willing to come forward: there was a long list, with addresses, all of which had been followed up, scattered though they were geographically. The policeman doing the checking up had recorded (with appropriate professional detachment) all the various frills and furbelows on the basic facts which the various witnesses indulged in: 'His eyes were glowing with maniac fury,' young Miss Vanessa Corbett had explained; 'he brandished a table knife in Jack Larkin's face, and then plunged it into the table,' said another romantic soul. The policeman reporting all this allowed himself the luxury of a few exclamation marks in the margin.

But what interested Meredith was mainly who was there at the time—and here the reports were not as satisfactory as he would have liked: they did not, that is, confirm a little guess he had made to himself. But he had often found that people who had a bit to drink could remember much more than they thought, if you could only find the thing to trigger their memories off. He would have, he thought, to find the right sort of trigger. He looked down the list, trying to select the most likely witness for the sort of experiment he had in mind.

It was nearly half past ten by the time they had driven into Wiltshire and found the village of Lorstone. Meredith left both his car and his driver at the little pre-war council house that doubled as a police station. He had seldom found that an ostentatious display of strength had a very positive effect on a witness, and he certainly didn't think it would have one on the witness he was going to interview now. He would, he told the local constable, walk to the cottage, if he would be so kind as to direct him.

It was only a few minutes' walk, and Meredith paused by a tree unseen to look at the cottage before he went up to the door. It was very unlike the Woodstocks' tarted-up little pair of labourers' dwellings. It was a single, one-storied cottage, and—as Meredith had guessed from the newspaper photograph—in a very dilapidated condition. The gate was swinging open on its hinges, the garden was a tangle of weeds and sprawling bushes, the roof lacked slates. If Ben Woodstock was the aspirant man of letters at the beginning of his career, with a cottage to match, this hovel was the mirror of such a career as it coughed and wheezed its way to a dispirited close.

As he watched, the owner came out. He locked the door, clumsily, as if it was not something he was used to doing, then he pottered along towards the front gate. Meredith looked at his watch. It was a couple of minutes to opening time.

Darcy Howard, when he came towards Meredith, looked no more impressive than he had in the newspaper picture: if the remains of an aristocratic manner were there at all, it was in so wispy and wraith-like a state as only to highlight the other dominant impressions to be gained from the man's face and clothes. Darcy Howard was not quite clean, and his clothes smelled of tobacco and tap-rooms. His walk was a shuffle, and he looked around with a sort of roguish furtiveness, as if for acquaintances who could still be touched for fifty pence. Underneath the general air of decay and seediness there was a little spark of light in his shifty eye. Meredith guessed he knew the reason: today, a rare occurrence, he had money in his pocket and another little nest egg in his cottage, and it came from Fleet Street.

He slipped out into Darcy Howard's path. 'I'd like to talk to you,' he said.

'Oh, would you?' Darcy Howard's face achieved something close to a cheeky schoolboy's smirk: he really was pleased with himself. 'Well, you'd better tell me what's it worth to you, hadn't you? People have to buy my time these days.'

Meredith pulled out his identification card. Howard peered at it, snuffling gently with disappointment. 'I've got a half of gin in my pocket,' said Meredith, patting it. Darcy Howard looked wistfully in the direction of the local and sighed. But, apparently deciding that a free drink ought to take precedence over a bought one—one of the few principles held fast to in these last decades of his life—eventually he turned and led the way back to his cottage.

'Bit of a mess in here,' he said, in perfunctory apology. 'The woman hasn't been in.'

No woman would want to. The place was a smelly slum.

Meredith sat down on a rickety wooden chair. 'I'm following up that article you did for the *Clarion*,' he said.

'Got paid for that,' said Darcy Howard, baring his old teeth in a great chuckle of self-satisfaction. 'Well, too.'

'It was extremely interesting,' said Meredith diplomatically.

'But of course you had to feed them some of the usual good stories
—the Oliver Fairleigh routine. I thought we might get a little
closer to what he actually was like at the time you knew him.'

Darcy Howard digested this slowly, and then looked at Meredith in his cunning, bloodshot way. 'Of course, you give them
what they want,' he said, grandly general. 'You don't tell the whole
truth. You lot do the same, don't you? "The police are following
up certain leads which they are convinced . . ." sounds better
than "The police are thrashing around in the dark." The newspapers wanted the usual routine, so I dredged up a few stories.
Made up one of them myself. It's natural. Especially as there was
money involved.' Darcy Howard cast his eye significantly around
his unattractive little piece of real estate. Then for the first time he
looked Meredith straight in the eye: 'You said you had a half of
gin,' he said.

With a sigh which said that he had hoped the interview might
be conducted with more of an eye to police standing orders, Meredith took out the bottle, and Darcy Howard jumped up with something close to alacrity and got two smeary glasses and a milk-jug of
water. Meredith made his a small one, but Darcy Howard didn't.

'The point is really,' said Meredith, sipping warily, 'that from
your point of view you knew Oliver Fairleigh at the wrong time,
didn't you? It was only later in life that he developed this . . .
personality that so fascinated everybody and you didn't in fact
have much contact with him in later years, did you?'

'Not a great deal,' said Darcy Howard.

'Not much after his marriage, I gathered.'

'Oh, we met, of course. But not a great deal, as I say.'

'That was odd, wasn't it? In view of the fact that he married
your—what—niece?'

'Not so odd. Eleanor comes from the respectable side of the
family. Nice people, but stiff, you know. I was always the black
sheep. They met at my place. Not here—' he gestured round,
again, as if to imply that even he would not sink to inviting his
niece to such a dump—'in London. After the war. Anyway, they
married. Good catch for Oliver. But they hadn't much use for me

after that. Oliver decided to become a country gentleman. I'd served my turn.'

'So you knew him mostly in the 'thirties and during the war?'

'That's it,' said Darcy, apparently relieved that the clock had been turned back to the period before his casting-off. 'Bright boy he was then. Up and coming. So was I. More than that. I had talent, by God I had.' He gestured towards the rough shelf full of books in the corner. 'Anthologies. Poetry of the 'thirties. There's hardly one of those that hasn't one of mine in it. Worth a mint of money today, some of those books.' His tone was as unconvinced as Meredith felt it ought to be. However he forbore to ask what went wrong. Lack of fulfilment is doubtless as painful to the untalented as to the talented. He just said: 'Of course, Oliver Fairleigh was a Socialist at that time . . .'

'Of course he was. We all were. All the bright boys. He had it worse than some. You'll find that when the old families go in for Socialism—' he turned his profile in Meredith's direction, as if it were distinguished enough to be stamped on coin of the realm— 'we do it with a bit of *style*, we keep our sense of proportion. Now Oliver, he was what I'd call industrial aristocracy, and when they get it, they tend to go the whole hog. Like Mr Benn, you know. Trade union banners in the living-room and eternal thick mugs of strong tea. Not a bit of discretion, had Oliver, no sense of the ridiculous. Which was as well,' he added, with Olympian spite, 'because he was ridiculous much of the time.'

'So he was very committed in the 'thirties, was he?'

'Oh yes—the Peace Pledge, Republican Spain, Jarrow marches —the lot.'

'When did you notice him changing?' Meredith sensed, so imperceptibly he couldn't be sure it was so, a slight stiffening in Darcy Howard.

'Well, of course we lost touch, naturally,' he said, not answering the question but gesturing grandly. 'We had quite a little group going in the 'thirties.' He reeled off a series of names that meant nothing to Meredith. 'We had the same sort of aims as the Auden group, but we were more hetero. Oliver kept in with us, and with them. Funny to think about it now. He was quite good at keeping in with people at that time. Must have been saving himself up.'

'But it was in the war he changed, wasn't it? And you did serve with him, didn't you?'

'If you like to put it that way. We lost touch round about nineteen-forty, when he joined up. Of course I did my bit in different ways. Anyway, we met up in Sicily in 'forty-three, and we kept bumping into each other on and off for the next few years. He was still a Socialist in 'forty-three, or called himself one. But I think the bloom was wearing off, even then.'

'Why?'

Darcy Howard hesitated. 'Well, he was always a drawing-room pinkie, you know. He could throw dogmas and slogans and theories around with the rest of us, but in point of fact he understood very little of them, and as far as contact with the working-class movement was concerned, he hadn't any. He knew nothing whatsoever about it. Well, in the army he met up with the workers.' Darcy Howard once more forced out his wheezy chuckle. 'I think he discovered they didn't know their place. He did some lecturing —on left-wing topics. They didn't accept his opinions as gospel. He didn't like it. He was always opinionated, was our Oliver from Brummagem.' Darcy Howard attempted a Birmingham accent, unwisely. Then he handed his glass over to Meredith to be refilled with the air of a man who is giving value for money, and then settled back with his glass into his chair, as if his side of the conversation were more or less over and he had told everything he knew.

'There was no incident, then, that was crucial to his change of mind?' asked Meredith. Perhaps he let a note of urgency creep into his voice; at any rate he sensed again a slight stiffening in Howard which suggested that he was walking carefully.

'No, no, not that I know of,' he said, sipping his gin. 'As I say, it seemed to have been coming on gradually. There was once—some time in 'forty-four it must have been—he was invalided back home, after Monte Cassino. There wasn't anything much wrong with him. It was really three months' leave to write propaganda pieces on the battle aimed at the popular market (and *that* didn't please our Oliver. He thought he was more of an *Observer* writer, but they'd got his measure). Anyway, he hadn't anywhere much to go. His father was in hospital—mental home, just between ourselves—and there wasn't any other family. I put my London flat at his disposal, but I believe he also spent some time up North—with a private in his regiment he'd struck up some kind of friendship with.' Darcy Howard chuckled again, but uneasily, as if aware that Meredith was looking at him very closely. 'It didn't work out, I believe. That was Oliver's first real taste of working-class life. It only lasted a few days. He told me later he loathed it. Loathed *them*. He never said much about the class struggle after that.' It was clear that Darcy Howard took immense spiteful pleasure from the story. But then he paused, and—as if thinking he'd gone too far—said: 'But as I say, he'd been re-thinking his position for a long time. Oh yes, I'd seen it coming on.'

Meredith looked at the cagey old crook, dissatisfied with the progress of the interview. Howard was giving away just so much, and no more. On the off-chance, he said: 'He had affairs too at this time, didn't he?' Howard opened his eyes quickly, then closed them again.

'Oh, Oliver always had the odd girl in tow, you know. There was always someone or other in the old days back in London. Pretty dire types, mostly—long matted hair and chunky beads, quoting Freud or Stalin or an unholy mixture of the two. Not my style at all, I can tell you. I'm afraid I can't help you there.'

'I meant in Italy,' said Meredith. 'Or perhaps when he was on leave.'

'Couldn't say, old man. You know what it was like then—well, no, you wouldn't—too young—but it *was*.' Seeing Meredith looking at him and perhaps feeling himself that he had been less than clear, he added: 'Well you'd meet up for a couple of days, have a bit of a ball, you know, and then he'd be posted to Rome, and you'd be sent to liaise with Pisa, and you wouldn't see each other for a couple of months. That's how it was. I didn't know anything about Oliver's private life. Didn't concern me. Had a real little Neapolitan spitfire myself at that time. Still get a Christmas card from her. Runs a tourist hotel near Naples. Such is life. I expect Oliver had something of that sort on the side too.'

'You certainly implied that the girl in the picture was—'

'Oh, one does. Have to make a good story for the press boys. Don't remember the girl from Adam—or Eve, rather.'

'But you must have *known*—'

'Good heavens man, why? Oliver was nothing special at that time. Whereas I—' Darcy Howard smiled with the irony and the sense of the ridiculous that he had also brought to his left-wing politics—'I was a promising poet.'

The ex-promising poet slid his glass in Meredith's direction. There was on his face a look of considerable self-satisfaction. He had established his story, and was intending to stick to it. If there was more to the relationship that he could tell (and Meredith was sure there was) he would doubtless have told it to the *Daily Clarion,* for money. Unless he could get something on Darcy himself, that was all he was going to be vouchsafed for this interview.

Meredith pushed the half-bottle of gin across the table, and abruptly took his leave. Darcy Howard hid the bottle of gin in the cupboard under the sink, and pottered off to the pub—late but not (these days) unwelcome. He felt he'd had a good morning.

16

TERMINAL

The General Hospital where Miss Thorrington was lay near the sea front, and as the West Indian nurse led Meredith along the corridors of the second floor he could see from the windows elderly couples walking on the promenade, greeting each other reservedly, or sitting in deckchairs on the shingle, contemplating the horizon.

It was in this genteel, old-fashioned community that Miss Thorrington had lived since she left the employ of Oliver Fairleigh, husbanding her limited means and attending to the observances of her religion. It was to the hospital here that she had been brought to die of cancer with such dignity as she could muster and in such haste as she could. She was, the nurse said, not far now from death.

Her little room was hardly more than a cubicle, but Meredith imagined she valued the cramped privacy of it. The nurse drew back the curtains to let the sunlight in, but the old body on the bed did not stir. Meredith studied the face. It was long and strongly marked, the face of a woman of character: it was, in fact, not unlike Lady Fairleigh's, but whereas her face had the unbeautiful individuality which bespoke Family, Miss Thorrington's face only told of firm middle-class principles of duty, reticence and keeping up standards—principles long held and not found to fail. He was not surprised that this woman had stood up to Oliver Fairleigh.

When, after a minute or two, she stirred and opened her eyes, the nurse said very quietly: 'This is Inspector Meredith, Miss Thorrington, come to have a little word with you. I told you about him last night, if you remember.'

Her eyes found it difficult to focus on anything for any length of time, and after registering Meredith's presence she closed them. But an expression of doubt flitted over her face. 'An inspector. Oh dear. I don't know how lucid I can be. I think you shouldn't really rely on anything I might say. It's the drugs, you know. They make you so unsure of everything.'

'I promise you I won't rely on it,' said Meredith.

'Then get down to it quickly, please. I'm best when I wake. Did she tell me what you wanted? I don't remember.'

'It's about Sir Oliver Fairleigh-Stubbs,' said Meredith, quickly, but clearly. 'You were his secretary for nine years, is that right?'

'That's right. I hope there isn't anything wrong at Wycherley Court.'

'Sir Oliver was murdered, last Saturday evening.'

'Dear me. I didn't know. I *try* to keep up with events . . . with the wireless . . . but I must have missed it, or forgotten. Poor Lady Fairleigh.' Something almost like a smile flitted over her face suddenly. 'But how *horribly* appropriate.'

'Do you remember the books you took down and typed while you were his secretary?'

'Oh yes. Or I could—before this. I'm really rather proud of them, as if they were partly mine. I've often discussed them with people here—he's very popular.' A wicked glint appeared in her clouded eyes. 'I *liked* them, you know. It doesn't do to say so, but I *enjoyed* them. I don't like detective stories that pretend to be real novels. And I don't like all those scientific details. "Damn forensic science," he used to say. I think he was right. People liked Oliver Fairleigh because his books were good entertainment, good fun.'

'But did you like him as much as his books?'

'Oh, *he* was another matter,' said Miss Thorrington.

'Did you take down a book called *Black Widow*?'

'Yes, I did. It was the last I did take down. I never got to clean-type it.'

'How did the murder in that one take place?'

'It was nicotine poisoning. I remember quite well because I've told a lot of people here. That's rather naughty, of course, but they were interested, knowing it wouldn't be published till after his death. Someone soaked a cigar in alcohol, and got enough poison to kill someone.'

'What were the circumstances of the murder, do you remember them?'

Miss Thorrington creased her brow with effort. 'I think it was a big businessman was killed, at an important dinner. It may have been the Lord Mayor's Banquet, or something like that. Sir Oliver rather went in for that sort of occasion.'

'Do you remember any more details?' asked Meredith. 'How it was done, who did it?'

'Oh dear. It was very ingenious and not very convincing as I remember it. I think the wife did it, but I couldn't swear. I think it was one of those where it was proved in advance that she couldn't have done it, because she was too far away—at the other end of the table, or not there at all, or something—but then it turned out that she did. But details—no—I'm sorry.'

'That's enormously helpful. Would you like to tell me how it was you didn't come to fair-type it? Why you left Sir Oliver's.'

'I'd *much* rather not say,' said Miss Thorrington, her voice firmer than it had been so far.

'There was no pressure put on you by anyone? No—blackmail, for example?'

'Goodness me, no. I am *not,* Inspector, the sort of person susceptible to blackmail. Whatever can have put that into your mind?'

'It's something that's sort of in the air. I've heard stories about one member of the family.'

'Terry, I suppose.' The voice suddenly lapsed into tiredness. 'Be careful of Terry, Inspector. I liked Mark: he put up with more than a child should have to. Even Bella, sometimes . . . But Terry . . . Terry was a *wicked* boy.' Then, pulling herself together with an almost physical effort of her frail body, she said: 'That's rambling, Inspector. Ignore that.'

'I will,' said Meredith. 'But I think you should tell me why you left Oliver Fairleigh.'

Miss Thorrington again seemed to be trying bodily to pull herself together. Meredith decided she was one of those people for whom the prime imperative was to do what was right. But the flesh was very, very weak, and its weakness made the decision more difficult. 'Why?' she said, remotely, at last. 'It will have died with him.'

'Perhaps,' said Meredith. 'Will you let me judge? If it is not to the purpose, I promise nothing that you say will go any further.'

'So difficult,' said Miss Thorrington, still, seemingly, a long way off. 'He was a bad man, a cruel, unfeeling one . . . But one owes one's employer loyalty—even after one has left his employ. So I have always felt.' Then, with what little strength she had, she seemed to come to a decision. 'But of course you are right. In a matter like this . . . murder . . . I *must* tell you, in case it should be relevant.' She swallowed, and fingered her coverlet in some distress. 'He liked to shock. To wake people up, hoping they'd make some sort of scene. You must know that by now. Over the years I cultivated . . . indifference. Unshockability they say, nowadays. But then, one day, he had a phone call. He told me to stay . . . deliberately, knowing who it was, and what it would be about. He had that look on his face, as if to say . . . "This will make you sit up." ' The voice, becoming very, very weak, at last faded almost to nothingness as Miss Thorrington sank into the drugged state which is the last blessing of the incurably ill. Meredith bent very close to her lined face, and caught a few more words.

'A woman . . . He said—dreadful things . . . disgraceful . . . "Your bastard" . . . "I've helped you enough"—'

The whispers withered away to nothing. Meredith stood up, drew the curtains to, and respectfully slipped out into the corridor. Down below on the beach the old people sat and slept and strolled, as if life were infinite, and death could be warded off, with care and sensible clothing.

* * *

Down once more in the police car, Meredith suppressed his constable's desire to get started, and sat shuffling through the sheaves of reports on Mark Fairleigh's activities. Finally he found the one he wanted—the report on the witnesses of Mark's disgraceful outburst at the Prince Albert, Hadley. It was not a pub Meredith had patronized more than once or twice, having too Welsh a concern for the quality of the beer. He did not know any of the patrons, and he studied their names and the notes on them with great interest. He knew the constable who had done that particular piece of footslogging. PC Thorpe, a bright tom-sparrow of a boy, with a sharp eye and a sense of humour. His reports were not quite the official thing, and all the better for it.

Scanning the list, Meredith noted by the name of one of the bar-proppers the succinct summary 'flabby windbag.' He paused, then shook his head. Not quite what he wanted. That type never noticed much—too busy waiting to get their word in. Then his eye caught one of PC Thorpe's inimitable abbreviations: 't.h.l.o.d.' It stood by the name of Mrs Jessie Corbett, and it meant—as Meredith knew from previous reports of the same constable—'Talks the hind leg off a donkey.' That was more the type. She had been in the Prince Albert that night two Saturdays ago now, with her husband, her elderly mother, and her teenage daughter. Just the thing: a family party where everyone had long ago said everything there was to say to each other and could sit back and watch the rest of the customers. He got on to Hadley on his radio phone.

'Tell her,' he said, in an inspired touch, 'I'll meet her tonight at eight-thirty, at the Prince Albert.'

Mrs Jessie Corbett, unused to going out for a drink without her husband, settled her substantial self (purple-rinsed and navy Crimplene suited) behind a table in the Prince Albert Saloon Bar, fingered her vodka and tonic, and said: 'Well, this is better than *Softly, Softly.*'

And her round, noticing eyes seemed to say: 'And you're better-looking than Barlow, and all.'

Chief Inspector Meredith, raising his pint, said: 'Cheers. To you!'

The atmosphere being so effortlessly cosy, Meredith got straight down to business (wiping the bottled light ale from his mouth on his sleeve) by asking her about her family party of two weeks before.

'Well, there was Mum, she usually comes with us of a Saturday, though George—that's my husband—always says couldn't we leave her at home, and for all the fun and laughter we get out of her we might just as well, then there was George, same as usual, not saying very much, and then there was Vanessa, that's our youngest, and she was in a foul mood and all, because she wanted to go to the disco, and George wasn't having any, says he knows what they get up to there—though *how* he knows *I* don't—and says he doesn't want her with a bundle of unwanted trouble before she's seventeen, though heaven knows that's how we got married, but perhaps that's what he means.'

She came to a breathy pause, sipped her vodka and tonic and looked at Meredith. I'm a very good bargain, taken all round, she seemed to be saying.

'Now,' he said, 'I want you to tell me exactly what happened when young Mark Fairleigh threatened his father. You've probably told it so often by now the odd little detail has crept in that's not really what you saw.' Mrs Corbett did not take offence, and her bright wide eyes told him she understood exactly what he meant. 'I want to hear just what happened, with no melodramatics. Okay?'

It was a test that Jessie Corbett passed with flying colours. She described Mark rather well ('the sort you wouldn't mind your daughter bringing home, but you'd want to look at a bit if it looked like getting serious'), described the two couples talking at the next table to her ('some people do talk'), described Mark glowering and drinking, and finally erupting unsteadily at the next table, where he and his father were being talked about. There was nothing about manic fury, or brandished knives, or any of the ludicrous details that had crept into other people's versions. It was admirably done—it was the basic version, as Meredith had extracted it from all the variations of the different reports. That was the test. Now came the serious bit.

Meredith led her on to the other customers in the bar. It was also an area that PC Thorpe had been over with her before, but Meredith had the advantage over him of being on the identical spot. He made her place each person she mentioned where they stood, and he forced her to conjure up the expressions on their face, and their reactions to the scene. It was a real exercise in total recall.

'There was that Colonel Redfern, standing at the bar, always here of a Saturday night, and most other nights from what I hear, all paunch and blarney he is, and he was drinking it in (along with the others) because anything for a good story, anything to be the centre of attention, then next to him was Albert Courtle, garage man, bit of a crook like they all are, but quite nice with it, then there was . . .'

And so on, through the pub, from table to table, from group to group around the bar. As she went on, the pictures in her mind's eye became more vivid, and more detailed:

'Then right in the corner, there was a man and his wife, never seen them before, didn't talk much, just sat and drank shorts. Oh yes, then behind them on the bench, didn't remember him before, was a chap on his own, reading the paper—'

'Oh yes,' said Meredith. 'Tell me more about him.'

17

DEATH COMES AS THE END

Arriving at Macpherson's elegantly decaying Queen Anne offices at eleven o'clock, Inspector Meredith found the Scottish dragon alone in the reception room on the ground floor, and meekly sent his name up to Gerald Simmington.

'He's in conference with Sir Edwin,' said the dragon. 'He would be obliged if you would wait five minutes.'

'Of course, no hurry at all,' said Meredith. Then to pass the time of day (though her expression did not encourage chat for the sake of chat) he said: 'I suppose you're all busy coping with the rush on Oliver Fairleigh's works?'

'Precisely,' said the dragon, her thin lips registering no pleasure. 'Last year's hardback will be top of the bestseller lists on Sunday again. Reprints ordered over the whole range of paperbacks. Talk of one of those all-star films. As if his death improved the quality of his books. I never cease to be surprised by the reading habits of people.' She threw a disapproving emphasis on the last word, as if the reading habits of dogs and cats were more rational and predictable.

'I was talking to Sir Oliver's old secretary yesterday,' said Meredith.

'Oh yes, Miss Thorrington.'

'She confessed to enjoying Sir Oliver's books. She obviously prefers her entertainment to be frankly enjoyable—doesn't like all these forensic details one gets these days.'

The Edinburgh Terror gave him a look which said that but for Loyalty to the Firm she would have told him what she thought of Miss Thorrington's literary opinions. She turned to go back to her ancient Olivetti, but Meredith said pleasantly:

'I suppose Sir Edwin is worried about the manuscript of the posthumous book?'

'That I couldn't say,' said the dragon.

'It must represent a great deal of money to him,' said Meredith.

'Sir Edwin is a good Scot,' said the dragon. 'He takes what the Lord provides.'

Meredith wondered in how active a sense one should understand the word 'takes'. He scanned the bookcases in the outer office which contained the various publications of Macpherson's— religious, educational and frankly unworthy. He was saved from having to incur the dragon's disapproval of his choice of browsing material by a call from upstairs.

'Mr Simmington will see you now,' said the dragon, as to a tradesman. She took him into the hall-way and gave him precise instructions how to find his office. As he made his way again through the labyrinth of small corridors and disconcerting steps Meredith saw the maze as an indisputably appropriate habitat for a publisher of detective stories. After various sudden blank walls and hairpin turns he came to the door marked 'Gerald Simmington,' knocked and went in.

The room was as neat and characterless as ever, the desk cleared for action, or perhaps abstract speculation, only the covers of the books on the shelves giving a modicum of colour. The only addition was a glass of whisky by Simmington's right hand. Meredith hadn't thought of Simmington as a mid-morning drinker, but doubtless his profession had its rigours and its *longueurs*. The editor of the Golden Dagger series looked as neutral and uninvolved as ever.

'I hear from your receptionist that the sales of Oliver Fairleigh are soaring,' Meredith said pleasantly.

'Incredibly,' said Gerald Simmington smoothly. 'He was always our best seller in the fiction line. Now he's beginning to outstrip the popular religious works.'

'It will compensate Sir Edwin for the loss of *Black Widow*—if it *is* lost.'

'Perhaps,' said Mr Simmington, shaking his head sceptically. 'Does that mean you've given up hope of finding it?'

'No, by no means,' said Meredith. 'If I'm any judge of character it should still be in existence.'

Gerald Simmington gestured him to a low seat by the door, and then, as if saying something he knew sounded naive, asked: 'And if it's found, will it solve Sir Oliver's murder?'

Meredith eased himself back in his chair. 'Not perhaps in the sense you mean,' he said. 'No, I'm afraid Oliver Fairleigh didn't have a literary premonition of his own end, and I don't think it was precisely used as a blueprint. The thing that's always been odd —and which everyone in one way or another has pointed to, whether charitably or otherwise—is that Oliver Fairleigh was a very slapdash writer, especially as far as plotting and scientific detail were concerned. Miss Thorrington—' he saw a flicker of recognition in Simmington's eyes—'says he was a fun writer. Miss Cozzens says she doesn't think anyone copying his methods would ever manage to kill anyone. Sir Oliver himself said "Damn forensic medicine." No—all in all, I haven't got too far with the idea that the method, in detail, was copied from the missing book. And as far as I can learn from Miss Thorrington, the actual situation was fairly remote from what actually occurred at Wycherley Court.'

'Fascinating, this,' said Mr Simmington in his bloodless way.

'One is left with the idea that perhaps someone felt that the mere fact of his or her having read it was enough to cast suspicion in his direction, since the method of poisoning—nicotine is decidedly unusual—was gained from Oliver Fairleigh's book.'

'I see,' said Gerald Simmington doubtfully. 'It doesn't seem to narrow the field very much, does it?'

'Oh, the field is enormous,' said Meredith cheerfully. 'Again and again I've come back to the sort of man Oliver Fairleigh was. They sent me a transcript of his broadcast at the BBC—fascinating? He obviously wanted more than anything in the world to shock or annoy as many people as possible. That's evident too from his behaviour at the Woodstocks'. Dreadful and quite unwarranted—and just to get attention to himself. With a man like that the net is inevitably wide.'

'And he must have been enormously difficult to live with,' said Mr Simmington, blinking sympathetically. He had not touched his drink, perhaps fascinated by the conversation, perhaps out of politeness because he felt he could not offer a police officer one.

'Of course, of course, hideously difficult,' said Meredith. 'Though there again, I have a very slight feeling that—how should one put it—his bark was worse than his bite.'

Meredith's diamond-sharp eyes noticed that Mr Simmington wasn't willing to accept this: his eyebrows rose a mere fraction, in polite scepticism. 'Of course, we here are not the best people to say,' he said doubtfully. 'There was no particular reason for him to bite us. But still—'

'Don't get the wrong idea,' said Meredith. 'As soon as one uses a phrase like that, people get the idea you're suggesting that underneath that rough exterior there lurked a heart of gold. Nothing of the sort, of course. I mean precisely what I say. Mostly Oliver Fairleigh's malice, desire for attention, enjoyment of outrage and chaos, exhausted itself in words. If he had created a scene, he was happy. He seldom took it further than that. He behaved appallingly to Mark, but he didn't change his will. He behaved appallingly at the Woodstocks', but he proposed to introduce the young man to Sir Edwin. He—but that's another matter. Of course, on the surface it would *seem* that those closest to him had the best motive for killing him. But it may well be that his family subconsciously appreciated how much of his awfulness was mere words.'

'You may be right,' said Simmington, still showing scepticism.

'As a matter of fact there are quite a lot of reasons for thinking the immediate family are not necessarily the most likely suspects in this case. If the poison was put into the decanter just before Sir Oliver drank the lakka, why was such a risky method chosen? The family would have had so many better opportunities than that, so many safer ones.'

'Possibly because there were outsiders present . . .' suggested Simmington, very tentatively.

'Only the Woodstocks. It would be a perverse policeman who would suspect them rather than the immediate family. Again, if the idea was to use Mark's outburst at the Prince Albert to make him prime suspect, the poison can surely not have been put in the decanter during the opening of the birthday presents, immediately before the toast. Because by then Mark was out to the world, and likely to be for some time to come. It would have to be done earlier—either earlier in the day (Bella arrived in the morning), or earlier in the week (Terence had been in the house some days).'

'I see,' said Simmington. 'That seems logical.'

Meredith, his eye resting on Simmington's whisky for no reason he could think of, felt he had got into his best expositional style. This was the kind of thing Simmington ought to like.

'Of course, leaving aside Lady Fairleigh (it is difficult to imagine her trying to implicate her eldest son), both Bella and Terence are very tempting, as suspects. Terry especially, perhaps.'

'There have been rumours,' murmured Simmington.

'There is one big factor against him, though. He was—we are pretty sure—trying to implicate his brother in the drug traffic, with a view to making a big stink that would finally settle his hash as far as his father was concerned. Not a nice young man, Terry, as Miss Thorrington said. Now, he hadn't succeeded in this, but he must surely still have had hopes that he might. He would hardly embark on a further project to involve him in something criminal so soon. More particularly, since the aim was to get Mark cut out of his father's will, he most certainly wouldn't involve him in the killing of his father—that really would be killing the goose that was intended to lay Terence's golden egg! The idea is quite crazy. By and large, neither Terence nor Bella could have wanted Sir Oliver dead until they were quite sure Mark was cut out of the will, and so far there had apparently been no discussion of it in the family, so they certainly couldn't know. Of course it's just possible the dose was not intended to be fatal. But I have the impression that both Terence and Bella would have calculated the dose to a nicety.'

'One comes back to the brute fact that it is Mark who benefits,' said Gerald Simmington. 'Though of course he's impossible.'

'Not *impossible*,' said Meredith. 'Oh, Mark is a wonderful suspect, no doubt about it. Everything perfect except opportunity. Only provide the opportunity, and—bingo! The five-card trick done again to perfection. But I haven't, as yet, found the opportunity. And you know, if I were Mark and my alibi depended on my congenital drunkenness—I don't think I would have sobered up so conspicuously the day after the murder, would you?'

'Not the family, then,' said Simmington.

'I'm a cautious policeman,' said Meredith, 'not Hercule Poirot relying on his little grey cells. Let's say I don't think the family are as good bets as I imagine most outsiders are thinking they are.'

'I confess, I have been thinking along those lines. I do take your point, though.'

'Perhaps the best approach to the whole case,' said Meredith, his eyes now straying to the colourful dustjackets on Simmington's shelves, 'is the practical one: who had a chance to poison the decanter? Did those people have a motive? Here again one encounters difficulties. There were two names that sprang to mind in answer to the first question. Unfortunately, the second question then becomes peculiarly difficult. On the surface the answer would seem to be: no motive at all.'

'But you can't accept that?'

'I can't accept it without a bit of background digging. And then again—how far is a *bit* of background digging going to get you? Sir Oliver's life was—how shall I say?—full of incident. I decided the best line to work on was the assumption that a motive for murder is not, as a rule, trivial. If it came from Oliver Fairleigh's past, it would probably be something big—perhaps, therefore, something he wanted to keep quiet, but by the same token very possibly something not irrecoverable, even today.'

'I see, the Ross Macdonald type of plot,' murmured Simmington.

'Something like that,' said Meredith, not quite sure what he was talking about. 'I wanted to bring a few things together: the people who had the most opportunity; the attempt to implicate Mark

Fairleigh; the motive; the fact that this seemed, somehow, a haphazard sort of crime—'

'Haphazard?'

'Improvised. More or less spur-of-the-moment. That all along was my impression. Not a murderer of devilish cunning at all—and therefore not one likely to have concocted any infallible plan. The poison did actually kill Sir Oliver, but equally it could well have killed someone else instead. So, anyway, what do I do? I look first of all at my two people with the best opportunity to poison the decanter. I look for a start at Surtees.'

'Surtees?'

'He had the key to the drinks cupboard in the study some minutes before the rest came in, and before Mark went out like a light. Surtees: thirty-eight years old, I found; one marriage in the past; running a nice little business selling information to Sir Oliver and screwing his daughter as a return for doing the same service. Did he have serious designs (as they say) on Bella? If so, he didn't know his girl. Did he kill Sir Oliver assuming Bella was his heir? Possibly, because he *did* think that. But it doesn't seem in character to go quite so far on such a rash assumption. No—unless there was something else in the background waiting to be dug out, one can only say Surtees would have to be a very impulsive, irrational murderer, and this doesn't seem to conform to his type.'

'I see. And—the other?'

'The other, Mr Simmington, is you.'

Meredith let his eyes rest on the man's face. There was no change there whatsoever, not a flicker of fear or chagrin. He remained what he had been since the interview began: a sandy-haired, opaque nonentity.

'I see,' said Gerald Simmington neutrally.

'Opportunity: the Sunday before the actual murder, when you both had liqueurs together. Sir Oliver broadcast it around fairly freely that under doctor's orders he drank liqueurs and spirits only at weekends. You could poison the lakka on Sunday and be fairly certain he would not drink it until the following Saturday.'

'No doubt that is true,' said Gerald Simmington, not departing from his civil-service tones. 'As I explained to you in our previous talk, we were together after dinner for a very short time, and Sir Oliver did not leave the room. However, I quite realize that is merely my own uncorroborated word.'

'Precisely. And you also say that Sir Oliver fetched the type-script of *Murder Upstairs and Downstairs,* all but the last chapters. Miss Cozzens tells me this was after dinner.'

'After dinner, but—oh, I'm sorry, I interrupted you.' He looked at Meredith courteously, his eyes blank of any other expression.

'So, I look into your background. Age—thirty-two. An Oxford second in nineteen-sixty-seven. Began working for Macpherson's in nineteen-seventy. Unmarried.'

'Not much to tell, I'm afraid,' said Gerald Simmington apologetically.

'I found the age interesting, though,' said Meredith. Mr Simmington had folded his fingers together in his characteristic little pyramid, and was showing no sign of emotion. Once again Meredith found his eyes being caught by the glass of whisky at his right hand. 'Your birthdate—nineteen forty-five—I had already found that rather an interesting period in Oliver Fairleigh's life. So I looked further into your background. Your mother—'

'My mother—' Mr Simmington's voice, astonishingly, came loud and clear, and he held up his hand in a gesture that was almost commanding. 'I would prefer to talk about my mother myself.'

'Please do,' said Meredith, adopting Simmington's old neutrality.

'My mother was a very remarkable woman. Only I was in a position to understand just *how* remarkable. If she hadn't fallen in the way of Oliver Fairleigh—anyway, as you will be able very easily to find out, she was a working-class girl, born in Bradford. Both her parents were mill-workers. She got to Grammar School, then to Domestic Science College. She had been there two years in nineteen-forty, but she joined up. She was with the ATS in Italy when she met up with Oliver Fairleigh in late nineteen-forty-three. He'd been lecturing—wonderfully ironic—on 'Towards a Classless Post-War Britain.' She asked a question, and they talked afterwards. They became friends, then lovers. They intended to get married as soon as the war ended—or she did. She did.'

Gerald Simmington's voice, which had been strong and convincing, faded into silence for a moment. But his whole manner had lost its air of apology and withdrawal—as if he were emerging blessedly into life after long years of hibernation. He took a breath, then went on:

'I don't suppose he ever intended it—marriage, I mean. At any rate, if he did, it didn't survive his visit to her home, my grandparents' home. He had leave in 'forty-four, to write about the Italian campaign. She wangled leave at the same time, and they were together in London. I don't think things were going too well between them even then. Then they went to Bradford. My grandfather was a fine man, an original. He was a mill-worker through and through—a Trade Union man, a Labour Party man. He had his views, he argued them, he never pulled his punches. He hated drawing-room radicals. He and Oliver Fairleigh loathed each other on sight. In fact, Oliver Fairleigh loathed everything about working-class life—the town, the food, the matiness, the manners. My mother said those days in Bradford—it was as if he were being physically sick every minute of the day.'

'And that was the end of the relationship?'

'Yes. They quarrelled. He'd been looking for an excuse for leaving. She was already pregnant, but she didn't tell him until later, till just before I was born. By then things were changing with him. The war was all but over, he'd had his first book accepted, he had changed his politics and was even looking for a constituency to adopt him, though none of the local Conservative Associations could stomach his swift conversion, so he didn't get one at that time. Anyway, he and my mother came to a financial arrangement, and he was rid of us both. I imagine very few apart from him and my mother knew about the episode at all.'

'I rather think someone called Darcy Howard knew,' said Meredith, 'and made a little bit out of Oliver Fairleigh as a reward for keeping his knowledge to himself.' He had noticed a flicker of recognition at the mention of the name, and decided that Darcy had already begun negotiations designed to continue his subsidy. At his age, presumably, one could afford to live a bit dangerously.

'That, anyway, was what happened,' said Gerald Simmington. 'I suppose it was a common enough sort of episode at the time.'

'Why do you bear such a grudge, then?'

Gerald Simmington looked quite steadily at Meredith. 'I've not said I bear a grudge. I'm telling you about my mother. Telling you things you can quite easily find out from others. Well, what more is there? My mother lived for a time with her parents, but it wasn't pleasant—with everyone knowing. And she thought about me growing up. She always thought about me. She was a saint. So we moved to London, where she passed as a war widow. We lived in a shabby area, near Alexandra Palace in fact, and we just about managed on the pittance she got from Fairleigh. It went less and less far as the years went by, of course, but when I began school she could take part-time jobs. There were always extras needed, of course: school uniforms, holidays for me abroad (I was good at languages). Then she might have to ring up Oliver Fairleigh.' His mouth twisted in distaste.

'Was that wise?' asked Meredith.

'Wise? She didn't think of whether it was *wise*. She did it for me. And of course the money always came. As you say, his bark was worse than his bite. But perhaps it would have been better not to have given the money and not to have barked either. She had to put up with—well, you can guess: revolting insults, innuendoes, abuse. He was a hateful bully. When I got to Oxford, of course, I had a grant, and she didn't need to go to him any more. Except once.'

The sharper, newly awakened eyes met Meredith's, and a hand went nervously towards the whisky glass, then drew back. 'Of course, you would know that. That would be easy enough to guess. I was teaching at the time. I'd got a good second, but teaching was about the only thing that seemed open. It was sheer misery, every minute of the day. I don't think there *is* any torture more awful than an incompetent teacher suffers. I was at the end of my tether. My mother rang Oliver Fairleigh and asked if he could get me a job in publishing. With the usual result. Outrage, insult, refusal. But of course in the end he did it—he got me in here.'

Meredith almost asked if he hadn't been grateful—but he realized at once that this had been the worst thing of all, the ultimate insult: he had had to take help from Oliver Fairleigh; he had put himself in a position where gratitude was in order.

'Two years after that, my mother died. She had overworked for years, and was not strong. She had influenza which developed into pneumonia, and it carried her off. That is the story of my mother, Inspector.'

'And since he got you in here, your relations with Oliver Fairleigh have been—?'

'Perfectly normal. When I saw him for the first time he treated me like any other junior employee of the firm. He's gone on doing that—getting perhaps marginally politer as I worked my way up.'

'I suppose it was early on when he gave you the manuscript of *Black Widow*?'

The new, liberated Gerald Simmington—no longer under the pressure of any personal emotion, and seemingly totally relaxed—leant back in his chair, and even grinned broadly. He looked almost happy. Meredith noticed suddenly that he was quite a large man, and rather a good-looking one.

'Come, come, Inspector. Surely senior police officers don't try to play childish tricks like that. I've told you some facts that you could very easily have found out for yourself—from public records, friends, Sir Edwin. If you wish to believe that I killed my —killed Sir Oliver, that's up to you. I admit no such thing. And I very much doubt whether you could put together any sort of case.'

'At the moment it would be mainly circumstantial,' admitted Meredith. 'Let me tell you, then, how I see the sequence of events. Some of my guesswork will be quite easy to check up on, I think. First of all, you were in the Wycherley area the weekend before the murder, but not necessarily with that intention in mind, not immediately. More or less by chance you happened to be in the Prince Albert at the time of Mark Fairleigh's outburst.'

'Oh really?' Gerald Simmington raised his eyebrows.

'I have one witness to a "sandy-haired man in the corner, with an evening paper," which I take to be you. I will arrange an identity parade to confirm that—if necessary separate identity parades in which you can be picked out by everyone who was in the pub that night.' Something of the old Gerald Simmington returned in the expression of fastidious distaste that crossed his face at the idea. 'As I say, I think the notion of killing your father was already in your mind, and had been since your mother died. I think hearing Mark Fairleigh threaten his father brought it to the forefront of your thoughts. I think you then rang Wycherley Court and were invited the next night to dinner.'

'I had a standing invitation,' said Gerald Simmington. 'He would always say: "If you're ever down our way . . ." You know how it is. But I knew the sort of pleasure it would give Fairleigh to have his bastard eating at the same table as his wife. He was a connoisseur of that sort of situation.'

'Fine, the picture is emerging,' said Meredith genially. 'You rang, then, said you were in the area and wanted to talk over *Murder Upstairs and Downstairs,* which was overdue. You were invited along to dinner. And you went prepared—with nicotine.'

'Which I just happened to have with me.'

'It's very easy to obtain, as you knew from reading *Black Widow.* Getting it needed no special measures on your part. And of course the victim already suffered from heart trouble, so no great amounts were needed. I think you already knew two things that turned out to be vitally important: Oliver Fairleigh's regime as far as drink was concerned—he was always broadcasting it around— and the fact that his birthday dinner was imminent, an occasion which all the family was accustomed to attend. You confirmed in your conversation that night that Fairleigh was unlikely to touch liqueurs or spirits between that night and the next Saturday, when all the family would be around. Just before you left you persuaded him to get the completed portion of *Upstairs and Downstairs,* so that you could begin editorial work on it. Did you see the mock bookcase then, with the references to your mother's story? Perhaps. Or perhaps Sir Oliver drew your attention to it himself. Anyway, while he was out you put the nicotine in the lakka. The poison was likely, over a period of time, to discolour it, make it brown, but it is already a deep yellow, and the study is badly lit. Oliver Fairleigh certainly wouldn't notice, and in fact our lab boys, though they *thought* it had been put in some little time before Oliver Fairleigh died, couldn't be sure. It was a very clever piece of work indeed.'

'I'm sure the murderer would be grateful to you for your good opinion,' said Gerald Simmington. 'It rather underlines the fact that so far you have no case whatsoever. Even a poor little editor glutted on garbled detective fiction can see that.'

'I don't think things went *quite* so well for you after that, though,' said Meredith, trying to keep up the tone of unabated geniality which had somehow crept into the conversation. 'Because it was a very hastily decided on murder—hence the feeling I get of improvisation. In that sort of circumstance, little things have a habit of going wrong.'

'Like, for example?'

'Well, like *Black Widow,* notably. I expect when you'd got the poison into the lakka you came home and hugged yourself on your cleverness in using one of Oliver Fairleigh's methods, and obtaining the poison as he told you. And then you thought: now which book of his was it where the nicotine was used and the details given? And you looked along your shelves, and you couldn't find it—and you realized it was in the book that you, and only you had read. Damning!'

'Hardly that, Inspector. Hardly more than mildly corroborative.'

'But it could never be published. Because people would read it, and comment, and the police would look into it. And they would be coming, inevitably, to you—and wondering who you were. Your great strength was how few knew that—not even, I suppose, Sir Edwin. So the book had to be suppressed. It had been given to you just after you started work, after Miss Thorrington left. I suppose you put it in the vaults here, or the Oliver Fairleigh archive.'

'They're chaos, the firm's records,' said Gerald Simmington disapprovingly.

'Luckily. So you got it out, and then had to pretend the manu-

script must be at Wycherley. Improvised, you see. A bit last-minute.'

'It would—taking your story as a piece of fiction—have worked
quite well if Oliver Fairleigh hadn't left the copyright to his wife.'

'It would have worked only until Sir Edwin started making
enquiries about the posthumous work,' corrected Meredith. 'And
that would have been soon enough, I dare say. Anyway, this little
detail panicked you, and then the plot to incriminate Mark misfired completely because he was so drunk, and then you started
thrashing around?'

'Come, come, Inspector, am I the type to thrash around?'

'Well, you did silly things. Like pretending no one here could
remember Miss Thorrington's name. I've just ascertained it is perfectly well remembered by the lady downstairs. You even managed
to throw a few dark hints in the direction of your employer,
though why *he* any more than the family should kill the goose that
laid the golden eggs is beyond comprehension. No, it was a good
plan, but it needed more care.'

Mr Simmington remained looking at him, still almost insouci-
ant. Meredith's eyes had lost their sparkle. The murderer of Oliver Fairleigh was not going to be the criminal he was most pleased
with himself for having caught. He wondered why Simmington
did not take a drink, and found his eyes returning to the whisky
glass as a fully formed idea suddenly pushed its way to the front of
his mind.

'Well,' said Gerald Simmington finally, with a broad smile.
'That's the plot outline. Now perhaps we can get on to the proof.'

'Very little so far, as I say, and mostly circumstantial,' said Meredith. 'But I shall get it. I have a warrant in my pocket to search
your flat. I shall search everywhere you've been in the last two
weeks, very carefully, I shall get you in the end. No doubt you've
destroyed anything you used to get the nicotine. But how did you
get it to Wycherley Court? Have you destroyed the clothes you
wore that evening?' A flicker crossed Gerald Simmington's face. 'If
you haven't there are sure to be traces the lab boys can pick up.
There always are. I'd be willing to bet you haven't destroyed *Black
Widow*. You're too good a servant of the firm of Macpherson.

Habit would die too hard for you to do that. We'll find it. You may find the process slow, but it will be sure.'

'Then I suppose the kindest thing for me to do, Inspector, would be to wish you good day—if not good luck,' said Gerald Simmington, standing. Once more he was the courteous representative of a well-established publishing firm. 'No doubt I shall be hearing from you again.'

But as Meredith began to get up, he seemed to make a sudden decision, and gestured him to sit again.

'One thing I will say,' he went on slowly, 'strictly off the record. I hated my—my *father*—there, I've said it—for what he did to my mother. I loathed him, and everything in me screamed out against the fact that *he* was responsible for *me*. When my mother died, my life was quite empty, quite meaningless. It has been ever since. The only thing that gave it shape, gave it an aim, was the thought of killing him. Thinking of ways to do it, that was a luxury, something that went with my profession.' He gestured at the gaudy, bloody covers dotted on the bookcases round the room. 'But the essential thing, all that mattered, was to kill him. If I did that, there was the victory. If I got away with it, I still had my meaningless life. If I didn't—' he shrugged—'what did it matter?'

Gerald Simmington smiled at the inspector.

'I couldn't lose,' he said, and his hand darted to the whisky glass and he drained it down. 'One way or another,' he added, as he lay dying.

ABOUT THE AUTHOR

ROBERT BARNARD, a seven-time Edgar nominee, is one of the mystery genre's most popular practitioners. He is the author of twenty-five novels, including *A Scandal in Belgravia*, *A City of Strangers*, *Death and the Chaste Apprentice* and *At Death's Door*. He and his wife live in England.